A Book That Was Lost

The Toby Press S.Y. Agnon Library
Jeffrey Saks, Series Editor

Books from this series

Illustrated:

A BOOK THAT WAS LOST
THIRTY-FIVE STORIES
EXPANDED EDITION, INCLUDING ALL STORIES FROM *TWENTY-ONE STORIES*

S.Y. Agnon

EDITED WITH INTRODUCTIONS BY
ALAN MINTZ &
ANNE GOLOMB HOFFMAN

ADDITIONAL STORIES EDITED BY
NAHUM N. GLATZER

PREFACE BY
JONATHAN ROSEN

The Toby Press

A Book That Was Lost: Thirty-Five Stories
by S.Y. Agnon
The Toby Press S.Y. Agnon Library Edition
© 2008 The Toby Press LLC
Revised Toby Press Edition 2017

These stories, published in arrangement with Schocken Publishing
House, Ltd., are available in Hebrew in the Collected Writings
of S.Y. Agnon—Kol Sippurav shel Shmuel Yosef Agnon, world
copyright © Schocken Publishing House, Ltd. (Jerusalem
and Tel Aviv, Israel), most recent edition 1998-2003.

Originally published as *A Book That Was Lost & Other
Stories* © 1995 Schocken Books, Inc. Portions of
this book were previously published in *Twenty-One
Stories*, Schocken Books, Inc. (New York, 1970).

Original publication data for each translation appears as part of the
Permissions Acknowledgments, pp. 583-584

Cover painting © Batnadiv Weinberg

The Toby Press LLC
POB 8531, New Milford, CT 06776-8531, USA
POB 2455, London W1A 5WY, England &
www.tobypress.com

ISBN 978-1-59264-254-0 *Paperback*

Printed and bound in the United States

Contents

v

vii

A Reader's Preface

For my Bar Mitzvah, a friend of my parents, a Jewish writer, gave me a small bundle of books that included a collection of Agnon tales. In those days I did not wonder much about the authors of the books I read. A friend had given me *The Hobbit* and I didn't know or much care that Tolkien was British, that his dark vision was shaped by a world war, that aspects of his imaginary world drew on Norse mythology. I merely plunged into the story of a small furry creature who follows a wizard and defeats a dragon.

It was the same with Agnon. I once read an interview with I.B. Singer where he talked about reading Dostoyevsky at the age of nine and simply assuming that Dostoyevsky—despite the anti-Semitism, or perhaps even because of it—was a Yiddish writer. This is how I read Agnon—I did not worry about translation, linguistic or cultural barriers. I did not think about Biblical, Mishnaic, Hasidic reverberations, or modern Hebrew interpolations. I just read. And so his stories entered through the same door that Tolkien, and that Dostoyevsky, enter when you read them as teenagers, which is actually the only door literature ought to go through, at least in the beginning.

Agnon's stories stirred very strong, disturbing feelings in me.

Looking back, I recognize these emotions as tinged with nascent historical and religious and political awakening, though I didn't recognize or have a name for this at the time. It was the dreamlike force of the stories that gripped me. In one, a man was looking for his father in a town where he no longer lived, Pesach was coming, the sun was going down, time and space were bent. I felt deep anxiety and displacement and longing without knowing why.

These stories stayed with me for many years, most especially the famous story, "Fable of the Goat," included in this collection, about the boy who follows a magical goat that leads him from his shtetl straight to the Land of Israel. The boy in the story follows this goat through a cave and comes out near Tzfat. He is so delighted he decides to stay. He sends the goat back to his father with a note tucked in its ear saying, essentially, "Follow the goat." But the father fails to find the note, and in grief and rage, butchers the animal. Only after the goat is dead does the little piece of paper fall out with its messianic message. The shortcut—and perhaps the bond between the father and son—is lost forever.

This story struck me with tragic force, even though re-reading it I recognize now it is half-ironic, a sort of Aliyah joke, as well as a serious mystical meditation.

But I first read this story without thinking of any of the things I would make myself think about now—the binding of Isaac, the way Jacob fooled his father with a goatskin and was in turn fooled with the blood of a goat, or the undertow of Hasidic mysticism and an overtone of Kafka's parable *Before the Law*, with its infinite waiting. Reading it at thirteen, there was a human ache, a Jewish ache, that stirred in me, ignorant as I was

As I got older, the story of the goat merged with a story I had long known about my own father.

My father went to Israel in 1954 to visit his sister, who had made Aliyah in the 1930s. My father, who had grown up in Vienna visiting Herzl's grave, announced that he was just going home to New York to pack his suitcase and would then return to Israel to live. He did not return to Israel for 30 years, when he was in his sixties, and I was in college.

The reasons why my father didn't return are less important—at least for the purpose of this preface—than the fact that Agnon had already taught me something about going to Israel with his simple fable. Later, when I read Agnon's novel *Sippur Pashut*—though I read it in English as "A Simple Story"—I recognized how good Agnon was at simple stories that wind up teaching you that in fact there *are* no simple stories.

In his great novel *Only Yesterday—T'mol Shilshom*—a character filled with Zionist dreams makes Aliyah only to have every illusion painfully beaten out of him, much as Don Quixote, his head full of novels of chivalry, sets out on his romantic road only to receive beating after beating. What a shock it was for me to read Agnon's Zionist adventure.

His hapless hero is harried by crazy orthodox Jews and cheated by Godless philistine Jews, brutalized by the weather and undone by his own romantic delusions about the land. With Zionism like that, I thought, who needs post-Zionism? Or at least I should say that Agnon made me realize that even after you went to the land, you were still traveling there, still making a sort of journey that never stopped. It was a simultaneously gloomy and oddly uplifting discovery, to know that Israelis were also in a constant process of Aliyah, much as all Jews are constantly choosing to be Jewish even after three thousand years of being chosen.

But by that point I could no longer overlook the fact that Agnon wrote in Hebrew. And I could not ignore the fact that I was cut off from the central element of his writing. The triumph, almost the punch line, of *Only Yesterday* is that it is written in Hebrew. This Jewish Don Quixote remains in the land of his dream, and, lo and behold, it is no dream, as the *Hebrew* account of his adventures attests. (Actually, he's destroyed by a mad dog, but that's another story.)

And so now I come to my great shame, of which Agnon is a constant reminder.

There is no magic tunnel to lead me to Agnon; translation may look like one but it leads you to a different place altogether. You have to take the long way around in reading Agnon, but my Hebrew stinks, despite many years of trying to learn it. And even if it didn't stink, it would be inadequate. And so I can only circle Agnon without ever quite arriving. I take some tiny comfort in the observation occasionally made to me that "even most Israelis can't understand Agnon anymore." There are, after all, multiple forms of literacy—and illiteracy. But it is very small comfort indeed.

I remember when the *New York Times* asked me to review *Only Yesterday* when it was finally translated, by Barbara Harshav, in 2000. I was delighted, but at the same time I felt, even more than is customary when reviewing a book, a deep sense of fraudulence. I kept thinking about Virginia Woolf's essay "On Not Knowing Greek." I can really only speak about not-knowing Agnon.

But there are lots of things I don't really know that I speak about—maybe the most important things in life. And I've come to the conclusion that if one waited for mastery before blundering out into the field, not only would it be impossible to be a writer, or a parent, or a believer in God—I don't think one could actually be Jewish. Agnon, easily mistaken as a touchstone of linguistic and religious and cultural authenticity, after all invented himself, and took his very name from one of his own stories.

He was born Shmuel Yosef Czaczkes in 1888, in the town of Buczacz in eastern Galicia, and though he spoke Yiddish and studied traditional Hebrew and Aramaic texts, he was tutored in German as a child and gained early access to European culture. He claimed to have been born on the Ninth of Av, the traditional anniversary of the destruction of both the first and second Temples, weaving brokenness into his very birth and pointing the way for the repair affected by his move to Palestine in 1907. On his father's side he was linked to Hasidic culture, but his mother was descended from mitnagdim, rationalist doubters of the ecstatic tradition of religious Judaism. Though devoted to Jewish scholarship, he was early on affected by the nascent currents of Zionism that often ran counter to the steadfast life of a traditional Jew. In short, his traditionalism was riven by the contradictions and tensions of modern Jewish life.

His first published work in Israel, "Agunot," derives its name from the Hebrew word *agunah*, describing the condition of a woman who cannot get divorced because the whereabouts of her husband are unknown. She is thus "chained," as the word literally means; legally, and in some sense spiritually, she floats unmoored in a world that no longer has a traditional place for her. Agnon, especially once he moved to Palestine, saw himself inhabiting a similar condition.

Without realizing all this it's easy to let Agnon terrify you since he seems to carry on his back the entire weight of unbroken tradition. But Agnon was himself a living embodiment of many of the contradictions of Jewish life.

Still, the world often took him as he presented himself at the Nobel ceremony in 1966, a stooped man with his head traditionally covered, reciting before the King of Sweden the blessing one is commanded to say on standing before a king, and claiming in his speech that people see in his work the influence of "authors whose names, in my ignorance, I have not even heard."

It's been instructive for me to discover how uncomfortable Agnon seems to have made other Jewish writers. There is the famous story Saul Bellow tells in his introduction to "Great Jewish Short Stories" about his meeting in Jerusalem with Agnon. Agnon was very keen to know if Bellow has been translated into Hebrew because only then, Agnon explained, would Bellow be safe, preserved in the only tongue that ultimately matters. Bellow appears to be laughing along with Agnon but in fact his revenge is swift. In the same volume, introducing Agnon's story "The Kerchief," Bellow says of Agnon: "Entirely immersed in Hebrew and Yiddish literature, he apparently has little interest in Western literary traditions." Bellow wrote this in 1963, just three years before Agnon received the Nobel Prize—and 13 years before he himself was awarded it. The falseness of this comment is staggering, especially from Bellow, who surely knew better. Even if Bellow had not read Agnon's correspondence, in which he asks his patron Zalman Schocken for a copy of *The Song of Roland* and rhapsodizes about Flaubert, a brief sampling of Agnon's works brings its western literary elements home, however braided through with Jewish sources.

It is as if Bellow—who after all wrote *To Jerusalem and Back*—

needed to persuade himself that Agnon's world and his own could not really overlap. That it was well and good that the goat, and even the dream of the goat, was dead. Bellow's American security somehow depended on it.

The same thing happened when I was talking once to Alfred Kazin, the great American Jewish literary critic and author of the landmark study of American literature, *On Native Grounds*. In passing, Kazin mentioned to me that his daughter was living in Israel.

"Well," I said, "she's really on native ground!"

Kazin flew into a rage. For him—and he was born in 1915, the same year as Bellow—the idea that native ground might not be where his own feet rested, and where his immigrant parents had toiled to belong, was too threatening, too anxiety provoking.

Even Isaac Bashevis Singer was made uncomfortable by Agnon—though perhaps it makes sense that a Yiddish writer would squirm a little at the prospect of a modern Hebrew one. I.B. Singer's son, Israel Zamir, tells a story in his memoir about going with his father to the 92nd Street Y to hear Agnon speak. It was 1967, the eve of the Six Day War. After Agnon's reading, Singer remarked to his son: "Too bad there aren't any translators so his books could be distributed widely."

It's one thing for the Nobel committee, in its citation to Agnon, to offer the unwittingly insulting observation that Agnon's work "has gradually penetrated linguistic barriers which, in this case, are particularly obstructive." It's another thing for the two other Jewish literary giants, all headed for the Nobel Prize, to feel a similar sense of obstruction and impossibility.

But these questions of language, like questions of national identity, are intimately bound up with Agnon's work, and he would hardly have been surprised by them. And my fascination with them, and Agnon, only grew stronger as I myself became a writer and wondered about the role of Jewish identity not merely in my life but in my writing life. In America, the pattern of Jewish writing established by critics like Kazin and novelists like Bellow was one of sailing out into the open culture of America from a Jewish immigrant origin that receded forever behind you. But a younger Jewish generation of writers has recognized that the journey back to Jewish identity, or at least to Jewish consciousness, is an equally heroic journey.

And for this journey Agnon also has a contribution to make.

Consider a novel like *A Guest for the Night* in which an Agnon-like character returns to his Galician town from the Land of Israel in the vain hope of making contact with some living element of Diaspora culture. Reading *A Guest for the Night* in college, I realized that for Agnon it was a sorrow not only that those in the Diaspora had no shortcut to the Land of Israel, but that those in the Land of Israel had no shortcut to the Diaspora. The Holocaust—or in the case of *A Guest for the Night*, published in 1939, the First World War—made the reverse journey impossible. But that doesn't mean it wasn't a dream for Agnon. Although at the end of *A Guest for the Night* the narrator returns to Palestine with the key to the Beit Midrash in his suitcase, that doesn't mean that Agnon didn't dream of opening that lost Diaspora door as much as he dreamed of passing through a modern Zionist gate.

More and more I've been moved to think about what a lonely figure Agnon seems. And how true he is to his self-invented name—an *agunah*, someone neither in one world or the other. But in a way, that might make him more accessible to the inhabitants of different worlds, not less, even if we have to work together to interpret him, and to repossess him.

We should no longer be asking whether it is in the Diaspora or Israel that the key resides. Israel exists. European Jewry is gone forever but American Jewry isn't going anywhere soon.

We should be trying to open up that cave again. It is perhaps more urgent than ever that we follow Agnon's goat—in both directions.

I've passed through many phases in my thoughts about Agnon but am perhaps thrown back most often on my earliest experience of him. If Agnon taught me that all simple stories are in reality complex, he also teaches, as all great writers do, that no matter how complex a story is, it also endures at a level of simplicity. Searching for my European-born father, who is no longer alive, and for my Israeli relatives—who are very much alive but who nevertheless elude me at times in mysterious ways—I return to that simple childhood fable about the goat. I feel more than ever that primal longing to belong, to stand in a place where all my worlds are joined.

And I feel that, much as Agnon lives in a world beyond my grasp, I need him more than ever.

Jonathan Rosen, 2008

Introduction

Many storytellers have arisen to tell the story of East European Jewry, but the achievement of S.Y. Agnon remains singular. His canvas is wider, his erudition vaster, his humor wittier, his irony subtler. Above all, like any great writer, his art transcends the limits of its ostensible subject. To be sure, Agnon's writing is inseparably entwined with the very particular culture of Polish Jewry and its continuation in the Land of Israel. At the same time, however, his art explores the universal questions that preoccupy great writing in all modern cultures: the fragmentary and fallen nature of human experience after the collapse of community and faith, and, as a counterbalance, the turn toward writing with its mythic possibilities and its linguistic and textual playfulness.

Perhaps the best way to comprehend Agnon is to invoke the examples of two modern masters in the English language whose lives were roughly contemporaneous with his: James Joyce and William Faulkner. Both writers are ultimately concerned with the experience of aloneness in the cosmos and with efforts to overcome that state; yet their exploration of these ultimate issues is undertaken entirely through the particular and unfamiliar—and often exotic and arcane—

materials of their national and regional cultures. In truth, the mores and speech habits of the American South and the geography and politics of Dublin at the turn of the century lie far beyond the competence of most of us. Yet we read Faulkner's *Absalom! Absalom!* and Joyce's *Ulysses* because it is only in such works of radical parochialness that we find the great themes of human fate and the quest for renewal most vividly portrayed. Agnon's art partakes in this same mysterious dependence of the universal upon the particular.

The immense achievements of writers such as Faulkner, Joyce, and Agnon are self-evident. So are the difficulties. If the way to the universal is through the particular, still one cannot be expected to glimpse the greatness if the path is strewn with opaque symbols and foreign references. In Agnon's case, the issue is not merely one of translation. Even the contemporary Israeli reader, fluent in Hebrew, is likely to miss key allusions to classical texts and to find the account of some ritual practices baffling, in much the same way that the contemporary English reader of *Ulysses* is likely to miss important allusions from Greek mythology and Irish politics.

How then does a reader of these supposedly great works get at their greatness? To begin with, one has a right to expect some help. Few would embark upon a reading of *Ulysses* without a reader's guide in hand or at least an edition with some annotation. Yet once we have plugged up some of the holes in our knowledge, we expect the larger message to become luminous. Lacking mastery of the culture in which a great work is embedded, we accept a certain level of unfamiliarity as inevitable, and we rely upon a common vocabulary of human emotions to get our bearings. But if we are given some help and the greatness still fails to shine through, then we must conclude that the work in question is too rooted in its time and place, and cannot transcend those boundaries to speak to readers either from other cultures or at least located at a cultural remove.

It is our conviction—and that of many longtime readers of Agnon in both the original and translation—that Agnon belongs in the company of the great modern writers and that, given some help, general readers who are not rooted in the culture about which he writes can find pleasure and illumination in his works. One of the purposes of this volume is to provide that crucial margin of help. Although the approach is not in itself revolutionary, it does represent a genuine departure from previous efforts to present Agnon in English. The assistance offered the reader is of two kinds. The first is presented through the glossary of recurrent terms from Jewish life and the notes to particular references in each of the stories, as well as through the general and section introductions. This explanatory material aims to supply the essential "cultural literacy" necessary for a good grasp of the stories. We have sought to avoid weighing down the stories with needless erudition. This moderate and selective level of annotation is intended to be of use both to the general reader, who wants central cultural allusions glossed, and to a reader more familiar with Jewish culture, who would welcome having specific textual references supplied.

The second kind of assistance has to do with the fact that this is a collection of short stories. Agnon wrote novels and novellas as well as short stories, but it is in the latter genre that he most characteristically distinguished himself, and it makes abundant sense that a new effort to present Agnon in English should begin here. The challenge is that Agnon wrote hundreds of short stories over seven decades in a wide variety of styles. To compile an anthology that is simply "The Best of..." would not help the reader find an orientation within the epic Agnon world. Our goal has therefore been, in accordance with a principle of overall excellence, to find a plan of organization that would deliver the best of Agnon in meaningful categories.

In searching for this shape, we let ourselves be guided by Agnon's own preoccupation with autobiographical self-invention. Throughout his long career, Agnon fashioned and refashioned the myth of himself as a writer. He told the story of his upbringing in Galicia, his journey to the Land of Israel, his extended sojourn in Germany, and his return to Jerusalem in many different versions, placing the persona of the writer at times at the center of the story and at times at the margins as a kind of ironic scaffolding. We have therefore chosen to organize the volume along a rough autobiographical-geographical axis, while making some exceptions for themes that profit from being taken separately. The introductions that preface the six sections of the volume establish a context for each grouping of stories and present some background as to how the texts have been read by previous readers.

> When it was his turn to be presented, Mr. Agnon jumped to his feet and enthusiastically shook the King's hand as he received the prize. Then, instead of the usual single bow to the King, he kept on bowing until he got back to his chair. He was obviously a very happy and flustered man. When he learned in October in Jerusalem that he had won the Nobel Prize, Mr. Agnon said that going to Stockholm would give him special pleasure "because there is a special benediction one says before a king and I have never met a king before." Tonight at the banquet, as the King looked on, Mr. Agnon, speaking in Hebrew, recited the blessing, "Blessed art Thou, O Lord our God, King of the universe, who has given of His glory to flesh and blood." The Israeli author said that "some see in my books the influences of authors whose names, in my ignorance, I have not even heard, while others see the influences of poets whose names I have heard but whose writing I have never read." The true sources of his inspiration, he went on, were, first and foremost, the sacred scriptures and, after that, the teachings of the medieval Jewish sages, and the spectacle of nature, and the animals of the earth.
>
> —The *New York Times*, December 11, 1966

The sight of the little round man in the black tails, white tie, and large velvet skullcap receiving an international prize from the king of Sweden was remarkable on a number of counts. Though a sophisticated participant in modern culture, Agnon presented himself as a pious and naive representative of the lost world of East European Jewry who is ignorant of European literature and has been instructed only by the Bible and the spectacle of God's Creation. No scene could provide a more powerful instance of the writer's ability to fashion and refashion his artistic persona. Agnon's construction of an autobiographical myth of the artist, with its deliberate blurring of the boundaries between life and art, is a key to understanding his work.

Over the years, Agnon shaped the narrative of his own beginnings to produce an image of the artist as a figure at once solitary and part of a community, both a rebel and a redeemer. He may not have left us a formal autobiography, but through his letters and public statements we do have evidence of his engagement in a remarkable process, carried out over most of a lifetime, that amounts to the fashioning of a public name and history of the writer.

The example of Joyce's artistic self-consciousness and his sense of a mythic renewal through language gives insight into the process through which Agnon created himself as a modern Jewish writer, linking significant markers in his own life to Jewish history and community. Among European modernists, Joyce offers a portrait of the artist who becomes his own father, an act of self-creation that also links him to his people. Like Joyce, Agnon saw himself as one whose life and art could shape new identities out of old traditions.

Born in eastern Europe in 1888, Shmuel Yosef Agnon died in Jerusalem in 1970. He offers us a life and an art that are emblematic of the century to which he was witness. If we think of him as a Jewish writer, it should be in the sense of a confrontation with history that encompasses destruction and rebirth, from the stirrings of national consciousness to the extermination of European Jewry and the establishment of the state of Israel.

In Agnon's account of himself, personal biography intertwines with national narrative through recurring themes of destruction, rebirth, and renewal. Most striking in this life story is his designation of the Ninth of Av as his date of birth. The Ninth of Av is a date deeply embedded in the history and eschatology of the Jewish people, as the date of the destruction of the first and second Temples in Jerusalem.

Its significance is reiterated in the collective memory of the Jewish people as the date of catastrophes throughout history. At the same time, we find the traditional belief that the Ninth of Av is the date on which the Messiah will be born. Agnon's choice thus carries the meanings of both destruction and redemption. The Ninth of Av holds an essential tension that comes to define the figure of the writer and to constitute a major theme in his work.

Along with the Ninth of Av, Agnon cited the Jewish holiday of Lag B'Omer as the date of his initial aliyah to the Land of Israel. (The term *aliyah* literally means "ascent," in the sense of "going up" to the Land of Israel.) In the Jewish calendar, Lag B'Omer marks the date of Bar Kochba's rebellion against Roman occupation of the ancient Land of Israel. A minor festival associated with a struggle for liberation, it is accompanied by a turn to the outdoors that marks the spring season in which it occurs. Evoking the spirit of that day, Agnon was fond of recalling one of his earliest Hebrew publications, "A Little Hero," a poem that pictures a small boy as the savior of his people on the occasion of Lag B'Omer.

In a similar association of life events with the history of a people, Agnon dated his second return to the Land of Israel in 1924 with a reference to the Torah portion of that week, *Lech lecha* ("Go forth"; Genesis 12:1–17:27). That portion of the Genesis narrative opens with God's commandment to Abraham to leave his birthplace and his family for the land that God would show him. Agnon thus intertwines his personal journey with the ancestral narrative. In letters and autobiographical statements, Agnon returned to such evocative coincidences, weaving them into a narrative frame for the life of a writer who lives out the story of his people.

The historical accuracy of these dates is less the issue than the function they serve as markers in a life story. Agnon may have constructed a biographical myth, but he also held onto the original documents, going back to 1908, that allow comparisons of the writer's story to the historical record. Why do both? This is Agnon the modernist, who offers us access to the making of a life as well as to the life that is made. He engages in the narrative construction of a myth while leaving traces of the materials out of which it is fashioned. We see him as the mythmaker, and he acknowledges his own artifice with a wink and a nod that invite us into his workshop.

Out of that workshop came embellishments to the portrait of the writer as a youth who revered his father. In a ceremonial letter to the municipality of Tel Aviv, Agnon observes that "I was born in the city of Buczacz in eastern Galicia to my father Rabbi Shalom Mordecai ha-Levi Czaczkes, of blessed memory, on the Ninth of Av." In the Jewish calendar, the year is signified by the letters of the Hebrew alphabet, each of which has a numerical equivalent. The notation of a date thus offers Agnon the opportunity for recombinations of letters that become the source of new meanings. With inveterate playfulness, he takes the Hebrew letters that designate the year in which he was born, t-r-m-h, and rearranges them to form the phrase "Zion will be merciful" ("Zion t-r-h-m"). Never losing the opportunity to heighten the personal with bits of exegetical play, Agnon fashions the public face of the writer out of bits and pieces, artfully constructing significance out of odds and ends of tradition.*

There is a considerable element of irony in Agnon's designation of dates and coincidences. He may draw upon biblical phrases or rabbinic exegesis in order to enlarge the horizon of meaning by linking the individual to the nation, but his relationship to his sources is never simple. Wordplays and historical associations work to inflate and deflate the figure of the writer, by connecting him to religious themes and simultaneously exposing his pretension. On occasion, Agnon takes these associations to a playful excess that suggests an element of self-mockery, as when he notes that he wrote his first poem on Lag B'Omer, made his first aliyah on Lag B'Omer, married his wife on Lag B'Omer, received the Swedish translation of one of his novellas on that day, was notified of the award of an honorary doctorate on Lag B'Omer, and so on. At such moments as this, Agnon jokingly exposes his game, even as he continues to play it.

Agnon's ongoing self-portrait connects the writer not only to the history of the people, but crafts a special relationship to Hebrew as the holy tongue, the language of Creation. Agnon's choice of Hebrew, after early experiments with Yiddish and Hebrew, links him with others of his generation who turned to Hebrew as a potent resource in the enterprise of national renewal. But while Agnon's writing draws

---

* This letter can be found in the autobiographical collection *Me'atzmi el atzmi* [From Myself to Myself] (Tel Aviv: Schocken Publishing House Ltd., 1976), p. 9.

upon the riches of language and makes us feel keenly the centrality of Hebrew to a worldview centered on Scripture, the relationship of the writer to that universe involves an intricate combination of reverence and subversion, piety and irony.

The very name "Agnon" is a fabrication, a central instance of the interpretive play that identifies the writer's art. It is a name that the writer, who was born Shmuel Yosef Czaczkes, invented by adapting the title of "Agunot," the first story he published in Palestine in 1908. To fashion both the title and his own name, Agnon used the Hebrew noun *agunah*, a term in Jewish law that designates a woman who is not free to marry because her husband has disappeared or left without divorcing her. The agunah is an indeterminate figure, at once connected to the community and separate from it. Interestingly, the story "Agunot" itself contains no agunah in the technical sense of the term. We must realize, then, the boldness of Agnon's imagination in taking a legal term and spiritualizing it, shaping it into a metaphor for the modern condition. Fertile with meaning, the name suggests an image of the artist as a soul without anchor. Thus, at an early point in his career, the writer arrived at a title and a name that express the longing for completeness amid the awareness of isolation and distance.

Picturing himself as one who maintains a connection to what he has lost, Agnon paints a portrait of the writer as a figure on the margins of tradition. In this passage from "The Sense of Smell," written in the 1930s, he maps out a mythic universe in which Torah—Jewish Scripture—occupies the center, while he defines himself by his distance from that language of plenitude and presence:

> For love of our language and affection for the holy, I darken my countenance with constant study of Torah and starve myself over the words of our sages. These I store up in my belly so that they together will be present to my lips. If the Temple were still standing, I would be up there on the platform among my singing brothers, reciting each day the song that the Levites sang in the Temple. But since the Temple remains destroyed and we have no priests at service or Levites at song, instead I

study Torah, the Prophets and the Writings, Mishnah, laws and legends, supplementary treatises and fine points of Torah and the works of the scribes. When I look at their words and see that of all the delights we possessed in ancient times there remains only this memory, my heart fills up with grief. That grief makes my heart tremble, and it is out of that trembling that I write stories, like one exiled from his father's palace who makes himself a little hut and sits there telling of the glory of his father's house.

Positioning himself as one who writes in the aftermath of destruction, Agnon subordinates himself to the priestly poets who are his predecessors and effaces his own individuality. Paradoxically, the effect of this denigration is to secure for the writer an affiliation to tradition: we have here a mythic portrayal of the writer as one who longs for return and restoration. What disappears from this picture is, of course, his more worldly or modernist face.

In the study of his house in Talpiyot, just outside of Jerusalem, Agnon preferred to write while standing at a lectern, a relic of an eastern European talmudic academy. He was fond of gesturing to the scores of volumes of Jewish learning to be found on the shelves lining the walls, noting in passing the presence of a modest shelf of twentieth-century literary works. This arrangement of books suggests an architecture of the imagination in which secular influences play a distinctly minor role. Indeed we might compare this denial of his own modernism to Agnon's public comments after accepting the Nobel Prize: he acknowledges sacred texts as the sources of his inspiration and disavows the influence of writers whose names he claims never to have heard. In both instances, we see the persona of the writer at play. Agnon, whose works display a range of literary experimentation that links him to the major modernists of our century, chose to minimize that affiliation and to present instead the image of the writer who subordinates himself to traditional texts. In so doing, he sought to fit his public image to a simpler notion of membership in a community unified by its history.

That mask was also real. Agnon devoted a large portion of his energies to insuring the survival of cultural documents of European communities that were ultimately destroyed. Indeed, even before the threat of the destruction of European Jewry became apparent, Agnon had come to play a major role as a collector of Jewish books and manuscripts and compiled several anthologies of Jewish lore. He was an important figure in Mekitze Nirdamim (Those Who Awaken the Sleeping), a group devoted to the retrieval, preservation, and dissemination of old Jewish manuscripts.

The cultural influences and traditions into which the writer was born all eventually found their way into an art that is encyclopedic in its references to Jewish life and texts.* Shmuel Yosef Czaczkes, son of Shalom Mordecai ha-Levi Czaczkes and his wife, Esther Farb, was born in 1888 in Buczacz, a town of some 12,000 inhabitants located in eastern Galicia, then part of the Austro-Hungarian Empire. Family lineage and traditions on both sides exposed him to a variety of currents in nineteenth-century Jewish life. From his mother's side, Agnon inherited ties to the Mitnagdim, the rationalist opponents of Hasidism, while his father's lineage included hasidic connections. Thus within his family he experienced the major currents of life in eastern Europe, from the joyous pietism of hasidic traditions to the rigorous intellectual commitments of the rationalists. With his father, who traded in furs, the boy Shmuel Yosef frequented a kloyz, a hasidic house of prayer, that belonged to followers of the Chortkover rebbe, the leader of a sizable community of Hasidim. It was also through his father that he first studied rabbinic texts.

By his own description, Agnon received a traditional education, studying in the traditional one-room Jewish school, the heder, then privately with a teacher and with his father, learning Bible, Talmud, and literature of the Haskalah (the Jewish Enlightenment). The family library was stocked not only with the Talmud and its commentaries but also with the works of Maimonides and the Galician

---

* For historical and biographical data, the editors are indebted to Arnold Band's *Nostalgia and Nightmare: A Study in the Fiction of S. Y. Agnon* (Berkeley and Los Angeles: University of California Press, 1968).

maskilim, the eighteenth-and nineteenth-century proponents of Jewish enlightenment. It was in this library and other local collections that as an adolescent Agnon freely educated himself. The comfortable circumstances of his family allowed him the leisure to do so. But the absence of more formal schooling was in fact a general trait of Galician-Jewish culture.

In a somewhat nontraditional departure, Agnon studied German with a tutor and gained access to European literature in German translation. Thus we see that a certain sophistication attaches to the young writer's early education. Nevertheless, his reminiscences tend to dwell on the traditions of Jewish learning in the town of Buczacz, traditions that he associates, most particularly, with his father. Marking an idealization of the father that recurs through his work, the son, in later years, painted a portrait of his father as a figure of radiant piety: "My father, my teacher, Rabbi Shalom Mordecai son of Zvi Aryeh ha-Levi, was a man of wondrous learning. Expert he was in the Mishnah and in early and late commentators. And as learned as he was in the Mishnah and its commentaries, so too was he expert in secular learning.... I was not worthy of acquiring even the slightest bit of his knowledge [Torah] or of his qualities. But he taught me love of Torah and of those who study it."* In a portrait that is already embellished with the touch of myth, the son underscores his own deficiencies through comparison with a father whose learning participates in the plenitude of the Torah.

This juxtaposition of son to father, lack to wholeness, present to past, enters into the writer's depiction of his birthplace, the town that he left as a young man. Destroyed in the Holocaust, the town of Buczacz retains in his imagination the accumulated richness of centuries of Jewish life in eastern Europe. *Sefer Buczacz* (The Book of Buczacz) is the memorial book of the town to which Agnon contributed. It belongs to a genre that was created in response to the Holocaust by the surviving members of communities that were obliterated. Along with histories, photographs, anecdotal memorabilia, *The Book of Buczacz* sketches a portrait of the writer as a young boy

* *Me'atzmi*, pp. 25–26.

of twelve, cataloguing the books on the shelves of the town's house of study, its Beit Midrash. The Beit Midrash functioned as a center for the study of classical Jewish texts and thus can be understood as a central structure in the maintenance of Jewish life.

Sefer Buczacz incorporates its native son into the town's tradition of study and commentary: "Wondrous was that old Beit Midrash—it was not just any Beit Midrash, but the capital of the Mitnagdim, a center for those antagonists of Kabbalah and Hasidism.... In this Beit Midrash Sh. Y. Agnon spent his time and nourished his spirit. Until the destruction his notes and comments could be found in the margins of pages of the books that he studied."* In this scene, the youthful figure of the writer-to-be takes an active role in continuing the traditions of study and commentary that distinguished the town, an enterprise of learning that found its physical and spiritual center in the Beit Midrash.

Compiled after the destruction, *Sefer Buczacz* is unambivalent in its attention to the history, the setting, and the lives of the inhabitants of Buczacz. By contrast, Agnon's maturation as a writer undoubtedly involved a resolution of his relationship to traditional Jewish texts and the communal structures that house them. That resolution produced an ironic stance, where the writing constantly plays out themes of rebellion and reconciliation. The disjunctions in Agnon's art are all the more sharply felt in light of the traditions that the writer draws upon so eloquently. Nowhere can this be better seen than in the quasi-autobiographical *A Guest for the Night.* This novel takes note of the writer's youthful rebellion as its first-person narrator describes his early preference for writing poetry rather than studying traditional texts in the Beit Midrash. That bit of personal history is then integrated into the narrator's account of his return for a yearlong stay during which he devotes himself to efforts to revive the dying town and to undo his own early rebellion through a newfound dedication to the study of old texts.

---

* Israel Cohen, ed. *Sefer Buczacz* (Tel Aviv: Am Oved, 1968), p. 95; Avinoam Barshai, ed. *Haromanim shel Shai Agnon* (Tel Aviv: Everyman's University, 1988), pp. 16–17.

Agnon builds this major novel around the Beit Midrash, which serves as the organizing structure for the efforts of its narrator to bring about a restoration that is both personal and communal. The key to the Beit Midrash provides a symbol for the lost potency of the town and its inhabitants. Nevertheless, the narrator's efforts to reverse that loss and to bring about a renewal of the town are treated with a wry combination of seriousness and irony. Agnon uses the novel to acknowledge the traditions of learning and piety that the Beit Midrash represents, but also to mark the futility of attempting to preserve them in eastern Europe. Written in the 1930s, *A Guest for the Night* is set in the period immediately following World War I. In a sense, it can be said to straddle history by recording the devastation of the period immediately following World War I, while in retrospect conveying a sense of the greater destruction that was yet to come.

For Agnon the writer, the ultimate destruction of the town in the Holocaust became the occasion for its recreation in art. Nowhere is this more apparent than in the posthumously published volume *Ir Umeloah* (A City and the Fullness Thereof).* Agnon arrived at the commitment to produce his own ongoing Book of Buczacz, a work of epic proportions that came eventually to include legends, folktales, family sagas, and grotesque renditions of popular culture. While this compendium has not yet been translated into English, the present anthology breaks new ground with its inclusion of "Pisces," "Buczacz," and "The Tale of the Menorah," all from *A City and the Fullness Thereof.*

At the turn of the century, Buczacz found itself responding to the rumblings of Jewish nationalism. Zionist congresses from 1897 on captured the imagination of the young Czaczkes. He would have been part of communal responses to the 1903 massacre in Kishinev, the death of Theodor Herzl in 1904, and the 1906 riots in Bialystok. A development of some importance occurred in the spring of 1906, when Elazar Rokeah came to Buczacz to publish *Der Yidisher Veker;* a Jewish weekly, and took on the young Czaczkes as his assistant. Rokeah's hiring must have given a significant boost to the youth's

---

* Tel Aviv: Schocken Publishing House Ltd., 1973.

literary ambitions. We have evidence through these early years in Galicia of numerous pieces in Hebrew and Yiddish published by the young writer. The Israeli critic Gershon Shaked has analyzed Agnon's maturation through the development of a more complex and ironic relationship to his early romantic tendencies.* In later years, Agnon distanced himself from his early romantic effusions, even occasionally inserting an early poem into a novel where it serves to demonstrate a character's youthful enthusiasm and naiveté.

The first manifest break in the writer's life took place in 1907, when Agnon left Buczacz for Palestine at the age of nineteen. Along the way, he passed through Lemberg and Vienna, where he encountered important figures in Jewish public affairs, such as the Hebrew writer Asher Barash and the Hebraist and educator Eliezer Meir Lifschütz. But while his visits with these men and others seem to have yielded opportunities for employment and study, Agnon appears to have kept his gaze fixed on the goal of reaching Palestine.

Indeed he appears to have sustained his resolve in the face of the astonishment of Galician Zionists, who were unaccustomed to actual decisions to emigrate to Palestine. For an insight into the period, we might consider Agnon's account of the aliyah of Yitzhak Kummer in the as-yet-untranslated novel *Temol Shilshom* (Only Yesterday): this youthful idealist sets sail for Palestine filled with expectations of fraternal solidarity. But despite his fervent echoing of the refrain *Kol Yisrael haverim* ("All Israel are friends"), he is set back by encounters with self-important Zionist functionaries in Europe and Palestine.

During his first sojourn in Palestine, from 1907 to 1913, Agnon encountered the pioneers of the Second Aliyah, who had come to work the land. While he never joined them in their physical labors, he came to know the land intimately over the years. In this first period, Jaffa was his preferred milieu, and he found work as a tutor, as secretary to the editor of a literary journal in which he published his first story, and as secretary to a variety of groups involved in Jewish settlement. The novella "Betrothed" gives us something of the cultural mix

---

* Gershon Shaked, *Shmuel Yosef Agnon: A Revolutionary Traditionalist* (New York: New York University Press, 1989).

of Jaffa in those years. In Jaffa, he extended his readings in European literature and, in a striking break with his background, abandoned Orthodox dress and practice. He also spent time in Jerusalem, where he drank in the lore of the city's neighborhoods.

These years bear evidence as to the impact of relationships with influential older men. In particular, the writer Yosef Hayim Brenner played an important role in the publication of Agnon's early stories in Palestine. Agnon looked up to Brenner as a man of uncompromising integrity. In later years, he described their first meeting in Lemberg, where he stopped on his way to Palestine and sought an introduction to the older writer whose work he so admired.* Noting the brilliance of Brenner that shone from the pages of contemporary journals, Agnon describes Brenner's utterly unassuming figure and mocks his own youthful expectations of the impressive figure of an author. As thoroughly secular a writer as Brenner came to figure for Agnon as the type of uncompromising authenticity.

It was during this first Jaffa period that Czaczkes first adopted the pen name Agnon. During these years, several long stories found serial publication in the Hebrew-language newspaper *Hapo'el Hatzair*. Despite these indicators of early success, however, the young writer apparently failed to find firm footing in the Land of Israel, and his abrupt departure for Berlin in 1913 remains something of a mystery. This is the second break in Agnon's development. Unlike the departure from Buczacz for the Land of Israel, this departure appears to be surrounded by confusion, rather than any clear sense of direction.

From 1913 to 1924 Agnon lived in Germany, and these years constitute the writer's major European period. Living in Berlin, with interludes in Munich, Leipzig, and a small town near Brückenau, Agnon absorbed a variety of cultural influences—secular and Jewish—that stayed with him, however he may later have chosen to represent his relationship to them. Gershom G. Scholem, the great scholar of Jewish mysticism, recalled his impression of the young Agnon in Berlin, "in the reading room of the library of the Jewish Community Council where he tirelessly leafed through the Hebrew

---

* See his reminiscence in *Me'atzmi*, pp. III–12.

card catalogue. Later I asked him what he had so intensively searched for there. 'Books that I have not read yet,' he replied with a guileless and yet ironic gleam in his eyes."*

In the fall of 1913, Agnon attended the Eleventh Zionist Congress in Vienna. Shortly after, he was called home because of the death of his father, but he arrived one day too late for the funeral. Whatever the circumstances, this delay suggests an ambivalence never to be fully overcome, an ambivalence that is as much a part of his character as the unqualified reverence for his father that he expressed elsewhere. Looked at retrospectively, in light of the proliferation in his fiction of themes of lateness and delay in fulfilling important obligations, Agnon's failure to arrive on time for his father's funeral takes on dramatic resonance. Literary reverberations of this theme can be felt in the stories that comprise the last section of this anthology; there you will find stories that vary from the dreamlike to the realistic but convey nevertheless a sense of lapses or losses that can never be made good.

The years of World War I saw the arrival in western Europe of large masses of refugees from eastern Europe. These "Ostjuden," or eastern Jews, met with ambivalence and hostility from some German Jews and were romanticized as "authentic" Jews by others, among them Martin Buber. Here we must try to imagine Agnon's double perspective: he was and was not one of the Ostjuden, given the acculturation to the West he had undergone. In a study of Agnon's German affiliations, the Israeli critic Dan Miron points out that Agnon's early years in Galicia brought him closer to Jewish-German influences than to contemporary developments in Russian Hebrew culture, so that he can be regarded as something of a liaison between the two segments of a divided Ashkenazic Jewry.**

Scholem describes the Agnon of this period as an extraordinarily sensitive young man, for whom the German Jews were an

---

* Gershom G. Scholem, *From Berlin to Jerusalem: Memories of My Youth* (New York: Schocken Books, 1980), p. 91.

** Dan Miron, "German Jews in Agnon's Work," *Leo Baeck Institute Yearbook 23* (1978): 265–80.

endless source of fascination. From our vantage point of the present, it seems clear that the differences between eastern and western Jews allowed for a cross-cultural fertilization that enriched immeasurably the scholarship of Scholem and the fiction of Agnon. The stories that Agnon set in Germany give us some indication of the cultural mix of this period. Those that we have selected for the "Germany" section of this anthology provide a sampling of Agnon's range, from haunting evocations of medieval Jewish communities to quite modern psychological dramas of divorce and postwar devastation.

Scholem shows us Agnon as a young writer who appeared to inhabit an imaginative universe of his own making: "Every conversation with him quickly turned into one or more narratives, stories about great rabbis and simple Jews whose intonation he captured enchantingly. The same magic could be found even in his colorful but completely incorrect German."* Over the many years of their relationship, from Berlin to Jerusalem, Scholem and Agnon would engage in bouts of scholarly banter, each outdoing the other in producing bits of exotic lore from actual or invented sources. Thus Scholem tells us that Agnon persisted in claiming that "Agnon" could not be considered his real name, since it was only an invention, with no roots in the holy books. In a bit of scholarly play, Agnon claimed that the name "Czaczkes" could be found among the mystical names of angels in the Book of Raziel, an ancient Hebrew book of angelology.

In Scholem's eyes, Agnon appears as something of an aesthete, an Ostjude who enjoyed friendships with German intellectuals. The young writer found himself developing his art amid a linguistic mélange of Yiddish, Hebrew, German, and Russian and an array of ideologies from socialism to Zionism, Jewish mysticism, and Continental philosophy. Here we see also the Agnon who would frequent the Frankfurt dealers in secondhand Hebrew books, and indeed it was a shared interest in old Jewish books that brought Agnon together with the older German-Jewish businessman and bibliophile Salman Schocken. Agnon and Schocken first met toward the end of 1915, when both were attending philosophy lectures in Berlin. Schocken

---

* 10. Scholem, *From Berlin to Jerusalem*, pp. 92–93.

drew on Agnon's bibliographic knowledge, while Agnon benefited from Schocken's familiarity with German and European literature. This remarkable relationship has been documented through the recent Hebrew publication of the correspondence between the two men.*

The relationship took shape at a time when Agnon's status as an Austrian citizen subjected him to the possibility of induction into the German army. At one point, in 1916, Agnon sought to fail his physical examination by consuming quantities of pills and coffee, and smoking incessantly. Not only did he succeed in flunking the physical, he made himself quite sick and ended up spending four months in the Jewish hospital near the town of Brückenau. During this time, Salman Schocken kept Agnon supplied with reading materials. Providing us with evidence of the scope of his literary interests, Agnon writes to Schocken that he has read Zola's essay on Flaubert in one breath, not because it was so beautiful, but because it was on Flaubert and anything on Flaubert "goes straight to my heart." He goes on to ask Schocken to send him the medieval *Chanson de Roland*, along with Jakob Burckhardt's writings on the Renaissance.

The relationship between Agnon and Schocken grew in importance for both, as the older man commissioned the younger writer to search for Judaica and rare manuscripts. Indeed, part of the uniqueness of Agnon's position in modern Hebrew literature must be understood through his relationship with Salman Schocken and the Schocken publishing house. Schocken became aware early on of the writer's talents and supported his development with a yearly stipend and a commitment to publish his work, although Schocken had not yet opened his publishing company. The publication agreement that Agnon signed with Schocken allowed the writer to devote himself completely to his art. The mutually enriching interaction of the young writer and the older patron and collector of Judaica offers an opportunity to study the mingling of East European, German-Jewish, and Zionist elements in the early decades of this century.

In 1920 Agnon married Esther Marx, the daughter of a Ger-

---

*   *Shai Agnon—Sh. Z. Schocken: Hilufe Igarot* 1916–1959, Emuna Yaron, ed. (Tel Aviv: Schocken Publishing House Ltd., 1991).

man-Jewish family prominent in Jewish scholarship and Zionist activities. Together with his wife, Agnon established a home in Homburg. Esther gave birth to a son and a daughter during these years. (Agnon's daughter, Emuna Yaron, is responsible for the publication of a major portion of her father's work in the years since his death.) While living in Homburg, Agnon participated in Franz Rosenzweig's Lehrhaus, a center for adult Jewish studies. Rosenzweig, who had briefly contemplated conversion to Christianity, turned instead to an exploration of Jewish learning and committed himself to developing the Lehrhaus, a place for European Jewish intellectuals to seek a deeper understanding of Judaism. During these years, Agnon also collaborated with Martin Buber on a collection of hasidic stories that was never published. (A volume of stories of the founder of Hasidism, the Baal Shem Tov, that draws on that collaborative work was published posthumously in 1987.)* Agnon also spent a great deal of time with Hebrew writers such as the poet Hayim Nahman Bialik and the Zionist theorist Ahad Ha'am, as well as the publisher Y.H. Ravnitzky. Bialik and Ravnitzky had collaborated on the mammoth project *Sefer Ha-Aggadah* (The Book of Legends), an anthology of rabbinic lore.** Agnon thus encountered the full spectrum of Jewish life in Germany, from assimilationist trends to the search for a more authentic Judaism through study of classical texts. In retrospect, it is possible to discern the contribution of all these currents to his art.

At the same time, stark themes of loss and destruction find their roots in Agnon's experience during these years. In 1924, he suffered a devastating loss when his home in Homburg was destroyed in a fire that consumed all of his books, along with the manuscript of an unpublished autobiographical novel. This fire registered as one of the decisive losses in his life, and its impact can be felt throughout his work in themes of destruction and loss.

---

*   *Sippure Habesht*, Emuna and Hayyim Yaron, eds. (Tel Aviv: Schocken Publishing House Ltd., 1987).

** *The Book of Legends/Sefer Ha-Aggadah*, Hayim Nahman Bialik and Yehoshua Hana Ravnitzky, eds., trans. by William G. Braude (New York: Schocken Books, 1992).

Agnon moved back to Eretz Yisrael in 1924 and his family followed him soon after. His letters to his wife during this time express
his concern with establishing a home for his family, a concern that
appears to coincide with the decision to extend the name Agnon to
his personal as well as public life. Through his letters to his friend
and publisher, Salman Schocken, over an eight-month period, we
can follow the gradual shifts in his signature from Sh. Y. Czaczkes to simply Sh. Y. and finally to Sh. Y. Agnon. In the letters that
date from this time, Agnon expressed his pleasure at resuming his
walks through the Old City of Jerusalem and at the recognition he
received. Perhaps most important, he looked forward to Schocken's
publication of a complete edition of his works. It was in 1931 that
the first four volumes of *The Collected Works of S.Y. Agnon* appeared
in Hebrew, inaugurating Schocken Verlag, the publishing house in
Berlin. Cumulatively, the developments of these years may be considered to be something of an inauguration, heralded by the name shift
that extends the domain of Agnon to personal as well as professional
life, as if to assimilate the writer to his story.

Following his return to Eretz Yisrael, Agnon returned to Orthodox ways. We can surmise a consolidation in the identity of the writer:
he has arrived at a sense of himself. There are signs of this settling in
to be discerned in his mythologized account of his relationship to
the Land of Israel. During a series of conversations that were later
published, Agnon told the young writer David Canaani that God had
punished him with the loss of the home he established in Germany
because he had abandoned the Land of Israel.*

Agnon was to lose his home once again, and the historical resonance of this twice-repeated loss with the destruction of the Temple
was significant to him. The year 1929 saw widespread Arab uprisings
against Jewish settlement, and Agnon suffered yet again the loss of his
home and library, this time in Talpiyot. The story titled "The Sign,"
which can be found in the closing section of this anthology, conveys
the multiple significances of loss and rebuilding. After this second

---

* As cited in David Canaani, *Shai Agnon be'al-peh* (Israel: Hakibbutz Hameuchad,
1971).

destruction, he built a new house for his family in Talpiyot and this was where he lived to the end of his life. Today, the house is open to the public: visitors can stand in the writer's study and examine the titles on his shelves.

With the passing of years, Agnon became the writer of Jerusalem. A sign on his street in Talpiyot, Rehov Klausner, warned visitors to be quiet because of their proximity to a WRITER AT WORK. The city occupies the central place in the map of Agnon's imagination, as in Jewish tradition, however much his writing may play with ambiguities and paradoxes in the relation of the individual to sacred space. For Agnon, the establishment of a home in Talpiyot acquired significance in terms of the relationship of the neighborhood to the city of Jerusalem. From the roof of Agnon's Talpiyot home, one used to be able to see the Old City. The location expresses something of the identity of the artist, whose vision is sustained by Jerusalem and yet who situates himself just outside its gates.

The awarding of the Nobel Prize to Agnon was rightly taken by many, especially in Israel, as a belated recognition of the achievements of Hebrew literature and the legitimacy of Israeli culture. As a modern literature, Hebrew had been producing impressive writing for two hundred years; and, since the turn of the twentieth century, a series of great modern writers had emerged (Hayim Nahman Bialik, Yosef Hayim Brenner, Uri Zvi Greenberg, and Natan Alterman, among others) who in no way suffered in comparison to the best artists in European languages. Yet it took the annihilation of the very subject matter of Agnon's epic art—the social and spiritual life of East European Jewry—to prompt international recognition of Hebrew.

Two decades before the Holocaust destroyed the European centers of Jewish culture, the scene of Hebrew writing had already largely shifted to the new Jewish settlement in Palestine, and thereafter it became fused with the fortunes of the state of Israel. Agnon, who settled permanently in Palestine in the 1920s, should be counted in every sense as an Israeli writer, yet not a typical one. His use of traditional Jewish sources, his appropriation of traditional Jewish storytelling techniques, his preoccupation with East European themes—all these choices set him apart from most of Israeli writing at the time, which was realistic in mode and devoted to the depiction of the secular actualities of the new society.

Such is the uniqueness of Agnon. There is no figure in modern Jewish culture in any language whose work is as suffused with the texts and symbols of classical Jewish learning and as steeped in the customs of a thousand years of Jewish life in eastern Europe. Yet at the same time, the genius of Agnon's achievement was unleashed only by the rise of modern Hebrew literature. To be sure, European romanticism and modernism contributed to his work. But in order to understand where Agnon came from and to grasp the cultural matrix that made his writing unique, one must first turn to the specific conditions of time and place. The time was a particular moment in the emergence of the new Hebrew literature after the first challenges of modernity to Judaism had exhausted themselves. The place was the Jewish community of Galicia, the southeastern provinces of Poland that were ruled before World War I by Austria-Hungary.

The origins of modern Hebrew literature entailed a two-phased assault against traditional Jewish culture. In the first phase, which was called the Haskalah and took place between approximately 1780 and 1880, the ideals of the Enlightenment in western Europe were domesticated within the sphere of Hebrew literature and culture, first in Germany and then in eastern Europe. The social program of the Haskalah called for Jews to cease being merchants and shopkeepers and to enter more "productive" occupations. The educational program sought to introduce the study of arithmetic, world history, and western languages into the exclusively religious curriculum of Jewish schools. The religious program sought to rid Judaism of superstitious beliefs and practices and to emphasize the foundations of reason in the Jewish creed. The literary program sought to confer prestige on the classical lineage of Hebrew over Yiddish and opened Hebrew writing to the novel, the lyric poem, the essay, and other western genres. Yet despite these multiple challenges to traditional Judaism, the world view of the Haskalah remained essentially hopeful: divine reason remained the underpinning of a world that would progress from folly to enlightenment.

This optimism could not be sustained by the events that over-took Jewish life in eastern Europe in the late nineteenth century. The pauperization of the Jewish masses, the widespread pogroms of 1881, the virulent anti-Semitic policies of the tsarist regime—these and other related causes prompted Jews to take measures ranging from emigration to the West to the more ideological forms of political awareness embodied in socialism, communism, and Zionism. Zionism broke with the Haskalah over the possibility of the Jews' acceptance into European society in exchange for the modernization of their culture. The Jews could realize their national identity, Zionism argued, only in a land of their own and in a language of their own. Zionism broke with religious tradition by rejecting transcendental messianism in favor of a this-worldly politics of self-redemption.

Beneath the political and communal turmoil of these years, an even graver ordeal was being enacted in the spiritual lives of a generation of young people. For many, the coherent world of the Torah, within which the experience of the individual had been securely inscribed for the thousand years of Jewish settlement in the cities and hamlets of eastern Europe, broke down in the last decades of the nineteenth century. The daily intimacy with holy texts, the deep texture of study and interpretation, the rhythm of sacred and profane time, the dense patterning of ritual gestures and symbols, the assured authority of teachers and sages—all these strands in the weave of tradition loosened in the course of a single generation. For some young people, the rejection of the religious tradition was the dialectical by-product of a principled espousal of a new faith in one of the revolutionary ideologies of the age. For others, the failure of Judaism had less to do with the adoption of new secular faiths than with a process of internal decline. In the face of modernity, the very plausibility of the religious tradition had suddenly collapsed, its authority neutralized and its relevance rendered mute. The world of the Torah had ceased to speak to them.

The crisis of these young people is one of the major themes of Hebrew literature at the turn of the century. The enormity of their loss was experienced on several levels. For the characters in the fictional world of Mordecai Ze'ev Feierberg, for example, the collapse of the tradition is experienced as nothing less than a catastrophe; in the sudden absence of the tradition that had both oppressed and nurtured them, they feel orphaned and hollowed out. For the characters in the fiction of Y.H. Brenner and U.N. Gnessin, the loss of faith is taken for granted as an inevitable rite of passage; the source of their suffering is the ensuing void with its coils of self-consciousness and its temptations to bad faith. For the fictional figures of M.Y. Berdichevsky, the void is invaded by the humiliations of erotic obsession. Taken together, these characters and their creators are members of a generation that was born too late for religious tradition to remain intact and too early for the new order of Jewish national life to delineate itself.

To be sure, the force of experience engendered extraordinary aesthetic gains. The depiction of life in the immediate aftermath of faith in all its existential extremity led these writers to abandon the decorative language and convention-bound techniques of their Haskalah predecessors and to fashion a Hebrew prose far more capable of representing the complexities of modern consciousness and experience. Yet for all these achievements, the loss of the past remained enormous. Thousands of years of Jewish cultural creativity had been rendered irrelevant, compromised, contaminated, and utterly unavailable to the reconstruction of the fractured modern Jewish mind.

Against this background, the significance of the precise moment at which Agnon entered the scene of modern Hebrew literature comes into view. Born in 1888, Agnon began publishing in Hebrew and Yiddish periodicals while still a teenager. Though not much younger than the other Hebrew writers just mentioned (he was twenty-three years younger than Berdichevsky and only seven years younger than Brenner), this was a sufficient interval in these revolutionary times to make a difference. The small-mindedness and intolerance of the insular Jewish society of the shtetl, the brutalizing medievalism of the heder, the repressive and superstitious religion of the fathers, the self-deluded rationalism of the Enlighteners—all the abuses of the old order had already been systematically laid out; the burden of critique had been discharged. For the majority of Hebrew writers, this settled the score with the past and enabled Hebrew writing to proceed to engage the troubling and hopeful realities of the twentieth century. For Agnon's genius, it had the effect of clearing a path to the past and making possible an ambitious examination of the present through the reappropriation of classical Jewish culture.

The area of Galicia in which Buczacz lay was part of the kingdom of Poland until Poland's partition in 1772; from that time until World War I, Galicia was an eastern province of the Austro-Hungarian Empire. That the great majority of Polish Jewry to the north came under the rule of the Russian tsars while Galicia was governed by the Hapsburgs is a fact of paramount importance. While life under the Hapsburgs was not easy for the Jews, it compared favorably to the grinding poverty and official anti-Semitism of the tsarist government. The Jews of Galicia were spared the kind of pogroms that were visited upon Russian Jewry in 1881 and 1903–5. The Austro-Hungarian administration was also less autocratic than the Russian imperial regime; on the provincial level, socialist and republican movements were allowed to play a role in local politics. When it came to language and culture, Galicia was particularly polyglot. The Jews spoke Yiddish and read Hebrew, the landowners Polish, the peasants Ukrainian, the government German. German was the language of culture, and many Jewish women, even from religious families—Agnon's mother included—read modern German literature.

In Jewish culture, Galicia had been the scene of great controversies. Earlier in the nineteenth century it had been a center of westernization and a home to such Haskalah writers as Nachman Krochmal, Yosef Perl, Yitzhak Erter, and S.Y. Rapoport; some of the fiercest battles between the Hasidim and their opponents took place here. But by the end of the century, when Agnon was growing up, these conflicts had been domesticated into a diverse and tolerant religious culture. Galicia lacked the great yeshivot (the talmudic academies) of Lithuania to the north in which young minds were either inducted into the rigors of rabbinic erudition or provoked by rabbinic authority into rebellion against the world of tradition. Galicia also proved fertile ground for the Zionist ideal. Even before Theodor Herzl created a mass movement, Buczacz boasted several proto-Zionist organizations and the Zionist cause enjoyed much support among the middle-class religious families of the city. Agnon's departure, at the age of nineteen, to settle in Palestine can be understood at one and the same time as fulfilling a widely held ideal and leaving behind his provincial origins through a sanctioned escape route.

Agnon did escape. He turned first to the heady milieu of young pioneers and cosmopolitan émigrés in Jaffa and then to Germany, where he gained intimate knowledge of the streams of modern European culture. Agnon never experienced the extremes of negation that characterized the spiritual world of his Russian counterparts. He was a modern man whose modernity could not be expunged, but the world of classical Jewish culture, in all its dimensions and manifestations, remained for him animated and animating in a way it did not for other modern Jewish writers in Hebrew or in any other language. Agnon's relationship to that heritage had little to do with nostalgia, and he was expert at dissecting the ways in which a man might use religion for self-serving purposes. For Agnon, the past exists for the sake of the present, and its stories and symbols exist for the sake of what they offer to the construction of a fuller Jewish self-understanding in the modern world.

New York, 1995
Alan Mintz
Anne Golomb Hoffman

The Signature Story

Our anthology opens with "Agunot," Agnon's first publication in the Land of Israel and the story whose title he adapted to form his own name. "Agunot" marks the artistic birth of the writer and shapes his unique relationship to the traditional Jewish world. The title "Agunot," derived from *agunah*, the legal term for a woman whose status in the community is indeterminate, highlights themes of disconnection and lack of wholeness. These themes enter indirectly into the story's account of souls who are set adrift and unable to find their anchors. The narrative is prefaced by an exquisite passage that draws on the imagery of the Song of Songs to depict the close relationship of God to Israel. We might almost think we were reading a classical midrash—a rabbinical expansion on the biblical text. Indeed the story opens with the traditional phrase "It is said," an expression used by the rabbis to introduce a quotation from Scripture. But rather than a biblical citation, "Agunot" crafts its own combination of images drawn from rabbinic commentary and mystical writings. This opening paragraph engages in an intricate piece of interpretive play, what we might call, following the critic Gershon Shaked, a pseudomidrash.

Endowing the relationship of God to Israel with a sense of radiant wholeness, the opening passage traces for the reader the tender desire with which God weaves a prayer shawl for Israel. The image of the prayer shawl portrays the interwoven relationship between God and Israel as an intimacy that is disrupted by the introduction of a "flaw" in the weave, a defect that appears to be the product of human error or frailty. This notion of the prayer shawl as a fabric woven out of many strands is a suggestive one: it can be taken further to suggest an emblematic image of Agnon's writing as a weaving out of many sources.

The image of the flawed prayer shawl and the loss of wholeness in the relationship of God to Israel provide a backdrop against which the kinds of loss that the story depicts can be measured. Thus we find in "Agunot" lovers who are mismatched or who undergo separation. We see the imbalance and disconnection that are the result of the excessive attachment of an artist to the holy ark he crafts, a woman's jealousy of the artist's commitment, and several pairs of mismatched lovers.

Desire figures prominently as a driving force in "Agunot," but the aims and objects of desire are quite varied. They include certainly the desire of one person for another, but the story also demonstrates the rivalrous desires for glory in Torah learning felt by Jews in the Diaspora and those in the Land of Israel, as well as the desire of the artist to complete the perfect work. Nowhere do these desires find fulfillment. And so desire itself becomes a subject of the writing in this delicately wrought tale of attraction, investment, and frustration. Agnon returned to "Agunot" over the years, revising it in 1921 and again in 1931, each time rendering it a more concise and highly crafted text. The story that we have before us, rewritten twice over, weaves elements of hasidic storytelling and European romanticism into a narrative mode that is uniquely Agnon's.

Agunot

It is said: A thread of grace is spun and drawn out of the deeds of Israel, and the Holy One, blessed be He, Himself, in His glory, sits and weaves—strand on strand—a tallit all grace and all mercy, for the Congregation of Israel to deck herself in. Radiant in the light of her beauty she glows, even in these, the lands of her exile, as she did in her youth in her Father's house, in the Temple of her Sovereign and the city of sovereignty, Jerusalem. And when He, of ineffable Name, sees her, that she has been neither sullied nor stained even here, in the realm of her oppressors, He—as it were—leans toward her and says, "Behold thou art fair, my beloved, behold thou art fair." And this is the secret of the power and the glory and the exaltation and the tenderness in love which fills the heart of every man in Israel. But there are times—alas!—when some hindrance creeps up and snaps a thread in the loom. Then the tallit is damaged: evil spirits hover about it, enter into it, and tear it to shreds. At once a sense of shame assails all Israel, and they know they are naked. Their days of rest are wrested from them, their feasts are fasts, their lot is dust instead of luster. At that hour the Congregation of Israel stays abroad in her anguish, crying, "Strike me, wound me, take away my veils from me!" Her beloved has slipped away, and she, seeking him, cries, "If ye find my beloved, what shall ye tell him? That I am afflicted with love." And this affliction of love leads to darkest melancholy, which persists—Mercy shield us!—until, from the heavens above, He breathes down upon us strength of spirit, to repent and to muster deeds that are pride to their doers and again draw forth that thread of grace and love before the Lord.

And this is the theme of the tale recounted here, a great tale and terrible, from the Holy Land, of one renowned for his riches—Sire Ahiezer by name—who set his heart on going up from the Diaspora to the holy city Jerusalem—may she be rebuilt and established—to work great wonders of restoration in the midst of her ruins, and in this way to restore at least a corner of the anteroom which will be transformed into our mansion of glory on the day when the Holy One, blessed be He, restores His presence to Zion—may it be soon, in our day!

And credit him kindly, Lord—credit him well for his wishes, and for his ministrations to his brethren, sons of his people, who dwell before Thee in the Land of the Living, and this though he ultimately failed.

Sire Ahiezer fathered no sons, but he praised the Ineffable sevenfold daily for the daughter who fell to his lot. He cherished her like the apple of his eye, and set maidservants and tirewomen to wait on her, that her very least wish might be honored. And, surely, she was worthy of all this respect, for she was the pattern of virtue, and all the graces were joined together in her person: princely the radiance of her countenance; like the matriarchs' her straitness of virtue; her voice pleasing as the harp of David; and all her ways modest and gentle. But all this pride was inward, and dwelt apart, in the innermost chambers, so that only the intimates of her father's house might behold her, at twilight, when, at times, she went down to walk in the garden, among the spice trees and the roses, where the doves fluttered about her in the twilight, murmuring their fondness in her ears and shielding her with their wings, like the golden cherubs on the ark of the sanctuary.

And when her season came, the season of love, her father sent couriers to all the dispersions of Israel, to spy out a youth that would be her match, such a paragon, a cluster of virtue, as had no peer in all the world. Here it was that the evil one intervened, and not in vain were the words bruited about, by the men of Jerusalem, to the effect that Sire Ahiezer had slighted all the seminaries and academies, all the seats of learning in the Land of Israel when he sent to find a match for his daughter among the sons of the exile abroad. But who might admonish so mighty a man—who might tender him counsel? They all began eagerly to await the match that the Holy One, blessed be He, would provide for this cloistered grace, glorious child, vaunted daughter of Jerusalem.

And then, months having passed, a scroll was received from the emissaries, declaring: "We hereby proclaim with joy: with the aid of the Lord we have found in Poland a boy, a wondrous lad, in virtue clad, with wisdom blest, head and shoulders above all the rest; pious, modest, pedigreed; model of virtue and good deed; paragon and worthy son, wreathed in blessings from the sages, who bless this match with all their hearts and wages." And so forth.

The grandee, Sire Ahiezer, seeing his designs were prospering, thought it only fitting that the above-mentioned bridegroom hold forth at a great academy in Jerusalem, that scholars might stream from the ends of the earth to hear the law from his lips. What did he do? He convened all manner of craftsmen, built a great mansion, adorned it inside and out—painted it and gilded it and furnished it with several cartloads of precious texts, no jot of godly wisdom lacking among them. And he designated a hall for prayer, adorned it with all manner of adornment, and called on the scribes to prepare the scrolls of the law, and on the gold- and silversmiths to design the ornaments of the scrolls—and all of this in order that the prayers of the sage might be neighbor to his studies, so that he might truthfully say, "Here is my God, and I will praise Him." The grandee, wishing to consummate his work of glorifying the sanctuary, set his heart on an ark for the scrolls—an ark such as the eye of man had never seen.

He began to ask after a proper craftsman. Among the journey-men he came on one said to be versed in the subtlest of crafts, one

Ben Uri by name—a man both modest and diffident, a mere craftsman as met the eye were it not for the spark that flashed from his
glance and was reflected in the work of his hand. Ahiezer took note,
and placed the work of the ark in his hand.

2

Sire Ahiezer took Ben Uri and lodged him by the garden at the bottom
of his house. Ben Uri brought his tools and readied himself for the
task. Immediately, another spirit possessed him. His hands wrought
the ark; his lips uttered song all the day.

Dinah, lovely child of Ahiezer, stood by her window, gazing
into the trees, and heard. Dreaming, she was drawn to the singer as
though—God save us!—a spell had been cast. So she went down,
she and her handmaidens with her went down, to examine the work
of the man. She peered into the ark, she stirred his paints, examined
his carvings, and picked up his tools. All the time Ben Uri worked,
singing as he worked, working even as he sang. Dinah heard his song
and did not know her heart. And he, even as he wrought, all the
time aimed his song at her heart, to wrap it in his rapture, so that
she might stand there forever, never depart.

But as Ben Uri pursued his work, he cleaved more and more
to it, until both eyes and heart passed into the ark; no part of him
was free of it. Memory of Dinah fled him; it was as though she did
not exist. Not many days passed before he stopped singing altogether;
his voice rang out no more. Ben Uri stood by the ark all day, carving figures on the ark and breathing the soul of life into them. Lions
mounted upon it, a mane of gold on each of the pair, their mouths
brimming with song, uttering the glories of the Lord. On the hang-
ings that draped the doors of the ark, eagles poised above, their wings
spread, to leap toward the sacred beasts above. At the sound of the
golden bells when the ark was opened, they would soar in their places,
flap their wings, and wrap the universe in song. Already the worthies
of Jerusalem awaited the day the ark would be borne up to the house
of the Lord the hand of the grandee had builded, when the scrolls of

the law, crowned with silver and lapped in gold and decked out in all the jewels of sanctity, would find their place within this ark.

Rapt, Ben Uri wrought, possessed by a joy he had never known before. In no kingdom, in no province, in the course of no labor had he exulted as he exulted here, in the place where the Shekhinah was revealed and then reviled, in the multitude of our transgressions. Not many days passed before his labors were ended. Ben Uri looked at the work of his hands and was astonished how the ark stood firm while he himself was like an empty vessel. His soul was sad and he broke out in tears.

Ben Uri went out to seek the air among the trees in the garden, to restore his spirits a little. The sun set in the west; the face of the heavens crimsoned. Ben Uri went down to the far corners of the garden, he laid himself down, and he slept. At just that moment Dinah left her chamber. Her robe clung to her flesh; fear was on her countenance. It was many days since she had heard Ben Uri's voice, since she had looked on the man. She went to his chamber to look at the ark. She came, but did not find him there. Dinah stood in Ben Uri's chamber, and the ark of God stood at the open window, where Ben Uri had worked. She stood near the ark and examined it. The evil one came and poured a potion of vengeance into her heart. He pointed at the ark and said, "It is not for nought that Ben Uri takes no thought of you; it is the ark that separates you twain." At that moment Dinah lifted her arms and smote the ark. The ark teetered and fell through the open window.

The ark fell, but no part of it was broken, no corner of it was blemished. It lay there among the trees in the garden below. Roses and lilies nodded over it, like mourners at the ark of the dead. Night drew a mantle of black silk over the ark. The moon came out of the clouds and, weaving its silvery web, traced a Star of David on the shroud.

3

On her couch in the night Dinah lies and her heart wakes. Her sin weighs heavily upon her: who could bear her burden of guilt? Dinah buries her head in her pallet, oppressed by sorrow, by shame. How can she look to Heaven, how call to it for grace? Dinah springs from her couch and lights the taper in her room. In the mirror opposite, light flares out in her eyes. It had been her mother's glass but held no trace of her mother's glance. Were Dinah to look into it now, it is only her own countenance she would see—the countenance of a sinner. "Mother, Mother!" her heart cries out. But there is no answer. Dinah rose and crossed to the window; she rested her chin on her hands and looked out. Jerusalem is cradled in mountains. The wind swept down and entered her chamber, extinguishing the light, as in a sickroom where some invalid sleeps. It played around her hair and through her ears, whispering sweet melodies, like the songs Ben Uri had sung. Where, oh where, is he now?

Among the trees in the garden he sleeps, like a lyre whose strings are rent, whose melodies have forsaken it. And the ark lies prone, in the garden. The Guardian of Night unfurls his pinions of darkness, and the lions and eagles in the ark nestle under his wings. An unspotted moon slips out of the clouds; another moon rises to meet her in the waters of the pond. They stand, face to face, like a pair of Sabbath candles. To what might the ark have been compared at that moment? To a woman who extends her palms in prayer, while her breasts—the Tables of the Covenant—are lifted with her heart, beseeching her Father in heaven: "Master of the Universe, this soul which Thou hast breathed into him Thou hast taken from him, so that now he is cast before Thee, like a body without its soul, and Dinah, this unspotted soul, has gone forth naked into exile. God! Till when shall the souls that dwell in Thy kingdom suffer the death of this life, in bereavement, and the service of Thy habitation sound out in suffering and dread?"

All Israel that was in Jerusalem had foregathered to consecrate the ark, to bear it up from Ben Uri's chamber to the synagogue. They thronged into Ben Uri's chamber, but the ark was not there. Bewildered, they cried, "Where is the ark?—the ark of the Lord?" "Where is the ark?" "The ark, where is it?" They were still crying out when they spied it, under the window, prone in the yard. Directly they began to heap abuse on its creator, saying that the ne'er-do-well, the scoundrel was surely an infamous sinner, quite unqualified for the hallowed work of the ark: having presumed to undertake it, he had surely called down the wrath of the heavens, which had overturned it. And, having revered the ark, they loathed it. The rabbi immediately condemned it to banishment. Two Ishmaelites came and heaved it into the lumber room. The congregation dispersed in torment, their heads covered with shame.

The morning star glimmered and dawned, lighting the skies in the east. The folk of Jerusalem awoke as from an evil dream. The ark had been banished, their joy had set, Ben Uri had vanished, none knew whither. Misery reigned in the house of the Sire.

Night and day Dinah keeps to her window. She raises her eyes to the heavens and casts them down again, like a sinner. Sire Ahiezer is dogged by worries. The synagogue his hands had builded stands desolate, without ark, without prayer, without learning. Sire Ahiezer bestirred himself and commissioned an ark to replace Ben Uri's. They installed it in the synagogue, but it stood there like an emblem of loss. Whoever comes to pray in the synagogue is at once struck by dire melancholy; he slips away from that place and seeks some place of worship, humble and poor, where he can pour out his heart before God.

4

The time of rejoicing is come; the wedding day is near, and in the house of Sire Ahiezer they knead and they bake and they dress all the viands, and prepare fine draperies to hang in the gateway, for the day his daughter will enter under the bridal canopy with her partner in joy, the esteemed and the learned Ezekiel, God preserve him.

And—see!—upon the hillsides the feet of a courier—a special emissary with scroll in hand: "'Twill be the third day hence!" They were preparing themselves to delight in the bride and the bridegroom on the day of their joy, saying, "A precious pearl it is the couriers have drawn from the sea of learning that is Poland, and the festivities will be such that as Jerusalem shall not have seen the likes of, since the day her sons were driven into exile." All the men of Jerusalem went forth to welcome the bridegroom, and they brought him into the city in great honor, with tabor and cymbal and dancing. They escorted him to the house of Sire Ahiezer, and the great ones of the city, assessing his virtues, were dazzled by a tongue dropping pearls, and by his regal presence. Then the wedding day arrived. They accompanied the bride to the house of the rabbi, to receive her blessing from his lips. Suddenly, she raised her voice in weeping and cried, "Leave us alone!" They left her with the rabbi. She told him all that had happened, how it was she who had overturned the ark. The rabbi stood mute with terror, his very vision was confounded. But, deferring to the eminence of the bride on this, her day of grace and atonement, he began to ply her with comfort. "My child," he said, "our sages of blessed memory tell us that when a person takes a wife to himself, all his sins fall away. Notice that it was 'person' they said, not 'man,' and thence we gather that it was not man, the male, that was meant, but mankind in general, so that man and wife are one in this, that on the day of their marriage the Holy One, blessed be He, pardons their sins. And should you ask, How is a woman to earn her absolution, on whom the yoke of works weighs so lightly?—know that the good Lord has called you to the greatest of all works. And should you ask, What could that be? I will tell you: it is the rearing of children in the ways of the Lord." And he proceeded to speak the praises of her bridegroom, to endear him to her and draw her heart to his virtues. And when the rabbi came to the matter of the ark, he intimated that silence would be seemly and held that the ark would be restored to its rightful place, to the synagogue, and that merciful God would grant Dinah forgiveness. After the bride had left the house of the rabbi, the latter sent Sire Ahiezer word regarding the restoration of Ben Uri's ark to the synagogue. They sought it, but did not find it. Stolen? Hidden? Ascended to heaven?—who could presume to say?

Day ebbed and the sun set. All the great ones of Jerusalem foregathered with Sire Ahiezer in his house to celebrate his daughter's marriage. Jerusalem glowed in precious light, and the trees in the garden were fragrant as spices. The musicians plied their instruments, and the servants clapped for good cheer. Yet nonetheless a sort of sadness has found a place among them. This sadness attacks the bridal canopy and rips it into shreds. They assemble at the grandee's table, to partake of the wedding feast. The throats of the scholars are filled with delicate viands and wines, with song and hymns of praise. The jester calls for a dance for the righteous, and they move out in a ritual ring to cheer the bride and the groom. But this dear pair are afflicted by some sadness; it drives a wedge between them and forces their elbows apart. And neither drew near to the other all that night, even in the seclusion of their chamber. The groom broods in one corner, his thoughts straying elsewhere. He dwells on his father's house, on Freidele, whose mother had tended his father and him since his sainted mother had died. And Dinah broods in the other, her thoughts going back to the ark and its builder who has vanished from the city, no one knowing where he has turned.

At morning prayers the young man stood wrapped in a prayer shawl and crowned with tefillin. He reigns as bridegroom all the seven days of the feast, and is not left alone, lest envious spirits assail him. But how to ward off the spirits that hold sway in his heart and afflict him greatly? Just when he is preparing to give himself over, heart and soul, to the Shema and shields his eyes with his palms in order to shut out anything that might intrude on his devotions—just then his Freidele slips into the palm of his hand and stands there before his eyes. And once she has accommodated herself there, she stays there till the end of the service, when he unwinds his phylacteries and lays them in their reticule. This reticule—Freidele has made for him with characters embroidered upon it! He folds the reticule, and wraps it in his tallit, and furtively puts it away. His father, come from Poland for the nuptials, watches him, angry and troubled. What might he be wanting in the house of Sire Ahiezer? If wealth he craved, here was wealth, so prodigal; if love of woman, his wife was comely and gracious; if a home, this one was fit for a king. Why, then, was he restless? They went in to breakfast, and chanted the seven blessings of nuptial felicity, and seated the couple side by side. Their bodies are close, but their hearts have been given to others.

5

And they never drew near. Month comes and month goes. In numbers the scholars assembled, to attend the law from Ezekiel's lips, and the academy was filled with holy lore. Gracious learning was on his tongue, and whatever his mode of expounding—simple or subtle or mystic—bright angels gathered around him, shedding the light of the law on his brow. But even as he teaches, anguish gnaws at his heart, as though—God forbid!—he lacks gratitude for having been deemed worthy to go up to the Holy Land.

And Dinah—Dinah sits, despondent. At times she goes out for a while, and stands by the spot where Ben Uri had wrought, and stares at his implements, which are gathering dust. She clasps her hands and murmurs some few of the songs Ben Uri had sung, sings until her eyes are dimmed by tears. Her soul weeps in secret for her pride. Once, as Rabbi Ezekiel was passing by, he heard a pleasing melody rising within that chamber. When he paused to listen, they told him that it was no mortal voice he heard singing, but rather the evil spirits that had been created out of Ben Uri's breath as he sat and sang at his work. Rabbi Ezekiel hastened away. Thenceforth, when forced to walk in that part of the house, he averted his head, in order to avoid lending his ears to the chants of such as these.

Toward evening, Rabbi Ezekiel goes to walk in the hills. The mighty ones of Israel walk out at that hour, and their retainers go before them, striking the earth with their staffs, and all the people hasten to rise in awe and deference before them, and the sun casts purple canopies over each of the righteous as it goes down to greet its Creator. The elect, who are deemed worthy of this, are granted the privilege of finding their place in the Holy Land in their lifetime, and not only this, but those deemed worthy of dwelling there in their lifetime are privileged to enjoy the Holy Spirit forever and ever. But Rabbi Ezekiel? His feet are planted in the gates of Jerusalem and stand on her soil, but his eyes and his heart are pledged to houses of study and worship abroad, and even now, as he walked in the hills of Jerusalem, he fancies himself among the scholars of his own town, strolling in the fields to take the evening air.

It is told once they found there Freidele sitting with her friends, singing:

They have borne him far away
To wed a dowered maiden.
His father did not care to know
Our hearts were heavy laden.

One day an emissary of the rabbis returned to Jerusalem from the Diaspora and brought a letter for Rabbi Ezekiel. His father was pleased to inform him that he had negotiated the home journey in safety and now, as ever before, was bearing up under the burdens of justice and learning in their town. In passing, he thought his son might care to know that Freidele had found her mate and had moved—together with her mother—to another city, so that the sexton's wife was therefore looking after his needs. Rabbi Ezekiel read the letter and began to weep. Here was Freidele, decently wedded, and here was he, fancying her still. And his own wife? When they pass each other she stares off in one direction, he in another.

Month comes, month goes, and the academy grows ever more desolate. The scholars, one by one, steal away. They cut a staff from some tree in the garden, take it in hand, and set off on their separate ways. It is obvious for all to see—Heaven help us!—that Rabbi Ezekiel's soul is tainted. Sire Ahiezer perceived that his works had not prospered, that the couple was ill-matched, that the marriage, in fact, was no marriage at all.

The couple stand silent before the rabbi, their eyes downcast. Rabbi Ezekiel is about to divorce his wife. And just as he did not look at her at the hour of their marriage, so he does not look at her in the hour of their parting. And just as Dinah did not hear his voice as he said to her, "Lo, thou art sanctified unto me," so she does not hear it as he says, "Lo, I cast thee forth." Our sages of blessed memory said that when a man puts his first wife away from him, the very altars weep, but here the altars had dropped tears even as he took her to wife. It was not long that Sire Ahiezer left Jerusalem with his daughter. He had failed in his settlement there; his wishes had not prospered.

He went forth in shame, his spirit heavy within him. His house was deserted, the house of study stood desolate. And the quorum that had gathered in the synagogue to honor Sire Ahiezer so long as he was there, now did not assemble there for even the first round of afternoon prayers on the day of his departure.

6

That very night, after the departure, the rabbi, seated at study, nodded over his Talmud. In a dream he saw that he would suffer exile. Next morning, following the counsel of our sages, he put the best possible interpretation on his dream, and fasted all day. After he had tasted a morsel and returned to his study, he heard a voice. He raised his eyes and saw the Shekhinah in the guise of a lovely woman, garbed in black, and without adornment, nodding mournfully at him. The rabbi started out of his sleep, rent his garments, again made good his dream, and sat fasting for a day and a night, and in the dark of the following evening inquired as to the signification of his dream. Providence disclosed to him a number of things concealed from mortal sight, and he beheld with eyes of spirit the souls of those bereaved of their beloved in their lifetime groping dismally in the world for their mates. He peered hard and saw Ben Uri. Ben Uri said to him, "Wherefore hast thou driven me out, that I should not cleave to my portion of the Kingdom?" "Is it thy voice I hear, Ben Uri, my son?" the rabbi cried, and he lifted his voice and he wept. Weeping, the rabbi woke out of his sleep and knew that his doom had been sealed. He washed his hands, drew on his mantle, took up his staff and his wallet, and, calling to his wife, said, "My daughter, seek not after me in my going forth, for the doom of exile has been levied upon me, to redeem the forsaken in love." He kissed the mezuzah and slipped away. They sought him, and did not find him.

They say he wanders still. Once an aged emissary from the Holy Land stopped at a house of study in the Diaspora. One night he nodded at his devotions, and in his sleep he heard a voice. He awoke and saw that selfsame rabbi holding a youth by the hem of his robe and trying to draw him away. Frightened, the emissary cried out, "Rabbi, are you here?" The rabbi vanished. The youth then confided to the emissary that when the house of study was emptied of its worshippers, he had begun to fashion an ornament for the easterly wall of the synagogue, and the emissary had borne witness to the loveliness of that ornament and to the craft with which it was fashioned. But as soon as he had begun, that old man had stood at his side, drawn him by the hem of his robe, and whispered, "Come, let us rise and go up to Jerusalem."

Since that time innumerable tales have been told of that rabbi and of his sojourning in the "world of confusion," Mercy shield us! Rabbi Nissim, of blessed memory, who traveled about in the world for many years, used to say, "May I forfeit my portion in the redemption of Israel, if I did not behold him once floating off into the Great Sea on a red kerchief, with an infant child in his arms. And even though the hour was twilight, and the sun was setting, I swear by all that we yearn for in prayer that it was he, but as for that child—I do not know who that was."

At the present time it is said that he has been seen wandering about in the Holy Land. The world-wise cavil and quibble, and even—some of them—mock. But little children insist that at times, in the twilight, an old man hails them, and peering into their eyes drifts into the gathering dusk. And whoever has heard the tale here recounted surely knows that the man is that rabbi, he, and no other. But God alone knows for a fact.

Translated by Baruch Hochman

Tales of Childhood

Agnon wrote a series of extraordinary autobiographical childhood stories. In addition to the two stories contained in this section, examples include "The Story of My Prayer Book," "My Grandfather's Talmud," and "My Bird." These are not children's stories, but rather stories about childhood written for adults. The strength of these fictions derives precisely from this double axis. On the one hand, the stories are told through the child's perception of the world, with all its disarming simplicity and disposition to wonder and delight. On the other, the symbols and allusions invoked in the stories point in the direction of weightier matters of the sort that trouble adult minds.

These are tales of initiation, and the two included here, "The Kerchief" and "Two Pairs," deal with the moment that epitomizes the passage from childhood to adulthood in the Jewish life cycle: the bar mitzvah. Yet readers will find in Agnon's stories little that reminds us of the lavish celebrations common to America. In the pious society of Eastern Europe, the bar mitzvah was less an occasion for festivity than a solemn marking of the boy's arrival at the adult responsibilities and prerogatives entailed in full observance of the commandments.

Agnon does something special in his fiction with the bar mitzvah that is a sign of his modernity. While the spiritual seriousness of the moment is taken for granted, the emphasis is shifted from the initiation into ritual obligation to the psychological and existential experience of leaving childhood behind and encountering the unredeemed reality of the world.

"The Kerchief" is Agnon's bar-mitzvah story *par excellence*. It was originally written on the occasion of the thirteenth birthday of Gershom Schocken, the son of Agnon's patron Salman Schocken. The story contains thirteen sections, and the first presentation edition was printed in thirteen copies with thirteen lines to the page.

"The Kerchief" indeed celebrates the successful transition from childhood to adulthood, yet at the same time the story makes it clear that the safe negotiation of the passage can by no means be taken for granted. The story operates along two thematic tracks that come together in the climactic scene. One track reflects the idealization of the Jewish family as symbolized by the gifts brought back by the father from the trade fair. The kerchief given to the mother, which she wears only on Sabbaths and holidays, represents the sanctity of the family felt in a heightened way on these special days. It is this structure of wholeness and integrity anchored in the tradition that gives the narrator a sense of being that cannot be effaced in later life.

The other track is linked to loss and the unredeemed state of the world. The time the father is away at the fair is likened to the days of semi-mourning preceding the Ninth of Av, the fast day that commemorates the destruction of the Jerusalem Temples (and which also happens to be the date Agnon took as his birthday). The Messiah, who will restore this loss, is the subject of the boy's nighttime fantasies as he lies in his father's bed during his absence. In the boy's imagination, the messianic era is grasped as a time when his father will no longer travel away from home and children like him will be freed from school to play in the Temple courtyards. The Messiah himself is imagined, according to talmudic legend, as disguised among the company of repulsive beggars. Though they be reviled and abused by most, the narrator imagines himself honoring and revering the beggars, "since among them were those who had dwelt together with the Messiah."

When the narrator encounters a real beggar on the day of his bar mitzvah, there is nothing redemptive about the sad and disgusting creature who stands before him. The man has been spurned by the townsfolk in violation of the high Jewish precepts of charity and hospitality. It is a marker of the boy's innocence that—until this point—he cannot recognize this hypocrisy; he resists admitting the existence of a reality that does not comport with his conviction of the holiness of the community in which he lives. Yet alone, face to face with the beggar, the boy meets the challenge presented to him: he loosens the precious silk kerchief that his mother had tied around his neck that day and hands it to the beggar, who winds it around his running sores.

The handing over of the kerchief does not mean the narrator rejects the family sanctity it symbolizes. The loving gaze of the mother upon his return home bare-necked only redoubles the sense that he has acted upon rather than betrayed the values of his family. What the boy has managed to do on this day of his coming of age is to acknowledge the existence of suffering and evil in the world and to accept some responsibility toward it. His gesture brings with it no dramatic transformation, but the act is real in a way entirely at odds with his childlike reveries of messianic deliverance.

The themes of family and unredemption are fused in the Hebrew text by the word *bayit*. *Bayit* means "home," "house," as well as the family that dwells in it; *bayit* also refers to the Jerusalem Temples, which served, while they stood, as the earthly seat of God's dwelling among the people of Israel. With the loss of the national home for the spirit, the family becomes the custodian of the spirit and the workshop within which individuals are prepared for engaging in the unfinished work of redemption.

The acceptance of loss achieved by the narrator of "The Kerchief" on the day of his bar mitzvah is not attained by the narrator of the next story, "Two Pairs," until much later in life. Both are bar mitzvah stories, and both feature an autobiographical narrator, but in "Two Pairs" it is the weight of retrospective wisdom that is most acutely felt. The adult narrator recalls the pair of tefillin written by a famous scribe that was given to him on his bar mitzvah and which was destroyed much later in the fire that consumed the narrator's home. He reconciles himself to the newly written pair he has to purchase as he tells the story of the beloved first pair and its meaning to him.

Tefillin, or phylacteries, are a pair of small black boxes with leather straps; one box is wound around the arm and the other placed on the forehead. They contain pieces of parchment on which verses from the Bible are written in calligraphy by a scribe. The origin of this practice lies in the interpretation of Deuteronomy 11, which is quoted in the story: "Bind them [the words of the Torah] as a sign on your arm and let them be a band between your eyes." In its original meaning, the verse was probably a figurative exhortation to be ever mindful of the words of the Torah. The rabbis gave a hyper-literal interpretation to the verse and took the signs to be bound on the arm and head as actual inscriptions to be contained in boxes and held in place with black straps. (Tefillin also play a crucial role in the story "Pisces" in this volume.) Tefillin and the tallit—the fringed prayer shawl—are worn in prayer only by adult males, and together they represent the most visible signs of the commandments acceded to by a boy at the time of his bar mitzvah.

In "Two Pairs," the tefillin as a symbol function on two very different dimensions. On one level, they serve as a naive religious fetish. The narrator is deeply attached to his tefillin and proud to own them; he loves to touch them and feels comforted by wearing them in times of trouble. On a deeper level, however, the tefillin are associated with the rabbi Elimelech, the scribe who had written them in an earlier age of spiritual plenitude. Like the kerchief, Elimelech's tefillin are associated with the wholeness of the family because of the scribe's power. Like the kerchief, which is never soiled, so the script inside the tefillin remains unfaded after many decades of use.

If the Hebrew word *bayit* gives unity to "The Kerchief," so the word *sofer*, which means at once a ritual scribe and a writer of modern literature, suggests the importance of the figure of Elimelech. As can be seen from a number of stories in this volume, especially "The

Tale of the Scribe," Agnon was preoccupied with scribes and their work, and even compiled an anthology of information and legends about them. His identification with scribes is unmistakable, as is his desire to see his literary enterprise as a continuation of theirs. So when the special tefillin written by Elimelech are lost in the fire, the calamity is painful but not devastating, because the spirit of sacred inscription lives in the figure of the writer who is telling the story of his growing up.

The Kerchief

I

Every year my father, of blessed memory, used to visit the Lashkowitz fair to do business with the merchants. Lashkowitz is a small town of no more consequence than any of the other small towns in the district, except that once a year merchants gather together there from everywhere and offer their wares for sale in the town's marketplace; and whoever needs goods comes and buys them. In earlier times, two or three generations ago, more than a hundred thousand people used to gather together there; and even now, when Lashkowitz is in its decline, they come to it from all over the country. You will not find a single merchant in the whole of Galicia who does not keep a stall in Lashkowitz during the fair.

2

For us the week in which my father went to the market was just like the week of the Ninth of Av. During those days there was not a smile to be seen on Mother's lips, and the children also refrained from laughing. Mother, peace be with her, used to cook light meals with milk and vegetables and all sorts of things that children do not dislike. If we caused her trouble she would quiet us, and did not rebuke us even for things that deserved a beating. I often used to find her sitting at the window with moist eyelids. And why should my mother sit at the window; did she wish to watch the passersby? Why, she, peace be with her, never concerned herself with other people's affairs, and would only half hear the stories her neighbors might tell her; but it was her custom, ever since the first year in which my father went to Lashkowitz, to stand at the window and look out.

When my father, of blessed memory, went to the fair at Lashkowitz for the first time, my mother was once standing at the window when she suddenly cried out, "Oh, they're strangling him!" Folk asked her, "What are you saying?" She answered, "I see a robber taking him by the throat"; and before she had finished her words she had fainted. They sent to the fair and found my father injured, for at the very time that my mother had fainted, somebody had attacked my father for his money and had taken him by the throat; and he had been saved by a miracle. In later years, when I found in the Book of Lamentations the words "She is become like a widow," and I read Rashi's explanation, "Like a woman whose husband has gone to a distant land and who intends to return to her," it brought to mind my mother, peace be with her, as she used to sit at the window with her tears upon her cheeks.

3

All the time that Father was in Lashkowitz I used to sleep in his bed. As soon as I had said the night prayer I used to undress and stretch my limbs in his long bed, cover myself up to my ears and keep them pricked up and ready so that in case I heard the trumpet of the Messiah I might rise at once. It was a particular pleasure for me to meditate on Messiah the King. Sometimes I used to laugh to myself when I thought of the consternation that would come about in the whole world when our just Messiah would reveal himself. Only yesterday he was binding his wounds and his bruises, and today he's a king! Yesterday he sat among the beggars and they did not recognize him, but sometimes even abused him and treated him with disrespect; and now suddenly the Holy One, blessed be He, has remembered the oath He swore to redeem Israel, and given him permission to reveal himself to the world. Another in my place might have been angered at the beggars who treated Messiah the King with disrespect; but I honored and revered them, since Messiah the King had desired to dwell in their quarters. In my place another might have treated the beggars without respect, as they eat black bread even on the Sabbaths and wear dirty clothes. But I honored and revered them, since among them were those who had dwelt together with the Messiah.

4

Those were fine nights in which I used to lie on my bed and think of Messiah the King, who would reveal himself suddenly in the world. He would lead us to the Land of Israel where we would dwell, every man under his own vine and his own fig tree. Father would not go to fairs, and I would not go to school but would walk about all day long in the courts of the House of our God. And while lying and meditating thus, my eyes would close of their own accord; and before they closed entirely I would take my fringed garment and count the knots I had made in the fringes, indicating the number of days my father stayed in Lashkowitz. Then all sorts of lights, green, white, black, red, and blue, used to come toward me, like the lights seen by wayfarers in fields and woods and valleys and streams, and all kinds of precious things would be gleaming and glittering in them; and my heart danced for joy at all the good stored away for us in the days to come, when our just Messiah would reveal himself, may it be speedily and in our days, Amen.

While I rejoiced so, a great bird would come and peck at the light. Once I took my fringed garment and tied myself to his wings and said, "Bird, bird, take me to Father." The bird spread its wings and flew with me to a city called Rome. I looked down and saw a group of poor men sitting at the gates of the city, and one beggar among them binding his wounds. I turned my eyes away from him in order not to see his sufferings. When I turned my eyes away, there grew a great mountain with all kinds of thorns and thistles upon it and evil beasts grazing there, and impure birds and ugly creeping things crawling about it, and a great wind blew all of a sudden and flung me onto the mountain, and the mountain began quaking under me and my limbs felt as though they would fall asunder; but I feared to cry out lest the creeping things should enter my mouth and the impure birds should peck at my tongue. Then Father came and wrapped me in his tallit and brought me back to my bed. I opened my eyes to gaze at his face and found that it was day. At once I knew that the Holy One, blessed be He, had rolled away another night of the nights of the fair. I took my fringes and made a fresh knot.

5

Whenever father returned from the fair he brought us many gifts. He was very clever, knowing what each of us would want most and bringing it to us. Or maybe the Master of Dreams used to tell Father what he showed us in dream, and he would bring it for us.

There were not many gifts that survived long. As is the way of the valuables of this world, they were not lasting. Yesterday we were playing with them, and today they were already thrown away. Even my fine prayer book was torn, for whatever I might have had to do, I used to open it and ask its counsel; and finally nothing was left of it but a few dog-eared scraps.

But one present that Father brought Mother remained whole for many years. And even after it was lost it was not lost from my heart, and I still think of it as though it were yet there.

6

That day, when Father returned from the fair, it was Friday, after the noon hour, when the children are freed from school. This fact should not be mentioned to children. Those Friday afternoon hours were the best time of the week, because all the week around a child is bent over his book and his eyes and heart are not his own; as soon as he raises his head he is beaten. On Friday afternoon he is freed from study, and even if he does whatever he wants to, nobody objects. Were it not for the noon meal the world would be like paradise. But Mother had already summoned me to eat, and I had no heart to refuse.

Almost before we had begun eating my little sister put her right hand to her ear and set her ear to the table. "What are you doing?" Mother asked her. "I'm trying to listen," she answered. Mother asked, "Daughter, what are you trying to listen to?" Then she began clapping her hands with joy and crying, "Father's coming, Father's coming." And in a little while we heard the wheels of a wagon. Very faint at first, then louder and louder. At once we threw our spoons down while they were still half full, left our plates on the table, and ran out to meet Father coming back from the fair. Mother, peace be with her, also let her apron fall and stood erect, her arms folded on her bosom, until Father entered the house.

How big Father was then! I knew my father was bigger than all of the other fathers. All the same I used to think there must be someone taller than he—but now even the chandelier hanging from the ceiling in our house seemed to be lower.

Suddenly Father bent down, caught me to him, kissed me, and asked me what I had learned. Is it likely that Father did not know which portion of the week was being read? But he only asked to try me out. Before I could answer, he had caught my brother and sisters, raised them on high, and kissed them.

I look about me now to try and find something to which to compare my father when he stood together with his tender children on his return from afar, and I can think of many comparisons, each one finer than the next; yet I can find nothing pleasant enough. But I hope that the love haloing my father, of blessed memory, may wrap us around whenever we come to embrace our little children, and that joy which possessed us then will be possessed by our children all their lives.

7

The wagoner entered, carrying two trunks, one large, and the other neither large nor small but medium. Father looked with one eye at us and with the other at the medium trunk; and that second trunk too seemed to have eyes and smile with them.

Father took his bunch of keys from his pocket and said, "We'll open the trunk and take out my tallit and tefillin." Father was just speaking for fun, since who needs phylacteries on Friday afternoon, and even if you think of the prayer shawl, my father had a special one for Sabbath, but he only said it in order that we should not be too expectant and not be too anxious for presents.

But we went and undid the straps of the trunk and watched his every movement while he took one of the keys and examined it, smiling affectionately. The key also smiled at us; that is, gleams of light sparkled on the key and it seemed to be smiling.

Finally he pressed the key into the lock, opened the trunk, put his hand inside, and felt among his possessions. Suddenly he looked at us and became silent. Had Father forgotten to place the presents there? Or had he been lodging at an inn where the inn people rose and took out the presents? As happened with the sage by whose hands they sent a gift to the emperor, a chest full of jewels and pearls, and when he lodged one night at the inn, the inn folk opened the chest and took out everything that was in it and filled it with dust. Then I prayed that just as a miracle was done to that sage so that that dust should be the dust of Abraham our father, which turned into swords when it was thrown into the air, so should the Holy One, blessed be He, perform a miracle with us in order that the things with which the innkeepers had filled Father's trunk should be better than all presents. Before my prayer was at an end Father brought out all kinds of fine things. There was not a single one among his gifts that we had not longed for all the year around. And that is why I said that the Master of Dreams must have revealed to Father what he had shown us in dream.

The gifts of my father deserve to be praised at length, but who is going to praise things that will vanish, and be lost? All the same, one fine gift that my father brought my mother on the day he returned from the fair deserves to be mentioned in particular.

8

It was a silk brocaded kerchief adorned with flowers and blossoms. On the one side it was brown and they were white, while on the other they were brown and it was white. That was the gift Father, of blessed memory, brought to Mother, peace be with her.

Mother opened up the kerchief, stroked it with her fingers, and gazed at Father; he gazed back at her and they were silent. Finally she folded it again, rose, put it in the cupboard, and said to Father, "Wash your hands and have a meal." As soon as Father sat down to his meal I went out to my friends in the street and showed them the presents I had received, and was busy outside with them until the Sabbath began and I went to pray with Father.

How pleasant that Sabbath eve was when we returned from the house of prayer! The skies were full of stars, the houses full of lamps and candles, people were wearing their Sabbath clothes and walking quietly beside Father in order not to disturb the Sabbath angels who accompany one home from the house of prayer on Sabbath eves: candles were alight in the house and the table prepared and the fine smell of white bread, and a white tablecloth spread and two Sabbath loaves on it, covered by a small cloth out of respect so that they should not feel ashamed when the blessing is said first over the wine.

Father bowed and entered and said, "A peaceful and blessed Sabbath," and Mother answered, "Peaceful and blessed." Father looked at the table and began singing, "Peace be unto you, angels of peace," while Mother sat at the table, her prayer book in hand, and the big chandelier with the ten candles—one for each of the Ten Commandments—hanging from the ceiling, gave light. They were answered back by the rest of the candles, one for Father, one for Mother, one for each of the little ones; and although we were smaller than Father and Mother, all the same our candles were as big as theirs.

Then I looked at Mother and saw that her face had changed and her forehead had grown smaller because of the kerchief wound around her head and covering her hair, while her eyes seemed much larger and were shining toward Father, who went on singing, "A woman of valor who shall find?"; and the ends of her kerchief which hung down below her chin were quivering very gently, because the Sabbath angels were moving their wings and making a wind. It must have been so, for the windows were closed and where could the wind have come from if not from the wings of the angels? As it says in the Psalms, "He maketh the winds His messengers." I held back my breath in order not to confuse the angels and looked at my mother, peace be with her, who stood at such a lofty rung, and wondered at the Sabbath day, which is given us for an honor and a glory. Suddenly I felt how my cheeks were being patted. I do not know whether the wings of the angels or the corners of the kerchief were caressing me. Happy is he who merits to have good angels hovering over his head, and happy is he whose mother has stroked his head on the Sabbath eve.

9

When I awakened from sleep it was already day. The whole world was full of the Sabbath morning. Father and Mother were about to go out, he to his little prayer room and she to the house of study of my grandfather, peace be with him. Father was wearing a black satin robe and a round shtreimel of sable on his head, and Mother wore a black dress and a hat with feathers. In the house of study of my grandfather, where Mother used to pray, they did not spend too much time singing, and so she could return early. When I came back with Father from the small prayer room she was already seated at the table wearing her kerchief, and the table was prepared with wine and cakes, large and small, round and doubled over. Father entered, said, "A Sabbath of peace and blessing," put his tallit on the bed, sat down at the head of the table, said, "The Lord is my shepherd, I shall not want," blessed the wine, tasted the cake, and began, "A Psalm of David: The earth is the Lord's and the fullness thereof."

When the ark is opened on the eve of the New Year and this psalm is said, the soul's awakening can be felt in the air. There was a similar stirring in my heart then. Had my mother not taught me that you do not stand on chairs and do not clamber onto the table and do not shout, I would have climbed onto the table and shouted out, "The earth is the Lord's and the fullness thereof"; like that child in the Talmud who used to be seated in the middle of a gold table which was a load for sixteen men, with sixteen silver chains attached, and dishes and glasses and bowls and platters fitted, and with all kinds of food and sweetmeats and spices of all that was created in the six days of Creation; and he used to proclaim, "The earth is the Lord's and the fullness thereof."

Mother cut the cake, giving each his or her portion; and the ends of her kerchief accompanied her hands. While doing so a cherry fell out of the cake and stained her apron; but it did not touch her kerchief, which remained as clean as it had been when Father took it out of his trunk.

10

A woman does not put on a silken kerchief every day or every Sabbath. When a woman stands at the oven, what room is there for ornament? Every day is not Sabbath, but on the other hand there are festivals. The Holy One, blessed be He, took pity on His creatures and gave them times of gladness, holidays and appointed seasons. On festivals Mother used to put on a feather hat and go to the house of prayer, and at home she would don her kerchief. But on the New Year and the Day of Atonement she kept the kerchief on all day long; similarly on the morning of Hoshana Rabbah, the seventh day of Tabernacles. I used to look at Mother on the Day of Atonement, when she wore her kerchief and her eyes were bright with prayer and fasting. She seemed to me like a prayer book bound in silk and presented to a bride.

The rest of the time the kerchief lay folded in the cupboard, and on the eves of the Sabbaths and festivals Mother would take it out. I never saw her washing it, although she was very particular about cleanliness. When Sabbaths and festivals are properly kept, they themselves preserve the clothes. But for me she would have kept the kerchief all her life long and would have left it as an heirloom.

What happened was as follows. On the day I became thirteen years old and a member of the congregation, my mother, peace be with her, bound her kerchief around my neck. Blessed be God, who has given His world to guardians. There was not a spot of dirt to be found on the kerchief. But sentence had already been passed on the kerchief, that it was to be lost through me. This kerchief, which I had observed so much and so long, would vanish because of me.

II

Now I shall pass from one theme to another until I return to my original theme. At that time there came a beggar to our town who was sick with running sores; his hands were swollen, his clothes were rent and tattered, his shoes were cracked, and when he showed himself in the street the children threw earth and stones at him. And not only the children but even the grownups and householders turned angry faces on him. Once when he went to the market to buy bread or onions the shopwomen drove him away in anger. Not that the shopwomen in our town were cruel; indeed, they were tender-hearted. Some would give the food from their mouths to orphans; others went to the forest, gathered twigs, made charcoal of them, and shared them free among the beggars and poor folk. But every beggar has his own luck. When he fled from them and entered the house of study, the beadle shouted at him and pushed him out. And when on the Sabbath eve he crept into the house of study, nobody invited him to come home with them and share the Sabbath meal. God forbid that the sons of our father Abraham do not perform works of charity; but the ministers of Satan used to accompany that beggar and pull a veil over Jewish eyes so that they should not perceive his dire needs. As to where he heard the blessing over wine, and where he ate his three Sabbath meals—if he was not sustained by humankind he must have been sustained by the grace of God.

Hospitality is a great thing, since buildings are erected and administrators appointed for the sake of it and to support the poor. But I say it in praise of our townsfolk, that although they did not establish any poorhouse or elect any administrators, every man who could do so used to find a place for a poor man in his own house, thus seeing the troubles of his brother and aiding him and supporting him at the hour of his need; and his sons and daughters who saw this would learn from his deeds. When trouble befell a man he would groan; the walls of his house would groan with him because of the mighty groaning of the poor; and he would know that there are blows even greater than that which had befallen him. And as he comforted the poor, so would the Holy One, blessed be He, in the future comfort him.

12

Now I leave the beggar and shall tell only of my mother's kerchief, which she tied around my neck when I entered the age of commandments and was to be counted a member of the congregation. On that day, when I returned from the house of study to eat the midday meal, I was dressed like a bridegroom and was very happy and pleased with myself because I was now putting on tefillin. On the way I found that beggar sitting on a heap of stones, changing the bandages of his sores, his clothes rent and tattered, nothing but a bundle of rags which did not even hide his sores. He looked at me as well. The sores on his face seemed like eyes of fire. My heart stopped, my knees began shaking, my eyes grew dim, and everything seemed to be in a whirl.

But I took my heart in my hand, nodded to the beggar, and greeted him, and he returned the greeting.

Suddenly my heart began thumping, my ears grew hot, and a sweetness such as I had never experienced in all my days took possession of all my limbs; my lips and my tongue were sweet with it, my mouth fell agape, my two eyes were opened, and I stared before me as a man who sees in waking what has been shown him in dream. And so I stood staring in front of me. The sun stopped still in the sky, not a creature was to be seen in the street; but He in His mercy sat in heaven and looked down upon the earth and let His light shine bright on the sores of the beggar. I began loosening my kerchief to breathe more freely, for tears stood in my throat. Before I could loosen it, my heart began racing in strong emotion, and the sweetness, which I had already felt, doubled and redoubled. I took off the kerchief and gave it to the beggar. He took it and wound it around his sores. The sun came and stroked my neck.

I looked around. There was not a creature in the market, but a pile of stones lay there and reflected the sun's light. For a little while I stood there without thinking. Then I moved my feet and returned home.

13

When I reached the house I walked around it on all four sides. Suddenly I stopped at Mother's window, the one from which she used to look out. The place was strange; the sun's light upon it did not dazzle but warmed, and there was perfect rest there. Two or three people passing slowed their paces and lowered their voices; one of them wiped his brow and sighed deeply. It seems to me that that sigh must still be hanging there.

I stood there awhile, a minute or two minutes or more. Finally I moved from thence and entered the house. When I entered I found Mother sitting in the window as was her way. I greeted her and she returned my greeting. Suddenly I felt that I had not treated her properly; she had had a fine kerchief which she used to bind around her head on Sabbaths and festivals, and I had taken it and given it to a beggar to bind up his feet with. Ere I had ended asking her to forgive me she was gazing at me with love and affection. I gazed back at her, and my heart was filled with the same gladness as I had felt on that Sabbath when my mother had set the kerchief about her head for the first time.

The end of the story of the kerchief of my mother, peace be with her.

Translated by I.M. Lask

Two Pairs

You can buy a pair of tefillin for eight crowns; if you prefer that the tefillin be made out of a single strip of leather, it will cost you ten crowns. Scribes who produce holy books, tefillin, and mezuzot are not looking to get rich from their righteous labor. And even if they would choose to get rich, the Men of the Great Assembly stipulated twenty-four restrictions that prevent scribes from getting wealthy from their work. In that case, why did my father, may he rest in peace, spend such an exorbitant amount for my tefillin? Was it their age that made them so valuable? No, these particular tefillin were written by Rabbi Elimelech the Scribe, and because my father, of blessed memory, admired him he spent a fortune on these tefillin. But wasn't Rabbi Elimelech bound by the restrictions of the High Court? Moreover, what did Rabbi Elimelech do with all that money? After all, he was poor and he lived in a primitive house that didn't even have a chair to sit on. Rabbi Elimelech, of blessed memory, used to say that since our blessed sages thought of this world as a passageway and the world hereafter as a magnificent ballroom, does a man rushing to a ballroom even need a chair to sit on in the hallway? But all cavils aside, when people had an opportunity to acquire a set of Rabbi Elimelech's tefillin they would happily come up with extraordinary sums of money.

2

On the day of my bar mitzvah I went to the mikvah and I was adorned like a bridegroom. They dressed me in a new jacket, a silk cummerbund whose two fringes extended down to my knees, a black hat, black shoes, and around my neck a silk kerchief with a pearl fastened to it. Any time I raised my head to say Amen to a blessing, it would radiate a flash of light. In my hand when I came to school were my tefillin in a carrying bag of black silk with filaments of pale silver spelling out a Star of David as well as my name and my father's name. The bag was tied with a reddish yellow drawstring and inside were my two tefillin. I took out my tefillin, and my schoolmates could see that they were antique. They gasped and asked: How much money did some father waste on this boy instead of buying plain new tefillin? They immediately started to tease me by saying that these tefillin must have belonged to the dead who were raised by the prophet Ezekiel; King Saul's daughter Michal used to wear them! I thought to myself that it was inappropriate to talk while praying so I didn't bother to answer them. After finishing my prayers I told my friends that my father had gone to the scribe with the intention of buying a plain new pair of tefillin. Oh, well, they said, when your father discovered that the scribe would charge him eight or ten crowns for them he took the old ones instead and brought them home. I asked them: How could they think that my father would balk at paying eight or ten crowns for a new pair when the old pair cost him many times that amount? So they asked me to explain. I told them that on his way to buy tefillin he happened on the opportunity to buy a pair written by Rabbi Elimelech. He said to himself that these were the most beautiful tefillin he had ever seen and he insisted on buying them for me. When they heard that, my friends bit their tongues and kissed my tefillin. On that day, my coming of age, my father set out a spread of cakes and wine, and everyone there praised my tefillin and offered me blessings. My friends were particularly proud of their own tefillin because they sparkled and smelled of new leather, but they expressed their admiration for my tefillin because even though they were old, they had been written by Rabbi Elimelech.

3

And just who was Rabbi Elimelech the Scribe? He was a transcriber of holy books and objects who lived during the time of the Tzaddik of Buczacz. But if I were going to tell you of the greatness of this holy man I wouldn't know where to begin. For someone who was eager to learn the laws of the Halacha, this righteous man of blessed memory would review eighteen laws every single day. And for one who wanted to hear about miracle workers, this Tzaddik of blessed memory would dwell on tales of miracles. And if it chanced that he heard it said about himself that he received revelations from the prophet Elijah, he would say that any man, after all, could receive such revelations from Elijah. How? By studying a chapter from Tana Devei Eliyahu. How wonderful for the righteous that they know whom to cling to and how equally wonderful for the righteous that they know whom to clasp to themselves. How fortunate for Rabbi Elimelech that he followed the Tzaddik of Buczacz and how fortunate for the Tzaddik that he embraced Rabbi Elimelech. The entire alphabet is insufficient to encompass his wonders. And I haven't gathered here more than can be contained in one small drop of ink.

4

Writers of holy books and tefillin also transcribe a get, a bill of divorce. And a scribe earns more from the latter than from the former. After all, someone who wants to be rid of his wife and asks a scribe to write a get doesn't bargain over pennies. One penny more, one penny less…just as long as he gets his divorce. We've heard of cases where a wedding was called off because the two sides could not agree on a dowry, but we've never heard of a case of a man who called off a divorce because he couldn't come to terms with a scribe on the cost of writing the get. So when a man in such a circumstance comes to a scribe, the scribe gathers his writing equipment and writes a get. But in the case of Rabbi Elimelech, before he would write a get he would fast all day, and that night he would approach in tears the involved couple and plead: I am a frail man. I can't prolong this fast.

Have pity on me and make peace between the two of you. If they agreed, he would make a party that very night; if they refused, he would continue his fast. It was said of Rabbi Elimelech that he would not budge until the couple reconciled and passed from gloom and confusion to peace and celebration. If they had had no children before, they subsequently had children; if they only had girls, then boys were born to them. And that's why, when someone is about to arrive at the age of commandments, the bar mitzvah, one seeks out Rabbi Elimelech to inscribe a pair of tefillin. It has been said that one who is fortunate enough to wear tefillin inscribed by a peacemaker will himself be a peacemaker and will live happily with his wife. Thus the tefillin of Rabbi Elimelech.

5

Mornings I would run to the synagogue. Sometimes I would arrive before the appointed hour for prayer and I would stare out the window at the sky to spot the sunlight when it would first appear so that I could then put on my tefillin. When prayer time arrived I would take out my tefillin, and a fragrance of prayer would emanate from them. As I lay the tefillah on my arm I could feel my heart pounding alongside them and I would then wind the warm straps around my arm until they pressed into my skin. And then I would circle my head with the other tefillah. When the cantor recites the prayer that thanks God for "girding Israel with strength and crowning Israel with splendor," I stand astonished that I myself am "girding" and "crowning" like a man of Israel and I am overjoyed. I ask my tallit not to be cross with me for being less enthusiastic about it. After all, when a holiday falls on the Sabbath, isn't it true that the standard Sabbath prayer of the Shemoneh Esreh is set aside in favor of a special prayer for the holiday?

That's how I used to stand in the old synagogue praying, one tefillah on my arm and the other on my head. Sometimes my praying would be soulful and plaintive, sometimes melodious and joyful. In either event, I would continually touch my tefillin—something like a shepherd making music out in the field who periodically remembers his charges and looks around to see if any of them have wandered off—until I completed my praying, removed my tefillin, and saw pressed in my arm's flesh the remaining evidence of the straps. I wouldn't eat or drink until the indentations on my arm had completely disappeared. Often I would spend time studying before I removed my tefillin. My eyes would focus on a book, accompanied by my tefillin, or would pause between the letters on a line, and the tefillin would pause with them. I was filled with sadness for having been born into this generation. If only I had been born during the time of the Talmud I would have worn my tefillin for the entire day. How I loved them. Maimonides, of blessed memory, had surely done the right thing when he included the regulations pertaining to tefillin in his Book of Love.

6

Now I know that some of you will claim that the story about the tefillin is nothing less than an allegory about God and the people of Israel. Rabbi Elimelech the Scribe represents the Lord, King of Kings, and the tefillin stand for Israel, which we learn from the fact that the blessings over the tefillin include the phrase "and who is like your nation Israel." And God is living in a simple dwelling because He had a desire to live among the earthlings. The absence of even a chair in His house signifies the absence of the Shekhinah. And He rushes to the parlor room because He anticipates the return of God's glory to Zion in our very own time. On the contrary, however, I tell you that far from being allegorical, everything is just as it appears. The tefillin are simply tefillin, as is stated in the Torah: "Bind them as a sign upon your arm and let them be a band between your eyes." I've got much to tell, but living at a time when the taste for performing the commandments has been lost, it's best that I simply do my part and let those who are enlightened remain silent.

7

My grandfather, of blessed memory, used to say that there are two things that a man never stints on: bread and tefillin. I am a descendant of good people and I was spoiled as a child. I used to think to myself: Grandpa, how do you compare bread and tefillin? After all, when my mother used to give me bread I would risk offending her by asking if I could have cake or pastries or wafers or pretzels (Heaven forbid!) rather than bread. But tefillin, on the contrary, have been dear to me every single day from the very first time that I wore them. When I was despondent I would put on tefillin in preference to a piece of bread which I was too distracted to look for. On my wall I hung my tefillin bag with the two tefillin tied securely inside; the aroma of my tefillin was contained within, and the Holy One did not smell it. My friends, you undoubtedly know the story of the son who left his father's table and ceased practicing good deeds and performing the commandments. Better that I should conceal my appearance within my tefillin bag and not parade my sins in public.

8

Did I really expect that my tefillin would remain mine for all time? After all, before they came to me they belonged to someone else and before that to yet another person, and in the same way, after one hundred and twenty years, they will pass from me to someone new. Someone once found in an old notebook a story of a Jew who, on his deathbed, wrote to the local rabbi a description of his specific place in the synagogue so that in the distant future, when all the synagogues and houses of study in the Diaspora are destined to be reassembled in the Land of Israel, his proper seat will be assigned to him. In that same future, who will inherit my tefillin? Maybe I myself, or the man who owned them before me, or the man before that. But I've always said: Don't be a dark cloud. It might very well be that in an earlier incarnation I was the man who owned these tefillin, and in a still earlier incarnation I was that other man who wore these tefillin. Since there is no proof to the contrary, it must be so, for, after all, the headband of the tefillin is fitted to a specific head. So in the distant future I will lift my head out of my coffin and flex my arm, and the two tefillin will fly to me like doves returning to their nest.

9

Much time has passed since my bar mitzvah, and I've traveled far since I first wore my tefillin. Many times, exhausted by the ravages of life, I was too rushed for deep prayer so I would put on my tefillin for a brief prayer. On my head the tefillah was like a tired bird wanting to perch quietly but who is forced to move by arrows that are aimed at it.

Once, during the Ten Days of Repentance—before the conflagration—I asked a scribe to inspect my tefillin. I never knew if Rabbi Elimelech, of blessed memory, had written them in his youth or in his old age, and in any event, since they were more than a hundred years old and had rested in plenty of tefillin bags and had been used by many hands, perhaps the writing had been effaced and the letters had become indistinct. When the scribe returned them to me, he said: I am astonished by the gentleman's tefillin. I asked why. He said: Even though the writing is old, it looks as though it were written today. Does the gentleman know who inscribed them? I said to him: And if I tell you his name, are you familiar with my locale? He said to me: Nonetheless, tell me. I said to him: Rabbi Elimelech the Scribe.

He said to me: Do you mean Rabbi Elimelech of Buczacz who lived in the days of the great Tzaddik of Buczacz, may their honor protect the people of Israel? I nodded yes. He said: Since I mentioned their names, let me tell you what I have heard about them. I said: After all, they're from my own city and it would please me greatly, since I love to hear even simple things about simple men from my home, all the more so about two righteous men like them. So the scribe told me a story about a righteous man on whose tombstone were inscribed the words ABRAHAM OUR FATHER THE TZADDIK and DAVID OUR KING as an allusion to the dead man, Abraham David, may his worthiness protect us. There was in town a wanton trouble-maker who went to the authorities and told them that the Jews had rebelled against them and had crowned a king for themselves. The authorities dispatched an agent to investigate. When the agent came to inspect the tombstone, instead of DAVID OUR KING he found written DAVID OUR FING, and the Jews were saved because to be imprisoned in Buczacz could be a catastrophe. And the Jews were well aware that a great miracle had occurred when the agent found "fing" instead of "king," since "king" was what had originally been written. Now, the residents of Buczacz are deep thinkers and they quite naturally love to do research and search for explanations for everything, so they started an inquiry to discover who had switched the *K* to an *F*. One man finally rose and said: Do you remember the handwriting of Rabbi Elimelech the Scribe, of blessed memory? The rest responded: Of course we recognize his handwriting. This very day we read in the synagogue from a Torah that was written by Rabbi Elimelech, and the *F* on the tombstone is identical to the *F*'s in his Torah. And so everyone then knew that even in the world hereafter Rabbi Elimelech had not forgotten his children. And the scribe also said to me: Does the gentleman know that it is a tradition among us that no man who wears tefillin written by Rabbi Elimelech ever suffers a divorce? I told him that I knew that. He asked me: Is the gentleman married? I answered: Thank God. He took a deep breath and sighed. I never knew why he sighed, whether it was because he did not have the pleasure of a peaceful house or because at that particular time his business of writing tefillin was dwarfed by the writing of divorces. In any event, not every scribe manages to be like Rabbi Elimelech and not every man is worthy of wearing the tefillin of Rabbi Elimelech.

10

One night I dreamed that I put on the tefillah for the arm but not for the head, and the dream upset me a bit. During the course of the day additional anxieties entered my life and I forgot my dream until the Master of Dreams caused it to recur. I went to a wise man and told him my worry. He said: Do you know what I would suggest? That you're getting signs that your tefillin have to be inspected for flaws. I said to him: I've had them inspected and there are no flaws. So he had no response. When the dream occurred a third time, I said to myself that there must be something to this. I convened a panel of three judges and told them my dream. I saw a look of concern on one of their faces but I paid it no heed. Some people are melancholy and some are cheerful. But in fact I couldn't get my mind off the tefillin even when I wasn't saying my prayers, like when I would see them hanging in their bag on the wall and I would go over and anxiously touch them to make sure that I had not placed them in their bag improperly. But they were always in their rightful place and in their proper order. One time I discovered that the bands of the head tefillah were not properly tied, so I stood there and tied them, as I always did, in the shape of a dove's wings. The next day I discovered that the wings were spread like the wings of a dove who wants to fly from its nest. A short time later my house burned down, and the tefillin burned with it. I don't know if I was a victim of the evil eye or one of those judgment decrees that comes upon a man suddenly. The Lord giveth and the Lord taketh away.

II

The day of perfection has not yet arrived in this world, so I went and bought new tefillin. Once again I did not buy a pair made out of a single piece of leather. In fact, I bought the first pair that I saw. My wife took some cloth that had not been consumed by the fire and made from it a kind of tefillin bag, not of silk this time, and with no silver lettering. No cakes and wine were offered in honor of the day; a piece of bread was sufficient. True, I did wear new clothes, but that was because all of my old clothes had burned in the fire.

When I came to the synagogue and put on my tefillin, my friends did not look on with disapproval, nor did they bombard me with words. On the contrary, they sympathized with one whose house had burned and who did not have a roof over his head. Pay no mind to his new clothes, his old ones all burned; even his tefillin burned and that's why he's wearing new ones. I folded my tallit over my head so as not to hear their comments. When I got to the prayer that tells of God opening His hand and satisfying all living beings, I raised my hands to feel my tefillin. I was reminded of how I used to touch my old tefillin, and I thought to myself that those old ones were like a charm that let me live peacefully, and the new ones were to make sure that no one would envy me. I took a breath and sighed. This too is for the best.

Translated by Walter Dubler

The Artist in the
Land of Israel

If Agnon can be said to have invented himself as a modern Jewish writer, then these stories define that identity. From a tale of the would-be writer as a young man in Jaffa to stories that contrast the figure of the writer to his peers and his predecessors, we see a variety of narrative self-portraits. These are "self-portraits" only in the broadest sense: they give narrative form to the writer's understanding of himself, his community, his art, and the Jewish past. These portraits are often heavily shaded by irony: the writer mocks his presumption in even designating himself with the title *sofer*, the Hebrew term for "writer," which also refers to the scribes responsible for the transcription of Scripture. How can he take on this title, he asks, when he does not devote himself to the full-time study of traditional texts? In the range of these stories, we gain access to a variety of personae of the writer, with the result that our portrait of the artist resists reduction to any one component.

In "Hill of Sand," a story set in Jaffa in the years of the Second Aliyah, we encounter the writer as a young man unable to write, to love, to work. ("Hill of Sand" went through a number of revisions, dating from the early story "Tishre," a tale of unrequited love, written in 1911 in Jaffa, and culminating in the 1931 text of "Hill of Sand" which is the basis for this version.) Agnon lets us feel the atmosphere of the period from the perspective of the youthful Hemdat, who witnesses the founding of Tel Aviv from afar, but does not engage in physical labor or join in the enterprise of Jewish settlement. Themes of ambivalence are signalled by Hemdat's repugnance for the physical side of life. He is drawn to Yael Hayyut, whose last name, derived from the Hebrew word for "life," suggests a vitality, a life force, that Hemdat longs to share.

Nor is Hemdat able to resolve an artistic identity for himself. He cites the stories of Rabbi Nahman of Bratslav and thus directs our attention to an important influence on Agnon's literary development: Rabbi Nahman (1772–1810) told dark tales of enigmatic beauty, which were recorded by his followers. On a more satirical note, Hemdat expresses his scorn for the poet Pizmoni (whose name means "rhymester"), a self-proclaimed leading light of Hebrew literature. Hemdat may lie in bed thinking of translating the nineteenth-century Scandinavian writer Jens Peter Jacobsen, another important influence on Agnon, but he is unable to put pen to paper. This portrait of the artist as a young man uses irony to sketch conflict and indecision, and to draw the contrast between the youth's vaulting ambitions and his inability to realize them.

"Knots upon Knots" gives us the writer at a later stage in his life, ill at ease in a series of encounters with a variety of individuals and groups, each of which has some connection to books and to writing. "Even I was invited to the craftsmen's convention," the opening line of the story announces, but the story that follows describes the failures of the protagonist to enter into any form of community. Indeed, he manages to offend and alienate all those he approaches, suggesting a singularly ambivalent relationship to his vocation. In contrast, the figure of the bookbinder, who stores all the narrator's unwanted articles and binds his books, suggests a level of integration and a kind of spiritual harmony in his careful preparation of the workroom and the hints that he is about to engage in prayer.

"Knots upon Knots" engages in some historical playfulness underscoring its ironies. The narrator meets in succession two leaders of rival schools of thought and distances himself from each with awkwardly offensive behavior. The interactions of the narrator with these two characters take on an intriguing complexity when we realize that they carry the surnames of two great eighteenth-century rabbis, Eibeschütz and Emden. These two prominent rabbis engaged in a drawn-out feud that split German Jewry. The split began when Jacob Emden accused Jonathan Eibeschütz of being a covert follower of Sabbatai Zvi, leader of the messianic movement that swept seventeenth-century Jewry and continued even after its leader's apostasy. That Agnon calls one character Eibeschütz and the other Emden, and gives to each one of his own names—Samuel and Joseph—suggests that the conflicts that energize this story are as much internal as they are external.

"Knots upon Knots" is one of the stories included in the Hebrew collection *Sefer Hama'asim*, which can be translated as both *The Book of Deeds* and *The Book of Tales. Ma'asim* is the Hebrew word for "deeds"; the Yiddish *mayses* refers to tales. Agnon's title capitalizes on the coincidence. These stories, written largely in the 1930s and 1940s, offer dreamlike scenes of encounters with suggestive figures who either lead the protagonist astray or rebuke him for unspecified lapses. During this period Agnon was sometimes in the habit of transcribing his own dreams and developing stories out of them. "Knots upon Knots" takes its place in this fictional category, demonstrating his capacity to craft a perfectly balanced structure out of suggestive pairs of oppositions.

A pair of stories from the 1930s, "On One Stone" and "The Sense of Smell," offer delicate portraits of the writer's relationship to Jewish traditions of writing. It should be noted that "On One Stone" is actually set in eastern Europe. It is in this section, along with "The Sense of Smell," because both stories highlight the writer's relationship to mystical traditions of writing. These stories approach the mythical as they position the figure of the writer in relation to wonder-working rabbis of the past and to a conception of writing as magical in its capacity to create worlds. This belief in the special potency of the Hebrew language goes back very far in Jewish tradition. At the beginning of Bereshit Rabbah, the midrash on the Book of Genesis, we find the belief that God looked into the Torah to find the blueprint for Creation. This conception of the special powers of the very letters in which the Torah was written held enormous appeal for Agnon, whose writing plays out a variety of positions in relation to the holy tongue.

With the model of the world-creating language of Torah before him, Agnon enacts the attempt and failure to attain the linguistic level of the sacred. Each story includes a brief moment of participation that appears to lift language beyond itself, but these are moments that cannot be sustained. The two stories offer tales of the writer that occupy a middle ground between the early stories of Hemdat, the artist as youth ("Hill of Sand"), and the stories that comprise *The Book of Deeds*, in which nothing happens but the act of telling itself.

"On One Stone," written in 1934, mimics a passage in *The Book of Praises of the Baal Shem Tov*, a compilation of stories of the Baal Shem Tov, the eighteenth-century holy man around whose life and works Hasidism developed. The Baal Shem Tov is a luminous figure in hasidic tradition, a wonder-worker whose miraculous deeds are told and retold by his followers. In the source passage in *The Book of Praises*, the Baal Shem Tov speaks directly to a stone, so that it opens up and he can place his writings in it. Without ever explicitly referring to the Baal Shem Tov, Agnon's story invokes this act of enclosure in a variety of ways that remind us of the story of the Baal Shem Tov as well as of other stories of wonder-working rabbis.

The first-person narrator of "On One Stone" is a writer, but he opens his story by referring to the days in which he devoted himself to writing about the wonder-working rabbi Adam Baal Shem, a predecessor of the Baal Shem Tov, who used the holy writings in his possession to bring about the redemption of souls in Israel. The narrator tells us how Rabbi Adam Baal Shem went to the forest and sealed his writings in a rock when the time for his death drew near. Emphasizing all the while the profound gap that separates him from the level of Rabbi Adam Baal Shem, the narrator of our story "inadvertently" reenacts a latter-day version of the moment at which the rabbi gave up his writings to a rock. Concerned about finding himself beyond the Sabbath boundary of the town, the narrator goes in search

of the writings he had left lying out in the open upon a stone, only
to see them swallowed up by that stone before his very eyes. What
follows is a scene of radiant wonder that mimics a mystical moment
in which word and world are fused. For that brief moment, it is as if
the narrator gains access to the language of Creation.

In "On One Stone," the speaker describes what could almost
be considered a wish: were he able to read the writings of Rabbi
Adam Baal Shem that were hidden in the rock, he would be able to
"join together" worlds out of them. The story thus implies levels of
linguistic activity, in order of descending strength, but on the model
of a world-creating use of language. "The Sense of Smell," written in
1937, enters this mythology of writing by building on the traditional
belief that language is prior even to Creation. "The Sense of Smell"
is a story in which the persona of the author figures as speaker. He
refers to himself as the *mehabber,* meaning "author," or more literally, "composer," in the sense of "joiner of words." And it is that very
activity of joining words that the story brings up for question, since
it is a dispute over proper linguistic usage that provides the stimulus
for the mock-heroic text. In actuality, the story constitutes an engaging response to an annoying incident in which Agnon was rebuked
for incorrect word usage by a member of the National Committee
on Language. Agnon uses this story to enact a particularly literary
form of revenge.

"The Sense of Smell" draws to an end with a two-sentence
paragraph that acclaims the greatness of the holy tongue. Ultimately,
it is Hebrew—the language of Creation—that joins together sages of
the past and the figure of the writer in a fantasy that establishes the
community of those who are devoted to the holy tongue. A Tzaddik (righteous man) leaves paradise, identified here as "the Academy
on High" or a heavenly yeshivah, in order to come to the aid of
the writer and to vindicate his use of the phrase that had brought
Agnon under attack. In this linguistic fantasy, Agnon's reference to
the Academy on High not only suggests the timeless community of
those who devote themselves to Torah, but it replaces the authority
of the Committee on Language, established in 1900, with that of a
much higher body.

Conflict is muted in these stories, as the figure of the writer effaces his own individuality in an effort to draw nearer to traditional uses of language. In each story, the writer achieves a moment of self-transcendence: the abrasive tensions of the present dissolve as he enters into moments of alliance with legendary sages and their writings.

"A Book That Was Lost" shifts the focus from the writer's own work to tell the story of his efforts to send a text of rabbinic commentary from Buczacz to Jerusalem. The story takes in the years from the writer's eastern European youth to his maturity in Jerusalem and places that time span within a larger compass of rabbinic commentaries, beginning with the Shulhan Arukh, the sixteenth-century code of laws written by Joseph Caro, and moving on to the seventeenth-century Magen Avraham, the commentary of a Polish rabbi on a section of the Shulhan Arukh. This is a story that charts its course via references to the public dialogue of rabbis, conducted over centuries through their written works. The Magen Avraham was considered to be a difficult and elusive work, and scholars were helped by the eventual appearance of Rabbi Samuel Kolin's commentary on it, Mahazit Hashekel. Agnon's story sketches out this extended network of rabbinic texts and adds its own account of the modest Rabbi Shmaria, a rabbinical judge of Buczacz, who refrained from publishing his commentary when he came upon Mahazit Hashekel and felt it superseded his own work.

Drawing the larger scope of history into a personal frame, Agnon depicts himself as a young man who happens to stumble upon the commentary of Rabbi Shmaria in the attic of the Great Synagogue in Buczacz. Agnon uses this glimpse of his youth to touch upon the history of Buczacz and to affirm the ongoing life of the works of its sages, which survived even the predations of Tartar invasions in the seventeenth century. It becomes, then, the mission of the youth to insure the survival of Rabbi Shmaria's commentary, first by ascertaining the originality of its contents and, second, by sending it to a newly founded library in Jerusalem.

Not so much a story of the writer as a story of the writer's devotion to the town, "A Book That Was Lost" uses its narrative frame to construct a home for the lost book, the book that never makes it to the new national library of the Jewish people. Along the way, the story pays tribute to Joseph Chasanowitsch, a Russian doctor who was not able to settle in Palestine himself but whose collection established the basis for the Jewish National and University Library in Jerusalem. Thus the narrative draws together threads of history to link Buczacz to the Land of Israel. But while it appears to organize itself around the Zionist shift from Europe to Palestine, a shift that includes the writer's own journey from Buczacz to Jerusalem, the story is as much a record of what has been lost or destroyed over the years as it is of Zionist achievement. With the account of the writer's arrival in Jerusalem on the Ninth of Av, the day of mourning the destruction of the Temple, the story draws to a close by incorporating a reminder of loss into the narrative of Zionist renewal. It becomes the mission of the writer to record loss—to continue to look for the book of Rabbi Shmaria of Buczacz—and thus to make a place for a traditional text in a new society, even if that "place" consists of the notation of its absence.

In the major novel *A Guest for the Night*, the first-person narrator leaves his eastern European hometown, taking with him the key to the town's Beit Midrash and citing the belief that in the future all houses of study will move to the Land of Israel. He resigns himself to waiting for that day. In "A Book That Was Lost," the writer depicts himself at the other end, waiting in the Land of Israel for the book that he sent from Buczacz to arrive.

This section of tales of the artist in the Land of Israel closes with "From Lodging to Lodging," a story that follows the moves of its first-person narrator from one residence to another as he claims to seek greater comfort and fresher air. In an expressionistic enactment of conflicts between illness and health, passivity and activity, death and life, "From Lodging to Lodging" moves through a variety of settings in the Land of Israel. From the noise and bustle of Tel Aviv to the seashore and from there to a rural setting, the narrator finds himself restless and ill at ease. His discomforts in each new setting suggest an inability to settle into anyone address or identification.

In the fourth section, then, when the narrator finds himself in a house on a hill that is described with the biblical imagery of the

Zionist return to the land, his response acknowledges the fulfillment of that return and yet distances himself from complete identification: "I was glad that a man in the Land of Israel had all this, and I had my doubts that this place was for me." The couple who live in this house recount stories that are the counterpart of the setting: of their own emigration to the Land of Israel and of their daughter, who willingly sacrifices comfort for the physical hardships of kibbutz life. The fulfillment in a relationship to the land that they express is something Agnon's fiction tends to acknowledge, but from a distance. In novels as well as short stories, Agnon acknowledges the need for community while positioning his protagonists as solitary figures. The daughter's commitment to collective life in "From Lodging to Lodging" finds its counterpart in several novels: in *A Guest for the Night*, we find the description of young Zionists who prepare themselves for aliyah to the Land of Israel by working on a farm in eastern Europe, and in the posthumously published novel *Shira* we have the involvement of the protagonist's daughter and her family in a collective farm.

In the logic of this particular story, the room to which the narrator returns suggests acceptance of a part of himself that he had sought to escape. The narrator returns to find the sickly child of his landlady on the doorstep, eager as ever to poke his dirty fingers into the narrator's eyes, in search of his own reflection there. It was the intrusive presence of this child that caused the narrator to go in search of quieter surroundings in the first place. His return to a reluctant involvement with the child thus evolves into an emblem of identity by suggesting acceptance of an aspect of himself he has hitherto sought to escape.

Through these stories of the artist, we encounter shifting identifications and transient affiliations, all of which comprise facets of the artist's identity. Whether by detaching the writer from the community of his peers or linking him to those who preserve tradition, these stories offer insight into the structures that define Agnon's fictional world. The stories position the writer on the margins, never wholly inside or outside of a traditional Jewish world view.

Hill of Sand

It was most curious, Hemdat's having agreed to give Yael Hayyut literature lessons. Yet since it struck him as being but one more insoluble psychological riddle, he took the moralist's advice and did not probe what was beyond him. You made a promise? Keep it.

The evening before their first lesson he happened to find out more about her. He had always considered her an empty-headed flirt who never did a day's work in her life, but now he discovered that she was terribly poor and hard up. She had more than her share of troubles. Although life had treated her well as a girl in Russia, she had not seen a cloudless day since coming to Palestine, and a stocking knitter's wages were all she could look forward to. Or rather, while she was learning to knit stockings, a wage was far from certain, since she had a bad arm and was not supposed to strain it. As sad as it was to see anyone down on his luck, it was sadder to see a girl from a good family who had to work for a pittance, a princess banished to the spinning wheel.

How unfair he had been. Thank God he could make up for it.

He opened his Bible as she opened the door of his room. He would teach her Hebrew. With a knowledge of the language she could be a nursery-school teacher instead of having to knit all her life. He had been providentially chosen to rescue her.

She was hungry, quite simply hungry. Not that she said so. But he could tell from the way she asked for a glass of water that she had not eaten lunch. Hemdat took out bread and wine. Oh, no, Yael said, she did not want anything. Just some water. In the end she took and ate a slice of bread, pecking at it like a bird. Exactly like a bird: that was all she touched. Pizmoni the poet once said that only birds ate aesthetically. Well put, Mr. Pizrmoni!

It was a fine time of his life, the one in which Hemdat tutored Yael Hayyut. The summer was over; the first rains had fallen and the days were no longer blistering deserts for the sun to beat down on. Hemdat liked to spend his afternoons in bed until clouds formed in the west. Beauteous were the evenings in Canaan.

One Wednesday Yael came late. When she arrived, she sat down on the divan instead of on the chair by the table. You could see she did not feel like studying. She looked at Hemdat and said:

"What makes you so quiet? I used to think you were happy, but now that I know you better I can see that you're not. Why don't you tell me about yourself?"

Hemdat bowed his head and said nothing.

Once, when he was more of a ladies' man, Hemdat had liked nothing better than talking about himself. He had had a happy childhood and his stories about it had won many hearts. Now that all this was behind him, however, he preferred silence. He picked up his Bible and sat down with Yael.

She was a good head taller than he was. He had noticed yesterday how this made her bend, and so he propped the Bible on another book for her. Yet though he had meant to be helpful, she now had to arch her neck like a swan. What did Yael's tutor think he was doing?

Hemdat took a small pillow and placed in on Yael's chair. "That's better, much better," she nodded. After two hours of study she could sit in comfort at last. She gave him a grateful look with her green eyes. Before they could return to their book, he said:

"If you have no objection, it's dinner time. I'd like to ask you to join me."

Yael shook her head. "Oh no, thank you."

"All right," said Hemdat, putting away the tablecloth he had taken out. "Let's get on with the lesson." He was not going to eat without her. In the end she agreed. She did not have much choice.

If you have never met Hemdat, you might as well meet his room. It stood in the dunes of Nevei Tsedek and had many windows: one facing the sea, and one facing the sand that Tel Aviv is now built on, and one facing the railroad tracks in Emek Refaim, and two facing the street. And yet by drawing the green curtains, Hemdat could cut himself off from the world and the bustle of Jaffa. The room had a table spread with green wax paper, which doubled as the desk he wrote his poems at. Next to it stood a small chest full of good things. There were olives, and bread, and oranges, and wine, and you could take whatever you wanted, and whatever you took was washed down with the coffee that Hemdat made on the alcohol stove on top of the chest. Bright beads of flame twinkled around the beaker while it cooked. Yael glanced up at them from her book. Hemdat looked at her and said:

"You can't say I'm not a good housekeeper."

Indeed, you could not. He kept house for himself and ate from his own table. He was not one of your room-and-boarders who lounge around gabbing all day and are sitting down to supper before they have risen from lunch. Not Hemdat. He came from a well-to-do, bourgeois home in which a day spent in idleness was a day stolen from its Creator.

Hemdat bent his curly head by the flaming stove. The light lent his face a charming flush. Yael stared dreamily at the picture over the table. Apart from its furniture, Hemdat's room had a portrait by Rembrandt on the wall, a picture of a bride and a groom. Yael saw her reflection in it. "I do believe," she smiled, "that I can see myself in the picture. It's a Rembrandt, isn't it?"

Hemdat nodded. "So it is. It's a Rembrandt, and it's called *The Bride and Groom*."

Hemdat's room had no mirror except for the glass frame of the picture. Once, when the fiancée of one of his friends was half in love with him, he had imagined himself as a third person in it. He didn't have such thoughts any longer. People should be happy with what they had and not crave what belonged to others. Hemdat thought of a friend who once said teasingly:

"You only like Rembrandt because he was a Casanova like yourself."

Who was that knocking? It was Shoshanna and Mushalam. Hemdat opened the door and said, "Come on in."

Yael jumped to her feet as if bitten by a snake. "Mr. Hemdat is behaving very oddly," she said. "He absolutely insisted that I stay for supper. It's too much for me, really it is."

She blushed all the way down to her throat and looked away from the table.

Shoshanna and Mushalam had just come back from Petach Tikva, where they had unexpectedly attended their own wedding. What happened was that a cousin of Shoshanna's had married off his youngest son and decided to make the most of the occasion by marrying off Shoshanna too. She and Mushalam were quite unprepared.

"Mazal tov, mazal tov!" said Hemdat and Yael in one breath. "Mazal tov, mazal tov!" they repeated in loud voices.

Hemdat kept thinking how happy he was for them. Such a story should be written in gold letters on unicorn horn. Shoshanna and Mushalam had come to invite him to their wedding party. Hemdat thanked them kindly but said he was busy. He would gladly come to their golden anniversary. Shoshanna and Mushalam were sorry to hear that but told him in leaving that they loved him anyway.

Yael sat there stunned. Shoshanna's getting married was a big surprise. Imagine two people, one here and one there, and before you know it they have met somewhere else and are joined for life. They were like the palm tree and the fir tree in the poem by Heine.

Yael was poor at literary comparisons. What did one thing have to do with the other? The tree in Heine's poem stood yearning at a distance of thousands of miles, while Shoshanna and Mushalam were now a married couple. "Some people," said Hemdat, gripping the edge of the table, "are under the wedding canopy before they know it and others wait to get there all their lives."

What had made him say a thing like that? Really, he was beginning to talk nonsense.

2

His friends' suspicions were groundless. "Yael is a nice looking girl," they said to him. "It's no wonder that you're taken with her." But Hemdat knew that he was only giving her lessons because he felt sorry for her. The two of them were poles apart, and he had never even touched her. Not that she wasn't attractive. Her tranquil bearing, fresh complexion, and tall, womanly way she held herself made him feel a kind of respect. And the odd thing was that before getting to know her he hadn't thought her pretty at all and had even called her "that beefsteak" behind her back.

She arrived one evening soaking wet and limping, her right shoe as full of water as a kneading trough. "It's raining," she said, standing in the doorway.

Hemdat brought a chair for her to sit on and took off her shoe. She had a surprisingly delicate foot. "What are you looking at?" she asked, following his glance.

"Excuse me for asking," he said, as though waking from a dream, "but did you make these socks?"

Yael smiled. "No, they're from home. But I could have made them."

Hemdat helped her out of her coat and spread it on the divan. How nice it would have been for there to be a warm stove in the corner and a samovar boiling on the table, so that he could dry out her coat and make her a glass of hot tea. He bent quietly to wring out the bottom of her coat. Yael put on a pair of his slippers, and he said with a smile:

"There's a belief that if the groom at a wedding makes the bride move her foot with his own, he'll be the boss. But if she makes him move his, she'll be."

Yael laughed. "Oh, my, I've gotten mud on you," she said. "I'm so sorry." She brushed off Hemdat's clothes and went to wash her hands.

He shook his head and said, "You needn't have bothered."

The next day he washed without soap. Yael's fingerprints were on his one bar. He knew he was being silly.

Yael was not a good student. She had managed to learn some writing and a few chapters from the Bible and Part II of Ben-Ami's grammar, but that was all. She had neither a quick grasp nor the time for it. Since she worked in the mornings and spent the afternoons with her sick mother at the hospital, she came unprepared to her lessons. Hemdat scolded her good-naturedly and did the best he could, but devoted teacher though he was, he was wasting his time. To think of all the things he could have done with it! Should he tell her he was stopping? But he did not want to stop. Often she came late. Once, when he asked her why, she said that she hated to take him away from his work. Another time she came and found him lying on the divan as though swimming in a sea of sadness.

Hemdat wondered what she saw in him. He knew that she liked him and valued his opinions. Once she even told him that the Bible verse "Your words uphold the stumbler" made her think of him. She had never met anyone like him who always knew the right thing to say. And yet he spoke haltingly. Every phrase began with a sigh and his warm voice was slow and monotonous. What did she see in him?

Yael saw that Hemdat was a poet. Poets took their time when they spoke. Pizmoni was a greater poet than Hemdat, but Bialik was even greater. She loved looking at Bialik when he visited Rehovot. He had worn a velvet jacket and walked with the almond-wood cane that he stood leaning on at the bonfire made in his honor. The whole town had turned out to see him. Not even a baby stayed home. What had he been thinking of? He seemed such a nice man. Yet in his photographs he bit his bottom lip as though annoyed. No two poets were the same. Hemdat bowed his head when he talked and shaded his right eye with his hand. Schiller needed the smell of rotten apples to write poetry. Not that she ever had read Schiller. Her father read him all the time. Why did no one read him anymore? Every age had its authors. Now there was Tolstoy and Sanin and Sholom Aleichem. Of course, Sanin was a character in a novel, not an author, but Yael was not a student of literature and had no way of knowing such things. She had her good points, Yael Hayyut, and was certainly very pretty.

Once Hemdat sat by the window as dusk fell. The door of his room was wide open. The branches of the eucalyptus trees cast long shadows and the world was fading into darkness. A poet might have said that Sir Day was departing and Fair Night was about to arrive. Yael came for her lesson. Hemdat did not hear her. His bowed head was wreathed in shadow. He felt dull, and all he could think of was a lone cow standing in a field.

What was on his mind? Yael stood there saying nothing. She was thinking of the evenings in the town where she grew up. It was more of a forest than a town, and the whole summer had been one long frolic, every tree a maypole. But as soon as summer ended, so did the good times. The forest grew ever so dreary and sunken in snow. If a boy and girl went off into it, their voices were heard from afar and their footprints stood out in the snow.

Yael felt a flush. She wanted to take Hemdat's head in her warm arms and hold it tightly. He had such fine hair. She thought of her own gorgeous head of rich hair with its auburn braids that had been like nothing else. Her friends could have told you about that hair. "Just imagine what it must do to a man," they said, staring at it, "if that's what it does to us."

Hemdat's eyes felt moist. Softly his hand grazed her short hair. Though he had never seen it long, he had heard of it. It had glowed like chestnuts half in shade and half in sunlight. Her old friends had burst into tears when she cut it because of the typhus. One, who was no longer even on good terms with her, woke from a dream crying out, "Oh, no, they're cutting Yael's hair!"

Hemdat sat up and looked at her like a man waking from his sleep. "Is that you, Yael?" he asked. She should forgive him for not having noticed her. Although this was an odd way of putting it, since he had just touched her hair, he was not conscious of telling a lie.

"Have you been here long?" he asked, rising in his confusion to offer her his chair while at the same time pointing to the divan. Yael retreated a step but did not leave. Even though she knew that he would rather be alone, she sat down. In fact, she sat down beside him on the divan.

Hemdat did not light the lamp as usual and sat with her in the dark. How afraid she once had been of him! But she was not anymore. They sat half-touching, and when the other half touched she took his head in her hands. He was so close that she could have bitten off the lock of hair on his forehead. What did he need it for? "What a fantastical idea," laughed Hemdat loudly. "Go ahead and try."

Yael leaned forward and bit off Hemdat's hair. He had never laughed so hard in his life. What a she-devil she was, this quiet, sedate young lady! It was incredible. Who would have thought she had such spunk? He would never have believed it if he hadn't felt it with his own head.

Although he had spent long hours with her, it only now struck him that she deserved a closer look. She was—with her green eyes, green hat, and green jersey—a living, breathing emerald. It thrilled him to see her so wild and full of life and youth. He gave her hand a friendly squeeze.

She looked at him and said, "I know why you did that."

"You do?" he asked with a smile.

"I suppose you think I haven't read my Forel. A handshake is a sexual release." Hemdat beamed at her lovely innocence. Let him meet the cads who spread stories about her and he would tear them to shreds.

What a shame time couldn't stand still. It was getting late. Yael rose to go. It was past her bedtime. Hemdat took his hat and set out to walk her home.

In the tender moonlight, the sand stretched for miles all around. The eucalyptus trees by the railroad tracks gave off a good smell, their branches whispering the heart's language in the wind. The surf sounded far away, and the bells of a departing caravan chimed to the singing of the camel drivers. Nothing stirred in the world without Hemdat seeing or hearing it. He had a sharp eye. How many times have you passed the tree poking through the wall of the garden near his house without noticing that it was whitewashed? Not Hemdat. It was a clever joke on someone's part to paint it white, as though that were its true color. You can't fool me, he thought, because I know what I'm looking at. He walked Yael home and headed back.

3

She lived in one room with her friend Pnina. Hemdat had never been there. One Saturday night Pizmoni talked him into going. Disorder reigned everywhere. All kinds of things lay untidily about, one on top of another, as if thumbing their noses at their owners. A few young men were sitting around. It was a Saturday and they had had the day off.

Dorban, the poet who had trekked the length and breadth of Palestine, was ridiculing the latest Hebrew poetry. Anyone who had heard the music of camel steps in a howling sandstorm could tell you that all that was written nowadays sounded like a creaky door. Dorban's meters were based on camel steps. You had to have heard them to appreciate his verse.

Seated opposite him was fat Gurishkin. Gurishkin had a bushy, waxed black mustache tilting up at the ends that he resisted the temptation to twirl by ordering his hand to rub his forehead instead, which gave him a philosophical look. His eyes were red from hauling sand to building sites by day and writing his autobiography by night. Not that it was a major work yet, since he was young and hadn't lived much, but it would be by the time he was finished. Gurishkin thought so far ahead that he had trouble keeping up with himself.

Gurishkin was no poet, and his imagination was not his strong suit. From time to time, he turned to look at Pnina. Pnina had a high opinion of him, but she never fell in love with her opinions. He was too big and fat. Not even his being a writer, that most spiritual of occupations, could make him less so.

Shammai was there too. Shammai was neither a poet like Dorban nor a workingman like Gurishkin but a student at the American College in Beirut. However, he thought highly of both poetry and work, having learned to admire them as a child from the Hebrew primers used by his teachers.

Apart from these three, several other young men were having an argument, gusting windily from politics to art to literature to the Hebrew press to the Ninth Zionist Congress and its consequences. Hemdat sat without joining them, alone with his thoughts. Now and then he glanced at Yael's bed, which was made of a board and some oil cans. It looked more like an instrument of torture than something to rest on.

After the argument they sat around chatting. Pizmoni joked with Pnina, and Shammai with Yael. Shammai spat into a cracked pail, then looked at it and said, "Of course, I could be wrong." Soon another argument broke out and lasted until everyone was hoarse. "How about a glass of tea?" Dorban asked. When he wasn't trekking through the desert, he liked his creature comforts. "With pleasure," said Yael and Pnina in one breath. Pnina lit the battered oil burner and Yael poured water in a kettle while Hemdat watched. Unless he imagined it, she took the water from the pail Shammai spat in. The smoke was too much for him.

Hemdat sat on an empty crate near the window, a wallflower in a garden of words. He had a headache and hoped the fresh air would help. "If you don't mind my saying so, Mr. Hemdat," said Yael, "you'll get a concussion from pressing your head against that window." The kettle began to boil. Pnina grabbed a handful of tea leaves and tossed them in. Presto, tea!

"And sugar too," said Yael from her heights. Hemdat sipped his tea. He could not help thinking that he was drinking someone's spittle. When he was done he put the empty glass on the shaky table. "More?" asked Pnina. Hemdat shook his head and said, "No." He sat there silently, answering any questions as though at gunpoint. Words did not come easily to him. He knew he was not clever or witty like the others, and he had no desire to be. In the end they fell flat beneath their own jokes, blank and burdened by weariness. How he yearned for a face that was free, for friends who did not peck at life's slops, who dreamed in the pallor of morning and saw through the noonday sun and ate the bread of unworriedness and spoke of themselves without banter! He threw an involuntary glance at the two girls sitting arm-in-arm on the edge of the bed: Pnina, so good and pure-faced, with her pretty tresses that bored him to tears, and dewier-but-just-as dull Yael. He rose and left.

Jaffa and its little houses stood soundlessly half-sunken in sand. Except for Hemdat, the town had gone to sleep. He walked on and on, his head heavy as a stone yet empty of all thought. He did not love her: he had told himself that a hundred times. He was bound to her by pity. She was misfortune's child and he worried for her like a father for his daughter. He had never once touched her. She did not even excite him. How did he know what she would do if he tried kissing her? He liked to look at her, that was all. It had nothing to do with the lures of sex.

On his way he met Mrs. Ilonit. Mrs. Ilonit was happy to see him, because she had gone out for a walk and was afraid to be alone. She didn't know what had possessed her to go out by herself in the middle of the night. Suppose she ran into an Arab. They were a loathsome people.

Mrs. Ilonit shook Hemdat's hand. Her thumb rested on his pulse. How happy she was to see him! They hadn't met in ages. Since the day of her visit, in fact. Hemdat had gone out that day because the cleaning woman had come, and as he was returning toward evening he met Mrs. Ilonit, who decided to walk him home. His room was a shambles. The table had been moved, and the washbowl left on top of it was full of books. Nothing was in its right place and there was nowhere to sit except the bed, on which a pair of his pants sprawled with its legs sticking out. He couldn't find the lamp or even a candle. The damned little Yemenite had mixed everything up. They were fine at scrubbing and scraping, the Yemenite girls, but they never put anything back. Hemdat lit a match that went out and another that did the same. The room looked as big as a dance hall. "Shall we dance, Mr. Hemdat?" asked Mrs. Ilonit, taking him in her arms. Before he could answer she was waltzing him around. Suddenly she stopped and picked up the pants on the bed. "If I ever have to play a man on stage," she said, "you can lend me these." He was lucky he was a man. What woman could take the liberties with him that she took with him? Mrs. Ilonit clutched his arm. How dark it was getting. She couldn't see a thing. Was that him? "Here, let me feel you." My goodness, she had stumbled right into his arms. Hemdat backed disgustedly away.

Yael, lovelier than ever, came to see Hemdat. She was not alone. Shammai came too. "I won't be a bother," he said, and Yael swore that he never was. In any case, it was the Lord's Sabbath and she hadn't come for a lesson. Shammai looked around and spied a full bottle of wine. "Wine, wine, I am overcome by wine," he cried biblically. He took the bottle and Hemdat gave him a glass. "You shouldn't," Yael said with a smile. "He's still a baby and much too young to drink. I would have thought you'd prefer brandy. There was a lady back home who drank brandy all the time. She was born with a glass in her mouth. She said it was good for toothache and her teeth always ached. The funny part was that she never got drunk. She knew how to hold her liquor. Why don't we go out for a walk?" Hemdat put on his hat and coat, and went for a walk with them.

They walked along the railroad tracks. The walls of Emek Refaim rose on either side of them, two green mattresses of fragrant grass. The tracks gleamed on their wooden ties as though polished. Shammai really was a baby. Suddenly he had a notion to walk on the tracks. Yael had to hold his hand to keep him from falling. Hemdat followed dotingly behind them. They both looked like babies now. Yael raised Shammai's hand and said, "Your hands are so gross, Shammai. Hemdat's hands are as smooth and pretty as a girl's. I do believe that Mr. Hemdat is giving a lecture at the public library tonight. What will you say, Mr. Hemdat? I mean, what will your lecture be about?"

"The stories of Rabbi Nahman of Bratslav," answered Hemdat in a whisper.

"I'll be there to clap for you. Shammai, you have the perfect hands for a standing ovation." Yael clapped her hands and said, "I'm just warming up. Wait until tonight. You better be there, Shammai. Oh, my, look how late it is." Hemdat gave a start. He had almost forgotten that the Mushalams were back in town and that he had promised to drop in on them.

Hemdat couldn't say what drew him to the Mushalams. Before their marriage he had not been especially close to either of them. Not that it wasn't nice to spend time in a tasteful house, even if it was lived in by newlyweds. Shoshanna Mushalam understood him. Unlike some people, she didn't think he had fallen for Yael Hayyut, and the apples she served were immaculately peeled and never came with bits of skin or knife mold. Shoshanna liked the early plays of Ibsen. It wasn't fair that Norway had all those mountains and glaciers when here there was nothing but a bit of sea beyond the flat roofs of the houses and a lot of pushy women playing Florence Nightingale. "That's all there is. Oh, look, the sun is going down. I've never seen anything so gorgeous. I wouldn't leave this place for the world. Happiness for me is going out to my backyard and seeing all the fig trees and dates. It's beyond me how Mrs. Ilonit goes around complaining all the time. Why, it's paradise here! Hemdat, look at all those shooting stars. Someone should give the sky a hanky. When did you last see Yaelchi? I mean Yael Hayyut. How is she? Such a lovely person. I can't believe you'll end up living here, Hemdat. You'll go abroad. You're always welcome to stay with us when you come back, though. Tell me, do you think those frames suit the paintings?"

"Of course, of course," Hemdat nodded automatically. He even found things to praise on his own. The furniture and the house matched perfectly. So did the flowers and the flowerpots. The Mushalams' home smelled of flowers all year long.

Although Mrs. Mushalam was happy to hear nice things about her house, she had too much to say to have time to listen. "Really?" she said and was off again. It was a miracle she had found those flowers. She was on her way to the souk when she saw a little Arab holding them. "Ma'am, ma'am," said the Arab, "buy my flowers." And so she did. "Would you like a glass of water, or some juice? Yael Hayyut loves this juice. Aren't those flowers just bursting with life? O my sweet little darlings!"

Mrs. Mushalam removed her head from the flowers and said to her husband, "Why didn't you tell Hemdat that you read his story 'The Shattered Soul'? Hemdat, I must know if it's about you. I can't believe that your father really walks around with a hasidic fur hat. Here, this flower is a present for you. You can give it to Yael Hayyut. Just don't abscond with it. My spies are everywhere."

Yael Hayyut had never brought him flowers. She couldn't afford them. Once, when a rose fell off her hat, she picked it up and stuck it in the Rembrandt. Although roses were not in season at the time and this one was not real, Hemdat was pleased by the gift. From each according to her ability.

4

Hemdat lay on the divan. Usually Yael arrived between five and six, but today she was late again. She would do him a favor if she didn't come at all. He needed to work and she wasn't letting him. She was taking up all his time. Perhaps he should stop tutoring her.

A gust of wind caught the papers on the table and sent them flying in all directions while riffling the green blotter. Hemdat remained seated. He had a feeling of foreboding. The sky had grown dark. Where was she? Just when he needed her, she hadn't come. His nights would be forlorn without her. There were days when he had to force himself to rise and only bothered to wash because of her. It was six o'clock and still no sign of her.

The wind was blowing harder. A storm was brewing. The street lamps sputtered in vain against the darkness. Swirls of dust spiraled upward, spiraling swirls of gritty dust. His hat nearly flew off his head. What was he doing out in a sandstorm? He began to run down the dark, narrow streets. The sand clung to his feet and lashed his face. He prayed he would make it to Yael's room.

Yael was not in. A small, smoky lamp gave off a dim light. When Pnina turned up the wick, which cast its sickly glare on Hemdat, the flame grew even weaker.

"Where's Yael?" Hemdat asked, looking down to hide his face.

Pnina looked down to hide the fact that she knew what it looked like. "She went to see her mother and stayed. Her bad arm is acting up and the doctor wants to keep her in the hospital."

Suppose it was blood poisoning and they had to amputate? The thought of her lovely body without an arm! He felt overcome by sorrow, but even though he wanted to, he could not cry. He went back to his room and lit the lamp. The night seemed endless. He did not do a single thing he had planned to do, and what he did would better have been left undone.

Pizmoni whistled as he climbed the front steps. He was coming from the hospital, where he had just seen Yael. There was nothing to worry about. It wasn't serious. Tomorrow or the day after, she would come home. After leaving the hospital he had decided to take a walk. What a lovely night it had turned out to be. An hour ago it was blowing like the devil, and now just look at the sky. That was Palestine for you! That was Pizmoni too: one minute with Yael in the hospital and the next minute here. He was in high spirits. A few days ago he had published his poem "The Song of the Strong," which was a new voice in Hebrew literature. Now he had made up his mind to go abroad. A poet without an education was like a candle without a wick. Next summer he planned to start at a European university.

Hemdat enjoyed their walk. The night glowed darkly. A light breeze blew good smells from the wet sand, and the sea murmured in the stillness. The conversation flowed. Pizmoni knew more about the oddest things than all your uncles and cousins combined. I don't know if Yael ever told you what made her come to Palestine, but Pizmoni knew the whole story. What happened was that a friend of hers in Russia had been arrested for subversive activities. When his house was searched, a letter from Yael was found, and although there was nothing against the government in it, she was thrown into jail with a lot of revolutionaries. It cost her father a pretty penny to get her out, and since the police kept following her even then, it was decided to send her to Palestine. Soon afterward her father lost his money and died in poverty, and the shame was so great that her mother packed her things and set out to join Yael. She had barely recovered from the voyage when she fell ill and had to be hospitalized.

Ah, wasn't it the loveliest night! You could walk forever and never tire of the murmur of the sea and the smell of the sand. And what in the whole world tasted better than the salt on your lips? If Pizmoni hadn't needed his sleep, Hemdat could have strolled with him all night.

The next day he put off going to the hospital. The hours passed in sleep. He wrote nothing new and revised nothing old. After parting from Pizmoni, he had stood looking out the window until the sunrise filled his room with light. Now he found himself at the gate of the hospital. Visiting hours were over, but the good-natured attendant let him in.

Outside the ward he found Gurishkin, who had come to see Yael too. Gurishkin was putting his time to good use, for he would have a few pages to add to his autobiography when he sat down later that night by his dim lamp. Although the hospital was a Jewish institution and deserved the public's support, it was so poor that it stood empty most of the year despite the illness going around. Whoever was sick had to go to the Christian hospital and pay ten francs for the pleasure of being preached at.

Yael lay in a bed spread with white sheets, her heavy body rumpling the bedclothes. Her hospital smock gave her an odd look. It was hard to say if she looked happy or sad, but she was glad to be lying in a real bed in a clean room and to be brought her meals without lifting a finger. Even when he stared down at the legs of her bed, Hemdat saw her image before him. So she would look when she gave birth. And that, Hemdat, was the most peculiar thought you ever had in your life.

Hemdat was sure that Yael would marry someone rich. She was not made for drudgery. One day, gaunt from suffering, he would return from afar and come see her. A swarm of children would greet him in the yard and run to their mother's arms. "It's a stranger, Ima," they would say. "Why, it's Hemdat," Yael would exclaim, jumping with joy. In the evening her husband would come home from work and sit down to eat with them. Hemdat would be far too frail to arouse his envy.

He was on his way to the hospital again when he was told that Yael had been released. She was planning to leave for Jerusalem the next day. It seemed that she needed a minor operation, and Mrs. Mushalam was going with her. Mrs. Mushalam had to go to Jerusalem to buy inlaid furniture from Damascus.

How would Yael pay for the trip? Hemdat felt his pocket. There was nothing in it, but he was owed some money by Dr. Pikchin. Dr. Pikchin was a leader of the Jewish community and Hemdat had served as his secretary. When he found him, he said:

"Doctor, I would appreciate it if you could give the money you owe me to Yael Hayyut."

Dr. Pikchin puffed silently on his pipe.

"You can tell her, Doctor," said Hemdat, who had to walk fast to keep up with him, "that the hospital is paying for her treatment. She doesn't have to know where the money came from. Have you heard that Efrati is back from Europe? They say that he did a lot for this country when he lived here."

Dr. Pikchin took his pipe from his mouth and said, "Everyone who comes back from abroad thinks he's done a lot for Jewish settlement."

"But he really did," said Hemdat eagerly. "When I was abroad I heard of him too."

Dr. Pikchin put his pipe back in his mouth and said, "Everyone who comes back from Europe says that he did a lot for this country."

"I was just making conversation," said Hemdat, his eagerness gone.

Hemdat ran into Yael. He was happy to hear she was all right. Yael gave him her cold hand to shake. She looked well but distracted. "Why don't we buy a herring," she said as they stood in the street.

Hemdat was glad that they had met, and that she wanted to eat with him, and that his room was nearby. She climbed the stairs to it with stately steps. He lit the lamp and set the table. There was butter and honey and jam. Who wanted jam, though? Yael was set on herring. She never ate preserves. Herring was what she craved.

III

The green-globed lamp gave off a tender light. On the green tinted walls the pots and pans gleamed larger than life. Shadow rubbed against shadow and pot against pan. Hemdat sat eating with Yael. Their shadows danced on the walls, barely touching. Yael poured Hemdat tea. "Why don't you drink your tea?" she asked. "Or didn't I pour you any?"

"You did," he said.

Yael said, "I'll bet you're afraid to gain weight and spoil your good looks. Is that it, Mr. Hemdat?"

Hemdat smiled and said nothing. Yael thought that writers never stayed good-looking for long. Their chests collapsed from sitting so much and their hair fell out from too many thoughts. Each time Hemdat spoke, his face clouded with romantic anguish. It was as though he were in one place and his mind in another. What was he thinking? "Thinking?" he said. "I was thinking how many hankies you need for one snotty nose." Writers could be a vulgar lot.

Yael was tired and stretched out on the divan. Hemdat offered her a pillow. She asked him to sit next to her and ran her hand along the wall. Back when her hair had been long, there had been a nail over her bed. She had slept on her side with her hair wrapped around it and her mother had woken her by undoing it and laying it on the pillow by her head. Everyone said it would grow back.

Yael lay on the divan. "Poets lose their hair on top," she said, "and philosophers in front. Some men are so bald that they don't have a single hair left." There was a man in Dostoevsky with hair on his teeth, but Yael had her doubts about that. "I'll bet he made it up," she said. How could anyone have hair on his teeth? However, she also had doubts about her doubts, because her best friend Pnina had a dark white spot right over her heart.

Hemdat's room was agreeably restful. Yael lay on the divan and Hemdat sat by her side. She opened her eyes, and when their eyes met both turned red as if a blush had passed between them. Hemdat rose determinedly and went to open a window to keep his flushed cheeks from being seen. The lamplight trembled. He hastened to trim the wick. The night blew sweetly through the open window. One summer Yael had spent moonlit nights like these in the lean-to of a field guard in the vineyards of Rehovot. Night cloaked the earth and the foxes barked and the wind blew through the vines and Pizmoni told legends of long ago on a straw mat in the vineyards of Rehovot.

"Tell me a story," Yael said to Hemdat. "Tell me something you remember." Right away she forgot what she had asked him and began telling him how hard her first days in Jaffa had been, when she lay ill by herself in a rented room until she was taken to the hospital.

Hemdat covered his eyes to hide his tears and a tear tumbled onto his fingers. How sorry he felt for her and how happy that she was telling him all this. Her eyes shone serenely in dark, green-tinted repose. Calmly she showed him the scar on her arm. The same arm that deserved to be covered with kisses bore the scrawl of a scar. Thank God she was going to Jerusalem, where there was a good hospital for her to get treatment.

Yael glanced at him and said, "Who knows when we'll see each other again? I want you to tell me something."

"And what, my child," asked Hemdat with a smile, "is that?"

Yael ran a hand over her hair. "What are you?"

Hemdat did not answer.

Yael pouted indignantly and said, "I'm not asking if you're a Zionist or a communist or anything like that. When I was a girl I had a friend who wrote in my class yearbook: 'Our lives are as pointless as a dead tree.' Isn't that a nice way of putting it? He used to say, 'I don't care what party you belong to, I care what you are.' What are you?"

"Me?" said Hemdat, letting his head fall back. "I'm a sleeping prince whose true love puts him back to sleep. I'm love's beggar walking around with love in a torn old bag."

5

Yael was still in Jerusalem, and Hemdat puttered about busy Jaffa. What was he doing there? What had brought him to this place? He twisted and turned inside himself, his torment unremitting. He was as lost on the dark plain of time as a solitary groan or a faded spark.

His shadow marched before him beneath a profuse sun, up and down winding streets without a blade of grass to relieve their harsh lines. How small it was and what tiny legs it had. A man's foot could cover the lower half of it.

Behind him, like a solid mirror, was the life he had lived, sunk in the doldrums of melancholy. And as in a mirror, he saw the days ahead, without change or the prospect of change. There was nothing to see but the endless, oppressive emptiness of a mirror reflected in a mirror. He wanted to cry and vent his sorrow, but the sun would have dried his unshed tears. Hope alone kept him going. The black mood would pass, he told himself. He would sleep for twenty-four hours, take a hot bath, and emerge a new man.

He longed for it to be winter. A cold wind would blow, the sea would pound, and he would rise cheerful and fit from a delicious sleep beneath warm blankets. Then would come days in which he would write his great novel. The kettle would boil and hot coffee would froth in his cup. In the garden the citron would flower beneath a brilliant moon, its branches dripping fragrance. The starry sky would sweeten the soft silence and Hemdat would pour the dew of his soul into the sea-blue night.

A caravan of camels plodded by, four-legged porters carrying twice their weight. Behind them came their driver, a two-legged camel crooning to Allah for strength. People passed, among them Mrs. Ilonit. A dentist drove by in a carriage and the coachman cried, "Cheap! Cheap! Cheap! Twelve bishliks a tooth, teeth pulled for twelve bishliks!" Men and women crowded around, and the dentist pulled their teeth.

The souk was teeming. Arabs stood selling cold drinks on crates filled with bottles and glasses. Here and there a white Panama hat gleamed amid the forest of red fezes. Shopkeepers sat in front of their shops, hawking bolts of fabric and colorful clothes in loud voices. Greek vendors hunched over their coals and spits of meat. A big beefsteak draped with gold tinsel hung before a butcher shop, glittering brightly despite the bugs and flies swarming over it. An old Arab straddled a basket of bananas, peeling them unhurriedly for customers who stood spitting out the seeds. Sailors from all over strutted with outthrust chests as if to embrace every female that their hungry eyes devoured. A semicircle of squatting women sold cut flowers and wild lilies.

Everyone was busy but Hemdat, alone in his own hapless world. I can't simply do nothing, he told himself. I had better go see Pikchin. Perhaps he'll give me some work or have news of Yael. There were two bishliks left in his pocket. He bought a bunch of roses with one and looked around for a shoeshine man. Two ran for Hemdat's shoes and started to fight over them. One took his shoeshine stand and hurled it at the other's head. While the blood was running down the second man's face, a third came along and grabbed Hemdat's feet. Hemdat threw him his last coin, and the man let out a whistle and scampered off with it.

Everyone, everyone, thought Hemdat self-improvingly, is doing something. How could he remain idle, faced with such a spirit of enterprise? He wanted to work, to accomplish. He would make lots of money before Yael returned to Jaffa. He had been a fool to throwaway a good job.

Hemdat entered Pikchin's office just as an armless man was carried in and laid on the couch in the waiting room, like a broken wagon wheel waiting to be fixed. Hemdat sat without moving, embarrassed to have the full use of his limbs. He crossed his legs and looked out to sea. A southbound ship was making for the harbor. Soon it would anchor with another group of immigrants, new faces with new hopes and the same old problems.

Dr. Pikchin attended to the amputee and then sat down with Hemdat and dictated a few letters. Hemdat reached home exhausted. His head ached and he could barely move his legs. Yet even when he flopped down weakly on his bed and fell asleep, his nerves kept crawling like worms. Something was the matter with his brain. Perhaps it needed to be pulled by a dentist. He sat upright in bed, terrified of going mad. What would become of him? One morning he would awake to find that he was out of his mind.

Although Hemdat came on his father's side from a distinguished old family, its vital force had run down in him, its last hope. Of course, he was young and had hardly lived yet. But did not Rabbi

Nahman say that some people had lived more by the age of eighteen than others at seventy?

Hemdat thought of a pretty cousin of his who also had rebelled and left home. She had had a lovely voice and wanted to be a singer, and when her parents objected she ran away to Vienna and got along there on nothing, studying as much and eating as little as she could while waiting for the day she could support herself. Yet her dreams proved greater than her strength, which soon gave out, so that on the night of her debut before a large audience blood spurted from her mouth with the first note. Her parents came to take her home and plied her with doctors and drugs, and now, her lovely voice stilled, she never left her bed. Her brain had been affected too, and she lay wrapped in white in a white room with white walls and white rugs. All this whiteness was reflected in a large mirror, and if a doctor happened to bring her red roses, she sprinkled them with white powder while gazing off into dim space.

Once, as darkness was falling, Hemdat came to visit her. At first, although her eyes clung to him, she did not know who he was. Then she rose from her bed, spread her long, cold fingers, and ran them over his face. "Hemdat," she said.

Hemdat jumped to his feet. He was certain that Yael Hayyut had called him. In this he was greatly mistaken, for he had imagined it. Grieving, he lay down again.

Hemdat lay in bed, his heart wide awake. Pikchin has nothing for you? Then sit down at your desk and get to work. You wanted to translate Jacobsen's *Niels Lyhne*? Then do. He rose to get some paper and a new pen nib. The old nib was rusty. That was as far as he got. Still, it was a start.

Every morning Hemdat stepped out onto his terrace and gazed down at the railroad tracks in Emek Refaim. They gleamed as though polished. The train passed twice a day. Yael Hayyut would be on it and look out the window at him. "Hello, hello!" she would call. He secretly dreamed of a warm kiss. Yael would come and find him hard at work, and his chaste lips would linger on her pretty face. Though he was no longer the Don Juan he once had been, her calm mien stirred a longing for the pure elixir of a kiss. Someday, when he was already an old man, such pleasures would be his by right. He knew that Yael had been kissed before, but each kiss was holy to her and no man had profaned her face.

Hemdat got nowhere with his work. The sun beat down, its flat rays stinging like gnats and sapping his will. It was too hot, his heart was too inflamed, to get anything done. He remembered the days when his soul dripped its leafy dew on the tender buds of his poems while coffee sputtered on the alcohol stove. He wanted them back again and went to light the stove. Hemdat drank coffee like water. Black coffee must be running in his veins.

For hours, his eyes open and his mind blank, he lay on the divan without boredom. Weary was what he was, with a harsh, prolonged weariness. Oh, Lord, he said aloud, annoyed by the languor of his voice. Oh, Lord, where can I find rest. He lay without moving hand or foot, like a man about to be flogged. He heard the rumble of a train. It whistled as it approached.

A frightening shriek tore the silence. The train rushed by and was gone, leaving behind a slanting corkscrew of dark blue smoke.

"Yael!" cried Hemdat, jumping to his feet. Quickly he tidied up, did the dishes, spread the table with new wax paper, washed, put on fresh clothes, and sat down. His body came to life, his fingers sapient. The pen began to move, distributing letters over the page that joined into words, lines, sentences. I do believe the translation went well.

The hours went by and Yael did not come. Hemdat feared he had been wrong. Perhaps she had not been on the train after all. He had not seen her face, only a green coat. Could she already be wearing winter clothes? What would his landlord's daughters say? The dowdy guests our tenant has! He had made a mistake. It was not Yael. Her face had been turned away from him. Surely she would not have ridden by in the train without a glance at his room.

Yael was back. She had not been seen looking so well since she arrived from Russia. Hemdat wondered if her hair had grown. You'll find out when you see her tomorrow or the day after, he told himself, having heard from Pnina that she would come then. She had first gone to visit her mother in Rehovot. Yael's mother was going back to Russia. An old woman like her was not meant for Palestine, nor was the country meant for her. Once, when Jews were more stalwart, coming to live out one's last years in the Land of Israel had been the thing to do, but nowadays no punishment was harder. The sky dripped sweat, the earth brimmed dust, and a person did not last long. Even the food was not fit to eat. Whatever Yael's mother ate went straight to her kidneys.

Hemdat, however, did not spend his time thinking about old people in the Land of Israel. He was twenty-two years old, Hemdat was, and not overly concerned with his digestion. If he had a bishlik he bought some bread, and if he had another, some figs, dates, or olives to go with it. "A land wherein you will eat bread without scarcity," the Bible called it, and it had everything anyone could want. If you have any doubts about that, just count the treats that Hemdat bought for Yael.

Every morning after rising he cleaned his room—in fact, sometimes every minute. He changed his clothes each day and glanced often at the glass frame of the picture—that is, in case you have forgotten, at Rembrandt's *Bride and Groom*. His room was spic-and-span, the table was freshly covered, and everything smelled good. He even scrubbed the floor all by himself. There was reason to suspect that he did it with eucalyptus water.

Having accomplished all this, Hemdat sat down at the table, picked up his pen, and guided it across the paper. How fine the tiny letters looked on the white page! Besides the page in front of him, two or three blank ones were laid on the edge of the table. Every few minutes he rose to open or close the window. Although he liked the breeze blowing through it, he also liked the quiet when it was shut, and since it was hard to decide, he kept changing his mind. Meanwhile, he heard Yael's voice. Hemdat ran to the window. Yael was standing below. She had only a minute.

"Why don't you come up," he called down.

"Why won't you come down," she called up.

"Come," said Hemdat.

"I can't," said Yael. "I have no time."

Hemdat glanced back at his room as he started down the stairs. Bright and shiny though it was, it looked in mourning.

6

She came that evening. Hemdat met her in the yard. He held out his hand to her and said, "Come. Let's go to my room."

"Why?" asked Yael. "We could take a walk."

They walked awhile, and Hemdat asked, "Why didn't you write me from Jerusalem?"

"I didn't think you would answer," Yael said. And when he looked at her in silence, she added, "Pizmoni's gone."

"Where is he?"

"At some university."

"What is he studying?"

"Zoology," said Yael. "He should have chosen botany." She would write him a long letter if she knew his address. Though, of course, he might not answer.

Hemdat broke his silence and began to talk. He hadn't talked so much since the day he swore off women. It was unwise of him to let Yael know how he had longed for such a conversation. The more things he told her, the more trivial, even illogical, she became. At first, she said, she had found him insufferable. There had been something ridiculous about him. A woman passing in the street could make him blush. She would be a happy person if she knew Hebrew. That was her one desire.

Hemdat knew it was just chitchat, but he listened and was sorry when they parted. Before that, they came to a dune called the Hill of Love. Yael's tall figure reached it first. Hemdat trailed behind her. He hadn't kept a thing from her. He swung his arms limply, nothing left to say.

The dune was a lovely place on which to sit at night. The sand was dry and fragrant. Hemdat bent and scooped up a handful of it and they sat together on a little hillock. The words trickled a while longer from the wellspring of his heart and stopped. His right hand played with the sand, squeezing the gritty grains between his fingers and letting them run out. His hands felt cold. A breeze blew from the sea. Hemdat made a half-fist and placed it over his mouth like an empty clam shell. Yael glanced at him and said, "Why are you growing a beard? You look better without it. Something is digging into me. Oh, it's the key." She took the key to her room and handed it to Hemdat. Hemdat stuck it in his pocket.

All at once Yael rose. "Home!" she said. Hemdat walked her back and handed her the key. Yael opened the door and shut it from within. Hemdat's pocket was empty. For a while he stood on the front stoop. He had thought she would turn around to say goodnight. Her firm footsteps rang in his ears. Hemdat smiled mockingly at himself and at his hopes, and went home.

*   *   *

Once she had come all the time, every evening of the week and twice on Saturdays, and now she had vanished.

"Why don't you come anymore?" Hemdat asked Yael when he met her in the souk.

"I don't want to keep you from your work," Yael said. He had to work. The Mushalams had asked her what he lived off.

Yael Hayyut found an easy job overseeing the woman workers in a small fabrics factory. Hemdat talked to the manager, who agreed to hire her. Yael would make twenty-five francs a month, perhaps even thirty. "To tell you the truth," said the manager, "I'm overpaying her at fifteen, but who can say no to a poet waxing eloquent?" Yael Hayyut had to pinch herself. She could rent a better room and buy a stove to cook on. She had already ruined her digestion. She thanked Hemdat for his efforts.

Hemdat went to get his hair cut. On the faded sign outside the barbershop was a man with a towel around his neck sitting in front of a barber. A small girl walked by, spat naughtily at the man, and ran off. Hemdat asked for a shave and a haircut. He was happy to have done Yael a good turn. The barber noticed his good mood and delivered a poetic speech about authors, who would sooner style their hair than their prose and cut their long locks than a word from their books. The scissors clicked and the barber's eyes peered shrewdly out from a sea of hair to see what impression he was making. Hemdat was looking at his own hair, which lay scattered on the floor. "Right you are, old man," said the barber. "The crown of your head's on the ground to be tread." When the barber was done, Hemdat looked in the mirror and saw his smooth, naked skull instead of his rich chestnut hair. He nodded and said, "There's nothing like a change."

That evening he went to see Yael Hayyut. The sight of what Hemdat had done to his beautiful hair nearly drove Yael crazy. His head came to a funny point. It was like a stand without a use. Hemdat took Yael's hand. Back in Europe he had taken his little sister's hand after shaving and run it over his cheek. "Ouch!" she had cried.

What more shall we tell you about Hemdat? All would have gone well with him had only it gone well with Yael Hayyut. Yael had a new worry. She had barely recovered before her arm got worse again. It wasn't the future that troubled her, it was the past that wouldn't go away. Yael had poor circulation and lived in fear of blood poisoning, and the slightest pain made her afraid that the arm would have to be amputated. Hemdat prayed for her health as though for a king's. He brought her milk and medicines, and sat by her bed all day. "Yael's brother," he was called by the children in the neighborhood, and he bore the name with pride. An angelic soul, said the neighbors, which made him blush and bow his head. His alcohol stove had been thoroughly ruined by Yael, but she was getting better and soon was out of bed again.

Hemdat tidied up his room and went to see Yael. On the way he met an elder colleague. It was kind of the elder colleague to walk Hemdat to Yael, since it was Hemdat's friendship with her that had caused him to stop seeing Hemdat—for Hemdat, thought his colleague, was spending too much time with Yael and not enough on his work. How pleased Yael would be to be visited by a famous author. She would tell all her friends that a famous author had been to see her.

The more was the pity, then, that Yael was not home. Tomorrow, thought Hemdat, she'll come to see me. But she did not.

Hemdat ran into Yael in the street and asked her why she hadn't come. She had wanted to, she said. Her room was like an oven. There was so little air that not a feather stirred in her torn pillow. "Then why didn't you come?" asked Hemdat. "I was embarrassed," said Yael, "because I don't have a good dress."

Next he met Mrs. Mushalam. Breezy Mrs. Mushalam was happy to see him. Dorban walked doubled over by her side, his hands gripping the ends of a rope. Although his meters were based on camel steps, he looked like anyone else beneath a load. Mrs. Mushalam had bought her husband the complete Brockhaus for his birthday, and Mr. Dorban had been kind enough to lend a hand. It wasn't the latest edition, but you could hardly tell the difference. An encyclopedia was an encyclopedia. Of course, each edition had something new, but in Palestine one learned to make do. You could find everything in it from Chrysanthemums to Vasco da Gama. Reading an encyclopedia was like taking a tour around the world. She had already learned that Wasserman's *Caspar Hauser* was based on a story from real life. "But why," said Mrs. Mushalam, "should I even be talking to a man who hasn't come to see my new furniture from Jerusalem? Didn't Yael tell you about the inlaid furniture that I bought?" She held out a bouquet of roses and said, "Here, smell this rose."

Hemdat apologized. "I've been meaning to come," he said, "especially since there was something I wanted to talk to you about."

Mrs. Mushalam pulled a rose stem from the bouquet as if reading his thoughts.

Hemdat buried his face in the rose. "When Yael's mother left," he said, "she gave me money for Yael to buy fabric for a dress. Yael can sew it herself." It was Hemdat's misfortune that he always blushed when he lied, but Mrs. Mushalam was a kind heart and did not hold it against him. "You needn't tell Yael who gave it to you," Hemdat said. "Any story will be fine. What a surprise it will be when she comes around in a new dress."

Hemdat jumped back and rubbed his forehead. He had been

stung by a bee. No, it was only a thorn. "The Revenge of the Rose," said Mrs. Mushalam, laughing.

Although Hemdat did not know what fabric Yael would buy, he tried picturing her in her new dress. And if it is possible to picture a scent, he imagined that too. All day long he waited for her to come. But she did not. What was keeping her? Surely not the lack of a dress. Toward evening he left his room for the first time. What had he done at home all day? He had waited for Yael. And why had he not gone to see her? Because he had cleaned his room for her and wanted to share its intimacy with her. Now that his hopes had waned with the day, he stepped out.

Sandy Jaffa was at rest. The whole town had gone to walk by the sea. Hemdat strolled among the mounds of sand. A sound of singing came from some houses. Old Jews were sitting over the Sabbath's last meal and singing the Sabbath's last hymns. Hemdat felt a twinge. Through an open window he heard the rabbi giving a sweet-voiced homily. He tore himself away and walked to the sea. When Yael's laugh reached him from a group of young people on the beach, he moved away and sat down by himself.

Hemdat sat facing the sea. The lacy waves raced in. Perhaps they bore Yael's image. Pnina spied Hemdat and called to him from afar. Yael joined in, bidding him to come. Hemdat rose and went over. Pnina and the others slipped away. Yael acquiesced and stayed with Hemdat.

Although evening had fallen, there was still a bit of light in the sky. Suddenly Yael got to her feet and said, "I've creased my dress."

Hemdat looked at her and said, "Wear it well. It's very nice fabric."

"My mother bought it. I sewed it," said Yael measuredly, running a hand over the dress as if to brush something away. What childish pride. She studied him as though comparing their clothes. His pants cuffs were frayed and loose threads stuck out of them. It was the fault of the pigeon-toed way he walked, which made his legs rub dolefully together.

Hemdat traced some letters in the sand. At first he did not realize that they spelled Yael Hayyut. Although it was banal, he wanted to show her her name. Along came a wavelet and washed it away. Hemdat watched the waves lick at the sand and fall silently back. Yael got to her feet. She was hungry and wished to go home. Hemdat knew she had no food there and invited her to eat with him. Not in his room but in a restaurant. Yael said no. Then she said yes. Then she said no and yes. Hemdat was in rare spirits. He would not have to eat by himself.

They went to Yaakov Malkov's inn. For once Hemdat was not his own housekeeper. Mrs. Malkov wiped the Sabbath wine from the table and Mr. Malkov spread a fresh cloth. Yael ordered meat, and Hemdat ordered dairy and fish. Hemdat did not eat meat. The truth was that he would have given up fish too, but he did not want to be labeled a vegetarian. Mrs. Malkov took away the big tablecloth and brought two smaller ones, one for meat and one for dairy. Hemdat regarded the plain strip of table between the two festive tablecloths.

As he was eating Malkov asked him, "If you're a vegetarian, how come you eat fish?" "Because," Hemdat said, "the fish didn't sin before the Flood and weren't punished by it."

Malkov did a doubletake. Today's young men had an answer for everything. What answer would they have on Judgment Day? He rose and went off singing an end-of-the-Sabbath hymn, and came back with a bowl full of almonds. Hemdat beamed at him. "That's my man, Reb Yaakov," he said, sliding the bowl over toward Yael.

The almonds had a tangy bitterness. Hemdat dipped one in sweet wine and watched Yael's jaws bulge as the strong teeth she had bitten off his hair with cracked almond after almond. Yael rose and went to the sink for a glass of water. Hemdat poured her some wine. She shook her head. "I want water," she said with a toss of her proud shoulders.

Mr. Malkov's little daughter came to remove the tablecloth and whispered to Hemdat, "She's so pretty."

Hemdat patted her fondly on the ear.

7

Hemdat enjoyed Shammai's visits. Shammai was a sight to see when he talked about Yael. He had visited her every day in the hospital, walking all the way to Jaffa. He had guarded her like a watchdog. And yet Yael could not stand him. She did not want him anywhere near her. Hemdat must remind her when he saw her that evening of everything Shammai had done for her. Really, Yael, what an ingrate you are.

Shammai's enthusiasms delighted him. He was so youthfully naive. What did Yael have against him?

A few days went by. Yael was nowhere to be seen. Shammai dropped by. He had a walking stick, a safari hat, high boots, and a full picnic basket. Where was he off to?

Shammai had rented a carriage and was inviting Hemdat to come on a trip to Rehovot. "Please do us the honor," he said. "Yael is coming too." Shammai's eyes came to rest on the Rembrandt and his reflection appeared between the couple there.

Hemdat removed the picture from the wall. As if Yael cared whether he came or not. "Yes or no," Shammai had said. "If you don't come, Mrs. Ilonit would like your place."

Who was Shammai to be chasing after Yael Hayyut? Shammai was the son of a Jewish businessman who owned land in Palestine and lived in America and supported a family left behind in Russia, plus Shammai, who was studying medicine at the American College in Beirut. On his vacations Shammai came to Palestine to acquaint himself with the site of his future practice. His coarse hands and jowly cheeks should not mislead you into thinking that he wasn't an idealist. Was it because he said, "Why don't you drop in on us?" that he blushed when urging Hemdat to visit Yael? It made Hemdat laugh to hear him declare boyishly, "I love what you write, Hemdat. Everything of yours is so perfect. I'll be damned if I know why Pizmoni is called a poet. I've never read a single line of his."

Really, Hemdat asked himself, why don't you go see Yael? After all, she invited you through Shammai. One evening he went. Yael's embarrassment was great. She was wearing Shammai's jacket, and

Shammai lay sprawled on the couch. His smooth jowls that looked like an extension of his swollen neck erupted in strained, triumphal laughter.

They both jumped to their feet and said, "Why, it's Hemdat! How about some seltzer and lemon marmalade? Or perhaps you would like an aperitif. There's nothing like a little drink before dinner. You'll stay to eat with us, of course."

How, Hemdat wondered, could they sit in a room with no air? The place was a mess. Shammai's ties hung over the back of the couch and a pair of slippers lay under each bed.

Hemdat did not judge Yael harshly. She had been hungry, and Shammai kept her not only in bread but in chocolates. When you came right down to it, she was a simple girl. Before you knew it she would be the fat wife of some businessman, with lots of children. He bore her no grudge. He did not mention her name anymore.

The summer was coming to an end. The days were muggy. An immense, relentless sun baked the city and there was not a breath of air. The best thing to do was to stay home and sweat as little as possible. Hemdat rarely went out. The coffee beaker bubbled all day and he drank cup after cup. It did not make him less lethargic but it did give him something to do. Not that there weren't other ways of taking one's mind off oneself. He could have gone to see the founding of Tel Aviv, for which there happened to be a party that day. All Jaffa celebrated with wine and cake except Hemdat, who stayed home drinking black coffee.

Hemdat's friends began dropping by again. It must have been the simmer of the coffee. Gurishkin was in fine fettle. He was now a founder of Tel Aviv and the chronicler of a city. Dorban was tipsy most of the time, which did not make him any less himself. The thought of the first Jewish metropolis left a desert rat like him cold. His muse was not about to be seduced by it. Gurishkin did not take him seriously. Dorban had yet to publish a thing. If Gurishkin was up in arms about anyone, it was Pizmoni, who had just come out with a new poem entitled "On the Banks of the Dnieper." How could you call yourself a Palestinian poet and write about Russian rivers? Hemdat kept filling their glasses. If the wine made them drunk, the coffee sobered them up. The conversation shifted from patriotism and poetry to women and love.

Hemdat, who had been sitting there quietly, stirred and said, "If you're in your right mind you shouldn't go out with a girl unless you take along a fat imbecile. She's sure to fall in love with him and spare you a messy romance."

Pnina hung her chaste head. She would never have thought that Hemdat could be so crude.

Hemdat stepped outside. In the street he bumped into Yael and Shammai. "How much did the meal at Malkov's cost?" they asked. Yael wanted to pay for her share. Hemdat smiled awkwardly. "It isn't fair of you not to answer, Hemdat," said Yael. "There's nothing to say," Hemdat said. "It's an insult to Yael not to tell her," said Shammai. "Why don't you visit me?" asked Yael. "Why don't you visit me?" asked Hemdat. "I did," said Yael. "You weren't in. If you don't believe me, your green jacket was on the chair by the table." "Then come now," Hemdat said. "No, you come first," said Yael. They changed the subject.

Hemdat had told Yael what he thought of Shammai, which was not very much. Shammai's father was sweating to put him through college, and Shammai was living high and growing a paunch at his father's expense. He could never make a woman happy. All he could do was stain her honor. And now that he was not in the best of mental states, Hemdat was a danger too. "If you value your peace and quiet," he told Yael, "stay away from me, because whatever I've got may be catching." He knew she would pass what he said on to Shammai. What else could you expect from a gossip like her? Shammai was sporting her ring. Where was Hemdat going? He was going to tell Shammai he hadn't meant it.

Hemdat was plagued once more by carnal desires. One sea-blue night followed another. He would have liked to run into Mrs. Ilonit. The summer was almost over. Although the girls still went about in short sleeves, in another week or two you would be able to touch them without feeling the clamor of the flesh. Hemdat had women on his mind. Being with them made him feel worse, though. Sometimes he still thought of the time he had kissed the hands of mothers in public and the lips of their daughters in private, and sometimes he no longer could imagine it.

When his loneliness was too much for him he left his room and went out, but it followed him everywhere. He shrank from the smell of humanity. He wanted to get as far away from it and into himself as he could, oblivious of others and even, in the quiescence of bone and blood, of his own self. And yet someone had only to lay a friendly hand on his neck to make him quiver with hidden bliss.

Hemdat roamed the streets of Jaffa. His days passed with no purpose and his nights with no rest. He must not let it get him down, his friends said. It was the lull before the creative storm. And indeed something great was brewing in the world. He could hear the tread of things to come. And whatever was heard by his dreaming ears was also heard, seen, and smelled by his other senses. Great events were afoot and the palpable world would step aside to make way for them. The dull, sweltering day was nearly over. Soon it would be night.

Hemdat's room was on the top floor and had five windows. They were open all day, and green curtains rippled on them like the waves of a river, checkering the floor with tufts of light and darkness. Hemdat paced the room, up and down and across and back. Although the windows were open in all directions, the door was shut tight. Hemdat knew that the Blessed Days had come to the world. You could not find him in the streets of Jaffa or down at the beach. He sat in his room in front of his faithful table. How was he celebrating the holiday? With the gift-offering of his poetry. The summer was gone and the winds were starting up again. The eucalyptus trees swayed in the gardens and shed their wilted leaves. A dry leaf flitted in a corner of the room. The wind had blown it in.

The sun was setting, and black clouds flew like birds at summer's end. Should he light the lamp? Why sit in darkness? Yael would come. He would be good to her. All was forgiven. They would sit close together on the green divan. She was his beloved.

How long have I known Yael? Hemdat wondered. For ages and ages, he told himself. Perhaps a year and perhaps more. On one of those light nights that flared in early summer he had gone for a walk to the dune. Some young ladies were out for a stroll. One of stately step kept laughing and tugging at her hat brim.

Hemdat rose and left his room.

Before he knew it, he had reached the dune.

He circled it at an even distance.

Then he was standing on top of it.

A chill, greenish moon lit the dune. Here, in this place, he first had seen her. Here he had walked with her. The Hill of Love, it was called. He felt a pressure in his heart. How close it all seemed. Her words lingered over the sand. That woman was born with a glass in her mouth. She never got drunk, though. She knew how to hold her liquor.

Hemdat stood on the dune. Just then he saw a shadow. It puzzled him, like an unfamiliar object found by a man returning home. He knew the dune and everything on it well. He tried to comprehend the shadow. Was it a bush or tree that had sprung up miraculously overnight? Perhaps it was a late stroller.

If it is the shadow of a tree, Hemdat told himself, our love is rooted and will last, and if it is the shadow of a person, it soon will be gone. He froze and did not move, willing himself between hope and despair. A sudden calm, like that between a baby's fall and its cry, came over him. The shadow stirred and moved in his direction. Ah, sighed Hemdat, it's a living creature. Was it a man or a woman? It was a woman. He took a deep breath and thought:

Thank God it's not Yael Hayyut, because if it were Yael Hayyut that would be a bad sign.

It was Yael Hayyut.

She did not look his way.

Hemdat came down from the dune.

Translated by Hillel Halkin

Knots Upon Knots

Even I was invited to the craftsmen's convention. Since they had invited me I said, I'll go. I gathered my overnight things and wrapped them in paper and took along several copies of my new book, for several of those who had requested copies of my book were sure to be at the convention, and by giving it to them I would not have to bother with the mails. It would have been good had I put my belongings in a satchel, except that a satchel is useful only as long as it carries your belongings. Once empty, it is simply a load to be carried.

I came to the city and left my things at the bookbinder's place as I always do when I come to town, and then I set out for the convention building.

The hall was filled to overflowing. With difficulty I found myself a cramped spot among the many visitors, some invited and some uninvited. When my eyes had become clear of the stuffiness in the air I saw Joseph Eibeschütz standing before me. And since he is smaller than I in height, it seemed to me that I was sheltering him. His ears were red out of the strain of his effort to listen closely. But don't be surprised, for at that moment the elder of the craftsmen was lecturing about all that had been introduced in his generation, and here Eibeschütz wanted to grasp the essence of the era's innovations.

I greeted him with a nod, but did not ask him, Surely you wanted to visit me, so why didn't you come? Nor did he apologize that he had not come. Others came and pushed their way between us, and I was pushed from my spot. And as long as I had been pushed, I left.

Since I had come for the sake of the convention but had not found myself anything to do, it appeared to me as if I had been blessed with a day that was entirely my own. I said to myself, As long as that's so, I'll take a little walk.

I took myself toward the Gates of Mercy and went down into the valley behind the houses, and from there I went up the hill that overlooks the valley.

The month of Heshvan was already over. Bands of clouds lay beneath the heavens and hung over the low trees on the hill. Their branches lowered themselves to the earth to form a kind of booth. And within that booth sat a group of men, among them Samuel Emden, who was striking out at adherents of the known craft. It was easy to understand his coming to the craftsmen's convention but difficult to understand why he was here and not there. Since I knew him I went up to him.

At that moment he was sitting and discussing a matter that as yet had no interpreters, although a few people had begun to be aware of it. As soon as he saw me he greeted me and made room for me at his side. And he went on speaking, setting forth hidden matters as if they were explicit. When he paused I said to him, "That was a nice letter you wrote me. Perhaps I was supposed to have answered it?" This question was hardly necessary, for there had been nothing in the letter that required an answer. But when I asked him his face whitened like that of one who has been insulted. And I knew that I had not done well to leave his letter unanswered.

After a short while he and all the members of the group stood up and went on their way.

I too stood up and went on my way.

It would have been good had I returned home, but the day was drawing to a close and my house is far from the city and the buses to my neighborhood had already stopped running. There was nothing for me to do but to look around for an inn to find myself a place for the night. I went to the bookbinder's to get my overnight things before he locked up the workroom.

Upon entering the bookbinder's place I found several members of Emden's group. From their manner it was apparent that they too had deposited their things there. And they whose feet were lighter than my thoughts had gotten there before me.

The old bookbinder stood in the entrance, twisting his sash on his loins in the manner of one who prepares himself for prayer. Afterward he took a bunch of keys and handed them over to him to whom he gave them and went on his way. When the one had gone, the other got up and gave each and everyone his belongings. Finally, with his keys in his hand, he showed me a many-chambered chest that held the articles I had brought today as well as those I had left there days and weeks and months before. Not only many articles, but numerous books that the binder had bound for me were piled in several places. I had no need of them at that moment, nor did I have a satchel or suitcase at hand to hold them. Consequently I kept my hands off them and took my overnight things.

Meanwhile the members of the group had gathered their things and were taking out their wallets to pay a storage fee. I was amazed that they were paying a storage fee, for the binder had never asked a fee of me for anything I had left with him. Since I saw that all were paying, I rummaged in my pocket and asked, "And how much must I pay?" And I thought, Without a doubt this fellow is going to ask a fee for each and every package. I became enraged that for the sake of one piece of rope with which I had not tied all the packages into one, I was to be charged who knows how much. He shook his head at me by way of saying no and did not request a fee. But he urged me to clear out my things, for the painter was to come the next day to paint the workroom and he could not guarantee that my things would not be lost, and even if they were not lost they were sure to be messed up.

I looked at the members of the group to see if they might leave with me. They left without me. And even the holder of the keys went out. Maybe he left to accompany them or maybe he went out for his own purposes. One who is not burdened with things is free to do whatever his heart desires.

I stood among my things and thought to myself, When did I ever have need of you and when will I ever need you? And there they lay, casting a shadow upon themselves, a thick and thickening shadow. And if there is no substance in a shadow, substance there is in those who cast shadows.

The holder of the keys returned to rap with the keys, whose sound became increasingly angry. But don't be surprised, for tomorrow's a hard day, the day they're painting the workroom, and he wants to rest and renew his strength and at the last minute he's held up by me. My hands weakened and my fingers became intertwined as if they had been tied with ropes.

I stretched out my hands to stir them from their sluggishness and took package after package and tied them one to another, because packages have a way of being easier to carry when they are tied together, which is not so when they are separate. When I noticed that fellow's eyes as he waited impatiently, my fingers lost all their strength and the packages fell from my hands. And even the books that were wrapped and tied ripped out of their cords. The paper that covered them tore and they fell.

I went over to the biggest of the packages and took the rope that was on it in order to tie one package to another. The rope was old and knotted in knots upon knots, and on every knot that I unraveled I bruised my hands and tore my fingernails. And when I had finally unraveled all the knots, the rope fell apart. Its mate that I untied from a different package was no better. I unraveled it and it weakened, I knotted it and it disintegrated.

I took the pieces that had separated themselves and joined one to another to make one long rope out of them. And once I had a long rope in my hands, I used it to tie one package to another, all together, until they formed one package. The man locked the workroom after me and went his way, talking to himself and saying, "I hope it doesn't rain tomorrow."

It would have been good had I found myself an automobile to take me to an inn, but it was time for the evening session and all the visitors who had come to the convention had grabbed all the vehicles in the city to get to the convention building. I bent my back to the package that weighed me down more and more. And as it was with the package, so it was with its shadow. I am not saying that the shadow weighed me down, but it is terrifying when it is thick and lacks a head. And don't be surprised, for the load reared itself up above the head of the one who carried it so that his head entered into his burden.

In the meantime I heard a dull noise and saw that my things were falling. The rope I had worked so hard to assemble had been weak from the start, and when I began to move, the package on my shoulders shook, the rope tore, and the articles scattered.

I bent down to the ground and began to collect my things. I would lift one thing and its mate would fall from my shoulders. I would lift it and it would fall again. I had nothing left but the rope with which I had tied my package. To add to this, drops of rain began to fall. The rains that had hidden by day in the clouds emerged from their hiding places. And there was no automobile around to take me to the hotel, nor was there anyone to help me. And don't be surprised, for the craftsmen's convention was a large convention and all who were able went to the convention and whoever didn't go to the convention hid at home from the rain.

The rains that had pattered softly at first began to descend heavily. And in the midst of the rain, as in a vision, two men ran in great haste. I am not saying that they were Joseph Eibeschütz and Samuel Emden. But if I were to say that one of them was one or the other, it would not be far from the truth.

Translated by Anne Golomb Hoffman

A Book That Was Lost

Rabbi Shmaria the dayan, one of the rabbinical judges of our town, was a man learned in the law and conversant with the Shulhan Arukh, particularly with the section on daily ritual, Orah Hayyim, with which not all rabbis concerned themselves too much. Of all the glosses on Orah Hayyim, he liked best the commentary of Rabbi Magen Avraham.

Of course, most of Magen Avraham's commentary is obscure and enigmatic due to overabbreviation. For though a man of great learning, he was poor, without the means to buy paper on which to write, and used to write his novellae on the face of the table and on the wall, and when a piece of paper came into his hands, he would compose his thoughts and jot down their essence in extremely concise language.

Out of fondness for the Magen Avraham, Rabbi Shmaria took upon himself to construe, interpret, and explain it for every student to learn and understand. I don't know for how many years Rabbi Magen Avraham was occupied with his work. As for Rabbi Shmaria, I heard that it took him twelve years to define, elucidate, and construe each and every expression. He left no difficult passage uninterpreted.

At the end of twelve years he checked and found nothing further to add or to detract.

He sent for a bookbinder to bind the sheets and delighted in the thought of printing and publishing his book.

The bookbinder came with a sheaf of pages in his hand.

Rabbi Shmaria picked up his work and said to the bookbinder, "Bind these sheets for me and make me a book out of them."

The bookbinder put aside the sheets he had brought with him and picked up those of Rabbi Shmaria. He looked at them the way bookbinders do, at their thickness and size, taking into consideration the boards he would use and what he would cover them with, whether with hide or with cloth.

While the bookbinder was attending to Rabbi Shmaria's sheets, Rabbi Shmaria became aware of the sheets the bookbinder had placed on the table and said, "What have you put down here?" The bookbinder replied, "A new book I was given to bind." Rabbi Shmaria said, "Let me take a look." The bookbinder put down Rabbi Shmaria's work and handed him the book he had brought.

That book was called Mahazit Hashekel, which the great scholar Rabbi Samuel Halevy Kolin wrote on the commentary of the Magen Avraham to the Shulhan Arukh, Orah Hayyim.

Rabbi Shmaria fixed his gaze on the book again and again, and said, "A most satisfactory commentary, most satisfactory; apt and with the ring of truth." He sighed and said, "I have been preceded by another; there is no need for my work."

He apologized to the master binder for having bothered him for nothing, left his work where it was, and had it neither bound nor published.

Four or five generations later the book came into my hands. How so? I was poking about the attic of the Great Synagogue in our town where the worn-out books were put away and whence they were brought to the graveyard for burial between the graves in earthenware urns. At first they used to bury them between the graves of the righteous, but later they began burying them between the graves of the stillborn, as I have related elsewhere.

I picked up the book and shook off the dust. I collected all the pages together and put them in order. I saw before me a complete work.

I went up to an embrasure in the wall through which rifle fire was once directed at the Tartars who came to wage war on the town. I stopped to thumb through the book and read a little here and there. I saw that it was a commentary on the commentary of Magen Avraham, and I knew that it was the work of Rabbi Shmaria the Dayan. I found in it nice distinctions not to be found in the book Mahazit Hashekel nor in the other books that I knew, which Rabbi Shmaria, so sorely grieved when he saw that all his efforts over twelve years were in vain, did not perceive in his own innovations.

I went into the old house of study in order to take a look at books that discuss the Magen Avraham, and I found that none of them contained the innovations of Rabbi Shmaria.

I showed some of Rabbi Shmaria's innovations to my father, my teacher and a righteous man of blessed memory, and to other scholars. After giving them their consideration they said, "Rabbi Shmaria's is a fine commentary. He has made nice distinctions. What he says deserves to be heard."

I was sorry for such a wise man who had labored so hard in the law and had not been found deserving enough for a dictum of his to be cited. I wanted to save his innovations from oblivion. It occurred to me to make up a copy of the book, but I said to myself, What good would that do? That would only mean another bundle of writings that would drift from place to place and at best would end up in a place where worn-out books were laid to rest.

About that time I read in the *Hamizpeh* about the Ginzei Yosef Library in Jerusalem (which heralded the Jewish National and University Library). There appeared in the paper a notice asking publishers and writers, etc., to send books to the library. It seemed to me that this notice was read all over the world and that people from all places were sending books to Jerusalem. I said to myself, People everywhere are contributing to Jerusalem and Buczacz contributes nothing, so let me send Rabbi Shmaria's book to Jerusalem.

Messengers with whom to send the book were not available; neither did I have any extra money to pay the cost of sending it by post. The little that my father, of blessed memory, used to give me from time to time was spent on payments I felt obliged to make, such as to the Jewish National Fund, anonymous poor, membership in the Zionist Society, and occasionally to buy a new book. But my ingenuity served me to find the money to send the book to Jerusalem. How so? When I was studying the law and would rise early and remain until evening at the house of study, my mother used to give me every Monday two kreutzers, so that if I was hungry I could buy a wafer or a piece of fruit. I said to myself, What my mother has done for the sake of her son's learning I will do for the sake of Rabbi Shmaria's teaching. So I said to my mother, "I have come to a very difficult passage and will not be home for lunch." My mother was sorry for me for denying myself a regular meal but was happy that learning the law had become dear to me once again. At that time my interest in the law had waned in deference to those little books that God does not deign to look upon. But to get the book to Jerusalem I used the law as a pretext. My mother took from the housekeeping money and gave to me. So she did on that day and for a number of days, so that if I was hungry I might buy a wafer or a piece of fruit. Fruit and wafers I did not buy, but put a penny to a penny until I had enough to send the book by post to Jerusalem.

I went to a shopkeeper who was one of the Zionists in our town and bought strong paper and brand-new twine. I didn't tell him what the paper and twine were for, lest he should think that I wanted a discount. God knows he didn't run his shop for charity.

After I had bought the paper and twine I went home and took the manuscript and looked it over once or twice, wrapped it in the paper, and bound the twine around it. Then I sat down and wrote on the paper the name of the curator of the Ginzei Yosef Library and the designation Jerusalem. This time the word Jerusalem was not written in vain. I added the name of the country, Palestine, and not the Land of Israel, in memory of the destruction of the Temple.

I surveyed the parcel and found it fair enough to send up to Jerusalem. I took it and went to the post office.

There are things you do out of love but nevertheless you do not hasten to complete them. So it was with Rabbi Shmaria's book.

I was like a child holding fast to a paper kite; although the kite was made to fly on high, nevertheless the child holds on to it and doesn't let it go. Why? Because as long as it stays in his hand, it belongs to him, but when he lets it fly, it disappears high up in the sky and he is left empty-handed. I knew that I had made up the parcel in order to send it up to Jerusalem, but for as long as it was in my hand, it bound me to Jerusalem. But if I let the parcel out of my hands it would go up to Jerusalem while I stayed in Buczacz. But my legs led me of their own accord to the post office.

I entered the post office and stood among the errand boys of the Buczacz merchants who send their goods to places all over the world, and although I was the only person in the whole town who was then about to send something up to Jerusalem, I was in no hurry and kept standing where I stood until the room was empty of all those who had come, and still I stayed where I was standing.

The clerk saw me and said, "And what have you brought?"

I raised my parcel from where I was standing. He beckoned me to approach and I did.

He took the parcel and looked kindly at me, for Jerusalem is still near to everyone's heart, even if he is a clerk. He even gave me a receipt with "Jerusalem" written on it.

Upon returning home from the post office I resumed doing the things I used to do, such as a little Zionist activity, and a little of all those other things done by most Jewish boys of that generation who were still dependent on their fathers. In addition to those, I composed poems about Zion and Jerusalem.

I can't tell whether the poems of Zion and Jerusalem brought me to Jerusalem or whether it was my longing for Zion and Jerusalem that brought me to compose poems about them. Either way, it was my good fortune to go and settle in the Land of Israel.

I spent a year in Jaffa before I settled in Jerusalem. In my own way I was persuaded that I was to be tested to see whether I was satisfied with Jaffa, so I was delayed there for a year until I went up to Jerusalem. Don't be surprised to hear me say so, as if I consider myself worthy of being tested. But as every man who does not live in the Land of Israel is put to the test to see whether he is worthy of settling in the Land of Israel, so every man in the Land of Israel is put to the test to see whether he is worthy of settling in Jerusalem. And so after staying a year in Jaffa and its suburbs, I took my staff and my knapsack and went up to Jerusalem.

On the eve of Shabbat Hazon (the Sabbath before the Ninth of Av) before sundown I entered the gates of Jerusalem. If God be with me I shall tell what happened at the time I was fortunate enough to come to Jerusalem. For now I shall relate what happened to the book.

And so on the Sabbath eve before sundown I came to Jerusalem. I laid down my staff and my knapsack, washed myself of the dust of the road, and put on my Sabbath clothes and ran to the Western Wall. From there to the Hurvah Synagogue, from there to other synagogues, from there to the hostel, and to the streets of Jerusalem which were lit up quite clearly. Though Jerusalem was desolate, the moon, by the grace of God, had not ceased to shine upon it.

After the Ninth of Av my friends in Jerusalem took me to some places for which Jerusalem is commended. In the end they brought me to the Ginzei Yosef Library, which in those days we believed was the depository for all the books of Jewry. How strong was our faith in those days!

On the way to the library I told my friends about Rabbi Shmaria's book which I had sent so many years ago to Ginzei Yosef in Jerusalem.

I was reminded of Buczacz and began telling about her. Perhaps I said too much and aroused their annoyance, because in those days which we now call the Second Aliyah every newcomer to the Land of Israel tried to forget his place of origin, and if he couldn't, he endeavored not to mention it, for a new focal point requires a new frame of mind.

One of my friends laughed at me and said, "Even before you came to the Land of Israel you had already made your mark in Jerusalem."

We went into the library and one of the two librarians who were there was kind enough to show us various books, and of each book he said, "It's the only one in the world, unique, a gift from

so-and-so." And more than anyone else he praised Dr. Joseph Chasanowitsch of Bialystok, who denied himself bread for the sake of
amassing a store of books in Jerusalem.

We looked at the books, everyone in his own way and everyone trying to say a word in expression of his feelings.

When we were about to leave I said to the librarian, "I too
sent a book to Jerusalem."

The librarian asked me for the name of the book. I told him,
"It doesn't have a name, but its description is just so, and in such-and-
such a year I sent it, addressed to the man in charge by the name of
So-and-so I sent it." There I stood, telling what I knew, without distinguishing between what was relevant and what was not. Had it not
been for my friends who wanted to see other things in town, I would
have put before the librarian some of the novellae of Rabbi Shmaria.
Those were the days when I still had such a formidable memory and
librarians were so keen to hear something of the wisdom of the law.

"I will go and see where the book is," said the librarian. He
went from room to room and from cupboard to cupboard. After he
had investigated all the cupboards, he said, "I have searched for it
but have not found it. If your book has reached us, I will find it. It
may be lying among the books that haven't been given out for binding. Due to lack of funds, piles and piles of books are lying around
that still haven't been given out for binding. All the same, I will look
for it and if I find it I will show it to you."

Gratefully I took my leave of the librarian. His eyes testified
to his good heart that was ready to oblige.

Many times did I go to the library and many times did I speak
to the librarian. When I didn't mention Rabbi Shmaria's book, the
librarian would, and he would say, "I still haven't found it, but if not
today, then tomorrow."

So the years passed. That librarian went the way of all flesh
and the librarian who succeeded him has also passed on, but the
book was not found.

What a pity the book was lost.

Translated by Amiel Gurt

On One Stone

Those were good days. I remained secluded in my house, writing the adventures of Rabbi Adam Baal Shem. This wise sage knew the Kabbalah in both theory and practice. He could recognize ghosts and demons as they set out upon their ways. He would throw a shawl over their eyes so that they could not see to do any harm. He was an expert on trees and could tell which ones grew by God's grace and which ones were formed from the bodies of sorcerers in order to trick people. These he would cut down, limb by limb. Thus he saved many of Israel from the depths of evil and restored them to their own root. All this Rabbi Adam did only by the word, for he possessed holy writings of an esoteric sort. And when the time came for Rabbi Adam to depart from this world, he hid the writings in a rock, upon which he cast a spell that it not open itself, so that no unfit person could study those writings and turn the world back to chaos and confusion.

As though in a vision I saw the rock and the writings inside it. I could discern every letter and word, every line, every page of writing, every leaf. Had these writings belonged to the root of my own soul, I would have read them, and out of them I would have fashioned worlds. But I didn't deserve to read them; I could only sit and look. My eyes would surround them like the metal settings in which precious stones are placed but which never combine with the stones themselves. Still, even if I didn't manage to read them, I can tell about them. If we come into this world to put in order those things that previous generations have left behind, I can claim a certain measure of success.

When I got around to writing the tale of the rock, I began to worry that I might be interrupted in the middle. Even though I dwelt cut off from the world, I suspected that once I got into this matter and began to write the tale itself, people would come and bother me. That's the way it is with people. They're never there when you look for them, but just when you don't want them, they come around. I took all that I needed for writing—ink, pen, and paper—and went to the forest near my town. I went in among the trees, and there I found a certain rock where I made myself a place. I laid my writings down on the rock, and there I sat and wrote. When I stopped my writing, I would see the trees, the birds, and the grass, as well as the river that flowed through their midst. My heart took great joy in hearing how the birds would speak their piece before their Father in heaven, how each shrub in the field would speak up before the Everpresent, how all the trees of the forest would bow down before Him. The river's waters flowed gently, never raising themselves up too high. I did this for several days, until I had finished writing the tale of the writings Rabbi Adam Baal Shem had possessed on the theory and practice of Kabbalah. When the day of his death came, he was afraid that they might fall into the hands of improper folk, so he got up and went to a certain rock. He opened the rock, hid his writings there, and closed it up. No one knows where that rock is.

I wrote a lot about this matter, and I had still more to write. But on the day when I was going to finish the story, a man came by and asked me the way to town. I saw that he was elderly and walked with some difficulty. The path was strewn with rocks and the sun was close to setting. Fearing that he might not make it to town while there was still light, I left my writings and went to his aid. I walked along with him until we were close to town.

After taking leave of the old man I stood in astonishment. The holy Sabbath was coming and I was outside the permitted domain. Not only that, but something I had worked hard on all week long I had now suddenly abandoned in the middle. Even worse, I had left it there, open to the wind, to beast or to bird. Even if I'd had to fulfill the commandment of honoring the elderly by walking with him, I could have picked up my writings and then walked into town. I could have fulfilled the commandment perfectly and still preserved my writings, and not have to go back to the woods on the eve of the Sabbath as night was falling. It was not regret or distress that I felt, but just a sense of shock, like a person who is astonished at himself, but not distressed.

Just then the sun set. The day turned to silver and the Sabbath light began to break forth. I stood still, not knowing where to go first. If I went to town, I'd be abandoning all I had done in six days. If I went to the forest, the holy Sabbath would be coming in and I would not be coming in with her. While I was still weighing the alternatives in my mind, my legs took themselves to walk into the forest.

When I returned to the forest I found my writings lying on the rock, just as I had left them. No wind had scattered them. No beast or bird had bothered them. Had it not been for that old man who had interrupted me and were it not for the darkness of this Sabbath eve, I would have gone over what I'd written and come away with a finished product. What a shame that I'd let the time go by and left my affairs in such a state.

While I was thinking this, the rock opened up, took in my writings, and closed up again. I left the rock and went back to town.

In that hour the blessed Holy One brought the moon, stars, and constellations out in the sky. The whole earth shone, and every rock that came up before me along the way gave off light. I could see every crack and crevice, every vein in the rock. I took all those rocks into my sight, my eyes serving as the soil that surrounded each rock, the setting in which each rock was placed. I loved and took delight in each and everyone. I said to myself: What difference is there between the rock that took in the writings and these rocks right here? They peered out at me, or at least they seemed to be peering. And perhaps they said the same thing I had just said, not in my language but in their own.

Translated by Arthur Green

The Sense of Smell

1. The excellence of the Holy Tongue

The holy tongue is a language like no other. All other tongues exist only by agreement, each nation having agreed upon its language. But the holy tongue is the one in which the Torah was given, the one through which the blessed Holy One created His world. Angels and seraphim and holy beings praise Him in the holy tongue. And when He comes to praise Israel, He also does so in the holy tongue, as it is written: "Behold thou art beautiful, my beloved, behold thou art beautiful." What language does Scripture speak? Surely the holy tongue. And when He longs to hear the prayers of Israel, what language is it that He longs to hear? The holy tongue, as He says: "Let me hear your voice for your voice is sweet." What voice is sweet to Him? The voice of Jacob, praying in the holy tongue. By the holy tongue He will one day rebuild Jerusalem and return the exiles to her midst. By the holy tongue He heals the mourners of Zion, their hearts broken by the destruction, and He binds up their wounds. Thus it is written: "The Lord builds Jerusalem, gathering the scattered of Israel; He heals the brokenhearted and binds up their wounds." For this reason all Israel should take care with their language, keeping it clear and precise, especially in these last generations so close to redemption, so that our righteous Messiah (may he be revealed speedily, in our own day!) will understand our language and we will understand his.

2. Against the scholars of our generation who write in every language except the holy tongue

But someone might object and say: "Is it possible to speak a language that has not been spoken for more than a thousand years?" as some stupid folk among the Jews have said. "Even most of the scholars in our generation cannot stand up to it, and they either make a mess of their language, even in the most simple things, or else they write in every other language except the holy tongue." Whoever says this hasn't paid attention to the most important fact. Even though speech passed from the lips, it never passed out of writing, and it is there for anyone who seeks it. How is this? A person reads Torah or studies Mishnah or learns Gemara and immediately all those treasures of the holy tongue that the blessed Holy One has stored up for His beloved are revealed to him. This is especially true on the Sabbath, when we are given an extra soul that understands the holy tongue just as well as do the angels.

Then why do certain scholars make such a mess of their language? Because they put worldly matters first and words of Torah second. If they would make Torah their basis, the Torah would come to their aid. As for those who write in every other language but not in the holy tongue, even a Gentile who writes in the holy tongue is more beloved than they, so long as he does not write words of folly. You can know this from the case of Balaam the Wicked. No man did such evil as the one who suggested that the daughters of Moab go whoring, by which one hundred fifty-eight thousand and six hundred of Israel were destroyed. But because he spoke in the holy tongue and in praise of Israel, he merited to have a section of the Torah called by his name, and to have all Israel open their prayers each morning with the verse "How goodly," which Balaam spoke in praise of Israel.

And if you should say, "But do we not find that some of our early sages composed a portion of their books in Arabic?" the early sages are different, because the people of their generations were made weary by exile and were far from Messiah's light. Therefore their sages wrote them letters of consolation in their own language, the same way you pacify a child in whatever language he understands. The language of Ishmael is also different, since the Land of Israel has been given over into their hands. Why was the Land of Israel entrusted to Ishmael? Because he had managed to wrest it from the hands of Edom. It remains entrusted to Ishmael until all the exiles are gathered and God returns it to their hands.

3. *The secret of writing stories*

For love of our language and affection for the holy, I darken my countenance with constant study of Torah and starve myself over the words of our sages. These I store up in my belly so that they together will be present to my lips. If the Temple were still standing, I would be up there on the platform among my singing brothers, reciting each day the song that the Levites sang in the Temple. But since the Temple remains destroyed and we have no priests at service or Levites at song, instead I study Torah, the Prophets and the Writings, Mishnah, laws and legends, supplementary treatises and fine points of Torah and the works of the scribes. When I look at their words and see that of all the delights we possessed in ancient times there remains only this memory, my heart fills up with grief. That grief makes my heart tremble, and it is out of that trembling that I write stories, like one exiled from his father's palace who makes himself a little hut and sits there telling of the glory of his father's house.

4. All that happened to the author because of a certain grammarian and all the suffering and woe that came upon the author

Since I just mentioned a hut, let me say something about one. It once happened that I had written a story about a sukkah, a festival hut. Using colloquial language, I wrote, "The sukkah smells." A certain grammarian rose up against me, stuck his pen into me, and wrote, "You cannot say: 'The sukkah smells.' Only a person smells the aroma of the sukkah." I was worried that perhaps I had strayed from proper usage and done harm to the beauty of the language. I went and looked in reference books but found no support for my usage. Most of the books either tell you what you already know or else tell you nothing at all. I went to the scholars of our time, and they did not know what to answer me. Scholars know everything except that particular thing you are looking for. Then I happened upon a certain Jerusalem scholar, and he brought support for my words from the book called Perfect Treatise by an early sage named Moses Taku, of blessed memory. I was somewhat consoled, but not completely. I still wanted further support. When I ran into people who were experts in the holy tongue, I would ask them, "Perhaps you have heard whether it is permitted to write: 'The sukkah smells.'" Some permitted while others forbade. Neither gave any reasons for their opinions, but just stated them, like a person who sticks his thumb out at someone and says, "Well that's my view," or someone who licks his lips and says, "That's my feeling." That being the case, I went to erase those two words against which the grammarian had raised a protest. But when I started to do so, the sukkah came and its aroma rose up before me until I really saw that it was smelling. I left the words as they were.

5. The righteous from paradise come to the author's aid

Once somebody came to ask me a favor. In the course of the conversation he revealed to me that he was a descendant of Rabbi Jacob of Lissa. I put aside all my other concerns and did him great honor. I took the trouble to offer him some honey cake and a glass of whiskey. I fulfilled his request gladly, out of respect for his learned ancestor whose Torah we study and out of whose prayer book we pray.

After I'd accompanied him on his way, I ran into a certain scholar who was carrying a book under his arm. I asked him, "What's that you've got there? Isn't that the prayer book of the Sage of Lissa?" He smiled and said to me, "Sometimes you get so clever that you forget a simple custom of prayer and you have to look it up in a prayer book." I said to him, "It shows a special quality of that true sage, one who had already written novellae and commentaries known for both sharp insight and breadth of learning, that he would take the trouble to briefly lay out the laws of prayer and other matters in such an accessible way. His is a book that anyone can use to find the law and its sources, written right there with the prayers themselves. Our holy rabbis have left us lots of prayer books, filled with directions and commentaries both hidden and revealed, with matters grammatical or sagacious, with permutations of letters, secrets, and allegories, all to arouse the hearts of worshippers as they enter the King's palace. But if not for my respect for our early teachers, I would say that the prayer book of the Sage of Lissa is better than them all. In many of those prayer books the light is so bright that most people can't use them, while this one appeals to any eye."

While I was talking, my own heart was aroused and I started to tell of some things that happened to that sage whose teachings had spread throughout the scattered communities of Jews, who in turn followed his rulings. I told of some of his good qualities, things I had heard from reliable sources and had found in books.

Finally we parted from one another, he with his prayer book and I with my thoughts. I went home and lay down on my bed to sleep a sweet sleep. Since I had done a Jew a favor and had gone to bed after telling tales of the righteous, my sleep was a good one.

I heard someone trying to awaken me. I was feeling lazy and I didn't get up. On the second try I awoke, and I saw an old man standing before me. The prayer book *Way of Life* lay open in his hand; his eyes shone and his face bore a special radiance. Even though I had never seen a picture of Rabbi Jacob of Lissa, I recognized him right off. It wasn't that he looked like any of the members of his family. The great among Israel just don't look like their relatives, because their Torah gives their faces a special glow.

When a person darkens his face over study of Torah, the blessed Holy One gives him that radiant glow and makes his face shine.

While I was still staring, the prayer book closed, the old man disappeared, and I realized it had been a dream. But even though I knew that, I said: There must be something to this. I washed my hands, got out of bed, and walked over to the bookcase. I picked up the prayer book *Way of Life*. In it I noticed a slip of paper serving as some sort of marker. I opened up to that place and there I read: "One uses lots of flowers that smell sweet to make the holiday joyous." It seemed that I had once been reading that page and had put the slip of paper there as a marker.

I thought to myself: He wouldn't have used such language on his own, without some authority in Torah. In any case, I took the prayer book *Pillars of Heaven*, by his uncle the sage Javetz, of blessed memory, and there I found the same expression. I was glad that I hadn't failed in my words and had done no harm to our holy tongue. If these two great pillars of the universe wrote this way, it must indeed be proper. The grammarian who had shot off his mouth at me would one day have to pay his due.

6. Reciting psalms
How Rashi, of blessed memory, interprets for the author a verse from the Psalms and lights up his spirit

It was hardly worth going back to bed, since most of the night had passed, but it wasn't yet time for morning prayers. I got up and took a Book of Psalms. Reciting psalms is good anytime, but especially early in the morning when the soul is still pure and the lips are not yet defiled by wicked chatter. I sat and read a few psalms; some I understood on my own, and the rest were explained to me by Rashi, of blessed memory, until I'd completed the first book of the Psalter. My soul still wanted to say more. I did its bidding and read psalm after psalm, until I got to the Psalm for the Chief Musician upon Lilies. This is a song in praise of the sages' disciples, those who are soft as lilies and pleasant as lilies, so that they come to love their learning.

That was a beautiful hour of psalm-saying. The lamp on the table was lit, crowning with light every word, every letter, every vowel point, every musical notation. Opposite it there was a window open, facing the south. Outside, the predawn breezes blew, but they didn't put out the lamp or even challenge its wick. The breezes danced about the trees and shrubs in the garden, and there wafted in a sweet fragrance of laurel and dew, smelling something like wild honey or perfume.

The light from the lamp had begun to pale. It seems that the night was over. It may be that God hangs up the sun in the sky at that hour for the sake of those simple folk who don't know the whole morning prayer by heart but who recite it out of the prayer book.

A sound was heard from the treetops, the voice of a bird reciting her song. Such a voice could interrupt a person's studies. But I didn't get up from my book to listen to the bird's voice, even though it was both sweet to the ear and attractive to the heart. I said: Here I am reciting the Psalms. Should I interrupt these to listen to the talk of birds?

Soon another voice was to be heard, even more attractive than the first. One bird had gotten jealous of another and had decided to outdo her in song. Or maybe she wasn't jealous and hadn't even noticed the other. She was aroused on her own to sing before her Creator, and her voice was just sweeter than the other bird's. In the end they made peace with one another, and each bird seemed to complement the other one's melodies. They sang new songs, the likes of which no ear had ever heard. Melodies and voices like these certainly could keep a man from studying, but I made as though I didn't hear. There is nothing especially wondrous or praiseworthy about this, because the psalm played itself like an instrument of many strings. A Song of Love, next to which all other songs are as nothing. I followed after its every word with melody.

"My heart overfloweth with a goodly matter...My tongue is the pen of a ready scribe;...ride on in behalf of truth, humility, and righteousness; let thy right hand teach thee awesome things." I understood as much as I could, and the rest was explained to me by Rashi, of blessed memory. When I got to the verse "Myrrh and aloes and cassia are all thy garments," I did not know what it meant. I looked in Rashi's commentary and there I read: "All thy garments smell like fragrant spices. And its meaning is that all your betrayals and foul deeds will be forgiven and will smell sweet before Me." My mind was eased, like a person smelling flowers that smell.

7. To conclude with praise as we opened with praise

Come and see how great is this holy tongue! For the sake of a single word a holy man troubled himself to come out of the Academy on High in the Garden of Eden, bringing his book before me, causing me to rise up at night to recite the Psalms, so that I might find something I'd been seeking for many days.

Translated by Arthur Green

From Lodging to Lodging

Not one good thing happened all winter. Before I was free of one illness I was seized by another. The doctor had become a steady visitor; two or three times a week he came to examine me. He felt my pulse and wrote out prescriptions, changing his medicines and his advice. The doctor was always on call, and the whole house was filled with all kinds of cures whose smell reminded one of death. My body was weak and my lips were cracked. My throat was sore, my tongue was coated, and my vocal cords would produce nothing more than a cough. I had already given up on myself. But the doctor had not given up on me. He was constantly piling up pill after pill and giving new names to my illness. In spite of it all, we saw no change for the better.

Meanwhile, the cold season passed. The sun began to rise earlier each day and each day it tarried longer in the sky. The sky smiled at the earth and the earth smiled at man, putting forth blossoms and flowers, grasses and thorns. Lambs rollicked about and covered the land, children poured from every house and every shack. A pair of birds came out of the sky, leaves and stubble in their beaks, and hopped from my window to a tree and from the tree to my window, chirping as they built themselves a home. There was a new spirit in the world, and the world began to heal. My limbs lost their stiffness; they became lithe and limber. Even the doctor's spirit had changed. His instruments seemed to be lighter and he was light-hearted and happy. When he came in he would say, "Well, now, spring certainly has arrived," and he would open a window, knocking over two or three bottles of medicine, not caring if they broke. He still would examine me in order to write out prescriptions. At the same time he would write down a woman's name and put it in his jacket or stuff it under the watch strap on his left wrist. After several days, he advised me to change my place of residence for a change of climate, to go down to Tel Aviv, for example, to enjoy the sea air.

When moving time came and I had to leave my lodgings, I decided to go down to Tel Aviv. I said to myself: He who changes his residence changes his luck. Perhaps the sea will help me get my health back.

The room I rented in Tel Aviv was narrow and low; its windows faced a street filled with people rushing back and forth. There were many shops on this street, dispensing soda and ice cream. And there was one further drawback: the bus station, noisy all day and not resting at night. From five in the morning until after midnight buses came and went, as well as all kinds of two-and four-wheeled vehicles. When this tumult stopped and the soda vendors' kiosks closed, an echo began to resound within my room, as when a stone is thrown against a brass drum, making its sides resound. Often I awoke from my sleep to the sound of clinking glasses and rolling wheels, as if all the soda vendors on the street had gathered within the walls of my house to pour drinks for their customers, and as if all the buses were racing on the roof of the house. Then again, perhaps these sounds were no mere echo but the real sounds of buses and of street cleaners going about their work at night, when people sleep. And as for the pouring of drinks, a neighbor had returned from a meeting and had opened a tap to douse his head in cold water, and it had seemed to me that the soda vendors were pouring drinks. Because of all this, my nights passed without sleep, my mornings without a dream. I gave up on sleep and tried to lie quietly awake, but the city's fish merchants came to shout their wares and the sun came to heat my room like Gehenna.

2

Because of lack of sleep I could not enjoy whatever is available for one to enjoy in Tel Aviv. I betook myself to the sea and took off some of my clothes. Even this exertion tired me, and I could not take off the rest. I took off one shoe; I was unable to take off the other. At times the waves of the sea would come toward me, inviting me in or driving me away. Finally I would return to my room, more weary than when I had left it. And my friends were already warning me, saying, "Leave your lodgings or you will come to a bad end." With fantasy and with words they portrayed all sorts of dangers that were likely to befall a person in such lodgings. Some spoke calmly with me, and some told me of bad things that had befallen them. If I retained any ability to think, I thought that they were right, that I must leave these lodgings. But not every thought leads to action. I remained where I was, until a new trouble appeared. What kind of trouble? The landlord had a child whose frail body was a meeting ground for all kinds of ailments. Before my arrival he had lived with his grandmother; after I arrived, his mother brought him home, because she longed for her son or because my rent enabled her to support the child. I do not know if he was better off with his grandmother; with his mother he was not well off. She was a do-gooder, attending to everyone's affairs with no time to attend to her own son. Each morning she would put him outside with a tomato or a roll in his hand, kiss him on the mouth, tell him what he should and should not do, and leave him. His father, too, was somewhat busy looking for work and did not have as much free time as he wanted. The child would lie around on the doorstep of the house and lick at dirt or scrape plaster from the wall and eat it. Didn't his mother feed him? But it is human nature to want what we don't have, and it is not human nature to be satisfied with what we do have. Whenever I walked by, he would stretch his thin arms and hang on to me, and not let go until I took him in my arms and rocked him back and forth. Why was he attracted to me? I certainly was not attracted to him. I treat children as I treat their parents. If I like them I get closer to them; if I do not like them I keep my distance from them. Humanity has invented many lies, nor am I free of them, but of one thing I can boast: where children are concerned I never lie.

All of this applied to daytime. Nighttime was worse. From the moment they put the child to bed until they wake him he cries and whimpers, stopping only to groan. When he neither cries nor groans it is even worse, for then he seems to be dead, Heaven forbid. I say to myself: Get up and wake his father and mother. Before I can get up I hear the sound of crying and groaning. Like everyone else, I dislike both sounds. But, in this case, the child's cries and groans are dearer to me than all the musical instruments in the world, for then I know that he is alive.

3

In short, this child was attached to me, perhaps because his father and mother did not take care of him and he longed for human companionship, perhaps because I rocked him back and forth. In any case, he would never let me pass the doorstep without taking him in my arms. When I did take him in my arms, he would poke his fingers into my eyes and grin. Throughout the day he smiled only when he stuck his fingernails into my eyes. Often his father and mother would scold him. "Bobby, no! Bobby, no!" But from their manner of scolding it was clear that they were pleased with his cleverness. I, who did not share the joy of his father and mother, could not understand: when flies and mosquitoes crawled over his sores he was too lethargic to chase them away, but whenever he caught sight of my eyes he immediately sprang into action.

I too began to act cleverly. When I had to leave, I checked first to see if Bobby was outside. If he was, I would wait in my room. But

since my room was not comfortable to sit in, I would be forced to go
out. When I went out, the child would climb on me with a double
measure of love, and would not leave me alone until I took him in
my arms and rocked him. And, while rocking, he would stick his
fingers into my eyes and grin. When I put him down he would shout,
"Moo, moo, oinkle, moo," which is to say, "More, more, uncle, more."
Who composed this jingle, the child or a nursery-school teacher? In
any case, the nonsense syllables were something that a nursery teacher
would compose. Man's superiority over animals lies in his power of
speech, but all of God's works require a process of "redemption" on
the part of man, and nursery-school teachers are the ones who do
this. Since he asked for more, I would take him in my arms again and
rock him, while he stuck his fingernails into my eyes and shouted,
"Bobby! Bobby!" He could see his reflection in my eyes and was trying to snatch it away.

When a man is suffering he should examine his deeds. If he
is humble and modest, he blames himself for his misfortunes; if he
is neither, he blames others. If he is a man of action, he tries to rid
himself of his trouble through action; if he is a man of contempla-
tion, he waits until his trouble ends by itself. Sometimes he goes away,
or another trouble appears, causing the first one to be forgotten. I,
who have attained neither the passivity of the humble nor the zeal of
men of action, would sit and ponder, Why do they make doorsteps
for houses? If there were no doorstep, the child would not lie around
there and I would not run into him.

I have already mentioned my friends; because of their affection
I shall mention them again. At first they warned me. When their pre-
dictions came true, they began talking to me as people talk to someone who is sick, and they would say, "The prime need for any man
is a place to live in, especially one who has come here to be healed."
Since it was difficult for me to change my quarters, I tried to shrug
off the matter with a talmudic saying: "A man should never change
his quarters." What did my friends say? "In spite of the Talmud we
shall rent another room for you." But talk is easier than action, let
alone than friendship. This being so, I stayed where I was.

There was one woman who did not argue with me, but took the trouble to find me a pleasant location with a pleasant climate, and she would not desist until I went with her to see it.

She told me that the owner of this house usually did not rent rooms. However, his daughter had gone to a kibbutz, her room remained empty, and he had agreed to rent it. And the rent was no more than what I was paying already. He had explicitly mentioned that "Money is not the main thing; it's the tenant. If a man is looking for rest, I will gladly open my house to him."

4

Among vineyards and orchards rises a hill surrounded on all sides by pleasant trees. On this hill stands a small house. One reaches it by walking up grass-covered steps. And a hedge of fruit trees surrounds the house, shading the house and the grass. One enters a yard wherein is a pool of water with small fish. When I saw the house and the yard, I was glad and I had doubts. I was glad that a man in the Land of Israel had all this, and I had my doubts that this place was for me.

The lady of the house came out. She greeted us gladly and looked approvingly at me. Then she led us into a pleasant room where the heat of the day was not felt, and brought us cool water to drink. The owner of the house came in, an aging man of about sixty, tall and lean, his head bent slightly to the left. His blue eyes were filled with sadness, but love of humanity shone in them. He greeted me and poured a drink for us. After we drank, he showed me the room I had come to rent.

A pleasant, square room suddenly stood open before me. Its wooden furniture was simple, but every piece appeared indispensable. This was also true of the picture on the wall, painted by the daughter, a picture of a girl alone in a field, looking at the setting sun. Sunset usually brings on sadness, but this one brought on sweet rest. And this was true of the breeze that blew from outside, and it was true of the entire room. After I rented the room, the owner of the house invited us to his garden for a glass of tea. A breeze was blowing from

the trees and from the sea, the tea kettle was steaming, and the repose
of peace and tranquility hung over the table and the people. As we sat
there the lady of the house told us about her daughter who had left
every comfort for the kibbutz. She was not complaining, but spoke
like a mother who loves to talk about her daughter. The owner of
the house was silent. But he looked at us with affection so that he
seemed to have joined our conversation.

5

I asked him how he had come here. He answered and said, "I came
here as most men in the Land of Israel came here. But some come
when they are young; they are happy with the land and the land is
happy with them. And some come when they are old; they are happy
with the land but the land is not happy with them. I did not have
the privilege of coming in my youth, but in my old age I came, even
though I had given serious thought to the land before I reached old
age. How did this come about? I was a grain merchant and once, in
a field, as I walked behind the reapers, I thought about the Land
of Israel and the Jews living on their own land, plowing and sowing and reaping. From that time on I could not stop thinking about
the Land of Israel. I thought: May I be found worthy of seeing it. I
did not intend to settle, but only to see it. During those years I was
preoccupied with my business affairs and I had no time to emigrate.
Then the war came and closed the road to us.

"When things calmed down and the roads were opened, I sold
everything I owned and I came to the Land of Israel, not just to see
it but to settle. For in those days, the land in which I had lived had
become like Gehenna for Jews, and they could not stand up against
their enemies.

"I did not buy land, for most of my life was over and I was
not fit to work the land. And I did not want to work through others,
since I did not want to be supported by their labors even if the land
were mine. I decided to buy some houses, and to support myself from
the rent. But I left that enterprise before I scarcely began. Why? The

night I reached the Land of Israel I could not sleep. I went outside, to sit at the door of my hotel. The sky was clear and pure, the stars sparkled, and a quiet, secure repose reigned above, but below, on earth, there was neither quiet nor repose. Buses dashed madly about and people rushed in excitement and boys and girls shuffled wearily along, singing, and all kinds of musical instruments screeched from every house, every window.

I considered my surroundings, and I did not know whether to be filled with anger or with pity, for it certainly was possible that they also wanted to sleep, and that their apartments were not made for rest, just as my hotel was not, but since I was an old man, I sat on a bench, while they, being young, milled about in the streets. After several hours, the noises of the city died away, and I thought that I would go to lie down. When I was about to go inside I heard a weary voice. I turned this way and that, but saw no one. The voice seemed to be coming out of the ground, and I was reminded of the followers of Korah who had been swallowed up by the earth. But they are said to sing, while this was a voice of suffering and cursing. I looked again and saw some light coming up underfoot and realized that a cellar was there, with people living in it. I thought: Is it possible that in a city in the Land of Israel, built by the great leaders of Israel to enhance the people of Israel with grace and greatness in the Land of Israel, people are living in a cellar? I got up and walked away, so that I could not steal any air from them. All that night I could not sleep because of the mosquitoes and because of disturbing thoughts. Finally I reached the conclusion that I could never buy houses in the city, since no one knows what will become of them, for certainly that landlord too had come to Israel out of love and ended up doing what he did.

"I began visiting the outskirts of the city, and I found this hill. But I did not buy it until I had thought about the neighbors first. When I was satisfied that they were not in the class of those who cut up our land like so many olives to make merchandise out of it, I built a house in which my wife, my daughter, and I could live. I planted a garden to appease the land, and the land was appeased, for it gives us fruit and vegetables and flowers."

The lady of the house added, "If people have money they usually travel abroad every year to mend their bodies and to be healed. For this purpose they leave their homes to travel for days by train and by ship. They come to a place with pleasant air, find cramped lodgings which are not pleasant and which have no air. But my husband has made our lodging in a pleasant place with pleasant air, and we do not need to wear ourselves out on the road. We live here in our house, enjoying everything with which the Lord has blessed us."

Before I left, I took out a one-pound note to give to the owners of the house as a deposit. He waved his hand and said, "If you like the room, you will come; but if you do not come, where will I find you to return your money?" I rejoiced that God had brought me to pleasant lodgings and an honest landlord, and I thanked my companion for having brought me here.

In short, I liked the room and the landlord and the location, and the rent was no higher than I was paying the father of the child. I rejoiced over the repose that awaited me in that house and over the sweet sleep in store for me there. Someone who has known neither sleep by night nor repose by day can imagine my joy over that room.

6

It is easier for a man to grow wings and fly from one lodging to another than to tell his landlord, "I am leaving your lodgings." For there is some embarrassment involved, as though it were repugnant for you to live with him—in addition to whatever you make him lose in rent.

Since I was thinking about leaving my lodgings, I paid no attention to the roar of the buses and the tumult of the street. And since I stopped thinking about them, sometimes I even slept. And since I slept, my heart slumbered, free of troubles. I thought to myself: There are people, like those living in cellars, who would be happy in a room like mine, and I didn't need to look for other lodgings. But since I had rented another room I had to move there. But, since I had not yet left my lodgings, perhaps there was no need to leave.

While I was debating whether or not to leave, my eyes began bothering me. I went to a doctor, and he wrote me a prescription for eyedrops and warned me against touching my eyes with my fingers lest they become worse.

When I am alone I can be careful. But whenever that child sees me he hangs on to me and pokes his fingers into my eyes. And it is not bad enough that his fingers are dirty; his own eyes are diseased. What good is it for a doctor to warn those who take heed if he doesn't warn those who don't?

But Heaven helped me. It so happened that I had to take a trip. Because of this, there was no fear of embarrassing the landlord, since he realized that I was going out of town. I took leave of him and his wife in friendship, and because of their friendship they even let me hold the child in my arms. As I left, they said, "If you should return to Tel Aviv, our house is open to you." I nodded to them, reciting silently, "Praised be He who has rid me of you." From this day on you will not have the privilege of seeing me under your roof.

For eight days I was on the road. I had much trouble and much trouble was caused to me. But since I knew that soon I would move into comfortable lodgings, I accepted all troubles gladly, looking forward to the day of my return to Tel Aviv.

I had much trouble and much trouble was caused to me. But I also took joy in much happiness. I passed through the land and I saw that we had several more villages. Places that had produced only thistles and thorns had become like a garden of God. And like the land, so too the people were happy in their labors and rejoicing in building their land, their sons and daughters healthy and wholesome. Their hands were not soiled, and their eyes were not diseased. It is a pleasure to take a child in your arms. He does not stick his fingers into your eyes, and when he touches you it is as though a pure breeze has blown across your face.

At one kibbutz I met the daughter of my new landlord. Had most of my years not been behind me, and had I not rented lodgings from the parents of this young woman, I might have remained in that kibbutz. I left her as one leaves a friend, happy that he will see him again.

7

I was very happy to return to Tel Aviv, happier than I had been for many years. I could already picture myself living in a pleasant room, in a pleasant climate, with pleasant furniture and pleasant people, and I would come and go with no child to stick his fingers into my eyes. But most important of all would be the sleep, uninterrupted by buses and vendors and crying and groaning. Between you and me, for many years now I have considered man's purpose to be sleep, and whoever has mastered sleep, and knows how to sleep, is as important in my eyes as if he knew why man was created and why man lives. Because of this, it is easy to understand my great joy at coming to occupy lodgings where sleep awaited me.

I do not know if that house is still standing, and, if it is, whether they have not made offices and stores and soda stands out of it, as they have done with most of the houses in Tel Aviv. In those days, it was unique among houses, the pleasantest of houses.

8

When the train arrived in Tel Aviv, my heart began to dance. At last I was entering the city and my room, to sprawl out on the bed for a good sleep. Praised be He who has preserved such satisfaction in His world for His creatures.

I called a porter and he took my baggage. Feeling very expansive, I asked him out of friendliness where he lodged and if he had pleasant lodgings, after the manner of a man whose mind is clear and open enough to ask after the welfare of his neighbor. And I told him all about my new lodgings. Moving from one subject to another, we spoke about the beginning of Tel Aviv, which had been a pleasant place to live. The porter sighed. "We will never be granted peace like the peace we had here at first, until the Messiah comes."

As we spoke we came to the new house. The green hill rose among its stately trees, and lovely flowers put forth their fragrance from every side. The porter stopped and looked around. It was obvious that never in his life had he seen such a pleasant place.

Silently we walked up the grassy steps. A breeze blew in from the garden, and with it every good smell. Small birds were flying swiftly through the air, and fish were swimming below them in the pool, chasing the birds' shadows.

The landlord came out, gave me a warm welcome, and said to the porter, "Bring up the baggage."

Suddenly my heart sank, and I looked at the doorstep of the house. I was clean and scrubbed, and shadows of flowers were playing upon it. But that child was not there and did not climb all over me and did not hang on to me and did not stretch his arms to me. Silently the shadows of the flowers waved upon the doorstep; there was no child there at all. The porter stared at me. Was he waiting for me to tell him to take the baggage elsewhere? The lady of the house came out, affectionately nodded her head to me, and said, "Your room is ready."

I bowed to her and I said something. Or perhaps I said nothing, and I retraced my steps. The porter trailed after me, my baggage on his shoulder.

9

I walked until I came to my first quarters. Truly, this porter be remembered for blessing, for he kept his silence and did not disturb my thoughts. Was he thinking about the peace to come in the days of the Messiah, or did his heart warn him not to disturb a man who returns to the place he has fled?

The child was lying on the doorstep, soiled with sores. His

eyelashes were stuck together, covered with some sort of green pus. It would surprise me if eyes like that could see anything.

But he saw me. And when he saw me he stretched his slender fingers and called out, "Oinkle," which is to say, "Uncle." His voice was strained, like that of a cricket whose wings were weak.

I took him in my arms and rocked him up and down, north and south. He hugged my neck and clung to me with all his might. He was lighter than a chick, and his body was very warm. He seemed to be feverish.

For a long time I held him in my arms, and he kicked at my stomach with both of his feet in inexpressible joy. Two or three times I stared at him, to remind him that his reflection was still in my eyes. But he did not stick his hands into my eyes, since during the eight days of our separation his eyes had closed from sobbing so much and he could not see his reflection.

The landlord came out. "Have you come back to us, sir?" And he looked upon himself with great importance. I embraced the child again and said nothing. Finally I put him down, and I paid the porter for his trouble. The child stretched his arms to me and said, "Oinkle, moo." I took him into my arms again. He put his head against my neck and dozed off.

I went into the house and I set him on his bed as his lips whispered, "Moo, moo, oinkle, moo," which is to say, "More, more, uncle, more."

The child's mother came in. She put down her bag and curled her lips. "So, you have returned to us, sir. Had we known we would have tidied up the room a bit." I nodded to her and went up to my room. There was so much dust there that the real dirt could not be seen.

I took off my clothes and stretched out on my bed. The buses roared in front of my window and sellers of soda poured and shouted. But all of these sounds gradually died away, except for an echo of the child's voice ringing in my ears. I made my ear into a funnel so that I could hear more.

Translated by Jules Harlow

The Ancestral World

Agnon's writing first came to the attention of western Jewry during the period of World War I, when the author was living in Germany. His work was embraced as an authentic recreation of the inner spiritual life of Polish Jewry and compared to the achievement of the German Romantics in retelling the legends of their national culture. Such powerful critics as Dov Sadan and Baruch Kurzweil would later demonstrate the sophistication of the subversions that lay beneath the pious surface of the text. Yet the earlier, more naive response to the stories remains an important clue to the process whereby one typically reads an Agnon story. If it is set in the ancestral world of eastern Europe and its mode of telling is traditional—this accounts for much though certainly not all of Agnon's oeuvre—then our attention is naturally drawn first to the conventions of pious storytelling. These include quotations (or pseudoquotations) from sacred texts, interpolated parables and anecdotes, and the use of such traditional expressions as "of blessed memory," "Mercy deliver us!" and the like. The narrator's measured tones and balanced sentences add to this effect, as does the subject matter itself: the world of scribes, sages, and the righteous and believing poor.

Yet a second, deeper reading usually reveals the behavior described in the stories to be more often than not at odds with the idealized code implied by the traditional mode of storytelling. Often the failure derives from the limitations of human nature or from the suffering that is man's lot or from the evil that is at large in the world. Sometimes the criticism is even directed back at the code itself, and God's expectations of man are implicitly found wanting. Whatever the case, a full appreciation of Agnon's art hinges on savoring the gap between the normative expectations spun by the reverent way in which the story is told and the more troubling events that are enacted within that framework.

The best and most subtle example of this paradox is "The Tale of the Scribe." The office of the scribe was an object of boundless fascination and veneration for Agnon. He compiled an anthology of legends and lore about scribes, and clearly identified his vocation with theirs. That relation is evident in the loving description of Raphael the Scribe, his devotion to his calling, and the daily round of his spiritual exercises. The sadness in the picture of his life is the barrenness of his pious and modest wife Miriam. She dies of sorrow at an early age, and Raphael copies out a Torah scroll in memory of her soul and the souls of his unborn children.

Now, on the surface of things, the tragic dimension of the story would appear to result from God's inscrutable will or, in a naturalistic framework, from the equally unfathomable accidents of biology. On closer inspection, however, the reasons for Miriam's childlessness lie closer to home. Raphael has abandoned himself so totally to the regimen of purity and sanctity required by his calling that he has left no room in their house for sexual desire and its fulfillment. Each month Miriam returns from the ritual bath purified and available to her husband for the kind of marital relations that are not only permitted but encouraged by Jewish law. Although they are drawn toward each other, their union never takes place. They catch a glimpse of scriptural verses embroidered on a wall hanging, and they are reminded of the fullness of God's presence in the world. They part from each other silently and return to their separate spiritual endeavors. In "The Tale of the Scribe" the problem is not the failure of human beings to live up to divine expectations, but rather a quality of excess at the heart of the tradition itself—at least within the ascetic mystical tendencies of Ashkenazic Jewry. This is a piety that, by sublimating the life force, sows the seeds of its own destruction.

In the case of "That Tzaddik's Etrog" and "Fable of the Goat," the burden rests more squarely on human weakness, and the gap between the pious conventions and the wayward outcomes is more explicit. In the former, the Tzaddik's quest for a beautiful etrog is revealed to be simply a higher form of spiritual selfishness. The old man's indulgence in grief in the second story clearly represents a generation that could not part with its sorrows in order to seize the opportunity for redemption in the Land of Israel.

The longing for the Land of Israel is used as an effective marker of dubious piety in the grotesque story "Paths of Righteousness, or The Vinegar Maker." The subject of the title is a poor old man who has suffered greatly in his life and whose only reason for living is to put aside some of the meager proceeds from his labors so that he can end his life in Zion. Once again we are in the reverential atmosphere of innumerable tales in Jewish literature about the righteous poor whose simple faith is extolled. Yet two themes in the story urge us toward a more ironic reading of the old man's situation. The first is his trade as a vinegar maker. Vinegar is the acidic reduction of wine, and in fact the rabbinic phrase for the unworthy son of a good family (*hometz ben yayin*), which is invoked later in the story, literally means wine that has become vinegar. The old man's life in exile has been eaten away by suffering to the point where it is nothing, and it is only this nothing that would be taken to the Land of Israel. The hallowed ideal of going to the Holy Land to die comes under scrutiny here as a macabre offering of the dead to the Land of the Living.

The second theme concerns the representation of Jesus, who is referred to euphemistically in this story, as in traditional Jewish literature, as "that man" (*oto ish*). The old man is so pathetically ignorant of the Polish-Christian society in which he lives that he has no notion that the charity box in which he places his savings belongs to the church. When he is apprehended trying to redeem his deposits, his imprisonment cannot even arouse indignation over gentile persecution among his coreligionists because his behavior was based on such dim stupidity. His dying vision of being embraced and then dropped by the Christian savior is an ironic and delusional extension of his ignorance and spiritual isolation.

"The Lady and the Peddler" also uses strongly marked conventions to set up readers' expectations, but in this case the conventions are distinctly non-Jewish. Agnon uses the familiar framework of the vampire story in which to set a fable summing up the historical experience of the Jews in European culture. The story was published during the Holocaust, and the prototypical names of the characters (Helen as the woman who launched the Trojan War and Joseph as Jacob's son who winds up in Egypt) identify them as allegorical counters for their respective civilizations. The easy recognizability of the vampire story and its conventions serves Agnon well by enabling him to create a classic case of dramatic irony. While the true motives of the lady's hospitality are obvious to the reader, the peddler remains doggedly innocent of her designs.

The story is hardly an ecumenical meditation on Jewish-gentile relations. Yet given the years during which it was written, the generalization of European society as predatory and homicidal is not surprising. It is the representation of the Jew here that is ferociously critical: his abject gratitude for being taken in out of the cold, his eagerness to forget God's commandments, his self-flattering need to believe that he is being loved for his own sake, his steadfast determination to learn nothing from his experience. This is a bleak and unsparing indictment, and it might have made the story into a grim allegorical tract were it not for the leavening of black humor. Within the grisly and campy conventions of the vampire story, the lady's tongue-in-cheek derision and the peddler's witless complacency make the message of the text all the more chilling.

The Tale of The Scribe

Dedicated To My Wife, Esther

I

This is the story of Raphael the Scribe. Raphael was a righteous and blameless man who copied Torah scrolls, tefillin, and mezuzot in holiness and purity. And any man in the household of Israel who was childless, Mercy deliver us, or whose wife had died, Mercy deliver us, would come to Raphael the Scribe and say, "You know, Reb Raphael my brother, what are we and what are our lives? I had indeed hoped that my sons and my sons' sons would come to you to have you write tefillin for them; but now, alas, I am alone, and my wife, for whom I had thought I would wait long days and years in the upper world, has died and has left me to my sorrows. Perhaps, Reb Raphael my brother, you can undertake to write a Torah scroll under the good guidance of God's hand, and I will compensate you for it. Let us not be lost both in this world and the next, my dear Reb Raphael. Perhaps God will be gracious unto me and the work of your hands will be found acceptable." And Raphael then would sit and write a Torah scroll to give the man and his wife a name and remembrance in the household of Israel.

What may this be likened to? To a man who travels far from his own city, to a place where he is not known, and the watchmen who guard that city find him and ask, "Who are you and where do you live?" If the man is wealthy and a property owner, then as soon as he says I am So-and-so, the son of Thus-and-so, from such-and-such a place, they check the record books and documents, and find out how much he had given to the king's treasury, how much in property taxes he had paid, and they welcome him immediately, saying, "Come in, you blessed of God, the entire land is before you, dwell wherever you wish." But if the traveler is an ordinary man, and has neither property nor wealth, then he shows them a document written and signed by officials of his own city, which states that So-and-so is a resident of our city. Then he is permitted to remain and they do not hurry him out.

Likewise, when a man comes to the next world, and the evil angels meet him and ask, "Who are you and where are you from?"; if in his earthly life he had been an upright and blameless man, and left behind him good deeds, or sons busy with Torah and commandments, then these certainly serve as his good advocates. But if he had had none of these, then he is lost. However, when Jews come to the synagogue to pray and take a Torah scroll out of the ark and read from it, if the scroll was written as a memorial for the ascent of this man's soul, then it is immediately known on high that he had been So-and-so, a resident of such-and-such a place, and that is his identification. They then say to him, Enter and rest in peace.

Raphael the Scribe sat and wrote, and his wife, most blessed among women, the pious Miriam, stayed home and made life pleasant for him in a fine house with fine utensils which she scrubbed and cleaned and purified, so that her husband would do his work in a clean and pure atmosphere. She delighted him with delicate foods and savory beverages, and for Sabbaths and holidays, and sometimes even for the New Moon, she would buy a goose, cook the meat in a pot, or roast it; and Raphael would prepare the quills for writing Torah scrolls, tefillin, and mezuzot. He sat at the Torah and at God's service in holiness and purity, wielding the scribe's pen and fashioning crowns for his Creator.

2

Before we begin telling part of the story itself, let us tell about his way in his holy work. This was his way in holiness:

At midnight he would rise, seat himself on the floor, place ashes on his head, and weep for the destruction of Jerusalem, for the death of the righteous, the burning of the Temple, the length of the exile, the exile of the Shekhinah, the suffering under enslavement, and all sorts of hard and cruel decrees that are inflicted on the people of Israel day in and day out, and for our just Messiah, who is held in iron chains because of the sins of our generation. After that he would study the Path of Life and the Book of Splendor until the morning light, thus tying together what is proper for the night with what is proper for the day.

In the morning he would go down to the ritual bath and immerse his thin body in the water, then recite the morning prayers, return home and eat a piece of honey cake dipped in brandy, and fortify his weak body with a very light repast. After that he would go back and immerse himself again in the ritual bath, and then turn his heart away from all worldly matters. All day he sat in his house communing with his soul in solitude, completely within the frame of Torah. He did not mingle with other human beings and was thus saved from any of the transgressions between man and man, and remained holy in his speech, thought, and deed, and was spared all temptation and distraction. He sat secluded and isolated, and no one was with him except His Name, may He be blessed, and he studied a portion of the Talmud in order to tie together the oral teachings with the written ones, and concentrated on all the sacred meanings hinted at in Scripture. He was careful never to write the Holy Name without first having purified his body. For this reason he often wrote an entire sheet of parchment but left blank the spaces for the Holy Name, and later he wrote the Name in the blank spaces only after having immersed himself again in the purifying ritual bath.

He may thus be likened to a craftsman making a crown for a king: does he not first make the crown and then set into it the diamonds and other precious stones? Thus Raphael sat and wrote, until the beadle came, knocked on the window, and announced that the time had come for the afternoon prayers.

3

How good is a word in its proper time. Having told of his way in his sacred work, let us now note the place of this work.

He lived in a small house close to the big synagogue and to the old house of study and to other houses of prayer, a few steps from—not to be mentioned in the same breath—the bathhouse that contained the ritual bath. His house was small and low. It had only one room, which was divided in the middle by a partition made of boards. On the other side of the partition there was an oven and a range for pots, and between oven and range the pious and modest mistress of his house sat, and she cooked and baked and preserved and wove and knitted and looked to the needs of her home. Children they had none. Because the Holy One, blessed be He, desires the prayers of the righteous, He closed her womb.

When she completes the tasks that a wife is required to perform for her husband, she takes out a used garment and remakes it into clothing for an orphan. She is especially fond of this task because it enables her to sit quietly, to pull thread after thread, and in her thoughts take stock of the world. And in order to avoid doubts, Heaven forfend, about God's ways, and not to complain, Heaven forfend, against Him, she recalls several pious tales of salvation. For example, the story of a childless woman like herself who saved money in a stocking to buy a ruby, which is a proven remedy against childlessness. Then she saw the officials of the Society for Clothing the Naked, and gave them all the money, and in addition sewed clothes for the orphan children. Not many days later her womb was blessed, and out of her came affluent men who served God in comfort.

Or another story about a woman who was making a small tallit for an orphan, and suddenly she felt that the ritual fringes were being pulled and drawn upward, and a fragrance like that of the Garden of Eden was all around her. When she looked up she saw

Reb Gadiel, the infant who had been born by virtue of his father's having taught Torah to Jewish children; Reb Gadiel was kissing the ritual fringes she had made, and she heard him say to her: "Know that your deeds are acceptable on high, and that you will yet merit making ritual fringes for your own sons and sons' sons." Not many days later she was rewarded and her womb was blessed, and out of her came righteous, God-fearing, good men, taken up with Torah and God's commandments. And this birth was out of the ordinary, because that woman had been barren by nature.

Thus the pious Miriam sits, drawing thread after thread, and a thread of mercy is drawn and extended on high, and good angels bring up before her various fantasies: for example, that she is preparing a garment for her son who is sitting in his schoolroom and studying Torah.

From time to time she raises her pure eyes toward Raphael, the husband of her youth, who sits on the other side of the partition, near the window, at the clean table covered with a tallit. Also on the other side of the partition are a wardrobe and a bed. The bed is covered with a colored, clean spread, and the wardrobe contains rolls of parchment and sacred implements. In it her white wedding dress hangs, and in it also earth from the Land of Israel lies hidden away.

Across the top of the room a dart beam stretches from one end of the house to the other. On top of the beam there are a number of sacred books: some new, some old; some thick, some thin; some bound in cured sheepskins and some in a plain binding.

Near the beam, to the right, on the eastern wall, is the embroidered wall hanging Miriam had made in her youth at her father's house. It depicts a garden full of fruit trees, with a palace in the garden, and two lions watching over the garden. The lions' faces are turned toward each other, lion facing lion, one tongue reaching out toward the other; and stretching from tongue to tongue there is an inscription in large letters of gold, which says, "The earth is the Lord's and the fullness thereof," as if it were one mighty roar. In each of the four corners of the embroidery there is a square that contains the words: "I have set the Lord always before me."

Facing the east-wall embroidery, on the opposite wall, there is a mirror, and on top of its frame lies a bundle of willow twigs. Each year, on Hoshana Rabbah, Miriam brings home a bundle of the twigs that had been beaten against the prayer lecterns in the synagogue as part of the liturgy. A number of women had already been helped at childbirth by water in which such willow twigs were boiled. Only she herself has never yet made use of that water. The willow twigs continue to wither, and leaf after leaf is shed into the web that the spider has spun over the amulet that is near the bed. Her mother had given her the amulet on her wedding day to help keep away from the house the evil spirits that prevent births.

The amulet is written in the letters of the sacred alphabet but in the tongue of the Gentiles, *Yak krova mloda*, etc., meaning, "When the cow is young and healthy, why should she not give birth to a calf?" It was written for her mother, peace be upon her, who had been childless for a number of years, by Rabbi Simon of Yaroslav during his stay at the inn operated by her mother. He wrote it at the insistence of several righteous rabbis, while she cooked red borsht and potatoes for them after they had gone without food for three days on their journey to their saintly rabbi, the Seer of Lublin. And since at that time Rabbi Simon had not yet been ordained, he did not write the amulet in the sacred tongue; but the Hebrew letters in which the amulet was written spelled out the name of the angel in charge of pregnancy, with the Holy Name interwoven among them. Miriam tied the amulet with seven threads from seven veils of seven women from whom had come sons and sons of sons, none of whom had died during the lives of their parents.

From time to time Miriam comes softly to her side of the partition, and stands there letting her pure eyes rest on her husband as he sits at his work in holiness and purity. And if Raphael should interrupt his work and notice her standing there, immediately the pallor leaves her face and a blush takes its place, and she offers him the excuse that she had only come to fetch the Sabbath candlesticks to polish them in honor of the Sabbath. This is the rule of the house. Outside of the house nothing unclean ever appears, because the schoolchildren drive away any dog or pig that may wander into the street. The only animal present is the cat, which was created for the purpose of keeping the house free of mice. Geese and other clean fowl wander around the house. And the birds of heaven, at the time of their migration to the Land of Israel when the Torah portion *Ki tavo* is read in the synagogue, and again at the time when they return on Passover to hear the recitation of the Song of Songs in the classroom, sing their own song at his window every morning.

4

Inside the house there is quiet and peace. A feeling like Sabbath rest prevails. And the beauty of the place is reflected in its dwellers. The beloved Miriam's head is always covered by a clean white kerchief knotted below her throat, with its ends resting upon her heart like a dove's wings. Unlike most women, she uses no pin in her kerchief so that not even the smallest part of the covered area may become exposed, Heaven forbid. And if her hands were not busy with her work, one might mistakenly think that every day is Sabbath unto the Lord.

At times a poor man comes to the house to ask for alms, or a traveler comes in to have his tefillin repaired, and they tell Raphael what they had seen and heard in the dispersion of Israel. "What shall we say and what shall we relate, Reb Raphael? If told it would not be believed. In the house of Thus-and-so the Scribe, I saw with my own eyes a number of young men sitting day and night writing Torah scrolls, tefillin, and mezuzot, thus making factory work of the sacred Torah. Not only this, but I have heard that another scribe even employs girls to sit and write."

Raphael listens respectfully and replies humbly, "Do not say this, my dear fellow Jew. Why should we slander the people of God? Indeed, we have reason to rejoice that we have reached a time such as this when the Torah is spread so widely that a single scribe for a city is no longer enough."

At times a woman neighbor comes in to consult Miriam on something related to cooking, or to ask when the new month will begin. And if there is a difficult birth in town, someone comes running to her to borrow her willow twigs. The woman says to her, "My dear Miriam, surely you wish to save two human souls, therefore please lend me your willow twigs. Tomorrow, God willing, I shall go from one end of the town to the other end and find other willow twigs to replace these." And Miriam answers with a sigh, "Take the willow twigs, my dear soul, and may they bring good fortune and long life. As for me, I am not worthy of your going to any trouble about me; for myself, what will these willow twigs give or add, even if they were boiled in tears?" And her neighbor replies, "Don't, Miriam, don't, my precious life, let us not give Satan a foothold by complaining. We have a mighty Father in heaven and His mercies are over all His works. Many barren women have given birth, and children have clung to their breasts. There is a women's prayer book that has been brought from the Holy Land; nothing I can say matters, but in that book you will discover God's acts and miracles, and in it also you will learn how to entreat God."

When Miriam visits the bathhouse Raphael remains in the house of study. When she returns home she dresses in fine clothes, like a bride on her wedding day, and stands before the mirror. At that moment it seems as if the days of her youth were returning to her. She recalls an inn on a main road, frequented by gentile lords and ladies, and cattle dealers sojourning there, and herself sitting with her father and mother, and with Raphael the husband of her youth. She recalls the crown her mother placed on her head on her wedding day, and at that moment the thought enters her mind to make herself beautiful for her husband. But then she sees reflected in the mirror the east-wall embroidery with its scenes and those two lions with their mouths open; immediately she is startled and shrinks back: "The earth is the Lord's and the fullness thereof."

And when Raphael returns home after the prayers and sees his wife in her true beauty reflected in the mirror, he is immediately attracted to her. He goes toward her to make some pleasing remark. But when he is near her, His name, may He be blessed, flashes before him out of the mirror. Immediately he stops and recites devoutly and in holiness: "I have set the Lord always before me," and shuts his eyes before the glory and awe of the Name. Both turn away silently. He sits in one corner and studies the Book of Splendor, and she sits in another corner reading the women's prayer book, until sleep invades their eyes. They take the large bucket of water with the large copper fish embossed on its bottom, and wash their hands in preparation for reciting "Hear, O Israel" before retiring.

5

When hope and patience came to an end and she no longer had the strength to weep and pray for children, she stood before her husband heartbroken and with great humility. Said Raphael to Miriam, "What is your wish, Miriam, and what is your request?" And Miriam replied, "My wish and my request, if I have found favor in my husband's eyes, and if it please my husband to do my wish and fulfill my petition, then let him write a Torah scroll for us also."

At that moment Reb Raphael took Miriam's head and placed it on his knees, then he placed his eyes upon her eyes, his face upon her face, his mouth upon her mouth, and said to her, "Please don't, my daughter, God has not yet withdrawn His mercy from us. We shall surely still behold seed upon the earth." Miriam lowered her eyelids and replied, "May the words of your mouth enter the ears of the Holy One, blessed be He." From then on her hands were busy making a mantle for a Torah scroll, and other sacred implements, as does a woman whose hands are busy making decorative ribbons, sheets, and coverings for the expected newborn baby.

6

"Good fortune is not forever." God chastises those He loves. One Sabbath morning Miriam returned from the synagogue, put down her prayer book, and, before she was able to remove her outer garment and prepare her heart and soul to greet her husband properly, a sigh escaped from deep within her, she began to feel alternately chilled and hot, her face turned green, her bones began rattling in their joints, and her whole skin sought to escape from her body. She lay down on her bed and remained there and never again rose or left her bed. She had not been inscribed on high for a long life, and was plucked while still in her youth.

Miriam died in the prime of her days and left her husband to his sorrows. She died in the prime of her days and left behind her neither son nor daughter.

7

At the end of the seven days of mourning, Raphael the Scribe arose, put on his shoes, went to the marketplace, and obtained sheets of parchment, bundles of quills, a string of gallnuts for ink, and soft gut-thread for sewing together the sheets of parchment, and set his heart to the writing of a Torah scroll in memory of the soul of his wife whom God had taken away.

What may this be likened to? To a great gardener who raised beautiful plants in his garden, and all the officials who were to see the king would first come to his garden and buy beautiful flowers to take with them. Once the gardener's wife was to see the king, and the gardener said, "All others who visit the king take flowers from my garden. Now that my own wife is to visit the king, it is only proper that I go down to my garden and pick flowers for her."

The comparison is clear. Raphael was a great gardener. He planted beautiful Torah scrolls in the world. And whoever was invited to appear before the King—the King over kings of kings, the Holy One, blessed be He—took a Torah scroll with him. And now that Miriam's time had come to appear before the King—the Holy One, blessed be He—Raphael immediately went down to his garden—that is, to his pure and holy table—and picked roses—that is, the letters of the Torah scroll he wrote—and made a beautiful bouquet—that is, the Torah scroll he had prepared. Thus the work began.

8

Raphael sat and wrote. He wrote his Torah scroll day and night, interrupting the work only for prayers with the congregation and for the recitation of the kaddish. A tallit was spread over the clean table, its fringes drooping below the table and getting intertwined with the fringes of the little tallit he wore. On the tallit lay a lined sheet of parchment dazzling in its whiteness as the sky itself in its purity.

From morning to evening the quill wrote on the parchment and beautiful black letters glistened and alighted on the parchment as birds upon the snow on the Sabbath when the Song of Moses is read. When he came to the writing of the great and awesome Name he would go down to the ritual bath and immerse himself.

Thus he sat and wrote until he completed the entire Torah scroll.

9

But the doing does not flow as fast as the words. Raphael sat at his toil a long time before he completed the writing of the scroll. His face shrank, his cheeks became hollow, his temples sunken, his eyes larger and larger, as he sat bewildered in the emptiness of his desolate house. Near its hole a mouse plays with a discarded quill, and the cat lies dejectedly on the abandoned oven. A month comes and a month goes, and time sprinkles his earlocks with gray. Raphael prods himself with the sage's saying: "Raphael, Raphael, do not forget death because death will not forget you." Month comes and month goes and there is no action and no work done. The sheet of parchment lies on the table and the quill lies in the sunshine, and the sun's reflection out of the quill shines as the hidden light from among the wings of the celestial creatures. Sunbeams come down to bathe in the scribe's inkwell, and when they depart in order to bid welcome to the shadows of the night, the sheet of parchment lies unchanged.

At times Raphael summoned strength, dipped the pen in ink, and wrote a word, but this did not lead to any more work because his eyes filled with tears. When he sat down to write a single letter in the Torah, immediately his eyes brimmed with tears which rolled down to the parchment.

> *In vain do builders build palaces*
> *If a flooding river sweeps away their foundations;*
> *In vain do people kindle a memorial candle*
> *If the orphans extinguish it with their tears.*

And when he swallowed his tears and said to himself, Now I will work, now I will write, he would reach such a peak of devout ecstasy that his quill spattered droplets of ink, and he was unable to write even a single letter properly.

It is told of the Rabbi of Zhitomir that he once asked the Rabbi of Berditchev about the biblical verse "And Aaron did so," on which the commentator Rashi, of blessed memory, commented that Aaron did not deviate from God's instructions. This is puzzling; how could it have been otherwise? The Holy One, blessed be He, told Aaron to kindle the lights; would it have been possible for Aaron to deviate? Had God instructed an ordinary man to do this, would that man have deviated? Therefore, what is so praiseworthy about Aaron's not having deviated? However, if the Holy One, blessed be He, had told the Rabbi of Berditchev to kindle the lights, he would surely have felt ecstasy and awe and fervor, and if he tried to kindle them he would spill the oil on the ground, and, because of his awe, would not succeed in kindling them. But Aaron, even though he surely possessed ecstasy and awe and fervor more than any other person, when he came to kindle the lights, he did as God commanded, without any deviation.

That winter it once happened that the bathhouse in Raphael's town was closed down by the authorities because it was near collapse, and when Raphael reached a place in the Torah scroll where the Name had to be written, he could find no bath of purification. He took an ax, went down to the river on the outskirts of the town, broke the ice, immersed himself in the water three times, and returned and wrote the Name with the joy of wondrous fervor. At that moment Raphael attained the merit of discovering the divine secret that before a man is able to rise to the height of joyous fervor he has to be like a man who stands in icy water on a snowy day.

From then on Raphael sat, physically weakened, in the joy of silence, and with emaciated hand he wielded the quill on the parchment until he completed his scroll. The wooden rollers on which the parchment sheets are rolled, and other sacred implements, he made himself. In this he may be compared to a host who always had guests in his house and had several servants waiting on them. Once he made a feast for the king. Who should properly wait on the king? Surely the host himself.

10

And now let us recall the custom—a custom in Israel is like a law— observed at the completion of the writing of a Torah scroll.

When a scribe is about to complete a scroll, he leaves several verses at the end unfinished, in outlined lettering, in order that any Jew who had not himself had the privilege to fulfill the biblical admonition "And now ye shall write down this song for yourselves" may be afforded the opportunity to come and fill in one of the letters of the Torah. And whoever is so favored takes a pen, dips its tip in ink, and fills in the hollow, outlined letter. Raphael put down his quill, having left several verses in outlined letters, and said to himself: I shall go and invite a quorum of ten Jews, so that the Torah will not be lonely, and saintly Jews may see and rejoice in the completion of a Torah. He walked over to the mirror to look into it and straighten out his earlocks and his beard in honor of the Torah and in honor of those who would come to rejoice with him.

The mirror was covered with a sheet. From the day of Miriam's death, peace be with her, no one had removed this sign of mourning. Raphael pulled aside the end of the sheet, looked into the mirror, and saw his own face, and the east-wall embroidery across the room, and the scroll he had written, with the hollow, outlined letters at its end. At that moment his soul stirred and he returned to the table, took the quill, and filled in the letters in the scroll he had written in memory of his wife's soul. When he completed the task he rolled up the scroll, raised it high, dancing with great joy, and he leaped and danced and sang in honor of the Torah. Suddenly Raphael stopped, puzzled about the melody he was singing in honor of the completion of the scroll. He felt sure that he had heard this melody before but could not remember where he had heard it. And now, even when he closed his lips the singing of the melody continued by itself. Where had he heard this melody?

II

Having mentioned the melody, I shall not refrain from relating where he had heard it.

It was the evening of Simhat Torah. That evening the rabbi's house of study was full of bright lights, every light fixture glowing with a radiance from on high. Righteous and saintly Hasidim clothed in white robes of pure silk, with Torah scrolls in their arms, circled the pulpit, dancing with holy fervor and enjoying the pleasures of the Torah. A number of Hasidim as well as ordinary householders get the privilege of dancing with them, and they cling to the sacred Torah and to those who selflessly obey the Torah, and they forget all anger and all disputes and all kinds of troublesome trivialities. And their young children form an outer circle around them, each child carrying a colored flag, red or green or white or blue, each flag inscribed with letters of gold. On top of each flag is an apple, and on top of each apple a burning candle, and all the candles glow like planets in the mystical "field of sacred apples." And when young boys or girls see their father receive this honor, carrying a Torah scroll in his arms, they immediately jump toward him, grasping the scroll, caressing, embracing, kissing it with their pure lips that have not tasted sin; they clap their hands and sing sweetly, "Happy art thou, O Israel," and their fathers nod their heads toward the children, singing "Ye holy lambs." And the women in the outer lobby feast their eyes on this exalted holiness.

When the seventh round of the procession around the pulpit is reached, the cantor takes a Torah scroll to his bosom and calls out to the youths, "Whoever studies the Torah, let him come and take a Torah scroll," and a number of fine youths come and take scrolls in their arms.

Then the cantor calls out again, "The distinguished young man, Raphael, is honored with the honor of the Torah, and with the singing of a beautiful melody."

Raphael came forward, went to the ark, accepted the scroll from the cantor, and walked at the head of the procession. The elders stood and clapped their hands, adding to the rejoicing. The children stood on the benches chanting aloud "Ye holy lambs" and waving their flags over the heads of the youths. But when Raphael began to sing his melody all hands became still and everyone stood motionless without saying a word. Even the older Hasidim whose saintly way in prayer and in dancing with great fervor is like that of the ancient sage Rabbi Akiba—of whom it is told that when he prayed by himself, his bowing and genuflecting were so fervent that "if when you left him he was in one corner, you found him in another corner at the next moment"—even they restrained themselves with all their might from doing this. They did not lift a hand to clap because of the ecstatic sweetness, even though their hearts were consumed with fire. The women leaned from the windows of the womens' gallery, and their heads hung out like a flock of doves lined up on the frieze of a wall.

Raphael held the scroll in his arm, walking in the lead with all the other youths following him in the procession around the pulpit. At that moment a young girl pushed her way through the legs of the dancers, leaped toward Raphael, sank her red lips into the white mantle of the Torah scroll in Raphael's arm, and kept on kissing the scroll and caressing it with her hands. Just then the flag fell out of her hand, and the burning candle dropped on Raphael's clothing.

After the holiday, Raphael's father brought an action before the rabbi against the girl's father in the matter of Raphael's robe that had been burned because of the girl. The rabbi, indulging himself in the pleasure of a wise remark, said to the girl's father, "God willing, for their wedding day you will have a new garment made for him." Immediately they brought a decanter of brandy and wrote the betrothal contract. And for Raphael's and Miriam's wedding a new garment was made for him. This is the story of the melody.

And Raphael continues to circle the pulpit, singing sweet melodies. His voice is lovely and sad, numbing the senses but wakening the soul to rise and dance the dance of the Shekhinah. That dance without sound or movement, in which even the earlocks and beard remain motionless, and only the fringes of the prayer shawl drip down to the knees. The house is still, the feet are stilled, and the hands unmoved. The girls come down from the women's gallery to the house of study to watch the youths dance. The youths continue to circle the pulpit, and the girls reach out with the tips of their fingers toward the Torah scrolls in the hands of the youths.

The sun has set, her last rays shine through the cracks in the shutters, and their light adorns Miriam's white dress. Raphael came toward Miriam and bowed before her with the Torah scroll held in his arm. He could not see her face because she was wrapped in her wedding dress. Silently Raphael stood and wondered where her wedding dress had come from, because he had taken it out of her wardrobe to have a curtain for the ark made out of it. He walked over to see whether her dress hung there, but when he got there he no longer remembered what he had come for. He stood facing the wardrobe and looked into its black void. Suddenly he noticed the little bag of earth from the Land of Israel. He had placed some of this earth on Miriam's eyes in her grave. Raphael took the little bag of earth in his hand and his heart trembled violently. His hand faltered and the earth spilled to the floor of the house. His heart became agitated as that of a man who stands on sacred soil.

The lamp flickers. Raphael is wrapped in his prayer shawl, a Torah scroll in his arm, and the scroll has a mantle of fine silk on which the name of Miriam the wife of Raphael the Scribe is embroidered. The house becomes filled with many Torah scrolls, and many elders dancing. As they dance they neither lift their feet nor bend their knees, but move as if they had no joints. They dance without motion, revolving their bodies, and Miriam stands in the center, her face covered, dancing with her shoulders, her arms raised into the emptiness of the room. She approaches Raphael's scroll. She takes off her veil and covers her face with her hands. Suddenly her hands slide down, her face is uncovered, and her lips cling to the mantle of the Torah scroll in Raphael's arms.

The Holy One, blessed be He, removed His robe of light, and the world stood in silent evening prayer. The lamp flickered and the wick sank into the oil. Suddenly a tongue of flame leaped up and illuminated the room. Its light framed the face of Raphael the Scribe, who sank down with his scroll. His wife's wedding dress was spread out over him and over his scroll.

Translated by Isaac Franck

That Tzaddik's Etrog

Y ou heard the story from whomever you may have heard it, whereas I heard it from a Hasid son of a Hasid who heard it from his teacher Reb Shlomo the Tzaddik of Zvihel, the direct seventh generation descendant of Reb Mikheleh the Holy Preacher of Zloczow. And there is no question that the way I heard it from that Hasid who heard it from his Rebbe, is exactly the way it happened, since that righteous Reb Shlomo of Zvihel had it from his fathers and in the very language of his fathers he told it, not adding a word except for clarification. So whatever he added was of the very stuff of the original.

Reb Mikheleh the Holy Preacher of Zloczow started out a pauper in a house devoid of material goods. Often he had nothing except the slice he had stashed away in the hat on his head for a beggar, so that in case a beggar should happen along he would not leave humiliated, for so devoted was that righteous man to his Maker that he neglected his own needs, paying attention only to the needs of the Shekhinah—that is Torah, prayer, and good deeds.

Doesn't Solomon tell us in his Proverbs that the righteous man understands the soul of his beast? Well, so, too, the wife of that righteous man understood the soul of her righteous husband. She did all she could to keep aggravation away from him and to protect him against all distractions from his holy work, unlike most women who, when the cupboard is bare, come muttering and nattering.

One year it was already hours before Sukkot and the rabbi's wife did not have a morsel in the house for celebrating the holiday. She thought, I will go tell my husband—he will hear and know my distress. She went to his solitude room, stood in the doorway, and said, "Sukkot eve is upon us and I still have no festival provisions."

That righteous man lifted himself from his chair, poked his head out from under his tallit, put his hand on his tefillin, and said to her, "You are worried about meat and fish, and I am worried about not yet having my etrog."

She kissed the mezuzah on the doorpost of his room and left dejectedly.

That righteous man stood up and went all over the house looking for something to sell and use the money to buy an etrog. He looked and looked but did not find a single thing worth an etrog.

He fondled his tefillin and mused, The nine festival days are approaching, and during the festival tefillin aren't worn, and my tefillin were written by a holy man of God, who writes each and every letter in holiness and purity, investing the most sublime and most awesome intents and purposes in the writing of each and every character. Tefillin of his make are much sought after and command a high price. I will sell them, and with the proceeds I will get an etrog.

Reb Mikheleh removed his tefillin and took them and went to his Beit Midrash and asked, "Who would like to buy my tefillin?" A certain man stood up and said, "I will buy them." He took out a gold dinar and gave it to the righteous man, and the righteous man handed him his tefillin.

The righteous man took the dinar and ran to the etrog seller to get an etrog. He saw a beautiful etrog and judged it to be kosher and perfectly formed. Now a truly righteous man, when he buys an object for performing a divine precept, doesn't bargain. All the more so when it comes to an etrog, about which it is written, "And on the first day [of Sukkot] you shall take a fruit of the beautiful tree…and rejoice before the Lord your God" (Leviticus 23:40).

Reb Mikheleh returned home happy that he had come by a beautiful etrog possessing all the qualities that are lauded in an etrog. He went into his sukkah to fix something and returned to his solitude room.

He sat down in his chair and placed the etrog before him and ruminated on this precept that God had given the Jewish people to observe during these holy days of Sukkot, a holiday adorned with a multitude of precepts to observe.

His wife the rebbetzin heard that her husband had been to market. She went into his room.

She saw the glow in his face and the ecstasy emanating from his entire being. The rebbetzin thought he had brought home all the festival victuals. She said to him, "I see that you are happy. You must have brought us the festival provisions. Give them to me and I will prepare them, for it is nearly time."

The righteous man rose from his chair and put his hand on his eyes and said, "Praised be the blessed and sublime Name for bestowing His grace on me and fulfilling my every need."

The rebbetzin stood there waiting for her husband to deliver. He sat back down in his chair and told her that he had been privileged to acquire a kosher etrog.

She asked him, "How did you have money to get an etrog?" He said to her, "I sold my tefillin for a gold dinar and bought an etrog." She said to him, "In that case, give me the change." He said to her, "They didn't give me any change. All the money they gave me for my tefillin, I gave for my etrog." He started to enumerate with steadily mounting enthusiasm all the virtues of the etrog.

The rebbetzin swallowed her tears and said, "I want to see this great find of yours." The righteous man took out the etrog and unwrapped it. It radiated its beauty and emitted its fragrance, a feast for the eyes and truly fit for the benediction.

The woman said, "Give it to me so I can have a good look at it." She reached out and picked up the etrog.

She thought of the pitiful state of her house and the distress of her children who had nothing to eat, and how the festival of Sukkot was nearly here and she had nothing with which to make it festive. Grief drove the strength from her hands, and the etrog slipped and fell. And having fallen, its stem broke. And the stem having broken, the etrog was no longer fit for ritual use.

The righteous man saw that his etrog was no longer fit for the benediction. He stretched out his two holy hands in despair and said, "Tefillin I have not and etrog I have not; all I have left is anger. But I will not be angry, but I will not be angry."

Now that Hasid who told me this story said to me: I asked my rebbe, "Is that really how it happened?" And my rebbe said to me, "That is how it happened, exactly as I have told it to you." And my rebbe also said to me, "This story—the daughter-in-law of the Holy Preacher, wife of Rabbi Yosef of Yampol, told it to the father of her son-in-law, Rabbi Baruch of Mezbizh. On the very day that this incident occurred she had been in the Holy Preacher's home and had seen it with her own eyes. And when she told it to Rabbi Baruch the Tzaddik of Mezbizh, Rabbi Baruch, father of her son-in-law, said to her, 'Mother of my daughter-in-law, tell me the story again from beginning to end. This is a story worth hearing twice.'"

Translated by Shira Leibowitz and Moshe Kohn

Fable of The Goat

The tale is told of an old man who groaned from his heart. The doctors were sent for, and they advised him to drink goat's milk. He went out and bought a she-goat and brought her into his home. Not many days passed before the goat disappeared. They went out to search for her but did not find her. She was not in the yard and not in the garden, not on the roof of the house of study and not by the spring, not in the hills and not in the fields. She tarried several days and then returned by herself; and when she returned, her udder was full of a great deal of milk, the taste of which was as the taste of Eden. Not just once, but many times she disappeared from the house. They would go out in search of her and would not find her until she returned by herself with her udder full of milk that was sweeter than honey and whose taste was the taste of Eden.

One time the old man said to his son, "My son, I desire to know where she goes and whence she brings this milk which is sweet to my palate and a balm to all my bones."

His son said to him, "Father, I have a plan."

He said to him, "What is it?"

The son got up and brought a length of cord. He tied it to the goat's tail.

His father said to him, "What are you doing, my son?"

He said to him, "I am tying a cord to the goat's tail, so that when I feel a pull on it I will know that she has decided to leave, and I can catch the end of the cord and follow her on her way." The old man nodded his head and said to him, "My son, if your heart is wise, my heart too will rejoice."

The youth tied the cord to the goat's tail and minded it carefully. When the goat set off, he held the cord in his hand and did not let it slacken until the goat was well on her way and he was following her. He was dragged along behind her until he came to a cave. The goat went into the cave, and the youth followed her, holding the cord. They walked thus for an hour or two, or maybe even a day or two. The goat wagged her tail and bleated, and the cave came to an end.

When they emerged from the cave, the youth saw lofty mountains, and hills full of the choicest fruit, and a fountain of living waters that flowed down from the mountains; and the wind wafted all manner of perfumes. The goat climbed up a tree by clutching at the ribbed leaves. Carob fruits full of honey dropped from the tree, and she ate of the carobs and drank of the garden's fountain.

The youth stood and called to the wayfarers: "I adjure you, good people, tell me where I am, and what is the name of this place?"

They answered him, "You are in the Land of Israel, and you are close by Safed."

The youth lifted up his eyes to the heavens and said, "Blessed be the Omnipresent, blessed be He who has brought me to the Land of Israel." He kissed the soil and sat down under the tree.

He said, "Until the day breathe and the shadows flee away, I shall sit on the hill under this tree. Then I shall go home and bring my father and mother to the Land of Israel." As he was sitting thus and feasting his eyes on the holiness of the Land of Israel, he heard a voice proclaiming:

"Come, let us go out to greet the Sabbath Queen."

And he saw men like angels, wrapped in white shawls, with

boughs of myrtle in their hands, and all the houses were lit with a great many candles. He perceived that the eve of Sabbath would arrive with the darkening, and that he would not be able to return. He uprooted a reed and dipped it in gallnuts, from which the ink for the writing of the Torah scrolls is made. He took a piece of paper and wrote a letter to his father:

"From the ends of the earth I lift up my voice in song to tell you that I have come in peace to the Land of Israel. Here I sit, close by Safed, the holy city, and I imbibe its sanctity. Do not inquire how I arrived here but hold on to this cord which is tied to the goat's tail and follow the footsteps of the goat; then your journey will be secure, and you will enter the Land of Israel."

The youth rolled up the note and placed it in the goat's ear. He said to himself: When she arrives at Father's house, Father will pat her on the head, and she will flick her ears. The note will fall out, Father will pick it up and read what is written on it. Then he will take up the cord and follow the goat to the Land of Israel.

The goat returned to the old man, but she did not flick her ears, and the note did not fall. When the old man saw that the goat had returned without his son, he clapped his hands to his head and began to cry and weep and wail, "My son, my son, where are you? My son, would that I might die in your stead, my son, my son!"

So he went, weeping and mourning over his son, for he said, "An evil beast has devoured him, my son is assuredly rent in pieces!"

And he refused to be comforted, saying, "I will go down to my grave in mourning for my son."

And whenever he saw the goat, he would say, "Woe to the father who banished his son, and woe to her who drove him from the world!"

The old man's mind would not be at peace until he sent for the butcher to slaughter the goat. The butcher came and slaughtered the goat. As they were skinning her, the note fell out of her ear. The old man picked up the note and said, "My son's handwriting!"

When he had read all that his son had written, he clapped his hands to his head and cried, "*Vay! Vay!* Woe to the man who robs himself of his own good fortune, and woe to the man who requites good with evil!"

He mourned over the goat many days and refused to be comforted, saying, "Woe to me, for I could have gone up to the Land of Israel in one bound, and now I must suffer out my days in this exile!"

Since that time the mouth of the cave has been hidden from the eye, and there is no longer a short way. And that youth, if he has not died, shall bear fruit in his old age, full of sap and richness, calm and peaceful in the Land of the Living.

Translated by Barney Rubin

Paths of Righteousness, or the Vinegar Maker

In one of the towns of Poland there lived an old man who used to make vinegar. His forebears were renowned wine merchants, but hard times impoverished them and they left him with no more than a shack and wine that had gone sour. Ne'er a happy day did he see there. His wife died when his children were small, and when they grew up they were pressed into military service and died in the wars. The old man would sit there all alone and make vinegar. For the first five days of the week he would engage in his trade, and on Fridays he would fill up a large can and make his rounds about town. Many times he would stop and think, What am I and what is my life? Five days a week I make vinegar to sell; when I have sold it I make some more and go out again to sell it. And for what reason? To sustain this enfeebled body. If my wife and children were alive, I would truly provide for them. Now that my wife is dead and my progeny is no more, why do I take such pains to draw my skin from my flesh? He would whine and sigh and moan about the course of his life so much that his work was discreditable in his eyes, and even the wearing of tsitsit and tefillin of little worth. But since the love of the Land of Israel was embedded in his heart, he made up his mind to go up to the Land of Israel, and if he were found worthy he would find for himself a grave in its dust. Not only was he sparing in his food and parsimonious in his pleasures, but he would even deny himself tasting the fruit that he had from which to make vinegar and would take his bread with weak brew, eating less than his due. On Mondays and Thursdays he would fast, until he got used to living on very little. And on Friday afternoons, after he had sold his vinegar and returned from town, he would sit on a stone and take the money out of his pocket, half of which he would take for sustenance and the other half he would put into a charity box which the Gentiles in this realm used to place at crossroads in the hands of *that man*. A simple man, he didn't know what the purpose of the box was, and thought that there was no place safer than that. Copper coins he would take for his immediate requirements and silver coins for his traveling expenses to the Land of Israel, and he would make a scratch on the can for a sign. From then on he labored with joy. Lo and behold, he would say to himself, up to now I disliked my trade and now I find it hard to give it up; the same utensils and the same vinegar, and before I know it the day is done. At midnight he would get up from his bed, take his can, and dance about with it until it was time for morning prayers. The more he was occupied with his calculations of how many scratches there were on the can and how much money he had put in the charity box, so his prayers suffered, becoming somewhat erratic. And so said he, "O God, it is plain for You to see that all the calculations I make are only so that I may go up to Your land. Take me there and there I will say to You a fine prayer."

And thus several years passed. The old man, out of love for his work, went around the town with his vinegar, after which he would apportion his earnings, one-half for his immediate requirements and one-half for his traveling expenses. Then he would make more vinegar to take around the town, apportioning his earnings, one-half for his sustenance and one-half for the charity box. So is the nature of simple people that, notwithstanding the passage of years, they do not change their ways. And thus several years passed. The inner walls of his house began to peel. The roof began to leak and cracks appeared in the walls. And when it rained he was soaked to the skin, even when he was under the covers. And the way taxes and rates were going up, if he were to remain either the state would take over his house or his house would be his grave. The vinegar maker would lie on his bed at night and listen to the sound of the plaster crumbling from the walls, bit by bit snapping off and falling away, almost without being heard due to the moisture. But the old man's heart quavered like a bell out of joy at God's mercy in keeping him alive and not letting him perish abroad.

At cockcrow, the old man would wash his hands and eyes, light the candle and sit by the front door and wrap himself up as one who mourns and bewails the exile, but as soon as he sees his can and how many scratches there are on it, he recalls immediately the money he had put into the charity box for his traveling expenses. He would pick up the can and drum on it with his fingers songs and praises, and then, placing one hand on his hip and raising one shoulder, he would count how many scratches there were on the can—two, three, forty, fifty, a hundred—dancing for joy. Not like those who dance over their heads and not like those who if they are put in one corner are to be found in another, but like those who dance around their shoulders, moving their shoulders to and fro. And so he would hop about until summoned by the beadle to services. Upon hearing the beadle's voice calling to services, he would say to himself softly, I will get up and go to prayers, abashed at being so happy in this world. And then he would get on his feet and take with him his tallit and tefillin. How tattered was his tallit, virtually disintegrating with tears. Thank God he is going to Jerusalem where one is buried without a tallit. When prayers were over, and unless it was a fast day, he would dip a slice of bread into a glass of weak brew and lick the dust with his tongue so as not to be tempted to indulge in meat and wine. Then would he get down to making vinegar. Five days a week he made vinegar, and on Fridays he would fill up the can and make his rounds about town. Upon his return he would apportion the money he had made, one half for his immediate requirements, and the other for his traveling expenses. And when no one was looking he would thrust his finger through the cobwebs that had gathered during the week around the slit in the charity box which was clasped between the hands of *that man*, and would put the coins into the box. He was a simple man and knew not the purpose for which the box served. Each time he put coins in the box he would add another scratch on the can for a sign.

And thus several years passed. His body became bent like a ram's horn and he groaned from the heart. The vinegar ate away half of his lungs and he breathed with difficulty. Most of the time he suffered and there was hardly enough left of him to fill his clothes. But each Friday afternoon he would add another scratch to the can, although there was barely room for one more. Now he was already saying that it was high time to go up to the Land of Israel, for, he said, last Friday afternoon when I put my money in the can, I could see the coins peeping out of the box. But as long as the can is whole it is hard to retire.

One day while the old man was pouring off vinegar the can burst. Whether he sold any more vinegar I never knew. But I heard that he went to the image of *that man* and took a stone to break open the charity box and take out his money. I also heard that on the same day Roman priests came to open the charity box and found him standing over the charity box with the stone in his hand. They seized him and put him in prison. No sooner had they seized him and put him in prison than the whole town was seething like hell. Some said, "The world is going to the dogs and there is no more faith," and others said, "The tradesman is but a product of his trade. For as vinegar is none other than fermented wine, so has this old man shown himself to be wicked." The former and the latter all ashamed sighed ruefully at such sacrilege, saying, "Oh, what an unworthy son born of a worthy father." The old man sat in jail chained in irons. But his wrists were thin and the irons did not press on them. When God brings an affliction upon a man, God relieves the bitterness so that he might cope with the suffering. The old man sat in jail and shook his chains, and hordes of bugs and the like went scurrying. He was afraid to lie on the floor. He put his head between his knees like the early mystics until he was brought before the judge.

The judge asked him, "Do you admit that you were about to open the charity box?" The old man replied, "I was about to open the box because the money…" Before he could finish what he was saying, the judge said to him reproachfully, "Does the accused admit that he wanted to open the box?" The old man wanted to explain to him that whatever he had done he had done lawfully, since the money in the box was his and a man cannot be guilty of stealing his own money. But the presumption in that jurisdiction was that the more one spoke the truth the more was he deemed to be lying. The judge called the witnesses. The priests came forward, each one in turn taking out his cross from under his vestments and kissing it, and testifying that on said day of said month at said hour they were about to open said box when they found a Jew with a stone in his hand about to smash the box. The judge then asked the witnesses, "Do you recognize this old man as the one who was about to smash the box?" And they repeated after him, "We testify on our oath against this old man that he was about to smash the box." The man was taken aback that men of such high order should take the oath where it is not required. He shook his hands and his chains rattled, making a loud noise. The judge turned to him and said, "Are you inferring that these high-ranking witnesses have perjured against you?" God forbid! It had never occurred to the old man to say so. It was true that he was about to open the box. And what did this judge see to indicate that he was lying? But he would not lie, all he wanted was his money back. He was chained hand and foot with chains of iron and he was incriminated out of his own mouth. But he was still well served by his eyes, which he raised and looked into the judge's and witnesses' faces. A weird state of affairs: all speak the truth and the truth gives rise to a miscarriage of justice. With one eye on his chains, the old man looked with his other eye about their heads. He saw the image of *that man* hanging on the courtroom wall and said to himself, You smile at me. He began rapping on the table with both hands until the sound of his chains was heard from one end of the building to the other, and cried out, "Leave me alone and give me back my money." But they beat him and put him back in jail.

The old man sat on the straw and complained, "O God, it

was plain for You to see how many years I have had to contend with this exile; I ate no good food, I wore no fine clothes, and I occupied no fine lodgings. All my years were sour to me as vinegar, and I accepted it all lovingly solely because I was to go up to Your Holy Land. And now that my time has come to go up, my captors have come and taken my money and put me in jail." So he sat and cried until he dozed off in the midst of his crying. At midnight he woke of his own accord. In the room of the jail there was no mezuzah and no can. He began shaking his chains and chanting in a sad voice some songs and praises which he was used to singing at night; and so he went on chanting until he fell asleep again. The jail door opened, and there appeared some apparition of a man with a stone box in his hand and a certain smile on his lips. The old man turned his eyes away from him and tried to fall asleep. That man put him on his feet and said, "Hold on to me and I will bring you to wherever you wish to go." The old man extended his arms toward that man and said, "How shall I hold on to you when my hands are in chains of iron?" And the latter replied, "Regardless thereof you shall." The old man opened wide the palms of his hand and clasped them around the neck of that man who smiled and said, "I shall promptly bring you to the Land of Israel." The old man embraced the neck of that man as the latter turned and faced in the direction of Jerusalem. On their first flight that man stopped smiling. On their second flight the old man's fingers turned cold. On their third flight he felt that he was embracing cold stone. His heart melted and his hands waxed weak. He was set loose and fell to the ground. On the morrow when his captors came in, he was not to be found.

That night a knocking was heard on the door of the Kolel in Jerusalem. Those who went outdoors saw a flight of angels which had come from the exile bearing a mortal form, which that very night they took and buried, in keeping with the custom in Jerusalem not to hold over the dead.

Translated by Amiel Gurt

The Lady and the Peddler

Acertain Jewish peddler was traveling with his stock from town to town and village to village. One day he found himself in a wooded region far from any settlement. He saw a lone house. He approached it and, standing before the door, he cried out his wares. A lady came outside and spoke to him. "What do you want here, Jew?" Bowing, he wished her well and said, "Perhaps you can use something of these lovely things I have?" He took his pack off his back and offered her all sorts of goods. "I have no use for you or your wares," she said to him.

"But look and see, perhaps even so? Here are ribbons and rings and kerchiefs and sheets and soap and fine perfumes that the noble-women use." She looked at his pack for a few moments, then averted her eyes from him. "There's nothing here. Get out!" Again he bowed before her and took things out of the pack to offer to her. "Just look, my lady, and don't say there's nothing here. Perhaps you might want this, or perhaps this lovely piece of goods pleases you. Please, my lady, look and see." The lady saw a hunting knife. She paid him for it and went back into her house. He put his pack on his shoulders and went on his way.

By that time, the sun had already set and he could no longer make out the road. He walked on, and on again farther, weaving his way in among trees and out and in among them once more. Darkness covered the earth and no moon shone in the sky. He looked all around and began to be afraid. Then he saw a light shining. He walked toward the light until he arrived at a house. He knocked on the door. The mistress of the house peered out at him and shouted, "Are you here again? What do you want, Jew?"

"Since I left you, I've been wandering in the darkness and I can't find any town."

"And so, what do you want from me?"

"Please, my lady, give me permission to sit here until the moon comes out. Then I'll be able to see where I'm going and I'll be off." She looked at him with an angry eye and granted him permission to spend the night in an old barn in her courtyard. He lay down on the straw and dozed off.

That night it rained heavily. When the peddler rose in the morning, he saw that the entire land was one great swamp. He realized that the lady was a hard person. Let me abandon myself, he thought, to the mercy of Heaven, and I'll ask no favors from ungenerous people. He put his pack on his shoulders and prepared to leave. The lady looked out at him. "It seems to me that the roof needs mending. Can you do anything about it?" The peddler set down his pack. "I'll be glad to jump right up and take care of it." She gave him a ladder and he climbed up to the top of the roof, where he found shingles torn loose by the wind. At once, he set them back in place, paying no heed to himself while all his clothes gushed water and his shoes were like two buckets. What difference does it make to me, he thought, whether I'm on the top of a roof or walking through the forest? There's as much rain in the one place as in the other. And perhaps because I'm helping her out, she'll show some kindness to me and let me stay in her house till the rains stop.

The peddler fixed the shingles, sealed the leaks in the roof, and climbed down. "I'm sure that from now on the rain won't get into your house," he told the lady. "You are a real craftsman," she answered. "Tell me what your fee is and I'll pay you." He put his hand over his heart and said, "God forbid that I should take a single penny from my lady. It is not my practice to accept payment for anything that is not part of my trade, certainly not from my lady, who has shown me the kindness of allowing me to spend the night in her house." She looked at him with suspicion, for she thought that he spoke in this manner in order to ingratiate himself with her and get more money out of her. Finally she said, "Sit down and I'll bring you some breakfast." He stood up to wring out his clothes, then he emptied the water from his shoes and looked all around. From the many antlers hanging on the walls, it was clear that this was a hunter's house. Or perhaps it wasn't a hunter's house at all, and those antlers were simply hung up for decoration, as is the custom of forest dwellers, who decorate their homes with the horns of wild animals.

While he was still standing and looking, the mistress of the house returned, bringing with her hot liquor and cakes. He drank and ate and drank. After he had eaten and drunk, he said to her, "Perhaps there is something else here that needs to be fixed? I'm ready to do whatever my lady wishes." She cast a glance around the house and told him, "Look and see." The peddler was happy that he had been granted permission to stay in the house until the rains passed. He began to busy himself, fixing one thing and then another, and he asked no payment. In the evening she prepared supper for him and made up a bed for him in a room where she kept old things no longer in use. The peddler thanked the mistress of the house for bestowing such bounties upon him, and he swore that never would he forget her kindness to him.

By the next morning, new rains were falling. The peddler looked first outside and then at the face of the lady: Who was prepared to have pity on him sooner? The mistress of the house sat huddled in silence, and a great feeling of desolation arose from the furniture all around. The animals' horns on the walls were enveloped in mist and they gave off an odor like the odor of living flesh. Perhaps she wanted to relieve that feeling of desolation which gripped the heart, or perhaps she was moved to pity for this fellow who would have to walk through rains and swamps. Whatever the reason, the lady began to speak to him.

About what did she speak and about what didn't she speak! About rains that did not stop and winds that blew without letup, about roads that were becoming impassable and grain that would rot, and much of the same sort. The peddler thanked her in his heart for every word because every word extended his time in the house so that he did not have to drag himself along the ways in rain and cold and storm. And she also was pleased that she had a living creature there. She took up her knitting needles and told him to sit down. He sat before her and began to tell of noblemen and noblewomen, of lords and ladies, of all that he knew and all that was pleasant for her to hear. In the meantime, they had drawn closer together. He said to her, "My lady lives all alone. Has she no husband or friend and companion? Surely there must be here many distinguished gentlemen to seek the company of such a fine lady."

"I had a husband," she said. The peddler sighed, "And he died." "No," she corrected, "he was killed." The peddler sighed over her husband who was killed and asked, "How was he killed?" She answered, "The police don't know, and now you want to know! What difference does it make to you how he was killed, whether an evil beast ate him or whether he was slaughtered with a knife? Don't you yourself sell knives with which it is possible to slaughter a man?"

The peddler saw that the lady was not inclined to discuss her husband, so he kept silent. And she too was silent. After a little while the peddler spoke again. "May the Lord grant that they find the murderers of your husband to exact vengeance from them."

"They won't find them," she said, "they won't find them. Not every murderer is meant to be caught." The peddler lowered his eyes. "I am sorry, my lady, that I have reminded you of your sorrow. If I only knew how I could cheer you up, I'd give half my life to do it." The lady looked at him and smiled a queer smile, perhaps in contempt or perhaps in gratification, or perhaps just an ordinary smile that one person smiles to another and the other interprets as he wishes: if he is naive, then he interprets it in his own favor. The peddler, who was a naive man, interpreted the laughter of that woman in his own favor and for his own benefit. And since he was sorry for this woman who, to judge by her age and beauty, should have had men courting her, he suddenly looked upon himself as just such a man. He began to speak to her the sort of things that the ear of a young woman loves to hear. God only knows where this simple peddler learned such a style of talking. He soon found courage and began to speak of love, and even though she was a lady and he was a poor peddler, she welcomed his words and showed him affection. And even when the rains had passed and the roads had dried, they did not part.

The peddler stayed with the lady. Not in the old barn and not in the room for old things that were no longer used. No, he stayed in the lady's room and slept in her husband's bed, while she waited upon him as though he were her lord. Every day she prepared him a feast from all that she had, in house and field, every good fowl and every fat fowl. And if she broiled the meat in butter, he did not hold back from it. At first, when he would see her twisting the neck of a bird, he would be shocked. Afterward, he ate and even sucked the bones dry, as is the way of worthless folk: at first they are unwilling to commit a sin and afterward they commit all the sins in the world with a hearty appetite. He had neither wife nor children, he had no one to miss, and so he lived with the lady. He took off his peddler's clothes and put on the garments of aristocracy, and he fell in with the people of the place until he was like one of them. The lady did not allow him to labor, neither in the house nor in the field. On the contrary, she took all the work upon herself while she treated him royally with food and drink, and if she was short-tempered with him in the daytime she was loving to him at night, as it is a woman's nature to be sometimes one way and sometimes the other. And so passed one month and then two months, until he began to forget that he was a poor peddler and she a lady. She on her part forgot that he was a Jew or anything of the sort.

And so they lived together in one house under one roof, and he ate and drank and enjoyed himself and slept in a properly made bed—in short, it would seem that he wanted for nothing. But about one thing he was amazed: all that time he had never seen her eat or drink. At first he thought she might think it degrading to eat with him. After he became used to her and had forgotten that she was a lady and he a Jew, he wondered more and more.

Once he said to her, "How is it, Helen, that I've been living with you several months and I've never seen you eat or drink? You haven't put a feeding trough in your belly, have you?" She said to him, "What difference does it make to you whether I eat or drink? It's enough that you don't want for anything with me and you have plenty to eat always." "It's true," he answered, "that I eat and drink and I lead a more comfortable life now than ever before, but even so I would like to know how you sustain yourself and how you nourish yourself. You don't eat at the same table with me, and I've never seen you eat away from the table either. Is it possible to exist without eating and drinking?" Helen smiled and said, "You want to know what I eat and what I drink? I drink men's blood and I eat human flesh." As she spoke she embraced him with all her might and placed her lips against his and sucked. "I never imagined," she said to him, "that a Jew's flesh would be so sweet. Kiss me, my raven. Kiss me, my eagle. Your kisses are sweeter to me than all the kisses in the world." He kissed her, thinking, This is the kind of poetic language that noblewomen must use when they address their husbands with affection. And she on her part kissed him and said, "Joseph, in the beginning, when you showed yourself here I wanted to set the bitch on you, and now I myself am biting you like a mad bitch, so much that I'm afraid you won't get out of my hands alive. O my own sweet corpse!" And so they would while away their days in love and affection, and there was nothing in the world to upset their affairs.

But that one thing kept gnawing away in the heart of the peddler. They lived together in one house in one room, and her bed was next to his, and everything she had she put in his hands, except for the bread which she did not eat at the same table with him. And she observed this to such a degree that she would not even taste from the dishes she prepared for him. Since this thing was gnawing away in his heart, he would ask about it again. And she would tell him.

"He who delves too deeply digs his own grave. Be happy, my sweet corpse, with everything that is given to you, and don't ask questions that have no answer." The Jew reflected on this. Perhaps she's really right. What difference does it make to me whether she eats and drinks with me or somewhere else? After all, she is healthy and her face looks fine and I want for nothing. He decided to keep quiet. He went on enjoying her board and all the rest of it. He neither pressed her with questions nor bothered her with excessive talk. Rather, he loved her even more than before, whether because he really loved her, or perhaps because of that enigma which had no solution.

Anyone who has to do with women knows that a love that depends upon the physical bond alone will come to an end before long. And even if a man loves a woman as Samson loved Delilah, in the end she will mock him, in the end she will oppress him, until he wishes he were dead. That is the way it was with this peddler. After a while she began to mock him, after a while she began to oppress him, after a while he began to wish he were dead. Nevertheless, he did not leave her. And she on her part did not tell him to get out. He stayed with her month after month: they would quarrel and make up, quarrel and make up, and he not knowing why they were quarreling and why they were making up. But he would reason thus to himself: Here the two of us are intimate with each other, living side by side, never apart from one another, and yet I know no more about her today than I knew yesterday, and yesterday I knew no more than I knew about her the day I came here for the first time when she bought the knife from me. As long as they continued to live together in peace, he didn't ask many questions, and if he asked, she would stop up his mouth with kisses. When the peace between them disappeared, he began to think more and more about it, until he said to himself, I won't let her be until she tells me.

One night he said to her, "Many times now I've asked you about your husband, and you've never said a thing to me."

"About which one did you ask?"

"You mean you had two husbands?"

"What difference does it make to you if there were two or three?"

"So then I'm your fourth husband?"

"My fourth husband?"

"Well, from what you say, that is what it comes to. Doesn't it, Helen?"

"Wait a minute and I'll count them all," she said to him. She held up her right hand and began counting on her fingers, one, two, three, four, five. When she had counted all the fingers on her right hand, she held up her left hand and went on counting. "And where are they?" he said to her.

"Now, didn't I tell you that he who delves too deeply digs his own grave?"

"Tell me anyway." She patted her belly and said, "Some of them perhaps are here."

"What do you mean, 'here'?" he asked. She narrowed her eyes and smiled. She looked at him for a few moments. "And if I told you," she said, "do you think you would understand? Mother of God! Look, see what a face this corpse has."

But from the moment she had begun to count on her fingers, he no longer had his wits about him. Now he lost the power of speech as well. He sat in silence. She said to him, "Darling, do you believe in God?" He sighed and answered, "And is it possible not to believe in God?"

"You're a Jew, aren't you?" He sighed "Yes, I'm a Jew."

"Well, the Jews don't believe in God, for if they believed in Him they wouldn't have murdered Him. But if you do believe in God, pray to Him that you won't end up the way they did."

"The way who did?"

"The way those you asked about ended up."

"You mean your husbands."

"Yes, my husbands."

"And how did they end up?"

"If you don't understand," Helen answered, "it doesn't pay to talk to you." As she said this she looked at his throat, and her blue eyes glittered like the blade of a new knife. He took a look at her and shuddered. She also looked at him and said, "Why did you turn so pale?" He touched his face and asked, "Did I turn pale?"

"And the hair on your head," she continued, "is standing up like pig bristles." He felt his hair. "My hair is standing up?"

"And the strands of your beard," she said, "are clotted together in patches like goose feathers. Pfui, how ugly the face of a coward is!" She spat in his face and left him. As she was walking away she turned her head back toward him and called out, "Take good care of your Adam's apple. Mother of God! It's trembling as though it saw the knife. Don't worry, my little sweetheart, I haven't bitten you yet."

The peddler was left sitting by himself. One moment he would feel his face with his hand and the next moment his beard. The hair on his head had already settled and was lying in place as before, half on one side and half on the other, with a part going down the middle that was as cold as though ice had been laid on it. From the next room he could hear Helen's footsteps. At that moment he neither loved her nor hated her. His limbs began to grow numb, as though he had lost control over them. His thoughts, on the other hand, became more and more active. I'll get up and take my pack and be on my way, he said to himself. But when he tried to leave, his limbs became even weaker. Again he heard Helen's footsteps. Then her feet were still and he heard the clattering of utensils and the smell of cooking. The peddler began to consider again. I have to get out of here. If not now, then tomorrow morning. How glad he was when he had been permitted to spend the night in the old barn. Now even the bed made up for him shrieked, "Pick up your feet and run!" By that time it had already grown dark. Despite himself, he decided to spend the night in that house. Not, however, in his wife's room, in the bed of her murdered husbands, but in the old barn or in some other room. When day broke, he would be on his way.

Helen came in and said, "You look as if I had already swallowed you." She took him by the arm and brought him into the dining-room, sat him down at the table, and told him, "Eat." He lifted up his eyes and looked at her. Again she said, "Eat." He broke off a piece of bread and swallowed it whole. "I see you need to have your bread chewed for you," Helen said. He wiped the remnants of bread from his hands and got up to leave. "Wait, and I'll go with you," Helen said. She put on a sheepskin coat and went outside with him.

Walking along, they spoke nothing either good or bad, but they just talked, like people who have quarreled and want to take their minds off themselves. As they were walking, they came upon a stone image. Helen stopped, crossed herself, stood and recited a brief prayer. Afterward she took Joseph by the arm and returned with him to their house.

During the night Joseph awoke from his sleep in terror and screamed with all his might. It seemed to him that a knife had been thrust into his heart, and not into his heart but into that stone image, and not into the stone image, but into another image made of ice, the kind the Christians make on the river during their holidays. And though the knife had not struck him, even so he felt pain in his heart. He turned over and sighed. Sleep fell upon him and he dozed off. He heard a clinking sound and saw that the bitch was pulling off the chain around her neck. He closed his eyes and did not look at her. She leaped up on him and sank her teeth into his throat. His throat began to spurt and she licked up his blood. He screamed with all his might and thrashed about in the bed. Helen awoke and shouted, "What are you doing, raising the house with your noise and not letting me sleep!" He shrank under his covers and pillows, and lay motionless until daybreak.

In the morning Joseph said to Helen, "I disturbed your sleep."

"I don't know what you are talking about."

"Why, you shouted at me that I wasn't letting you sleep."

"I shouted?"

"Then you must have been talking in your sleep." Helen's face paled and she asked, "What are you saying?"

That night he moved his bedding to the room where old things were kept that were no longer in use. Helen saw and said nothing. When it was time to go to sleep, he said to her, "I haven't been sleeping well and I keep turning and tossing in bed, so I'm afraid that I'll disturb your sleep. That's why I've moved my bed into another room." Helen nodded in agreement. "Do whatever you think is best for you."

"That's what I've done."

"Then good."

From then on they spoke no more of the matter. Joseph forgot that he was only a guest and continued according to his practice. Every day he thought of leaving her house, of abandoning all her favors. A day passed, a week passed, and he did not leave her house. And she on her part did not tell him to get out.

One night he was sitting at the dinner table and Helen brought in a dish. Her mouth gave off an odor like the smell of a hungry person. He grimaced. She noticed and said to him, "Why are you twisting your mouth?"

"I didn't twist my mouth." She smiled a queer smile. "Maybe you're bothered by the way my mouth smells?"

"Take a piece of bread and eat," he entreated her. "Don't worry about me, I won't go hungry," Helen answered. And again a queer smile played over her face, worse than the first one.

After eating and drinking, he went off to his room and made his bed ready. It occurred to him suddenly to recite the bedtime Shema. Since there was a crucifix hanging on the wall, he got up and went outside to recite the Shema.

That night was a winter night. The earth was covered with snow and the sky was congealed and turbid. He looked up to the sky and saw no spark of light; he looked to the ground and he could not make out his own feet. Suddenly he saw himself as though imprisoned in a forest in the midst of the snow around him that was being covered over by new snow. And he himself was also being covered over. He uprooted his feet and began to run. He bumped into a stone image that stood in the snow. "Father in heaven," Joseph shouted, "how far away I have gone! If I don't return at once, I am lost." He looked one way and then another until he got his bearings. He directed himself toward the house and went back to it.

A tranquil stillness prevailed. No sound could be heard except for a muffled sound like snow falling on piles of snow. And from that arose another sound of his feet sinking in the snow and struggling to get out. His shoulders grew very heavy, as though he were carrying his heavy pack. After a while he reached the house.

The house was shrouded in darkness. There was no light in any of the rooms. "She's sleeping," Joseph whispered and stood still, his teeth clenched in hatred. He closed his eyes and entered his room.

When he came in he sensed that Helen was in the room. He put aside his hatred for her. Hurriedly, he took off his clothes and began to grope among the covers and pillows. He called out in a whisper, "Helen," but received no answer. Again he called and received no answer. He got up and lit a candle. He saw his bedding filled with holes. What's this? What's this? When he had left his room, his bedding had been undamaged, and now it was filled with holes. There could be no doubt that these holes were made by human hands, but for what reason were they made? He looked and saw a blood spot. He stared at the blood in wonder.

Meanwhile, he heard the sound of a sigh. He looked and saw Helen sprawled on the floor with a knife in her hand. It was the hunting knife that she had bought from him the day he came there. He took the knife out of her hand, lifted her from the floor, and stretched her out on his bed. Helen opened her eyes and looked at him. As she looked at him, she opened her mouth wide until her teeth glittered.

Joseph asked Helen, "Do you want to say something?" And she said not a word. He bent down toward her. She pulled herself up all at once, sank her teeth into his throat, and began to bite and suck. Then she pushed him away and shouted, "Pfui, how cold you are! Your blood isn't blood. It's ice water."

The peddler took care of the lady a day, and two days, and another day. He bound her wounds, for on the night that she came in to slaughter him, she wounded herself. He also prepared food for her.

But whatever food she tried to eat she would throw up, for she had already forgotten the science of eating ordinary human food, as it was her practice to eat the flesh of her husbands whom she slaughtered and to drink their blood, just as she wanted to do with the peddler.

On the fifth day she gave up the ghost and died. Joseph went to look for a priest but found none. He made her a coffin and a shroud, and dug in the snow to bury her. Since all the land was frozen over, he could not manage to dig her a grave. He took her carcass, placed it in the coffin, and climbed up to the roof where he buried the coffin in the snow. The birds smelled her carcass. They came and pecked away at the coffin till they broke into it, and then they divided among them the carcass of the lady. And that peddler took up his pack and traveled on from place to place, traveling and crying out his wares.

Translated by Robert Alter

Tears

It was told to me by Rabbi Shmuel Arieh: In my youth I lived in the village of Koshilovitz, the same Koshilovitz that gained world renown because the Baal Shem was a shohet there before his greatness was revealed. I met a shohet there, an old man over eighty. I asked him, "Did you perhaps know someone who knew the Baal Shem?" Said he, "I have never met a Jew who saw the Baal Shem, but I have met a Gentile who saw him. When I was a young man I used to lodge with a Gentile farmer. Whenever I would pour water on a stone before whetting my slaughtering knife, the farmer's grandfather, an old man of ninety or a hundred, would shake his head. I used to think it was due to his age. One time I sensed that he was doing it out of disapproval. I asked him, 'Why do you shake your head while I work?' Said he, 'You are not going about your task in a nice way. Yisroelki, before he whetted his knife, would dampen the stone with tears.'"

Translated by Jules Harlow

Buczacz: The Epic Life of One Town

During the last decade of his life, Agnon was busy compiling a volume of stories about his hometown Buczacz which was published after his death under the title *The City and the Fullness Thereof* (*Ir Umeloah*). Agnon combined stories of various genres that he had published previously with new stories written for the volume. He then took these heterogeneous narratives and arranged them like brilliant pieces of mosaic tiles to create a whole that was greater than its parts: nothing less than an epic portrait of one Jewish town in eastern Europe.

The creation of this volume tells us something very important about Agnon's relationship to modern Jewish history. Because Agnon is the great Hebrew writer of European Jewry, one is surprised by how little his work directly engages the destruction of European Jewry in the Holocaust. To be sure, there are a limited number of stories that deal with the Holocaust (three are included in this collection: "The Lady and the Peddler," "The Sign," and "At the Outset of the Day"). Agnon's great novel *A Guest for the Night*, which anatomizes the devastating effects of World War I on Galician Jewry, and was published on the eve of World War II, might be thought of as the writer's statement on the destruction of Jewish life. Yet his reticence on the Holocaust itself remains perplexing.

The fashioning of *The City and the Fullness Thereof* provides something of an answer. Instead of undertaking to represent the atrocity of the Holocaust, with all the ethical and aesthetic dangers inherent in the depiction of evil, Agnon chose another path. He spent the last years of his life mounting a coherent imaginative evocation of the lost world of East European Jewry as represented by Buczacz. He chose, in a sense, the representation of life over death. He reasoned, one supposes, that it was a greater calling—and perhaps a better use of his own gifts as a writer—to summon up the fullness of the culture that was lost than to document the throes of its heartbreaking annihilation.

Despite their memorializing function, the stories in this volume are not fixed in a uniform gloss of nostalgia. They are as various in style and technique as the whole range of Agnon's work, and, despite Agnon's evident love for his hometown, the literary simulacrum of Buczacz is not spared. The three stories in this section represent this diversity.

The story "Buczacz," which opens the collection, plays a special role in laying down the foundational myth of the town. Stories recounting the origins of great cities are no less common in Jewish literature than they are in world culture. Just as the wandering Aeneas founded Rome after the Trojan War, so too, according to legend, the great Diaspora of Spanish Jewry was begun by four shipwrecked talmudic sages from Babylonia. In the case of Galician communities such as Buczacz, the facts behind the myth are these: in the fourteenth and fifteenth centuries, Jews who had long lived in the Rhine Valley began to move east and south into Poland and the Ukraine in search of better living conditions and at the invitation of Polish landowners who valued their commercial and managerial acumen.

In the mythic mode in which "Buczacz" is told, this narrative of immigration is given a different emphasis. The motives of the Jews' journey eastward are ennobled and presented as an expression of the millennial longing for the Land of Israel. Because this longing is unsupported by any practical preparation for the trip, the party of

Jews becomes stranded in the deep snows and virgin woods of distant lands. Salvation, it turns out, comes not from above but from the protection extended by Polish landowners, who delight in the Jews' success in developing the lands that they are colonizing. For many practical reasons, the journey to the Land of Israel is abandoned, and, with the approval of the gentile gentry, the Jews set about establishing the institutions of a permanent community, which in time becomes the center of piety and learning called Buczacz.

Harmony between the Jews of Buczacz and their rulers is the starting point of the second story, "The Tale of the Menorah." The Chmielnicki massacres in the seventeenth century nearly destroyed the town; Buczacz was gradually rebuilt under the rule of the kingdom of Poland until Poland was partitioned at the end of the eighteenth century. The new rulers were the Austro-Hungarians, who held sway until World War 1. The changing relations between the Jewish community of Buczacz and its temporal rulers are traced in this story through the fortunes of a candelabrum, a menorah, given to the community as a token of gratitude by an early monarch.

The menorah is altered, lost, found, smashed, rebuilt, and lost and found again in a way that mirrors the vicissitudes of the Jewish-gentile political connection. The intertwined nature of this relationship is represented by the changes the Jews of Buczacz make in the menorah, which stands in the synagogue recalling the Jerusalem Temple of antiquity. When the town is ruled by Poland, the national insignia, a white eagle, is patriotically placed in the center of the menorah. When Austria takes over, the Polish eagle is publicly smashed and the two-headed Austrian eagle ceremoniously established in its stead.

The story concludes with the pious observation: "One kingdom comes and another kingdom passes away. But Israel remains forever." The people Israel, like the menorah, endures, however battered and decimated. Yet, the story implies through its believing chronicler, the source of this endurance is not the politics of accommodation but trust in God, "whom alone we desired."

"Pisces" illuminates a different aspect of the Buczacz myth. Written late in Agnon's life (1956), "Pisces" is ambitious both in its proportions—somewhere between a short story and a novella—and in its thematic horizon. It is less an account of Buczacz than a statement about the human enterprise as a whole. The story is also a wonderful repository of many of the features that make Agnon's writing distinctive: the stance of the detached storyteller-chronicler, the serious playfulness with learned sources, the frequent digressions, and the antic intermixing of the sacred and the profane.

The grotesque quality of the story, as analyzed in illuminating studies by Gershon Shaked, results from the mixed feelings of amusement and anxiety that are aroused when the distinctions between animals and human beings are blurred. "Pisces" narrates the parallel lives of Fishl Karp, a famous Buczacz glutton, and an enormous fish, which Fishl buys from a gentile fisherman and proposes to make into a feast. The two occupy positions of dominance in their respective domains. Fishl is a coarse moneylender of enormous appetites who flouts communal edicts (the Jews are boycotting fish to combat price gouging) and who uses Jewish law to justify his gluttony. For its part, the fish is a lordly denizen of the oceans whose hubris leads it to explore the lesser rivers, including Buczacz's modest Strypa, where it is snared. The nobility of the fish's mien and the vast freedom of its movements contrast sharply with Fishl's venality and his self-satisfied rationalizations. Yet because of the supposed superiority of man over beast, it is the netted fish, quivering in its death throes, that is taken possession of by the hungry Fishl.

The desired repast never takes place. Fishl is separated from the object of his desire and, like the fish, soon ends up in the grave. The story wastes no opportunity to underscore the fishlike qualities of human beings and the human qualities of the fish. The latter are evident in the very personification of the fish and the pathos of its ordeal. The former are evident in the fish-derived names of the characters and the vast number of intertextual references to fish taken from the Bible and the Talmud. The most grotesque linkage concerns Fishl's tefillin. Tefillin (singular: tefillah) are small black boxes containing scriptural passages held in place on the forearm and head by leather straps which are worn by adult males in prayer. In his haste to despatch both his morning prayers and the fish, the head tefillah becomes separated from the arm tefillah; one ends up on Fishl's arm and the other, in an act of hilarious sacrilege, on the head of the fish. Thus man's capacity for spiritual consciousness, which marks him off from the animals and which is ritually symbolized by the tefillin, is decisively effaced.

The message of "Pisces" is inescapably pessimistic. Literally, with every pun intended, big fish eat little fish, and man's sensual appetites do not exempt him from this grim journey toward death. There is one exception in the story, however; this is the figure of the poor orphan Bezalel Moshe, whom Fishl orders to carry the fish home to his wife to be prepared for cooking. Bezalel Moshe, whose name recalls the master biblical craftsman of the desert tabernacle in Exodus, is a true hunger artist who subsists by drawing plaques (mizrahim) for the eastern wall of the synagogue and other small jobs of folk illustration. His stock-in-trade includes the astrological signs for the months, including the wreathed fishes of Pisces, the sign for the carnival month of Adar. His figures, however, are stylized and unconvincing because he has only had faded old books to copy from. Contemplating the glorious specimen Fishl has put in his hands, Bezalel Moshe is transformed as he experiences the vital original that stands behind the pallid model. Long after Fishl and the fish have passed from this world, the vitality of Bezalel Moshe's experience continues to energize and enrich his art.

Buczacz

When was our city founded, and who was its founder? Long have all the chroniclers labored to find this out in vain. But some few facts have been revealed to us, and I am herewith setting down a faithful record of all I know.

There once was a band of Jews who were moved by their own pure hearts to go up to the Land of Israel, together with their wives and their sons and their daughters. They sold their fields, their vineyards, their male and female servants, their houses, and all of their movable chattels that could not be transported. They obtained the governor's permission to leave their city. They purchased provisions and set forth on the road.

They did not know the road to the Land of Israel, nor did anyone they met along the way know where the Land of Israel was. They only knew that it was in the east; so they turned their faces eastward, and that was the way they went. Whoever had a mount to ride rode his mount; whoever had no mount went by foot, leaning on his staff.

They passed by many towns and villages and castles and Jewish settlements and long stretches of forest and places inhabited by packs of wild animals and bandits. But since the Lord loves to see His children in His home, He made the Gentiles look upon them favorably, so that they let them pass unharmed. Even the brigands who lie in wait for wayfarers and ambush passersby and seize their lives and goods did them no harm; they were content with tribute in the form of money or a silver goblet or a ring or such jewelry as the pilgrims gave them.

They set out toward the end of April, when the highways are merry and the fields and vineyards full of people, but as they proceeded, people became scarce, vineyards and fields vanished, and all the roads led through forests that never seemed to end, with birds and beasts and kine. If they came upon a person, he would not know their language or they his. Even had they had understood his tongue, the Gentiles in those lands could not show them the way, for they were ignorant; they had no idea of any town or province other than their birthplace, certainly not of the Land of Israel. If anybody there had heard of it, he thought it must be in the skies.

In this way they passed the summer and reached the end of August. They made a halt and set up camp for the month of holidays: New Year, Atonement, and Sukkot.

They made their camp in a place of forests and rivers, with no sign of habitation for several days' march in any direction, and they fashioned booths from the forest's trees. They celebrated the Days of Awe in prayer and supplication, and the Days of Joy in feasting and delight, trusting in the faithful mercy of God that in the year to come they would observe these days before Him in the holy city of Jerusalem. For the rites of Sukkot, they used the old palm branches, citrons, and myrtles that they had brought with them upon setting out; the fourth species, willows, they gathered new each day of the festival. These willows were the best that they had ever seen, for the place where they had made their camp was thoroughly damp, with many rivers, ponds, and streams.

In those regions, as in most of the lands of the Slavs, winter comes on early. They were already suffering from the cold when they arrived, but particularly so during Sukkot, when they could hardly observe the ritual of dwelling in booths. At the holiday's end, when they ought to have set forth, the snow began to fall, fitfully at first, and then nonstop, until the roads were blotted out and they could not distinguish land from water or tell where it was solid and where it was river or pond. Like it or not, the pilgrims had to linger in their camp.

They brought wood from the forest and fixed up their booths into something more like cabins, and in them they set up various kinds of ovens for cooking their meals and for keeping themselves warm during the cold season. Out of the bark of trees they made themselves shoes, for their leather shoes were all tattered from their march. They also made new staves and waited for the time when the Lord would restore the sun's strength and the roads would be clear of snow and they could set forth again. Huddled they sat in their booths in the snow, snug and secure from storm winds and bears and other wild beasts that would come alone or in packs right up to their doors and let out their awesome roar.

One day, when they were sitting as usual in their booths, some reading the Psalms, others doing their work, one of them cocked his head, perked up his ears, and said, "I think I hear a trumpet's call." Another said, "No, it is the sound of horses." A third said, "No, it is the sound of people."

So they sat arguing about the sounds so suddenly heard in the forest. At length they all yielded: the one who had called it the sound of a trumpet agreed that it was the sound of a dog, and the one who had called it the sound of a dog agreed that it was the sound of people. At last they realized that there were actually three different sounds: the sound of a trumpet, the sound of a dog, and the sound of people. Then they found themselves surrounded by strange people who seemed to them like animals, with huge and fearsome dogs at their heels and great trumpets at their lips. But these people had not come to them with evil intent but only to hunt animals. They were great and distinguished noblemen, and it is the way of noblemen to go to the forests to hunt game.

One of the noblemen asked them in Latin, "Who are you and what are you doing here?" They told him their whole story, how they had purposed to go up to the Holy Land and had been overtaken by winter and had made camp there until the winter should be over and the cold should pass. The noblemen began to ask them what they had seen along the way and what was the news of the day and who were the rulers that governed those lands, and the pilgrims answered all their questions in such detail that the noblemen were struck by their cleverness and eloquence. So enchanted were they that they forgot the game and gave up the hunt and began to urge them to come with them and to live with them, arguing that winter is very hard in that land, that many people fall sick from the great cold, that not everyone is built to bear it, and that these Rhinelanders would certainly never survive a winter in the forest. The pilgrims saw that the noblemen's counsel was right. They agreed to go and live with them until the end of the winter season; then, with winter gone and the snow cleared, they would reassemble and set out on the road again. Each nobleman took with him an individual or a family and brought them home, treating them with every courtesy. The pilgrims stayed with the noblemen throughout the winter.

The noblemen who had taken the Jews into their homes enjoyed prosperity in whatever they did. They realized that their success was due to the Jews. Each one began to worry and fret: "What shall I do when the Jews leave us? They will certainly take their blessing with them, or the blessing will go away of its own accord." They began to urge them to stay, saying, "The whole land is yours; make your home wherever you like. If you want to engage in commerce in the land, better yet, for no one here knows anything about commerce." Some of the pilgrims paid no attention to them and wanted to be on their way; but others let themselves be won over by the noblemen, for they were weary, and many were sick and fearful of the rigors of the road. And because they were not of one mind, even those who wanted to go did not, for they were but few, and the roads were presumed too dangerous to be traversed by any but a large band.

In the meanwhile, the Days of Awe returned. The entire band gathered in a certain place for communal prayer, and there they remained until after Sukkot. They did the same the following year and for several years thereafter: throughout the year each one would live in his own place by his nobleman, and on the Days of Awe and the three festivals they would assemble to observe the holidays by holding prayers, reading Scripture, and performing all the other statutory observances.

One year, at Simhat Torah, when they were all in good spirits because of the joy of the Torah and the great feast that they had made to celebrate its completion, one of them said with a sigh: "Now we are content, for we are together, worshiping as a community and reading the Torah; but what about tomorrow and the next day and the next? Winter is here, and again we shall go without the reading of the Torah and without communal prayer." They thought about it and began to discuss what to do. To leave where they were and go to the Land of Israel was out of the question; for by now they had acquired property in the land and built houses and were in favor with the nobility. As for the women, some were pregnant, some were nursing, some were worn out and weak. And the elders were even older than before, so that traveling would have been hard on them. But to stay where they were, without Torah or communal prayer, was certainly not acceptable as a permanent arrangement. It would have been better if they had not given in to the noblemen and had gone their way right after the snow had cleared and were now settled before the Lord in Jerusalem; but having yielded and not made the pilgrimage, they now had to take active steps to enable themselves to perform all the rites of God that we are commanded to perform. After much discussion, they agreed unanimously to establish a permanent house of prayer and to hold services on every weekday when the Torah is read, and of course on the Sabbath and New Moon and Hanukkah and Purim. Whoever was able to attend the services would attend, and whoever was not able on account of illness or some other impediment would try to have someone attend in his stead. The building in which they had been holding services on the festivals they designated as the synagogue.

When word reached the local nobleman, it so pleased him that he gave them the building and everything in it as an outright and perpetual gift. Before he died, he ordered his sons to treat the Jews with benevolence, for God had granted him prosperity on account of the Jews, and from the Jews had come whatever he was leaving them.

They turned the building into a synagogue, and there they would come to pray on all the days when the Torah is read, including especially the Sabbaths and festivals and other days of distinction. Occasionally they would hold communal prayer even on days when the Torah is not read; for if someone happened to be in the vicinity, he would say, "I think I'll go and see if enough Jews happen to be there to hold services, so that I can hear Barekhu and Kedushah. Thus, with one coming from one way and one coming from another, they would come together and hold a service. The place came to be a favorite, for whoever was hungry for the word of the Lord or whoever yearned to see his fellow Jews would turn to it. And whoever could afford to do so built himself a house nearby, so that, living near the place of prayer, he would be able to participate in communal prayer.

Little by little the entire place came to be settled by Jews. They built themselves a ritual bath and whatever else a community needs. Whenever they needed a rabbi to answer a ritual question, or a teacher for their children, or tsitsit, or to have their tefillin examined, they would turn to that place. Even the noblemen and their retainers would come there for advice or business, knowing that they would find Jews there. The place acquired a reputation; people began to come from far and wide on the days of their festivals, both to see and to be seen. Noblemen and noblewomen came, too, riding on their horses. Then the local nobleman built himself a stone house; eventually he built a castle up on the mountain facing the Strypa, a great castle befitting one of the great princes of the land. This castle was for many years the defense and refuge of the lord of the town and his retainers, until the Tartars attacked it, and, on defeating him, compelled him to destroy it. The ruins are there to this day.

That is how Buczacz began. Formerly it was not called Buczacz but Biczacz, and at the very first it was called something very like.

As to the name and its meaning, there are many opinions and conjectures, some of which, though plausible, remain conjectures nonetheless. I am setting aside the *ifs* and *maybes* and writing only the truth as it actually is.

Eventually the holy community of Buczacz was joined by a number of Jews from other places, especially from Germany. Disaster had overtaken the people of God, the holy community of Worms, Mayence, Speyer, and other distinguished communities in Germany, because of the filthy infidels whose arrogance moved them to go up to the Holy Land to fight the king of Ishmael and to conquer the land. Wherever they encountered Jews along the way they murdered them, killing them in cruel and unusual ways. Many of the people of God valiantly sanctified His Name; they were killed and slaughtered as martyrs to the unity of God's terrible, unique Name. Most of the communities in the land of Germany were destroyed; the few survivors wandered from one nation to another until they reached the lands of the Slavs, and of them, some reached our town. In our town they dwelt in safety and in peace. On minor ritual matters they consulted their own sages, and on major ritual matters they consulted our sages in Germany until from among the townspeople emerged some great and authoritative masters of the Torah who illuminated the world with their learning. Now they were completely supplied with religious wisdom and knowledge of God. They were secure in their wealth and dignity, their piety and righteousness, until, struck by divine justice, they nearly all perished in God's rage through the persecution of Chmielnicki's thugs.

When some quiet was restored after the riots and rebellions and killing and breakdown, some of those who survived the sword returned to their towns and their settlements. So did those who had been dispersed from Biczacz. They built themselves houses and shops, but first they built houses for study and prayer. There they dwelt for many generations in security and tranquility, except in years of war and revolution. Their first protector was the kingdom of Poland, later Austria; then Poland reestablished its kingdom and engaged in conquest and destruction, until the Enemy came and eradicated them all.

May God return the remnants of His people from wherever they are; may He assemble our Diaspora from among the nations; may He bring them to Zion, His city, in song, and to Jerusalem, His temple, in lasting joy; may no enemy or foe enter the gates of Jerusalem from this day forth. Amen. Selah.

Translated by Raymond P. Scheindlin

The Tale of the Menorah

Rabbi Nahman, the keeper of the royal seal, was a man of great importance in the eyes of the king. Whenever he came to the royal court, the palace attendants gave him an audience with the king, for they knew how beloved Nahman the Jew was to the king.

It happened one day that Rabbi Nahman came to the royal court, for he had a matter about which he had to speak to the king. The king, too, had a certain matter that he had concealed from his closest counselors, his company of advisors. The moment he saw Rabbi Nahman, the king said, "This is the man I shall consult." So the king related to Rabbi Nahman the matter that he had not wished to tell a single one of his counselors. But he did tell it to Rabbi Nahman, the keeper of the royal seal.

The Almighty bestowed wisdom upon Rabbi Nahman, and he responded with intelligent advice. The king listened and did as Rabbi Nahman had advised. And it turned out to be a blessing for the king. Then he knew how excellent was the advice Nahman had given him.

After this Rabbi Nahman was summoned to the palace court.

When the king heard that Nahman was in the royal courtyard, he commanded, "Bring him to me."

Rabbi Nahman entered the king's chamber. The king said to him, "The advice you gave me was excellent. Ask of me now whatever you desire, and I will grant it to you."

Rabbi Nahman replied, "Blessed be the Lord who has shared His wonderful counsel with the king." But for himself Rabbi Nahman did not ask for a single thing. He said to the king, "I am unworthy of the least of all your kindnesses." These were the very words that Jacob our forefather spoke to Esau, and Rabbi Nahman said them to the king.

The king replied, "Because you have not asked for a single thing for yourself, I will make a holy donation to your God." Rabbi Nahman did not ask the king what it was he promised to give. And the king did not tell him.

2

It came to pass in those days that Buczacz built itself a Great Synagogue. Its community of Jews had grown to nearly two hundred and fifty householders, in addition to the women and the children and all the servants of the wealthy who had come from other towns and now lived in the city. So the people of Buczacz built themselves a large synagogue in which to worship. That is the same building that the Gentiles living in the city made into a church for their gods after the city fell into the hands of Chmielnicki and he had slain every Jew who had not fled in haste from the sword of his wrath.

The king commanded his metalworkers to make him a great brass menorah to place in the synagogue in Buczacz in honor of Nahman, the keeper of the royal seal and the leader of the community of Israel in Buczacz.

The king's metalworkers made a great menorah out of brass. There were seven branches in the candelabrum, the same number of branches that we had in ancient days in the holy candelabrum in the Temple, the house of our glory. The artisans did not know that it is forbidden to make a vessel identical to one that had been in the Temple.

When they brought the menorah, which was a gift from the king, to the synagogue, the Jews saw it and they beheld its seven branches. They said, "We cannot place this menorah in the synagogue." If we do, they said to themselves, we will sin against God; on the other hand, if we do not set it in the synagogue, we will insult the king and his gift." They did not know what counsel to take for themselves. Even Nahman, the counselor to the king, had no solution. He said, "This has all befallen us because I frequented the court of the king."

But God saw their distress, and He set the idea in their heads to remove one branch from the menorah and thus make it into an ordinary candelabrum. Then, if they placed the menorah in the synagogue, there would be no sin for them in doing so. And if someone mentioned it to the king, they could say, "From the day that our Temple was destroyed, we make nothing without marking upon it a sign in remembrance of the destruction."

So they removed the middle branch. Then they brought the menorah into the house of God and placed it on the ark and lit its candles.

The menorah stood in the synagogue. The six candles in the six branches of the menorah lit up the building on the eve of every Sabbath and holiday. And on Yom Kippur and on those holidays when the memorial prayer for the departed is recited in synagogue to remember the souls of the departed, they shone during the day as well. A Gentile watched the candles lest one fall out.

So the menorah stood there, and so it shone for the entire time this house of God was indeed a house *for* God, until the day Israel was driven out by Chmielnicki and the town's Gentiles made the house of God into a church for their gods. Then the Gentile who watched the candles, who was a millworker, took the menorah and hid it in the River Strypa, which was near the mill. The menorah lay at the bottom of the Strypa's waters, and no one knew where it was. As for the millworker, he died after his body got caught in the millstone's wheel; he was ground up and cast away, and his flesh became food for the fish in the River Strypa.

3

After some years, those who had survived Chmielnicki's sword returned to their homeland and towns. The few survivors from Buczacz also returned to the town, and there they built themselves a small sanctuary in place of the Great Synagogue, which the Gentiles had plundered and made into a house for their gods.

That year, on a Saturday night at the close of the Sabbath, on the night that was also the first night for reciting the Selihot, the penitential hymns, the young children were shining candles over the surface of the Strypa. They were doing this in order to make light for the slain martyrs who had drowned in rivers, streams, and lakes. On the first night of Selihot all the dead whom our enemies have drowned come to pray to the eternal God in the same synagogue in which they prayed during their lifetimes. The other nights of Selihot are dedicated respectively to those martyrs who died by fire, to those who were stabbed to death, to the ones who were strangled, and to those who were murdered. For on account of their numbers, the building could not contain all the slain at once. As a result, they divided up the nights between them, one congregation of martyrs for each night of prayer.

Now while the children were on the banks of the Strypa shining their candles, a great menorah such as they had never seen before suddenly shone forth from beneath the water. They said, "That must be the menorah of the dead; for the dead bring with them their own menorot when they come to pray." Their hearts quaked in fear, and the children fled.

Some grownups heard the story about the menorah that the children had told, and they said, "Let's go and see for ourselves!" They went and came to the Strypa. And indeed, there was a menorah in the Strypa. "The story is true," they said. "It is a menorah." But not a person knew that it was the menorah that the king of Poland had given to the old Great Synagogue before the Gentiles of the city took it over and made it into a church for their gods.

The Jews retrieved the menorah from the waters of the Strypa and brought it to the synagogue. There they placed it upon the reading table, for another menorah already stood on the stand before the ark, and they had promised the donor of that menorah that no one would ever replace it. Besides, the stand before the ark was too small to hold the large menorah. And so they placed the menorah they had drawn from the waters on the reading table.

The menorah illuminated the house of God with the six candles that stood in its six branches. And for a long time the menorah lit up the house of God on the evenings of the Sabbath and the holidays. The candles of the menorah shone on the holidays during the daytime as well, and on the Twentieth of Sivan when the souls of the departed are remembered in the service. And when the sun came out in all its strength and reached into the house of God, then the menorah shone with the luster of burnished brass in sunlight.

4

Many days later, after that entire generation had died, a new generation arose that did not know all that had happened to their forefathers. After looking at the menorah day after day, one of them said, "We should repair the menorah; it shouldn't look like a vessel that is missing something." And they did not realize that their forefathers had already repaired the menorah when they cut off one of its branches to avoid sinning against either God or the king.

They made an eagle of glittering brass, and they placed a large amount of lead in the brass so that it would appear to be a white eagle. For a white eagle is the national insignia of Poland. They placed the eagle beneath the spot where their forefathers had removed the branch. Originally, it had been a menorah with seven branches, but our forefathers had repaired the menorah when they removed one of its branches. But the members of the next generation, those who brought the national insignia of Poland into our synagogue, said to each other, "Now we will let Poland know how truly attached we are to our country and homeland, the land of Poland. Out of our love for the homeland, we have even placed the national insignia of Poland in our house of worship!"

So the menorah stood on the holy reading table on which they used to read from the Torah of God. And the eagle—the Polish eagle—lay between the branches of the menorah. So stood the menorah: three branches on one side, three branches on the other, with the candles in the menorah shining on one side toward the reader's stand and on the other side toward the holy Torah ark. And in the center, the white eagle, the national insignia of the Polish kingdom, stood between the candles. So stood the eagle in the menorah in the synagogue for all the time Poland was a sovereign state ruling over the entire land of Poland.

5

Sometime later, Poland was conquered. The country was divided up among its neighbors, each neighbor taking for itself all that it could, and Buczacz fell to the lot of Austria. The Austrian forces camped across the city—the soldiers, their officers, the entire army that had conquered the territory of Buczacz.

After summoning the town's rulers, the army generals ordered them to make a holiday now that the city had come under the rule of the Austrian emperor. They commanded the Jews to gather in their Great Synagogue to praise and glorify their Lord, the God of Israel, who had bestowed upon them the emperor of Austria to be their ruler. The heads of the city and of the Jewish community listened and did just as the generals said. For no one disobeys the orders of an army general; whoever does, disobeys at the risk of his life.

And so everyone in the city came to make a holiday that God had given them the Austrian emperor to protect them beneath the wings of his kindness. Many of the Jews offered their gratitude innocently and sincerely, for God had indeed liberated them from the oppressiveness of Poland and from the priests who handed Israel over to despoilment through the libels and plots they had devised against them, so as to persecute the Jews and take their money and lead them astray from God's statutes. Not a year had passed that righteous and innocent men were not murdered because of blood libels and every other type of false accusation.

And so all the Jews of Buczacz came and filled the synagogue, even its women's section. Many of the city's leaders who were not Jews also attended, and at their head came the generals of the Austrian army.

The synagogue's cantor and his choir chanted from the psalms of David, from those psalms that David, king of Israel, had sung to the God of Israel when the people of Israel lived in their land and when David, our king, reigned in the city of God, in Israel's holy Zion. The generals and the city's rulers sat there and gazed at the synagogue building and its walls and the ceiling and the candelabra that hung from the ceiling. All of them were of burnished brass, the handiwork of artisans. They gazed at the holy curtain covering the holy ark of the Torah, and at the covering over the holy curtain, and at the lectern, and at the cantor and his choir standing in front of the lectern. They gazed at the raised platform made of hewn stone which stood at the center of the synagogue, and at the steps leading up to the platform, and at the table on the platform. Then they saw the great menorah that stood on the table with its branches and flower-shaped cups. And they saw how beautiful it was.

And as they were looking, the officers suddenly saw the Polish eagle on the menorah. They immediately became incensed at the Jews.

The synagogue president rushed off, grabbed the gavel that the synagogue's sexton used to rouse the congregants for morning services, and smashed the white eagle with the gavel. He hit the eagle with the gavel and knocked it off the synagogue menorah. And thus he removed the national insignia of Poland from the house of worship. The officers said to him, "You acted well. If you hadn't done this, we would have imprisoned you and the elders of the community, and we would have fined the Jewish community as punishment." Then the army officers ordered that a two-headed eagle be set on the menorah in place of the eagle they had removed. For the two-headed eagle is the Austrian eagle.

They immediately sent for Yisrael the Metalworker, summoning him to come. This was the same Yisrael the Metalworker whose wife received seven copper pennies every Friday, so that she could buy herself sustenance for the Sabbath during the period that the Austrian emperor imprisoned her husband and she had literally nothing with which to celebrate the Sabbath, as I related in my tale "My Sabbath."

Yisrael the Metalworker made a brass eagle with two heads, and they set that two-headed eagle on the menorah in place of the one-headed eagle. The young boys took the eagle that Yisrael the Metalworker had discarded, and they brought it to him to make dreidels for them to play with during Hanukkah. And those are the very same dreidels that our grandfathers told us about—the dreidels of burnished brass that Yisrael the Metalworker made for the children of Buczacz.

The menorah stood in the Great Synagogue for many days. With its six candles in its six branches the menorah lit up the synagogue. On Sabbath nights and the nights of the holidays, the menorah's candles were lit, as they also were on the Austrian emperor's birthday, which the country celebrated as a holiday, because he was a beneficent ruler. And so the two-headed eagle vanquished the menorah and its branches.

But the Polish people never reconciled themselves to the Austrian rulers who had stolen their land. They prepared war against them. They came out of every town and village to wage a war on behalf of their nation and homeland.

6

Buczacz, like the other towns and villages, supported the uprising. Many Jews were also among those fighting on behalf of Poland. They held a heavy hand over their own brethren; indeed, they were particularly hard upon all those who sought peace and quiet, and upon all who remained loyal to Austria.

Certain Jews passed through the land of Galicia to rouse up their brethren in every town and make them come to the rescue of Poland. They spoke of all the wonderful things Poland had done for the Jews, but they did not recall the wicked things. One of these men came to Buczacz. He was wearing a hammer on his belt just like those firemen wear when they go out to fight a fire. On the Sabbath morning he came to the Great Synagogue. The Jews there paid him much honor; they seated him next to the eastern wall of the synagogue and they called him up to the Torah.

And so it happened, as he was standing before the Torah, that the man saw the two-headed eagle. He began to scream: "This is an abomination! An abomination!" Then he grabbed the hammer from around his waist and struck at the two-headed eagle. He paid no attention to the other worshippers, not even when they pleaded with him to stop and not desecrate the Sabbath. He did not listen to them until he had broken the Austrian eagle from off the menorah and cast it to the ground.

The young boys took the eagle that had been removed from the menorah and brought it to one of the metalworkers to make into dreidels for Hanukkah, for they had heard that their forefathers had made dreidels for themselves from brass. But the metalworker did not make dreidels for them, because it is very difficult to make dreidels from brass. But he did make them dice, which children also play with on Hanukkah.

And all the days of the uprising, the menorah stood there with the eagle cut off.

7

Eventually the uprising was put down and Austria returned to ruling over the country. Now, though, its rulers cast a wary eye upon every matter, large and small, in enforcing the law of the land and its ordinances.

It was then that the synagogue treasurers hastened to make for themselves an eagle with two heads, which they set on the menorah in place of the eagle that had been cut off and discarded.

The eagle stood there between the six branches of the menorah, its one head turned to the three branches to the right, and its second head toward the three branches to the left. All the years until the Great War broke out, until Austria and Russia became enemies, the eagle stood there on the menorah, and the menorah stood on the holy reading table, the table on which the Torah was read.

8

As conditions in the war grew more difficult, it became harder for the soldiers to find weapons to shoot. So they took metal utensils, large and fine utensils, and they melted them down in order to make out of them weapons with which to destroy the country. These soldiers came as well to the Great Synagogue in Buczacz. They took the brass basin in which every man who entered the sanctuary washed his hands. They took the brass pitcher that the Levites used to pour water over the hands of the priests before they went up before the congregation on holidays to bless them with the priestly blessing. They took every utensil made of brass and lead. They took the charity box that was made of gold, the box in which people made secret contributions to charity. And the officers also fixed their eyes upon the great menorah. A certain metalworker was with them. For they had brought a metalworker in order to take the utensils from the synagogue and melt them down into weapons.

But just as they were about to seize the menorah, the sound of Russian tanks was heard. The Austrian forces immediately fled for their lives, and left behind all they had taken.

But the metalworker, the one who had come with the army officers when they came to take the brass utensils—he did not flee.

He took the menorah and hid it in a place that only he knew. No one else knew its place. And no one gave a thought to the menorah, for all anyone cared about was saving his own life from the Great

War and from the heavy shellfire that fell continuously through the war until its conclusion.

Then the war ended, and the land of Poland that had been fought over came under Polish rule. And the town of Buczacz was also given over to Poland.

9

A number of the former inhabitants of Buczacz returned to the town. Many villagers from around Buczacz also settled in the town, for their houses had been stolen by their neighbors with whom they had fought on behalf of their homeland. They all came to worship in the Great Synagogue for, of all the prayer houses, the Great Synagogue alone survived the war.

And so it happened, when they could not find a single lamp to light up the house of worship at night, that they took some stones from the place, they bored holes in them, and then they set the stones on the lectern in order to place candles in them to make light for themselves when they stood in prayer before the Lord. Later, they made for themselves menorot out of tin and wood, because they were very poor. For they had been unable to recover anything of all they had owned. Whatever the war had spared the enemy had taken; and whatever the enemy had spared, the Poles took. So it was not within their means to make for themselves menorot from brass or from lead as they once had.

10

One man, who had been born in Buczacz, came home after being a captive in Russia. And it happened that, when he came to the Great Synagogue on Friday night and saw the menorot of tin and wood that were without any beauty, he remembered how he happened to be in the trenches with a metalworker, and how that metalworker had told him that, when the Russians advanced upon Buczacz, he had hidden the town's great menorah to keep it from falling into the Russians' hands. But before the metalworker was able to tell him where he had hidden the menorah, a cannon hit the trench and the two never saw each other again. And now, when the man saw the synagogue, he remembered the metalworker and the trench that the cannon had blown up. For if the cannon had not blown up the trench, he would now have known the place where the metalworker had hidden the menorah.

The next morning, on the Sabbath day, the man was called to the Torah, for it was the first Sabbath since he had returned to his hometown. The Torah reading for that Sabbath was the portion called *Terumah*, which begins with Exodus 25. As the Torah reader read aloud the section in Scripture describing the making of the menorah that was used in the tabernacle, he came to the verse "Note well, and follow the patterns for them that are being shown you on the mountain" (Exodus 25:31). At that instant the man knew that the menorah was hidden on a mountain!

The town of Buczacz is surrounded by mountains; it sits on a mountaintop itself. And the man had no idea which mountain it was that held the menorah.

The man began to wander the mountains. There was not a mountain of all the mountains around Buczacz that he did not search. The man did not reveal to anyone that he was searching after the menorah, for he feared the riffraff that had joined the town and that, if they heard about the menorah, they would take it away. Every day the man went in search of the menorah, through cold and heat, until summer and winter had both passed. But he still had not found the menorah.

Now the days of cold, the winter season, returned, and the man did not return from his daily labors in the mountains. At the end of several days, after wandering in the mountains, he said to himself: Let me return home and no longer search after the menorah. For I am not able to find it.

II

And it came to pass that, as the man was returning home, another man was standing on the road, a man crippled in his legs and missing an arm. The two of them stood there. They looked at each other in astonishment and exclaimed, "Blessed be He who resurrects the dead!"

Then the man who had been searching after the menorah said, "I told myself that you were blown up in the trench, and now I see you are alive!"

The metalworker said to him, "I too thought you were among the dead. Blessed be the Lord who has saved us from the Russian cannons and who has left us alive after the horrible Great War."

The man who had been searching for the menorah asked him, "Didn't you tell me that when the Russians first came to Buczacz you hid the great menorah? Well, where did you hide it?"

The metalworker replied, "That is why I have come."

"Where is it?" the other asked.

"It is hidden in the ground beneath my house," he answered.

"Where is your house?"

"It is destroyed," the metalworker said. "It no longer exists. But the place is still there. It is beneath a pile of snow. If I only had a shovel in my hand, I could already have cleared away the snow and the earth beneath it and dug the menorah out."

The two of them went off. They brought a shovel and worked there all day and all night and all the next day, for a huge amount of snow covered the mountains, until, finally, they had cleared the snow and the earth, and they found the menorah.

They removed the menorah and brought it to the Great Synagogue, where they stood it on the reading table where the menorah had once stood. And so the menorah stood on the reading table as it had in earlier days, in the days when there was peace in the land. The metalworker said, "Now I will cut off that bird with two heads, for Austria has ceased to rule over Buczacz. And if there are young boys in town, I will make dreidels from the brass eagle for them to play with during Hanukkah, just as our grandfathers did for our fathers." He added, "Let us also not make a one-headed eagle, like the eagle that is the national insignia of Poland. I have heard that the Ruthenians have revolted against Poland. If they see the eagle of Poland in our synagogue, they will say that we have prepared to go to war against the Ruthenian nation."

The two men said to each other, "One kingdom comes and another kingdom passes away. But Israel remains forever." And they said, "O Lord! Have pity on Your people. Let not Your possession become a mockery, to be taunted by nations! How long shall they direct us however they wish? You, our God, are our rock and refuge forever. You alone we have desired; let us never be ashamed."

Translated by David Stern

Pisces

Prologue

Seeing that most people do not know the story of Fishl Karp, or they may know part of it but not all of it, or they may know the story in a general way—and indeed there is no greater enemy to wisdom than superficial knowledge—I have taken it upon myself to recount things exactly as they happened.

I know that I myself have not managed to verify all the details or to reconcile everything, and, needless to say, others would have told it better than I. But I say that full detail is not the main thing, nor is beauty nor the reconciling of inessential matters. The main thing is truth. In that wise every word spoken here is true.

I
A Solid Citizen

Fishl Karp was a householder. Householders like him are not found in every generation nor in every place. Tall was he, and as his height, so was his breadth. That is, his height equaled his circumference. Of similar amplitude were his limbs. His neck was fat and, as they say among us in Buczacz, it measured up to the forearm of Eglon, the king of Moab. This, apart from his belly, which was a creature by itself. Such a belly is not to be found in our generation, but even in Fishl's generation it was numbered among the city's novelties.

Two merchants once came from Lemberg to Buczacz to buy groats, and Fishl Karp happened upon them. They looked at him and said, "Even among the gizzard eaters and mead drinkers in Lemberg, a belly like that would command respect." It was ample, like a cauldron for cooking prune jam. Not for nothing was it said that his double chins compared to his belly like a bird's gullet to its body, and his double chins were fat like a goose before Hanukkah. Hence he honored his belly and cared for it and saw that it lacked for nothing. Be it meat and fish, let there be meat and fish; be it gravy and groats, let there be gravy and groats; and if you want a prune compote, let there be a prune compote, aside from carrot wrapped in tripe stuffed with flour and toasted with fat and raisins, not to mention the dishes that come before the meal.

Ordinarily people eat sauce before meat and meat before prunes and carrots. Fishl Karp would eat the meat before the sauce and the carrots and prunes before the sauce, so that if the Messiah should come he could give him what he was eating and not deprive his belly. Otherwise, while all the Jews were taking joy in the Messiah, his belly would be miserable and sad. If things were thus during the six days of the week, on Sabbaths and festivals it was even more so. What Reb Fishl ate at the optional fourth meal of Rabbi Hidka would be enough for ten Jews for an entire Sabbath, and what he used to eat on the eve of Yom Kippur would be enough for anyone for all the three festivals. Even those holidays that are not mentioned in the Torah but which were ordained by Ezra and his court he honored with food and drink, as well as all the other special days when it is one's religious duty to eat a copious meal.

To make them noteworthy, he would prolong his meals until midnight, and in the same manner he would prolong the banquet to bid farewell to the Sabbath Queen. For a person has a bone called *luz* which enjoys no food except at the banquet for the departure of the Sabbath, and from that bone the Holy One, blessed be He, will make the entire body sprout in the world-to-come. Fishl intended to provide it with much pleasure so it would remember him in the afterlife when there will be Leviathan and Wild Ox.

The child is father to the man. Even as a lad it was evident that he would be a man of substance. It once happened that a man held a yahrzeit. After prayers he gave out cakes and brandy, for in those days some people had already taken up the hasidic custom of bringing cakes and brandy to the house of prayer on the occasion of a yahrzeit to drink to the living and to bless the dead for the ascent of his soul. Fishl saw an old man slice a piece and abandon the rest. He was astonished. The old man said to him, "What are you looking at me for?" He said to him, "I'm observing the little slice that's wobbling between your gums and not getting any smaller." He said to him, "And you would swallow a slice like that in the wink of an eye?" He said to him, "Even if they gave me all the cakes, I wouldn't leave a single crumb." The old man's son heard this. He grabbed Fishl by the ear and said to him, "Here, the cakes are yours if you eat them in front of us, but if you leave even one of them, you must stretch yourself out upon the table and receive forty lashes plus one." He listened and agreed.

Twenty-four cakes there were, each as thick as the nose of the official who collects excise taxes on taverns. They were in three layers and kneaded with eggs, and Fishl ate them all. Finally, for fear of even numbers, he ate yet another. The next day he bet a man who held a yahrzeit that he could drink a jug of brandy without a morsel of food. He downed it all and quaffed another cupful for good measure, and no change was noticeable in his face.

On Sabbaths and festivals Fishl used to pray with the first minyan, but on ordinary days he would pray with the second or third, and sometimes he prayed by himself. For on Sabbaths and festivals a man's table is set and a feast is ready for him when he returns home. His plate and cup greet him, one with food and one with drink. But on ordinary days many things delay a man before he stands up to pray. For the market swarms with a multitude of fowl, and the butcher shop is full of meat. Sometimes on his way to synagogue a gentile man or woman would meet him bearing good things to eat. Such was Fishl Karp's custom: he would take his stick in his right hand and his tallit and tefillin in his left, and he would cross the market and peer into the butcher shop, sending his eyes in front of him. He might see a fat hen, a fine piece of meat, a fruit worthy of a blessing, or a vegetable that would be good to add to his meal, and he would purchase them, before anyone else preempted him. If his tallit and tefillin bag was large enough, he would secrete them there and bring them home after his prayer, and if there were too many things for his tallit and tefillin bag to hold, he would send them off with someone else, such as a little orphan boy who had come to say kiddush or anyone else who was at hand to run his errand.

2
A Fish He Found

One day Fishl arose early, as was his wont on the six days of the week. He boiled a kettle and drank hot tea with honey. He filled his pipe with tobacco and saw to his bodily needs. Afterward he peeked into the cupboard where all sorts of victuals lay ready, and in his thoughts he tasted their flavors and in his mind he exchanged one food for another and one drink for another, since not all times and not all tastes are equal. You hunger for one thing and something else comes and appeals to your palate. The manna that fell from heaven for the Israelites had all the tastes in the world. If they wished, it tasted like bread or like honey or like oil. Our foods, alas, have merely the memory of taste.

Once he had made up his mind about what he would eat after prayers—what first, what last, and what in the middle—he took his tallit and tefillin bag and went to pray. His tallit and tefillin bag was not made of satin nor of the leather of an unborn animal. Rather, it was made from the skin of a calf, from which he had not removed even enough to make a little strap for lashes on the eve of Yom Kippur. This was the calf that Fishl consumed at a single meal before he was required to report to the army officials who had come to take able-bodied men to military service. For by then the custom had been abolished, by which one could redeem oneself from the king's service by hiring one soul for another. Instead, anyone found worthy was taken to serve the king. Some Jewish lads would starve themselves so as not to be fit to serve the king. Fishl was a fleshy man and said, "Even if I sit and fast for a whole year, I'll still be fitter than five men together, so why should I deprive my soul? I'd do better to eat a lot and drink a lot and treat myself well and put on a lot of weight, for they account ample flesh a flaw." And because a miracle happened for him on account of the calf that he ate, in that he fell sick and they excused him from the king's army, he made a bag out of its skin for his tallit and tefillin.

Fishl gathered himself up to go to the house of prayer. As he left, he said, "I won't linger there long," to announce that he didn't have it in mind to prolong his prayers, so they would hurry and prepare his morning meal, so that upon his return he would find his table laid and he would start his meal without delay. Finally he kissed the mezuzah, thinking: Something new has just become clear to me. If you eat some fruit preserves before going to sleep and kiss the mezuzah in the morning, you can find a bit of sweetness on it.

He said, "I won't linger long," and Hentshi Rekhil his wife knew that he was just talking nonsense, because even if he intended to return immediately, he would not, since it was his practice on the way to the house of prayer to stroll through the market and look into the butcher shop and to go out to the crossroads and meet the Gentile men and women who brought poultry and vegetables to town. So it was on that day. He set out for the house of prayer, but his feet brought him to the center of town to see the foodstuffs with which the villagers supplied the town.

He met a fisherman with his net coming from the Strypa. He was stooped under the weight of the net, and the net was shaking itself and its bearer. Fishl looked and saw a fish quivering there in the net. In all his days Fishl had never seen such a large fish. When his eyes settled down after seeing the new sight, his soul began to quiver with desire to enjoy a meal made from the fish. So great was his appetite that he didn't ask how such a stupendous fish had found its way into waters that do not produce large fish. What did Fishl say when he saw the fish? He said, "The Leviathan knows that Fishl Karp loves large fish and sent him what he loves." Though he had still not made up his mind how he would eat it, whether stewed or grilled or fried or pickled, in his thoughts he gathered together all the tastes that the white flesh of that water wolf was likely to give him.

Fishl's lips quivered with hunger, like a mullet with its many scales and fins. His eyes dimmed, and he did not see the fish. As the saying goes in Buczacz: One sees the Purim goodies, but not their sender.

The fisherman saw a Jew staring at the fish without saying a thing. He took his mind off him and went on his way.

Fishl was alarmed and raised his voice in a shout, "Hey, fellow, where to?" The fisherman replied, "To sell the fish." He said to him, "And I, am I nothing?" He said to him, "If you want to buy, buy."

He said to him, "How much?" He answered, "This much." He said to him, "And if I give you so much, will you write your will and die?" Fishl knew that the fish was worth twice what the fisherman asked, but if you can lower the price, you lower it. In short, the one swore he would not reduce the price by even a farthing, and the other swore that he would not pay half a farthing more. One swore by his God and all his saints, and the other swore on his own head. One raised, the other lowered; one added, and the other subtracted. Finally they came to terms. Fishl opened his purse and got his bargain.

The fisherman went on his way and Fishl stood there, devouring the fish alive. Not that he ate it alive, but he was like a man who sees a fat goose and says, "On your life, I'd swallow you just as you are." Though Fishl was used to fish, such an enormous one had never come into his hands. Even though they bring fish from all the great rivers, from the Dniester and from the Danube, a fish this big had never appeared in our city, or if it had, someone else had beaten him to it.

He looked at the fish again, and then at his own belly, at his belly and at the fish, and he said to them, "You see, you gluttons, what's waiting for you. Right after we finish morning prayers we'll sit down together and eat." He raised his eyes upward, thinking to himself: The Holy One, blessed be He, knows that in the whole city there is no one who makes as many blessings over food as Fishl. When they make their blessings, they bless on the measure of an olive or an egg, but when I make a blessing, it's over a satisfying meal. So may it be Thy will that there's a bridegroom or the father of a child about to be circumcised in the synagogue, so we won't be delayed by saying the prayers for divine mercy.

One good idea brings another. From thoughts of the prayers for mercy he turned his mind to the entire service, when it is long and when it is short, when one recites many verses and when one recites fewer. He began to be amazed at the wisdom of Moses, our teacher, who arranged everything in timely fashion. You find that on Yom Kippur, when it is forbidden to eat and drink, you spend all day in prayer. So it is with the other fasts: since there is no eating and drinking, one recites many penitential prayers. But on the eve of Yom Kippur, when you are commanded to eat and drink, you don't say the prayers for mercy, you don't add "He shall answer you on this day of affliction" to the Eighteen Benedictions, and you skip the Psalm of Thanks. The same holds true for the day before Passover, when you give a banquet to honor the completion of a tractate, and you eat a lot of cakes and biscuits left over from Purim. True, a slight difficulty is presented by the Fast of Esther on the day before Purim, a day of baking and cooking, a day when savory odors waft from oven and range. Yet if you only delve deeply into the matter, you find that even the Fast of Esther has something good about it, for by starving yourself during the fast, you double your pleasure in the food and drink taken after the fast, just as meat eaten on Sabbath during the nine days of mourning preceding the Ninth of Av gives double pleasure. So why does the eve of Yom Kippur come before the day? So that a man will prepare himself for it with food and drink.

What good thoughts would Fishl Karp have savored in his heart were it not for that fish. Consider the matter: the very same fish that taught him the ways of the world put an end to his thoughts. Why? Because not all views are the same. The man thought: I'll bring him to make a fish meal for me. And the fish wondered: How long will I be stuck in this man's hands? The man stroked its fins and savored the taste of fish, and the fish grew angry like a bird in a hunter's hands. The man was at peace, the fish at war. At last the fish tightened all its scales like a suit of mail and lifted one of its fins, nearly slipping out of Fishl Karp's hands.

Fishl noticed and said, "If that's how you are, I'll show you that I'm no worse than you are." He pressed his two hands together, clamping the fish between them. Its scales stood still as its fins opened, and its eyes were about to pop out when they saw the extent of human wickedness. Fishl looked at the fish and said, "You evil scaly thing, now you know that Fishl is not one of those self-righteous folk who pretend to be merciful while they're waving about a rooster that's going to be slaughtered for Yom Kippur."

Though he had reason to be angry at the fish, he dismissed all resentment toward it. On the contrary, he looked at it benevolently and spoke nicely to it. He said to it, "Now that you've left off your wild ways, I'll treat you well in return and conceal you from people's view, so they won't give you the evil eye. For there's nothing harder to eat than the evil eye. As my grandmother used to say, 'A stranger's eye on food is like bones on a full stomach.' You might say that a man is valued according to the foods and beverages that come to his table. But you should know that just as people honor the rich for their money, although they lock it away from others, so it is with food and drink. If you have them, you'd better not show yourself at mealtime or display what you're preparing for dinner." Another reason why Fishl promised to hide the fish from people's view was because in those days Buczacz had forsworn the eating of fish. Since the fishermen had raised the price of fish, the entire city was refusing to buy fish, even for the Sabbath, except for one family that didn't share in the public grief, as I've told you elsewhere. Therefore he comforted the fish, saying he would hide it from public resentment. Just as he was about to keep his promise, he found it hard to do so. Why? Because he couldn't find any place to hide the fish. He thought to hide it between his belly and his clothing, like a smuggler, but they who are skinny because of all the pains they take to make a living can do so, whereas his belly was so ample that it would not tolerate any external addition. He thought to stuff the fish against his chest, but his double chin wouldn't permit it. He looked at the fish like a man asking advice of a friend. The fish, which was mute by nature, was all the more mute at that time because of its sorrows, and it did not answer him. Were it not for his tallit and tefillin bag, Fishl could not have kept his promise, and people would have given the fish the evil eye.

As I have said, his tallit and tefillin bag was made of the skin of an entire calf, and to my eye it resembled those musical instruments that the musician inflates out to make a sound. But while the instrument makes a sound and does not absorb anything, the bag is silent and accepts whatever you put into it. Were that not so, how could he put in it meat and fish and fruit and vegetables and sometimes even a pair of pigeons or a hen or a goose that he purchased on his way to synagogue? At any rate, that sack had never in all its days seen a creature as rebellious as that scaly, finny one. When the fish was only a year old, its length was already close to that of Fishl's arm, and since then it had further increased itself by a third and half a third.

The tallit and tefillin huddled together and acted hospitably, as did the prayer book. Fishl shoved the fish in among them and the bag stretched itself to receive the fish. The fish, which was weak because of the change in place, the rigors of travel, and Fishl's manhandling, accepted its torments in silence and did not say: The place is narrow for me. But unwittingly it took revenge against Fishl, since it was very heavy and hard for Fishl to carry.

3
A Man's Emissary

Fishl got himself to the synagogue and found that even the latest service was over. He said to himself: It would be worth knowing what breakfast was waiting for them, putting them in such a hurry to pray. Now I'll pray without a minyan and I won't hear Kedushah and Barekhu. In any event he did not pin the blame on the fish or say to it: You are the one that made me late for public prayer and deprived my soul of Kedushah and Barekhu and the privilege of responding Amen. On the contrary, he thought well of the fish. He would make such a breakfast meal out of it that even the books that heap condemnation on eating and drinking would sing its praises. Since he always took great care to eat breakfast, a meal that the sages praise extravagantly, humility gripped him. He said, "It makes no difference to the fish who hands it over to be cooked, whether it's me or someone else."

He found Bezalel Moshe, the son of Israel Noah the House Painter, who, as was his habit, was sitting in the synagogue. The house painter had been killed when he fell from the church roof while he was repairing one of their statues, and broke his neck, and his only son, Bezalel Moshe, was left an orphan. The beadle of the synagogue took him to the synagogue and found a few householders who took it upon themselves to give him food, each on a different day of the week. He used to live in the synagogue and eat day by day with different householders. Whatever he lacked in food, the beadle supplied, and what the beadle lacked, he supplied with his own hands. For he would make mizrahim, plaques for the eastern wall of the home, indicating the direction in which one prays, and rotating plaques for counting the omer, and he would draw letters and drawings for the cloths that girls embroider to cover challot and matzot. He also made playing cards for Hanukkah and, by contrast, for Christmas Eve, when it is forbidden to study Torah, and in payment he would take a penny or a farthing or something to eat. Even the tombstone engraver would use him occasionally to draw the hands of Aaron the Priest on the stone, or a pitcher for a Levite, twins for someone born under the sign of Gemini, or fish for someone born under Pisces. Bezalel Moshe would draw on the stone in ink, and the engraver would engrave it on the monument.

At that moment Bezalel Moshe was sitting in the corner behind the pulpit, next to the holy ark, a spot hidden from all eyes. He was busy making a mizrah and was in the midst of the sign of Pisces. Said Fishl, "He's sitting there like someone who got a saucer of jam and hides so he won't have to share with others." Fishl inspected the beasts and animals and fowl and fish that the orphan had drawn. Fishl was astonished that this poor son of poor folk had it in him to draw offhandedly what the Holy One, blessed be He, had taken six days to create. And I—Fishl went on to reflect—and I, if I've got to sign my name, I distrust my fingers all day. Fishl chirped with his lips, "Pish, pish, pish," as though to say: Miracle of miracles I see here. The orphan heard and was startled. He covered the mizrah with his hands.

Said Fishl to Bezalel Moshe, "What are you sitting around for, you idler? On a sheet of paper that size we could write the names of all the portions of the Torah with compound interest on each and every portion. Show me what you've heaped together here. What's that, the fruits of the tree in the Garden? Don't be afraid that I'll take one to eat. They're not even worth sending to the judge and the cantor as Purim gifts. And what's this? The sign of Pisces? Fish you call those miserable things?" He extended his finger toward the two fish that were drawn on the mizrah, the head of one against the tail of the other, and the fins of one against the fins of the other. Great sadness bubbled up from the eyes, as if they didn't know that Pisces was the constellation of Adar, the month in which we are meant to rejoice. Fishl laughed and said, "You call those fish? If you want to see what a fish is, I'll show you."

He took his tallit and tefillin bag and removed the fish, saying, "I reckon that in your prayer book you won't find a blessing for a fish like this! From now on, picture to yourself how lovely it will be, stewed or roasted or fried or pickled. Now take it to Hentshi Rekhil my wife and tell her, 'Reb Fishl desires a fish meal.' You can count on her to catch the hint, and I promise you that before I finish my prayers, the meal will be ready."

Bezalel Moshe looked at the fish, which was quivering in Fishl's hands the way his father Israel Noah had quivered after falling from the church roof. At that moment the fish mustered its last strength and tried to escape from the hands of that human being, who was torturing him with words as harsh as wormwood. Fishl grasped him powerfully and said, "You're shivering, you're cold, a chill has gripped you. I'll send you to my house right away, and Hentshi Rekhil my wife will make a fire and warm up a hot drink for you, and she'll feed you onions and peppers to warm you up and abate the chill."

The fish closed its eyes in grief, and at that moment they showed it the death that was awaiting it. Then it sang a dirge for itself. If we translate its words to our language, this is approximately what they said:

Not in mighty waters did I end my allotted days;
Nor in ancient rivers shall I wend my destined ways;
  In a wicked man's hand I perish indeed;
Though I offer much prayer, he will not heed.

After the fish vomited out the last remnant of its strength, Fishl laid it on the reading table and removed his prayer things from the bag. He picked up the fish and stuffed it back into the bag. The fish, whose strength was gone and who was already half dead, submitted to suffering in silence and offered no protest against Fishl, Fishl opened his tallit and tefillin bag again, to show his face to the fish before sending it away. He laughed to himself contentedly and said, "I shall recite some of your praises to your face. You are fit for me and worthy to be eaten by me. Karpl Shleyen and Fishl Fisher and, need it be said, Fishl Hecht, the half-brother of Fishl Fishman can all envy us."

After giving praise to the fish, he said to the orphan, "How many feet do you have, all in all?" "Two." "If so, pick up both of them at once and run swiftly to tell Hentshi Rekhil my wife what I told you, that is, 'Reb Fishl, long may he live, desires a meal of fish. Hurry and cook the fish and make him tasty victuals such as he loves.'"

Bezalel Moshe gazed at him and asked permission to conceal the mizrah first. Fishl laughed and said, "Fool, what are you scared of? Not even a mouse would nibble at it, but if you wish, hide it then and hurry, for Reb Fishl craves the taste of this fish."

Bezalel Moshe put away the mizrah and the tools of his trade, and took the fish, which was ensconced in Fishl's tallit and tefillin bag, for Fishl had emptied the bag and stuffed in the fish.

The fish lay in the bag and its soul yearned to die, for it had come to loathe this world to which no creature comes but to die. Even if it has brought forth great things, its end is death. And how did the fish cogitate, since it was already dead? It was dead, let us say, but its torments were still alive.

Were it not for the fish's ignominious end, it would be worth recounting all its deeds and celebrating each and every detail. Now that it has plunged to the deepest abyss, it is enough for me to recall some of its deeds and to include the deeds of its fathers and also what befell it before reaching Fishl Karp. And don't be surprised that I do not call it by name. It had no name, since no fish is called by a given name, due to the great honor they accord to the Leviathan, their king. Moreover, until the time the Talmud was written, no species of fish even had a general name. This should be evident, for when the Bible speaks of fish, it never mentions the species.

4
Lords of the Water

His fathers and his fathers' fathers were among those venerable fish whose lineage extended back to the fish who were with Jonah in the belly of the Great Fish, and since their souls clung to Jonah's prayer in the belly of the Great Fish, they followed him until the Great Fish vomited him forth, as ordered by the Holy One, blessed be He. Hence there is no doubt that Jonah prayed inside the belly of the Great Fish, contrary to those commentators whose forced interpretation maintains that Jonah did not pray until after he went forth on dry land, since it is written, "And he prayed, et cetera, *from* the belly of the fish," and not "*in* the belly of the fish."

How did the fish come to our rivers, which are far from the place where Jonah was? But where was Jonah's prayer offered? Was it not in the place where the sea joins the river, as he said, "And Thou didst cast me into the deep, in the heart of the seas, and the river surrounded me."

These fish left the sea and came to the river and tossed in the fresh water from river to river, sometimes willingly and sometimes unwillingly. There are no bounds to the rivers they crossed and no end to the waters they swam in, nor is there any measure to the roiling water they passed through at peril of their lives, nor is there a limit to the snares and nets that caught them. Finally they came to the least of our waters, the River Dniester, which traverses the lands of His Majesty the Kaiser, as did the members of the Kiknish family, who came from the seed of Jonah the Prophet, as their name indicates. For Kiknish comes from *kikayon* the Hebrew word for "gourd," which is the gourd that the Lord appointed for Jonah to shade him from the sun. I do not know if there are still any members of the Kiknish family alive, but some of them are buried in the Lemberg cemetery.

Nonetheless, it is fitting that you know that what was once accepted as undeniable truth has now come to be challenged. And some people already say that these are legends and that the lineage of this fish is made up. Not that the fish is not the son of its ancestors, but that they are not the sons of their ancestors—meaning those ancestors from whom they claim descent, that is, the fish who were with Jonah in the belly of the Great Fish. And by now every schoolboy is scornful. Using ichthyological terminology, they claim that the descendants of all the fish that were with Jonah in the belly of the Great Fish have become extinct, and that not one of them remains. So that anyone who says that he comes from the belly of Jonah's fish is an imposter. But I say, if we do not have ancestral honor here, we have honor itself. And if you wish to know what that is, I shall tell you in a manner comprehensible to human understanding, just as the early sages put human words in the mouths of beasts and animals and birds. True, they were great sages, and all their deeds were done for the sake of wisdom and morality, and to endow the simple with insight, on the strength of the verse "Who teaches us by the beasts of the earth." But for me, who have not even come so far as the pupil of their pupils, things as they were are enough.

In its youth, when it was still a light greenish color, the fish had already made a name for itself among the lords of the waters. Fish both great and small were in awe of it. Before it reached them, they glided toward it and entered its mouth alive. Fish that float on their bellies and those fish that swim on their ribs, left-handed ones and right-handed ones—they all came on their own to be his food. Not to mention snouty fish and those with eyes in their heads. Our fish, whose heart was close to its cheeks, let no rings be put through its gills and opened its mouth to dine upon them. Indeed, never in our lives have we heard that a fish like this one was to be found in our rivers, but because of its power and might, the others exaggerated, saying that even the fish in the sea were its subjects.

Cruising mighty waters, dreaded by fin and scale,
Here minnows gulping and there large fish devouring,
When it holidayed, ah, then did its foes all quail.
When it sallied forth with legions noble, scouring

The enemy's scales. Then did they savage and blast
The vanquished adversaries' heads. One day it called
For banquet and gluttony, then declared a fast.
Sometimes it did fierce battle, other times it brawled.

Now it crammed its huge mouth with seaweed's denizens,
Now it bloodied streams but swam not all the long day.
Now it tripped and capered with the Leviathan's
Daughters, now like a groom, having with them its way.

Here passed it hours in banqueting and pleasure,
Dining with counselors, the shellfish sagacious,
Now crowning players and singers at leisure,
Discharging advisors when feeling pugnacious.

Every white-fleshed fish to its pointed teeth fell prey,
Until done eating, never calling for a pause,
Ruthless, killing whatever swam into its way,
In secret and in public view, by its own laws.

Its dread voice withered the Dniester's watery flora,
Earning it a blessing from everybody's mouth.

For it saved the carp from Sodom and Gomorrah.
You know that carp are lazy fish and quite uncouth.

Hounding and hunting them without surcease, it saved
Them from death by indolence. Hardly lovable,
We might well say—as of those whose life's path is paved
With splendid fortune—that all it lacked was trouble.

After traversing the Dniester and surveying its length and breadth, the fish wanted to see the rest of the waters and to know its relatives, for there is no river in Europe without members of this fish's tribe. This is not a matter of merit or of blame but simply the way things work out, sometimes one way, sometimes another.

Thus, after surveying the Dniester, the fish betook itself to the place where the Strypa falls into the Dniester. It did not stop and return to the waters of the Dniester, but rather it said, "I shall go and see what there is in the Strypa."

We cannot know whether this took place in the Strypa at the village of Khutzin or in the Strypa at the village of Kishilivitz. In any event, the fish did not remain there. For it coasted with its fins all the way to the Strypa of Buczacz, that is, Buczacz that sits upon the River Strypa.

It arrived at Buczacz and said, "Here I shall dwell, for this is my desire." The other fish of the Strypa saw it and were alarmed. Never in their lives had they seen such a large fish. They erred in thinking that it came from the seed of Leviathan, from those who were born before the Holy One, blessed be He, castrated it and killed the female and salted it away for the righteous in the future. Some paid tribute to the fish and brought it presents. There were so many presents that the waters of the Strypa began to empty of fish. Though we are not dealing with history, this most likely transpired in 5423 or 5424, for in those years the fishermen raised the price of fish exorbitantly, and the whole city came to the head of the rabbinical court and asked him to ostracize anyone who bought fish until the fishermen lowered the price.

Thus the fish swam in the waters of the Strypa, and all the fish

of the Strypa in Buczacz accepted its dominion over them and paid
it ransom for their lives, one delivering its brother, another handing
over its friend, and yet another, its relative.

With high hand did it rule in the Strypa's waters,
Eating every fish, the parents, sons, and daughters,
Serene, consuming water folk, it put on flesh,
A delight to the eye, comely, speedy, and fresh.

Everyone scurried like slaves to do its bidding;
Before it knew, its will was done. So, from eating
And drinking in excess its will was lost.
The fish
Believed that everything they told it was his wish.

As its willpower faded, so increased its fame:
All the Strypa's wisdom was spoken in its name.

The fish lived in the lap of luxury and lacked for nothing.
    One day it rained. Although fish grow in water, they greet a
drop that falls from above as thirstily as though they had never tasted
water in their life. Our fish, too, floated up to snatch a drop.
    After slaking its thirst from the upper water, which is the best
water, for it irrigates and quenches and enriches the body and gives
it purity, the fish lay contentedly with its fins relaxed, like a fish with
a mind in repose.
    At that moment those who sought its favor stood and pointed
to it with their fins, swishing their scales. If I may transpose their
gestures to human language, this is approximately what they said: "It
sees what is between the upper and the lower waters, and apprehends
the higher wisdom from which all other wisdom derives."

5
A Day of Grief

People have a saying that it is good to fish in muddied waters. That day the water of all the rivers and streams and lakes was turbulent because of the rainwater, which drew with it tangled weeds, dirt, and mud puddles. All the fishermen went out and set traps in the great and small rivers, in the brooks, the ponds, and lakes, in the Weichsel and the Dniester rivers and in the Prut, the Bug, the San, and in the Donets and the Podhortsa and in the Strypa River, and in all the rivers of their countries and towns. In the Strypa at Buczacz, too, the fishermen let down their nets, even though at that time none of the Jews would leap to buy fish, except for one man. Since we have already mentioned him elsewhere, we shall not mention him again.

Thus a fisherman cast his net in the waters of the Strypa. Our fish had never seen a net of that kind, for in its home waters, that is, the Dniester, the fishermen's nets are different from those in the Strypa. Every river follows its own custom.

The fish glided up toward the net and wondered: If this is a mountain, since when has a mountain grown up here? The fish had happened by there many times and had never seen a mountain. And if it is a reef, when was it brought here, and who made it full of holes? Or perhaps it is a kind of animal, and these holes are its eyes. If so, what is it, so full of eyes? Perish the thought that it might be the Angel of Death, whom everyone dreads. The fish, too, began to feel dread, and it raised one of its fins to flee. Once it saw that no one was in pursuit, it said, "Not even the Angel of Death wants to kill me." Once its terror departed, the fish returned to find out who that creature was and what it was doing here.

It backwatered with one of its fins and began paddling toward the thing that seemed to it like a mountain, a reef, or a living creature. Not even in its imagination did the fish envision what it really was.

The other fish saw it running toward the net. Fear fell upon them, and they panicked, since of those who enter that net, none returns. They wanted to shout, "Stay away! Keep your distance from the snare!" Terror froze their tongues in their mouths. They did not lose their panic until it gave way to wonder: did the fish not know that was the evil snare in which fish are seized? But in their innocence some of them believed that the fish was such a great hero that even a snare was child's play for it. They began to glory in its heroism and to scorn the snare, since they had a hero who was not frightened of the snare. They still called the net a snare, that is, a fishhook that is nothing more than a needle, an expression used by King Solomon, may he rest in peace, when he sought to portray human weakness, as he said: "For a man cannot know his time, as fish are enmeshed in an evil snare," et cetera. While some fish were praising the fish's heroism, others sought to warn it: "Pick up your fins and flee for your life, for if you draw close sudden disaster will befall you." They held a council and agreed unanimously to get rid of it completely. They played dumb and told it nothing. Those who did not shut their mouth in great joy on seeing a murderer's impending disaster embraced a language of flattery and lies, and told it things that in our tongue go approximately as follows: "Our lord, you are worthy to make yourself a greater palace than that, but this is a time of distress, for the people of Buczacz have forsworn all pleasure from fish, and they won't even buy a fish for the Sabbath." The fish was seduced into thinking that they had prepared a palace in its honor. It flashed its scales to them and opened its eyes as though to say, "Let us go and see." Some of them began to be remorseful and reflective: "Alas, what have we done? It will see immediately that we wanted evil to befall it, and it will take its revenge upon us." But the fish had already been fated to die. Its foolishness trapped it, and it entered the palace, that is, the net.

The fisherman's hand began to be pulled downward. The fisherman was used to the small fish of the Strypa at Buczacz, and he thought it was not a fish tugging at him and his net but a corpse, a bastard's corpse. He cursed all the wanton women who endanger his nets with the infants they throw into the river. He wanted to leave the net in the river, so that if the baby were still living, it would die a long death and exact its torments from its mother. His hand began to tire and was pulled downward. He gathered that the corpse was conspiring to pull him into the river. He quickly drew in his net.

Our fish felt itself being pulled up. It began to wonder: Is this not the ascent of the soul? Since nothing like this had ever happened to it in its life, and all its life it was used to having everything its way, our fish came to the conclusion that this was the ascent of the soul that all the righteous gloried in. It began to see itself as righteous, in addition to all the praises that had been offered it from the day it had begun to rule over the tides of the Strypa, and it was angry at its ministers and servants for not calling it righteous.

Even if we had no books of moral teachings, we could learn the nature of temporary success from that fish. It was a great creature whose dread oppressed all the creatures in the Strypa, who were all prepared to render up the souls of their brothers and relatives to it, and there was no end to the words of flattery they would utter. Suddenly disaster befell it, and after that, no one could be found to stand by it in its troubles, not even to console it, not even insincerely. At that time all the swamp fish raised their voices and began to mock it, saying, "They are raising you up in order to crown you king on high, just as you ruled as a king below." Come see these tiny ones, as our sages of blessed memory said, "The smallest of the small," who had never opened their mouths in their lives, and who saw themselves only as food for the big ones, and whom the big ones took note of only for a snack. Suddenly they became heroes and mocked the fish to its face. Of this type of thing I say, with a slight change in the wording to satisfy the demands of the present subject, what they said in the Gemara: "Everything on dry land is also in the water."

6
Ascent that is Descent

The fisherman drew in his net and found a big fish. He had not seen its like in the waters of the Strypa in his entire life. It was huge in flesh and fat, and its fins were crimson with blood, and its scales glistened like fine silver. The fisherman began to think well of himself and see himself as a wise man and hero. But what can wisdom and heroism offer if they are not accompanied by wealth?

At that time in Buczacz people refrained from buying fish, even for the Sabbath, which one is commanded to make pleasant with fish. And why did Buczacz refrain from buying fish even for the Sabbath? Because the fishermen had raised the prices higher than their due. Even though the eminent rabbi, the head of the court, had not declared a ban upon fish, everyone refrained from buying fish, except for one man, as I have recounted elsewhere.

The fisherman began to grumble about the fish that had come his way when people were not jumping to buy fish. If it had come in normal times, he would have made a good name for himself and made money and drawn girls' hearts after him. Now it was doubtful whether he would find a customer aside from the priest, who paid with words and not with coin.

The fisherman reflected about what to do, but he came to no thought leading to action. The fish's lodging in the net was hard for it. It began to flop around and to tug the net. The fisherman was afraid the fish would escape. He ran and fetched a basin and filled it with water and took the fish out of the net and placed it in the basin.

The fish was consigned to the basin. Never in its life had it been relegated to such a narrow place, and never in its life had its thoughts been so expansive. Needless to say, not when it was a king and exempt from thinking, for it is the way with kings that their ministers think for them, but even before being crowned it had not been used to thinking. Now, confined in the basin, it was thinking, and the world grew ever smaller: In the days of my forefathers, fish swam in the sea, then in the big rivers which spread out over every land, and then in the Strypa, which is called a river only in honor of Buczacz, and finally the world has been reduced to a basin of water.

Come and see how great the power of thought is. Not only does one thought lead to another, but it also passes from creature to creature. You see, while the fish was in the basin of water, gathering up its entire world in its thoughts, the fisherman laid himself down on his sack and his straw, wanting only to sleep, but thoughts came and visited him. As I have said, the fish was thinking about seas and rivers, about its forefathers and itself, and the fisherman was thinking about the Jews and the fish and himself. God may have graced him and sent him a fish worth a lot of money, but what did the Jews do? They stopped eating fish even on their Sabbath, when they are commanded to do so. And were it not for the pact the Jews had made among themselves not to buy fish, he would have sold the fish to a Jew and drunk wine and offered others a drink and hired a musician to play. The girls would have heard and come out to dance with him. He would have chosen one of the pretty ones and done with her what his heart desired. When he thought about what the Jews had done to him, rage blazed within him. He rolled on his bed and could not fall asleep. He rose and poured a full bottle into his mouth. When the bottle was empty, he threw it against the wall. The bottle broke and its fragments rang like church bells. The priest heard and said, "Thus they ring the bells for a priest who has died. Therefore I am dead, and I have to prepare a death banquet." And because it was Lent, when it is forbidden to eat meat, he sent to the fisherman to have him bring him the fish. The fisherman was sad. Every single one of the fish's scales is worth a penny—why must he part with it for nothing? He pounded his head against the table and wept. The innkeeper saw and asked him, "Why are you weeping?" The fisherman kicked his belly and scolded, saying to him, "Jew, don't stick your tongue into things between me and the church. If you don't shut up, I'll say that your wine is mixed with Christian women's blood, that you pierce the nipples of their breasts and kill their children and throw them into the river, and they get into my nets and ruin them." The innkeeper was alarmed and frightened. He began to console him with a bottle as big as the wall. The wine entered and softened his heart. He revealed his trouble. The innkeeper said to him, "It's a difficult problem. If the priest has asked you for the fish, you can't put him off with a scale or two. I have an idea." But he did not need the Jew's advice, for meanwhile another Jew had come along and bought the fish.

7
Damp Thoughts

In the morning the fisherman removed the fish from the basin and put it back in his net, for if people see a fish in a net, they believe there was no delay from the moment it came from the river, and they are fonder of nothing more than a fish that comes right from the place where it lives to the market.

When the fish saw itself lying in the net, it mistakenly thought that the fisherman intended to return it to the river. This is the mistake that most people make, for the greater the trouble is, the more they think erroneously that salvation will arise from it.

The fisherman's thoughts were unlike those of the fish. The fish thought it would be returned to the place where it lived, while the fisherman desired its price. One looked forward to salvation, and the other despaired of salvation. One looked forward to salvation because it had been removed from the basin, and the other despaired of salvation because of the Jews who had conspired not to buy fish. But what was in store for them was unlike the thoughts of both fish and fisherman. You see, as they reached town, there came toward them a certain fleshy man with his bag and put out his hand to the net and took the fish and stuffed it into his bag. Not only was the bag smaller than the basin, but it was also wiped dry of all the moisture.

The one responsible for a miracle does not recognize it. If instead of Fishl Karp there had come someone who puts on two pair of tefillin or someone whose bag was full of those writings by which one seeks to approach our Father in heaven, such as *Hok Leyisrael* or *Hovot Halevavot* or *Reshit Hokhmah*, it would have been more crowded.

The fish extended one of its fins and bumped into a tefillah. I do not know whether it was for the head or for the arm, and what I do not know, I do not say. It also banged its mouth on the prayer book. If the fisherman had been in the place of the fish, he would have hollered, "What do you want from me? Am I a Jew? Am I required to pray and wear tefillin?" But the fish shut its mouth and kept silent.

It shut its mouth but not its thoughts. What were its thoughts at that moment? That fleshy man bought me with scales of silver. If I make a reckoning, my silver scales are more numerous than the scales of silver he gave to the one who delivered me into his hands, and, needless to say, mine are finer. Thus, what made the one deliver me to the other? Perhaps because I am heavy to carry. If so, if I had deprived my soul of good, would that have improved anything? One way or another, it makes no difference in whose hands I am. Neither one intends to return me to the place where I live, but one gives me water for my thirst and the other does not even give me a drop of water.

Having touched upon Reb Fishl with the tip of its thoughts, the fish's mind now wandered from him to Reb Fishl's nation. Damp were its thoughts, and most of them nonsensical. If I were to reproduce them, they would be approximately thus:

The Jews are like fish and they are unlike fish. They are like fish in that they eat fish as fish do, and they are unlike fish since fish eat fish at every meal, and Jews—if they wish, they eat fish, and if they wish, they do not eat fish. It is difficult for the Jews to eat fish, for they have to take great pains before they bring the fish to their mouths. They rise early to go to market, and each grabs the fish out of the other's hands. One shouts out, "In honor of the Sabbath." The other taunts him, saying, "Don't say it's in honor of the Sabbath. Say it's in honor of your belly." In the end they take it and cut it and salt it like those who prepare salt fish, and they light a fire under it. Finally they eat it, some with their fingers and some with a pronged stick. And their pleasure is not complete, for they are afraid lest a bone catch in their throat. Whereas fish need nothing but their mouth. The Holy One, blessed be He, loves fish more than Jews, for the Jews weary themselves with every single fish, but while the fish swims in the water, the Holy One, blessed be He, sends it a fish that enters its mouth on its own. You know that this is true, for when you find a fish inside a fish, how else could it come to lie in a fish's stomach with the head of one toward the other's tail? Why is that? Because it enters the other's mouth headfirst, and if it had been fleeing, you would find its tail facing the other fish's tail.

The fish recalled times when it was in the water, and many good fish used to swim up and enter its mouth, and it would eat and drink all the delicacies of the rivers and streams and lakes, and the other fish all flattered it and were anxious to do its will. So our fish never imagined that the world was likely to change until it entered the net, which it had been seduced into believing was good for it. Those who had said that they themselves had been created only for our fish were the first to lead it to ugly death, beginning with imprisonment and ending with fire and salt and pepper and onions, and after all of those troubles it would not have the privilege of a watery grave. What would be done to it? It was to be buried in the bellies of human creatures. Wealthy men drink wine after the burial and poor men drink brandy after the burial, avoiding mention of water, in which the fish had lived. They drink to each other's life and are not fearful of dishonoring the dead.

The fish set its death before its eyes, no longer knowing whether or not it desired life. The image of its ministers and workers came to the fish's mind in its grief. Then it despised its world and began to spit in disgust. Were it not for the life force, which did not abandon the fish, it would have spit out the remnant of its life.

Little by little its salivation ceased, as did all its thoughts. Its thoughts ceased, but its torments did not cease. Finally its thoughts returned and traded places with its torments, and its torments with its thoughts. This is something the mind cannot grasp. The fish lay there as though inanimate, and it is in the nature of an inanimate object not to have thoughts, yet here its thoughts raced about and created torments. It girded up the remnant of its strength and drew its eyes into its head, gathering up scraps of thoughts and reflecting: Perhaps this is the gathering up spoken of in connection with fish: "And even the fish of the sea will be gathered up." Because the fish was kosher, the heavens had mercy upon it, and its spirit was gathered up with a verse from the Prophets.

8
Between One Fish and Another

At the moment when the fish began to depart from the world, Bezalel Moshe was dragging his feet with difficulty because of the weight of his burden and the weight of his thoughts. While he was sitting in the synagogue his heart had been one, bent upon the work of making a lovely mizrah. Once he went outside, his heart become two. Thinking about the mizrah, he remembered his hunger. Thinking about food, he remembered the mizrah.

He nodded his head to himself and said: What is the use of thinking about a mizrah if the mizrah is in the synagogue and I am outside, and what is the use of thinking about eating if I don't have a slice of bread to sate my hunger? The fish is heavy. Who knows how much it weighs? Certainly the soul of a great Tzaddik has been reincarnated in it.

He went and sat by the side of the road to rest from the effort of carrying the fish. He put down the tallit and tefillin bag, which had become the temporary home of the fish, and he sat, weary of his burden, weary of hunger, and weary of being a poor orphan. If people wished, they gave him food; if they did not wish, they did not. And if he had something to eat, rather than satisfying him, the food only made him hungry, for he feared lest the next day his soul should languish from hunger and ask to depart, and no one would think of inviting him to a meal or of giving him a penny to buy bread. Maybe that is the meaning of the verse "For the earth was full of knowledge"—in the future everyone would be of the same mind, so that if one person asks for bread, the other gives it to him. Bezalel Moshe knew there was no knowledge but the knowledge that there was no bread but the bread of Torah. However, a hungry man removes Scripture from its literal meaning and interprets "bread" as meaning actual bread. The greatness of bread is that even saints who fast constantly cannot live without eating. Some break their fasts on the Sabbath, on festivals, and on days when one is not supposed to fast, and from fast to fast they break their fast with a banquet for the fulfillment of a commandment, such as serving as the godfather at a circumcision. Whereas he fasted without fasting, for even when he fasted all day long, the fast did not count, since he did not fast of his own free will, but rather because he had nothing to eat. Were it not for the drawings that he drew, he would have seemed to himself like a beast whose only thoughts were about eating and drinking.

He began to be ashamed of his thoughts and tried to repress them. When he saw that they were stronger than he, he began to lose himself in them. Since he could not draw food to satisfy himself, though he knew some people can do that, his mind took leave of him and journeyed off to those who eat their fill and do not refrain from eating fish, not even on a weekday, not even when people seek to boycott them. In normal times everyone is used to eating fish, everyone but him, for in his life he had never seen a living fish nor even a cooked fish, except for those in old holiday prayer books next to the prayers for dew and rain. These had provided him with a model to draw fish on the mizrah and had given Fishl Karp reason to open his mouth and laugh at them.

He began comparing one form to another, that is, the fish he had drawn to the fish he was bringing to Fishl's wife. He admitted without shame that Fishl's was handsomer than those he himself had drawn. In what way? This is impossible to portray in words, something that needs a visual demonstration. He looked all about. He saw no one. He put his hand into the fish's dwelling and removed the fish. He picked it up and looked at it. I would be surprised if any fish eater in the world ever looked at a fish the way that orphan did at this time. His eyes began to grow ever larger to encompass the fish, its fins, its scales, and even its head—it and its eyes, which its Creator had made to see the world with.

The fish began to shed one form and don another, until it left behind the image of the fish that Fishl had bought for a tidy sum and began to resemble the fish that had been in the will of the Holy One, blessed be He, to create when He created the fish. But He had not created it. He had left it to artists to draw. And since this is one of those wonders that we are not permitted to interpret, I shall be brief.

9
Torments of the Will

When an artist wants to draw a form, he detaches his eyes from everything else in the world aside from what he wishes to draw. Immediately everything departs except that very form. And since it regards itself as unique in the world, it stretches and expands until it fills the entire world. So was it with that fish. When Bezalel Moshe set his mind to drawing it, it began to enlarge and expand to fill the entire world. Bezalel Moshe saw this, and a chill seized him. His heart began to flutter and his fingers trembled, as it is with artists who quiver with torments of the will and desire to recount the deeds of the Holy One, blessed be He, each in his own way—the writer with his pen and the painter with his brush. Paper he had none. Now picture to yourselves a world whose essence had been blotted out because a single form was floating in space and occupying all of existence, and there was not a piece of paper to draw on. At that moment Bezalel Moshe felt similar to that mute cantor whose heart was stirred to sing a melody. He opened his mouth and moved his lips until his cheeks crumpled and shattered from his torments. The mute cantor was given the inner sensation of a melody and denied its expression with his voice, whereas Bezalel Moshe was capable of drawing, but he was denied paper. His eyes expanded like nets fish are caught in and like ornamental mirrors into which one gazes. The form of the fish came and settled there, taking on an extra portion of life—more than was in the fish while it was living. Bezalel Moshe fumbled in his pockets again. He found no paper, but he did find a piece of black chalk. Feeling the chalk, he looked at the fish. The fish too looked at him. That is, its form rose up and gripped him.

He grasped the chalk and kneaded it with his fingers, like someone who kneads wax with his fingers, which is useful for memory. He looked at the fish and he looked at the chalk. A model for drawing was there. There was chalk for drawing. What was lacking? Paper to draw on. The torments of his will intensified. He looked at the fish again and said to it, "If I want to draw you, I can only shed my skin and draw on my skin." He could have drawn on the fish's skin, just as Yitzhak Kummer drew on Balak's skin, but Balak was a dog, whose skin absorbs color, which is not true of a damp creature full of moisture, where the color spreads in the moisture and will not register a form.

Bezalel Moshe yielded and returned the fish to the bag. He was about to walk to Fishl's wife, for the time had already come to prepare the fish for the meal.

Without doubt Bezalel Moshe would have brought the fish to make a meal of it, were it not that the fish was destined for greater things. What greater things? Why use words if you can see with your own eyes?

Now when Bezalel Moshe put the fish into the tallit and tefillin bag, his hand happened upon a tefillah for the head. He saw the tefillah and was surprised. What was that tefillah doing here? One cannot say that it had remained in the bag with Fishl's knowledge, for what would Fishl do without a tefillah for the head? One cannot say that it had remained in the bag without Fishl's knowledge, for does a man who has a head remove his tefillin in order to pray and take the one for the arm but not the one for the head? You must conclude that Fishl had another. But if so, what was this one doing here? He had found a flaw in it and ceased using it, and perhaps the parchment with the verses had even been taken out, and there was only an empty case here.

Had Bezalel Moshe known that it was a kosher tefillah, he would have kissed it and run to the synagogue and given it to Reb Fishl, and Reb Fishl would have placed it on his head and prayed and finished his prayer and returned home to eat breakfast and examine his accounts and lend to borrowers in their hour of need and eat the day's dinner and lay himself upon his bed and sleep until the fourth meal and eat and attend afternoon and evening prayers and return and eat the evening meal and gratify the Holy One, blessed be He, with blessings for pleasures and with the grace after meals. But now, since Bezalel Moshe did not know that the tefillah was kosher, he did not run to the synagogue and did not return the tefillah to Reb Fishl, and Reb Fishl was prevented from praying and from eating his fill, and so on.

And why was the head tefillah left in the bag? Because of Reb Fishl's craving for a fish dish. When he sent the fish to his wife and cleared out his tallit and tefillin bag, he did not take care about what he removed, and the head tefillah had been left there. And what caused Bezalel Moshe to suppose that it was flawed? Because the straps were dirty, like the cords used to tie up chicken legs, and they were tattered, and the paint on them had crackled, for it is a commandment revealed to Moses on Mount Sinai that the straps of tefillin must be black. The tefillah itself was wrinkled and colored like a goose's bill. The rim was broken and it was coated with a finger's thickness of grease.

Bezalel Moshe said to the fish, "Since a cat, which is not a kosher animal, had the merit of wearing tefillin, you, who are kosher, and who are a Sabbath dish, and who are perhaps even the reincarnated soul of a saint—so much the more so are you worthy of the commandment of wearing tefillin. But what can I do? Your Creator did not create you with a head for wearing tefillin, for your head is narrow and long, like that of a goose. In any event, I'll tie the tefillah on you with its straps, and if you don't take your mind off the tefillah, you shall be garbed in splendor."

What was that story about the cat and the tefillin which Bezalel Moshe mentioned to the fish? If you do not know, I shall tell you.

At that time all of Galicia was in an uproar about a certain Enlightener of the age who wanted to get rid of his wife, but she refused to accept a bill of divorce. He went and took a cat and placed his head tefillah on it. The woman's father saw what sort of a man he was and forced his daughter to accept her bill of divorce.

Thus a head that was not required to wear tefillin merited tefillin, and Reb Fishl, who was required to wear tefillin, was kept from the commandment of tefillin. Why? Because he had not been careful to make certain that his tefillin were tidy and that their straps were black. For had he made sure that they were tidy and that the straps were black, the orphan would not have been sure that he had found a flawed tefillah, and he would have run to return it to Reb Fishl, and Reb Fishl would have prayed and returned home and eaten breakfast and sat and examined the accounts of his loans and he would have made loans to merchants in their hour of need, and he who needed to be repaid would have been repaid, and thus a religious duty would have been done, for it is said that the payment of a debt is a religious duty.

10
The Form of a Man

While the fish was being ornamented with the head tefillah, Fishl was looking for his head tefillah and not finding it. That is the essence of the story, and the entire story is as follows. After sending the fish to his wife and preparing himself to pray, he filled his pipe with tobacco and saw to his bodily needs. He stayed there as long as he stayed and washed his hands to recite the blessing one recites after using the toilet, and then he went to wrap himself in his tallit and tefillin and pray. His thoughts began to race about within him. One said: Good-for-nothing, again you've forfeited the Kedushah and Barekhu. And one said: Since you're praying by yourself, you're the master of your own prayers, and you're not dependent on the prayer leader, who waits for the old men who take a long time to recite the Shema and the Eighteen Benedictions. Since Fishl did not like the thoughts that were racing about, he removed his mind from them to make room for the prayer itself. He said: Well, while I pray, Hentshi Rekhil will be preparing the fish, and if she has not managed to prepare it for the morning meal, I shall be content with those things that open up the gut, and I shall eat the fish at noon. All of those foods came and settled in his mouth. He hurriedly shook out his tallit and placed it on his shoulder and examined the fringes and wrapped himself in it and recited the blessing and recited all the appropriate verses in the prayer book. Then he reached out his arm and took the hand tefillah and placed it correctly on his upper arm, on the distended flesh over the bone, which was swollen because of all the fat, until a good part of the tefillah sank into it. I do not know whether he was accustomed to bind the strap around his arm seven times or nine times, and what I do not know, I do not say. Then he reached out his hand for the head tefillah and did not find it. And why did he not find it? Because it was bound around the fish's head. He sought and searched and groped, and there was nothing he did not look under. But he did not find it. He stooped to look under his belly. Perhaps it had fallen on the floor. And even though had it fallen on the floor he would have to fast all that day—and what a day, a fish day like this he still bent over to the floor and did not find it.

Reb Fishl stood alone in the synagogue, wrapped in his tallit and adorned with his arm tefillah, and he shouted, "Nu, nu!" That is, "Give me a head tefillah." But there was no one there to hear him shouting. Had the orphan been in the synagogue, he would have heard and brought him a head tefillah, and Fishl would have recited the blessing for tefillin and prayed, and so on. Since he had sent the fish with the orphan, Reb Fishl was alone in the synagogue, and even if he shouted all day, his shouts would not be heard. When would they be heard? In any event not before afternoon prayers. Since it was a hasidic synagogue, they recited afternoon prayers late, just before the stars came out.

An expedient occurred to him, and he opened the box under the reading stand, for men who come to pray every day customarily leave their tallitot and tefillin in the synagogue. He found a torn prayer book and flawed tsitsit and the case of an arm tefillah and an old calendar and a broken shofar and the *alef* made of tin that is hung up for a firstborn who is not yet redeemed, and a scribe's pen. But tefillin were not to be found. And why didn't he find any? Because people had stopped leaving their tallitot and tefillin in the synagogue. Why? Because of a drunken beadle in the town who had been discharged. He had looked for a teaching job and found none. He used to take tallitot and tefillin, and sell them cheaply to people from the villages, and he would drink up the profits in brandy. Now, picture this: a man has recited the blessing for the arm tefillah but has no head tefillah. Talking is forbidden between putting on the

arm tefillah and the head one, and he could not find a head tefillah.
Even had he stood there all day, the day would not have stood still,
and there was reason to fear the time for prayer might pass.

He rummaged through the box under the table and found what
he found: ritual articles that were no longer fit for use. But what he
wanted, he did not find. Now you see how expert a person must be
in the necessary religious rules. For had Fishl known, he would have
followed the rule for someone who only has a single tefillah: he puts
it on and blesses it, since each tefillah is a separate commandment in
itself. This is the law when a person is under duress: if he can only
put on one, he puts on the one he can.

At that moment, while Reb Fishl's world was falling in on him,
Bezalel Moshe was sitting in the shade of a tree and playing with the
fish and with the tefillah on the fish's head. To avoid dishonoring the
dead, I shall not repeat all the words that Bezalel Moshe said to the
fish, such as, "Brow that never wore tefillin," and the like. Finally he
changed his mind and said to the fish, "Now we shall remove the
tefillah from your head, so that Satan won't come and accuse those
Jews who sin with their bodies. For you are not commanded to put
on tefillin but do so, and they, who are commanded, do not put on
tefillin."

As he touched the fish to remove the tefillah from its head, his
fingers began to tremble again with desire to draw, like all artists whose
hands are eager to work. For if they have succeeded in making one
form, they wish to make another lovelier still. And if they have not
succeeded, they are even more avid to do so, as many as seven times,
a hundred times, a thousand times. As you know, Bezalel Moshe
had drawn the sign of Pisces that day, and it had not come out well,
because he had never seen a fish in his life. Now that a fish had been
shown to him, his soul truly yearned to draw a fish. Out of desire
for action his fingers trembled, nor did he take note of the nature of
the fish, for it is not the way of fish to absorb color.

He passed the piece of chalk across the fish's skin the way artists do before they draw. They mark a kind of guideline, and that
line shows them what to do. Thus Bezalel Moshe drew a line and
went back and drew another line, and between one line and another

the form of Reb Fishl Karp emerged, until the image of the fish was effaced beneath that of Reb Fishl Karp. And this is something quite unusual, for Reb Fishl's head was thick and round, and the head of that fish was long and narrow like the head of a goose.

And how did Bezalel Moshe come to draw the form of a man, when he had intended to draw the form of a fish? When he reached out his hand to draw, the form of the fish was transmuted into the form of Reb Fishl, and the form of Reb Fishl was transmuted into the form of the fish, and he drew the form of Reb Fishl on the fish's skin. Strange are the ways of artists, for when the spirit throbs within them, their being is negated and they are acted upon. They are directed by the spirit, which obeys the commandment of the God of all spirit and flesh. And why was Reb Fishl transformed into a fish? Because he was a lover of fish.

II
Between an Arm Tefillah and a Head Tefillah

I return to Fishl Karp—not to the Fishl Karp whom the artist drew, but to the Fishl Karp whom his Maker created.

Even before the time came to eat, his mind was driven to distraction by hunger. This is a virtue of man over fish. A fish can subsist without eating for up to a thousand days. A man can remain without eating no longer than twelve days. And Reb Fishl Karp not even a single day.

Bezalel Moshe heard the sound of passersby. He was frightened lest they ask him, "What is that in your hand?" And that they would see what he had done and tell Reb Fishl, and Reb Fishl would scold him, and everyone would say that Reb Fishl was saintly, for it is the way of the world that if a householder scolds a poor orphan, everyone joins in scolding him. He quickly concealed the fish and directed his feet toward Reb Fishl's house.

If the passersby had not interrupted him, he would have removed the head tefillah from the fish and erased the picture of Reb Fishl he had drawn on the fish's skin. Since the passersby did interrupt him, he did not manage to do even one of the things he ought to have done. He neither removed the tefillah nor erased the picture of Reb Fishl from the fish's skin, and he trusted that the tefillah would fall off the fish's head by itself. As for the picture, he expected that moisture would ooze out of the fish's damp skin and erase it.

Bezalel Moshe arrived at Hentshi Rekhil's and handed her Reb Fishl's tallit and tefillin bag. And in the bag lay the fish, glory bound to its head and the face of the fish like that of Reb Fishl. Hentshi Rekhil was of her husband's mind. She comprehended that if Fishl had sent her his tallit and tefillin bag, certainly something important to eat was concealed within it. The smell of the fish came and told her, You are not mistaken. She quickly took it and hid it so that her neighbors would not notice what had been brought her, and she sent the bearer off without any food, letting him go off far hungrier than when he set out on Reb Fishl's errand.

The orphan left Reb Fishl's house hungry, and his hunger walked with him. It would have been good had Reb Fishl's wife given him some food, which he would have eaten, and then he would have returned to the synagogue and saved Reb Fishl from hunger. But she dismissed the errand boy without food. And since hunger plagued him, he wanted to eat, for he had long since learned that if you put off hunger, it grows ever more importunate.

He had a penny which he had received in payment for drawing a memorial dedication for the abandoned woman's orphan daughter. He had written her relatives' dates of death in her prayer book. He had kept the penny in his pocket to buy paper or paints or red ink. Now that hunger seized him, he put his victuals before his art.

He went to buy bread. A peddler appeared with baskets of his fruit. The orphan thought to himself: Half the summer has already passed, and I still haven't tasted a fruit. I'll buy myself a few cherries. He bought a penny's worth of cherries and went out of the city, sat under a tree, and ate the cherries and threw the stones at the birds, watching to see how they flew. He forgot Reb Fishl and the fish and delighted his eyes with the birds' flight. He began to perfume their flying with the verse "As the birds fly," to the melody of Rabbi Netanel the Cantor. His heart filled with the force of the melody, and he began to think of the power granted to human beings. Some are given a melodious voice, like Rabbi Netanel, who stirred people's heart with love of the Lord when he opened his mouth in song, and some are given power in their fingers to make skilled handiwork, like Israel Noah, his father. Rabbi Netanel had the merit of emigrating to the Land of Israel, and Israel Noah his father had enjoyed no such merit but had fallen from the church roof and died. Some people say that the non-kosher wine that he had been given made him fall down and die, and others say he went out to work without eating first, because they had finished all the bread in his home, and hunger had seized him, and he had collapsed and died.

His father's death oppressed his heart, and he was sad. The birds came, and with their flight they carried his mind away from its gloom. He looked at the way the birds fly and sing and how they trace shapes in the sky with their flight. Although the shapes were not visible, nevertheless they were engraved before his eyes and upon his heart. The birds are beloved, since the power to fly is given to them. If the power to fly were given to man, his father would not have died. Now that he was dead, other artisans had come and painted the walls of the Great Synagogue.

The orphan set aside his grief over his father for grief over the Great Synagogue. Ugly drawings had been imposed upon its walls. Far worse were those that had been imposed upon the Tailors' Synagogue, where they had heaped up pictures of birds that did not even look like a likeness. If the painters had raised their eyes upward, they would have seen what a bird was. If so, why did the people of Buczacz praise the artists and their paintings? Because the people of Buczacz walk stooped over all their lives and never raise their eyes above their heads, and they do not see the creatures of the Holy One, blessed be He, except for the fleas in their felt boots. Therefore those drawings look pretty to them. But I shall show them how the creatures of the Holy One, blessed be He, look and how it is fitting to draw them.

From the birds in the sky he returned to the fish he had drawn.

At that moment he was grateful to Fishl Karp, without whom he would not have seen the form of a fish. From now on, said the orphan to himself, if I come to draw the sign of Pisces, I won't look in old festival prayer books, but I'll draw as my eyes instruct me.

At that moment there was no one happier in Buczacz than Bezalel Moshe, the orphan, and no one in Buczacz was sadder than Reb Fishl, the moneylender. This is indeed a wonder: here is a poor person without enough food for a single meal, and here is a rich man who could have held banquets and celebrations all his life with the interest on his interest. The one was happy because of the birds in the sky, and the other was grieved because of his fish, which he was kept from eating.

Fishl saw there was no point in standing in the synagogue and shouting "Nu, nu" when there was no one to hear his "nu, nus." The thought came to him that perhaps he had left the head tefillah in his tallit and tefillin bag when he had sent off the fish. Without further delay he removed his tallit and covered the arm tefillah with the sleeve of his garment and rushed home. He already visualized himself with the head tefillah adorning his head, praying swiftly and washing his hands for a meal. He swallowed his saliva and planned to double each of his steps and not to delay for anything in the world.

I too shall do as Fishl did and I shall not tarry until I reach the end of the story. For everything that has a beginning has an end. Happy is he whose end is finer than his beginning. Here, with the story of Fishl, though its beginning is apparently fine, its end is certainly not fine. If you wish to know, here it is before you.

12
The Thoughts of a Hungry Man

Indeed Fishl charged his legs according to the saying taught in the midrash: The belly charges the legs. However, our sages of blessed memory meant that by the power of eating the body has the power to charge its legs, whereas I interpret the teaching thus: Because he craved food, he found the power in his legs to bear the charge of his belly.

Thus Fishl hurried and did not tarry. He did not tarry, but the fortune of his meal tarried. He was not delayed; others delayed him. Where did they delay him? Close to his home, right next to the door of his house. So many people were there that he could not find the door. What did all of those people want at his house, and why had they gathered there, and why were they noisy and turbulent, and what caused them to besiege his house? Go and ask them when you are forbidden to speak, because you are in between the head and arm tefillin. As much as his soul clamors to know, no one tells him. Of such a situation it is fitting to say: There is no servant woman who has not got six mouths. Yet when you want to hear something, there is not one mouth to tell you.

He had a little girl whom he loved more than all of his other daughters, and she loved him too. She saw her father. She came and rose up on her tiptoes and wrapped his neck in her two arms and said, "Oy, Papa, oy, Papa." He could no longer restrain himself and asked her, "Why has the whole town gathered in front of our house?" The girl repeated, "Oy, Papa, don't you know?" And she said no more. Being small, she believed that her father knew everything and that he had asked in order to test her. If it's something that everyone knows, does her father not know more than they? She answered him in kind, "Papa, don't you know?" Fishl saw that the world was conspiring against him, and even the daughter of his old age, whose voice chattered on and on without stopping, would not tell him. Nor were his astonishments finished yet. While he was aching to know what had happened, he heard people saying, "He did well to lie down and die. In any event, he must be buried." Fishl understood that someone had died, but he was puzzled about why they said he had done well. Is death a fine thing? There is nothing better for a man than to eat and drink, and if one is dead, not only does one neither eat nor drink, but one becomes food for maggots. He stooped in sadness and lowered his eyes to the earth. The earth raised itself up and whispered to him, "Now you are treading upon me with your feet. Tomorrow

I shall cover you." It also whispered, "You may believe that I am sad because of you. I am sad for those who will bear your coffin, who will have to carry such a big-bellied man as you."

As he looked at the earth, he saw that the earth was dry. He began to converse with himself. He said, If a man dies, the neighbors pour out their water, and here, besides sewage, there is no sign that they have poured out water. Little by little his mind reached the truth—that no person had died here. When his mind reached that truth, it did not know what to do with it. For if no person had died, why must there be a burial? But they had explicitly said that he must be buried. And if there is no dead person, why need there be a burial? One way or another, did they not say that he had laid himself down and died?

Had Fishl been full, he would not have wasted time with such thoughts, but he would have entered his house, washed his hands, and sat down to eat, and after the meal he would have wiped his mouth and said, "What is that rumor that I heard, that someone died there? Who died?" Now that he was weak from hunger he turned his thoughts to death. He thought again: Since they mentioned burial, that means there is a dead person there. If so, if there is a dead person there, why isn't the beadle calling, Come out and accompany the dead? His thoughts began to devolve from person to person. He was alarmed lest someone who owed him money had died.

The thoughts that did him ill now turned kinder to him, for the idea came to mind that no person had died, for had a person died, they would have poured out water, and the beadle would be summoning people to the funeral. If so, what had died? A firstborn beast had died, which had to be buried, as is the law for a firstborn animal that dies. In any event, Fishl was somewhat puzzled as to why it had died at his house and not elsewhere. In any event, it had done a good deed in dying, for the city was released from its mischief. That it died at his house was a coincidence.

Although Fishl said that it was by chance, his mind was nevertheless disturbed, lest the animal had purposely chosen to die at his house, as in the story of the ewe and the old man.

What is the story of the ewe and the old man? It happened

in our city that when the flock went out to graze every day, one ewe would leave the rest and go and stand before a certain house and bleat. One day the owner of the house fell ill. The ewe came and bleated. Every day its voice was thin, but this day its voice was strong. Every day its voice was short, and this day its voice was long. People saw that the patient's face was changing because of his great suffering, for his heart was tormenting him because of his misdeeds, and his torments were etching themselves in his face. They believed that his face had changed because of his pains, and were he to sleep without disturbance, his torments would abate. They went out to drive away the ewe, but it would not move. They hit it with a stick, and it would not move. That day a soothsayer came to town. He heard and said, "You are struggling to drive it away in vain." "Why?" He said, "I shall tell you a story. There were two friends in the town. One fell ill and was about to die. At the time of his death he deposited a purse full of coins in his friend's hands and said to him, 'My daughter is young and does not know how to keep money. Keep these coins for her until she reaches maturity. And when she finds a good match, give her her coins as a dowry.' One man took the coins and the other turned his face to the wall and died. The orphan girl was close to maturity, and the holder of the deposit did not deliver the coins to her, but he buried them for himself under the threshold of his house. He said, 'No one was present when the coins were transferred. If I don't deliver them to the dead man's daughter, no one will claim them.' No one was present when the orphan girl's coins were transferred. Just a creature of the Holy One, blessed be He, was present to see and to hear. It was a ewe from the flock. And when the orphan girl reached maturity, the ewe pitied her and came to bleat and remind the man that the time had come for him to keep his word to his dead friend and return the money that the orphan girl's father had deposited with him for a dowry. As long as he doesn't return the orphan girl's money, the ewe won't leave the threshold of his house." They went and asked the dying man, "The money that your friend deposited with you—where is it?" He did not manage to tell them before he died. And the ewe died too. They sought to remove its body from the house, but they could not. The miracle worker said to them, "Dig beneath it and remove it with the earth." They dug and found a purse full of coins. They went and handed the coins over to the rabbi for the orphan girl. The ewe relinquished its place and they buried it.

Fishl began to fear that the ram had died in front of his house to remind him of some sin. He scrutinized his deeds and could find nothing in himself except that once he had lent someone money in his hour of need and he had forgotten to remind him that the loan was subject to the permitted form of interest. He began to add up how much interest he had received. His presence of mind returned immediately, and he cleared a way for himself to his house.

13
A Homily on Reincarnation and the Conclusion

Upon entering his house he saw a kind of dirty creature that gave off the smell of a fish lying on the floor, and on it was some object that would not have been recognizable as a tefillah were it not for its straps. Fishl shouted a great shout, "Oy, my fish!" He shouted a second shout, "Oy, my tefillah!"

The fish was squashed and spotted. Fishl's face, which Bezalel Moshe had drawn with chalk on the fish's skin, had already been effaced by the damp skin and nothing remained of it but the dirtiest dirt. Stranger than that was the tefillah. Until it landed on the fish's head, it had been yellow. Once it had sat on the fish's head, the color of the chalk with which Bezalel Moshe had drawn Fishl's face had clung to it and blackened it.

Before Fishl was freed of one fear, he saw that his head tefillah had been thrown down on the ground. Grief seized him, and he feared that the fish, in revenge, had thrown his head tefillah on the ground to force him to fast until after evening prayers to delay his enjoyment. He grew furious at that ingrate: had he not bought the fish from the fisherman, it would have descended into the priest's belly without a benediction. In his great anger a fit of apoplexy gripped him.

After stripping off his clothes and letting his blood, they found the arm tefillah on his upper arm and stood in astonishment. Could it be that a man with a brain in his skull would put on the arm tefillah but not the head tefillah? Before they could resolve the matter of Fishl, they were perplexed by the matter of the fish. For never in their lives had they heard that you could catch tefillin-laying fish in the Strypa, and even the most absolute of fish eaters in Buczacz said, "Never in our lives have we seen a fish crowned with tefillin."

There was in our city a research society called The Sons of Chance, because they used to say that everything happened by chance. For example, if Reuben ate bread, it was by chance that Reuben had found bread to eat—otherwise why is it that others seek bread but do not find it? Thus it was by chance that the fish found a tefillah. How? For example, a Jew had fallen into the river, and his tefillin tumbled out of his baggage, and the head tefillah caught on the fish's head. No chance event transcends its simple meaning; it is a happenstance like any other.

However, you would do well to know that opposing them there was an elite circle in our city concerned with the wisdom of truth; some of its members met during the ten fateful days between Rosh Hashanah and Yom Kippur, and others regularly after midnight penitential prayers, both in deepest seclusion. They heard the story of the fish and said what they said, but they, too—that is, the sages of truth—failed to discover the truth. However, from their words we have learned some of the secrets of Creation, including information about the reincarnation of souls. Some of what the mind can grasp, I shall reveal to you.

We have learned in mystical works that there are seventy souls, which are reincarnated in several animals, and they are called the Sign of the Lion, the Sign of the Ox, the Sign of the Eagle, the Sign of the Virgin, the Sign of the Scorpion, the Sign of the Ram. For we have found that the Twelve Tribes are compared to animals: Judah to the Lion—"A lion's cub is Judah"; Joseph to the firstborn ox; Issachar to a strong ass; "Dan shall be a serpent"; "Benjamin is a ravenous wolf." Clearly the whole secret of reincarnation is that the evil impulse alters everyone according to his deeds, and some are like a lion, a serpent, a donkey.

If so, why are saintly people reincarnated as fish? Because a fish's entire life is in water, and water is a place of purification. When they are removed from the water, their life ceases. Similarly, the righteous live all their lives in purity. Furthermore, the eyes of the saintly are open to their deeds just like fish, who have no lids on their eyes, which are always open; and through the merit of the righteous the Eye on high is ever open upon us for good. Also, the righteous are scrupulous not to be gripped by sins, but we are like fish caught in a net. Another thing: the righteous always pour out their hearts in repentance like water before the Lord, which is how the Targum translated the verse "And they drew water and poured it out."

We have also learned which are the fish in which the souls of the righteous are reincarnated; and what is the fate of those who make a show of righteousness but are not righteous—whether they are also reincarnated as fish; and what is the fate of those whom the world sees as righteous but are neither righteous nor evil.

Know that there are three classes: one consists of utter saints; one of those who pretend to be righteous and are neither righteous nor wicked; and one of the utterly wicked who pretend to be saintly. Absolute saints are reincarnated as kosher fish. The righteous who are neither saintly nor wicked are reincarnated as fish whose kashrut is debatable, for in some places they are permitted and in some places they are absolutely forbidden. And those who pretend to be righteous and are utterly wicked are reincarnated as non-kosher fish, since they are many and multiply and are fruitful like the fish, and they send forth progeny who are similar to them. Therefore the non-kosher fish are more plentiful than the kosher ones. They—that is, those evildoers whose countenance is saintly—are acolytes of Dagon, the Philistine god, who from his waist down was in the form of a fish and from his waist up was in the form of a man. Job prayed concerning them: "Let them curse it who curse the day, who are ready to rouse the Leviathan," which Rashi of blessed memory interpreted to mean: "To be childless in their joining together, to isolate their company from the society of man and wife, with no children."

We have other dread and marvelous secrets such as the reason why a fish has the merit of being eaten on the Sabbath and festivals. Moreover, there is a fish that has the merit of being eaten on the eve of Yom Kippur and a fish that is eaten at the Purim banquet, and there is a fish that is placed on the table of absolute saints, and there is a fish that descends into the belly of the utterly wicked. That is why some are cooked in vinegar and, in contrast, some are cooked in sugar. And also why it is that there is a fish we eat on the first day of the festival and one that we eat on the second day. Most profound are these matters, and I shall reveal only the tiniest bit here: a righteous man who possesses the sanctity of the Land of Israel has the merit of being reincarnated as a fish that we eat on the first day of the festival, and the soul of a righteous man who does not possess the sanctity of the Land of Israel is reincarnated in a fish that we eat on the second day. This is the secret of the saying of the rabbis of blessed memory: the second day compared to the first day is like an ordinary day.

Why did they not ask Fishl what the reason was for his wearing the arm tefillah and why his head tefillah was on the fish? In truth, they did ask him, but just as a fish does not answer, so, too, Fishl did not answer, because his tongue, may the Merciful One preserve us, was taken from him and he became mute.

I do not know what the end of the fish was. Fishl's end was thus: from then on he grew ever weaker until he died. But some say this is not so, that he regained his vigor, and that he even grew stronger, but on the Sabbath of Hanukkah, which was also the New Moon, between one pudding and another, he suffered a stroke once again and gave up the ghost. I do not know whether he died between the Sabbath pudding and the Hanukkah pudding, or whether he died between the Hanukkah pudding and the New Moon pudding. And, as you know, what is not clear to me, I do not say.

After he died his daughters built a great monument on his tomb, to honor the man lying beneath it. Since Fishl's Hebrew name was Ephraim, who was blessed with the phrase "And they shall abound

like fish"—the fish who are fruitful and multiply, and the evil eye
has no power over them—and since he was born in Adar, the month
of the constellation Pisces, the stonecarver carved a pair of fish on
his grave. Such fine-looking fish you will not find on the graves of
other Fishls or others born in the month of Adar, because the stonecarver used the orphan Bezalel Moshe to draw the form of the fish
on the stone before carving them. Since before they carve letters or
forms, stonecarvers customarily draw them on the stone, and since
Bezalel Moshe became a specialist in the form of fish, having examined so intently that fish which Fishl had sent with him, he drew
the fish well.

Years went by and the monument sank into the earth. Not
only do the living finish beneath the earth, so, too, do the dead, and
so, too, the things we fashion in their memory. Some people have
the merit of having their monuments stand for one generation, and
other monuments stand for two. In the end they gradually sink until
they are swallowed in the earth. So, too, Fishl Karp's monument sank
and was swallowed in the earth, but its tip did not sink. One can still
see a pair of fish there. In another city people would say that a fish is
buried there, and they would make up alarming stories, such as that
once, while a fish was being prepared for the Sabbath, it raised its
head and called out, "Remember the Sabbath day and keep it holy."
So it was known that the soul of a Sabbath observer had been reincarnated in it, and the rabbi ordered it to be buried in the cemetery. In
Buczacz people would not tell such a story. Just as Buczacz is full of
Torah, so, too, is it full of wisdom, and it does not like wonder tales
that are not consistent with nature. Buczacz likes things as they really
happen, and just as they happened, so does Buczacz tell them.

And since I was born in Buczacz and raised in Buczacz, mine
are the ways of Buczacz, and I tell nothing but the truth. For I say
that nothing is finer than truth, since aside from being beautiful in
itself, it also teaches men wisdom. What does the story of Fishl Karp
teach? That if you are going to pray, do not set your eyes upon meat
and fish and other delicacies, but let your path be holy. Lest you say
that Fishl is one matter and you are another, He knows that if you are
not avid in the pursuit of meat and fish, you are avid for other things.

The question of which is better is still open. We recite a blessing on fish and meat, both before and after eating them. Which of your other desires merits a blessing? May all our actions be for a blessing.

Translated by Jeffrey M. Green

Stories of Germany

The involvement of Jews in German life and their identification with German culture constitute a rich history, a history that is reflected in and refracted through Agnon's fiction. From his eastern European beginnings and a six-year sojourn in Palestine, Agnon came to Germany and immersed himself in the intellectual currents of both secular European and Jewish culture. The stories set in Germany convey keen absorption in the diverse and often conflicting styles of the people and the ideas he encountered.

These stories depict periods and settings that range from medieval Jewish communities in Germany to the period immediately following the Holocaust. Agnon makes us feel the paradoxical identification of Jews with German culture and society, as well as the inevitable strangeness of Jews within a social world that never completely accepted them. Through a variety of narrative modes from the realistic to the fantastic, these stories engage us in a complex cultural fabric. It is worth taking note of their assimilated milieu, because it runs counter to the general mold of Agnon's fiction. A number of these tales can be read as explorations of the realm of the senses and sentiments in a world emptied of sacred time, space, and meaning.

"The Doctor's Divorce" (1941) offers us the psychological portrait of a relationship as it takes shape and then dissolves. The narrative dramatizes the mind of the doctor whose desires and jealousies involve him in fantasies of a third person, his wife's former lover. This long story belongs to the domain of Agnon's psychological fiction, a literary terrain that includes "In the Prime of Her Life" (1923) and "Metamorphosis" (1941). Agnon demonstrates his skill at fashioning a central character whose point of view shapes the world of the fiction, however distorted it may be by passion or jealousy. If one is to question the reliability of the protagonist's perspective, then one must assemble clues suggestive of an alternative view of circumstances and events. Like other modernist texts, among them the stories of Joyce's *Dubliners*, "The Doctor's Divorce" requires a level of suspicious interest combined with sympathetic involvement in the dilemma of the protagonist.

Through the eyes of the narrator, the unnamed doctor, we first encounter the woman who is the object of men's desire. Set in Vienna, this story opens with a description of the "blonde nurse who was loved by everyone." The doctor's account of his own response suggests that his desire is first aroused by the sight of the nurse's devotion to the patients in the hospital: "From the moment I saw her eyes, I was just like the rest of the patients." (His attraction is reminiscent of the infatuation of Herbst, the middle-aged protagonist of the novel *Shira*, with the nurse Shira; not the least of Shira's attractions is her response to human suffering.)

The doctor's account of his infatuation with the nurse Dinah contains within it the seeds of the tormenting jealousy that will destroy the relationship, as he demonstrates repeatedly the role that others play in his attraction to her. Critic Dan Miron notes that the doctor is from eastern Europe, while Dinah is from a well-off Viennese family, an observation that underscores the dimension of cultural difference in this narrative of jealousy and desire. We come to realize that the presence of an invisible third party, most obviously Dinah's former lover, forms an integral part of the relationship of the doctor and his wife. "The Doctor's Divorce" creates a psychological drama through the consciousness of its central character. We can work through the character's thoughts and responses to reach a level of insight and understanding that the character himself never achieves.

"On the Road," which was written in 1944, appeared as part of *The Book of Deeds* and it shares with the stories of that collection its focus on a first-person narrator, one who finds himself lost on the eve of a holy day and is keenly aware of his disconnection from any form of Jewish community. (The translation that appears here was abridged, with Agnon's permission, for its original publication in *Twenty-One Stories*.) The story takes its narrator through a series of encounters with a group of Jews in ceremonial dress, who speak to him in archaic German and recount to him the slaughter that destroyed the surrounding Jewish communities. In the company of these Jews, the narrator visits settings that bear the signs of communal martyrdom. His experience is dreamlike: he seems simultaneously to remain asleep in the cleft of a rock and to move his limbs as he joins the ghostly company on their walk "to the house of God." The effect is to amalgamate catastrophic events in the remote past and the destruction of German Jewry in the twentieth century.

Agnon's protagonist, Samuel Joseph the son of Shalom Mordecai the Levite, joins this mysterious group of elderly Jews to complete the quorum of ten needed for public prayer. In doing so, he takes the place of one of their number, Samuel Levi, who has just died. We have here one of those instances in which Agnon sets up his own form of identity play, using the names of the living and the dead, his own and his father's.

Ghostly confusions give way to something of the atmosphere of a folktale as the narrator steps into the community like a lost son who has found his place. The particular customs of this community have been shaped by their shared history. The narrator describes the lives of these people with a combination of affectionate understanding and anthropological observation, as he notes the variations in their liturgy that reflect the massacres they endured. When the narrator leaves the community, the Ten Days of Repentance between the New Year and the Day of Atonement have passed. Through his journey real or imagined—he has absorbed the lived experience of a community.

"On the Road" ends with the narrator's concluding note of thanks to the Almighty who has "restored me to my place" in the Land of Israel. The concept of "my place" now includes within it the history of the community that vanished into the mist as he left it. That history displaces the emphasis from the narrator to the ghostly communities of Germany's past. The story evokes their traditions and beliefs with an exquisite clarity, all the more haunting in light of events in Germany at the time of the story's composition in the 1940s.

Studded with German names for people and places, "Between Two Towns" (1946) offers the reader poignant social comedy in a symmetrically constructed tale of two Jewish communities in neighboring towns in Germany. Here Agnon crafts a story of family separation in time of war, conveying to us the patriotism of Germany's Jews in World War I, as well as the strength of their communal practices. Never questioning their place in the larger society, these characters go through their daily lives. The narrator of the story takes a delicately pious tone as he notes that God has granted the residents of Katzenau "a resting place among the nations from which to serve Him and to earn a livelihood, be it meager or ample." Yes, the narrator acknowledges, in the past there may have been "countless edicts, attacks, murders, expulsions," but that time has passed and now "Israel is no longer despised because of matters of faith." The narrator's wish to believe that good times have arrived at last supplies a poignant irony that makes us aware of the limited horizon of the world of this story.

Agnon has created for us a third-person narrator who is totally absorbed in the daily lives of the inhabitants of the two towns named Katzenau and who is blissfully ignorant of any Final Solution to come in the lives of German Jewry. It is we as readers who cannot escape the burden of a historical consciousness that casts a shadow over the world of the fiction. "Between Two Towns" bears comparison in this respect to the as-yet-untranslated novella "Ad Hena" (Until Now). Both are set in the Germany of World War I and, in both, the horizon of the narrative is limited to the vision of the characters themselves. This limitation of vision jars us; we cannot help but supply the larger historical perspective that the narrative so resolutely excludes. The effect is to heighten our sense of a terrible gap between the complacency and innocence of German Jews and their ultimate fate.

"Between Two Towns" takes a gently ironic view of its characters, in particular the schoolteacher who repays the hospitality of the townspeople with a pedantic correction of their practices that introduces a measure of suffering into their lives. Agnon has recreated for us here the daily lives of communities, with a full portrayal of the intricacies of their attachments and their idiosyncrasies. These are habits and practices that develop over time in relation to a setting, here the rustic German milieu of mountains, forests, and waters. This story might be read as elegiac or ironic in light of subsequent history. Nevertheless, that dimension does not detract from the full absorption of Agnon's narrative energies in the substance of the lives that he creates.

The Doctor's Divorce

When I joined the staff of the hospital, I discovered there a blonde nurse who was loved by everyone and whose praise was on the lips of all the patients. As soon as they heard her footsteps, they would sit up in bed and stretch their arms out toward her as an only son reaches for his mother, and each one of them would call, "Nurse, nurse, come to me." Even the ill-tempered kind who find all the world provoking—as soon as she appeared, the frown lines in their faces faded, their anger dissolved, and they were ready to do whatever she ordered. Not that it was her way to give orders: the smile that illuminated her face was enough to make patients obey her. In addition to her smile, there were her eyes, a kind of blue-black; everyone she looked at felt as if he were the most important thing in the world. Once I asked myself where such power comes from. From the moment I saw her eyes, I was just like the rest of the patients. And she had no special intentions toward me, nor toward anybody in particular. That smile on her lips, however, and that blue-black in her eyes had the further distinction of doing on their own more than their mistress intended.

One indication of the degree of affection in which she was generally held was the fact that even her fellow nurses liked her and were friendly toward her. And the head nurse, a woman of about forty, well born, thin and wan as vinegar, who hated everyone, patients and doctors alike, with the possible exception of black coffee and salted cakes and her lap dog—even she was favorably disposed in this case. Such a woman, who couldn't look at a girl without imagining her half wasted away, showed special kindness to this nurse. And one hardly need mention my fellow doctors. Every doctor with whom she happened to work thanked his stars. Even our professor, accustomed as he was to concern himself less with the suffering of the sick than with the orderliness of their beds, made no fuss if he found her sitting on a patient's bed. This old man, the master of so many disciples and the discoverer of cures for several diseases, died in a concentration camp where a Nazi trooper tormented him daily by forcing him to go through exercises. One day the trooper ordered him to lie flat on his belly with arms and legs outstretched, and as soon as he was down, he was commanded to get up. As he was not quick about it, the trooper trampled him with his cleated boots until the old man's thumbnails were mutilated. He contracted blood poisoning and died.

What more can I say? I took a liking to this girl just as everyone else did. But I can add that she also took a liking to me. And though any man could say as much, others did not dare while I dared, and so I married her.

2

This is how it came about. One afternoon, as I was leaving the dining hall, I ran into Dinah. I said to her, "Are you busy, nurse?"

"No, I'm not busy."

"What makes today so special?"

"Today is my day off from the hospital."

"And how are you celebrating your day off?"

"I haven't yet considered the matter."

"Would you allow me to give you some advice?"

"Please do, doctor."

"But only if I am paid for the advice. Nowadays you don't get something for nothing."

She looked at me and laughed. I continued, "I have one good piece of advice which is actually two—that we go to the Prater and that we go to the opera. And if we hurry, we can stop first at a cafe. Do you agree, nurse?" She nodded yes good-humoredly.

"When shall we go?" I asked.

"Whenever the doctor wants."

"I'll take care of what I have to as soon as possible and I'll be right over."

"Whenever you come, you'll find me ready."

She went to her room and I to my responsibilities. A little while later, when I arrived to pick her up, I discovered that she had changed clothes. All at once she seemed a new person to me, and with the metamorphosis her charm was doubled, for she had both the charm I felt in her when she was in uniform and that which was lent her by the new clothes. I sat in her room and looked at the flowers on the table and by the bed, and after asking her whether she knew their names, I recited the name of each flower, in German and in Latin. But I quickly became apprehensive that a serious patient might be brought in and I would be paged. I got up from my seat and urged that we leave at once. I saw she was disturbed.

"Is something bothering you?" I asked.

"I thought you'd have something to eat."

"Right now, let's go, and if you are still so kindly disposed toward me, I'll come back to enjoy everything you give me, and I'll even ask for more."

"May I count on that?"

"I've already given you my word. Not only that, but, as I said, I'll ask for more."

As we left the hospital court, I said to the doorman, "You see this nurse? I'm taking her away from here." The doorman looked at us benevolently and said, "More power to you, doctor. More power to you, nurse."

*   *   *

We walked to the trolley stop. A trolley came along, but turned out to be full. The next one that arrived we thought we would be able to take. Dinah got onto the car. When I tried to climb up after her, the conductor called out, "No more room." She came down and waited with me for another car. At that point I commented to myself, Some people say that one shouldn't worry about a trolley or a girl that has gone because others will soon come along. But those who think that are fools. As far as the girl is concerned, can one find another girl like Dinah? And as to the trolley, I regretted every delay.

Along came a suburban trolley. Since its cars were new and spacious and empty of passengers, we got on. Suddenly (or, according to the clock, after a while), the trolley reached the end of the line and we found ourselves standing in a lovely place filled with gardens, where the houses were few.

We crossed the street talking about the hospital and the patients and the head nurse and the professor, who had instituted a fast once a week for all patients with kidney ailments because someone with kidney pains had fasted on the Day of Atonement and afterward there was no albumen in his urine. Then we mentioned all the cripples the war had produced, and we were pleased by the setting for our walk because there were no cripples around. I threw up my arms suddenly and said, "Let's forget about the hospital and cripples and speak about more pleasant things." She agreed with me, even though from her expression one could tell she was concerned that we might not find any other subject for conversation.

Children were playing. They saw us and began to whisper to each other. "Do you know, Fraulein," I asked Dinah, "what the children are talking about? They are talking about us."—"Perhaps." "Do you know what they're saying?" I went on. "They're saying, 'The two of them are bride and groom.'" Her face reddened as she answered, "Perhaps that's what they are saying."

"You mean you don't object to it?"

"To what?"

"To what the children are saying."

"Why should I care?"

"And if it were true, what would you say?"

"If what were true?"

I summoned my courage and answered, "If what the children say were true, I mean, that you and I belong together." She laughed and looked at me. I took her hand and said, "Give me the other one, too." She gave me her hand. I bent over and kissed both her hands, then looked at her. Her face became still redder. "There is a proverb," I told her, "that truth is with children and fools. We've already heard what the children say, and now listen to what a fool has to say, I mean, myself, for I have been touched with wisdom."

I stuttered and went on, "Listen, Dinah..." I had hardly begun to say all that was in my heart before I found myself a man more fortunate than all others.

3

Never was there a better time in my life than the period of our engagement. If it had been my opinion that marriage exists only because a man needs a woman and a woman a man, I now came to realize that there is no higher need than that one. At the same time, I began to understand why the poets felt it necessary to write love poems, despite the fact that I would have no part of them or their poems, because they wrote about other women and not about Dinah. Often I would sit and wonder, How many nurses there are in the hospital; how many women in the world; and I am concerned with one girl alone, who absorbs all my thoughts. As soon as I saw her again, I would say to myself, The doctor must have lost his wits to put her in the same category as other women. And my feelings toward her were reciprocated. But that blue-black in her eyes darkened like a cloud about to burst.

Once I asked her. She fixed her eyes on me without answering. I repeated my question. She pressed against me and said, "You don't know how precious you are to me and how much I love you." And a smile spread across her melancholy lips, that smile which drove me wild with its sweetness and its sorrow.

I asked myself, If she loves me, what reason could there be for this sadness? Perhaps her family is poor. But she said they were well-to-do. Perhaps she had promised to marry someone else. But she told me she was completely free. I began to pester her about it. She showed me still more affection, and she remained silent.

Nevertheless, I began to investigate her relatives. Perhaps they were rich but had been impoverished and she felt bad about them. I discovered that some of them were industrialists and some were people of distinction in other fields, and they all made comfortable livings,

I grew proud. I, a poor boy, the son of a lowly tinsmith, became fastidious about my dress, even though she paid no attention to clothes, unless I asked her to look at them. My love for her grew still greater. This was beyond all logic, for, to begin with, I had given her all my love. And she, too, gave me all her love. But her love had a touch of sadness in it which injected into my happiness a drop of gall.

This drop worked its way into all my limbs. I would ponder, What is this sadness? Is that what love is supposed to be like? I continued to beleaguer her with questions. She promised an answer but persisted in her evasiveness. When I reminded her of her promise, she took my hand in hers and said, "Let's be happy, darling, let's be happy and not disturb our happiness." And she sighed in a way that broke my heart. I asked her, "Dinah, what are you sighing about?" She smiled and answered through her tears, "Please, darling, don't say anything more." I was silent and asked no more questions. But my mind was not at ease. And I still awaited the time when she would agree to tell me what it was all about.

4

One afternoon I stopped in to see her. At that hour she was free from her work with the patients and was sitting in her room sewing a new dress. I took the dress by the hem and let my hand glide over it. Then I lifted my eyes toward her. She looked straight into my eyes and said, "I was once involved with somebody else." She saw that I didn't realize what she meant, so she made her meaning more explicit. A chill ran through me and I went weak inside. I sat without saying a word. After a few moments I told her, "Such a thing would have never even occurred to me." Once I had spoken, I sat wondering and amazed, wondering over my own calmness and amazed at her for having done a thing so much beneath her. Nevertheless, I treated her just as before, as though she had in no way fallen in esteem. And, in fact, at that moment she had not fallen in my esteem and was as dear to me as always. Once she saw that, a smile appeared on her lips again. But her eyes were veiled, like someone moving out of one darkness into another.

I asked her, "Who was this fellow who left you without marrying you?" She evaded the question. "Don't you see, Dinah," I pursued, "that I bear no ill feelings toward you. It's only curiosity that leads me to ask such a question. So tell me, darling, who was he?" "What difference does it make to you what his name is?" Dinah asked. "Even so," I persisted, "I would like to know." She told me his name. "Is he a lecturer or a professor?" I asked. Dinah said, "He is an official." I reflected silently that important officials worked for her relatives, men of knowledge and scholars and inventors. Undoubtedly it was to the most important of them that she gave her heart. Actually, it made no difference who the man was to whom this woman more dear to me than all the world gave her love, but to delude myself I imagined that he was a great man, superior to all his fellows. "He's an official?" I said to her. "What is his job?" Dinah answered, "He is a clerk in the legislature." "I am amazed at you, Dinah," I told her, "that a minor official, a clerk, was able to sweep you off your feet like that. And, besides, he left you, which goes to show that he wasn't good enough for you in the first place." She lowered her eyes and was silent.

From then on I did not remind her of her past, just as I would not have reminded her what dress she had worn the day before. And if I thought of it, I banished the thought from my mind. And so we were married.

5

Our wedding was like most weddings in these times, private, without pomp and ceremony. For I had no family, with the possible exception of the relative who once hit my father in the eye. And Dinah, ever since she became close to me, had grown away from her relatives. During that period, moreover, it was not customary to have parties and public rejoicing. Governments came and governments went, and between one and the next there was panic and confusion, turmoil and dismay. People who one day were rulers the next day were chained in prisons or hiding in exile.

And so our wedding took place with neither relatives nor invited guests, except for a bare quorum summoned by the beadle, miserable creatures who an hour or two ago were called for a funeral and now were summoned for my wedding. How pitiful were their borrowed clothes, how comic their towering high hats, how audacious their greedy eyes that looked forward to the conclusion of the ceremony when they could go into a bar with the money they had gotten through my wedding. I was in high spirits, and as strange as the thing seemed to me, my joy was not diminished. Let others be led under the bridal canopy by renowned and wealthy wedding guests. I would be married in the presence of poor people who, with what they would earn for their trouble, could buy bread. The children we would have wouldn't ask me, "Father, who was at your wedding?" just as I never asked my father who was at his wedding.

I put my hand in my pocket and pulled out several shillings which I handed to the beadle to give to the men over and above the agreed price. The beadle took the money and said nothing. I was afraid they would overwhelm me with thanks and praise, and I prepared myself to demur modestly. But not one of them came up to me. Instead, one fellow bent over, leaning on his cane, another stretched himself in order to appear tall, and a third looked at the bride in a way that was not decent. I asked the beadle about him. "*That one*, the beadle replied, and he bore down emphatically on the "th" sound, "that one was an official who got fired." I nodded and said, "Well, well," as though with two well's I had concluded all the fellow's affairs. Mean while, the beadle chose four of his quorum, put a pole in the hand of each of the four, stretched a canopy over the poles, and, in doing that, pushed one man who bent forward and thus brought the canopy tumbling down.

Afterward, while standing under the bridal canopy, I recalled the story of a man whose mistress forced him to marry her. He went and gathered for the ceremony all her lovers who had lived with her before her marriage, both to remind her of her shame and to punish himself for agreeing to marry such a woman. What a contemptible fellow and what a contemptible act! Yet I found that man to my liking, and I thought well of what he had done. And when the rabbi stood and read the marriage contract, I looked at the wedding guests and tried to imagine what the woman was like and what her lovers were like at that moment. And in the same way, just before, when my wife put out her finger for the wedding ring and I said to her, "Behold thou art consecrated unto me," I knew without anyone's telling me what that man was like at that moment.

6

After the wedding we left for a certain village to spend our honeymoon. I won't tell you everything that happened to us on the way and in the station and on the train; and, accordingly, I won't describe every mountain and hill we saw, nor the brooks and springs in the valleys and mountains, as tellers of tales are accustomed to do when they set about describing the trip of a bride and groom. Undoubtedly there were mountains and hills and springs and brooks, and several things did happen to us on the way, but everything else has escaped me and been forgotten because of one incident which occurred on the first night. If you're not tired yet, I'll tell you about it.

We arrived at the village and registered at a little hotel situated among gardens and surrounded by mountains and rivers. We had supper and went up to the room that the hotel had set aside for us, for I had telegraphed our reservation before the wedding. Examining the room, my wife let her eyes dwell on the red roses that had been put there. "Who was so nice," I said jokingly, "to send us these lovely roses?" "Who?" asked my wife with genuine wonder, as though she thought there were someone here besides the hotel people who knew about us. "In any case," I said, "I'm taking them away, because their fragrance will make it hard to sleep. Or perhaps we should leave them in honor of the occasion." "Oh, yes," my wife answered after me in the voice of a person who speaks without hearing his own words. I said to her, "And don't you want to smell them?"—"Oh, yes, I want to." But she forgot to smell them. This forgetfulness was strange for Dinah, who loved flowers so much. I reminded her that she hadn't yet smelled the flowers. She bent her head over them. "Why are you bending down," I asked her, "when you can hold them up to you?" She looked at me as though she had just heard something novel. The blue-black in her eyes darkened, and she said, "You are very observant, my darling." I gave her a long kiss; then with closed eyes I said to her, "Now, Dinah, we are alone."

She stood up and took off her clothes with great deliberation, and began to fix her hair. As she was doing that, she sat down, bending her head over the table. I leaned over to see why she was taking so long, and I saw that she was reading a little pamphlet of the kind one finds in Catholic villages. The title was *Wait for Your Lord in Every Hour That He May Come.*

I took her chin in my hand and said to her, "You don't have to wait, your lord has already come," and I pressed my mouth against hers. She lifted her eyes sadly and laid the pamphlet aside. I took her in my arms, put her in bed, and turned the lamp wick down.

The flowers gave off their fragrance and a sweet stillness surrounded me. Suddenly I heard the sound of footsteps in the room next to ours. I forced the sound out of my mind and refused to pay attention to it, for what difference did it make to me whether or not there was someone there. I didn't know him and he didn't know us. And if he did know us, we had a wedding and were properly married. I embraced my wife with great love and was happy beyond limit with her, for I knew she was entirely mine.

With Dinah still in my arms, I strained attentively to make out whether that fellow's footsteps had stopped, but I heard him still pacing back and forth. His footsteps drove me to distraction: a strange idea now occurred to me, that this was the clerk my wife had known before her marriage. I was horror-stricken at the thought, and I had to bite my lip to prevent myself from cursing out loud. My wife took notice.

"What's wrong, sweetheart?"

"Nothing, nothing."

"I see something's troubling you."

"I've already told you nothing is."

"Then I must have been mistaken."

I lost my head and said to her, "You were not mistaken."

"What is it, then?"

I told her.

She began to sob.

"Why are you crying?" I said.

She swallowed her tears and answered, "Open the door and the windows and tell the whole world of my depravity."

I was ashamed of what I had said, and I tried to mollify her. She listened to me and we made peace.

7

From then on that man was never out of my sight, whether my wife was present or not. If I sat by myself, I thought about him, and if I talked with my wife, I mentioned him. If I saw a flower, I was reminded of the red roses, and if I saw a red rose, I was reminded of him, suspecting that was the kind he used to give my wife. This, then, was the reason she refused to smell the roses on the first night, because she was ashamed in her husband's presence to smell the same kind of flowers that her lover used to bring her. When she cried, I would console her. But in the kiss of reconciliation I heard the echo of another kiss which someone else had given her. We are enlightened individuals, modern people, we seek freedom for ourselves and for all humanity, and in point of fact we are worse than the most die-hard reactionaries.

Thus passed the first year. When I wanted to be happy with my wife, I would remember the one who had spoiled my happiness, and I would sink into gloom. If she was happy, I asked myself, What makes her so happy? She must be thinking of that louse. As soon as I mentioned him to her, she would burst into tears. "What are you crying for?" I would say. "Is it so difficult for you to hear me talk against that louse?"

I knew that she had long since put all thought of him out of her mind, and if she thought of him at all, it was only negatively, for she had never really loved him. It was only his supreme audacity together with a transient moment of weakness in her that had led her to lose control and listen to his demands. But my understanding of the matter brought me no equanimity. I wanted to grasp his nature, what it was in him that had attracted this modest girl raised in a good family.

I began to search through her books in the hope of finding some sort of letter from him, for Dinah was in the habit of using her letters as bookmarks. I found nothing, however. Perhaps, I thought, she has deliberately hidden them somewhere else, inasmuch as I have already searched all her books and found nothing. I could not bring myself to examine her private things. And that made me still angrier, for I was pretending to be decent while my thoughts were contempt-ible. Since I had spoken with no one else about her past, I sought counsel in books and began to read love stories in order to understand the nature of women and their lovers. But the novels bored me, so I took to reading criminal documents. My friends noticed and jokingly asked me if I were planning to join the detective squad.

The second year brought no mitigation or relief. If a day passed with-out my mentioning him, I spoke about him twice as much on the following day. From all the anguish I caused her, my wife fell sick. I healed her with medicines and battered her heart with words. I would tell her, "All your illness comes to you only because of the man who ruined your life. Right now he's playing around with other women, and me he has left with an invalid wife to take care of." A thousand kinds of remorse would sting me for every single word, and a thousand times I repeated those words.

At that time I began visiting my wife's relatives together with her. And here a strange thing occurred. I've already mentioned that Dinah came of good family and that her relatives were distinguished people. In consequence, they and their homes gratified me, and I began to show favor to my wife because of her relatives. These people, the grandchildren of ghetto dwellers, had achieved wealth and honor: their wealth was an ornament to their honor and their honor an ornament to their wealth. For even during the war, when the great figures of the nation made money out of people's hunger, they kept their hands clean of all money coming from an evil source, and, accordingly, they refused to stuff themselves with food and accepted only their legitimate rations. Among their number were the kind of imposing men we used to imagine but never really saw with our own eyes. And then there were the women. You don't know Vienna, and if you know it, you know the sort of Jewish women the Gentiles wag their tongues over. If they could only see the women I saw, they would stop up their own mouths. Not that I care what the non-Jewish peoples say about us, for there is no hope that we'll ever please them, but inasmuch as I have mentioned their censure of us, I also mention their praise, because there is no higher praise for a brother than that which he receives from his sisters, through whom he is commended and extolled.

Before long I thought of my wife's relatives without connecting them with her, as though I and not she were their relation. I would think to myself, If they only knew how miserable I make her. And I was just about ready to unlock my lips and to open my heart to them. When I realized that my heart was urging me to talk, I stayed away from them, and they quite naturally stayed away from me. It's a big city and people are busy. If someone avoids his friends, they don't go hunting after him.

The third year my wife adopted a new mode of behavior. If I mentioned him, she ignored what I said, and if I connected his name with hers, she kept silent and didn't answer me, as though I weren't speaking about her. Infuriated, I would comment to myself, What a miserable woman not to take notice!

8

One summer day at twilight she and I were sitting at supper. It hadn't rained for a number of days, and the city was seething with heat. The water of the Danube showed green, and a dull odor floated over the city. The windows in our glass-enclosed porch gave off a sultry heat that exhausted body and soul. Since the day before, my shoulders had been aching, and now the pain was more intense. My head was heavy, my hair was dry. I ran my hand over my head and said to myself, I need a haircut. I looked across at my wife and saw that she was letting her hair grow long. Yet ever since women adopted men's haircuts, she always wore her hair close-cropped. I said to myself, My own head can't bear the weight of the little hair it has, and she's growing herself plumes like a peacock without even asking me if it looks nice that way. As a matter of fact, her hair looked lovely, but there was nothing lovely about my state of mind. I shoved my chair back from the table as though it were pushing against my stomach, and I ripped a piece of bread from the middle of the loaf and chewed it. It had been several days since I last mentioned him to her, and I hardly have to say that she made no mention of him to me. At that time, I was accustomed to saying very little to her, and when I did speak to her, I spoke without anger.

All at once I said to her, "There's something I've been thinking about." She nodded her head. "Oh, yes," she said, "I feel the same way."

"So you know what is in the secret corners of my heart. Then, go ahead, tell me what I was thinking of." In a whisper, she said, "Divorce."

As she spoke, she lifted her face to me and looked at me sadly. My heart was torn from its moorings, and I felt weak inside. I thought to myself, What a pitiful creature you are to treat your wife this way and cause her such pain. I lowered my voice and asked, "How do you know what is in my heart?"

"And what do you think I do with all my time? I sit and think about you, my dear."

The words leaped out of my mouth: I said to her, "Then you agree?"

She lifted her eyes to me. "You mean the divorce?"

I lowered my eyes and nodded in affirmation.

"Whether I want to or not," she said, "I agree to do whatever you ask, if it will only relieve your suffering."

"Even a divorce?"

"Even a divorce."

I was aware of all that I was losing. But the statement had already been made, and the desire to turn my wrath against myself drove me beyond reason. I clenched both hands and said angrily, "Well and good."

Several days passed, and I mentioned to her neither the divorce nor the one who had brought down ruin upon us. I told myself, Three years have passed since she became my wife. Perhaps the time has come to wipe out the memory of that affair. If she had been a widow or a divorcee when I married her, would there be anything I could have held against her? As things are, then, let me consider her as though she were a widow or a divorcee when I took her to be my wife.

And having reached this conclusion, I upbraided myself for every single day I had tormented her, and I resolved to be good to my wife. During that period I became a completely new person, and I began to feel an awakening of love as on the day I first met her. I was soon ready to conclude that everything is the result of man's will and desire: if he so wills it, he can introduce anger and hatred into his heart; if he wills it, he can live in peace with everyone. If this is so, I reasoned, what cause is there to stir up anger and bring evil upon ourselves when we are capable of doing good for ourselves and being happy? So I reasoned, that is, until something happened to me that set things back right where they were before.

9

What happened was this. One day a patient was brought to the hospital. I examined him and left him with the nurses to be washed and put to bed. In the evening I entered the ward to make my rounds. When I came to his bed, I saw his name on the card over his head, and I realized who he was.

What could I do? I'm a doctor, and I treated him. As a matter of fact, I gave him an extraordinary amount of care, so that all the other patients grew jealous of him and called him doctor's pet. And he really deserved the name, for whether he needed it or not, I treated him. I told the nurses that I had discovered in him a disease that hadn't been adequately studied yet, and that I wanted to investigate it myself. I left instructions for them to give him good food, and sometimes to add a glass of wine, so that he would get a little enjoyment out of his hospital stay. Further, I asked the nurses not to be too strict with him if he took certain liberties and didn't follow all the hospital regulations.

He lay in his hospital bed eating and drinking and enjoying all sorts of luxuries. And I came in to visit him and examine him again and again, asking him if he had a good night's sleep and if he was given all the food he wanted. I would order medication for him and praise his body to him, telling him that it would in all probability last to a ripe old age. He on his part listened with enjoyment and basked in pleasure before me like a worm. I told him, "If you're used to smoking, go ahead and smoke. I myself don't smoke, and if you ask me whether smoking is a good thing, I'll tell you it's bad and harmful to the body. But if you're used to smoking, I won't stop you." And in this way I gave him various special privileges, just so he would feel completely comfortable. At the same time I reflected: Over a man for whom I wouldn't waste so much as a word I am going to all this trouble, and it's all because of that business which is difficult to speak of and difficult to forget. Not only that, but I watch him and study him as though I could learn what rubbed off on him from

Dinah and what rubbed off on her from him—and from devoting so much attention to him, I was acquiring some of his gestures.

At first I kept the whole matter secret from my wife. But it burst forth when I tried to suppress it, and it told itself. My wife listened without the slightest sign of interest. On the surface, one would have thought that this was just what I wanted, but I was not satisfied, even though I realized that if she had responded differently I would certainly not have been pleased.

After some while he was cured and had recuperated, and it was high time for him to leave the hospital. I kept him day after day and ordered the nurses to give him the best of treatment, so that he would not be anxious to leave. And that was the period right after the war, when it was hard to get provisions for the sick, not to speak of the convalescent, and certainly not to speak of the healthy, so I gave him from my own food which the farmers used to bring me. He sat in the hospital eating and drinking and gladdening his heart, reading newspapers and strolling in the garden, playing with the patients and laughing with the nurses. He put on some weight and was healthier than the people who took care of him, so that it became impossible to keep him any longer in the hospital. I gave instructions that a proper final dinner be prepared for him, and I discharged him.

After the dinner, he came to say goodbye to me. I looked at the double chin he had developed. His eyes were embedded in fat, like those of a woman who has given up everything for the sake of eating and drinking. I stood by my desk rummaging through the papers on it as though I were looking for something I had lost. Then I took a stethoscope to examine him. As I was trying to appear busy, two nurses came in, one to ask me something and one to say goodbye to the doctor's pet. I pulled my head back suddenly, as though I had been reminded that someone was waiting for me, and I let out a brief exclamation of surprise, the way Dinah does when she sees that someone has been waiting for her. As I did that, I looked at the healthy patient with his double chin and I said to myself, You don't know who I am, but I know who you are. You are the man who brought ruin down on me and wrecked my wife's life. Anger surged within me, and I became so furious that my eyes ached.

He extended his hand to me in special deference and began to stutter words of thanks about my saving him from death and restoring him to life. I offered him my fingertips to shake, in an impolite and deprecatory manner, and immediately I wiped them on my white coat, as though I had touched a dead reptile. Then I turned my face away from him as from some disgusting thing, and I walked away. I sensed that the nurses were looking at me and knew the reason for my behavior, even though there were no grounds for such apprehension.

After a little while I went back to work, but my head and heart were not with me. I went up to the doctors' lounge and looked for a friend to take my place. I told him that I had been summoned to court to give testimony about a certain criminal, and that it was impossible to postpone the case. A nurse came and asked whether she should order a cab. "Certainly, nurse, certainly," I answered. While she went to the switchboard to telephone, I ran out of the hospital like someone who had gone berserk.

I passed by a bar and considered going in to drown my sorrows in drink, as embittered men are accustomed to say. I grew a bit calmer and told myself, Troubles come and go, your troubles will also pass. But I had only grown calm temporarily, and only to lose control again. I began walking. After an hour or so, I stopped and saw that I had gone all around myself and completed a circle around the same spot.

10

I came home and told my wife. She listened and said nothing. I was infuriated that she should sit there in silence, as if she had heard nothing of significance. I bowed my head over my chest the way he did when he stood before me to thank me, and, imitating his voice, I said, "I wish to thank you, doctor, for saving me from death and restoring me to life." And I told my wife, "That's the way his voice sounds and that's the way he stands," in order to show her how low he was, what a pitiful creature was the man whom she had preferred to me and to whom she had given her love before she knew me. My wife looked up at me as though the whole thing were not worth her while to care about. Rising, I scrutinized her face in the hope of finding some indication of joy over that good-for-nothing's recovery, but just as I had seen no signs of sorrow when I told her he was sick, I saw now not the slightest sign of joy over his recovery.

After two or three days, the experience lost its sting and no longer disturbed me. I treated patients, talked much with the nurses, and immediately after work went home to my wife. Sometimes I would ask her to read to me from one of her books, and she would agree. She read while I sat looking at her, thinking, This is the face that had the power to drive away the frowns and dissipate the anger of whoever saw it. And I would run my hand over my face in gratification as I continued to look at her. Sometimes we had a friend over for coffee or for supper. And once again we talked about everything people talk about, and once again I realized that there were things in the world other than woman trouble. Often now I climbed into bed at night with a feeling of contentment and gratification.

One night this fellow came to me in a dream: his face was sickly and yet just a little—just a little—likable. I was ashamed of myself for thinking evil of him, and I resolved to put an end to my anger against him. He bent down and said, "What do you want from me? Is the fact that she raped me any reason for you to have it in for me?"

* * *

The next night we had as dinner guests two of our friends, a married couple, whom we both particularly liked—him because of his admirable qualities, her because of her blue eyes filled with radiance, and because of her high forehead which deceived the eye into thinking that she was unusually intelligent, and because of the golden curls trembling on her head, and also because of her voice, the voice of a woman who suppresses her longings within her. We sat together some three hours without being aware of the time. He discussed the questions of the day, and she helped him with the radiance from her eyes.

After they left, I said to my wife, "Let me tell you a dream."

"A dream?" cried my wife in surprise, and fixed her eyes on me sorrowfully and repeated in a whisper, "A dream." For it was not my way to tell dreams, and it seems to me that all those years I had not dreamed at all.

"I had a dream," I told her. And as I said it, my heart suddenly quaked.

My wife sat down and looked into my face intently. I proceeded to tell her my dream. Her shoulders shook and her body began to tremble. She stretched out her arms all of a sudden and, placing them around my neck, she embraced me. I returned her embrace and we stood clinging together in love and affection and pity, while all that time this fellow never left my sight, and I could hear him saying, "Is the fact that she raped me any reason for you to have it in for me?"

I pushed my wife's arms away from my neck, and a terrible sadness welled up within me. I got into bed and thought over the whole affair quietly and calmly until I fell asleep.

The next day we got up and ate breakfast together. I looked over at my wife and saw that her face was the same as always. I thanked her in my heart for bearing no grudge against me over the night before. At that moment, I recalled all the trouble and suffering I had caused her since the day she married me, how time after time I drained her lifeblood and insulted her in every possible way, while she took everything in silence. My heart swelled with love and tenderness for this miserable soul whom I had tortured so much, and I resolved to be good to her. And so I was for one day, for two days, for three days.

II

And I was quite prepared to conclude that everything was being set right. In point of fact, nothing had been set right. From the very day

I made peace with myself, that peace was robbed from me through another means. My wife treated me as though I had become a stranger to her. Yet all the efforts I was making with her were for her sake. How this woman failed to take notice! But she did notice.

One day she said to me, "What a good thing it would be if I were dead!"

"Why do you say that?"

"Why, you ask?" And in the wrinkles around her lips there was visible a sort of smile which made my heart jump.

"Don't be a fool," I scolded her.

She sighed. "Ah, my dear, I am not a fool."

"Then I am a fool."

"No, you're not a fool either."

I raised my voice and challenged her. "Then what do you want from me?"

"What do I want?" she answered. "I want the same thing you want."

I brushed one palm off with the other and said, "There's nothing at all I want."

She looked into my face intently. "There's nothing at all you want. Then everything must be all right."

"All right?" I laughed scornfully.

"You see, my dear," she said, "that laugh does not sit well with me."

"What am I supposed to do, then?"

"Do what you've been wanting to do."

"Namely?"

"Namely, why should I repeat something you yourself know?"

"I'm afraid I don't know what that something is. But since you know, you can tell me."

She pronounced in a whisper, "Divorce."

I raised my voice as I answered. "You want to force me into giving you a divorce."

She nodded. "If you think it's proper for you to put it that way and say that I want to force you, then I agree."

"Meaning what?" I asked.

"Why do we have to repeat things when there's no call for it? Let us do what is written for us above."

In anger, I mocked her. "Even heaven is an open book for you, as you know what's written there. I am a doctor and I can only go by what my eyes see, while you, madam, you know what is written on high. Where did you pick up such knowledge, maybe from that louse?"

"Be still!" Dinah cried. "Please, be still!"

"You don't have to get so angry," I told her. "After all, what did I say?"

She rose, went to her room, and locked the door behind her.

I came to the door and asked her to open it for me, but she refused. "Look, I'm leaving," I said to her. "The whole house is yours, and you don't have to lock the door." When she still did not answer, I began to be afraid that she had taken sleeping pills and, God forbid, committed suicide. I began to beg and plead for her to open the door, but still she did not open. I peeked through the keyhole, my heart pounding me blow after blow, as though I were a murderer. Thus I stood before the locked door until evening came on and the walls darkened.

With darkness, she came out of her room, pale as a corpse. When I took her hands in mine, a deathly chill flowed out of them that made my own hands cold. She made no effort to pull her hands away from me, as though she had no feeling left in them.

I laid her down on her bed and calmed her with sedatives, nor did I move from her until she had dozed off. I looked at her face, a face innocent of any flaw, without the slightest blemish, and I said to myself, What a lovely world in which such a woman exists, and what difficult lives we have to live! I bent down in order to kiss her. She turned her head in sign of refusal. "Did you say something?" I asked. "No," she said, and I couldn't tell whether she was conscious of me or simply was talking in her sleep. Thoroughly disconcerted, I kept my distance from her. But I sat there all night long.

The next day I went to work and came back at noon. Whether out of prudence or for some other reason, I made no mention to her of what had happened the day before. She on her part did not speak of it either. So it was on the second day, so again on the third day. I was ready to conclude that matters were returning to their previous state. Yet I knew that though I might try to forget, she would not forget.

During that period her appearance became more vigorous and she changed some of her habits. Where she was accustomed to greet me as I came in the door, she no longer greeted me. Sometimes she would leave me and go off somewhere, and there were times when I came home and did not find her.

The anniversary of our engagement fell at that time. I said to her, "Let's celebrate and take a trip to the place we went to when we were first married."

"That's impossible."

"Why?"

"Because I have to go somewhere else."

"Pardon me, but where is it you are going?"

"There's a patient I'm taking care of."

"Why this all of a sudden?"

"Not everything a person does is all of a sudden. For a long time now I've felt that I ought to work and do something."

"And isn't it enough for you that I am working and doing something?"

"Once that was enough for me. Now it's not enough."

"Why not?"

"Why not? If you yourself don't know, I can't explain it to you."

"Is it such a complicated issue that it's difficult to explain?"

"It's not hard to explain, but I doubt if you would want to understand."

"Why are you doing it?"

"Because I want to earn my own living."

"Do you think you're not supported adequately in your own home, that you have to go look for a living elsewhere."

"Right now I'm being supported. Who knows what will be tomorrow?"

"Why all of a sudden such ideas?"

"I already told you that nothing happens all of a sudden."

"I don't know what you're talking about."

"You understand, all right, but you prefer to say, 'I don't understand.'"

I nodded my head in despair and said, "That's how it is, then."

"Really, that's how it is."

"This whole dialectic is beyond me."

"It's beyond you, and it's not particularly close to me. So it would be better if we kept still. You do what you have to do, and I'll do what I have to."

"What I do, I know. But I have no idea what it is you want to do."

"If you don't know now, you'll soon find out."

But her efforts did not succeed. And however they may have succeeded, she failed to make a penny out of them. She was caring for a paralyzed girl, the daughter of a poor widow, and she received no payment for her work. On the contrary, she helped the widow financially, and she even brought her flowers. At that time Dinah's strength drained from her as though she were sick, and she herself needed someone to take care of her instead of her caring for others. Once I asked her, "How long are you going to continue working with that sick girl?" She fixed her eyes on me and said, "Are you asking me as a doctor?"

"What difference does it make whether I ask as a doctor or as your husband?"

"If you ask as a doctor, I don't know what to tell you, and if you ask for other reasons, I see no need to answer."

I tried to act as if she were joking with me, so I laughed. She averted her face from me, and, leaving me where I was, went off. The laughter immediately died on my lips, nor has it yet returned.

It's just a mood, I told myself, and I can put up with it. Yet I knew that all my optimism was completely baseless. I recalled the first time she spoke to me about a divorce, and I remembered what she said: "Whether I want it or not, I am prepared to do whatever you ask, if only it will relieve your suffering—even a divorce." Now I thought, However you look at it, there's no way out for us except a divorce. As soon as this idea occurred to me, I dismissed it, as a man will dismiss something painful from his thoughts. But Dinah was right when she said we had to do what was written for us above. Before long I saw with my own eyes and I grasped with my own understanding what at first I had not seen and I had not grasped. At once I decided that I would grant Dinah the divorce. We had no children, for I had been apprehensive about begetting children for fear they would look like him. I arranged our affairs and gave her the divorce.

And so we parted from one another, the way people will part outwardly. But in my heart, my friend, the smile on her lips is still locked up, and that blue-black in her eyes, as on the day I first saw her. Sometimes at night I sit up in bed like those patients she used to take care of, and I stretch out both hands and call, "Nurse, nurse, come to me."

Translated by Robert Alter

On the Road

The train was lost among the mountains and could not find its way. All the travelers who were with me had got out. I remained alone. Apart from the guard and the driver of the train, not a soul was left. Suddenly the train had stopped and stood still, and I knew that I was done with the train and would have to go on foot among strange places and alien people whose language I did not know and with whose customs I was not familiar. Another day I would have had no regrets. On the contrary, I would have been pleased at the unexpected opportunity for a pleasant stroll. But that evening I was not pleased. It was the evening of the penitential hymn "Remember the Covenant," and next day was the New Year. How should I spend this sacred festival without public prayer and hearing the ram's horn? I got up and looked outside. The hills were silent, and all around was an awesome darkness.

The guard came up and said, "Yes, sir, the train has stopped and can't move." Seeing my distress, he took my satchel, put it on the seat, and went on, "Lay your head on your satchel, sir, and perhaps you will fall asleep and gather strength, for you have a long way

ahead." I nodded and said, "Many thanks, sir." I stretched myself out
on the seat and laid my head on my satchel.

Before daybreak the guard came back. He scratched his temples
and said, "We're far from any inhabited place, so I have to wake you,
sir, for if you want to get human company before nightfall you'll
have to hurry." I got up and took my staff and satchel, he showing
me whither to turn and where to go.

The dawn had risen and the stars had set. The mountains were
beginning to doff the covering of night, and the springs gleamed as
they emerged. The mountains raised their heads, and narrow paths
wound their way among them. The dew rested on them and the birds
pecked at the morning dew. I looked this way and that. Far and near,
mountains and rocks; near and far, not a place of habitation. The
road was long, and my feet were heavy, and the day was short, and
the hour was pressing. God knew when I would reach an inhabited
town and whether I would see a human face that day.

I do not know whether I followed the road the guard showed
me or strayed from it. In any case, the day passed and the sun soon
set. The mountains darkened, and awesome forms took shape in the
space of the world. There was still a trace of day, but night was drawing on: the day that belonged to a year that has passed and the night
that belonged to a new year. And between day and night, I stood,
a wayfarer, with my staff and my satchel, not knowing where to go
and where I would lay my head.

The night was overcast and the moon did not shine. The springs
still gleamed a little, but they too began to be covered. I looked this
way and that. The whole land was like one block of darkness. I went
into a cleft in the rock and laid myself down to sleep. The birds of
heaven nested above my head, and all around were the beasts of the
earth. The birds were already asleep and the beasts had not yet come
out. Silence reigned, the silence of mountain rocks at night. From
far and near came the sound of the spring waters, flowing as in a
land at peace.

I lie on the ground and look at the dark skies. This is the night
of the New Year, when all the multitudes of Israel stand in prayer,
and the women have already lit candles before nightfall in honor of

the day, so that they should enter the new year with light and joy. And here I lie in a dark country among the beasts of the earth, and if I reach an inhabited place tomorrow, I doubt if I will find a Jew there. Israel is like scattered sheep; wherever a Jew goes he finds Jews; but here all the communities have been destroyed and the Jews have not returned.

So I lay in the cleft of the rock and waited for morning. My feet moved off on their own and started walking. I reached a great park full of fine trees. I wanted to enter, but was afraid I might be rebuked by the wardens, who look askance at wayfarers. I entered—I do not know how—and they did not say a word. I walked from tree to tree and from flower bed to flower bed, until I was tired out, and fell down from the effort. Oh, those beautiful parks we see in dreams. They are larger than any parks in the world, and their fragrance is sweeter than all the sweet odors, and we walk in them without end or limit. What is the purpose of our walking in these parks? Only that in the end we should collapse in exhaustion? But the fragrance that clings to us is worth all that effort. This is the fragrance that refreshes our souls when we merely mention it.

The sound of my fall woke me, and I heard a man's voice. Since I knew that I was far from any inhabited place, I said to myself: I am dreaming; but since I longed to see a man I said to myself: Perhaps, after all, I am awake. I raised my eyes and saw two men, and then, behind them, two women. The morning mists hung below the mountains and the men and women were walking above the hills, above the mist.

I got up and went to meet them. Two more came and another two: those from behind the mountain and these from the lower slopes. And their wives came after them, two on this side and two on that, joining up and going on together, two by two. Their clothes were modest; they wore white gowns over their clothes, and white caps on their heads, with a band of silver, two fingers broad, surrounding the cap and tied at the back, and tallitot hanging over their shoulders, and belts over their clothes; they were distinguished by beard and sidelocks, and they had old, black books, festival or weekday prayer books, in their hands. Like the men, the women were clad in modest, humble clothes. Their heads were covered with white coifs, shaped like the Hebrew letter *kaf*, covering the head and the forehead and partially surrounding face and chin. I greeted them and they returned my greeting.

"Where do you come from, brothers, and where are you going?" I asked them. They pointed to the mountains and said, "We are going to the house of God," they said, pointing to the mountains. "And are there Jews here?" I said to them. "In days gone by," they replied, "all these places here were covered with sacred congregations, but because of our manifold sins and the malice of the Gentiles, all the congregations were burned and killed and destroyed and laid waste, and none were left but one Jew here and one there. On the three pilgrimage festivals—on the New Year and the Day of Atonement, and also at the New Moon of Sivan, which was the day of the great slaughter—we assemble and make a quorum, and recite the congregational prayers." They spoke an antique German, but the voice of Jacob somewhat sweetened the language. And their beautiful dark eyes gazed in grief and concern, like men who stand at sunset awaiting a tenth for the quorum.

We reached a ruined building of great stones. On the walls inside, there were visible signs of congealed blood, from the blood of the martyrs who slaughtered themselves, their wives and their sons and daughters, to prevent their falling into the hands of the accursed ones. And the smell of burning emanated from the ruin, for after the martyrs had slaughtered themselves, the accursed ones set fire to the synagogue over them. Above the sanctuary hung a heavy curtain. Once it was white, but now it was black. And marks of congealed blood were visible upon it: the blood of the martyrs.

When we entered, we found three men who had come before us. Among them was an old man, standing bowed, with his head resting on the old black festival prayer book that lay on the lectern. He was clad like the other people of the place, but they wore gray trousers, while his were white. He had the small fringed garment over his clothes, with a mantle over it and his tallit drawn up over his cap. Because of the sanctity of the day and the sanctity of the place, they did not speak, either in the profane or in the holy tongue.

The old man raised his head from the lectern and looked into the house of prayer. He rapped on the prayer book and said, "People, we now have a quorum. Let us pray." They replied, "Samuel Levi has not yet come." "Why does he not come," said the old man, "and why is he holding up the prayer?" One of them pricked up his ears and said, "I hear the sound of footsteps, here he comes." But no, those were not his footsteps. An old gentile woman came in and asked, "Who is the gravedigger here?" One of them removed the tallit from his face and asked her, "What do you want?" "The Jew Levi is about to die," she said, "and perhaps he is already dead. He sent me to tell you to come and see to his burial." The whole congregation sighed deeply and looked at each other, as people look at a little orphan who has suddenly lost his parents. And each and everyone of them looked as if he had been bereaved and he was the orphan.

"People, what does the Gentile woman want in the holy place?" the old man asked. They told him. "He was a good Jew," he said with a sigh. "Alas that he is dead, alas that he is dead." Then the old man looked at me and said, "Blessed be the Almighty who has brought you here. Surely He has brought you to complete the quorum." He rapped on the prayer book and said, "The dead praise not the Lord, neither any that go down into silence. People, we have a quorum, praise the Lord. Let us rise and pray." He let down his tallit over his face and began to recite the blessings. Immediately they all raised their tallitot and covered their heads. They recited the blessings, the hallelujahs, the "Bless ye," and the hymns. They recited the "Hear, O Israel" and then the Prayer of Benedictions. They took out the scrolls from the sanctuary and read the Torah. And I, Samuel Joseph, son of Rabbi Shalom Mordecai the Levite, went up to the lectern for the reading of the Torah in place of Samuel Levi, who had passed away. After the blowing of the ram's horn and the Additional Service, we went down to accompany our friend to his last resting place.

So that they should not be deprived of congregational prayer on the Day of Atonement, I postponed my departure until after the Day. Since I was idle and free to my own devices, I walked about during the intervening days from house to house and from man to man. Their houses were small, and as low as the stature of an ordinary man; each consisted of a small room with a courtyard surrounded by a stone wall. Attached to the room was a wooden hut, which they called the summer house all the year around and sanctified to serve as a festival booth at Sukkot, but they had to rebuild it every year, for the winds sent the boards flying a Sabbath day's journey and more. The doors of their houses were all made in the same measure and of the same width, for their fathers, when they built the houses, used to make the doorways the width of a bier, so that when they brought them out on the way to their last resting place, they should be able to take them out without trouble. Every householder had a milk goat, and four or five fowls, and plant pots in which they grew onions to flavor their bread and sweeten the Sabbath stew. Because of scanty resources and the pangs of poverty, the sons went out to the big cities and drew their sisters after them, and sent for the parents to come to their weddings. Some of the parents agreed and went, but immediately after the wedding they would leave quietly and go back home on foot. Old Mrs. Zukmantel told me, "At my son's wedding banquet, which was held with great splendor, I went outside for a breath of air. I saw my husband sitting on the steps with his head resting on his knees. 'Is that the way to sit at your son's wedding?' I said to him. 'I can't stand all that noise,' he replied. 'In that case,' I said, 'let us go back home.' 'Let us go,' he said, sitting up. So we got up straightaway and set off. We walked all night, and in the morning our feet were standing on the ground of our house." A similar tale I heard from Mistress Yettlein, the wife of Mr. Koschmann, son-in-law of Mr. Anschel Duesterberg, nephew of old Rabbi Anschel, who was cantor and ritual slaughterer, as well as rabbi.

To fulfill the precept of hospitality, which they had not been privileged to carry out for many years because they got no visitors, they took much trouble with me, and everyone devoted himself to me in love and affection and honor. Since they do little work on the Ten Days of Penitence, which they treat, as far as work is concerned, exactly like the intermediate festival days, they were all free to their own devices and free for me. They went out with me to some of their holy places, where they have a tradition that the bones of the martyrs who were slaughtered and killed and burned are interred. Most of the graves have no stones upon them, but only signs to warn the descendants of the priestly family to keep away. On the other hand, there are tombstones and fragments of stones without any inscription on them strewn all over the hills and valleys. On one of them I found the inscription: MY BELOVED IS GONE DOWN INTO HIS GARDEN; on another: GLORIOUS IS THE KING'S DAUGHTER, and on another I found the inscription:

They slandered the Jew,
And vilely slew
Numbers untold,
Both young and [*old*].
On every hill
Our blood they [*spill*].

Among the fragments I saw the fragments of one gravestone bearing a verse from the Song of Songs: THOU THAT DWELLEST IN THE GARDENS, THE COMPANIONS HEARKEN TO THY VOICE. They told me that there was a certain distinguished woman, Mistress Buna, who composed hymns for women, and they have a tradition that this was the tombstone of Mistress Buna. She died a year before the massacre, and after her death she would come in a dream to the leaders of the community and sing, "Flee, my beloved..." and the rest of the verse. They did not know what she meant, until the unbelievers came and slaughtered most of the communities, and those who were not slaughtered by the unbelievers slaughtered themselves so that they should not fall into their hands. And those who did not succeed in taking their own lives went to the stake with gladness and song, and sanctified the heavenly Name in the sight of the Gentiles, so that the uncircumcised were astonished when they saw it, and some of them cried, "These are not sons of man, but angels of God."

On account of the massacres they have special customs. They do not recite the hymn "It is for us to praise" after the prayers, whether individual or congregational. And if a man longs to recite it, he covers his face and says it in a whisper, because with this song of praise their martyred forefathers went to the stake, singing the praises of the Holy One, blessed be He, out of the fire. It is their custom to recite the prayer in memory of the slaughtered communities every Sabbath, even when there is a wedding. And they recite the Supplication in the month of Nisan, from the day after Passover. They fast on the New Moon of Sivan until after the afternoon service, and recite penitential prayers and the Song of Praise, and visit the tombs of the martyrs. At the Afternoon Prayer they recite the Supplication of Moses, because on that day the entire community was killed, and before the open scroll they pray for the souls of the martyrs who were killed and slaughtered and burned alive in those evil days. Another custom they once had: on the first day of Shavuot, before the reading of the Torah, one of the young men would lay himself on the floor of the synagogue and pretend to be dead, in memory of the giving of the law, of which it is said, "My soul failed when He spake." They would say to him, "What aileth thee? Fear not. The statutes of the Lord are right, rejoicing the heart." Immediately the young man opened his eyes, like a man who has come back to life, and there was great rejoicing; they surrounded him, dancing and singing and crying, "He liveth forever, awesome, exalted and holy!" This custom has been abolished, for once a certain illustrious scholar, Rabbi Israel Isserlin, who wrote a famous book, happened to visit them; he rebuked them angrily and said, "Pfui, ye shall not walk in their ordinances, neither shall ye do after the doings of the Gentiles." For the Gentiles used to behave in this way for several years after the disappearance of the sickness called the Black Death: they used to gather together and eat and drink until they were intoxicated; then they would choose one of their young men and lay him on the ground, and little girls and old women would dance around him, and they would sniff at each other, and say, "Death is dead, death is dead!" Then they would take a girl and lay her down, and old men and boys would surround her, knock their heads together, and dance around her, screeching, "Death is dead, death is dead!" so as to notify the Black Death that it was dead, for in those days there was a spirit of madness abroad, and people did strange things.

Blessed be He that distinguishes Israel from the Gentiles. Let us return to the Jewish customs. They do not perform the ceremony of casting away sins either at rivers or at wells, because the Gentiles used to say that the Jews dropped poison into the water and polluted it; but anyone who has a well in his yard recites the prayer beside the well. And although the suspicion has disappeared, the custom has not been changed. And it was an ancient custom among them to recite the blessing "Who hast not made me a Gentile" twice. They have evening hymns and morning hymns and hymns of redemption and penitential hymns that are not in our festival prayer book. The melodies of their prayers resemble ours, but ours are according to the taste of this generation, while theirs are as they have inherited them from their fathers, may they rest in peace. Sometimes their voices are terrifying, and sometimes a cry, as of a man whose soul struggles to escape, is wrenched from them. But when they stand up to pray, they recite in a sweet voice: "O my dove, that art in the clefts of the rock..." and so forth; "My dove, my undefiled is but one..." and so forth; "She is the choice one of her that bore her." Never in my life have I heard a melody so sweet. And I saw an excellent custom that they observed on the Day of Atonement: they do not leave the house of prayer, or speak, from the approach of night until the end of the Day of Atonement, either in the secular or in the sacred tongue, and even the women are very careful in this. And they do not interrupt the reading of the Torah to pronounce a blessing on those who are called up for the reading, but after it is over the reader blesses them all together. On festivals when they read the passage "Every firstborn," the leader of the congregation rises after the last reader has finished the final blessing, goes up to each one, carrying a scroll of the Torah, and blesses him, saying, "He that blessed our forefathers, etc., may He bless thee for giving a donation in honor of the Almighty, etc.," and the people contribute voluntarily to the cost of wine for the sanctification and lamps for the lighting and other needs of the congregation. Their scrolls of the law are tall; when they elevate the scroll they spread it out as far as their arms can reach. You have never seen a finer sight than a broad scroll held by tall Jews, for all of them are stalwart and powerful men. The one who elevates the scroll holds it firmly, while everyone looks at the Torah and puts together, from it, the letters of his name. Their ram's horns are kept in their cases. On some of the cases, beautiful shapes are engraved, and on others verses of the services connected with the sounding of the horn are written. They have no particular melody for reading the Scroll of Esther, but the reader reads it like an ordinary story. And when Master Moses Molin, the son-in-law of Reb Jacob Slitzstat, was good enough to read me a few verses, I felt as if I were hearing the story of Esther for the first time.

It is their way to mingle words of the holy tongue in their conversation. When it is warm they say *hamima* and when it is cold they say *karira*. They do not say *Soehne*, but *banim*, and not *Toechter*, but *banot*. But in the singular, they say *Sohn* and *Tochter*. When I asked them the reason, they could not answer, and I quoted to them in jest, "Ye are sons (*banim*) to the Lord your God." As for the daughters, I quoted, "Many daughters (*banot*) have done worthily." Most of the names of their articles of food and drink are in the holy tongue, such as *lehem*—bread, *basar*—meat, *dagim*—fish, *yayin*—wine, and *mayim*—water. A dish that is neither meat nor of milk, they call *lavlah*, from the initials of *lo vasar lo halav*. I found several beautiful words in use among them, which I have not found in our dictionaries, and no doubt they come from the festival prayer book, for they often recite the hymns. And most of the names of animals are in the holy tongue, except the calf, which they call *Kalb*, so as not to recall the sin of the Golden Calf. And if a man calls someone a calf, he makes his life a misery.

Their favorite entertainment at festival meals is to ask riddles about the laws, such as, "How can we prove so-and-so?" Another hallowed custom they have is to assemble in the synagogue on the Seventh of Adar and spend the day in fasting and prayer and the reading of the Torah, and I do not remember if they told me that they read the Supplication of Moses or "And Moses went up…" from the end of Deuteronomy. They recite the Memorial for the Departed, and every one kindles lights in memory of his relatives who have died, as on a yahrzeit, because no one can go to the synagogue all winter because of the tempests and snowfalls, so they decided to assemble on the Seventh of Adar, the day of the passing of Moses, our teacher, blessed be his memory. At night, after midnight, they hold a meal, and all eat together, and they have special penitential hymns for that day and special songs for that meal, which they sing to special melodies, and afterward they go home in peace. They also have several other customs. Happy is the man that follows them.

In the morning of the day after the Day of Atonement I went on my way. When I left, the entire community came out to see me on my road, standing on the hilltops. Five or six times I turned my head to look back at them, until they were swallowed in the blue mists. I kept to the road and walked on until I reached the railroad, which had been repaired in the meantime by craftsmen brought for the purpose. I traveled by rail to the port, and from there I traveled by ship to the haven of my desire, the Land of Israel. Blessed be the Almighty who has restored me to my place.

Translated by Misha Louvish

Between Two Towns

The town of Katzenau is situated among the mountains of lower Franconia. Its small houses are scattered among gardens, fields, hills, and valleys. Some of its inhabitants are craftsmen; others serve as clerics, teachers, and functionaries, foresters, hunters, and cattle breeders. In the center of this town, between the courthouse and the revenue offices, there is a street lined with two rows of buildings, across from each other, which house the stores that belong to Jews. Like their fathers and the generations that preceded them, they struggle for a meager profit and provide the local people with all sorts of goods, some necessary and some unnecessary. The Holy One, blessed be He, arranged the world as He saw fit. To some He granted fields and gardens, and, being generous and true to His people, Israel, He granted them a resting place among the nations from which to serve Him and to earn a livelihood, be it meager or ample. He is blessed and His Name is blessed, for every Jew is sustained according to his needs. In the past there were countless edicts, attacks, murders, expulsions. But in time this changed so that Israel is no longer despised because of matters of faith. Nor are we victimized for our positive qualities.

So the few families who live in the town support themselves, each family according to its needs, struggling to please God and humanity, seeking nothing for themselves beyond what they earn with their labor and beyond what they need to survive. They provide for their households with integrity, perform the commandments received from their forebears unquestioningly, grasping their essence while fulfilling them. About folks such as these was it said that "man was born to toil"—both for a livelihood and to perform the commandments.

The Sabbath comes, bringing peace. From noon on Friday very little business is done. The women prepare for the Sabbath; men tend their beards, pulling out hair after hair with a special implement. The Sabbath doesn't begin until everyone is in the synagogue, wearing Sabbath clothes and a Sabbath face, occupying an inherited seat. The old teacher, who is also the ritual slaughterer and cantor, stands before the holy ark chanting melodies received from generations back, which are, no doubt, pleasing to God. After these prayers the wine is blessed and a feast is served: white bread, meat, other dishes that grace the table only on the Sabbath and holidays. In winter there are songs. In summer, when the nights are short, it is the custom to delight one's table with a special psalm before saying Grace. Those familiar with the Five Books of Moses read the weekly portion; others read *Der Israelit* or *Das Familienblatt* until they fall asleep.

Morning prayers are early. The old teacher and cantor stands before the holy ark and chants the Torah. The privilege of participating in this part of the service is assigned carefully to avoid controversy, for there was once a feud that all but destroyed this community. A system of turns was thereupon instituted, which applied to everyone, with the exception of Herr Gundersheimer and old Neidermeir the Butcher, who were called up to the Torah every week when they were in town. (One of them being of priestly descent, the other from the tribe of Levi, they were granted this special privilege bestowed by the Torah.) After the service, everyone goes home in peace, blesses the government, indulges in the array of dishes that adorn the table only on the Sabbath and holidays. In winter, when the days are short, the Sabbath passes without much ado. By the time the afternoon prayers are concluded it is time for the evening round. The cycle of ordinary days, given not for rest and pleasure but for sorrow and toil, begins again.

2

But in the summer Katzenau changes its aspect, somewhat for the better. This small village, situated among mountains, locked in by forests, isolated from the world four or five months a year by snow, storms, and winds, has a twin sister: Bad Katzenau, with medicinal springs flowing through its soil. From all over the country people throng to drink the water and bathe in it. Local landowners built villas which they rented out, planted gardens, built a hall and hired musicians to entertain their guests. People came there from Katzenau to promenade and to hear the music. When Old Man Gundersheimer and Neidermeir the Butcher opened inns in Bad Katzenau, guests who observe dietary laws could go there too. And people from the neighboring community went there to meet their fellow Jews.

Herr Gundersheimer and Herr Neidermeir live together in peace. And when necessary they help each other, either because they are inundated with guests and have no reason to envy one another or because they are in the habit of cooperating. The one, a Kohen, is of priestly lineage; the other, a Levite, is trained to pour water on the hands of the priest when he goes up to the pulpit, while the Kohen is trained to include the Levite with the rest of Israel in his priestly blessing.

From the time Bad Katzenau became a health spa, and travelers—among them, Jews—began to come there for a cure, the people of Katzenau began to go there too. On weekdays they were occupied with business and were not free. But on the Sabbath, the day being long and idle, a man would take his wife, sons, and daughters, and go for a walk among the trees, gardens, and flowers, passing guests, seeing new faces, and hearing worthwhile conversation. Occasionally a rabbi would come there to mend his body. The people of the town of Katzenau, who were not numerous enough to hire their own rabbi, would come to meet him. One of the town elders would sometimes kneel to kiss the rabbi's hand and, noting how soft and delicate it was, would wonder about the benefits of this occupation. All week long everyone waited eagerly for the hour on the Sabbath when the entire community would set out for the spa. The distance between the two towns of Katzenau was not great. A sizable pine forest provided shade, and it was not a strain even for women, old people, or children to walk from one town to the other. As they passed through the forest, whose trees offered shade along with a fine fragrance and frolicking birds, they began to feel expansive. Their tongues came to life; their bodies, bent by the weight of merchandise and bowed by dealings with customers, became erect. All the more so upon returning from the spa and remembering a bon mot gleaned from one of the guests. The good Lord created a vast world, with many people in it whom He scattered wide, giving each place its singular quality and endowing every man with singular wisdom. You leave home and meet people from another place, and your mind is expanded by what you hear.

3

The great war, a blow to the wicked and the good alike, did not bypass Katzenau—least of all its Jews, who, from the onset of the war, were eager and anxious to defend their land. Those who were of age were called to serve in the ranks of the military; those who were too young volunteered, leaving behind only women, children, the elderly, and several citizens whose services were essential to the town. The community was overcome with sadness, now that all of its youths were gone. Some small comfort was derived from the weekly excursions, on the Sabbath afternoons, to the watering place, where there were new faces as well as information and commentary on the progress of the war.

In truth there was a further advantage in being there. In most areas of the country there were food shortages, whereas Katzenau was located in Bavaria, where bread, meat, milk products, and fruit were abundant. People would come from all over to this watering place to restore their bodies and eat their fill.

For this same reason and at this very time, one Isidor Shalthier, of Frankfurt, arrived in Katzenau. Herr Isidor Shalthier taught young children in a local elementary school, but he had great aspirations. The great things, however, had already been done by others, leaving nothing for Herr Shalthier to discover. He had no choice but to avert his mind from great things and deal with his frail, declining body, for teaching is a difficult profession, all the more so in wartime, when fathers make war and children do as they please. Herr Gundersheimer, the old innkeeper, treated him graciously and was generous with all manner of food and drink, beyond what he was paid for. The teacher spent his time sleeping, drinking, eating. Between meals he would sit on a lounge chair in the garden, coaxing his eyes to sleep. After a few days, his body feeling heavy with food, drink, and sleep, he began to walk between meals to speed up digestion and ready himself for new nourishment. It was wartime and most city dwellers had already forgotten what proper food is like. Finding himself in a place where food was plentiful, he needed many strategies to absorb his ample diet. So Herr Shalthier took walks between meals to relax his body. He was also careful not to tax his mind and, rather than think about anything that required the slightest strain, he would count either his footsteps or the telegraph wires. For the soul is not content with earthly matters and tends to elevate itself, soaring to the heights of the universe.

In the course of these walks, Herr Isidor Shalthier found himself in the town of Katzenau. He sniffed the scent of warm bread, followed his nose, and arrived at the door of a Jewish baker. He knocked, entered, and, as he was obviously a decent fellow, was welcomed warmly. The baker, hearing he was a teacher and furthermore that he was from Frankfurt, was extremely respectful. He was served cold milk, cake, bread, butter, and cheese, which he ate, drank, and enjoyed even as he bemoaned the plight of his wife and tender children who, while he was eating bread, butter, and cheese, and drinking rich milk, had barely enough dry crusts to eat—for in the big cities anyone who isn't well connected has nothing to eat. Moved by the plight of the teacher's wife and children, the baker and his wife took a dozen eggs, a pound of butter and cheese, and various other goods, wrapped them in paper, and said: There is a post office nearby and, if it isn't too much trouble, he could mail the package to his family. And, if the distance isn't too great for him, he could come every week and this effort would surely be rewarded. As they spoke, Herr Dingsfelder, the baker's neighbor, appeared. He was envious and said, "Absolutely not. Next week the teacher must do me the honor, for a package is ready and waiting. It was prepared for my son but I can't send it. My son, Rheinholdi, may his life be long, is a prisoner in the hands of our accursed enemies the French. We don't know just where he is. But the honored teacher must promise not to divulge this agreement to anyone." Herr Dingsfelder was afraid others in the town would snatch this good deed out from under him. And he was right to worry. For, in those sorrowful times, many hands were seeking out acts of charity and generosity. But his joy betrayed him. Two or three hours later all of Katzenau was aware that a man had appeared through whom good deeds could be done. Every householder searched and found things to give the teacher. Henceforth, Herr Shalthier was a regular guest in the town. Not a week passed without his coming to Katzenau nor was there anyone in Katzenau who did not give him a portion of his bread, butter, eggs, and other foodstuffs. As he walked to Katzenau and back, Herr Shalthier thought many thoughts about what he had been given to eat and drink, also about his wife who was lucky to have such a husband, one who remembers her from afar with packages laden with goodies.

4

There are people who occupy themselves with a single thought for several days, whereas others tend to drift from one thought to another. Herr Shalthier, being a teacher, with a single subject to impart, was in the habit of dwelling on a single thought for a long time. Now that he wasn't enslaved by students, he pursued other thoughts. But all significant thoughts having already been bestowed on others, he was left only with thoughts of food and drink. All that remained for him was to do with his feet what his mind couldn't do. Herr Shalthier began counting his paces again. When he was bored, he counted telegraph wires. When he was tired of counting telegraph wires, he counted paces again. Then he began calculating distances. After two separate calculations, he was puzzled: the distance from Katzenau to Bad Katzenau was more than two thousand cubits, yet it was the custom to walk from the town to the watering place every Sabbath, exceeding the distance one is allowed to traverse on the Sabbath. Could an entire God-fearing and observant community be violating such a major restriction? Furthermore, many Orthodox rabbis had already been in Katzenau to drink and immerse themselves in its waters. Could it be that they were unaware of this situation and that they had failed to correct it? He counted again, alternating broad and narrow steps, only to confirm that the distance exceeded the Sabbath limits. Still, he didn't presume to declare himself the first and only person to realize this. He reasoned that it could be fatigue, from so much food and drink, that was shrinking his paces. He resolved to test this out the following day, before ingesting any food or drink. The next day he measured the distance again and found that it hadn't changed. He stopped and marked the boundary of the Sabbath limits.

It was already dark and there wasn't time for him to retrace his steps. But the next morning, first thing, he went to Katzenau to impart what he had to impart. When the people saw the teacher, they were somewhat surprised, for he had already collected his weekly share and they had nothing more to give him. He said to them, "Listen here, friends. I have come not on my own behalf and not because of the sort of things that are consumed and lost, but for your good and benefit, to protect you from a serious transgression. On what grounds have you allowed yourselves to walk to the other Katzenau on the Sabbath, a distance that exceeds the Sabbath limits?" They heard this and were crushed. They stammered in response, "We were following our parents' ways. Even our teacher, an old man and an expert in the law, raised no objection. In the past he used to walk with us and we never heard that we exceeded the limit." Herr Shalthier said to them, "Listen to me, friends, what was is past. Henceforth you are forbidden to walk to the watering place on the Sabbath, for I have measured and determined that it is beyond the Sabbath limits. Now let us go to your teacher and I will discover his reason for not interfering with you."

They went to the elderly teacher and told him all. The old man said to them, "There is a Russian church in that town. The Russian guests pray there, their religion being different from that of the local people. On the outskirts of the town there is a house occupied by their beadle, which constitutes an extension of the town and is the spot from which our Sabbath limit was calculated." Their faces turned red and they responded, "If so, the reason is no longer valid, as their beadle left when the war began and his dwelling place is now a heap of rubble." The old man said to them, "In that case, the town limits have diminished and it is no longer permissible to go from Katzenau to Bad Katzenau on the Sabbath. The community elders felt faint when they realized how many times they had violated this prohibition by taking this walk on the Sabbath." They showered the teacher, Shalthier, with praise and gratitude for having taken the trouble to spare them further transgression. From here on, no one walked beyond the point marked by the teacher. Before Herr Shalthier's arrival in Katzenau, people used to stroll as they pleased. Now they took pleasure in stopping at the boundary.

5

The bathing season was ending and it was time for Herr Isidor Shalthier to return home. His face was full, his bags stuffed with provisions for the journey, given to him by the people of Katzenau. From the time he emerged from his mother's womb he hadn't been treated as well as during his stay in Katzenau. Every day he ate more than he needed and every week he remembered his family with butter, cheese, eggs, and fruit bestowed by admirers, free of charge—though they would be rewarded in the world-to-come, for he had prevented them from desecrating the Sabbath.

The bathing season was over and the resort town was empty. Some of the innkeepers left to stay with relatives and rest from the summer's work, while those who remained at home sat counting the income derived from their guests. At night they would exchange visits and play cards. In the town of Katzenau there was also a perceptible difference. Those who used to go to the resort and stroll on the promenade now sat in the tavern drinking whiskey and cider, discussing the events of the war and Germany's victories. Agitators came and went, teachers and officials deliberated continually about ways to finance the war. The Jews, being the first to give, gave and gave again. And it is right that they give—more so in bad times, when their neighbors' circumstances have declined and on the face of it nothing has changed, though any Jew who deals with the authorities finds them more demanding than usual.

Again it is winter. Days are short; nights are long. Even worse than the struggle to get through the day's unrewarding business is the struggle to get through sleepless nights filled with bad dreams. Every person has his troubles: a son who is a prisoner of war, a son-in-law who was its casualty. This small community, abandoned by its young men at the outset of the war, is engulfed by sorrow and mourning. Those who return home come only because they are crippled.

A great misfortune befell the family of Miersheim the Baker. He had an only son, long awaited and prayed for, born, raised, and sustained by miracles. When war broke out, the youth assumed the manner of a hero and said, "I am going off to war." The officers were kind to him, ignoring his frailties, and sent him to the front lines. He was wounded and spent several months in a hospital. When he recovered, he returned to the front. When both his legs froze in the trenches, he was sent home, with many honors and decorations, but with no legs.

6

There was yet another misfortune, the misfortune of Liesl, Mrs. Miersheim's sister. Liesl was married to Mr. Siegfried Speyer, a leather merchant in Offenbach. The two sisters missed each other but were unable to visit, one being busy with her store, the other with her oven. They expressed their longing in letters and dreams, hoping for a miracle that would bring them together. The miracle did occur, but in an unfortunate way. Liesl's husband was killed in the war. She was now a widow with three children to support. A small quantity of merchandise had been left to her, which she sold. But, her profit being meager, she was unable to replenish her stock and remained without a means of support. Her brother-in-law, Miersheim, found her work. Neidermeir, who was from their town, hired her to be a maid in the hotel he owned in Katzenau, the resort. She sent her children to her husband's relatives and moved to Katzenau. Liesl worked all day in Neidermeir's hotel and even at night she didn't rest, for the hotel was filled with guests and there was endless work. Liesl couldn't even spend an hour with her sister, though the distance was a mere cat's leap. Nor was Mrs. Miersheim free to visit Liesl though she was her own boss, for she had to deal with ration cards, render constant accounts to the authorities, tend her crippled son—a body with no legs. It is a miracle that we have such a thing as Sabbath and holidays, when people are free. But Liesl wasn't free of her work even on the Sabbath or on holidays, because of the guests.

On the second day of Shavuot the guests from Poland had their own service with memorial prayers for the dead, according to the custom of that land. Liesl went to pray with them. When the prayers were over, she spoke to herself as follows: I have already spoken with the dead; when will I speak with the living? A friend overheard her and said, "If you want to see your sister, go to her and I will do your work." Liesl informed her sister, through a Gentile messenger, that she would be in the forest in the afternoon.

Liesl dressed in holiday clothes and went to the forest to see the sister she hadn't seen for years, except for the one day when she came to Katzenau to hire herself out as a maidservant in the hotel that belonged to Neidermeir, her fellow townsman. Liesl stood in the forest where in her childhood she used to pick mushrooms and berries. The trees were much older, as were the young boys born after she left for Offenbach. Here, in these woods, Liesl used to walk with her Siegfried, and here among these green trees he had revealed his love to her. Now his bones are rotting in a distant land and she doesn't know where he is buried. Her three children are also far away. She hasn't seen them since she came to Katzenau. Here she has only her sister Margarete. Liesl paces this way and that. Then she stands still as if fixed to the ground, not knowing why she is standing there rather than running toward her sister—for her heart is racing and leaping toward her. Liesl perked up her ears, straining to hear if anyone was coming. She heard only the sound of a hunter and his dogs. But mixed with these sounds, she heard footsteps. Liesl lifted her eyes and saw children running, their parents following behind. She began to run toward them and was puzzled, for she had sent a messenger to inform Margarete that she would be free for two or three hours, yet Margarete was nowhere in sight. Liesl studied every woman's face and said to herself: They all came, everyone but Margarete. Oh, Margarete, why did you do this to me? Why didn't you come? When Liesl had despaired of seeing her sister, she placed her hand on her heart sadly, thinking: Not only did Margarete fail to come, but not even her husband has come.

Meanwhile, the women noticed Liesl. And as soon as they noticed her, they welcomed her, saying, "Aren't you Elise? Of course you're Elise and you're looking for your sister." Liesl nodded and said nothing. Mrs. Dingsfelder, who was Mrs. Miersheim's neighbor, said, "Don't worry, Elise. Margarete didn't forget you, but she was delayed by her son. She'll be here soon. Her husband agreed to take care of him. May we all enjoy good things as surely as you will soon enjoy seeing Margarete. How are you doing, Elise? How is the work in the hotel? Neidermeir knows he won't find your equal among a thousand women. And where are your children? How many are there? Three? We heard what happened to you, my dear. But in these times, is there anyone who can say, 'I'm all right'? Oh, this awful war! It punishes good people and bad people alike. Look up, Elise—what do you see? She's fast as a squirrel. Slow down, Margarete. Elise is standing right here."

7

Margarete was already there, thin as a wafer, her face aflame. She never realized she could cover such a distance in such a short time. But it wasn't her legs that raced; it was her heart, and her legs merely followed. It was a miracle that her heart hadn't expired in longing. When the two sisters saw each other, they embraced and kissed tearfully, their cries carrying from one end of the woods to the other. How they had yearned for each other all this time, being so close to one another yet unable to get together even for a brief visit.

After drying one another's tears, they looked at each other and said, "What is there to cry about." Then they began to cry again. They finally withdrew from the group and sat together, talking—about Speyer, who was killed, and about the children dispersed among Speyer's relatives; about Moritz, the long-anticipated son, who lost his legs and had no control of his body. They also talked about the work in the hotel, the work in the bakery, about Neidermeir and Neidermeir's wife, about the guests, who expected to be treated like only sons, for whom no amount of effort was sufficient. They talked about the ration cards, about tax accounts, about the authorities that swallow everything up. Whatever they said and whatever words they spoke did not seem to express what was in their mind. Nonetheless, they felt relief and began to recall forgotten times, when they were both young girls. Liesl said, "Remember, Margarete, how I was the envy of Katzenau because I married my Siegfried and went to live in Offenbach? Now every cat deserves my envy, for a cat has a place to rest its tail and I don't have a place of my own. Why did Siegfried leave me? I don't even know where he is buried. And my children are scattered. When the resort season is over, where will I put myself?"

Her sister meant to offer words of comfort but merely added to her sorrow, as sufferers often do, recounting their own troubles by way of comfort. Margarete said, "Now I will tell you something. You, of course, know what happened to my only son. But you don't know that my husband took sick and that what we earn in a few days is snatched up by the inspector. It's just as well that he takes it, because he represents the authorities and he could cast an evil eye on the bakery, which hasn't been repaired since the war began. So much for money matters. There are other things. If you want to listen, then listen. Look at me. If the Angel of Death were to come to me today and say 'Margarete, come with me,' I would kiss his fingers. But who will care for my son? My husband is half dead. What is the sound I've been hearing all day? Those hunters keep shooting, without a stop. What can you expect from Gentiles? If they don't manage to kill people, they devise ways to kill animals or birds."

The two sisters sat together telling each other about themselves and about others, not realizing that the day was declining, cherishing the holiday, a time when sisters can be together and share their heartfelt sorrows.

Everyone else began to think of returning to the town, for the day was done and it would soon be time for evening prayers. Yet they lingered in their place in the woods, urging each other to move on, as the sun had set and it was time to go. There was a time, not so long ago, when they used to come and go to the resort town, stroll in its gardens, hear music, see new faces, learn new things—unaware that, having exceeded the limits of a Sabbath walk, their pleasure would be costly. Thus was the teacher from Frankfurt remembered favorably, for he had marked the proper Sabbath limits and saved them from further transgression.

After a while, the agile ones bestirred themselves. They got up and prodded the dawdlers. Finally they too made a move to leave. They remembered Mrs. Miersheim, who was sitting with her sister, and went to call her. When Liesl heard that her sister was about to leave, she grew sad. She had so much to say to her sister. So far she had told her barely half of what she had in mind. Suddenly, remembering the friend who had undertaken to do her work, she tore herself from her place and helped her sister up. Margarete placed her hand on her ears to shield them from the cry of a bird wounded by the hunter. She then moved her hands away and waved them in despair. Finally she looked up and said, "Time to go."

The two sisters wept and fell on each other's necks, unable to utter a word. Finally one of them overcame her sorrow and said, "The holiday is over." The second sister said, "The next holiday is a long way off." The first one said, "When will I see you again? I am enslaved to others and I can't come and go freely." Her sister said, "And I, even if I do leave my house, I wear out my feet paying taxes and doing all the other chores that shorten our lives." Liesl said, "Then when will I see you?" Margarete said, "And when will I see you?" They turned away from each other and dried their eyes.

Day was done, and everyone began to go. The two sisters were still standing there, silent. Finally one turned toward home, as did the other. Between them, the forest and all its trees loomed dark. Then stars began to appear, lighting the road for these two sisters who had been together briefly on this final day of the holiday, who now took leave of each other and would not be together for many days, not until the next holiday—one of them heading this way, the other heading that way.

Translated by Zeva R. Shapiro

The Search for Meaning

gnon's stories over a thirty year period combine a sense of personal confusion with a more pervasive sense of existential dislocation. These narratives find their starting point within the psyche, but their effect quite often is to blur the distinction between inner and outer worlds. Most striking is their use of culturally specific terms to create dramas of impulse and inhibition, desire and constraint, longing and isolation. But these are versatile narratives that can also be read as responses to crises of Jewish modernity from the Emancipation to the present day. Through a focus on individual dilemmas, they draw us into narrative situations that carry resonances on multiple levels of experience.

Among these stories are some that have been described as Kafkaesque, a label Agnon always resisted and some of his critics have decried. These stories may remind one of Kafka's tendency to portray the impotence of the individual in a world he or she cannot completely decipher. However, Agnon's stories always retain suggestions of an identifiably Jewish frame of reference, along with lingering suggestions of possibilities of redemption. These dimensions are hardly ever to be found in Kafka's universe.

The first two stories, "To the Doctor" and the well-known "A Whole Loaf," were published in periodicals in the 1930s and form part of *The Book of Deeds*. Both place the protagonist in ostensibly mundane situations, but each offers the reader cues that suggest broader spiritual implications. The title "To the Doctor" opens the story to the possibility of a cure for unspecified ills. The story places the narrator between Mr. Andermann—a character whose name suggests a German rendering of the Sitra Ahra, the demonic "other side"—and a baal tefillah (one who leads communal prayer), who offers the protagonist the opportunity to participate in the collective confession of the Day of Atonement.

Like "To the Doctor," "A Whole Loaf" organizes itself around a conflict. The protagonist is caught between the desire to fill his belly after a day without food and the obligation to mail the letters entrusted to him by Dr. Yekutiel Ne'eman. The letters of Dr. Ne'eman carry with them the potential to bring words of cure to those who are ill, just as Dr. Ne'eman's book is said to have improved the lives of those who read it. Thus, the request that Dr. Ne'eman makes of the narrator—to deliver his letters to the post office before it closes—carries with it the sense of a higher ethical mission.

It is a short interpretive step from the bearded sage Dr. Ne'eman and his letters of spiritual uplift to the figure of Moses and the giving of the Torah, a step that is supported by a reading of Dr. Ne'eman's name. As the Israeli critic Baruch Kurzweil pointed out, Yekutiel—which means "listens to God"—is a name that has been applied to Moses, and the epithet *ne'eman*—"faithful"—is used to describe Moses as the faithful servant of God. Going further, we can note the dispute about Dr. Ne'eman's book. Did he simply write it himself or was it, as he claims, dictated by an unseen master? That dispute brings to mind the split between those who view the Torah as the product of revelation and those who see it as the product of human inspiration. The story is replete with cues that invoke the broader framework of communal values and traditions, but in a way that makes them part of the situation of a modern everyman.

That everyman is a fellow who wants to sit down and enjoy a good meal but is impeded in fulfilling his wish by a commission that recalls him to a spiritual dimension he is in danger of forgetting. Imaginative participation in this conflict does not require any particular acquaintance with Jewish learning. Some awareness of what Agnon has packed into the text, however, gives the reader access to a kind of learned gamesmanship that the text conducts with rabbinic injunctions and midrashic tales. Agnon is a master of this kind of erudite fun, and nowhere is it better illustrated than in "A Whole Loaf."

Consider the title of the story. What is this "whole loaf"? Is Agnon reminding us that the Sabbath blessing over bread may be recited only over a loaf that is whole, not cut? Are we meant to interpret the phrase in light of the rabbinic injunction to make a Sabbath blessing over two loaves? Or should we interpret the whole loaf as an indication of the greedy and egotistical nature of the narrator who will settle for nothing less than "a whole loaf"? Agnon is playing a particular kind of teasing game here, in which hints at rabbinic sources add an additional dimension to our reading.

Take the moment, late in the story, at which the protagonist finds himself sitting in the deserted restaurant amid the greasy plates and remains of others' meals. He checks his watch and sees that it is half-past ten. "Half-past ten is just a time like any other, but in spite of this I began to shake and tremble." Why shake and tremble? Critic Avraham Holtz tells us that Agnon may well be thinking of a famous midrash that recounts the story of Adam, from his creation to the forbidden fruit and expulsion from Eden, in the narrative framework of a twelve-hour day. At ten, according to the midrash, Adam sinned, and at eleven he was judged. Read in light of the midrashic narrative, then, Agnon's protagonist is caught at a moment of spiritual reckoning. What Agnon's story does is to take that moment and expand it into a kind of Chaplinesque comedy in which the fumbling protagonist fails to find *either* fulfillment *or* judgment.

In a different mode, "At the Outset of the Day," published in the early 1950s, places the narrator and his daughter in a scene of postwar devastation, but it moves back in time immediately as they seek refuge in the Great Synagogue of Buczacz, the town that no longer exists. Like other stories in this volume—"A Book That Was Lost" and "On the Road," for instance—"At the Outset of the Day" tells a story of destruction. But it also focuses on the dilemma of its narrator, who teaches his daughter to combine the letters of the prayer book to form *av*, the Hebrew word for "father," and yet fails to shelter and clothe his child after her dress is consumed by flames from the memorial candle lit for the Day of Atonement.

We can see in the young daughter a symbol of the soul, so that the narrator's parental failure becomes an emblem of his spiritual state. Little wonder, then, that he seeks and does not find a covering for his daughter in the geniza, the part of the synagogue where worn-out fragments of sacred texts are stored.

The narrator seeks a home and a past that he has abandoned: he approaches a group of old people, among them Reb Alter, who circumcised him and brought him into the community he now wishes to recover. While Reb Alter offers a reassuring presence that suggests continuity of the generations, the signs of the disintegration of that community are manifest. The narrator thinks of his friendship with Reb Alter's grandson Gad and remembers the account of a dream Gad's wet-nurse had just before Gad disappeared. The dream image pictures Gad in what the critic Gershon Shaked has identified as a nineteenth-century student's cap, with a plume that carries letters of the Latin alphabet, a hint that Gad has abandoned the traditional Jewish world for secular culture. The story thus responds not only to the destruction caused by "our enemies," but to the erosion from within of communal values.

The ending of "At the Outset of the Day," however, lends itself to varying and even opposing readings. From one angle, it can be argued that the story lifts both narrator and reader beyond the devastation it has recorded to achieve one of those moments of redemptive clarity that Agnon excels in creating. That concluding moment is achieved in this instance by virtue of the Torah scroll that the narrator himself inscribed, a writing that joins him to an ongoing tradition. On the other hand, the ending could be viewed as solipsistic, in the sense that the narrator can purify his soul after the destruction only by citing the scroll that he wrote for the souls of days departed. In this reading, the scroll constitutes his own body of work devoted to the world before the catastrophe.

In a different way, "The Sign" takes up the position of the writer in the world after the destruction of European Jewry. Published in 1962, this story uses shifts between past and present to communicate simultaneously a sense of the creation of a structure and of the impossibility of integration or wholeness after the Holocaust. Structure refers most obviously here to the narrator's house. But his efforts to establish a home for his family in the Land of Israel are opposed by the news of the destruction of Buczacz, the town of his beginnings. The story thus marks the impossibility of regarding the building up of the Land of Israel as compensation for the loss of the European Jewish community.

The drama in "The Sign" hinges on the narrator's emotional dilemma. Constricted emotionally, he is unable to weep for the destruction of his townspeople and at the same time afraid to face the enormity of his grief. Caught in this conflict, he finds himself unable to join in the celebration of the giving of the Torah, the holiday of Shavuot on which the story is set. Instead he absorbs himself in the physical setting of his neighborhood in Talpiyot, just outside of Jerusalem, where he feels the sea wind and the desert wind, and enumerates with love the flowers and shrubs that surround his house. Inevitably, however, he becomes the vehicle for powerful experiences of memory, which compete with ongoing ties to loved ones in the present. The attention of his imagination oscillates between past and present as he seeks the resolution that eludes him.

Working his way toward the expression of grief, the narrator recalls the coming of spring when he was a child in Buczacz: he remembers the recitation of Hallel at the New Moon, a moment that coincided with the thawing of the river. It is the interpenetration of these worlds that becomes the "sign" of the writing. The luminosity of the text is the result of grief transmuted into the activity of memory, which writes itself into the very landscape of Israel as the writer sees it.

In a bold gesture, Agnon summons up the figure of the medieval Jewish poet Solomon Ibn Gabirol to sanctify the memory of Buczacz and to signal its inscription in the heavens. The medieval payyetan (religious poet) who weaves his name into his poems promises the narrator a poem that will carry the name of Buczacz in its verses. The narrator's soul melts in response to this memorializing gesture of the poet, which produces a heavenly writing to which he alone is witness. The poem "sings itself in the heavens above, among the poems of the holy poets, the beloved of God." The dead of Buczacz now number among that heavenly company, while the writer remains below. He is the survivor, unable to evade the responsibility of memory, which animates his writing.

To the Doctor

Father lay ill, and a moist cloth was bound about his head. His face was weary from illness, and a heavy worry dulled his blue eyes—like a man who knows his death is near but doesn't know what will happen to his young sons and daughters. Opposite him, in another room, lay my little sister. Each was ill with a different illness for which the doctor had not yet given a name.

My wife stood in the kitchen and shelled peas from their pods. After she placed them in the pot she put on her wrap and went with me to the doctor.

As I was leaving the house, I stumbled upon some peas, for when my wife was busy preparing them for eating they had rolled out of her hands and scattered on the stairs. I wanted to sweep them away before the mice would smell them and come, but I was rushed; it was already past eight-thirty, and at nine o'clock the doctor used to visit his friends and drink with them all night, while at home there lay two sick persons who needed special attention—particularly my little sister, who used to caper and sing, exciting our anxiety lest she fall from her bed or disturb Father from his sleep.

Those peas began to bother me because they turned into lentils, and lentils are a food of trouble and mourning. It is easy to under-stand the sorrow of a man who has two sick persons at home, and things put this kind of thought into his heart.

It is not proper to tell that I was a bit resentful toward my wife and I thought to myself: What good are women? She had toiled to prepare a meal for us and at the end all the peas had scattered. When I saw she was running and knew why she was running, my resent-ment disappeared and love entered my heart.

On the way, right next to the black bridge, Mr. Andermann met me and greeted me. I returned his greeting and wanted to leave him. He held my hand and told me that he had just arrived from the city of Bordeaux in England and today or tomorrow he and his father would come to see our new house. "Ay, Ay, Ay," said Mr. Andermann, "they tell all sorts of wonders about your house." I contorted my face to give it a pleasing expression and reflected, Why does he say he will come with his father? Does Mr. Andermann have a father? And I reflected further: Couldn't this excessive attempt to give my face a pleasing appearance leave an impression after it? I remembered the peas which had turned into lentils and I began to worry about ret-ribution.

So that Mr. Andermann might not realize what was in my heart, I put my hand into my pocket and took out my watch; I saw that nine o'clock was near, and at nine the doctor used to go to his club and get drunk, while there at home lay two sick persons whose illness had no name. When Mr. Andermann saw I was in haste, he understood in his usual way that I was hurrying to the post office. He said, "The postal arrangements have changed and you don't have to hurry."

I left Mr. Andermann in his error and I didn't tell him about the sick persons lest he bother me with advice and detain me.

There came a stately old man in whose house of study I used to pray on the High Holy Days. I have heard many cantors, but I have not heard a baal tefillah like him whose prayer is beautiful and clear even during his crying. I had wanted to speak to him many times, but I never could. Now he set upon me his eyes which were bleary from crying and looked at me affectionately, as if he were saying, "Here I am; let us talk, if you wish." Mr. Andermann grasped my hand and didn't let me go. Actually, I could have removed my hand from his and gone off, but on that very same day a dog had bitten me and torn my clothes, and had I turned my face from Mr. Andermann and gone he would have seen the tear.

I remembered the time when the old man stood before the reader's desk during the prayer "And because of our sins…" and beat his head on the floor until the walls of the house of study quaked. My heart quaked and I was drawn toward him, but Mr. Andermann grasped my hand. I stood and twisted my face and tried to give it a pleasing expression.

My wife crossed the bridge and reached the doctor's house, which was next to the post office and stood before the entrance of the house, her shoulders twitching from sorrow and waiting. I removed my hand from Mr. Andermann's hand and went toward my wife. The black bridge quaked under my feet and the waves of the river swelled and rose, rose and swelled.

Translated by Arnold J. Band

A Whole Loaf

I had not tasted anything all day long. I had made no preparations on Sabbath eve, so I had nothing to eat on the Sabbath. At that time I was on my own. My wife and children were abroad, and I had remained all by myself at home; the bother of attending to my food fell upon myself. If I did not prepare my meals or go to hotels and restaurants, I had to put up with hunger inside me. On that particular day, I had intended to eat at a hotel; but the sun had flamed like a furnace, so I decided it was better to go hungry than to walk about in that heat.

In all truth, my dwelling did not keep the heat from me either. The floor was as hot as glowing fire, the roof fevered like piercing fire, the walls simply burned like fire, and all the vessels simply sweated fire, so that it was like fire licking fire, fire of the room licking at the body, and the fire of the body licking against the fire of the room. But when a man is at home, he can soak himself in water if he likes, or take off his clothes when he wants to, so that they do not weigh on him.

Once the greater part of the day had passed, and the sun

weakened, I rose and washed myself and dressed, and went off to eat. I was pleased to think that I would be sitting at a well-spread table with a clean tablecloth on it, and waiters and waitresses attending to me while I ate properly prepared food that I had not needed to exhaust myself about. For I was already tired of the poor food I used to prepare for myself at home.

The day was no longer hot, and a gentle breeze was blowing. The streets were filling up. From the Mahaneh Yehudah Quarter to the Jaffa Gate or nearby, the old men and women and the lads and girls were stretching their legs all the way. Round fur hats and caps and felt hats and turbans and tarbooshes shook and nodded, on and amid hairy and hairless heads. From time to time fresh faces joined them, coming from Rabbi Kook Street and from the Sukkat Shalom and Even Yisrael and Nahlat Shiva quarters, and from the Street of the Prophets which people have the bad habit of calling the Street of the Consuls; as well as from all the other streets to which the authorities had not yet managed to give names. All day long they had been imprisoned in their homes by the heat. Now that day was past and the sun was losing its strength, they came out to glean a little of the atmosphere of Sabbath twilight which Jerusalem borrows from the Garden of Eden. I was borne along with them till I came to a solitary path.

2

While I was being carried along, an old man knocked at his window to draw my attention. I turned my head and saw Dr. Yekutiel Ne'eman standing at the window. I hurried over with great pleasure, for he is a great sage, and his words are pleasant. But when I came there, he had vanished. I stood looking into his house until he joined me and greeted me. I greeted him in return, and waited to hear some of those great thoughts we are accustomed to hearing from him.

Dr. Ne'eman asked me how my wife and children were. I sighed and answered, "You have reminded me of my trouble. They are still abroad and want to come back to the Land of Israel."

"If they want to come back," said he, "why don't they come?"

I sighed and said, "There's some delay."

"Verily the delay comes from a crooked way," said he, rhyming on my word. And he began to scold me. "There's some laziness about you," said he, "so that you have not devoted yourself to bringing them back; and the result for you is that your wife and children are wandering about without father or husband while you are without wife and children."

I looked down at the ground in shame and said nothing. Then I raised my head and turned my eyes to his mouth, in the hope that he would say something consoling. His lips were slightly open, and a kind of choked rebuke hung from them, while his fine, gray-shot beard had creased and grown wavy, like the Great Sea when it rages. I regretted having brought his wrath down on me and causing him to bother about such trifles. So I took counsel with myself and began to talk about his book.

3

This was a book about which opinions were largely divided. There are some scholars who say that whatever is written in it as from the mouth of the Lord (....) was written by Yekutiel Ne'eman, who neither added nor took away anything from His words. And that is what Yekutiel Ne'eman declares. But there are some who say this is certainly not the case, and that Ne'eman wrote it all himself and ascribed his words to a certain Lord whom no man ever saw.

This is not the place to explain the nature of that book. Yet this I must add, that since it first became known the world has grown slightly better, since a few people have improved their behavior and somewhat changed their nature; and there are some who devote themselves body and soul to doing everything in the manner described there.

In order to make Dr. Ne'eman feel more pleased, I began proclaiming the virtues of his book and said, "Everybody admits that it is a great work and there is nothing like it." Then Yekutiel turned his face from me, let me be, and went his way. I stood eating my heart with grief and remorse for what I had said.

But Dr. Ne'eman did not remain annoyed with me for long. As I was about to go away, he returned with a packet of letters to be taken to the post office and sent by registered mail. I put the letters in my breast pocket and placed my hand on my heart as a promise that I would perform my mission faithfully.

4

On the way I passed the house of study and entered to recite the evening prayers. The sun had already set entirely, but the beadle had not yet kindled the light. In view of the mourning of Moses, the congregation did not engage in the study of the Torah, but sat discoursing and singing and taking their time.

Stars could already be seen outside, but complete darkness still held sway within the building. At length the beadle lit a light, and the congregation rose to recite the evening prayers. After the Havdalah ceremony, which brings the Sabbath day to a close, I rose to go to the post office.

All the grocery stores and other shops were open, and people crowded around the kiosks on every side. I also wished to cool myself with a glass of soda water, but since I was in a hurry to send off the letters, I kept my desire in check and did without drinking.

Hunger began to oppress me. I considered whether I should go and eat first. After starting, I changed my mind and said, Let me send off the letters and then I shall eat. On the way I thought to myself, If only Ne'eman knew that I am hungry, he would urge me to eat first. I turned myself about and went toward the restaurant.

Before I had taken more than two or three steps, the power of imagination arrived. What it imagined! What did it not imagine! All of a sudden it brought a sickbed before me. There's a sick man somewhere, I told myself, and Dr. Ne'eman has been told about it and has written down a remedy for him; and now I have to hurry and take the letter containing it to the post office. So I got set to run to the post office.

In the middle of my running I stopped and thought, Is he the only doctor there is? And even if he is, does he promise that his remedy is going to help? And even if it does help, do I really have to put off my meal, when I haven't eaten anything at all the whole day long? My legs grew as heavy as stone. I did not go to eat because of the force of imagination, while I did not go to the post office because of my reasoning.

5

Since I was standing still, I had time to consider my affairs. I began to weigh what I ought to do first and what I ought to do later, and reached the decision to go to an eating place first, since I was hungry. I turned my face at once to the restaurant and marched off as quickly as I could before some other thought should strike me; for a man's thoughts are likely to delay his actions. And in order that my thoughts should not confuse me, I gave myself good counsel, picturing all the kinds of good food for which the restaurant was well known. I could already see myself sitting, eating and drinking and enjoying myself. The force of imagination helped me, producing more than an average man can eat or drink, and making good to my taste each article of food and drink. Undoubtedly the intention was for the best, but what pleasure does a hungry man have when he is shown all kinds of food and drink but is given no chance to enjoy them? Maybe he can find satisfaction from this in dream, but it is doubtful if he will do so when awake.

This being the case, I went back toward the restaurant, thinking over what I should eat and drink. At heart I was already happy to be sitting in a pleasant building at a spread table, among fine folk busy eating and drinking. Then maybe I would find a good acquaintance there, and we would spice our repast with pleasant conversation which satisfies the heart and does not weigh on the soul; for I would have you know that Dr. Ne'eman had weighed somewhat on my heart.

Remembering Dr. Ne'eman, I remembered his letters. I began to feel afraid that I might be so carried away by my talk with my friend that I would not send the letters off. So I changed my mind and said, Let us go to the post office first and be done with the job, so that afterward we can sit comfortably and the letters will not keep on burdening my mind.

6

If only the ground had moved along under me, I would have done my mission at once. But the ground stood still, and the way to the post office is hard on the feet, because the ground is broken and uneven with heaps of earth and stones; while when you do get there the postal clerks are not in the habit of hurrying but keep you hanging about, and by the time they finish whatever it is they are doing, all the food will get cold and you will find no hot dishes, so that you are bound to remain hungry. But I gave no thought to this and went to the post office.

It is easy to understand the state of a man who has two courses in front of him: if he takes one, it seems to him that he has to follow the other; and if he takes the other, it seems to him that he ought to go along the first one. At length he takes the course that he ought to take. Now that I was going to the post office, I wondered that I could possibly have had any doubt for a while and wished to give my own trifling affairs precedence over the affairs of Dr. Ne'eman. And within a short while I found myself standing at the post office.

7

I was just about to enter when a carriage came along and I saw a man sitting in it. I stood and stared in astonishment: now, when as much as a horseshoe is not to be found in town, a man comes along in a two-horse carriage. And what was still more surprising, he was mocking the passersby and driving his horses along the pavement.

I raised my eyes and saw that he was Mr. Gressler. This Mr. Gressler had been the head of an agricultural school abroad, but there he used to ride a horse and here he drove a carriage. When he was abroad he used to joke with the peasants' daughters and the simple folk, and here in the Land of Israel he fooled about with anybody and everybody. Yet he was an intelligent and polite person, and although he was a fleshy fellow, his fleshiness was not noticed by reason of his wide learning.

This Mr. Gressler had something about him that attracted all who saw him. So it is not surprising that I was also affected. On this occasion Mr. Gressler sat leaning back in his carriage, the reins loose in his hand and dragging below the horses' legs, as he watched with pleasure while people passed on either side and returned to the place from which they had run, and jumped about in front of the horses, the dust of their feet mingling with the dust of the horses' hooves; all of them alike as cheerful as though Mr. Gressler were only out to please them.

This Mr. Gressler was my acquaintance, one of my special acquaintances. Since when have I known him? Possibly since the days I reached a maturity of knowledge. Nor do I exaggerate if I say that from the day I met him we have never ceased to have a liking for one another. Now, although all and sundry like him, I can say that he prefers me to all of them, since he has taken the trouble to show me all kinds of pleasures. When I used to tire of them he would amuse me with words of wisdom. Mr. Gressler is gifted with exceptional wisdom, of the kind that undermines all the wisdom you may have learned elsewhere. Never did he ask for any compensation, but he gives of his bounty and is happy to have people accept it. Ah, there were days when I was a lad and he went out of his way to divert me; until the night my house was burned down and all my possessions went up in flames.

The night my house burned, Mr. Gressler sat playing cards with my neighbor. This neighbor, an apostate Jew, was a dealer in textiles. He lived below with his wares, while I lived above with my books. From time to time my neighbor told me that there was no great demand for his goods, that all his textiles were like paper since they were made in wartime; now that the war was over, textiles were being made of proper wool and flax again, and nobody wanted to make a suit out of the substitute stuffs which wear through and tear as soon as they are put on, if he could get himself real material. "Are you insured?" Mr. Gressler asked him. "Insured I am," he answered. While they were talking Mr. Gressler lit a cigar and said, "Drop this match in this rubbish heap and collect your insurance money." He went and set his goods on fire, and the whole house was burned down. That apostate who was insured received the value of his goods, while I, who had not insured my possessions, came out of it in a very bad way. All that I had left after the fire I spent on lawyers, because Mr. Gressler persuaded me to take action against the municipality for not saving my home and, what was more, making the fire worse. That night the firemen had had a party and grown drunk, filling their vessels with brandy and beer, and when they came to put the fire out, they made it burn even more.

For various reasons I kept my distance from Mr. Gressler after that, and it almost seemed to me that I was done with him for good and all, since I bore him a grudge for being the cause of my house burning down, and since I was devoting myself to Yekutiel Ne'eman's book. Those were the days when I was making myself ready to go up to the Land of Israel and neglected all worldly affairs; and since I was neglecting these worldly affairs, Mr. Gressler let me be. But when I set out for the Land of Israel the first person I ran across was Gressler, since he was traveling by the same ship as I was; save that I traveled on the bottom deck like poor folk do, while he traveled on the top deck like the rich.

I cannot say that I was very happy to see Mr. Gressler. On the contrary, I was very sad for fear he would remind me of my onetime deeds. So I pretended not to see him. He noticed this and did not bother me. Then it seemed to me that since our paths did not cross on board ship, they would do so even less on the land. But when the ship reached the port, my belongings were detained at the customs, and Mr. Gressler came and redeemed them. He also made things easier for me in my other affairs until we went up to Jerusalem.

Thenceforward we used to meet one another. Sometimes I

visited him and sometimes he visited me, and I don't know who followed the other more. Particularly in those days when my wife was away from the country. I had nothing to do at that time, and he was always available. And when he came he used to spend most of the night with me. His was pleasant company, for he knew all that was going on and had the inside story even before the things happened. Sometimes my heart misgave me, but I disregarded it.

8

Seeing Mr. Gressler in front of the post office, I signaled and called him by name. He stopped his carriage and helped me up.

I forgot all about the letters and the hunger and went along with him. Or maybe I did not disregard the hunger and the letters, but I put them aside for a little while.

Before I had begun talking to him properly, Mr. Hophni came toward us. I asked Mr. Gressler to turn his horses to one side, because this Hophni is a bothersome fellow, and I am afraid to have too much to do with him. Ever since he invented a new mousetrap, it has been his habit to visit me two or three times a week, to tell me all that is being written about him and his invention. And I am a weak person, I am, who cannot bear to hear the same thing twice. It is true that the mice are a great nuisance, and the mousetrap can greatly correct the evil; but when this Hophni goes gnawing at your brains, it's quite likely that you would prefer the mice to the conversation of the trapmaker.

Mr. Gressler did not turn his horses away, but on the contrary ran the carriage up to Hophni and waved to him to get in. Why did Mr. Gressler think of doing this? Either it was in order to teach me that a man has to be patient, or because he wanted to have some fun. Now I was not at all patient at that time, nor was I in the mood for fun. I stood up, took the reins out of his hands, and turned the horses off in a different direction. Since I am not an expert in steering horses, the carriage turned over on me and Mr. Gressler, and we both rolled into the street. I yelled and shouted, "Take the reins and get me out of this!" But he pretended not to hear and rolled with me, laughing as though it amused him to roll about with me in the muck.

I began to fear that a motorcar might pass and crush our heads. I raised my voice higher, but it could not be heard because of Mr. Gressler's laughter. Woe was me, Mr. Gressler kept on laughing, as though he found pleasure in dusting himself with the dust of the horses' feet and fluttering between life and death. When my distress came to a head, an old carter came along and disentangled us. I rose from the ground and gathered my bones together and tried to stand. My legs were tired and my hands were strained and my bones were broken, and all of my body was full of wounds. With difficulty I pulled myself together and prepared to go off.

Although every part of me was aching, I did not forget my hunger. I entered the first hotel that came my way, and before entering the dining hall I cleaned off all the dirt and wiped my injuries and washed my face and hands.

This hotel has an excellent name throughout the town for its spacious rooms and fine arrangements and polite and quick service and good food and excellent wine and worthy guests. When I entered the dining hall, I found all the tables full, and fine folk sitting, eating and drinking and generally enjoying themselves. The light blinded my eyes and the scent of the good food confused me. I wanted to snatch something from the table in order to stay my heart. Nor is there anything surprising about that, as I had tasted nothing all day long. But when I saw how importantly and gravely everybody was sitting there, I did not have the courage to do it.

I took a chair and sat at a table and waited for the waiter to come. Meantime I took the bill of fare and read it once, twice, and a third time. How many good things there are which a hungry man can eat his fill of, and how long it seems to take until they are brought to him! From time to time I looked up and saw waiters and waitresses passing by, all of them dressed like distinguished people. I began to prepare my heart and soul for them, and started weighing how I should talk to them. Although we are one people, each one of us talks ten languages, and above all in the Land of Israel.

9

After an hour, or maybe a little less, a waiter arrived and bowed and asked, "What would you like, sir?" What would I like and what wouldn't I like! I showed him the bill of fare and told him to fetch me just anything. And in order that he should not think me the kind of boor who eats anything without selecting it, I added to him gravely, "But I want a whole loaf." The waiter nodded his head and said, "I shall fetch it for you at once, I shall fetch it for you at once."

I sat waiting until he came back with it. He returned carrying a serving dish with all kinds of good things. I jumped from my place and wanted to take something. He went and placed the food in front of somebody else, quietly arranged each thing separately in front of him, and chatted and laughed with him, noting on his list all kinds of drinks which the fellow was ordering for his repast. Meanwhile he turned his face toward me and said, "You want a whole loaf, don't you, sir? I'm bringing it at once."

Before long he came back with an even bigger tray than the first one. I understood that it was meant for me and told myself, That's the meaning of the saying: the longer the wait, the greater the reward. As I prepared to take something, the waiter said to me, "Excuse me, sir, I'm bringing you yours at once." And he arranged the food in front of a different guest most carefully, just as he had done before.

I kept myself under control and did not grab anything from others. And since I did not grab anything from others I told myself, Just as I don't grab from others, so others won't grab my share. Nobody touches what's prepared for somebody else. Let's wait awhile and we'll get what's coming to us, just like all the other guests who came before me; for it's first come, first served.

The waiter returned. Or maybe it was another waiter and, because I was so hungry, I only thought it was the same one. I jumped from my chair in order to remind him of my presence. He came and stood and bowed to me as though mine were a new face. I began wondering who this waiter could be, a fresh fellow or the one from whom I had ordered my food; for if he were a fresh waiter, I would have to order afresh, and if it were the same one, all I had to do was to remind him. While I was thinking it over, he went his way. A little later he returned, bringing every kind of food and drink, all for the fellows sitting to the right or the left of me.

Meanwhile fresh guests came and sat down and ordered all kinds of food and drink. The waiters ran and brought their orders to them. I began to wonder why they were being served first when I had been there before them. Maybe because I had asked for a whole loaf and you could not get a whole loaf at present, so they were waiting till they could get one from the baker. I began to berate myself for asking for a whole loaf, when I would have been satisfied with even a small slice.

10

What is the use of feeling remorseful after the deed? While I was bothering my heart, I saw a child sitting holding white bread with saffron of the kind that my mother, peace be with her, used to bake us for Purim, and which I can still taste now. I would have given the world for just a mouthful from that bread. My heart was standing still with hunger, and my two eyes were set on that child eating and jumping and scattering crumbs about him.

Once again the waiter brought a full tray. Since I was sure he was bringing it for me, I sat quietly and importantly, like a person who is in no particular hurry about his food. Alas, he did not put the tray in front of me but placed it in front of somebody else.

I began to excuse the waiter with the idea that the baker had not yet brought the whole loaf, and wanted to tell him that I was prepared to do without it. But I could not get a word out of my mouth because of my hunger.

All of a sudden a clock began striking. I took my watch out of my pocket and saw that it was half-past ten. Half-past ten is just a time like any other, but in spite of this I began to shake and tremble. Maybe because I remembered the letters of Dr. Ne'eman which I had not yet sent off. I stood up hastily in order to take the letters to the post office. As I stood up, I bumped against the waiter fetching a tray full of dishes and glasses and flagons and all kinds of food and drink. The waiter staggered and dropped the tray, and everything on it fell, food and drink alike; and he also slipped and fell. The guests turned their heads and stared, some of them in alarm and some of them laughing.

The hotel keeper came and calmed me down and led me back to my place, and he asked me to wait a little while until they fetched me a different meal. From his words I understood that the food that had fallen from the waiter's hands had been intended for me, and now they were preparing me another meal.

I possessed my soul in patience and sat waiting. Meanwhile my spirit flew from place to place. Now it flew to the kitchen where they were preparing my meal, and now to the post office from which letters were being sent. By that time the post office doors were already closed, and even if I were to go there it would be no use; but the spirit flew about after its fashion, even to places that the body might not enter.

II

They did not fetch me another meal. Maybe because they had not yet had time to prepare it, or maybe because the waiters were busy making up the accounts of the guests. In any case, some of the diners rose from the table, picking their teeth and yawning on their full stomachs. As they went out, some of them stared at me in astonishment, while others paid me no attention, as though I did not exist. When the last of the guests had left, the attendant came in and turned out the lights, leaving just one light still burning faintly. I sat at a table full of bones and leavings and empty bottles and a dirty tablecloth, and waited for my meal, as the hotel keeper himself had asked me to sit down and wait for it.

While I was sitting there I suddenly began to wonder whether I had lost the letters on the way, while I had been rolling on the ground with Gressler. I felt in my pocket and saw that they were not lost; but they had become dirty with the muck and the mire and the wine.

Once again a clock struck. My eyes were weary and the lamp was smoking and black silence filled the room. In the silence came the sound of a key creaking in the lock, like the sound of a nail being hammered into the flesh. I knew that they had locked me into the room and forgotten about me, and I would not get out until they opened next day. I closed my eyes tight and made an effort to fall asleep.

I made an effort to fall asleep and closed my eyes tight. I heard a kind of rustling and saw that a mouse had jumped onto the table and was picking at the bones. Now, said I to myself, he's busy with the bones. Then he'll gnaw the tablecloth, then he'll gnaw the chair I'm sitting on, and then he'll gnaw at me. First he'll start on my shoes, then on my socks, then on my foot, then on my calf, then on my thigh, then on all my body. I turned my eyes to the wall and saw the clock. I waited for it to strike again and frighten the mouse, so that it would run away before it reached me. A cat came and I said, Here is my salvation. But the mouse paid no attention to the cat and the cat paid no attention to the mouse; and this one stood gnawing and that one stood chewing.

Meanwhile the lamp went out and the cat's eyes shone with a greenish light that filled all the room. I shook and fell. The cat shivered and the mouse jumped and both of them stared at me in alarm, one from one side and the other from the other. Suddenly the sound of trotting hooves and carriage wheels was heard, and I knew that Mr. Gressler was coming back from his drive. I called him, but he did not answer me.

Mr. Gressler did not answer me, and I lay there dozing until I fell asleep. By the time day broke, I was awakened by the sound of cleaners, men and women, coming to clean the building. They saw me and stared at me in astonishment with their brooms in their hands. At length they began laughing and asked, "Who's this fellow lying here?" Then the waiter came and said, "This is the one who was asking for the whole loaf."

I took hold of my bones and rose from the floor. My clothes were dirty, my head was heavy on my shoulders, my legs were heavy under me, my lips were cracked, and my throat was dry, while my teeth were on edge with a hunger-sweat. I stood up and went out of the hotel into the street, and from the street into another until I reached my house. All the time my mind was set on the letters that Dr. Ne'eman had handed over for me to send off by post. But that day was Sunday, when the post office was closed for things that the clerk did not consider important.

After washing off the dirt I went out to get myself some food. I was all alone at that time. My wife and children were out of the country, and all the bother of my food fell on me alone.

Translated by I.M. Lask

At the Outset of the Day

After the enemy destroyed my home I took my little daughter in my arms and fled with her to the city. Gripped with terror, I fled in frenzied haste a night and a day until I arrived at the courtyard of the Great Synagogue one hour before nightfall on the eve of the Day of Atonement. The hills and mountains that had accompanied us departed, and I and the child entered into the courtyard. From out of the depths rose the Great Synagogue, on its left the old house of study and directly opposite that, one doorway facing the other, the new house of study.

This was the house of prayer and these the houses of Torah that I had kept in my mind's eye all my life. If I chanced to forget them during the day, they would stir themselves and come to me at night in my dreams, even as during my waking hours. Now that the enemy had destroyed my home, I and my little daughter sought refuge in these places; it seemed that my child recognized them, so often had she heard about them.

An aura of peace and rest suffused the courtyard. The Children of Israel had already finished the afternoon prayer and, having gone home, were sitting down to the last meal before the fast to prepare themselves for the morrow, that they might have strength and health enough to return in repentance.

A cool breeze swept through the courtyard, caressing the last of the heat in the thick walls, and a whitish mist spiraled up the steps of the house, the kind children call angels' breath.

I rid my mind of all that the enemy had done to us and reflected upon the Day of Atonement drawing ever closer, that holy festival comprised of love and affection, mercy and prayer, a day whereon men's supplications are dearer, more desired, more acceptable than at all other times. Would that they might appoint a reader of prayers worthy to stand before the ark, for recent generations have seen the decline of emissaries of the congregation who know how to pray; and cantors who reverence their throats with their trilling, but bore the heart, have increased. And I, I needed strengthening—and, needless to say, my little daughter, a babe torn away from her home.

I glanced at her, at my little girl standing all atremble by the memorial candle in the courtyard, warming her little hands over the flame. Growing aware of my eyes, she looked at me like a frightened child who finds her father standing behind her and sees that his thoughts are muddled and his heart humbled.

Grasping her hand in mine, I said, "Good men will come at once and give me a tallit with an adornment of silver just like the one the enemy tore. You remember the lovely tallit that I used to spread over your head when the priests would rise up to bless the people. They will give me a large festival prayer book filled with prayers, too, and I will wrap myself in the tallit and take the book and pray to God, who saved us from the hand of the enemy who sought to destroy us.

"And what will they bring you, my dearest daughter? You, my darling, they will bring a little prayer book full of letters, full of all of the letters of the alphabet and the vowel marks, too. And now, dearest daughter, tell me, an *alef* and a *bet* that come together with a *kametz* beneath the *alef*—how do you say them?"

"*Av,*" my daughter answered.

"And what does it mean?" I asked.

"Father," my daughter answered, "like you're my father."

"Very nice, that's right, an *alef* with a *kametz* beneath and a *bet* with no dot in it make *av*."

"And now, my daughter," I continued, "what father is greater than all other fathers? Our Father in heaven, who is my father and your father and the father of the whole world. You see, my daughter, two little letters stand there in the prayer book as if they were all alone, then they come together and lo and behold they are *av*. And not only these letters but all letters, all of them join together to make words and words make prayers and the prayers rise up before our Father in heaven who listens very, very carefully, to all that we pray, if only our hearts cling to the upper light like a flame clings to a candle."

Even as I stood there speaking of the power of the letters, a breeze swept through the courtyard and pushed the memorial candle against my daughter. Fire seized hold of her dress. I ripped off the flaming garment, leaving the child naked, for what she was wearing was all that remained of her lovely clothes. We had fled in panic, destruction at our heels, and had taken nothing with us. Now that fire had consumed her dress, I had nothing with which to cover my daughter.

I turned this way and that, seeking anything my daughter could clothe herself with. I sought, but found nothing. Wherever I directed my eyes, I met emptiness. I'll go to the corner of the storeroom, I said to myself, where torn sacred books are hidden away, perhaps there I will find something. Many a time when I was a lad I had rummaged about there and found all sorts of things, sometimes the conclusion of a matter and sometimes its beginning or its middle. But now I turned there and found nothing with which to cover my little girl. Do not be surprised that I found nothing. When books were read, they were rent; but now that books are not read, they are not rent.

I stood there worried and distraught. What could I do for my daughter, what could I cover her nakedness with? Night was drawing on and with it the chill of the night, and I had no garment, nothing to wrap my daughter in. I recalled the home of Reb Alter, who had gone up to the Land of Israel. I'll go to his sons and daughters, I decided, and ask clothing of them. I left my daughter as she was and headed for the household of Reb Alter.

How pleasant to walk without being pursued. The earth is light and comfortable and does not burn beneath one's feet, nor do the heavens fling thorns into one's eyes. But I ran rather than walked, for even if no man was pursuing me, time was: the sun was about to set and the hour to gather for the evening prayer was nigh. I hurried lest the members of Reb Alter's household might already be getting up to leave for the house of prayer.

It is comforting to remember the home of a dear friend in time of distress. Reb Alter, peace be with him, had circumcised me, and a covenant of love bound us together. As long as Reb Alter lived in his home I was a frequent visitor there, the more so in the early days when I was a classmate of his grandson Gad. Reb Alter's house was small, so small that one wondered how such a large man could live there. But Reb Alter was wise and made himself so little that his house seemed large.

The house, built on one of the low hills surrounding the Great Synagogue, had a stucco platform protruding from it. Reb Alter, peace be with him, had been in the habit of sitting on that platform with his long pipe in his mouth, sending wreaths of smoke gliding into space. Many a time I stood waiting for the pipe to go out so I could bring him a light. My grandfather, peace be with him, had given Reb Alter that pipe at my circumcision feast. "Your grandfather knows pipes very well," Reb Alter told me once, "and knows how to pick just the right pipe for every mouth."

Reb Alter stroked his beard as he spoke, like one well aware that he deserved that pipe, even though he was a modest man. His modesty showed itself one Friday afternoon before sunset. As he put out the pipe, and the Sabbath was approaching, he said, "Your grandfather never has to put out his pipe; he knows how to smoke more or less as time necessitates."

Well, then, I entered the home of Reb Alter and found his daughter, together with a small group of old men and old women, sit-

ting near a window while an old man with a face like a wrinkled pear
stood reading them a letter. All of them listened attentively, wiping
their eyes. Because so many years had passed, I mistook Reb Alter's
daughter for her mother. What's going on? I asked myself. On the
eve of the Day of Atonement darkness is falling, and these people
have not lit a "candle of life." And what sort of letter is this? If from
Reb Alter, he is already dead. Perhaps it was from his grandson, my
friend Gad, perhaps news had come from Reb Alter's grandson Gad,
who had frequented the house of study early and late. One day he
left early and did not return.

It is said that two nights prior to his disappearance, his wet-
nurse had seen him in a dream sprouting the plume of a peculiar
bird from his head, a plume that shrieked, "A, B, C, D!" Reb Alter's
daughter folded the letter and put it between the mirror and the wall.
Her face, peeking out of the mirror, was the face of an aged woman
bearing the burden of her years. And alongside her face appeared my
own, green as a wound that has not formed a scab.

I turned away from the mirror and looked at the rest of the old
people in Reb Alter's home and tried to say something to them. My
lips flipped against each other like a man who wishes to say something
but, upon seeing something bizarre, is seized with fright.

One of the old men noticed the state of panic I was in. Tap-
ping one finger against his spectacles, he said, "You are looking at our
torn clothing. Enough that creatures like ourselves still have skin on
our flesh." The rest of the old men and old women heard and nodded their heads in agreement. As they did so, their skin quivered. I
took hold of myself, walked backward, and left.

I left in despair and, empty-handed, with no clothing, with
nothing at all, returned to my daughter. I found her standing in a
corner of the courtyard pressed against the wall next to the purification board on which the dead are washed. Her hair was loose and
wrapped about her. How great is Thy goodness, O God, in putting
wisdom into the heart of such a little girl to enable her to wrap herself in her hair after her dress has burned off, for as long as she had
not been given a garment it was good that she covered herself with
her hair. But how great was the sadness that enveloped me at that

moment, the outset of this holy festival whose joy has no parallel all the year. But now there was no joy and no sign of joy, only pain and anguish.

The stone steps sounded beneath feet clad in felt slippers and long stockings, as Jews bearing tallitot and ritual gowns streamed to the house of prayer. With my body I covered my little girl, trembling from the cold, and I stroked her hair. Again I looked in the storeroom where the torn pages from sacred books were kept, the room where in my youth I would find, among the fragments, wondrous and amazing things. I remember one of the sayings, it went approximately like this: "At times she takes the form of an old woman and at times the form of a little girl. And when she takes the form of a little girl, don't imagine that your soul is as pure as a little girl; this is but an indication that she passionately yearns to recapture the purity of her infancy when she was free of sin. The fool substitutes the *form* for the *need*; the wise man substitutes *will* for *need*."

A tall man with a red beard came along, picking from his teeth the last remnants of the final meal, pushing his wide belly out to make room for himself. He stood about like a man who knew that God would not run away and there was no need to hurry. He regarded us for a moment, ran his eyes over us, then said something with a double meaning.

My anger flowed into my hand, and I caught him by the beard and began yanking at his hair. Utterly astonished, he did not move. He had good cause to be astonished too: a small fellow like me lifting my hand against a brawny fellow like him. Even I was astonished: had he laid hold of me, he would not have let me go whole.

Another tall, husky fellow came along, one who boasted of being my dearest friend. I looked up at him, hoping that he would come between us. He took his spectacles, wiped them, and placed them on his nose. The whites of his eyes turned green and his spectacles shone like moist scales. He stood looking at us as though we were characters in an amusing play.

I raised my voice and shouted, "A fire has sprung up and has burned my daughter's dress, and here she stands shivering from the cold!" He nodded his head in my direction and once more wiped his spectacles. Again they shone like moist scales and flashed like green scum on water. Once more I shouted, "It's not enough that no one gives her any clothing, but they must abuse us, too!" The fellow nodded his head and repeated my words as though pleased by them. As he spoke he turned his eyes away from me so that they might not see me, and that he might imagine he had made up the story on his own. I was no longer angry with my enemy, being so gripped with fury at this man: though he had prided himself on being my friend, he was repeating all that had befallen me as though it were a tale of his own invention.

My daughter began crying. "Let's run away from here."

"What are you saying?" I answered. "Don't you see that night has fallen and that we have entered the holy day? And if we were to flee, where would we flee and where could we hide?"

Where could we hide? Our home lay in ruins and the enemies covered all the roads. And if by some miracle we escaped, could we depend upon miracles? And here were the two houses of study and the Great Synagogue in which I studied Torah and in which I prayed and here was the corner where they had hidden away sacred books worn with age. As a little boy I rummaged about here frequently, finding all sorts of things. I do not know why, on this particular day, we found nothing, but I remember that I once found something important about *need* and *form* and *will*. Were it not for the urgency of the day I would explain this matter to you thoroughly, and you would see that it is by no means allegorical but a simple and straightforward affair.

I glanced at my little girl who stood trembling from the cold, for she had been stripped of her clothing, she didn't even have a shirt, the night was chill, and the song of winter birds resounded from the mountains. I glanced at my daughter, the darling of my heart, like a father who glances at his little daughter, and a loving smile formed on my lips. This was a very timely smile, for it rid her of her fear completely. I stood then with my daughter in the open courtyard of the Great Synagogue and the two houses of study which all my life stirred themselves and came to me in my dreams and now stood before me, fully real. The gates of the houses of prayer were open, and from all three issued the voices of the readers of prayer. In which direction should we look and whither should we bend our ears?

He who gives eyes to see with and ears to hear with directed my eyes and ears to the old house of study. The house of study was full of Jews, the doors of the ark were open, and the ark was full of old Torah scrolls, and among them gleamed a new scroll clothed in a red mantle with silver points. This was the scroll that I had written in memory of the souls of days that had departed. A silver plate was hung over the scroll, with letters engraved upon it, shining letters. And even though I stood far off I saw what they were. A thick rope was stretched in front of the scroll that it might not slip and fall.

My soul fainted within me, and I stood and prayed as those wrapped in tallitot and ritual gowns. And even my little girl, who had dozed off, repeated in her sleep each and every prayer in sweet melodies no ear has ever heard.

I do not enlarge. I do not exaggerate.

Translated by David S. Segal

The Sign

In the year when the news reached us that all the Jews in my town had been killed, I was living in a certain section of Jerusalem, in a house I had built for myself after the disturbances of 1929 (5629 which numerically is equal to "The Eternity of Israel"). On the night when the Arabs destroyed my home, I vowed that if God would save me from the hands of the enemy and I should live, I would build a house in this particular neighborhood which the Arabs had tried to destroy. By the grace of God, I was saved from the hands of our despoilers and my wife and children and I remained alive in Jerusalem. Thus I fulfilled my vow and there built a house and made a garden. I planted a tree, and lived in that place with my wife and children, by the will of our Rock and Creator. Sometimes we dwelt in quiet and rest, and sometimes in fear and trembling because of the desert sword that waved in fuming anger over all the inhabitants of our holy land. And even though many troubles and evils passed over my head, I accepted all with good humor and without complaint. On the contrary, with every sorrow I used to say how much better it was to live in the Land of Israel than outside the land, for the Land of Israel has given us the strength to stand up for our lives, while outside the land we went to meet the enemy like sheep to the slaughter. Tens of thousands of Israel, none of whom the enemy was worthy even to touch, were killed and strangled and drowned and buried alive; among them my brothers and friends and family, who went through all kinds of great sufferings in their lives and in their deaths, by the wickedness of our blasphemers and our desecrators, a filthy people, blasphemers of God, whose wickedness had not been matched since man was placed upon the earth.

2

I made no lament for my city and did not call for tears or for mourning over the congregation of God whom the enemy had wiped out. The day when we heard the news of the city and its dead was the afternoon before Shavuot, so I put aside my mourning for the dead because of the joy of the season when our Torah was given. It seemed to me that the two things came together, to show me that in God's love for His people, He still gives us some of that same power which He gave us as we stood before Sinai and received the Torah and commandments; it was that power which stood up within me so that I could pass off my sorrow over the dead of my city for the happiness of the holiday of Shavuot, when the Torah was given to us, and not to our blasphemers and desecrators who kill us because of it.

3

Our house was ready for the holiday. Everything about the house said: Shavuot.

The sun shone down on the outside of the house; inside, on the walls, we had hung cypress, pine, and laurel branches, and flowers. Every beautiful flower and everything with a sweet smell had been brought in to decorate the house for the holiday of Shavuot. In all the days I had lived in the Land of Israel, our house had never been decorated so nicely as it was that day. All the flaws in the house had vanished, and not a crack was to be seen, either in the ceiling or in the walls. From the places where the cracks in the house used to gape with open mouths and laugh at the builders, there came instead the pleasant smell of branches and shrubs, and especially of the flowers we had brought from our garden. These humble creatures, which because of their great modesty don't raise themselves high above the ground except to give off their good smell, made the eye rejoice because of the many colors with which the Holy One, blessed be He, has decorated them, to glorify His land, which, in His loving-kindness, He has given to us.

4

Dressed in a new summer suit and new light shoes, I went to the house of prayer. Thus my mother, may she rest in peace, taught me: if a man gets new clothes or new shoes, he wears them first to honor the holiday, and goes to the synagogue in them. I am thankful to my body, which waited for me, and did not tempt me into wearing the new clothes and shoes before the holiday, even though the old ones were heavy, and hot desert winds ran through the country. And—if I haven't reached the heights of all my forefathers' deeds—in these matters I can do as well as my forefathers, for my body stands ready to fulfill most of those customs which depend upon it.

5

I walked to the house of prayer. The two stores in the neighborhood were shut, and even the bus, which usually violates the Sabbath, was gone from the neighborhood. Not a man was seen in the streets, except for little errand boys delivering flowers. They too, by the time you could look at them, had disappeared. Nothing remained of them except the smell of the flowers they had brought, and this smell merged with the aroma of the gardens in our neighborhood.

The neighborhood was quietly at rest. No one stopped me on the street, and no one asked me for news of the world. Even if they had asked, I wouldn't have told them what had happened to my city. The days have come when every man keeps his sorrows to himself. What would it help if I told someone else what happened to my city? His city surely had also suffered that same fate.

6

I arrived at the house of prayer and sat down in my place. I kept the events in my city, as they appeared to me, hidden in my heart. A few days later, when the true stories reached me, I saw that the deeds of the enemy were evil beyond the power of the imagination. The power of the imagination is stronger than the power of deeds, except for the evil of the nations, which goes beyond all imagination.

I opened a Mahzor and looked at the evening prayers for the first night of Shavuot. People outside the Land of Israel generally add many liturgical poems, especially in those ancient communities that follow the customs of their forefathers. Although I think of myself as a resident of the Land of Israel in every sense, I like these piyyutim, which prepare the soul for the theme of the day. Our teachers, the holy writers of the piyyutim, are good intermediaries between the hearts of Israel and their Father in heaven. They knew what we need to ask of God and what He demands of us, and they wrote hymns to open our lips before our Father in heaven.

The people who come to the house of prayer began to gather. Even those whom one usually doesn't see in the synagogue came, to bring their children. As long as a child is a child, he is drawn after his father and draws his father with him. That is, he is drawn after his Father in heaven and draws with him the father who gave him birth. In my town, all the synagogues used to be filled with babes like these. They were good and sweet and healthy; now they are all dead. The hand of the enemy has finished them all. There is no remnant, no one left. And if a few of them do remain, they've been captured by Gentiles and are being educated by Gentiles. Let's hope that they too will not be added to our enemies. Those about whom it is written "I shall bear you on the wings of eagles and bring you unto Me" are given over to others and are trampled under the feet of human filth.

7

Although on the Sabbath and festivals one says the evening prayers early, on Shavuot we wait to say Maariv until the stars are out.

For if we were to pray early and receive the holiness of the festival, we would be shortening the days of the Omer, and the Torah said: "There shall be seven full weeks."

Since they had already finished Minhah and it was not yet time for Maariv, most of the congregation sat talking with one another, except for the children, who stood about in wonder. I know that if I say this people will smile at me, but I'll say it anyway: The same thing happened to those children at this season of the giving of our Torah as happened to them when their souls stood before Mount Sinai, ready to receive the Torah the following day.

While the adults were sitting and talking, and the children were standing about in amazement, the time came for the evening prayer. The gabbai pounded on the table and the leader of the prayers went down before the ark. After a short order of prayers, including neither piyyutim nor "And Moses declared the festivals of the Lord," they greeted one another and went home in peace.

8

I came home and greeted my wife and children with the blessing of the holiday. I stood amazed to think that here I was celebrating our holiday in my home, in my land, with my wife and children, at a time when tens of thousands of Israel were being killed and slaughtered and burned and buried alive, and those who were still alive were running about as though lost in the fields and forests, or were hidden in holes in the earth.

I bowed my head toward the earth, this earth of the Land of Israel upon which my house is built, and in which my garden grows with trees and flowers, and I said over it the verse "Because of you, the soul liveth." Afterward I said kiddush and the blessing "Who has given us life," and I took a sip of wine and passed my glass to my wife and children. I didn't even dilute the wine with tears. This says a lot for a man; his city is wiped out of the world, and he doesn't even dilute his drink with tears.

I washed my hands and recited the blessing over the bread, giving everyone a piece of the fine challot that were formed in the shape of the Tablets, to remember the two tablets of the Covenant that Moses brought down from heaven. The custom of Israel is Torah: if the bread comes from the earth, its shape is from the heavens.

We sat down to the festive meal of the first night of Shavuot. Part of the meal was the fruit of our soul, which we had turned with our own hands and watered with our own lips. When we came here we found parched earth, as hands had not touched the land since her children had left her. But now she is a fruitful land, thankful to her masters, and giving us of her goodness.

The meal was good. All that was eaten was of the fruits of the land. Even the dairy dishes were from the milk of cows who grazed about our house. It is good when a man's food comes from close to him and not from far away, for that which is close to a man is close to his tastes. Yet Solomon, in praising the woman of valor, praises her because she "brings her bread from afar." But the days of Solomon were different, for Solomon ruled over all the lands and every man in Israel was a hero. And as a man's wife is like her husband, the women of valor in Israel left it for the weak to bring their bread from nearby, while they would go to the trouble of bringing it from afar. In these times, when the land has shrunk and we all have trouble making a living, bread from nearby is better than that which comes from afar.

9

The meal which the land had given us was good, and good too is the land itself, which gives life to its inhabitants. As the holiday began, Jerusalem was freed from the rough desert winds, which rule from Passover to Shavuot, and a soft breeze blew from the desert and the sea. Two winds blow in our neighborhood, one from the sea and one from the desert, and between them blows another wind, from the little gardens that the people of the neighborhood have planted around their houses. Our house too stands in the midst of a garden where there grow cypresses and pines, and, at their feet, lilies, dahlias, carnations, snapdragons, dandelions, chrysanthemums, and violets. It is the way of pines and cypresses not to let even grass grow between them, but the trees in our garden looked with favor upon our flowers and lived side by side with them, for they remembered how hard we had worked when they were first beginning to grow. We were stingy with our own bread and bought saplings; we drank less water in order to water the gentle young trees, and we guarded them against the wicked herdsmen who used to send their cattle into our garden. Now they have become big trees, which shade us from the sun, giving us their branches as covering for the sukkah, and greens for the holiday of Shavuot, to cover our walls in memory of the event at Sinai. They used to do the same in my town when I was a child, except that in my town most of the greens came from the gardens of the Gentiles, while here I took from my own garden, from the branches of my trees and from the flowers between my trees. They gave off a good aroma and added flavor to our meal.

10

I sat inside my house with my wife and little children. The house and everything in it said: Holiday. So too we and our garments, for we were dressed in the new clothes we had made for the festival. The festival is for God and for us; we honor it in whatever way we can, with pleasant goods and new clothing. God in heaven also honors the holiday and gives us the strength to rejoice.

I looked around at my family, and I felt in the mood to tell them about what we used to do in my city. It was true that my city was dead, and those who were not dead were like the dead, but before the enemy had come and killed them all, my city used to be full of life and good and blessing. If I start telling tales of my city I never have enough. But let's tell just a few of the deeds of the town. And since we are in the midst of the holiday of Shavuot, I'll tell a little concerning this day.

II

From the Sabbath when we blessed the new month of Sivan, we emerged from the mourning of the days of the Omer, and a spirit of rest passed through the town: especially on the New Moon, and especially with the saying of Hallel. When the leader of prayer said, "The heavens are the heavens of God, but the earth hath He given to the children of men," we saw that the earth and even the river were smiling at us. I don't know whether we or the river first said, "It's all right to swim." But even the heavens agreed that the river was good for bathing, for the sun had already begun to break through its coldness; not only through the coldness of the river, but of all the world. A man could now open his window without fear of the cold. Some people turned their ears toward the sound of a bird, for the birds had already returned to their nests and were making themselves heard. In the houses arose the aroma of dairy foods being prepared for Shavuot, and the smell of the fresh-woven clothes of the brides and grooms who would enter under the bridal canopy after the holiday. The sound of the barber's scissors could be heard in the town, and every face was renewed. All were ready to welcome the holiday on which we received the Torah and commandments. See how the holiday on which we received the Torah and commandments is happier and easier than all the other holidays. On Passover we can't eat *whatever* we want; on Sukkot we can't eat *wherever* we want. But on Shavuot we can eat anything we want, wherever we want to eat it.

The world is also glad and rejoices with us. The lids of the skies are as bright as the sun, and glory and beauty cover the earth.

12

Now, children, listen to me: I'll tell you something of my youth. Now your father is old, and if he let his beard grow as did Abraham, you'd see white hair in his beard. But I too was once a little boy who used to do the things children do. While the old men sat in the house of study preparing themselves for the time of the giving of the Torah the following morning, my friends and I would stand outside looking upward, hoping to catch the moment when the sky splits open and everything you ask for (even supernatural things!) is immediately given you by God—if you are worthy and you catch the right moment. In that case, why do I feel as though none of my wishes has ever been granted? Because I had so many things to ask for that before I decided what to wish first, sleep came upon me and I dozed off. When a man is young, his wishes are many; before he gets around to asking for anything, he is overcome by sleep. When a man is old, he has no desires; if he asks for anything, he asks for a little sleep.

Now let me remove the sleep from my eyes, and I'll tell a little bit about this day.

Nowadays a man is found outdoors more than in his house. In former times, if a man's business didn't bring him out, he sat either in his house or in the house of study. But on the first day of Shavuot everybody would go to the gardens and forests outside the town in honor of the Torah, which was given outdoors. The trees and bushes and shrubs and flowers that I know from those walks on the first day of Shavuot, I know well. The animals and beasts and birds that I know from those walks on the first day of Shavuot, I know well. How so? While we were walking, my father, of blessed memory, would show me a tree or a bush or a flower and say, "This is its name in the holy tongue." He would show me an animal or a beast or a bird and say to me, "This is its name in the holy tongue." For if they were worthy to have the Torah write their names, surely we must recognize them and know their names. In that case, why don't I list their names? Because of those who have turned upon the Torah and wrought havoc with the language.

13

I saw that my wife and children enjoyed the tales of my town. So I went on and told them more, especially about the Great Synagogue—the glory of the town—the beauty of which was mentioned even by the gentile princes. Not a Shavuot went by that Count Pototsky didn't send a wagon full of greens for the synagogue. There was one family in the town that had the special rights in arranging these branches.

I also told them about our little kloyz, our prayer room. People know me as one of the regulars in the old house of study, but before I pitched my tent in the old house of study, I was one of the young men of the kloyz. I have so very very much to tell about those times but here I'll tell only things that concern this day.

On the day before Shavuot eve, I used to go out to the woods near town with a group of friends to gather green boughs. I would take a ball of cord from my mother, may she rest in peace, and I would string it up from the roof of our house in the shape of a Star of David, and on the cord I would hang the leaves we had pulled off the branches, one by one. I don't like to boast, but something like this it's all right for me to tell. Even the old men of the kloyz used to say, "Fine, fine. The work of an artist, the work of an artist." These men were careful about what they said, and their mouth uttered no word that did not come from their heart. I purposely didn't tell my wife and children about the poems I used to write after the festival—sad songs. When I saw the faded leaves falling from the Star of David I would be overcome by sadness, and I would compose sad poems.

Once my heart was aroused, my soul remembered other things

about Shavuot. Among them were the paper roses that were stuck to the windowpanes. This was done by the simple folk at the edge of town. The respected heads of families in town did not do this, for they clung carefully to the customs of their fathers, while the others did not. But since the enemy has destroyed them all together, I shall not distinguish between them here.

I told my wife and children many more things about the town and about the day. And to everything I said, I added, "This was in former days, when the town stood in peace." Nevertheless, I was able to tell the things calmly and not in sorrow, and one would not have known from my voice what had happened to my town—that all the Jews in it had been killed. The Holy One, blessed be He, has been gracious to Israel: even when we remember the greatness and glory of bygone days, our soul does not leave us out of sorrow and longing. Thus a man like me can talk about the past, and his soul doesn't pass out of him as he speaks.

14

Following the Blessing after Meals I said to my wife and children, "You go to sleep, and I'll go to the synagogue for the vigil of Shavuot night." Now I was born in Buczacz and grew up in the old house of study, where the spirit of the great men of Israel pervaded. But I shall admit freely that I don't follow them in all their ways. They read the Order of Study for Shavuot night and I read the book of hymns that Rabbi Solomon Ibn Gabirol, may his soul rest, composed on the six hundred thirteen commandments.

There have arisen many poets in Israel, who have graced the order of prayers with their poems and strengthened the hearts of Israel with their piyyutim, serving as good intermediaries between the hearts of Israel and their Father in heaven. And even I, when I humbly come to plead for my soul before my Rock and Creator, find expression in the words of our holy poets—especially in the poems of Rabbi Solomon Ibn Gabirol, may his soul rest.

I have already told elsewhere how, when I was a small child, my father, of blessed memory, would bring me a new prayer book every year from the fair. Once Father brought me a prayer book and I opened it to a plea of Rabbi Solomon Ibn Gabirol. I read and was amazed: Was it possible that such a righteous man as this, whose name was written in the prayer book, did not find God before him at all times and in every hour, so that he had to write "At the dawn I seek Thee, my rock and tower"? Not only did God make him seek Him, but even when the poet found Him, fear fell upon him and he stood confused. Thus he says, "Before Thy greatness I stand and am confounded."

As I lie down at night I see this saint rising from his bed on a stormy windblown night. The cold engulfs him and enters into his bones, and a cold wind slaps at his face, ripping his cloak and struggling with its fringes. The Tzaddik strengthens himself to call for God. When he finds Him, terror falls upon him out of the fear of God and the majesty of His presence.

For many days that saint wouldn't leave my sight. Sometimes he seemed to me like a baby asking for his father, and sometimes like a grownup, exhausted from so much chasing after God. And when he finally does find Him, he's confused because of God's greatness.

After a time, sorrow came and added to sorrow.

15

Once, on the Sabbath after Passover, I got up and went to the great house of study. I found the old cantor raising his voice in song. There were men in Buczacz who would not allow the interruption of the prayers between the Blessing of Redemption and the Amidah for additional hymns. Thus the cantor would go up to the platform after Mussaf and recite the hymns of redemption. I turned my ear and listened to him intone: "O poor captive in a foreign land." I felt sorry for the poor captive girl, who must have been in great trouble, judging from the tone of the cantor. It was a little hard for me to understand why God didn't hurry and take her out of captivity, or why He didn't have mercy on the poor old man who stood, his head bowed, begging and praying for her. I also wondered at the men of my city, who were doing nothing to redeem her from captivity.

One day I was turning the pages of the big prayer book in my grandfather's house, and I found those same words written in the prayer book. I noticed that every line started with a large letter. I joined the letters together, and they formed the name "Solomon." My heart leaped for joy, for I knew it was Rabbi Solomon from my prayer book. But I felt sorry for that Tzaddik. As though he didn't have enough troubles himself, searching for God and standing in confusion before Him, he also had to feel the sorrow of this captive girl who was taken as a slave to a foreign country. A few days later I came back and leafed through the prayer book, checking the first letters of the lines of every hymn. Whenever I found a hymn with the name Solomon Ibn Gabirol written in it, I didn't put it down until I had read it through.

16

I don't remember when I started the custom of reading the hymns of Rabbi Solomon Ibn Gabirol on Shavuot eve, but since I started this custom, I haven't skipped a year. It goes without saying that I did it while I lived in Germany, where they like piyyutim, but even here in the Land of Israel, where they don't say many of these poems, I haven't done away with my custom. Even in times of danger, when the Arabs were besieging Jerusalem and machine-gun fire was flying over our heads, I didn't keep myself from the house of study, where I spent most of the night, as has been done everywhere, in all generations, in remembrance of our fathers who stood trembling all night in the third month after going out of Egypt, waiting to receive the Torah from God Himself.

17

My home is near the house of prayer; it takes only a little while to get there. You walk down the narrow street on which my house stands, and you turn down the wide street at the end, till you come to a little wooden shack which serves as a house of prayer. That night the way made itself longer. Or maybe it didn't make itself longer, but I made it longer. My thoughts had tired out my soul, and my soul my feet. I stopped and stood more than I walked.

18

The world and all within it rested in a kind of pleasant silence: the houses, the gardens, the woods; and above them the heavens, the moon and the stars. Heaven and earth know that if it weren't for Israel, who accepted the Torah, they would not be standing. They stand and fulfill their tasks: the earth to bring forth bread, and the heavens to give light to the earth and those who dwell upon it. Could it be that even in my hometown the heavens are giving light and the earth bringing forth its produce? In the Land of Israel, the Holy One, blessed be He, judges the land Himself, whereas outside the land He has handed this supervision over to angels. The angels' first task is to turn their eyes aside from the deeds of the Gentiles who do evil to Israel, and therefore the heavens there give their light and the earth its produce—perhaps twice as much as in the Land of Israel.

19

I stood among the little houses, each of which was surrounded by a garden. Since the time we were exiled from our land, this area had given forth thorns and briers; now that we have returned, it is rebuilt with houses, trees, shrubs, and flowers.

Because I love the little houses and their blossoming gardens, I'll tell their story.

A young veterinarian from Constantinople was appointed to watch over the animals of the sultan. One day he was working in a village in the midst of the desert sands. On his way home, he stopped to rest. He looked up and saw the Dead Sea on one side and the Temple Mount on the other. A fresh breeze was blowing, and the air was better and more pleasant than any place in the land. He got down from his donkey and began to stroll about, until he found himself making a path among the thorn bushes, briers, and rocks. If only I could live here with my wife and children, he thought. But to live here is impossible, as the place is far from any settlement, and there's no sign that anyone lives here, nor is there any form of life, except for the birds of the sky and various creeping things. The doctor remained until it began to get dark and the time came to return to the city. He mounted his ass and went back to the city. A few days later he came again. A few days after that he came once more. Thus he did several times.

It happened that a certain Arab's cow became sick. He brought her to the doctor. The doctor prepared some medicine for her, and she got well. After a while, another one got sick. She too was brought to the doctor. Again he prepared some medicine and she became well. The Arab heard that the doctor wanted to build a summer house outside of town. The Arab said to him, "I have a piece of land near the town. If you like it, it's yours." It turned out to be just the spot the doctor had wanted. He bought thirty dunams of land from the Arab, built a summer house, dug a well, and planted a garden and an almond grove. All the clever people in Jerusalem laughed at him and said, "He's buried his money in the desert." But he himself was happy with his lot, and whenever he was free from work he would ride out there on his ass and busy himself with planting. Sometimes he would take along his young wife and small children to share in his happiness.

The word got around. There was a group of people that worked for the settlement of the land. They went and bought a piece of land near his. They divided their section up into lots and sent messengers to other lands to offer Zionists the purchase of a share in the inheritance of the Land of Israel. A few among them bought.

The Great War came, bringing death on all sides, and destroying in one hour that which had been built up over many generations. If one was not hurt bodily by the war, it hurt one financially. And if neither one's body nor one's money was hurt, it damaged one's soul. The war was harder for the Jews than for anyone else, as it affected their bodies, their money, and their souls. Thus it was in the place we are discussing. Turkey, which also entered the war, sent her legions to wherever she ruled. One legion came to Jerusalem and camped there, in this place, on the land of the doctor. The soldiers ripped out the almond trees to make fires to cook their food and to warm their bodies, and turned the garden into a lair for cannons.

From out of the storm of war and the thunder of cannons, a kind of heralding voice was heard—a voice that, if we interpreted it according to our wishes and desires, heralded the end of troubles and the beginning of good, salvation, and comfort. The war, however, was still going strong. Neither the end of the troubles nor the beginning of salvation could yet be seen.

Slowly the strength of those who had started the fighting wore out, the hands of war were broken, and they could fight no more. The bravery of the heroes had been drained, so they left the battlefronts. Behind them they left destruction and desolation, wailing and tears, forever.

20

After the war Jerusalem awoke, bit by bit, from her destruction. A few people began to think of expanding the city, for even if there were a few places left that had not been damaged by the war, they were crowded and overpopulated. Even before the war, when Jerusalem lay in peace and her inhabitants were satisfied with little, the air had become stifling. How much more so after the war. Even before the war there was little room left in Jerusalem; after the war, when the city was filled with new immigrants, how much more so.

People formed little societies to buy land in and around Jerusalem, and began to build new neighborhoods. These were small and far from town, and the sums owed were always great. People ran from bank to bank, borrowing in one place to pay off in another, paying in one place and borrowing in another. If it weren't for the bit of peace a man finds in his home and garden, they would have fallen by the way.

21

That stretch of barren desert also had its turn. They remembered the lands the doctor had bought and asked him to sell them part of his holdings. He liked the idea, sold them a section of his land, and helped them to buy from others. The news got around, and people began to flock. They bought twenty-one thousand dunams, each dunam equaling a thousand six hundred Turkish pik, at the price of a grush and a half a pik. Some bought in order to build, and some bought in order to sell.

Now I shall leave the real-estate agents who held back the building of Jerusalem. If a man wanted to build a house, they asked so much money that he was taken aback and went away. And if he agreed to come the next day to sign away his wealth, it would happen that overnight the lot had been sold to someone else, who had more than doubled his bid. The agents used to conspire together. Someone would ask to have a house built, and either they wouldn't build it for him or they'd build it in the wrong place. So his lot stood empty, without a house, along with the rest of the fields to which the same thing had happened.

The neighborhood was finally built, but its residents were not able to open a school or a post office branch or a pharmacy or any of the institutions that people from the city needed, except for two or three stores, each of which was superfluous because of the others. During the disturbances it was even worse. Since the population was small, they could not hold out against the enemy, either in the disturbance of 1929 or in the War of Independence. And between 1929 and the War of Independence, in the days of the riots and horrors that began in 1936 and lasted until World War II began, they were given over to the hands of the enemy, and a man wouldn't dare to go out alone.

Of the Zionists outside the land who had bought plots before the war, some died in the war and others wound up in various other places. When those who were fortunate enough to come to the land saw what had happened to the section, they sold their lots and built homes in other places. Of those who bought them, perhaps one or two built houses, and the rest left them until a buyer would come their way, to fill their palms with money.

22

Now I shall leave those who did not build the neighborhood and shall tell only about those who did build it.

Four men went out into the dusts of the desert, an hour's walking distance from the city, and built themselves houses, each in one spot, according to lots. The whole area was still a wilderness; there were neither roads nor any signs of habitation. They would go to work in the city every morning and come back an hour or two before dark, bringing with them all that they needed. Then they would eat something and rush out to their gardens to kill snakes and scorpions, weed out thorns, level off holes in the ground, prepare the soil, and plant and water the gentle saplings, in the hope that these saplings would grow into great trees and give their shade. As yet there were neither trees nor shrubs in the neighborhood, but only parched earth which gave rise to thorns and briers. When the desert storms came, they sometimes lasted as long as nine days, burning our skin and flesh, and drying out our bones. Even at night there was no rest. But when the storms passed, the land was like paradise once again. A man would go out to his garden, water his gentle young trees, dig holes, and add two or three shrubs or flowers to his garden.

From the very beginning, one of the four founders took it upon himself to attend to community business: to see that the Arabs didn't send their beasts into the gardens and that the garbage collector took the garbage from the houses; to speak with the governor and those in charge of the water so that water wouldn't be lacking in the pipes, and to see that the bus would come and go on schedule, four times a day. What would he do if he had to consult his neighbors? There was no telephone as yet. He would take a shofar and go up on his roof and blow. His neighbors would hear him and come.

After a while, more people came and built homes and planted gardens. During the day they would work in the city, and an hour or two before dark they would come home to break earth, weed, pull up thorns, plant trees and gardens, and clear the place of snakes and scorpions. Soon more people came, and then still more. They too built houses and made gardens. Some of them would rent out a room or two to a young couple who wanted to raise their child in the clear air. Some of them rented out their whole houses and continued to live in the city until they paid off their mortgage. After a time I too came to live here, fleeing from the tremors of 1927, which shook the walls of the house where I was living and forced me to leave my home. I came to this neighborhood with my wife and two children, and we rented an apartment. Roads had already been built, and the buses would come and go at regular times. We felt as though this place, which had been barren since the day of our exile from our land, was being built again.

23

Automobiles still came but rarely, and a man could walk in the streets without fear of being hit. At night there was a restful quiet. If you didn't hear the dew fall, it was because you were sleeping a good, sweet sleep. The Dead Sea would smile at us almost every day, its blue waters shining in graceful peace between the gray and blue hills of Moab. The site of the Temple would look upon us. I don't know who longed for whom more; we for the Temple Mount, or the Temple Mount for us. The king of the winds, who dwelt in a mountain not far from us, used to stroll about the neighborhood, and his servants and slaves—the winds—would follow at his feet, brushing through the area. Fresh air filled the neighborhood. People from far and near would come to walk, saying, "No man knoweth its value." Old men used to come and say, "Here we would find length of days." Sick people came and said, "Here we would be free from our illnesses." Arabs would pass through and say, "Shalom"; they came to our doctor, who cured them of their ills. The doctor's wife would help their wives when they had difficulty in childbirth. The Arab women would come from their villages around us, bringing the fruits of their gardens and the eggs of their hens, giving praises to Allah, who, in His mercy upon them, had given the Jews the idea of building houses here, so that they would not have to bring their wares all the way into the city. As an Arab would go to work in the city, taking a shortcut through these streets, he would stand in wonder at the deeds of Allah, who had given the Jewish lords wisdom to build roads, mend the ways, and so forth. Suddenly, one Sabbath after Tisha b'Av, our neighbors rose up against us to make trouble for us. The people of the neighborhood could not believe that this was possible. Our neighbors, for whom we had provided help at every chance, for whom we had made life so much easier—buying their produce, having our doctor heal their sick, building roads to shorten the way for them—came upon these same roads to destroy us.

24

By the grace of God upon us, we rose up and were strong. As I said in the beginning, I built a house and planted a garden. In this place from which the enemy tried to rout us, I built my home. I built it facing the Temple Mount, to always keep upon my heart our beloved dwelling which was destroyed and has not yet been rebuilt. If "we cannot go up and be seen there, because of the hand which has cast itself into our Temple," we direct our hearts there in prayer.

Now I'll say something about the house of prayer in our neighborhood.

Our forefathers, who saw their dwelling in this world as temporary, but the dwelling in the synagogue and the house of study as permanent, built great structures for prayer and study. We, whose minds are given over mainly to things of this world, build great and beautiful houses for ourselves, and suffice with little buildings and shacks for prayer. Thus our house of prayer in this neighborhood is a wooden shack. This is one reason. Aside from this, they didn't get around to finishing the synagogue before the first disturbance, the riots, or the War of Independence, and at each of those times the residents had to leave the neighborhood. It was also not completed because of the changes in its congregants, who changed after each disturbance. That's why, as I've explained, our place of prayer is a shack and not a stone building.

Now I shall tell what happened in this shack on that Shavuot night when the rumor reached us that all the Jews in my town had been killed.

25

I entered the house of prayer. No one else was in the place. Light and rest and a good smell filled the room. All kinds of shrubs and flowers with which our land is blessed gave off their aroma. Already at Maariv I had taken note of the smell, and now every blossom and flower gave off the aroma with which God had blessed it. A young man, one who had come from a town where all the Jews had been killed, went out to the fields of the neighborhood with his wife, and picked and gathered every blossoming plant and decorated the synagogue for the holiday of Shavuot, the time of the giving of our Torah, just as they used to do in their town, before all the Jews there had been killed. In addition to all the wildflowers they gathered in the nearby fields, they brought roses and zinnias and laurel boughs from their own garden.

26

I shall choose among the words of our holy tongue to make a crown of glory for our prayer room, its candelabra, and its ornaments.

The eternal light hangs down from the ceiling, facing the holy ark and the two tablets of the Law above it. The light is wrapped in capers and thistles and bluebells, and it shines and gives off its light from between the green leaves of the capers' thorns and from its white flowers, from between the blue hues in the thistles, and from the gray leaves and purple flowers around it. All the wildflowers that grow in the fields of our neighborhood gather together in this month to beautify our house of prayer for the holiday of Shavuot, along with the garden flowers that the gardens in our neighborhood give us. To the right of the holy ark stands the reader's table, and on the table a lamp with red roses around it. Six candles shine from among the roses. The candles have almost burned down to the end, yet they still give off light, for so long as the oil is not finished they gather their strength to light the way for the prayers of Israel until they reach the gates of heaven. A time of trouble has come to Jacob, and we need much strength. Opposite them, to the south, stand the memorial candles, without number and without end. Six million Jews have been killed by the Gentiles; because of them a third of us are dead and two-thirds of us are orphans. You won't find a man in Israel who hasn't lost ten of his people. The memorial candles light them all up for us, and their light is equal, so that you can't tell the difference between the candle of a man who lived out his days and one who was killed. But in heaven they certainly distinguish between the candles, just as they distinguish between one soul and another. The Eternal had a great thought in mind when He chose us from all peoples and gave us His Torah of life. Nevertheless, it's a bit difficult to see why He created, as opposed to us, the kinds of people who take away our lives because we keep His Torah.

27

By the grace of God upon me, those thoughts left me. But the thought of my city did not take itself away from me. Is it possible that a city full of Torah and life is suddenly uprooted from the world, and all its people—old and young; men, women, and children—are killed, that now the city is silent, with not a soul of Israel left in it?

I stood facing the candles, and my eyes shone like them, except that those candles were surrounded with flowers, and my eyes had thorns upon them. I closed my eyes so that I would not see the deaths of my brothers, the people of my town. It pains me to see my town and its slain, how they are tortured in the hands of their tormentors, the cruel and harsh deaths they suffer. And I closed my eyes for yet another reason. When I close my eyes I become, as it were, master of the world, and I see only that which I desire to see. So I closed my eyes and asked my city to rise before me, with all its inhabitants, and with all its houses of prayer. I put every man in the place where he used to sit and where he studied, along with his sons, sons-in-law, and grandsons—for in my town everyone came to prayer. The only difference was in the places. Some fixed their places for prayer in the old house of study and some in the other synagogues and houses of study, but every man had his fixed place in his own house of prayer.

28

After I had arranged all the people in the old house of study, with which I was more familiar than the other places in town, I turned to the other houses of prayer. As I had done with the old house of study, so I did with them. I brought up every man before me. If he had sons or sons-in-law or grandsons, I brought them into view along with him. I didn't skip a single holy place in our town, or a single man. I did this not by the power of memory but by the power of the synagogues and the houses of study. For once the synagogues and houses of study stood before me, all their worshippers also came and stood before me. The places of prayer brought life to the people of my city in their deaths as in their lives. I too stood in the midst of the city among my people, as though the time of the resurrection of the dead had arrived. The day of the resurrection will indeed be great; I felt a taste of it that day as I stood among my brothers and townspeople who have gone to another world, and they stood about me, along with all the synagogues and houses of study in my town. And were it not difficult for me to speak, I would have asked them what Abraham, Isaac, and Jacob say, and what Moses says, about all that has happened in this generation.

I stood in wonder, looking at my townspeople. They too looked at me, and there was not a trace of condemnation in their glances, that I was thus and they were thus. They just seemed covered with sadness, a great and frightening sadness, except for one old man who had a kind of smile on his lips, and seemed to say, *Ariber geshprungen*—that is, We have "jumped over" and left the world of sorrows. In the Conversations of Rabbi Nahman of Bratslav, of blessed memory, something like that can be found. He heard about a certain preacher in Lemberg who, in the hour of his death, gestured with his fingers and said that he would show them a trick. At that moment he passed from the world of sorrows. And the Tzaddik enjoyed those words.

29

Bit by bit the people of my town began to disappear and go away. I didn't try to run after them, for I knew that a man's thoughts cannot reach the place where they were going. And even if I could reach there, why should I prevent them from going, and why should I confuse them with my thoughts?

I was left alone, and I wandered back to former days, when my town was alive, and all those who were now dead were alive and singing the praise of God in the synagogues and the houses of prayer, and the old cantor served in the Great Synagogue, while I, a small child, saw him standing on the platform intoning "O Poor Captive," with the old prayer book containing all the prayers and hymns open before him. He didn't turn the pages, for the print had been wiped out by the age of the book and the tears of former cantors, and not a letter could be made out. But he, may God give light to his lot in the world to come, knew all the hymns by heart, and the praise of

God together with the sorrow of Israel would rise from his lips in hymns and in prayer.

30

Let me describe him. He was tall and straight-backed; his beard was white, and his eyes looked like the prayer books published in Slavita, which were printed on blue-tinged paper. His voice was sweet and his clothes were clean. Only his tallit was covered with tears. He never took his tallit down from his head during the prayers. But after every prayer of love or redemption he would take it down a little and look about, to see if there was yet a sign of the redemption. For forty years he was our city's messenger before God. After forty years he went to see his relatives in Russia. The border patrol caught him and threw him into prison. He lamented and begged God to take him out of captivity and return him to his place. God did not let the warden sleep. The warden knew that as long as the voice of the Jew was to be heard in his prison, sleep would not return to him. He commanded that the cantor be set free and returned home. They released him and sent him to our town. He came bringing with him a new melody to which he would sing "O Poor Captive."

31

The first time I heard that hymn was the Sabbath after Passover when I was still a little boy. I woke up in the middle of the night, and there was a light shining into the house. I got out of bed and opened the window, so that the light could come in. I stood by the window, trying to see from where the light was coming. I washed my hands and face, put on my Sabbath clothes, and went outside. Nobody in the house saw or heard me go out. Even my mother and father, who never took their eyes off me, didn't see me go out. I went outside and there was no one there. The birds, singing the song of morning, were alone outside.

I stood still until the birds had finished their song. Then I walked to the well, for I heard the sound of the well's waters, and I said, "I'll go hear the water talking." For I had not yet seen the waters as they talked.

I came to the well and saw that the water was running, but there was no one there to drink. I filled my palms, recited the blessing, and drank. Then I went to walk wherever my legs would carry me. My legs took me to the Great Synagogue, and the place was filled with men at prayer. The old cantor stood on the platform and raised his voice in the hymn "O Poor Captive." Now that hymn of redemption began to rise from my lips and sing itself in the way I had heard it from the lips of the old cantor. The city then stood yet in peace, and all the many and honored Jews who have been killed by the enemy were still alive.

32

The candles that had given light for the prayers had gone out; only their smoke remained to be seen. But the light of the memorial candles still shone, in memory of our brothers and sisters who were killed and slaughtered and drowned and burned and strangled and buried alive by the evil of our blasphemers, cursed of God, the Nazis and their helpers. I walked by the light of the candles until I came to my city, which my soul longed to see.

I came to my city and entered the old house of study, as I used to do when I came home to visit—I would enter the old house of study first.

I found Hayyim the Shammash standing on the platform and rolling a Torah scroll, for it was the eve of the New Moon, and he was rolling the scroll to the reading for that day. Below him, in an alcove near the window, sat Shalom the Shoemaker, his pipe in his mouth, reading the Shevet Yehudah, exactly as he did when I was a child; he used to sit there reading the Shevet Yehudah, pipe in mouth, puffing away like one who is breathing smoke. The pipe was burnt out and empty, and there wasn't a leaf of tobacco in it, but they said that just as long as he held it in his mouth it tasted as though he were smoking.

I said to him, "I hear that you now fast on the eve of the New Moon (something they didn't do before I left for the Land of Israel; they would say the prayers for the "Small Yom Kippur" but not fast). Hayyim said to Shalom, "Answer him." Shalom took his pipe out of his mouth and said, "So it is. Formerly we would pray and not fast, now we fast but don't say the prayers. Why? Because we don't have a minyan; there aren't ten men to pray left in the city." I said to Hayyim and Shalom, "You say there's not a minyan left for prayer. Does this mean that those who used to pray are not left, or that those who are left don't pray? In either case, why haven't I seen a living soul in the whole town?" They both answered me together and said, "That was the first destruction, and this is the last destruction. After the first destruction a few Jews were left; after the last destruction not a man of Israel remained." I said to them, "Permit me to ask you one more thing. You say that in the last destruction not a man from Israel was left in the whole city. Then how is it that you are alive?" Hayyim smiled at me the way the dead smile when they see that you think they're alive. I picked myself up and went elsewhere.

33

I saw a group of the sick and afflicted running by. I asked a man at the end of the line, "Where are you running?" He placed his hand on an oozing sore and answered, "We run to greet the rebbe." "Who is he?" I asked. He moved his hand from one affliction to another and, smiling, said, "A man has only two hands, and twice as many afflictions." Then he told me the name of his rebbe. It was a little difficult for me to understand. Was it possible that this rebbe who had left for the Land of Israel six or seven generations ago, and had been buried in the soil of the holy city of Safed, had returned? I decided to go and see. I ran along and reached the Tzaddik together with them. They began to cry out before him how they were stricken with afflictions and persecuted by the rulers and driven from one exile to another, with no sign of redemption in view. The Tzaddik sighed and said, "What can I tell you, my children? 'May God give strength to His people; may God bless His people with peace.'" Why did he quote that particular verse? He said it only about this generation: before God will bless His people with peace He must give strength to His people, so that the Gentiles will be afraid of them, and not make any more war upon them because of that fear.

I said, "Let me go and make this known to the world." I walked over to the sink and dabbed some water onto my eyes. I awoke and saw that the book lay open before me, and I hadn't yet finished reciting the order of the commandments of the Lord. I went back and read the commandments of the Lord as composed by Rabbi Solomon Ibn Gabirol, may his soul rest.

34

There was nobody in the shack; I sat in the shack alone. It was pleasant and nicely fixed up. All kinds of flowers which the soil of our neighborhood gives us were hung from the wall between branches of pine and laurel; roses and zinnias crowned the ark and the reader's table, the prayer stand, and the eternal light. A wind blew through the shack and caused the leaves and flowers and blossoms to sway, and the house was filled with a goodly smell; the memorial candles gave their light to the building. I sat there and read the holy words God put into the hands of the poet, to glorify the commandments He gave to His people Israel. How great is the love of the holy poets before God! He gives power to their lips to glorify the laws and commandments that He gave to us in His great love.

35

The doors of the holy ark opened, and I saw a likeness of the form of a man standing there, his head resting between the scrolls of the Torah, and I heard a voice come forth from the ark, from between the trees of life. I bowed my head and closed my eyes, for I feared to look at the holy ark. I looked into my prayer book and saw that the letters that the voice from among the scrolls was reciting were at the same time being written into my book. The letters were the letters of the commandments of the Lord, in the order set for them by Rabbi Solomon Ibn Gabirol, may his soul rest. Now the man whom I had first seen between the scrolls of the Torah stood before me, and his appearance was like the appearance of a king.

I made myself small, until I was as though I were not, so that he should not feel the presence of a man in the place. Is it right that a king enter one of his provinces, and he not find any of his officers and slaves, except for one little slave?

But my tricks didn't help any. I made myself small, and nevertheless he saw me. How do I know he saw me? Because he spoke to me. And how do I know that it was to me he spoke? Because I was alone in the house of prayer; there was no one there with me. He did not speak to me by word of mouth, but his thought was engraved into mine, his holy thought into mine. Every word he said was carved into the forms of letters, and the letters joined together into words, and the words formed what he had to say. These are the things as I remember them, word for word.

36

I shall put down the things he said to me, the things he asked me, and the things I answered him, as I brought my soul out into my palm, daring to speak before him. (But before I say them, I must tell you that he did not speak to me with words. Only the thoughts that he thought were engraved before me, and these created the words.)

And now I shall tell you all he asked me, and everything I answered him. He asked me, "What are you doing here alone at night?" And I answered, "My lord must know that this is the eve of Shavuot, when one stays awake all night reading the Order of Shavuot night. I too do this, except that I read the hymns of Rabbi Solomon Ibn Gabirol, may his soul rest."

He turned his head toward me and toward the book that stood before me on the table. He looked at the book and said, "It is Solomon's." I heard him and was astonished that he mentioned Rabbi Solomon Ibn Gabirol and did not affix some title of honor before his name. For I did not yet know that the man speaking to me was Rabbi Solomon Ibn Gabirol himself.

37

Now I shall tell the things that transpired after these former things. The memorial candles lit up the shack, the thronged flowers that crowned the eternal light before the holy ark and the other flowers gave off their aromas, and one smell was mixed with another—the aroma of the house of prayer with that of the roses and zinnias from the gardens. A restful quiet was felt on the earth below and in the · heavens above. Neither the call of the heart's pleas on earth nor the sound of the heavens as they opened could be heard.

I rested my head in my arm, and sat and thought about what was happening to me. It couldn't have been in a dream, because he specifically asked me what I was doing here alone at night, and I answered him, "Doesn't my lord know that this night is the eve of Shavuot, when we stay awake all night and read the Order of Shavuot eve?" In any case, it seems a little difficult. Rabbi Solomon Ibn Gabirol is the greatest of the holy poets. Why did he see fit to descend from the Palace of Song to this shack in this neighborhood to talk with a man like me?

38

I took my soul out into the palms of my hands and raised my head to see where I was, for it was a little hard to explain the things as they had happened, though their happening itself was witness to them, and there was no doubt that he was here. Not only did he speak to me, but I answered him. Maybe the thing happened when the heavens were open. But for how long do the heavens open? Only for a moment. Is it possible that so great a thing as this could happen in one brief moment?

I don't know just how long it was, but certainly not much time passed before he spoke to me again. He didn't speak with his voice, but his thought was impressed upon mine and created words. And God gave my heart the wisdom to understand. But to copy the things down—I cannot. I just know this: that he spoke to me, for I was sitting alone in the house of prayer, reading the commandments of the Lord as composed by Rabbi Solomon Ibn Gabirol. For ever since I was old enough to do so, I follow the custom, every Shavuot eve, of reading the commandments of the Lord by Rabbi Solomon Ibn Gabirol, may his soul rest.

39

I was reminded of the sorrow I had felt for Rabbi Solomon Ibn Gabirol because God made him search for Him, as he says, "At the dawn I seek Thee, my rock and my fortress," and when he finally found Him, awe fell upon him and he stood confused, as he says, "Before Thy greatness I stand and am confounded." And as if he didn't have enough troubles himself, he had to add the sorrow of that poor captive girl. I put my finger to my throat, as the old cantor used to do, and raised my voice to sing "O Poor Captive" in the melody he had written. I saw that Rabbi Solomon, may his soul rest, turned his ear and listened to the pleasant sound of this hymn of redemption. I got up my courage and said to him, "In our town, wherever they prayed in the Ashkenazic rite, they used to say a lot of piyyutim. The beauty of each piyyut has stayed in my heart, and especially this 'O Poor Captive,' which was the first hymn of redemption I heard in my youth." I remembered that Sabbath morning when I had stood in the Great Synagogue in our city, which was now laid waste. My throat became stopped up and my voice choked, and I broke out in tears.

Rabbi Solomon saw this and asked me, "Why are you crying?" I answered, "I cry for my city and all the Jews in it who have been killed." His eyes closed, and I saw that the sorrow of my city had drawn itself to him. I thought to myself, since the rabbi doesn't know all of the people of my town, he'll weigh the glory of all of them by the likes of me. I bowed my head and lowered my eyes and said to him, "In my sorrow and in my humility, I am not worthy. I am not the man in whom the greatness of our city can be seen."

40

Rabbi Solomon saw my sorrow and my affliction and the lowness of my spirit, for my spirit was indeed very low. He came close to me, until I found myself standing next to him, and there was no distance between us except that created by the lowness of my spirit. I raised my eyes and saw his lips moving. I turned my ear and heard him mention the name of my city. I looked and saw him move his lips again. I heard him say, "I'll make a sign, so that I won't forget the name." My heart melted and I stood trembling, because he had mentioned the name of my city and had drawn mercy to it, saying he would make a sign, so as not to forget its name.

I began to think about what sign Rabbi Solomon could make for my city. With ink? It was a holiday, so he wouldn't have his writer's inkwell in his pocket. With his clothes? The clothes with which the Holy One, blessed be He, clothes His holy ones have no folds and don't take to any imprint made upon them from outside.

Once more he moved his lips. I turned my ear and heard him recite a poem, each line of which began with one of the letters of the name of my town. And so I knew that the sign the poet made for my town was in beautiful and rhymed verse, in the holy tongue.

41

The hairs of my flesh stood on end and my heart melted as I left my own being, and I was as though I was not. Were it not for remembering the poem, I would have been like all my townsfolk, who were lost, who had died at the hand of a despicable people, those who trampled my people until they were no longer a nation. But it was because of the power of the poem that my soul went out of me. And if my town has been wiped out of the world, it remains alive in the poem that the poet wrote as a sign for my city. And if I don't remember the words of the poem, for my soul left me because of its greatness, the poem sings itself in the heavens above, among the poems of the holy poets, the beloved of God.

42

Now to whom shall I turn who can tell me the words of the song? To the old cantor who knew all the hymns of the holy poets? I am all that is left of all their tears. The old cantor rests in the shadow of the holy poets, who recite their hymns in the Great Synagogue of our city. And if he answers me, his voice will be as pleasant as it was when our city was yet alive and all of its people were also still in life. But here—here there is only a song of mourning, lamentation, and wailing, for the city and its dead.

Translated by Arthur Green

Additional Stories

To Father's House

I

Close to the Passover holiday it happened. I was far away from my father's house and my home town, and I was going about my work, which has neither beginning nor end, work which you start to no advantage and which never sets you free. Two men smeared with plaster and paint arrived, one of them holding a ladder. Actually I should say that the ladder stood by itself and he, that is, this man with the ladder, weaved his arms through the rungs. I asked them, "What do you want?" They told me, "We were sent here to white-wash the room."

I was involved in my work, and it was difficult for me to stop. Yet I was bothered not so much by the interruption as by the dirt, for these painters certainly would not go out of their way to spread a sheet over the books, and protect them from being soiled.

To avoid their reading my thoughts, I pretended not to see them and stared at a hole in the wall, near the ceiling. Straw and palm—branches hanging down from the ceiling covered the hole, and flies and mosquitoes clustered there. I said to myself, What do you gain with your windows screened if flies and mosquitoes come in through that hole?

I left the workers and went up to the attic, to clear away the straw and palm—branches so that the hole would be readily visible until I could find a board to cover it.

My little niece came to help me. For some reason which is beyond me, I scolded her: "I don't need you and the likes of you!" She shrugged her shoulders and disappeared.

Meanwhile, the workers began acting in my room as if it belonged to them. I thought to myself, I'm superfluous here, and I can't do my work, so I'll go to my home town, to my father's house. I haven't seen my father for many years now, and I haven't fulfilled the commandment of respect for Father. At the railroad station I boarded a train going to my town. Through no fault of my own, the train was delayed on the way, and when I reached town the festival had already begun; it was Passover night.

2

Passover night had come, and I had come to my home town. Since it was time for prayer, I went to pray, but I did not go where my father usually prays, for if he should see me so suddenly it would confuse his praying.

When I reached the courtyard of the House of Prayer I hesitated slightly, because I saw a lighted candle suspended in the air in a bottle swinging in the wind but not extinguished, and because at that moment one of the men whose avocation is interpreting the Bible—Isaac Euchel by name—came over to show me an explanation of a difficult verse at the end of the book of Joshua, or perhaps it was the beginning of the book of Hosea. Isaac Euchel's explanation was a bit forced, and medieval commentators had already interpreted the verse in a simple style and in clear, lucid language. Nevertheless, I nodded my head, as if the world needed his interpretation.

While talking, he took out a cigarette and asked for a light. A child came over to light a match, but it went out. He took another match and gave it to me, saying "Give it to that gentleman there." I told Isaac Euchel, "Your generation, with all its expertise in grammar, didn't know how to adorn this splinter with a word as suitable as 'match.'" And when I had said this it occurred to me he would answer that since there had been no matches in his day there had been no need for this word. Euchel took the match and said, "Now, then, we can make a flame with this metch" (he said "metch," with an "e" not an "a"). "But what good is a metch which goes out before serving its purpose?"

Alas, I tried to outsmart him and I was outsmarted.

3

I do not remember how we took leave of each other. When I left him, I found myself standing in a large room which had a set table, with bottles, jars, and glasses on it. And two women were standing there, one old and one young. And a candle was suspended in the air in a bottle, like the one I had seen in the courtyard of the House of Prayer. Or perhaps there were two candles which seemed to be one. The room opened directly onto the street, with two doorways facing each other. I turned to the doorway facing my father's house and started to leave.

The old woman said, "Is that the way it's done, coming in and going out?" I realized that I had come upon an inn and that they had made no profit from me. Placing my hand over my heart as an oath and a promise, I said, "Believe me, I'll come again."

The old woman's face lit up. "I know, sir, that you will keep your promise." I nodded my head, saying to myself, "I only hope I don't forget, I only hope I don't forget," even though it is difficult to keep such a promise. First of all, I had come to my father's town and my father certainly would insist that I stay at home, and not allow me to go to inns or hotels. And second—I've forgotten the second reason.

When I took leave of the old woman I started to run, for it was Father's custom to sit down to the Passover meal immediately following services. While I was running, it occurred to me that I might have passed his house. I raised my eyes to see. My eyes shut themselves firmly, and I did not see a thing. With great effort I opened them just a narrow crack, and saw three or four men running in haste and confusion. I meant to ask them where my father's house was, but they were strangers, even though they were dressed like the men of my town. I let them pass, without asking them.

Time does not stand still, but I was standing still, seeking my father's house, not knowing where it was. For I had not been in the town in many years and I had forgotten many of its roads, and the town itself had changed somewhat. Then I remembered that Father lived next to a man who was known by everyone.

I looked for someone who would tell me where the house was. My eyes shut themselves again. With all my might I struggled to open them. They opened just a narrow crack again. The moon came out, to shine upon them dust and ashes. I saw a little girl. Pointing with her finger, she said, "That's it." I wanted to ask her, "How do you know what I am looking for?" My eyes opened and I saw Father, holding his cup of wine, about to chant the blessing over the wine, hesitating, waiting.

Afraid that I might disturb the quiet of the house, I wanted to explain to Father, letting my eyes speak for me, telling him why I had delayed coming for so long. My eyes closed again. Struggling, I opened them. Suddenly I heard a noise like that of a sheet being torn. Actually, no sheet was being torn, but one small cloud high above was being torn, and once it was torn the moon came out, splitting the clouds, and a sweet light shone upon the house and upon Father.

Translated by Jules Harlow

The Document

Three days I spent in the office of the gray bureau. A certain relative, whose name I didn't even recognize, had written to me from a certain city I'd never heard of, asking me to go to a certain office and obtain for him such-and-such a document on which his whole life depended.

My throat was sore—and my whole body. Just the same, I got up very early and went to get my relative's document—thinking all the time that I would find it immediately and then go back to bed. I was fighting a cold which had troubled me all winter and which had returned that day with renewed force. I entered the office humbly and timidly. As I had gotten up early and not a soul was there before me, I was sure there would be no long delay before they gave me the document.

At that hour the cleaning woman was sweeping the building and raising clouds of dust. My lungs became blocked and my voice choked off. I said to myself, I'd better wait a minute until my throat clears; otherwise the official won't know what I want, and all my efforts will be wasted.

As I was standing, the office suddenly filled with hordes of people pushing one another, standing in angry, sullen compliance, and looking avidly toward the men and women clerks who sat at their battered desks scratching away with gray pens on pads and ledgers. I too was pushed first to this clerk and then to another, and I kept my head lowered timidly in the hope they would turn to me and ask what I want. But they paid no attention to me and of course asked me nothing. This was all to the good, for had they asked I doubt whether I could have said a word with all that dust clogging my throat.

So one day passed and so a second. From dawn to dusk I stood in that office. My feet became leaden and my spirit exhausted. Occasionally I was moved from one spot to another, from one room to another; I stood before this clerk or that clerk; I was pushed again and returned to the room from which I started. The clerks sat on— their faces bent over their papers and their pens writing automatically, incessantly. The clock ticked gloomily away. Its hand moved slowly, and a dead fly was stuck to it and moved along with it.

On the third day things got a little better for me. A new clerk came in to replace one of the clerks who had died. This new clerk, by the name of Nahman Horodenker, was a blond, well-built youth with clear spectacles over his good eyes. From his name and facial expression, as from his bear-like movements, I could tell that he was a countryman of mine. All I had to do was announce publicly that he was a Galician Jew, and immediately I would have had the upper hand. But some indefinable misgiving, something like conscience, stopped me. I swallowed my words and was silent.

Meanwhile I was getting sicker and sicker, and I could think of nothing else. I had been ill twice that winter, and each time the first symptoms had been the same—a swelling of the tongue, a tickle in the throat, dry and cracked lips. Now the symptoms were appearing again. My eyes blurred, my forehead began to sweat, and my throat became hoarse. I took a cigarette from my pocket and lit it. Without waiting to finish, I lit another. I had already forgotten why I had come to this office, and why I was standing here, and why I was being pushed and was running from room to room and from clerk to clerk.

Suddenly I heard a noise and felt my left foot expanding in its shoe. I looked down and saw that the shoe lace had snapped, but before I had a chance to tie it, they called my name. Looking up, I saw a man sitting alone at a small table covered with a soiled black oilcloth, and with files of papers to his right and left; his eyes smiled in his bent head.

I relaxed and rejoiced as one does in recognizing a man one knew before the war. It was the druggist of the municipal hospital in my home town, who always had a glass of soda to offer me whenever I came to visit a sick friend. The druggist looked up and motioned me to be seated. This gesture of compassion touched me, yet I didn't feel right about sitting down because of the papers that were on the chair. He took out a bar of chocolate and offered it to me.

I said to myself, It's now three days and three nights that I haven't seen my wife and children, and they're undoubtedly complaining about me; now I'll be able to placate them with some chocolate.

As I stretched out my hand to take it, though, I saw that the druggist had not intended to give me the whole piece. I became ashamed of my greediness, I blushed and lowered my eyes.

Slowly looking up I saw some professor sitting to the right of my acquaintance. He had a short, blond beard, a cane rested between his knees, and a hidden sneer played on his lips. I nodded and greeted him.

At this he grasped my hands and informed me that he had ingeniously solved a great problem. That letter "L" in a certain word, which everyone mistakenly believes to be part of its root, is not etymologically related to the word and should be substituted with another letter.

The professor's pronouncement was clear to me and the word he was talking about was completely explained. Yet, I was puzzled by a different problem of phonology…

In the meantime the day had cleared up, and I knew that in a certain spot near the edge of the table my acquaintance had left me a piece of bread—except that I couldn't tell where it was. But in any case, the mass of people had begun once again its squeezing and shoving. I was pushed outside and found myself standing on a large balcony floating on an endless ocean.

Translated by Joseph Moses

Friendship

My wife had returned from a journey, and I was very happy. But a tinge of sadness mingled with my joy, for the neighbors might come and bother us. "Let us go and visit Mr. So-and-so, or Mrs. Such-and-such," I said to my wife, "for if they come to us we shall not get rid of them in a hurry, but if we go to them we can get up and be rid of them whenever we like."

So we lost no time and went to visit Mrs. Klingel. Because Mrs. Klingel was in the habit of coming to us, we went to her first.

Mrs. Klingel was a famous woman and had been principal of a school before the war. When the world went topsy-turvy, she fell from her high estate and became an ordinary teacher. But she was still very conscious of her own importance and talked to people in her characteristic patronizing tone. If anyone acquired a reputation, she would seek his acquaintance and become a frequent visitor in his house. My wife had known her when she was a principal, and she clung to my wife as she clung to anyone who had seen her in her prime. She was extremely friendly to my wife and used to call her by her first name. I too had known Mrs. Klingel in her prime, but I doubt whether I had talked to her. Before the war, when people were not yet hostile to each other, a man could meet his neighbor and regard him as his friend even if he did not talk to him.

Mrs. Klingel was lying in bed. Not far away, on a velvet covered couch, sat three of her woman friends whom I did not know.

When I came in I greeted each of them, but I did not tell them my name or trouble myself to listen to theirs.

Mrs. Klingel smiled at us affectionately and went on chattering as usual. I held my tongue and said to myself: I have really nothing against her, but she is a nuisance. I shall be walking in the street one day, not wanting anyone to notice me, when suddenly this woman will come up to me and I will ask her how she is and be distracted from my thoughts. Because I knew her several years ago, does that mean that I belong to her all my life? I was smouldering with anger, and I did not tell myself: If you come across someone and you do not know what connection there is between you, you should realize that you have not done your duty to him previously and you have both been brought back into the world to put right the wrong you did to your neighbor in another incarnation.

As I sat nursing my anger, Mrs. Klingel said to my wife, "You were away, my dear, and in the meantime your husband spent his nights in pleasure." As she spoke, she shook her finger at me and said, laughingly, "I am not telling your wife that pretty girls came to visit you."

Nothing had been further from my thoughts in those days than pleasure. Even in my dreams there was nothing to give me pleasure, and now this woman tells my wife, "Your husband had visits from pretty girls, your husband took his pleasure with them." I was so furious that my very bones trembled. I jumped up and showered her with abuse. Every opprobrious word I knew I threw in her face. My wife and she looked at me in wonderment. And I wondered at myself too, for after all Mrs. Klingel had only been joking, and why should I flare up and insult her in this way? But I was boiling with anger, and every word I uttered was either a curse or an insult. Finally I took my wife by the arm and left without a farewell.

On my way out I brushed past Mrs. Klingel's three friends,

and I believe I heard one saying to the other, "That was a strange joke of Mrs. Klingel's."

My wife trailed along behind me. From her silence it was obvious that she was distressed, not so much because I had shamed Mrs. Klingel but because I had fallen into a rage. But she was silent out of love, and said nothing at all.

So we walked on without uttering a word. We ran into three men. I knew one of them, but not the other two. The one I knew had been a Hebrew teacher, who had gone abroad and come back rich; now he spent his time stuffing the periodicals with his verbiage. These teachers, even if their pupils have grown up, still treat them as schoolmasters do and teach them things of no importance. But in one of his articles I had found a good thing, and now we had met I paid him a compliment. His face lit up and he presented me to his companions, one of whom had been a senator in Poland, while the other was the brother of one of Mrs. Klingel's three friends—or perhaps I am mistaken and she has no brother.

I should have asked the distinguished visitors if they liked the city, and so forth, but my wife was tired from the journey and still distressed, and it was hard to stop. So I cut the conversation short and took my leave.

My wife had already gone off without waiting for me. I was not angry at her for not waiting. It is hard for a young woman to stand and show herself to people when she is sad and weary.

While I was walking, I put my hand in my pocket and took out an envelope or a letter, and stopped to read: "The main trial of Job was not that of Job, but of the Holy One, blessed be He, as it were, because He had handed over His servant Job to Satan's power. That is, God's trial was greater than Job's: He had a perfect and upright man, and He placed him in the power of Satan." After reading what I had written, I tore up the envelope and the letter, and scattered the pieces to the wind, as I usually do to every letter, sometimes before I read it and sometimes at the time of reading.

After I had done this, I said to myself: I must find my wife. My thoughts had distracted me and I had strayed from the road; I now found myself suddenly standing in a street where I had never been before. It was no different from all the other streets in the city, but I knew I had strayed to a place I did not know. By this time all the shops were locked up, and little lamps shone in the windows among all kinds of commodities. I saw that I had strayed far from home, and I knew I must go by a different road, but I did not know which. I looked at a stairway bounded on both sides by an iron fence and went up until I reached a flower shop. There I found a small group of men standing with their backs to the flowers, and Dr. Rischel standing among them, offering them his new ideas on grammar and language.

I greeted him and asked: "Which way to…" but before I could say the name of the street I started to stammer. I had not forgotten the name of the street, but I could not get the words out of my mouth.

It is easy to understand a man's feelings when he is looking for the place where he lives but, when he is about to ask, cannot pronounce the name. However, I took heart and pretended I was joking. Suddenly I was covered in a cold sweat. What I wanted to conceal I was compelled to reveal. When I asked again where the street was, the same thing happened again.

Dr. Rischel stood there amazed: he was in the midst of expounding his new ideas, and I had come along and interrupted him. Meanwhile, his companions had gone away, looking at me mockingly as they left. I looked this way and that. I tried to remember the name of my street, but could not. Sometimes I thought the name of the street was Humboldt and sometimes that it was West Street. But as soon as I opened my mouth to ask I knew that its name was neither Humboldt nor West. I put my hand in my pocket, hoping to find a letter on which I would see my address. I found two letters I had not yet torn up, but one had been sent to my old home, which I had left, and another was addressed poste restante. I had received only one letter in this house where I was living, and I had torn it up a short time before. I started reciting aloud names of towns and villages, kings and nobles, sages and poets, trees and flowers, every kind of street name: perhaps I would remember the name of my street— but I could not recall it.

Dr. Rischel's patience had worn out, and he started scraping the ground with his feet. I am in trouble and he wants to leave me, I said to myself. We are friends, we are human beings, aren't we? How can you leave a man in such distress? Today my wife came back from a journey and I cannot reach her, for the trivial reason that I have forgotten where I live. "Get into a streetcar and come with me," said Dr. Rischel. I wondered why he was giving me such unsuitable advice. He took me by the arm and got in with me.

I rode on against my will, wondering why Rischel had seen fit to drag me into this tramcar. Not only was it not bringing me home, but it was taking me further away from my own street. I remembered that I had seen Rischel in a dream wrestling with me. I jumped off the tramcar and left him.

When I jumped off the car I found myself standing by the post office. An idea came into my head: to ask for my address there. But my head replied: Be careful, the clerk may think you are crazy, for a sane man usually knows where he lives. So I asked a man I found there to ask the clerk.

In came a fat, well-dressed man, an insurance agent, rubbing his hands in pleasure and satisfaction, who buttonholed him and interrupted him with his talk. My blood boiled with indignation. "Have you no manners?" I said to him. "When two people are talking, what right have you to interrupt them?" I knew I was not behaving well, but I was in a temper and completely forgot my manners. The agent looked at me in surprise, as if saying: What have I done to you? Why should you insult me? I knew that if I was silent he would have the best of the argument, so I started shouting again, "I've got to go home, I'm looking for my house, I've forgotten the name of my street, and I don't know how to get to my wife!" He began to snigger, and so did the others who had gathered at the sound of my voice. Meanwhile, the clerk had closed his window and gone away, without my knowing my address.

Opposite the post office stood a coffeehouse. There I saw Mr. Jacob Tzorev. Mr. Jacob Tzorev had been a banker in another city; I had known him before the war. When I went abroad, and he heard I was in difficulties, he had sent me money. Since paying the debt I

had never written to him. I used to say: Any day now I will return
to the Land of Israel and make it up with him. Meanwhile, twenty
years had passed and we had not met. Now that I saw him I rushed
into the coffeehouse and gripped both his arms from behind, clinging to them joyfully and calling him by name. He turned his head
toward me but said nothing. I wondered why he was silent and
showed me no sign of friendship. Didn't he see how much I liked
him, how much I loved him?

A young man whispered to me, "Father is blind." I looked
and saw that he was blind in both his eyes. It was hard for me not
to rejoice in my friend, and hard to rejoice in him, for when I had
left him and gone abroad there had been light in his eyes, but now
they were blind.

I wanted to ask how he was, and how his wife was. But when
I started to speak I spoke about my home. Two wrinkles appeared
under his eyes, and it looked as if he were peeping out of them. Suddenly he groped with his hands, turned toward his son, and said, "This
gentleman was my friend." I nodded and said, "Yes, that's right, I was
your friend and I am your friend." But neither his father's words nor
my own made any impression on the son, and he paid no attention
to me. After a brief pause, Mr. Tzorev said to his son, "Go and help
him find his home."

The young man stood still for a while. It was obvious that he
found it hard to leave his father alone. Finally the father opened his
eyes and gazed at me. His two beautiful eyes shone, and I saw myself
standing beside my home.

Translated by Misha Louvish

Metamorphosis

I

She was wearing a brown dress, and her warm, brown eyes were moist.
As she came out of the rabbi's house with the bill of divorcement in
her hand, she found fair-haired Svirsh and Dr. Tenzer waiting for
her, two bachelors who had been friendly with her since the first year
of her marriage. Through the tears on her lashes, she could see how
overjoyed they were: not even in their dreams had they pictured the
happy day when Toni Hartmann would be parted from her husband.
They both sprang eagerly toward her and clasped her hands, Then
Svirsh took the parasol, hung it from her belt, and, taking both her
hands in his, swung them affectionately back and forth. Next Tenzer
took them in his large, clammy hands and gazed at her with the cold,
furtive look of a sensualist who is uncertain of his pleasures. Toni
withdrew her tired hands from them both and wiped her eyes.

Svirsh took her arm in his and prepared to accompany her.
Tenzer stationed himself on her right and thought: That albino has
got in first. But never mind; if it's him today it'll be me tomorrow.
And he derived a kind of intellectual satisfaction from the thought

that tomorrow he would be walking with Toni, who had been Hartmann's yesterday, and who was Svirsh's today.

As they were about to go, Hartmann emerged from the rabbi's house. His face was lined and his forehead furrowed. For a moment he stood there looking about him like someone who has just come out of the dark and is wondering which way to go. Catching sight of Toni with the two men, he looked at her with his hard, tired eyes. "Going with them?" he asked. Toni lifted her veil to her forehead and said, "Don't you want me to?" Her voice sent a tremor through him. He linked his thumbs one in the other and said, "Don't go with them." Toni crumpled her handkerchief in her hand, raised her sad eyes, and stood looking at him helplessly. Her entire appearance seemed to say, "Do I look as if I could go alone?"

He went up to Toni. Svirsh drew back and let her arm fall. Tenzer, who was taller than Hartmann, drew himself up bravely to his full height. But he soon lowered his head and relaxed his posture. He said to himself, "After all, it wasn't from me that he took her." Waving his hat, he walked off as his friend Svirsh had done—humming a little impromptu tune as he went.

As they went, they looked over their shoulders at the man who had been Toni's husband. Svirsh mumbled petulantly: "I've never seen anything like it in my life." Tenzer broke off his tune and wiped his heavy spectacles. "By the Pope's slipper," he said, "it's enough to make Mohammed wag his beard." Svirsh shrugged his shoulders and pursed his lips, but at Hartmann's anger rather than at Tenzer's levity.

Left alone with Toni, Hartmann made as if to take her arm, but desisted, so that she should not feel his agitation. For a moment or two they stood silently together. The whole business of the divorce had suddenly become very real, as if they were still standing in front of the rabbi, and the old man's bleating voice were still ringing in their ears. Toni gripped her handkerchief tightly and checked her tears with an effort. Hartmann removed his hat for relief. Why are we standing here? he asked himself. Once again he heard bleating in his ears—not the rabbi's voice, but that of the scribe who had read out the bill of divorce, and he thought there was a mistake in it. Why was the wretched man in such a hurry? Because Toni and I...

The whole thing was so strange. But as Hartmann could not define exactly what it was that was so strange, he became confused. He felt he must do something. He crumpled his hat and waved it about. Then he smoothed out the creases, crumpled it again, put his hat back on his head, and passed his hands over his face, from temples to chin. He could feel the stubble on his face: in his preoccupation with the divorce, he had forgotten to shave. What a disgusting sight I must look to Toni, he thought. *Ausgerechnet heute*—today of all days, he muttered between his teeth. He consoled himself with the thought that, although the greater part of the day was over, his beard was not yet noticeable. At the same time he was dissatisfied with himself for seeking lame excuses for his negligence. "Let's go," he said to Toni. "Let's go," he repeated, not certain whether he had uttered the words the first time or, if so, whether she had heard them.

The sun betook itself elsewhere. A spirit of gloom brooded over the street, and a harsh melancholy groaned among the paving stones. The windows looked out from the walls of the houses, strangers to themselves and to the houses. Hartmann fixed his gaze on a window being opened across the way, trying to remember what it was he had wanted to say. He saw a woman peeping out. That's not what I meant, he thought, and he began talking, not about what he'd been thinking, but about something quite different. And after every two or three words he waved his hand despairingly at the things that were coming into his mouth and that he was laying before Toni. Toni fixed her eyes on his mouth and thought: What is he trying to say? Her gaze followed his hand as she tried to fathom his meaning. His conversation was generally not beyond her understanding; if only he would speak coherently and calmly, she would understand everything. Her mouth quivered. The new crease on her upper lip, near the right hand corner, twitched involuntarily. As she smoothed it with her tongue she thought: God in Heaven, how sad he is. Perhaps he has reminded himself of his daughters.

Hartmann had indeed reminded himself of his daughters: they had not been out of his thoughts all day. Although he had not mentioned them to Toni, not even indirectly, he was constantly thinking of them, now of the two of them together, now of each one separately.

Beate, the elder, was nine, and she was old enough to realize that Daddy and Mummy were angry with one another. But Renate, who was only seven, had not yet noticed anything. When the atmosphere at home had become too strained, Toni's aunt had come and taken the children to live with her in the country, and they didn't know that Daddy and Mummy…. Before Hartmann could pursue his thought to the end, he saw Beate's eyes, the way they had looked when she had seen Daddy and Mummy quarreling for the first time, Her childish curiosity had been mingled with dull surprise at the sight of grownups quarreling. Hartmann had hung his head before his daughter's eyes as they grew dark with sorrow and her mouth assumed an expression of voiceless anguish. Then she had lowered her eyelashes and gone out.

Once again Hartmann felt the need to do something. Not knowing what to do, he removed his hat, mopped his brow, wiped the leather band inside his hat, and put it back on his head. Toni grew sad: she felt as if she were responsible for all his troubles. She took the parasol which Svirsh had hung from her belt and toyed with it. Meanwhile Hartmann had begun talking again. He made no reference whatever to the day's events, but they were all reflected in his voice. Toni answered him vaguely. If she were aware of what she was saying, she would have noticed that she, too, was talking to no particular purpose. But Hartmann accepted her replies as if they were to the point.

A little girl approached them and held out a bunch of asters to Hartmann. Perceiving her intention, he took out his purse and threw her a silver coin. The child put the coin in her mouth but did not move. Hartmann looked at Toni inquiringly: What could the child be wanting now? Toni stretched out her hand and took the flowers, inhaled their scent, and said, "Thank you, my dear." The girl twisted one leg around the other, rocked back and forth, and then went away. Toni looked affectionately at her retreating figure, a sad smile on her lips. "Ah," said Hartmann smiling, "she's an honest little trader. If she gets money, she has to give goods in exchange. Well, this is one transaction I've emerged from safely."

Toni thought: He says, this is one transaction he's emerged

from safely; that means there was another transaction he didn't emerge from safely. She raised her eyes to him, even though she knew that he was not in the habit of talking to her about his business affairs. But this time he opened his heart, and without any prompting began discussing business. He was involved in transactions he had entered into unwillingly, and now he could not extricate himself. These had led to disputes, quarrels and fights with partners and agents, who had bought merchandise with his money and, on seeing they were likely to incur a loss, had debited the amount to him.

Hartmann had started in the middle, like one who is preoccupied and talks of the things that are weighing on his mind. A person unfamiliar with the world of commerce could not have made head or tail of what he was saying, and Toni certainly knew nothing about business. But he ignored this and went on talking. The more he talked, the more confused he made matters sound, until his patience gave way completely, and he began to vent his anger on his agents, on whom he had relied as he relied on himself and who had betrayed his trust, causing him financial loss and involving him in degrading fights and disputes. He still didn't know how to get rid of them.

Realizing that Toni was listening now, he went back and began from the beginning, carefully explaining each point to her. He now clarified what he had left unexplained in the first telling, and what he did not explain as he went along, he made clear later. Toni began to get the drift of his story, and what she did not grasp with her mind, her heart understood. She looked at him with concern, and wondered how he could bear so many worries without anyone to share them. Hartmann became conscious of her gaze and recounted the entire story in brief. Suddenly he realized that he was seeing his affairs in a new light. Although he had not intentionally set out to prove himself in the right, matters now seemed clearer to him, and he saw that the problem was after all not so insoluble as he had thought.

Toni listened attentively to all he said and realized that his angry mood had been due entirely to his business worries. She applied her new knowledge to the other matter, to the divorce. It was as if he had said, "Now you know why I have been so short-tempered, now you know why we have come to this, to getting divorced, I mean."

Toni was thinking about the divorce and the period leading up to it, but she did not divert her attention from what he was saying. She lifted her brown eyes, which were full of trust and confidence, and said, "Michael, I'm sure you'll find a suitable way out of it." She looked at him again, trusting and submissive, as if it were not he but she who was in trouble, and as if it were she who was seeking help from him. He looked at her as he had not looked at her for a long time past, and he beheld her as he had not beheld her for a long time past. She was a head shorter than he. Her shoulders had grown so thin that they stuck out. She was wearing a smooth brown dress, open at the shoulders but fastened with rings of brown silk through which two white spots were visible. With difficulty he kept himself from caressing her.

2

Hartmann had not been in the habit of talking to his wife much, least of all about business. From the day he had built his house he had tried to keep home and office completely separate. But business has a way of not letting itself be shaken off. Sometimes he would enter the house looking worried. At first, when their love was still strong, he would fob Toni off with a kiss when she asked him to tell her what was worrying him. At a later stage, he would change the subject. Later still, he would scold her: "Isn't it bad enough that I have worries outside? Do you have to go and drag them into the house? When a man's at home he wants to take his mind off business worries."

But a man cannot control his thoughts, and they would come crowding in on him, turning his home into a branch of his shop. The difference was that when he was in the shop, his business affairs got the better of his thoughts, while at home his thoughts got the better of him. His father had not left him any inheritance, nor had his wife brought him a dowry; whatever he had acquired had been the result of his own exertions. He applied himself to business and kept away from other matters. That is how it: had been both before and after his marriage. While still a bachelor he had thought: I'll get married, build a home, and find contentment there; but when he did get married and built a home, he found himself stripped of all his expectations. At first he had solaced himself with hope, but now even that was gone. True, his wife did her best to please him, and the daughters she had borne him were growing up. On the face of it, he had no complaints against his home; the trouble was that he did not know what to do with himself there. At first he had numerous friends, but as time went on he had lost interest in them: it seemed to him that they only came on Toni's account. At first he used to look at the books Toni read and tried to keep up with them. But after reading three or four books, he stopped: the love affairs, dresses, plots, and sentiment with which they were filled—what need had an intelligent man to know of such matters? Would I care to hob-nob with such characters?

From the books he drew inferences about Toni, and from Toni about the whole house. Since he knew only his shop and was not in the habit of frequenting clubs, he had no recourse after locking up his shop but to return home. And since, once at home, he did not know what to do, he grew disgusted with himself. He began to find solace in smoking. At first he smoked in order to smother his thoughts; and he went on smoking because they were smothered. He began with cigarettes, and went on to cigars. At first he smoked in moderation, but later took to smoking continuously, until the whole house was filled with the smell of tobacco. He did not consider that he was in any way harming himself; on the contrary, he congratulated himself on the fact that he was sitting quietly by himself and not demanding anything of others. Every man has his form of pleasure: I derive mine from smoking, she derives hers from other sources. And since he didn't trouble to discover what her form of pleasure was, and he failed to find satisfaction in his own, he became troubled at heart and began to be jealous on her account of every man, woman, and child—in fact, of everything. If he saw her talking to a man or chatting with a woman or playing with a child, he would say: Has she no husband or children of her own that she has to chase about after others?

Michael Hartmann was a merchant, and he sold his goods by weight and by measure: he knew that to waste a measure meant losing it. Eventually he reconciled himself to the situation, not because he condoned her activities, but because she had come to assume less importance in his eyes.

3

The sun was about to set. In the fields the wheat swayed silently, and the sunflowers gazed one-eyed out of their darkening yellow faces. Hartmann stretched his hand out into the vacant air and caressed Toni's shadow.

All around him the silence was complete. Toni took the parasol and poked at the ground in front of her. Her action seemed devoid of both purpose and grace, and that bothered him. Once again he extended his hand and caressed the air. By now the sun had ended its course and the sky had become dulled. The countryside took on an appearance of desolation, and the trees in the field grew dark. The air began to grow cool, and the cucumber beds were fragrant. High up in the sky was a tiny star, the size of a pinhead. Behind it another star made its way through the clouds and began shining, and other stars followed.

The houses and barns stood in comfortable silence, and the smell of burnt weeds and of cattle rose from the pasture. Michael and Toni walked along silently. A boy and a girl sat with their arms twined about each other, talking; then their voices broke off abruptly, and the scent of hidden desire hung in the air. A light breeze sprang up, but no sound was heard. A little boy ran past holding a burning torch. He too had run like that in his childhood once, when his mother had found herself without matches and had sent him over to the neighbor's to fetch a light. He took out a cigarette and was about to light it; but the scent of the fields took away his desire to smoke. He crumbled the cigarette between his fingers and threw it away. He smelled his fingers and wrinkled his nose.

Toni opened her handbag, took out a bottle of scent, and sprinkled her hands with it. The scent reached his nostrils and put him in a good mood. So, so, he said to himself, by way of assent or as a question.

After his talk with Toni, in which he had told her all about that business, he began chiding himself for never, in all those years, discussing his affairs with her. If he had not snapped at her every time she wanted to know something about his doings, perhaps her interests would have grown closer to his, and they would not have come to regard themselves as such strangers to one another. This lesson was good for him at the moment, since it enabled him to blame himself and to justify Toni.

Again he folded his thumbs together and said, "I can't stand that Svirsh."

Toni hung her head and said nothing.

Hartmann repeated: "I simply can't stand him."

"And Dr. Tenzer?" Toni asked softly.

"Dr. Ten-zer?" said Hartmann angrily, stressing each syllable of the name. "I hate all the Tenzers of this world. They never seem to try and get anything for themselves. All they ever do is lie in wait for things meant for other people. I know what that fellow Svirsh is after. Whenever I see those pink eyes of his and his manicured nails, I know at once what he wants. But with Tenzer you never know where you are. He makes himself out to be in love with the whole world, but in reality he doesn't love anything. He runs after women, but he doesn't love any woman for herself, because she's pretty, or because she's this or that, but because she's another man's wife. The very fact that someone else has an interest in her makes her desirable to Tenzer."

Toni lifted her face toward Michael. It was night, and he could not see her eyes, but he felt that they were thanking him, as if he had taught her things she could never have learned by herself. Hartmann, who had been angry with himself for mentioning Svirsh and Tenzer, now experienced a feeling of relief, and he looked about him with a sense of freedom and happiness. He saw a light glimmering in the darkness. He stretched out his arm and, beckoning Toni with his finger, said: "Do you see the light?" Toni looked and said: "Where?" "Really, really, I can *see* the glimmer of a light over there," he said. "It's the lamp of an inn." "Is that so," Toni replied, "I thought it was a firefly."

A slight shudder ran through Toni, giving her a mysteriously pleasant sensation. Hartmann's saying it was the lamp of an inn and not a firefly suddenly set her musing about the first firefly she had ever seen. She had been on a visit to her aunt's in the country. It was Sabbath, and she was sitting in the garden at dusk. A spark darted through the gloom and settled on her aunt's hat. Not knowing it was a firefly, she thought it was fire and became frightened. How old had she been at the time? About seven. Now Beate and Renate were at her aunt's, and she, Toni, was here walking with their father.

"We can rest there and have something to eat," Hartmann said. "You must be hungry: you had no lunch. We won't get roast duck there, but at least we can have a meal and rest."

Toni nodded in agreement. She was thinking, When did I recollect the firefly: when Michael pointed to the light, or when I said I thought it was a firefly? But she felt she must have been thinking about the firefly before, as she had been thinking about her daughters in the country. She shivered, as if the incident had taken place only now.

The road twisted and turned, now to the right, now to the left. The inn lamp kept on vanishing and reappearing. A moist smell rose from the earth. Toni shivered a little, though she did not actually feel cold. She gazed silently into the darkness which was shrouding both her and Michael. Once more the inn lamp came into view, only to disappear a moment later. Toni drew in her shoulders, and a breeze passed across her body.

"Cold?" Hartmann asked solicitously.

"I think I see people coming."

"There is no one here, but perhaps."

"I've never seen such a tall person before," said Toni, "Do look." A man with a ladder came toward them. Placing the ladder on the ground, he climbed it and lit a lamp. Toni blinked her eyes and drew in her breath. "Was there something you wanted to say?" Michael asked her. She looked down and said: "I didn't say anything."

Hartmann smiled. "That's strange, I fancied you wanted to say something."

Toni blushed. "Did I want to say something?" She looked at her shadow in silence.

Hartmann smiled again: "So you didn't want to say anything. But I thought you did."

Toni walked on silently at Michael's side.

Two shadows became visible. The head of one of them was close to Toni's, while the other was close to Hartmann's. Two young people came in sight, a boy and a girl. The whole air became charged with their unfulfilled desires. Hartmann looked at them, and they at him. Toni lowered her head and looked at her wedding ring.

4

A little later they came to a garden fenced on three sides. The gate was open, and to the right of it shone a lamp. Some smaller lanterns, in the shape of apples and pears, hung from the trees in the garden. Hartman looked at the sign and said: "I wasn't mistaken, this is a restaurant. We'll get something to eat here." Taking Toni by the arm, he walked in with her.

A plump, loose-limbed girl was sitting in front of the house, cleaning vegetables and occupying half the width of the bottom step. She greeted them in a loud voice and lowered her skirt. Hartmann thought: She's red-haired and freckled. Although I can't see her in the dark, I've a feeling that's the type she is. Toni shook her head at him. He gazed at her in astonishment. Could she possibly have sensed what I was thinking? He took her parasol and laid it on a chair, and placed his hat on top of it. "Let's sit in the garden," he said, "or would you prefer to eat indoors?" "No," Toni replied, "let's eat out here."

A waiter came up, wiped the top of the table, spread a cloth on it, and handed them a menu. Then he fetched a glass of water and put the flowers in it, and stood waiting until they were ready with their order. Hartmann saw that most of the dishes listed in the menu had been struck out. He grumbled: "Most of the dishes have already been eaten up." Looking over Hartmann's shoulder, the waiter said: "I'll bring you some others immediately." "You're hiding your wares under a bushel," said Hartmann. The waiter bent down and said: "The dishes we have struck out have all been eaten. Others have been cooked instead, but we haven't had time to enter them in the menu." "In that case," observed Hartmann, "we ought to be glad that we shall be getting fresh dishes." "Your pleasure is our happiness," the waiter replied. "Will you have brown bread or white?" "When you eat in the country," Toni said, "you must have brown bread." "And what wines do you care for, sir?" the waiter asked. "Wine," exclaimed Hartmann happily, as if rejoiced to discover that such a thing still existed for people's delectation. He studied the wine list and placed his order.

"We're in luck," he said to Toni. "This is far better than we expected." Toni smoothed the crease on her upper lip with her tongue, either because she was hungry or maybe because she could think of nothing to say in reply. The waiter returned with their order. Michael and Toni drew up their chairs and began eating. Toni was ashamed to eat too heartily, but her bashfulness failed to blunt her appetite.

The potatoes, spinach, eggs, meat, turnips, and other things that the waiter brought them were all excellently prepared. Toni ate with relish. The stars winked at them from the sauce, and from the bough of a tree came the song of a bird. Hartmann covered his knees with his napkin and listened to the bird.

The girl they had seen on their arrival passed by. She gave them a glance of recognition. Hartmann looked at her and said, "Didn't I say she was a red-head with freckles?" though in fact he did not manage to see whether she had freckles or not.

Toni lifted the glass with the flowers, looked at them and then smelled them. She had always been particularly fond of asters, they were so modest and lovely. She had planted some on her mother's grave, and those asters, not particular about growing in the best soil necessarily, would look at her gratefully when she came for a visit.

Again the girl passed by, this time carrying a basket of plums with both hands. The juice of the overripe plums gave off an odor of cloying sweetness.

5

Taking his wineglass in his hand, Hartmann mused: Since the day I married her I never behaved so decently toward her as when I gave her the divorce. Unconsciously raising his glass higher, he continued: If a man quarrels with a woman, he has no right to live with her. Marriage without love is no marriage at all. Divorce is preferable to a quarrelsome marriage. He put down the glass, moved the cruet-stand, and selected a toothpick. Following the same trend of thought, he reflected: If a man marries a woman and does not love her, he has to give her a divorce. If he doesn't divorce her, he has to love her. And that love has to undergo constant renewal. "Did you say anything?" Toni stretched out her hand, pointed to the tree, and said: "A bird."

Hartmann looked at the tree.

"Is that the one that was singing," Toni asked, "or was it another one?"

"Of course it was," Hartmann replied with great animation, although his certainty rested upon insecure ground.

Toni leaned her head on her left shoulder and thought to herself, That little creature sits hidden in a tree, and its voice brings a thrill to one's heart.

Hartmann clenched his fingers and looked at Toni as she sat with her head resting on her shoulder. Her shoulders seemed to him to be hidden, and two white specks peeped at him through the openings in her dress where her blouse had slipped down, exposing one shoulder. Now, Hartmann thought, we shall see the other one. Unconsciously he rapped on the table. The waiter heard and came up to them. Once he had come, Hartmann took out his purse, paid the bill and tipped him. The waiter thanked him and bowed profusely: either he was drunk, or else the tip was larger than he had anticipated.

The meal had been a good one, and it had cost Hartmann less than he had expected. He sat with a feeling of contentment and ordered a quarter-bottle of brandy for himself and a sweet liqueur for Toni. He took out a cigar and trimmed it with his knife. Then he offered his cigarette case to Toni. They sat opposite one another, the smoke from the cigar and cigarette mingling. Above them shone the little lanterns, and above the lanterns shone the stars. Toni parted the smoke with her fingers and went on smoking tranquilly. Hartmann looked at her and said: "Listen, Toni." Toni raised her eyes to him. Hartmann put down his cigar and said: "I had a dream."

"A dream?" Toni closed her eyes as if dreaming herself.

"Are you listening?" Hartmann asked. She opened her eyes, looked at him, and closed them again.

"I don't remember whether I had this dream last night or the night before," he went on. "But I remember every detail of it, as if I were dreaming it now. Are you listening, Toni?" She nodded her head.

"In this dream I was living in Berlin. Suessenschein came to visit me. You remember Suessenschein? At the time he had just returned from Africa. I'm always glad to see him, for he brings with him an atmosphere of the far-off places I used to dream of in my child-hood. But that day I wasn't glad. Perhaps it was because he came in the morning, when I like to sit by myself. Perhaps it was because in dreams we aren't always happy to be with the people we enjoy when we're awake. He had someone else with him, a young man to whom I took a violent dislike the instant he walked in. He acted as if he had wearied himself with Suessenschein on all his travels. But for Suessenschein's sake I treated him civilly. Are you listening?" "I'm listening," Toni whispered, as if afraid that the sound of her voice would interrupt his story. Hartmann continued:

"Suessenschein looked around at my flat and said: If I found a flat like yours, I'd take it; I want to stay here awhile, and I'm tired of hotels. I replied: I've heard of a very nice flat that's going in Charlottenburg. To which he rejoined: All right, let's go there. Wait, I suggested, let me phone up first. No, he said, we'll go there straight away. I went along with him."

Toni nodded, and Hartmann went on:

"When we got there, the landlady was nowhere to be seen. I wanted to tell him off for being so impulsive, but I stopped myself, as my temper was very frayed, and I felt I was in danger of going too far. His companion urged the maid to go and call the landlady. The maid looked at him suspiciously, or maybe she just looked at him without any particular expression, but I hated him so much that I thought she looked at him with suspicion. As she went, the landlady came in. She was dark, neither young nor old, on the short side, eyes a trifle filmy, and one leg shorter than the other, though this did not seem like a blemish in her. On the contrary, she seemed to dance along rather than walk. A secret joy twinkled on her lips, a hidden, yearning joy, a virginal joy."

Although Hartmann was aware that Toni was listening with interest, he nevertheless asked, "Are you listening, Toni?" and went on.

"The rooms she showed us were very nice. But Suessenschein turned away from them and said: I wouldn't advise you to take this flat. Winter is approaching, and there is no stove. I gazed at him in astonishment: Who was it that wanted to rent a flat, I or he? I have a fine one of my own; I'm very pleased with it, and I have no intention of exchanging it for another. Suessenschein repeated: A place without a stove, a place without a stove, if I were you I wouldn't take it. Here the landlady put in: But there is a stove. But Suessenschein interrupted her: Where is the stove? In the bedroom. But the study, madam, is all of glass. Are you looking for somewhere to live, or for an observatory from which to view the frozen birds? His words depressed me so much that I began to feel cold. I looked around and saw that the study did indeed consist more of windows than walls. I nodded and said: That's so. The landlady looked at me with her filmy but charming eyes, and straightened herself with a caper. I turned away from her and thought, How shall I ever get away from this cold? My skin was already clinging to my bones. I woke up and found that the blanket had slipped off my bed."

After Hartmann had finished, he had a feeling that perhaps he ought not to have recounted his dream; and yet at the same time he experienced a sense of relief. In order, therefore, to give expression to both emotions, he assumed a tone of banter and said: "That was a fine story I told you. The whole thing really wasn't worth telling." Toni licked her lips, and her eyes grew moist. He looked at her involuntarily, and it seemed to him that it was with just such eyes that the landlady had looked at him. Now there was nothing wrong with her, except…except for something whose meaning he did not understand, but he felt that if Toni were to get up, she, too, would turn out to be lame. However, since that would not seem like a blemish—as he knew from the woman in the dream it followed that even if Toni were lame, she would not seem crippled to him. He got up, took his hat, and said: "Let's go."

6

Toni stood up, removed her flowers from the glass, shook the moisture off them, and wrapped them in paper. She inhaled their scent and paused a moment or two in the hope that Michael might sit down again: she was afraid lest on the way back something should happen to disturb their atmosphere of calm. The waiter came up, handed Toni her parasol, bowed them out, and followed them until they were out of the garden. When they had gone, he extinguished the lanterns. The garden and its surroundings became dark. A frog jumped in the grass. Toni dropped her flowers in alarm.

The croaking of frogs rose from the banks of the stream. The electric wires were giving off sparks: something had obviously gone wrong with them. After a few paces the wires and poles disappeared from view, and other sparks could be seen: they were the fireflies, which dappled the darkness with their glitter.

Hartmann stood wondering. What has happened here? he asked himself. His mind was tranquil, as if his question had furnished the answer.

Gradually they reached the stream. It lay there in its bed, its waters gently rocking. The stars cast their reflection upon its formless ripples, and the moon floated on the surface. The cry of a bird of prey was heard in the distance, and its echo pierced the air.

Toni crossed her feet and leaned on her parasol. She lowered her eyelids and drowsed. The waves raised themselves up and fell back exhausted. The frogs croaked, and the river plants exuded a tepid smell.

Toni was tired, and her eyes dropped. The river willows whispered, and the waters of the stream undulated languidly. Toni was no longer able to control her eyes, and they began to close of their own accord. But Michael was awake.

Never in his life had he been so wide awake. The tiniest movement set his mind working, and he looked about him searchingly, lest anything of what was happening should escape him. It was good, he felt, that Toni existed for him in this world and at that hour. But what was good for him was not good for her. She was exhausted, and her legs were incapable of supporting her body.

"Tired?" he asked her. "I'm not tired," she replied; but her voice belied her words.

Michael laughed, and Toni looked at him in surprise. He laughed again and said: "One day I was out walking with the girls. I asked them if they were tired, and Renate answered: 'I'm not tired, but my legs are.'"

"The sweet chick," said Toni with a sigh.

Hartmann was sorry he had mentioned the girls. He looked around to see if he could find a conveyance to take them back to town. But the earth was silent: no sound of a carriage wheel or motor. He looked in all four directions, to see if he could discover a telephone booth. He was filled with pity for this small woman who had not the strength to walk. Once or twice he supported her with his arm. Her dress was damp from the moist air, and she shivered a little. If he did not get her under a roof, she would certainly catch cold.

But the city was far away, and the air was dank. He wanted to take off his jacket and wrap it around Toni. But he was afraid she might refuse; and he did not want to do anything that would evoke her refusal.

Perhaps, Michael thought, there would be a bed for her at the inn where they had eaten. Taking her arm, he said: "Let's go back to the inn." Toni dragged after him, bereft of strength.

7

They took the same road by which they had come and found their way back to the garden. Hartmann shoved the gate open, and they went up the stone steps. The house was silent. The waiter was not to be seen, neither was the girl. Obviously the household was asleep, and no guests were expected. Every step they took cried out at the intrusion.

Hartmann opened the door to the house and stepped inside. He spoke a greeting into the room, but there was no reply. He found an old man sitting bent over a table, pipe in mouth, an expression of annoyance on his face.

"Is there any room to sleep here?" Hartmann asked. The old man looked at him and at the woman by his side. It was clear from the old man's expression that he was not pleased to see a couple who had turned up after midnight to seek a haven of love. He took his pipe from his mouth, laid it on the table, and, giving them a look of annoyance, said severely: "We have one room vacant." Toni blushed. Hartmann crumpled his hat and said nothing. The landlord took his pipe, turned it upside down, knocked it against the table, and removed the ash. Putting aside the ash and the burnt shreds, he gathered the remnants of tobacco and put them back in the pipe. Pressing them down with his thumb, he said: "We'll prepare the room for the lady." Finally, raising his eyes, he said: "We'll find a place for the gentleman as well. When we're full we usually make up a bed on the billiard table."

Toni inclined her head toward the landlord and said: "Thank you very much indeed." Said Hartmann: "Would you show us the room?"

The landlord got up and lit a candle. Opening a door for them, he followed them into a spacious room in which there were three beds, one of them made up. There was a washstand with two basins and two jugs filled with water, and a large decanter half-full of water covered with an inverted tumbler. Above the made-up bed hung a broken horn with a bridal wreath on it, and a ram's head and the head of a wild boar with eyes of red glass hung upon the walls. The innkeeper took the tumbler, examined it, stood it upside down, and waited for Hartmann to leave.

Hartmann put out his hand to test the mattress. Seeing him do so, the innkeeper said: "No one has yet complained of not getting a good nights sleep in this house." Hartmann paled, and his hand remained dangling. The innkeeper placed the candle next to the made-up bed and said: "Now sir, if you'll come with me, I'll make your bed for you." And he waited for his guest to accompany him.

Finally Hartmann grasped the innkeeper's intention. Taking Toni's hand, he wished her goodnight. Her hand clung to his, and her eyes enfolded his heart.

A few moments later the innkeeper was making up Hartmann's bed on the billiard table and chatting to him as he did so. His annoyance gave way to affability. Now that the guest was without the woman, he considered him respectable. He asked his guest how many pillows he liked to sleep on, and whether he preferred a heavy blanket or a light one, and did he wish to take anything to drink before he retired for the night. Finally he gave him a lighted candle and a box of matches and left the room. A few moments later, Hartmann went out into the garden.

The lanterns had gone out, but a light from heaven illuminated the darkness. The grass and the mandrakes gave off a damp, refreshing scent. A chestnut dropped from a tree and burst. Another chestnut fell sharply and burst.

Hartmann stood reviewing the night's events. After a brief pause he went across to the table at which he had dined with Toni. The chairs had been leaned against it, and the dew glistened on the bare tabletop. Underneath the table lay a thick cigar. It was the cigar that he had put down on the table when he began telling Toni his dream.

"Now we'll have a smoke," he said. But before he could take out a cigar he had forgotten what it was he had meant to do.

8

"What was I going to do?" he asked himself. "To get up on this little mound in front of me." He had not really intended to do so, but once he had told himself, he went and did it.

The mound was dome-shaped, wide at the base and narrow at the top and not far across, and it was surrounded by bushes. He drew in his breath and considered: I expect each thorn and thistle has a different name. How many names of thorns do I know? More than I thought. I wonder if the gardener doesn't lavish more care on the thorns than on the flowers. Those gardeners destroy the thorns where they normally grow and plant them in the wrong places. Perhaps the names I know are the names of the thorns growing here... Suddenly he smiled: That innkeeper doesn't know what Toni and I are to one another. How annoyed he was when we asked for somewhere to sleep. Now let me see what's here.

He looked down on the mound and recalled an incident of his childhood. He had gone for a walk with some friends, and, seeing a mound, he had climbed it, then slipped and slid down to the bottom. He imagined himself back in the same situation, and began to be afraid he would fall; no, it was rather a wonder he had not already slipped to the bottom. And if he had not already slipped and fallen, he was bound to do so; although there was no real danger of his falling, his fear itself would make him fall; though he was still on his feet, his legs were beginning to give way and to slip, he would roll down, his bones would get broken.

He took heart and climbed down. When he reached the bottom he was amazed. How high was the mound, a foot or eighteen inches? Yet how it had frightened him! He closed his eyes and said, "I'm tired," and returned to the inn.

An air of calm pervaded the entire house. The innkeeper sat by himself in a little room, rubbing his ankles together and drinking a beverage to help him sleep. Hartmann slipped in quietly, undressed, stretched out on the billiard table, covered himself, and looked at the wall.

Strange, he thought, all the while I stood on the mound, I was thinking only about myself, as if I were alone in the world, as if I did not have two daughters; as if I did not have—a wife.

Hartmann loved his daughters the way a father does. But, like any other father, he did not forego his own interests for the sake of his children. The incident of the mound had opened his heart. He was both ashamed and surprised. And he proceeded once more to occupy his thoughts with himself.

What had happened to him on the mound? Actually, nothing. He had got onto the top of the mound and imagined he was slipping down. And what if he had fallen? He would have lain on the ground and picked himself up again. He stretched out on the bed and thought, smiling: How ridiculous Tenzer looked when I took Toni away from that albino! There are still things left in the world to make one laugh. But let me get back: What happened on the mound? Not the one I was standing on just now, but the one I fell from. One day I went for a walk with my friends. I climbed onto the top of the mound, and suddenly I found myself lying in the ditch. He did not remember himself actually falling, only that he was lying in the ditch. Something sweet was trickling into his mouth, his lips were cut, his tongue swollen, and his entire body bruised. But his limbs felt relaxed, like those of a man who stretches himself after throwing off a heavy burden. He had often fallen since then, but he had never experienced such a feeling of tranquility in any other fall. It seems that one does not have to taste such an experience more than once in a lifetime.

9

He extinguished the candle, closed his eyes, and sought to recollect the event. The details of it were confused, as in a dream. From the walls of the house a cricket sounded, then stopped, and the silence became twice as intense. His limbs relaxed, and his mind grew tranquil. Once more the cricket chirped. What I want to know, said Hartmann to himself, is how long he's going to go on chirping. As he framed the question, he began thinking of Toni. He could see her face, and her movements, and also the two white spots where her skin showed through the brown dress…There's no doubt about it, she isn't young. Even if her hair hasn't turned gray, she has many more wrinkles, The worst of them all is that crease in her upper lip. Has she a tooth missing?

He still thought of Toni critically, as he always had, but now he felt that all those shortcomings in no way detracted from her. With a sweet feeling of adoration he summoned up her face, that wonderful face; but then it began to fade away from him, against his will. How thin her shoulders were, but her figure was that of a pretty girl. Hartmann embraced the air with his arm and felt himself blushing. As he was talking to himself he heard a sort of moan. Since he was thinking about his wife, it seemed to him that the sound came from her room. He opened his eyes and, lifting his head, listened intently. Help me, O Lord, help me. Has anything happened? In reality he could have heard nothing, for there was a thick wall between them. Nor was it a moan of distress he had heard. Nevertheless, he sat upright on his bed in case he should hear anything, in case anything of her vital being should reach his ears. Perhaps he might be able to help her.

Once again she appeared before him the way she had looked that day—lifting her veil onto her forehead, raising the asters to her face, digging her parasol into the ground, parting the cigarette smoke with her fingers. Gradually the parasol vanished, the smoke dispersed, and the asters grew more numerous, until they covered the whole mound. Astonished and puzzled, he gazed in front of him. As he did so his eyes closed, his head dropped on the pillow, his soul fell asleep, and his spirit began to hover in the world of dreams, where no partition separated them.

Translated by I. Schen

The Face and the Image

Naomi had washed the floor, arranged the furniture, watered the flowers, and wiped the inkwells; and the room was filled with peace. I waited for Naomi to finish all her work, and then I would sit down to do mine. For it was a great work I wanted to do, to write down in a book my thoughts about polished mirrors. This device, which shows you whatever you show it, aroused my wonder even in childhood, perhaps more than the thing itself. And now that I have grown old, and seen the deeds that pass, and some of the deeds that last, I have continued to ponder on the qualities of mirrors. They are flat, and thin, and smooth as ice, and there is nothing inside them. But they store up whatever you put before them, and before them there is no cheating, or partiality, or injustice, or deceit. Whatever you show them, they show you. They do not expunge or amplify, add on or take away—like the truth, which neither adds nor takes away. Therefore I said: I will tell of their virtues and their perfect rectitude.

"Finished," said Naomi, and a smile of satisfaction seemed to play on her chaste lips. Naomi was really entitled to be satisfied with her work, and I should have been satisfied too, but for a sudden sadness that enfolded my heart.

But I took no notice of this sadness, though it was heavier today than it had been yesterday, for that is how it goes: anything that lives continues to grow. So I took a chair to sit down and begin my work. A paper fell off the chair, and I saw it was a telegram. I looked at Naomi. "When they brought the telegram I was busy wiping the table," she said, "and I left it on the chair so it wouldn't get soiled."

For tidiness' sake I took the telegram and laid it on the table. Then I took a knife to open it. At that moment there appeared before me the image of my grandfather, my mother's father, in the year he died, lying in his bed and reading his will all night. His beard was bluish silver and the hair of his beard was not wavy but straight, every single hair hanging by itself and not mingling with the next, but their perfect rectitude uniting them all. I began to calculate how old my grandfather had been when I was born, and how old my mother had been when she bore me and it turned out that her age today was the same as my grandfather's age at that time, and my age was the same as hers when I was born.

Many other thoughts passed through my mind, but I set them aside and went back to the telegram. I opened the telegram and read: "Mother sick, awaiting you." Mother sick, waiting for me. Taking the plain sense of the words, they meant: Mother is on the point of death; or perhaps she was already dead and they were waiting for me before burying her.

I quickly took my traveling kit and put it in my valise; I gazed at the room, and at the table where a few moments before I had longed to do my work. I stood there all alone with myself, like a man who is shown a clenched hand and thinks that what he wants is inside, but when the hand is opened it turns out to be empty.

"Naomi," I said to her, "I am going away, and I do not know how long I shall stay. Close up the house behind me, lock it up thoroughly, and take the key with you until I come back."

Naomi nodded her head with its two plaits and looked at me. I saw from the look in her eyes that she disapproved of a man going to see his mother in the patched trousers in which he was in the habit of doing his work; it was not respectful to his family to come to them like that. What would people say? How many years he has spent in the world, and he has not managed to buy a whole garment!

I closed my eyes to Naomi's apprehensions. When Mother might be on the point of death, could I worry about my dress? By the time I took off my old clothes and put on new, Mother might have breathed her last. I waved my hand deprecatingly and said, "No, I am going as I am. In any case, I shall take another pair of trousers with me." But the valise was small and did not hold much. And my other valise was in the attic, and to get up there I needed a ladder, and if I found a ladder and climbed up, the valise might well be locked, and if it was locked, I might not find the key. So, since there were more doubts than certainties, I took my little valise in my hand and went out, dressed as I was in my patched trousers.

Thinking about the way ahead, I said to myself: I am going to my mother and I do not know whether she is alive or dead, for when I last left her she was sick, and she cried and said, "My heart tells me that I shall never see you again." And it is known that the sick see with a third eye, which the Angel of Death lends them.

I took a short cut through a certain old courtyard, like the one where I used to play hide-and-seek in my childhood. The same sensation I felt in my head during this game came back to me. Picture to yourselves a large, old courtyard, full of many corners, and every corner full of corners, besides various articles and bits and pieces deposited by their owners in case they might need them, the owners are dead, the articles are rusty, and the rust glows with a kind of damp light which terrifies but does not illuminate, And as I am a little child with my little friends, I hide from them and they hide from me. We stand and wait, and none of us knows whether he wants to be found or not. Finally, none of us looks for the others. We run about looking for a secret corner more secluded than the first, and my head goes around and around, and the rust that glimmers from the junk makes my flesh creep.

They were taking a body out of the yard, and a man I knew was carrying the bier, exerting all his strength and pushing his feet into the ground until they were getting flattened with the weight.

The very nails of his hands and toes cried: Come and carry with me. His eyes were weary; he seemed to be carrying them on his shoulders, from which they were looking out in entreaty, I began to worry in case he told me with his mouth what his eyes were entreating, when I was hurrying to Mother. I slipped through into a cranny, and from there to another, from there to the street and then to the railroad station, and from the station into a carriage.

Thank Heaven I had reached the train and got my ticket, and no longer had to push and be pushed, but could sit and leave my time at the disposal of the train, which knew when to depart and when to arrive. And since I was always engrossed in my work and had no time to look at myself, I thought: Now that I have set aside all my affairs, let me think about myself a little. It is good for a man to think about himself a little and not think what he is always thinking. I looked at myself and saw myself standing in the station on the carriage step. The station was full of people and luggage, some carrying their belongings in their hands and some pulling at the porters to carry their luggage. The guard was waving his flag and all of them were slipping from their places, some this way and some that, returning as they ran to the place they had come from.

Suddenly, I felt eyes staring at this man who is already taking his place in the train. I began to be afraid they might give me the evil eye. I turned my head toward the wall and found a notice there, stating that every traveler to this place needed a travel permit. I realized that this place where I was going was in a military area, and I had left my travel permit at home. This place where I was born, and where my mother was dying, was in a military area, and I had to go there, and I did not have my travel permit with me.

What was to be done? There was nothing to be done but to go back home, get my travel permit, and set off on tomorrow's train, for the guard was already blowing his whistle and the train was on the point of departure. I hastily jumped out of the carriage. Those who had come to see travelers off looked at me, startled, and those who had come to travel and had not arrived in time began to run in haste and confusion, as if I had left a place vacant for them. I held up my hands, as if begging their pardon, and felt that my hands were empty, for my valise was still in the compartment.

I fixed my eyes on the train, which had set out on a long journey and taken my valise with it. The train chugged on, emitting a heavy trail of smoke. My eyes were smothered in the smoke and covered with the smoke, and out of the smoke slipped the man who had been carrying the bier. Strange to say, he was no longer carrying his eyes on his shoulders, but his eyes were in his head, and his hands were empty, and on his lips there was a kind of smile. "Where are you going?" he said to me. "Home," I said to him. He passed his hand over his beard, blew a hair at me, and said, "Home?" And again he was looking at me from between his shoulders. How people can change! A short time before, he had been looking at me face to face, and a short time later he was looking at me from the back of his neck.

I took no short cuts on my way back, for you did not know what was hidden in that courtyard and what lay in store for you there. When I reached my house, I found it locked; the key was still in my valise, and my valise was still in the railway carriage. There was one more key, and Naomi had it. And You, O God, made me send Naomi on leave until my return.

I went to Naomi's house but did not find her. Where was Naomi? Naomi had gone to visit her uncle. Which uncle?

Some of the neighbors said her uncle on her father's side, and some said her uncle on her mother's side. If she had gone to her father's brother, he lived in Shaarayim; if to her mother's brother, he lived in Sdeh Shalom. If I went one way, it would take half a day; if I went the other way, it would take half a day; if I did not find her and had to go after her again, that would be a day gone, and I would be late for tomorrow's train. And after all, I could not tear myself in two—sending one part this way and one the other. Whether I liked it or not, I must go one way or the other. And my heart was pulling away from me, wanting to go to Mother; and it was right, for all the trouble I had taken had only been for Mother's sake, and if I did not hurry and set off at once, I might never find my mother and reach her before her burial.

Suddenly an idea came into my mind: perhaps Naomi had not gone away, and if she had not gone away she was still in the city, and if she was in the city, she might have gone to one of her relatives. I must go there and find her. It is a happy man who finds a new idea when all his ideas are exhausted. I began to inquire which of her relatives here Naomi was in the habit of visiting, and they told me: She has one relative here, a carpenter; perhaps she has gone to him.

I went to the carpenter and found him on his knees fitting a mirror into the door of a wardrobe. I greeted him and he returned my greeting from between his knees, without raising his head an inch for my sake. Almost certainly he had looked in the mirror and seen that my trousers were old, and he had understood in his own way that a man like this was not worth troubling his head over. "Is Naomi here?" I asked him; but he did not reply. "Where is Naomi?" I asked again. He looked at me over his shoulder and replied angrily, "What do you want of Naomi?" "Naomi works for me," I said, "and I need her."

When he heard I was Naomi's master, he stood up and started to treat me with deference. He snatched a chair and then another, set them before me and asked me to sit down, and began to say how fond of me Naomi's family were. And, since he was a relative of Naomi's and now had the privilege of seeing me in his home, I must eat something to bring a blessing on his house. So he called his wife and told her to bring refreshments. His wife came and brought some sweetmeats. She spread her hands in front of her eyes and kissed the tips of her fingers, as simple women do when the scroll of the law is taken out of the Ark. So sacred was the virtue of hospitality in her eyes. She started persuading me to eat and drink, while her husband begged me to drink and eat, she on one side and he on the other.

My lips were sealed and my hands were numb; they would not obey me and take some food or drink. I overcame them and replied in speech and gesture: "Impossible, I am in a hurry. I cannot stay here. I have to rush away." But Naomi's relatives turned a deaf ear, repeating their invitation over and over again. So I took something of what they offered me.

So there I sat against my will, eating and drinking whatever

Naomi's relatives gave me. At first I ate and drank against my will, without enjoyment, and then willingly, for hunger had begun to torment me. My house was locked, the key in the valise, the valise in the railway carriage, and the carriage on the way to its destination, and all my thoughts were with my mother; perhaps while I was filling my gullet they were sealing her grave. I turned my head aside so as not to look at what I saw. My image rose before me from the mirror in the wardrobe, which the carpenter had been fixing an hour before. The mirror stared at me face to face, reflecting back every movement of the hand and quiver of the lips, like all polished mirrors, which show you whatever you show them, without partiality or deceit. And it, namely, the revelation of the thing, surprised me more than the thing itself, perhaps more than it had surprised me in my childhood, perhaps more than it had ever surprised me before.

Translated by Misha Louvish

The Orchestra

I had been busy that entire year. Every day, from morning until midnight, I would sit at my table and write—at times out of habit, and at times stimulated by the pen. We sometimes dare to call this divine inspiration. I therefore became oblivious to all other affairs; and I would recall them only to postpone them. But on the eve of Rosh ha-Shanah I said to myself: A new year is approaching, and I have left many letters unattended. Let me sit down and reply to them, and enter the new year without obligations.

I proceeded on that day as on every other, save that I am regularly accustomed to arise at dawn, and that day I arose three hours earlier. For this is a night when one arises especially early for penitential prayers on the theme of "Remember the Covenant."

Before I sat down to take care of the letters, I reflected: A new year is approaching, and one ought to enter it clean, but if time does not permit me to go and bathe in the river, because of these letters, I will take a hot bath.

At that moment Charni happened to be visiting us. The same old Charni who usually boasts to me that she served in my grandfather's house long before I was born. Charni said: "Your wife is busy with holiday preparations, and you are placing extra burdens upon her. Come to our house and I will prepare you a hot bath." I liked her suggestion; after all, I needed a haircut in honor of the Rosh ha-Shanah festival, and on the way to the barber I would stop off and bathe.

I examined the letters and weighed which of them ought to be answered first. Since they were many and the time was short, it was impossible to answer in one day all that many men had written to me in the course of an entire year, and I decided to pick out the most important ones, then to deal with those of middling importance, and afterwards with the least important. While I stood deliberating, it occurred to me that I should get rid of the trivial letters first, in order to be free for the more important ones.

Trivia tend to be frustrating. Because a matter is trivial and has no substance, it is difficult to handle. If there is a trace of substance, it lies in what the author of the letter had in mind and what answer he expected. As much as I knew that I had nothing to say in reply, my desire to answer increased, for if I left them unattended, they would trouble me. Their very existence is a burden, for I remember them and come to trivial thoughts.

I picked up a pen to write, but my mind was blank. How strange! The entire year I write effortlessly, and now that I have to write two or three inconsequential lines, my pen refuses to cooperate. I put that letter down and picked up another.

This letter was no letter, but a ticket to a concert conducted by the king of musicians. I have heard that the minds of those who hear him are transformed. There actually was a man who used to go to all the concerts but got nothing out of them; he used to think that he did not appreciate music until he chanced upon a concert of this conductor. He said afterward: "Now I know that I do understand music, but that all musicians whom I have heard until now do not know what music is." I took the concert ticket and put it in my pocket.

2

The days before a holiday are brief—some of them because sundown is early and others because holiday preparations are heavy. All the more so the day before Rosh ha-Shanah, which is short in itself and is sped by preparations for the Day of Judgment. By noon I hadn't managed to answer so much as a single letter. I put the letters aside and said to myself that what I had not managed to do before Rosh ha-Shanah I would do in the days between Rosh ha-Shanah and the Day of Atonement. It would have been good to enter a new year free of obligations, but what was I to do when trivial letters did not instruct me how they were to be answered.

I got up and went to my grandfather's house to bathe before the holiday, for Charni had prepared me there a hot bath. But when I got to the house, I found the door locked. I walked around and around the house, and each time I reached the door, I stopped and knocked. A neighbor peeked out from behind her curtains and said: "Are you looking for Charni? Charni went to the market to buy fruit for the holiday benediction." I continued walking around the house until Charni arrived.

By rights the old lady should have apologized for making me wait and robbing me of my time. But not only didn't she excuse herself, she stood and chattered. If I remember correctly, she told about finding a pomegranate which was partly squashed, yet its seeds had not separated.

Suddenly three sounds were heard from the tower of the Council house. I looked at my watch and saw that it was already three o'clock. My watch is always in dispute with the tower of the Council house, and today it made peace with it. And it seemed that the Heavens were agreeing with them. Had I tarried so long on the way, and been detained walking around the house? In any case, three hours had passed and scarcely two and a half remained before the New Year's festival began. And this old woman was standing and chattering about a pomegranate that was squashed and about its seeds that had not separated.

I interrupted her and asked: "Have you prepared the bath

for me, and is the water heated?" Charni set down her basket and exclaimed: "God in Heaven, I had intended to prepare a bath for you!" I said: "And you haven't done it?" She replied: "Not yet, but I will do it right away." I urged: "Hurry, Charni, hurry. The day doesn't stand still." She picked between her teeth with her finger and said: "You don't have to rush me. I know that time doesn't stand still, and neither will I. Look, I am already on my way in to make the fire and warm up some water. You practically have your hot bath." I took a walk in front of the house while waiting for the water to heat.

The old judge passed by me. I remembered a question that I had meant to ask him, but I was afraid to get involved with him and so not manage to cleanse myself for the holiday; for this judge, once you turn to him, will not let you go. I postponed my question for another time, and did not turn to him. In order to occupy myself, I took out the ticket and noticed that the concert was for the eve of Rosh ha-Shanah. Isn't it strange that I who am not a concert-goer, should be invited to a concert on the eve of Rosh ha-Shanah!

I put the ticket back in my pocket, and resumed pacing in front of the house.

Ora, my little relative, came by, whose voice was as sweet as the sound of the violin, and who looked like a violin which the musician had leaned against an unstable wall, and the wall collapsed upon it. I looked closely at her and saw that she was depressed. I asked her: "What have you been doing, Ora? You look like a little fawn that went to the fountain and found no water." Ora said: "I'm leaving here." I asked: "Why are you leaving? What's your reason? You have always wanted to see this magnificent conductor, and now that he has come to conduct our orchestra, you are leaving." Ora burst into tears and said: "Uncle, I don't have a ticket." I laughed good-heartedly and said to her: "Let me wipe away your tears." I looked at her affectionately, and thought how lucky I was to be able to gratify this dear child, who found music more delightful than all the delights in the world, and was most enthralled with the famous conductor who was this evening conducting the great chorus. I put my hand in my pocket to take out the ticket and give it to Ora. And again I smiled good-heartedly, like one who has the power to do good. But Ora, who did not know my generous intentions, threw herself about my neck and kissed me goodbye. I became distracted, forgot what I was about, and didn't give Ora the ticket. And while I was standing there, bewildered, Charni came and called me.

The oven was flaming, the bath clean and clear, and the bath water leaped and rose to meet me. But I hadn't the strength to bathe. Even my time was not with me. I said to my brother: You bathe, for I am a weak person, and if I bathe in hot water, I have to rest afterwards, and there isn't enough time. I left the bath and went home. In order to be more comfortable, I removed my hat from my head and carried it in my hand. A passing wind mussed my hair. Where were my brains? For in the hour that I stood and waited for the bath, I could have gone to the barber's. I lifted my eyes and looked up at the sky. The sun was already about to set. I went home with a heavy heart. My daughter came out to meet me, dressed in her holiday best. She pointed her finger into space and said: "Light." I thought to myself: What is she saying? The sun has already set, and hasn't left a trace of light behind. Or perhaps she meant the candle that was kindled in honor of the festival. I looked at the candles and realized that the festival had already begun, and I had better run to the House of Prayer. My daughter stared at my old clothes and put her little hands on her new dress to cover it, so as not to shame her father in his old garments. And her eyes were on the verge of tears, both for herself who wore a new dress when her father was dressed in old clothes, and for her father who wore old clothes at a time when the New Year had arrived.

3

After dinner I went outside. The heavens were black, but many stars glittered in them and lit up their darkness. Not a man was outdoors, and all the houses were sunk in sleep. And I too started to doze off. But this sleep was not really sleep, for I could feel that my feet were walking. And I kept walking and walking like this until I arrived at a certain place and heard the sound of music, and I knew I had reached the concert hall. I took out my ticket and entered.

The hall was full. Men and women violinists, men and women drummers, trumpeters, and players of a variety of instruments all stood, dressed in black, and played incessantly. The great conductor was not to be seen in the hall, but the musicians played as if someone were standing over them and waving his baton. And all the men and women musicians were my friends and acquaintances, whom I knew from all the places I had ever lived. How did it happen that all my acquaintances came together in one place and in one chorus?

I came upon a place, sat down, and concentrated. Each man and woman was playing for himself. However, all the melodies joined to form a single song. And every man and woman was bound to his instrument, and the instruments were fastened to the floor, and each one thought that he alone was bound, and was ashamed to ask his neighbor to release him. Or perhaps the players knew that they were fastened to their instruments, and their instruments fastened to the floor, but thought that it was by their free choice that they and their instruments were so bound, and it was by their free choice that they played. One thing was clear, that though their eyes were on their instruments, their eyes did not see what their hands were doing, for all alike were blind. And I fear that perhaps even their ears did not hear what they were playing, and that from much playing they had grown deaf.

I slid out of my seat and crept toward the door. The door was open, and a man whom I had not noticed upon entering was standing at the entrance. He was like all other doorkeepers; but there was about him something like the air of that same old judge, who, once you have turned to him, does not let you go.

I said to him: "I would like to leave." He plucked the word out of my mouth and replied in my voice: "To leave? What for?" I said to him: "I have prepared myself a bath, and am in a hurry lest it grow cold." He replied in a voice that would have terrified even a man stronger than I, and said to me: "It's flaming. It's flaming. Your brother has already been scalded by it." I replied, apologetically: "I was occupied with correspondence, and didn't have time to take my bath." He asked: "With what letters were you occupied?" I took out a letter and showed him. He bent over me and said: "But I wrote that letter." I replied: "I intended to answer you." He looked at me and asked: "What did you intend to answer?" My words hid because of his voice, and my eyes closed, and I began to grope with my hands. Suddenly I found myself standing before my house.

My daughter came out and said: "Let me bring you a candle." I answered her: "Do you really think the candle will light my darkness?" By the time she had gone to bring it, the fire escaped from the furnace and blazed around about. And some woman stood before the furnace heaping wood on the fire. Because of the fire and the smoke, I could not look on. And I didn't see if it was old Charni who stood before the furnace, or if it was my young relative Ora who heaped up the fire.

A terror descended upon me, and I stood as if fixed to the earth. My spirit grew despondent within me that, at the time when all who sleep were sleeping, I should be so awake. In truth, not I alone was awake, but also the stars in heaven were awake with me. And by the light of the stars of heaven I saw what I saw. And because my spirit was lowly, my words hid in my mouth.

Translated by Judah Stampfer

The Letter

I

All that day I was busy writing a letter of condolence to the relatives of Mr. Gedaliah Klein. Mr. Gedaliah Klein had been one of the most prominent men in our city, well-born and wealthy like his fathers before him, liked by the authorities and respected by the community, blessed with a long life and a full one. He had married his daughters to the most learned men of his time; he had taken wealthy wives for his sons; and he had lived to see them producing shrewd and gifted sons and daughters, fit for anything the country needed. In short, he had achieved in this world every temporal success, and no doubt all good things awaited him in the world to come, through legacies he had left behind for works of charity and mercy.

When good men are successful in life, it is good for them and good for the world; moreover, they provide convincing testimony that virtue pays, for everyone can see that a man does not toil for nothing or waste his strength in vain. The whole world, therefore, mourns the passing of successful men. Relatives and friends, companies and charities, banks and business firms, managers and administrators, householders and craftsmen, speculators and agents, authors

485

and teachers—all proclaimed their grief in public: in the press and on every wall. The newspapers also praised him at great length, and if they exaggerated, the exaggeration itself showed that the deceased was a great man, for if anyone is praised, he must be praiseworthy.

I too put aside my work to sympathize with his relatives and write them a few words of condolence, for I had been his friend and acquaintance for thirty years. It started when I arrived in the Land of Israel with nothing in my possession but love of the land and love of labor. I went to Mr. Klein to ask his advice, because I had heard that he was an amiable man and one could get advice and assistance from him; but since he had his hands full with the general good, he could not manage to deal with each individual, and he put me off time and again. Several years later, when I had married into a good family and become a family man, he took notice of me and showed me affection and friendship, as if we had been friends all the time. He honored me in the presence of my neighbors and visited me at home; and he used to rebuke me, saying: "I was the first you came to, as soon as you arrived in the country, and now you do not show me your face." He remembered that I had waited at his door, but forgot that he had put me off. Because he was a great doer and was always doing good to people, he thought he had done good to me as well, like all the public benefactors, who feel as if they have worked for each and every man. I, too, felt as if I had benefited from him. Anyone who has asked another man for a favor, even if it is not granted, feels in his bones an attachment to him, as if he had received a benefit from him.

At the time when Mr. Klein was friendly to me, he had given up all his business and was busy only with his body, treating it with baths and medicines and taking a walk every day. But even during his walks he did not ignore the public needs, like a man of property who surveys his possessions to learn what they require. And during his walks he would call over anyone he met by the way, like those who are accustomed to company and do not like to walk alone. Often he would summon me and walk with me. It is not my way to boast, but I may be permitted to boast of this, because it shows Mr. Klein's affection, for he took the trouble to tell me all that had been done in Jerusalem during the years of his life. Sometimes he repeated himself, like an old man who is fond of his memories, and sometimes he changed a little, according to the needs of the time and the place.

We used to stroll in the streets and neighborhoods of Jerusalem, Mr. Klein straight as a cedar and I swaying like a reed. As he walked, he would lift his stick and point to a house or a ruin, and tell me how much money had been sunk in the ruin, or how often the house had passed from hand to hand, from bank to bank, from speculator to speculator, from creditor to creditor, and it was still doubtful whether the creditor had acquired permanent possession, for one of the ten things said of Jerusalem is that no house can be held in absolute ownership there. So in every neighborhood he used to tell me how many lives had been spent there and how much Jewish money had gone down the drain. This is how it used to happen: When a Jew wanted a plot of land, the speculators would immediately raise the price. But Jews are stubborn by nature, and stubborn by heredity; they say that real estate can never be overvalued. So they go to the owner of the land and raise their bid. But the trouble is that the speculators are also Jews, stubborn by nature and heredity; so they raise their bids too, until a speck of dust costs a golden pound. Humble people have no option but to withdraw from the deal in disappointment, and but for him there would be no neighborhood here, not even a house. But this is a story within a story, and every story is longer than the earth—and any one of them would take a thousand and one nights to tell. And as he told me about the building of Jerusalem, so he would talk to me about the land and its worthies. Mr. Klein used to say that by the nature of things every great man was small to begin with, so small that he needed a godfather at his circumcision, and he had been privileged to be godfather to most of the leaders.

During the year in which Mr. Gedaliah Klein died, and half a year before as well, I had been separated from him somewhat by reason of distance, because he lived in town and I had gone out to live in a distant neighborhood, and when I came to town I did not happen to see him. Now that he had passed away I said to myself: I will write a letter of condolence to his relatives.

2

When I sat down to write I did not know whom to write to, for of all his household I knew only one daughter, and she had no great respect or regard for me, for she remembered the early days when I would shuffle my feet on the threshold of her father's house and he would pay me no attention, though she did not know that in the meantime Mr. Klein had changed his attitude to me. So I girded up my intellectual loins, as the literary men say, wrote a few words of condolence, and put the letter aside till the next day to check it.

I felt depressed and sad. I always feel sad whenever I am distracted from my work. Some people can do many things at a time without worrying, but as soon as I interrupt my work my heart feels sad, like a bookcase empty of books, or a field riddled by ants. For a year and a half I had set aside every other occupation to study the works of our later sages. I gave up the pleasures of the time and cut down my sleep, but not all dreamers see in sleep the good dreams I saw in waking. Days gone by and communities uprooted would come and appear before me, as at the time when Israel clung to the fear of God and were deeply in love with the wisdom of the Torah. And sometimes I was privileged to see the great men of Israel, the princes of the Torah in that generation; to perceive, if not the depths of their words, at least the fragrance of their teaching. There were times and periods when we had patriarchs and elders, judges and kings, heroes and men of war, seers and prophets, men of the Great Synagogue and Hasmoneans, sages of the Mishnah and the Talmud, scholars and eminences, nobles and princes, rabbis and codifiers, hymnalists and poets, who exalted the glory of Israel and sanctified the Divine Name in the world. But I love our later sages. Like a child in the darkening Sabbath, who comforts himself with the thought that the Sabbath still delays its departure, so I would comfort myself with the words of our later sages, which showed that there was still a little left of the Torah. For love of the Torah I would sit and study until the second watch of the night, and if I went to bed I would rely on the Divine Mercy to raise me up in the morning so that I could go back to my studies. Until the affair of that letter, when I put aside my studies.

I took a book, to restore my equanimity with the study of the Torah. The book slipped and fell out of my hand. I picked it up and opened it, but forgot what I had opened it for. When I remembered and looked into it, the letters skipped about in confusion and did not combine to make any sense. And I, too, skipped from one subject to another until I returned to the subject of Mr. Klein. The image of Mr. Klein rose before me, as when he and I used to stroll in the streets and neighborhoods of Jerusalem. I said to myself: I will go out and stroll a little, and recover my peace of mind.

3

I had not managed to cross the road before Mr. Gedaliah Klein tapped me on the shoulder and asked, "Where have you been and where are you going?" "I am having a stroll," I replied. Mr. Klein stroked his handsome beard and said, "I only came out to stroll too. So let us stroll together."

The sunny days had passed; and a cold wind was blowing. No rain had fallen as yet, but clustering clouds in the sky foreboded the approach of winter. Mr. Klein was dressed in a fine fur coat, with a collar of silver fox over his shoulders and around his neck, and a fine cane with a silver knob in his hand. The white hair of his head and his white beard gleamed like the silver knob in his hand, and his face gleamed out of the collar of his coat like polished copper.

I began to apologize for not having come to see him for several days. He held up his hand to my mouth, as a person does who wants to speak and bids his companion be silent. And immediately he started talking and talking. Even if a bird had come from Paradise to teach us its talk, he would not have stopped his. Many things Mr. Klein told me on that occasion, and more than he told he hinted. From all he said I understood that, had he not raised up Jerusalem out of the dust, nothing worth a row of buttons would have been done.

The sun stood on the tops of the hills and enveloped the rocks with clouds of gold. Mr. Gedaliah Klein's beard glowed even more than that gold, and so did the silver knob in his hand.

So we strolled. He talked and I listened. The streets darkened, and the houses hid in their shadows. Old men and women ran by, as they do close to the time of the afternoon prayer. As they passed, they looked at Mr. Klein in wonderment and moved their lips. I looked after them in surprise, for they and their clothes were different from those of the other old people of Jerusalem.

After we had made the rounds of several places we came back to my house.

I began to be afraid that Mr. Klein might want to go up to my room—and the letter of condolence I had written to his daughter lay open on my table.

I began to shiver.

"Are you worried about anything?" he said. I was silent and did not answer. "I see you are shivering," he said. I thought it would not be polite to tell him what I was worried about, so I said to him, "Yesterday my grandfather appeared to me in a dream." "Is your grandfather dead?" said he. I nodded in assent. "Well?" he said. "I will go and kindle a light in the House of Study," I replied. He put his hand to his forehead and said, "You have reminded me where I was going." He stretched out his cane, made a kind of circle in the air, and whispered, "I am going to the House of Study too."

I said to myself: What will he do when the Divine Name is uttered during the prayers and in answering *Amen*? Is he not afraid they might realize that he is dead, and he will be put to shame? As in the case of the dead cantor, who used to slur over the Name when he prayed, because the dead cannot utter the Heavenly Name. Once a sage happened to be there, who sensed that the cantor was dead—and it is said: "The dead shall not praise the Lord." He examined him and found that the Sanctified Name was sewn into his wrist. So he took a scalpel, cut into his flesh, and took out the Name—and immediately the body collapsed, and they saw that the flesh was already decomposed.

Mr. Klein did not perceive what I was thinking, and walked on. This is the greatness of Mr. Klein: if he decides to act, he pays no attention to anyone.

I dragged my feet and stopped at every step; perhaps the

Almighty would find him some other topic on the way and distract his mind from the House of Study. He saw that I was lingering, and said with a smile: "If you had not told me your grandfather was dead, I would have thought I was walking with him." I wanted to answer, but did not know what to say. To tell him the truth was impossible, but nothing else came into my mind.

The streetlamps had been lit, and the lights peered out feebly from the latticed windows. I breathed deeply and said, "It is late for the afternoon prayer." He breathed deeply too, and said, "I feel warm—no, but..." He wrapped himself up better and began to fumble with his cane like a blind man, saying, "Do me a favor, see if there is not a House of Study here. Yes, there is one here."

The worshippers stood bowed with their faces toward the wall. Mr. Klein went up to the most prominent place, and I remained standing by the door. Wherever they go, people like Mr. Klein find their places at the top. One old man turned his head from the wall and fixed his eyes on me. Mr. Klein gripped his cane. The cane trembled, and so did his hand. He was old, and his hands quivered.

A dim light shone from the four or five candelabra, of copper, of tin, of iron, and of clay. A peace not of this world pervaded the room, The worshippers finished their prayer and took two steps backwards, but the cantor still delayed the recitation of the final kaddish until the last of them should finish.

I looked around to see whom he was waiting for, and saw an old man standing in the southeastern corner, wrapped in his prayer shawl, covered in a fur coat up to above his neck. I did not see his face because it was turned toward the wall, but I saw his weary shoulders, those shoulders which the Holy One, blessed be He, has chosen to bear the burden of His Torah. My heart began to throb and fill with sweetness. The Almighty has still left us men who fill the heart with sweetness when we see them.

The old man turned his face, and I saw he was one of the princes of the Torah whose books I had been studying. I rushed forward and stood beside him. I knew that this was not a courteous thing to do, but I could not control myself. And I still wonder where I took the strength to do it.

Mr. Klein tapped me on the shoulder, took me by the hand, and said, "Come." I looked at that illustrious scholar and went with Mr. Klein.

Mr. Klein noticed the president of the House of Study. So he left me and went up to him.

That illustrious scholar left the House of Study. As was always his way, so he behaved at that moment, not looking beyond the four cubits, either in front of him or behind him. Devoted as he was to the Torah, he saw nothing but the affairs of the Torah. As I looked at him, I saw that a deep hole was open at his feet. While he had been engrossed in prayer and study, a band of children, playing in front of the House of Study, had dug the hole and left it uncovered. I ran up and bowed before him, so that he should lean on me and pass over the hole.

But he, in his deep devotion to the Torah and the fear of God, saw neither the hole nor me, who had come to save him from it. I did not have the heart to raise my voice and warn him against the danger, in case I might distract him from his thoughts. I stood still, making myself like a staff, a stick, a block of wood, a lifeless object. The Almighty put it into the saint's mind to lean on me. His body was light as an infant's. But I shall feel it until they put dust on my eyes.

4

I went back home and lit the light. I opened a window and sat down to rest. The wind blew and threw the letter at my feet. I looked at the letter, and at my feet, and was too lazy to lift it, for I was so weary that my limbs had begun to fall asleep. I undressed and went to bed, thinking about the things that had happened to me and that saint I had seen, and I knew that a great event had happened that day. No greater event will ever happen to me again. I do not remember whether I was sad or joyful, but I remember that another feeling, to which no term of joy or sadness can apply, moved my heart. If I had departed this world at that hour I would not have been sorry.

I lay in bed and thought: Why do we fear death? Something whispered to me: Raise the blanket. Immediately my fingers were filled with that thing to which no term of joy or sadness applies. And it too, namely, that thing, spread gradually to my shoulders, and the nape of my neck, and the crown of my head. I still belonged to this world, but I knew that if I raised the blanket and put it over my head I could enter into another world in the twinkling of an eye. May all my well-wishers be privileged to experience such a good hour.

The wind blew again and moved the letter. The letter began to roll this way and that. I said to myself: If I die, the letter will remain without anyone to send it. I pushed off the blanket.

The moon peeped into the room, illuminating the floor, and a pale light covered my letter. I raised my right hand and made a kind of circle in the air. When I opened my eyes a second time I heard a bird twittering at my window. It noticed me and fell silent. Then it raised its voice and flew away.

A pleasant languor spread throughout my limbs, a languor that filled them with a pleasure beyond compare. My bones seemed to dissolve in my body and my spirit was light. Although I was lying among pillows and covers and blankets, I imagined that I was not lying among them, but was one of them, inanimate as they. I closed my eyes and lay still.

As I lay like this, a band of Arabs passed by; they sounded as if they were quarreling with each other, and the silence of the street doubled and redoubled their voices. I covered myself up to my head and over with my blanket, but the voices pierced the blanket. My peace had been interrupted, so I got out of bed.

Remembering my letter, I lifted it from the floor and spread it before me; then I put it aside and picked up a book to read, but I did not read it. I set aside my studies and sat down to copy out the glosses I had discovered, like those students of the Torah who write down comments and glosses in their notebooks. I dipped my pen in the ink, arranged the sheet of paper in front of me, and concentrated my thoughts in order to set them down. An hour passed, but nothing happened. Apart from the shadow of the pen, there was no shape of a letter to be seen on the paper. I bent my head over the sheet and looked at the shadow of my pen, which was coupled with the shadow of my fingers, like two different species who cannot be fertile.

I rose and picked up the pages I had written a few days before. As I read them, I began to feel a kind of writer's itch in my hand, that sweet tingling one gets before starting work. I stretched out my hand over the paper and clothed my ideas in words. But the ideas disintegrated, like the snowman a child has made and wants to cover with a garment, which melts away as he tries to clothe it.

I read over again what I had written a few days before. When I started to read it, I thought I had got into the subject. I picked up the pen again. And again the pen cast a pale shadow on the blank paper.

As I found it hard to sit idle, I looked for something to do. I began to shake my books free of dust. Once I had started to shake a book, I began to regret the waste of time, for while I was shaking the dust off the book I might have studied it. When I sat down to study, it all started up again from the beginning. Things that used to refresh my soul turned to ashes in my mouth. An hour passed and another hour. I was trying to impress the words of the Torah on my heart, and my heart was giving me idle thoughts.

I went back to my writings and sat down to copy out what I had written recently; perhaps, while doing that, I could add something. And indeed I did not labor in vain. The pen moved on of its own accord, and added more and more.

When I examined what I had written, I saw that it did not add up to anything at all. I held the pen upright and made circles in the air with it. I remembered I had meant to kindle a light in memory of my grandfather. So I got up and went into town.

Before I went out I read the letter and saw that it was no worse than any other epistle of condolence. If Job said to his companions, who were privileged to have their words recorded in the Holy Scriptures, "How then comfort ye me in vain?" what can we write? I put the letter in an envelope and sent it off.

I went into town and walked from street to street and lane to lane until I reached the yard of the House of Study where I had been the evening before with Mr. Gedaliah Klein, and I heard a voice emerging from inside the yard saying, "Blessed be the glory of the Lord from His place." I went into the yard and asked: "Where is the House of Study?"

A girl replied, "There's no House of Study here."

An old woman came out and asked, "What are you looking for?" I told her. "There is no House of Study here," she said with a sigh. "But I was here last night," I said to her. "Last night?" The old woman struck her forehead and said, "Well, Lord Almighty, now I remember! When I was a little girl, they used to show this place; they said there used to be a big House of Study here, and they used to study in it and pray, but because of all our sins it had disappeared."

I bade her farewell and went to another House of Study.

This one was built many years ago, and it was built with the aid of a gentile king. His forefathers had destroyed Jerusalem and he helped to rebuild it, and we heard from the righteous men of that generation that when the righteous Messiah comes he will come and pray there. Some say this meant the gentile king, who would be converted and come to pray, but others said it meant the King Messiah. And it seems that those who applied the words to the King Messiah were right, for converts are not accepted in the world to come. When this synagogue was built, books and candelabra and Ark-cloths were donated from many countries, and the sages of Jerusalem used to adorn it with teaching and prayer. Now the house is empty, the plaster has peeled off the walls, the furnishings are broken and the books torn, the Ark-cloths are tattered and the candelabra rusted, and the students of the Torah have passed away. Hardly a bare quorum assembles there. And if the gates of Heaven are still open, nothing reaches them but a pennyworth of prayer.

I went in and found a blind old man sitting at a rickety table, shaking his head and muttering verses from the Psalms.

"Where is the sexton?" I asked.

"I am the sexton," he replied.

I asked him to kindle a light in memory of my grandfather.

The sweet, clear smile of the blind gleamed in his two blind eyes, and he nodded, saying "I will."

He went up to the lectern, took out a glass and raised it to the light, put in some oil, cut a length of wick and put it in the glass, set it on the lectern again, and said, "I will light it for the prayer."

I took out four small coins and gave them to him. He took three and left one.

"I gave you four," said I.

"I know," he said, nodding.

He took the coin and put it into a charity box.

"Are you wary of even numbers?" I said to him.

He smiled and said, "A charity box should not be empty."

I kissed the *mezuzah* and went out.

In the morning, when I sat down to study, my mind was not at rest. I stopped, and said: If I had looked longer for that House of Study I would have found it. I knew that this had come into my mind only to confuse me, but I thought of nothing else.

I tried to remember the faces of the worshippers who had appeared to me the night before in the House of Study. Apart from that illustrious scholar, whom I had recognized from a drawing, I knew no one there. And even he was not like any picture I knew.

To gather up enthusiasm for my work, I reminded myself how our recent sages, of blessed memory, devoted themselves to the Torah. For instance, there was the story of the author of the *Face of Joshua*, whose disciples once arrived late. "Why are you late?" he asked them when they came. "We were afraid to go out because of the cold," they replied. He raised his face from the book—and his beard was frozen hard to the table. "True," he said, "it is cold today." Or like the story of Rabbi Jacob Emden, who hired a servant to announce to him every hour, "Woe, another hour has gone," so that that illustrious scholar should give himself an account of what he had put right during that hour. But the acts of the righteous did not bring me to the point of action.

Since I was sitting idle, I became a breeding place for strange reflections, for idle men beget idle thoughts. My study lost its savor, and I felt my work was of little worth. I began to ask myself: What is the point of this work when the land is being regenerated, when a new generation is regenerating the land by its deeds?

I rebuked myself and said to myself: Go and rake over your

own dunghill. And I started again to read the words of our sages, of blessed memory, but I found no contentment in their teachings.

I remembered the days when I dedicated myself to the Torah, but the memory did not bring me to the point of action.

I tried to arouse myself by idle acts. I started to arrange my books, one day according to the date when they were written and the next day according to subject, or in alphabetical order. I also prepared handsome notebooks and other accessories. Every day I invented something new. But before I managed to do it, I set it aside.

During that year and a half when I had dedicated myself to the Torah, I had received letters, books, and brochures which I had not taken the trouble to read. Now that I was idle, I looked at them.

I set aside all the books and brochures, and all the futile epistles, and turned to the letters of individuals I had left behind in exile in Poland and Germany, where they bewailed their exile and begged me to help them come to the Land of Israel.

I rested my hand on my table and spoke to myself: How shall I bring you up, how shall I bring you here, when you have no money to show the authorities?

I do not know whether it was in waking or in a dream, in vision or fancy, or perhaps it is neither dream nor fancy. Once a certain man wanted to come to the Land of Israel, and he did not have a thousand pounds to show the authorities. He took his wife and his sons and daughters, and wandered with them for several years until he reached the boundary of the Land of Israel, but the officers of the law would not let them in, so they threw themselves down before the gates of the land and wept. Sleep overtook them and they slumbered. Trees grew up around and concealed them, and they slept a long time. When they awoke, the father said to his son, "Take a coin and bring some bread."

He went out and saw people plowing and sowing in gladness, with never a policeman or an officer. He came back and told his father, who took his wife and his sons and daughters, and they entered into the land. The whole city was astonished at them, for they thought all the exiles had already arrived, and there was no Jew left who had not come. They gave them a dwelling and food and a field to plow and sow. The father took out money to pay. "What are these scraps of metal?" the people said to him. "You call these scraps?" he replied. "If I had had a thousand like them, I would have been with you long ago." Immediately it became a great joke throughout the city: for the sake of such things Jews had been prevented from entering the land, and the sons of the land had not been allowed to return. How foolish the world had been to torment the Jews for scraps of metal and paper notes.

The letters lay before me, and I had to answer them. I stretched out my hand and took the pen. I set a clean sheet before me and started to write, but apart from greetings and apologies I could not write a thing. I could not study the Torah, because of my confused mind: I could not stay at home for boredom. What could I do? I got up and went out to wander for a while in the streets of Jerusalem.

5

I walked about the streets of Jerusalem. Jerusalem, which had been still, gave voice. Buses and automobiles raced about as if pursued by demons; the noise of them rose into the heart of the heavens, and people dodged out of the way to avoid being run over. Every street and corner was full of soldiers, policemen and detectives, tarbushes red as blood and eyes angry and black with hatred. And the precious sons of Zion—some of them were dressed in velvet and satin, but others lay in the dunghills.

Even as the streets of Jerusalem have changed, so have its houses. Not all the prophecies have yet been fulfilled in the city, but some of its ruins have been rebuilt. The Lord buildeth Jerusalem, at any rate, even through gentiles, even through speculators. And there are houses that rise up to the sky. In the past, when the sons of Israel were lowly in their own eyes, He would, as it were, lower all the seven firmaments to be close to them; today, when they are proud and He is getting further away from them, they build their towers up to the sky.

There are other buildings in Jerusalem where you can find anything, whether you want it or not: shops where no one knows the use of the utensils they sell, or banks and coffeehouses and places of amusement and entertainment. If you find the night hangs heavy on your hands, and you do not know what to do with it, borrow money in a bank and go to a cinema or a coffeehouse or some other place of entertainment. And if you find it hard to wait until evening, stand at the side of the street and you will hear choruses on the gramophone. When Elijah, of blessed memory comes to bring tidings of redemption, we can only hope his voice will be heard above the noise of the automobiles and the screeching of the gramophones.

I stand in front of a large building full of shops selling clothing and foodstuffs, jewelry and ornaments for males and females. Signs hanging over the shops proclaim their wares in every possible tongue, and the building emits a vapor like the vapor of foreign lands.

"And I will make thy windows of agates, and thy gates of carbuncles, and all thy borders of pleasant stones." And the sages say: "One day the Holy One, blessed be He, will make Jerusalem of precious stones and diamonds." And even now we can see in Jerusalem something like a pattern of the days to come, for its mountains are covered with all kinds of pleasant colors, were it not for the tall buildings that conceal the face of Jerusalem.

I wandered in the streets and squares of Jerusalem without seeking anything, and when I recalled that House of Study and those old men I had seen there, I knew that I would never find it and never see it.

But I saw new faces. These were the immigrants from Germany who had lately arrived. Where was their dignity, their property, their wisdom, their power? Those who had displaced the Divine Presence with their pride now walked along bowed with care. From time to time the Holy One, blessed be He, shows favor to one of the tribes of Israel and gives it wealth and honor, that they may help their brethren, but they ascribe all their good fortune to their own merits, to their clever behavior, to the masters of the land who have given them good laws because they are better and more honest than the rest of their brethren. When the Holy One, blessed be He, sees this, He, as it were, turns His face away from that tribe. Immediately the wicked men among the gentiles bring down ruin upon them and they go down into the dust.

As I was walking, I met one of the German immigrants whom I knew. I stopped and asked how he was.

He began to tell me the same things he had told me recently, all that the wicked men had done to him there in Germany, what he had suffered, how much money they had taken from him, and how at last he and his wife and his children had escaped without a penny.

I comforted him as I had comforted him before. "You are fortunate to have come here," I said, "for from now onwards, no wicked hand has power over you."

Now that I had mentioned the Land of Israel in his presence, he began to abuse the nation and the population, their behavior and demeanor; his room was minute, and the rent, to boot, would not be too small for a baronial hall; the maid downstairs put on lady-like airs; the workers were all Left, and the merchants bent on theft. The phones had gone crazy, the children were lazy; immigrants from many lands talked with their hands; the trains were always late, the beer was second rate. People didn't know how to pray, and they spat on the floor; the politicians made you pay, always asking for more; the men at the top talked and talked without a stop; mosquitoes were a pest, and gave you no rest; at funeral rites there were barbarous sights. In short, life was vile at home and outside, above and below, whatever you tried.

I said: 'And thou shalt see the good of Jerusalem,' the Scripture said. A Jew ought to see the good of Jerusalem and not its evil." And I went on: "Perhaps you have heard from the old men of Jerusalem how many troubles our fathers found in the Land of Israel, for the land was in ruins at that time, and they were plagued by diseases; when they got out of one trouble, along came another, worse than the first. But they paid no heed to their troubles; they were happy to live in the land and gave praise and thanks to the Creator of all the worlds for choosing us out of all the nations and giving us the Land of Israel."

He took the cigar out of his mouth and said, "Those people had God in their hearts."

I said to him in a whisper, "God exists now too."

"But not within us," he said.

I said to him: "A certain hasidic master was asked where the Holy One, blessed be He, dwells. He told them: Wherever He is allowed to enter, there He dwells."

6

In these days I visited some of the new neighborhoods at whose dedication ceremonies I had rejoiced. Most of the little houses were rickety; their builders no longer lived in them, for they had built them with loans and could not pay, so the banks had sold their houses to others. The same thing happened to the purchasers: they borrowed from the banks—borrowed from one bank and paid to another, so they had to go to the moneylenders—and anyone who falls into their hands never recovers. But so long as they paid the interest they were allowed to stay.

One day I found myself in a certain neighborhood in Jerusalem which Mr. Gedaliah Klein had an affection for, because he had helped some of its people with a loan at one or two per cent less than the banks usually take.

I walked about in the neighborhood. A row of houses on one side and a row of houses on the other, with a kind of road winding between, producing weeds and growing thorns, and a broken-down car sunk in the ground. Some of the houses are unpainted; others have their walls calcimined to look like slabs of marble. Some are on the point of collapse; the builders did not want to invest their money in deepening the foundations, for if they had sunk deeper foundations they would not have had enough to build the houses. The soil of Jerusalem, which was accustomed to sanctuaries, does not like the light houses, so it undermines them until they collapse. Another thing this soil does is to grow bushes and trees inside the houses. Usually, bushes and trees that are planted need care; here they flourish and grow of themselves, and break up the floor and the walls. And why does the soil not make the gardens grow around the houses? Because if the people of the neighborhood plow and hoe and water to grow a little greenery, their bad neighbors come along and loose their goats on them. From the Talmud we learn that the wicked Titus laid waste our land, but the evidence of our eyes teaches us that the goats are laying it waste, and it is still far from clear which did more damage.

I walk about in the neighborhood. Peace and quiet everywhere; not a living soul but goats and cats and dogs. Those who have work in town have gone to town, and those who have nothing to do have gone to look for work. And there are some people who have despaired of work, so they stay at home and recite psalms, or study Mishnah or Midrash. As for the women, some of them have kinds of shops in towns and some have gone to buy vegetables in the market, for the two shopkeepers in the neighborhood have nothing to sell and are going around the town to plead with their creditors. And where are the children? Those who have shoes for their feet have gone to town to study, and those who have no shoes are playing with their brothers at home, for the rainy days have come, and if their clothes are tattered and they have no shoes they cannot play outside.

I walk through the neighborhood, in the length of it and in the breadth of it, looking at the rickety windows with their slackly hanging shutters. On one house at the top of the neighborhood hangs a tin sign bearing the name of a certain benefactor after whom the street is named. The rains and winds of two or three winters have obliterated the name of the man who has taken to himself the name of a street in Jerusalem, and left him no name, but only a buckled sign.

As I walked through the neighborhood the silence was broken by the arrival of a bus full of people. They stretched their limbs as they got off, some to collect taxes and some to collect charity, and some to examine the houses to see which were fit to be security for loans. As they found no one, they started to pester me. As I could tell them nothing, they insulted me. If Mr. Gedaliah Klein were alive and I were walking with him, no one would dare to speak to me like that.

The driver went into one of the houses to rest awhile from the fatigue of the journey, for part of the way from the main road to the neighborhood is covered with holes and pitfalls, and part with spikes and stones; the bus is also rickety, and unless the driver lent it some of his strength it would not go more than a yard or two. Since the visitors wanted to leave and could not find him, they went in to have a look at the synagogue.

The synagogue is a fine building outside and inside. Pious women in America donated the money to build it, but they left one place unfinished, for in the course of construction a great deal of money was wasted to no purpose, and when the donors were asked to make up the difference they could not do it, for America was short of money at the time. So one corner was left uncompleted, but if you do not look in that direction you do not see what is missing.

The synagogue rises higher than any of the houses in the neighborhood—a fine building outside and inside. The floor is made of large stones, and the ceiling is white as the whitewash of the Temple. The walls are straight, and there are twelve windows in them, like the number of the gates of prayer in the Heavens. Our father Jacob, on whom be peace, produced twelve tribes, and the Holy One, blessed be He, correspondingly opened twelve windows in the firmament to receive the prayers of each tribe. But the seed of the tribes were fruitful and split up into Sephardim and Ashkenazim, Perushim and Hasidim—and the Hasidim, too, are split up according to their rabbis, each group praying in a different style. But the Heavens are still intact and no new gates are opened in them, and every worshipper wants the prayers to be recited in his own style, so that there is great confusion, and quarrels break out.

At last the driver came out, sat down in the bus, hooted and blared and hooted again. The travelers pushed their way in. The driver hooted and blared, started up the bus, and set off for town. Again the neighborhood was silent, and were it not for the thick, heavy smell of burnt gasoline which defiled the air there would be no sign that human beings had been here.

I saw a man sitting beside his house and reading the *Book of Legends*. I went up to him and talked to him, praising the late Mr. Gedaliah Klein, without whom there would be no one living here. The man put down the *Book of Legends*, sighed and smiled, and said, "It's a hopeless mess. Half my house is a wreck and the other half a ruin—and the whole of it is mortgaged. If it were sold to pay the debt, not even a small part of the debt would be settled, and if it remains in my hands—where will I get the money to repair it? And so far I've only been talking about myself. The others are in the same predicament, and there's another difficulty: we're far from town, where the people work, and to get to town we need the bus. The bus isn't always there, and the money's not there either. So we go on foot, but you cannot be sure you will get there safely. In times of peace our bad neighbors threaten your money, and in times of stress they threaten your life."

"Well," I asked him, "what will you do?" "What we ought to do we certainly shall not do," he replied with a smile. "But I only hope the future is no worse than the past, for nothing is so bad that there's nothing worse. Master Gedaliah Klein, may he rest in peace, was a great man and meant to help the builders of the neighborhood. He came forward when they were in difficulties and found them money at a low rate of eight per cent when people pay nine or ten and up to twelve. But anyone who gets into debt has to leave his house in the end."

"And is there no hope for your neighborhood?" I asked. "There is one hope," he replied. "And what is it?" I asked. "When the Messiah comes," he said, "and the wolf dwells with the lamb, we shall no longer be afraid of our bad neighbors, and the goats will do no more harm either." "And until the Messiah comes?" I said. He smiled and replied, "The Old Man of Shpoli used to say, 'Master of the universe, I can assure Thee that the world will go on degenerating in this way until the coming of the Redeemer.' True, there was once a chance to put things right. You see the two rows of houses, on the road to our neighborhood, that separate us from the town and the next neighborhood? All these houses, as you see them, are new, recently built. But before they were built, that was virgin soil, and we could get from one neighborhood to the other in a short time. The owners of the land offered to sell it to us, and we agreed. So we went to our wealthy neighbors and said to them, 'This land is up for sale; buy it, and both of us will no longer be surrounded by the Arabs, who terrorize us so long as we are few. And we will pay our share for the bus and the watchmen and all the other public facilities that every Jewish community must have to survive.' But our neighbors sent us away empty-handed. After all, they had moved away from the town and its paupers, and then paupers come along and propose to get closer. We started going around from one institution to another, but they put us off, some for budgetary reasons and some for economic. 'It isn't enough that you haven't succeeded,' they said, 'but you want to drag other people into this mess.' So we were in despair. Meanwhile, along came Syrians from Syria, bought the land, and built themselves large houses. So we are still living in fear and trembling, and we can't keep up any public facility, not even a grocery. Our dignified neighbor has also suffered for its pride, for the Arabs have surrounded it, and it is far from any Jewish settlement, and the bus hardly comes for lack of passengers, for anyone who has no house of his own moves to town, and new houses are not being built there, for no one builds his home in a neighborhood whose people are leaving. And even those who own their own houses would be glad to leave, and this garden city, builded in beauty, is gradually being abandoned."

As we were talking, a bus came from town and the whole neighborhood went out to meet it. Women and children got off, carrying torn and tattered baskets, with a little cabbage, a little beet, a little turnip, a little garlic and onion in them, and a loaf or two on top—all those things a poor man covets. They set down the baskets and sacks, got into the bus again, and threw out bundles of rusty spikes and old iron hoops they had bought in town to reinforce their tottering houses; some brought out crates and some cradles.

The neighborhood began to hum and bustle. Even those who had been hidden in their houses came out and asked what news there was in town and when they would say the afternoon prayer. Little by little, the rest of the people returned from town with their sons, the young ones from the *heder* and the older ones from the *yeshivah*. And from end to end of the neighborhood, people came running to the synagogue.

In the meantime, Arabs came by, on their way back from their work in town to the neighborhood villages. They were followed by shepherds with their flocks, who stirred up clouds of dust. The people of the neighborhood pushed their way through the sheep, groaning and panting.

It was time for me to return to town, so I got into the bus. An hour passed but it did not move. I asked the driver when he would start. "What's wrong with staying here?" said the driver. I said to him, "If you are not going, tell me and I will go on foot." "Do you think I'm a prophet, that I should know if I'm going?" he said. "If you're not afraid of tiring out your legs, get up and walk. If I find passengers and start off, I'll pick you up on the way and take you in; if I don't, I'll stay the night here. Nice neighborhood, isn't it? Refreshing air! Pity you can't live on air."

I got off the bus and set out on foot. Fine, big houses accompanied me most of the way. When were they built? We did not read about them in the papers; we were not invited to the dedications, but there they are, sound and solid. Every house is surrounded by a garden, with an iron fence around it, so that no goat can get in. The Lord buildeth Jerusalem, sometimes by means of Jews and sometimes by means of gentiles.

7

Once I was going to and fro, as usual, in the streets of Jerusalem, when I saw large posters announcing a memorial meeting that night on the thirtieth day after the passing of Mr. Gedaliah Klein. Ah, thirty days had passed since the day I wrote the letter of condolence.

I took out my watch to see if the time had not yet come for the commemoration, and I saw that the time had not yet come. To pass the time I went from wall to wall and from poster to poster. I doubt if there was a man in Jerusalem that day who was so well versed as I in the names and titles of the eulogists.

I began to be afraid I might have made a mistake in the order of the days, and the day of the commemoration had passed. I went into a bookshop to buy a calendar tablet.

The shopkeeper said, mockingly, "We are just going to print a calendar for next year and you are looking for yesteryear."

"I am content with the old tablets," I said.

To pass the time I bought a newspaper. Since I had the paper, I read all the articles that were printed on the thirtieth day of Mr. Gedaliah Klein's passing. In the past, all the deeds of men were included in a single verse, such as "And Enoch walked with God: and he was not; for God took him," but now that knowledge has expanded and the deeds of men have multiplied, we cannot complete all their praises in one sentence.

It is almost eight o'clock. The shopkeepers are locking up their shops, with double locks, for fear of the thieves who have multiplied in Jerusalem. Buses race by, and so do passersby. As they run, they bump into peddlers and broom-sellers, beggars and flute-players, reformers, crazy men and crazy women, distributors of leaflets and advertisers of merchandise, a dog who has lost his master and a mistress who has lost her dog.

As you escape from these, the shoeshine boys take hold of your feet. While they are sharing out your feet, paperboys offer you their newspapers. As you stand and read, agitators come up and fill your hands with pamphlets. If you get rid of them, women come along and pin all kinds of tags on you. You stop to pay, but your pocket is empty, for in the meantime pickpockets have extracted your purse. As you stand in despair, wanting to go home, along comes a procession of boys. While you wait for them to pass, a bus goes by and runs over an ass. You run to lift it; along come the police and strike you with their batons for obstructing the populace and holding up the traffic. When you run away and find a place to hide, you come across a girl who has been attacked by zealots. While they are punishing her because they saw her going with the English, a young man throws vitriol in another girl's face and blinds her. The gramophone shrieks, "How goodly are thy tents, O Jacob," while the radio sings back, "Happy are ye, O Israel." Meanwhile, the whole street lights up, revealing the picture of a naked woman, and a loudspeaker proclaims to the heavens, "Come and see the enchantress!"

The streetlamps, square and round and semicircular, illuminate the streets of the city, in addition to the moon and the stars. I walk in their light and read all kinds of placards about new productions of plays like *Thy People* and *Hard to be a Jew*. And the gramophone screeches, "How goodly are thy tents, O Jacob," while the radio replies, "Happy are ye, O Israel," and the loudspeakers drown their voices, and the smell of *falafel* permeates the air. Little by little the street returns to normal. Buses rush and people push; some of their heads are hairy, and some of their chins are double; some of them float on air, and some are always in trouble; men with serious mien and women with delicate hands chatter in all the tongues of all the far-off lands; every stalwart lad and every maiden ripe puffs at a cigarette or pulls away at a pipe. The coffeehouses are full of people young and old; the men make eyes at the girls, and the girls are just as bold; the men drink beer and whiskey, the women paint their faces—O Muse, what have you to do with such peculiar places? The bars are full of soldiers, the British Mandate's men—"Drink up and then bring up, my lads, and fill your mugs again!" And now I go to mourn a man who is no more—O Muse, be silent now, and do not weep so sore.

8

The platform is draped in black, and a candelabrum draped in black illuminates a picture of the deceased hanging over the platform. His face is the face of a successful man, unmarred even by death.

The assembly hall is full and still the people come. The first arrivals have been seated by the ushers on the middle benches, while the latecomers are seated above, near the platform. Last come those for whom the platform is waiting.

Mr. Schreiholz mounted—he is the principal speaker everywhere. He made a sad face and started in a whisper, like a man who cannot speak for grief. Suddenly he raised his voice and stretched his hand upwards with his fingers spread, seeking a word to express the full depth of his thought. When he found the word he began to spout with growing fluency, declaiming at the top of his voice: "The deceased was…, the deceased was…," describing, between one "was" and the next, his recollections of where he had seen the deceased, and all the rest of it.

When he had finished, he got off the platform, pressed the hands of the mourners, climbed onto the platform again, and sat down, like an orator who knows his place.

Next came a teacher who had become a banker. As a man who knew the taste of learning and the value of money, he emphasized the virtues of the deceased, who had combined learning with trading, and by virtue of his talents had succeeded in setting several of Jerusalem's alms-hunting institutions on a sound financial basis and making them into national institutions, which added to the national capital and increased the strength of the nation.

After he had finished, he got down off the platform, pressed the hands of the mourners, and found a place to stand, like a man who seeks no more than a station for his feet.

Next came a townsman of the deceased. He recalled the honor of his house abroad, which was a place of assembly for Lovers of Zion and devotees of the Hebrew tongue. And first and foremost of all the deceased's achievements in his town was the splendid edifice of the modernized *heder*, which was the archetype of the Hebrew school, whose waters we drink and in whose shade we shelter.

After he had finished, he got down off the platform, pressed the hands of the mourners and pushed his way in somewhere, for during his eulogy someone else had taken his place.

Next came the last of the eulogists, Mr. Aaron Ephrati, a dignified old man respected by all. He started to sing the praises of the deceased, who had served the entire community without distinction of rich or poor, for since he had grown up in wealth and lived all his days in wealth, he regarded wealth as a matter of course, and not as a special virtue that entitles its possessors to make distinctions between rich and poor. And when he had set up the modernized *heder*, he had not behaved like those wealthy men who have their sons and daughters educated in the schools of the gentiles and leave the modernized *heder* for the common people, but sent his sons and daughters to the same modernized *heder*, so that they should get a plain Jewish education. And so as to combine the light of Judaism with the beautiful and the useful, he had sent them to high school and the university, so that they might fulfill the maxim: "Be a man and a Jew both in your tent and outside." Finally, Mr. Ephrati turned to the sons and daughters of the deceased and said to them: "Your father has still left you things to do, for his aspirations were in keeping with his greatness. Though he is dead, you are alive, and the sons must add to the deeds of their fathers."

After Mr. Ephrati had finished speaking, the cantor of the synagogue climbed onto the platform, took out a hexagonal velvet biretta, bent down and put the biretta on his head, took out a cantor's tuning fork and put it in his mouth, bent and struck the tuning fork on the table, stuck it in his mouth again, put it close to his ear, and began to sing "O God, full of mercy."

Since I am no judge of music, I was free to think my own thoughts. This prayer used to make my heart throb, I mused as I stood there, but today it just bores me. And another thought occurred to me: there are theater melodies which sound, when sung by the performers, like prayers and supplications, but sometimes prayers and supplications, when they are sung by the cantors, sound like theater tunes. On the cantor's head the biretta quivered; on his throat his Adam's apple shivered; around the hall the echoes rolled, over consolers and consoled; while biretta and pate, with every nod, invoked the infinite mercy of God.

I stand looking at the distinguished people who have come to pay their respects to the memory of Mr. Gedaliah Klein. Although I would not compare my work with theirs, I feel sorry that I do not succeed in doing my own work. And the man with the biretta, with his cantor's tongs, warbles his notes like a bird's sweet songs, stretching his throat toward God on high, emitting each word with a groan or a sigh; and everyone listens to the lamentation—wiping his tears, or his perspiration.

All the people are on their feet, including the daughter of the deceased. Her black veil quivers over her comely features, and she is surrounded by important people, whose faces are pink with satiety and complacency, like practical men rooted in the life of the nation, who can adapt their behavior to the nation's needs, or the nation's needs to their behavior. Fine clothes like theirs were never seen in

Jerusalem until Hitler started killing the Jews, so that all the great craftsmen fled, and some of them settled in the Land of Israel.

I look at the clothes and say to myself: I will get some clothes like these too; perhaps I will raise my spirits. But I am afraid the great tailors may see how humble I am and not take much trouble with such a fellow; they may not even make me as good a garment as this one, which was made by the Jerusalem tailor. And if they make me a fine garment, my friends and relatives will be ashamed of their clothes when they meet me, as I am ashamed to be seen by these men with their fine clothes. But all these were futile thoughts, for to get fine clothes you need money, and to get money you need the desire for money, and to have the desire, you must have a desire for the desire. And where will I get the strength for those desires?

The memorial light was still burning there, when the cantor finished the memorial prayer. He doffed his biretta and wiped his pate, and put on his hat, brooding on his fate: "If I sang in the theater, at home or abroad, all the beautiful women would applaud; but here not a soul has a word to say—that's your reward when you sing to pray."

After the recital of the mourners' kaddish, the audience mingled with each other, shook out their clothes, which had got wrinkled with sitting, and took out cigarettes for a smoke. "If anyone tells you there's such a thing as free will," said Mr. Schreiholz, "don't believe him. For two and a half hours I was waiting to smoke, but I didn't do it out of respect for this solemn occasion."

People from the suburbs who were in the hall started to push their way out to get their buses. I should have hurried, too, and run for my bus, but I wanted to pay my respects to Mr. Gedaliah Klein's daughter.

She sat like a mourner, her black hat adding to her charm; a peaceful sadness covered her face, like a well-bred woman who has been bereaved, but has not been bereft of her distinction. Public leaders, men and women, came up to her one after another and pressed her hand, and she pressed the hands of them all.

I bowed my head and greeted her. But she did not notice me.

I bowed and greeted her again. Perhaps she nodded slightly, and perhaps she did not nod to me at all. I felt no grudge against her. Why should she have to move her head in return for two or three lines I had written her? Countless letters of condolence had been sent her, and they were still being sent.

I left the assembly hall. The entire square was full of cars for Mr. Klein's family and the eulogists. A little while later, nothing was left of them but the odor of burnt gasoline and cosmetics and dust.

I set off for the bus station, but when I reached it the bus had gone. I waited for the next, but it did not come, so I gave up the idea of riding home and set out on foot.

An old carriage came along. The coachman reined in his horses and said to me, "Get in." I felt no desire to get in. The horses set off without me. Silently, silently, they moved off without lifting their feet, and, if I am not mistaken, the motion of the carriage was not visible either.

The air was clear; the moon and the stars shone. The earth was soft; it would have been easy to open it and cover oneself up with it like a blanket. How tired I was, how I wanted to rest. The coachman came back and rode around me with his coach. I looked up at him, hoping that he might take me into the coach, but he took no notice and did not take me in. The horses lifted their feet; not a sound was heard as they moved, but the echo quivered in my ears until I reached home and went in.

9

When I entered, I found Mr. Gedaliah Klein sitting at my table. His head was bowed toward his breast, and his cane lay between his knees. He stirred, raised his head, and whispered: "You here?" "I have just come," I replied in a whisper. He rubbed his eyes. "I felt sleepy and dropped off," he said.

His face was weary and aged. Since I last left him, he had suddenly become very old. Apart from the fox-fur coat he wore, there was nothing about him that was not old.

I pretended not to notice that he had aged considerably, for Mr. Gedaliah Klein desired the honor of age coupled with the vigor of youth, and not the old age which is a burden and a shame. He looked at me and said, "I have not seen you for decades. Tell me now, my dear friend, why do you not come to visit me? Or perhaps I have seen you in the meantime? Where have you been all the time? And where, for instance, did you spend the whole evening?" I could not bring myself to tell him where I had been, so I was silent.

He pricked up his right ear, supported it on his right hand, and said, "I did not hear what you said. Now for another matter: Where did I leave you that night I saw you last? If I am not mistaken, there was an old courtyard, and candles were burning low, and some man, a sexton, pestered me. Don't you remember, my dear friend?" I told him.

"One thing is clear," said Mr. Klein; "there was a House of Study there. You see, my dear friend, I forget nothing. What did we go to that House of Study for? If I remember rightly, you wanted to kindle a light for the repose of your grandfather's soul. I hear the sound of horses. Did you come home in a carriage?"

"No, I came on foot."

"So what is the carriage doing here?"

I said to him, "Perhaps you know where that House of Study is? I am looking for it but cannot find it."

Mr. Klein smiled at me as people do at a child who is trying to get something easy. He raised his hands to his eyes to settle his spectacles. Then he pried open his eyes with his fingernails and looked straight at me. "Did you put out the light?" he said. "You didn't? So why don't I see? What did you say? You are looking for the…What are you looking for? Speak into my ear. When one's eyes are affected, all one's limbs are weakened."

I went up close to him and said, "I am looking for the House of Study."

"You are looking for the House of Study?" he repeated in a tone of surprise. "Which House of Study are you looking for? Perhaps the one where you were with me? Give me my cane and I will draw you where it is."

I took his cane from between his knees and put it in his hand.

He took the cane and began to grope with it like a blind man in an unfamiliar place. The cane in his hand quivered, his hands quivered, and he quivered with the cane. He gripped the cane with all his strength, but his strength was gone. His face was no longer the same, and he, too, began to change, until he was entirely changed, and no longer resembled himself. And perhaps it was not he, but that old man, that blind old man who had kindled the memorial light for my grandfather, may he rest in peace.

I waited for him to look kindly on me, as he had done at first in the Great Synagogue when he whispered verses from the psalms. But his face was frozen and his eyes devoid of laughter. I felt it hard to stand in front of a man who used to be courteous to me but now paid me no attention, so I turned my face away from him. When I turned my face away, he stood up over me with his cane. I felt afraid of him and closed my eyes. He took hold of the cane and began to draw with it, making six marks. A house emerged and rose up, like that House of Study. I tried to enter but could not find the door. The old man raised his cane and knocked twice on the wall. An opening appeared, and I went in.

Translated by Misha Louvish

Fernheim

When he returned he found the house locked. After he rang once, twice, and then a third time, the doorkeeper appeared, folded her hands on her stomach, leaned her head on her shoulder, and stood gaping a moment. "Well," she said, "who do I see? Mr. Fernheim! Bless my soul, it *is* Mr. Fernheim. So, then, Mr. Fernheim's come back. Then why did they say he wouldn't come back? And all this ringing—it's really quite useless, because the house is empty and there's no one to open it for him, because Mrs. Fernheim left and locked the house and took the keys with her. She didn't imagine there'd be any need for keys, like now, for instance, that Mr. Fernheim's back and wants to get into his house."

Fernheim felt he had better say something before the woman inundated him with more derision. He forced himself to speak, but his reply was short, stammering—and meaningless.

The doorkeeper went on, "After the baby died, her sister Mrs. Steiner came, and Mr. Steiner with her too. They took Mrs. Fernheim with them to their summer home. My son Franz, who carried her bags for her, heard that the Steiners plan to stay there in the village until the big Israelite holy days at the end of the summer, right before the fall, and I'd guess Mrs. Fernheim won't come back to the city before then. Why should she hurry, now that the baby's gone? Does he need a kindergarten? Poor little thing, he kept getting thinner and thinner till he died."

Fernheim pressed his lips together tightly. Finally he nodded at the doorkeeper, stuck his fingertips into his vest pocket, took out a coin, and gave it to her. Then he turned and left.

Fernheim spent two days in the city. He left no cafe unvisited, nor did he neglect to speak to each and every one of his acquaintances. He went to the cemetery to his son's grave. On the third day he pawned the present he had bought for his wife, went to the railroad station, and bought himself a round-trip ticket to Lückenbach, the village where Hans Steiner, his brother-in-law, had a summer home. There, years back, Fernheim had met Inge when he was friendly with Karl Neiss, who had brought him along to see her. But Karl Neiss had not realized what was to come of it all.

2

When Fernheim entered the villa, Gertrude, his sister-in-law, was standing on the porch in front of a basket of laundry, folding linens she had taken down from the line. She greeted him politely and poured him a glass of lemonade, but without the least show of joy, as if he had not returned from prison camp, as if years had not passed without her having seen him. When he asked her where Inge was, she looked shocked, as if that were too personal a question. Finally, when he looked at the door opening to another room, Gertrude said, "You can't go in; Zigbert's bed is there. Remember Zigbert, the child of my old age?" As soon as she mentioned Zigbert she smiled inwardly for calling him "the child of my old age" when at that very moment a new child was stirring inside her. As she was speaking, Zigbert entered.

Gertrude stroked her boy's head, arranged the curls tumbling over his forehead, and said, "Moved your bed again? Now didn't I tell you, 'Don't move the bed'? But you, Zigbert, you don't listen, and you went and moved it again. You shouldn't have done that, my son."

The little boy stood wondering what bed his mother was talking about. And if he had moved the bed, why shouldn't he have moved it? But there wasn't any bed in the first place. And if there really had been a bed and he had moved it, why, his mother should have been proud that he was big and strong enough to move a bed if he wanted to! But everything that Mother was saying was strange, because there wasn't any bed. Zigbert wrinkled up his face at this yoke he had to bear. Nevertheless, he was ready to overlook it if there were the least bit of truth in what his mother had said.

By this time Fernheim realized nothing was in the way, but because he respected Gertrude and did not want to make a liar of her, he did not open the door.

Hans must be told that Fernheim is here, thought Gertrude, but if I leave Fernheim alone he could open the door, cross the room, and go right into Inge's room; and it won't do for him to see her before Hans talks with him. Anyway, it's not good that he came just today, with Inge sitting there waiting for Karl Neiss. Maybe Neiss has arrived already, maybe he's sitting with Inge. There's no need for these two to come across each other right in front of her.

She saw Zigbert standing by. "Go to Daddy and tell him that…"

"Whom do we have here?" Fernheim stretched his arms out to the little boy and began speaking affectionately. "Why, this is young Steiner of the house of Starkmat and Steiner. What's this, Zigbert, you don't say hello to your dear uncle, Uncle Werner, as though you weren't happy that he came back from prison where the enemy fed him live snakes and gave him snake poison to drink? Come, Zigbert, my sweet, let me kiss you." He caught hold of the child, lifted him up, and kissed him on the lips.

Zigbert wrinkled up his mouth and glowered. Fernheim took out half of a cigar, lit it with his lighter, and said to Zigbert, "Don't you want to put the flame out? Open your mouth and blow on it; it goes out almost by itself."

Gertrude addressed her son. "Go, sweetheart, and tell Daddy that—that Uncle Werner has come and would like to see him."

As he was leaving she called him back. Gertrude wanted to warn the child not to tell anyone, least of all Aunt Inge, that Fernheim had come, until he told his father first. But realizing that it was impossible to speak in front of Fernheim, she sent him off.

Zigi stopped, waiting for his mother to call him back as she had the first time. Seeing that she remained silent, he left.

"Daddy, Daddy," he called, "Mommy wants you. A man is here."

"Who's here?" Steiner called down from the attic.

"A man," the child repeated, saying nothing more.

"Go on and tell Mother that I'm coming."

"I don't want to," said the child.

"You don't want to what?" asked the father.

"I don't want to go to Mother."

"Why don't you want to go to Mother?"

"Because."

"Because why?"

"That man."

"What about that man?"

"Because."

"You're acting stubborn, Zigbert; I don't like stubborn people."

The child went off crying.

Fernheim sat himself down, as did Gertrude. While she folded her linens, he clenched a cigar stub between his lips. She sat quietly, uttering not a word, while he was astounded at himself for sitting next to his wife's sister and saying nothing. She waited for her husband to come; he puffed away furiously.

The cigar stub had almost vanished, but still he gripped it between his lips. I see, thought Gertrude, that the new laundress does a good job. The sheet is sparkling white. It needs scrubbing, though. Werner's coming back—it's not good. But now that he's come, maybe there can be an end to this business. The towels gleam more than the sheets, but their edges are crumbled. Obviously, the laundress ironed two towels as though they were one. What's this, pigeon droppings?

Doesn't she know you have to clean the rope before hanging the wash? Hans still hasn't come, and I can't make up my mind whether or not to invite Werner to lunch, since we've already invited Karl Neiss. But just so he shouldn't feel insulted, I'll pour him another glass of lemonade. He's looking for an ashtray. He's already thrown the cigar into the garden.

3

The footsteps of Hans Steiner resounded, and the aroma of the fine cigar in his mouth wafted into the room. He had a vexed look, the kind he wore regularly when having to appear before a stranger. As soon as he came in and saw Fernheim, his pent-up anger doubled. Utter amazement covered his face. Scratching his moustache and scarcely opening his lips, he muttered, "You're here?"

Fernheim, trying to look cheerful, answered, "There's a good deal of truth in that, Hans," immediately extending both hands in greeting.

Hans presented him with two fingertips and said something indistinguishable, without moving lips or tongue. "You're back," he added.

Fernheim replied jokingly, "That, we must admit, is correct."

"When did you come back?"

"When did I come back? I came back two days ago; to be precise, three days ago."

Hans flicked the cigar ashes into the glass of lemonade. "You've been here three days. Then I would assume you've come across some people you know."

"What if I did?" answered Fernheim heatedly.

"If you happened to meet some people you know," said Hans, "maybe you happened to hear a little something."

"'A little something,' meaning—"

"Meaning there have been some changes made."

"Yes," said Fernheim, "lots of things have changed. I wrote that I would come on a certain day, at a certain hour, on a certain train;

and when I got there I found the railroad station empty. Actually it wasn't empty. On the contrary, it was filled with mobs of noisy people who had come to welcome their brothers and sons and husbands returning from the war; but Werner Fernheim, who shed his blood in the war, who was a prisoner of war, who spent a year in a prison camp—no one was available to come welcome him."

Steiner raised his head above Fernheim's. "In your opinion, Werner, who should have come?"

"Heaven forbid that I meant you," he replied. "I realize that Mr. Steiner is an important personage, a man weighed down with serious business, so serious it even exempted him from army duty; but there is someone here who, had she come to greet her husband, would not have been acting altogether outrageously. What do you think, brother-in-law, suppose Inge had come? Does that sound so very unreasonable?"

Steiner tried to smile, but, as he was not used to smiling, his face assumed a look of surprise. He made a fist of his left hand, looked at his fingernails, and said, "If my ears aren't liars, Inge should have rushed to the railroad station to meet you. Is that it, Werner?"

"Why are you so surprised?" asked Fernheim. "Isn't it usual for a wife to greet her husband returning from a distant country? And what a distant country I'm returning from! Anyone else in my place would have died a hundred deaths by now and wouldn't have lived to see the face of his loved ones." Suddenly he raised his voice and asked fiercely, "Where's Inge?"

Steiner looked straight at his brother-in-law and then turned his eyes away. Then he looked at him again and calmly flicked off the cigar ash. "Inge is on her own; we don't pry into her affairs. And let me advise you, Werner: don't be prying into her affairs."

Gertrude sat thinking, This is a man, this is a man. This is a man who can handle anyone. Tonight I'll tell him my secret—that I've got a new child ready for him. But now I'll leave them alone.

The whites of Fernheim's eyes reddened as though they had been pricked and blood were trickling out. "What do you mean," he shouted, "'Don't be prying into her affairs'? It seems to me I still have some authority over her."

Gertrude rose to leave.

"Sit down, Gertrude," said Hans. "If you don't want to hear what this fellow has to say, maybe you'd like to hear what I have to say. Now, you, Werner, look here. If you haven't told it to yourself, I'll tell you. The world you left behind when you went to war has changed, and what concerns us most has changed, too. I don't know just how clear these things are to you, or just how pleasant you find them. If you like, I'm ready to explain them to you."

Fernheim raised his eyes and tried to look straight at his brother-in-law, whose face at that moment was not pleasant to look at. He lowered his head and his eyes and sat despondent. Steiner shouted suddenly, "Is there no ashtray here? Excuse me, Gertrude, if I say that here, on this spot, there should always be an ashtray."

Gertrude rose and got an ashtray.

"Thanks very much, Gertrude. The ash has already dropped onto the rug. What were we talking about? You want an explanation, Werner. In that case, let me begin at the beginning. Once there was a daughter of a well-to-do family who was engaged to a certain man; only the ceremony had not yet taken place. It chanced to happen that a certain fellow started to frequent this man's company. The man who was engaged to the girl disappeared, and this other fellow who had been trailing along after him came and started courting the girl, until finally he won her and she married him, Why did he win her and why did she marry him? This I leave to riddle solvers. I can't say why. From the very start the match was no match, but what happened happened. At any rate, there's no need that it be so forever. Do you understand, my dear fellow, what I'm driving at? You don't understand? Amazing. I'm speaking quite frankly."

"Is that the only reason?" said Werner.

"What I've said seems trivial?" Hans replied.

"At any rate," said Werner, "I'd like to know if that's the only reason."

"There's that and there's another reason..."

"And what's the other reason?"

Steiner fell silent.

Werner went on, "I beg of you, tell me what that other reason is. You say, 'There's that and there's another reason.' What is that other reason?"

"What you speak of as another reason," said Steiner, "is something else again."

"And if I want to know?"

"If you want to know," said Steiner, "I'll tell you."

"Well?"

"Well, the same man to whom the young woman was engaged was found alive, and we trust that you won't go about setting up obstacles. You notice, Werner, that I'm not bringing up your absconding with the funds and staining the firm's reputation."

Fernheim whispered, "Karl Neiss alive?"

"Alive," repeated Steiner.

"Have the dead revived already, then? I myself, everybody with me—we all saw him disappear beneath a landslide and I never heard of his having been pulled out of the debris. Hans, my dear fellow, you are joking with me. And even if they did get to him, he couldn't possibly have come out alive. Tell me, Hans, what led you to say such a thing? Didn't—"

"Story-telling is not my business," clipped Steiner, "but I'll tell you this: Karl is alive and well, alive and well. And, let me add, Inge is counting on you, on your not setting yourself as a barrier between them. And as to your coming back empty-handed, we've taken that into consideration; we won't send you away empty-handed. I haven't as yet set aside a definite sum for you, but at any rate you can be sure it will be enough to set you on your feet, unless you mean to go idle."

"Won't you let me see Inge?" pleaded Fernheim.

"If Inge wants to see you," said Steiner, "we won't stand in her way."

"Where is she?"

"If she hasn't gone out for a walk, she's sitting in her room."

"By herself?" asked Fernheim derisively.

Steiner did not catch Fernheim's derision and answered calmly, "She may or may not be by herself. Inge is on her own and may do

as she pleases. At any rate, she can be asked if she is free to receive
visitors. What do you think, Gertrude? Shall we send Zig to her?
What was wrong with Zig that he was acting so stubbornly? Doing
nothing is good for no one, especially children."

4

Inge greeted Fernheim politely. If we did not know what we do know,
we would think that she was glad to see him. A new light, a deep
contentment shone from her eyes. Happiness is a wonderful thing:
even when it is not intended for you, you bask in its light. At that
moment, all that he had to say fled him. He sat looking at Inge in
silence.

"Where were you all these years?" she asked. "That I know
perfectly well," said Werner, "but were you to ask me where I am
now, I doubt that I could answer." Inge smiled as though she had
heard a joke.

Werner moved uncomfortably in his chair. He leaned his right hand
on the arm of the chair, lifted his left hand to his nose, smelled his
fingernails, yellowed from smoking, amazed all the while that after
all the years that he had been away from Inge he was once more sitting beside her, even looking at her while she looked at him—but
not one of the thoughts that filled his heart reached his lips, even
though his heart urged him to say something.

"Tell me," said Inge, "I'm listening."

Werner stuck his hand into his pocket and started groping
about. But the present he had bought for Inge had been pawned for
travel expenses to Lückenbach. He smiled painfully and said, "You
want to know what I did all that while?"

She nodded her head. "Why not?"

As soon as he started speaking he saw that she was not listening.
"And how did the Bulgarians treat you?" asked Inge.

"The Bulgarians? The Bulgarians were our allies."

"But weren't you a prisoner of war? I thought I heard that you had been captured."

"I was a prisoner of war of the Serbs," Fernheim answered. "You fail to distinguish between friend and foe. I heard he came back."

Her face reddened and she did not reply.

"You suspect me of having purposely deceived you when I came and told you that I saw Karl Neiss buried in a landslide. I was ready to tell a hundred lies in order to win you. But that was true."

"True and not true."

"True and not true? What's not true about it?"

"It's true that a landslide fell on top of him, but it didn't bury him."

"Then where was he all those years?"

"That's a long story."

"You're afraid to tell me," said Werner, "for fear I'll stay here with you that much longer."

"I wasn't thinking of that."

"But rather—"

"Rather—I don't know how to tell stories."

"At any rate," said Werner, "I'd like to know what happened and what didn't happen. With my own eyes I saw a landslide bury him, and you say there was a landslide, but not on him. Forgive me if I repeat myself, but where was he, then, all those years? He wrote no letters, he wasn't inscribed among the living. Suddenly he comes and says, 'Lo and behold, here I am, and now, now all we need to do is pluck Werner Fernheim out of the world and take his wife.' Right, Inge?"

"Please don't, Werner."

"Or it would be better were this same Werner, this same Werner Fernheim, Inge's husband, to pluck himself out of the world, so that Mr. Karl Neis might take to wife Mrs. Inge Fernheim, excuse me, Miss Ingeborg of the house of Starkmat. This is the woman Werner took in holy matrimony, who even bore him a child, and though God did take him, his father is still alive, and means to go on living; yes, to go on living after all the years he was half dead. But this same Werner Femheim, this unlucky fellow, doesn't want to pluck himself out of the world. To the contrary, he seeks new life. Yesterday I was at our son's grave. Do you think that with him we buried everything that was between us? Don't cry, it's not tears I'm after."

Suddenly he changed his tone. "I didn't come to force myself on you against your will. Even the lowest of the low isn't utterly lacking in honor. But you do understand, don't you? I had to see you, I have to speak to you; but if you don't want me to, I'll go. And maybe the future will be brighter for me than Mr. Hans Steiner and Miss Ingeborg of the house of Starkmat think. My black fate isn't sealed forever. Not yet. Tell me, Inge, is he here? Don't be afraid of me, I don't want to do anything to him. What could I do, if even mountains make a fool of me?"

Inge sat silently sorrowful. Werner looked at her two or three times. Since he had last seen her she had put on a little weight. Or maybe she looked that way because she was wearing black. The black skirt she had on went with her slender figure and her shiny blonde hair. The white of her neck shone, but the radiance that had beamed from her eyes had dimmed. Fernheim knew that this happiness had not come on his account, on his returning from the prison camp; no, her happiness had been held in readiness for the coming of Karl Neiss. And even though at first he had been saddened by the cause, her happiness had made him happy. Now that all happiness had left her, he was overwhelmed with pity for her.

Again he looked at her. She sat hunched over, her face in her hands, wet with tears. Suddenly she shook herself in alarm, as if a hand had touched her shoulder. She extended her hands as if to defend herself and looked at him angrily.

"Well, now I'll leave," he said.

"Goodbye, Werner."

He returned. "You won't give me your hand?"

She gave him her hand in farewell. Clasping it, he said, "Before I leave, I want to tell you something."

She removed her hand and shook her shoulders in refusal.

"Still, maybe it would be worth your while to listen. And if not for the sake of the Werner standing here as an uninvited guest, then for the sake of that Werner who was lucky enough to stand under the wedding canopy with Ingeborg. But if you refuse, I won't impose upon you. And now—"

"And now, goodbye," said Inge.

"So be it. Goodbye, Ingeborg, goodbye."

Seeing her turn to go, he stood up.

She stared at him, wondering why he was not leaving.

"At any rate," said Werner, "it's rather strange that you don't want to hear a little of what I went through."

"Haven't you told me?"

"When I started to tell you, your ears were already in another place."

"My ears were in their proper place, but you didn't say a thing. Really, I don't recall that you said a thing."

"Would you like me to tell you?" asked Werner.

"You must have told Hans or Gertrude or both of them," she replied.

"And if I did?"

"If you did, they'll tell me."

"If I understand what you're really getting at," said Werner, "you don't want to hear it."

"Why do you say that? I expressly said that Gertrude or Hans would tell me, so I do want to hear it."

"And if I myself were to tell you?"

"What time is it?" said Inge.

Werner smiled. "So goes the proverb doesn't it? *Dem Glücklichen schlägt keine Stunde*: the happy person is beyond time."

"I don't know what answer to give to that sort of question," said Inge.

"And are you ready to answer other questions?" he countered.

"That depends on your questions. But now my head aches and I can't keep talking on and on, and anyway—"

"Anyway what?"

"You have a strange way of latching on to every word," said Inge.

"Does it seem strange to you that after all the years I haven't seen you I'm drawn by what you say?"

Inge clutched her temples. "My head, my head! Don't be difficult, Werner, if I ask you to leave me alone."

"I'm already leaving," he said. "Are you looking at my shoes? They're old, but easy on the feet. You're quite a la mode, though; you've even cut your hair. I can't say it's unattractive, but when you had all your hair it was prettier. When did the baby die? I was at his grave and I saw his stone, but I forget the date. Are you crying? My heart cries too, inside of me, but I get hold of myself. If you look at my eyes you won't find even a trace of a tear. Tell the fellow who's knocking at the door you can't get up and open it for him because of your headache. Zigi, are you here? What do you have to say, Zigi? Come here, sweetheart, let's make up. What's this in your hand, a letter? You're a mailman, are you, my dear nephew?"

Zigi gave a note to his aunt and left.

Inge took the note while looking at Werner with a furrowed brow, trying her best to understand why on earth the man would not go away. He should have left long since.

After a while she stopped thinking about him and began saying to herself, I have to leave, I simply must leave, it's impossible for me not to leave, every wasted minute is precious.

Her mind came back to Fernheim. Can't he see that I have to go? She looked at him and said, "Excuse me, Werner, but I'm wanted and I have to go."

"How do you know you're wanted? The note is still folded in your hand and you haven't looked at it."

Inge dropped her shoulders. It seemed that she abrogated her will before his, and that it did not matter whether she went or stayed. Her eyes were extinguished, as it were, and her lids fell down over them.

"Are you tired?" Werner whispered.

Inge opened her eyes. "I'm not tired," she replied.

A new spirit clothed Werner. "Good, good," he said, "it's good that you're not tired and we can sit and talk with each other. You can't imagine how I've longed for this moment when I should see you. Had it not been for this hope, I would have died long since. Now I see that all that longing is nothing compared to this moment when you and I are seated here together as one. I have no words to express it, but I think you read some of it in my face. You see, my darling, how my knees bend of themselves and kneel before you. So did they bend whenever I thought of you. How lucky I am to be with you once again under the same roof. I'm not an eloquent man, but I tell you this: From the moment that I stepped over the threshold of your room, my soul was stirred as on that day when you placed your hand in mine and agreed to become my wife. Do you remember that moment, when you rested your head on my shoulder while we sat together as one, your hand in mine? Your eyes were closed, as were mine, as I close them now and pass before me all the events of that matchless day. Throwaway the note, Inge, and give me your hand. My eyes are closed, but my heart sees how good you are, how good you are to me."

Inge shrugged her shoulders and left.

Fernheim opened his eyes. "Inge!" he cried.

But Inge had vanished. Fernheim was alone. What now? he thought. Now I have no choice but to leave this place. That's clear; but everything else is "something else again," as my worthy brother-in-law would put it.

His mind was already vacant of thought, and his former tension began to dissolve. But his toes were burning and the soles of his feet as well. It seemed that the shoes he had said were comfortable were not so comfortable after all.

He put his hand into his pocket and took out his ticket: one half had allowed him to visit his wife and the other half would allow him to return. Holding the ticket in his hand he thought, Now I'll go to the railroad station and leave. And if I've missed the afternoon train I'll take the evening train. Not only the happy ones stand beyond time, but the unfortunate, too. All times are ripe for misfortune.

For a little while he stood in the room that Inge had left. Then he turned around and went to the door. He looked about the room, walked out, and shut the door.

Translated by David S. Segal

528

The Night

When night fell I went home; that is, I went to the hotel room I had taken for my wife and myself. I was hurrying, as I knew that my wife was tired out by all the travel and wanted to sleep, and I had no intention of disturbing her.

There was a multitude of people in the streets, mainly new immigrants, who were arriving here from all over the world. For many years they had wasted away in the death camps, or wandered aimlessly over hill and valley, and through forests, all this time without seeing so much as the flicker of a candle, and now that they'd stepped from the dark into this sudden brightness, they seemed puzzled and somewhat suspicious, not being able to grasp whether all the lights had been left burning by an oversight, or whether it was part of some scheme of the authorities.

An old man came toward me, wearing a greenish coat that came down to his knees, exactly like the coat Mr. Halbfried, the bookseller in our town, used to wear for as long as I remember. The coat had lost most of its color, but had kept its original shape. Short coats are better at keeping their shape than long ones, because long coats sweep the ground and get frayed, whereas short coats flutter in the air, and the ground cannot harm them in any way. Even though their appearance might have changed, their hems remain as the tailor finished them and seem to have retained their perfection.

While I was wondering whether this was really Mr. Halbfried, he ran his weary eyes over me and said: "From the day that I arrived here I've been looking for you, and now that we've met I'm happy twice over, once because I've found someone from my home town, and twice because that someone happens to be you." The old man was so excited that he forgot to greet me properly, instead of which he straightway reeled off a string of names, people he'd asked about me, and after each name he'd express his amazement that So-and-so didn't know me, and had he himself failed to recognize me the moment he saw me, he could have passed me as if we were not fellow townsmen. Having come around to mentioning our town, he began talking about the past, the time when we were neighbors, and his bookstore was filled with books that united all the learned people of the town, who were passing in and out of the shop all day, and having heated discussions about what was going on in the world, and about the future, and coming to the conclusion that the world was evolving into a better place, and there was I, a small boy, fingering the books, climbing the ladder, standing at the top reading, not realizing that I was endangering myself; for had someone blundered into the ladder by mistake, I could very easily have fallen off. But as if the large stock of books which he kept were not sufficient for me, I had asked him to get me *The Poem of Jerusalem Liberated*. However, he couldn't remember any more whether he'd placed the order before I emigrated to the Land of Israel, or whether I did so before he'd placed the order.

Another thing he was reminded of, said Mr. Halbfried, was the time they showed my first poems to that old mystic who had written two interpretations of the prayerbook, and the old man had looked at them and murmured, *"Kehadin kamtza dilevushe mine uve"* ["like the snail whose garb is a part of it"], and the learned listeners tried hard to understand the meaning of these words, and did not succeed. He, Mr. Halbfried continued, was still puzzled that they never took the trouble to look them up in a dictionary, and that he himself did not do so, although he had a number of dictionaries in stock, and could have done so quite easily, yet somehow never did.

He broke off his story and asked me was I angry with his brother?—Why? His brother had just passed us and greeted me, and I made as if I didn't see him.

Mr. Halbfried's last words shocked and saddened me. I had not noticed anyone greeting me; as for the man who had passed us, I was under the impression that it was Mr. Halbfried himself. As I didn't wish him to think that I would turn my eyes away from people who greet me, I said to him: "I swear I didn't notice your brother; had I noticed him, I would have been the first to greet him." So Mr. Halbfried began talking once more of the good old days, of his bookshop and the people who came to it. Every time Mr. Halbfried mentioned a name, he did so with great warmth, the way we used to talk about good friends in those long-lost days before the war.

After a while, Mr. Halbfried stopped and said: "I shall leave you now, as I do not want you to keep a man waiting who wishes to see you." With that he shook my hand and went away.

The man Mr. Halbfried had mentioned was not known to me, nor did he seem to be waiting for me; however, Mr. Halbfried's mistake came in handy, as it enabled me to shake the old man off politely, and so avoid disturbing my wife's sleep.

But Mr. Halbfried had not been mistaken; after I'd gotten rid of him, this man barred my way, then poked his stick into the ground and leaned on it with both hands, while looking at me. Then he lifted his hand in greeting, lifted it to his cap, a round cap of sheepskin leather, and while he was doing so, he said: "Don't you know me?" I said to myself: Why tell him I don't know him? So I gave him a warm look and said: "Certainly I know you, you're none other than—" He interrupted me and said: "I was sure you'd know me, if not for my own sake, then for the sake of my son. What do you think of his poems?" From this I realized that he was the father of someone or other who had sent me his book of poems. I said to myself: Why tell him that I haven't looked at them yet? So I gave him a warm look and said whatever it is one says on these occasions. Yet he didn't seem satisfied with it. So I said to myself: Why not add a few nice words? So I added a few compliments; but he was still unsatisfied, and began singing his son's praises himself, and I kept nodding my head in agreement, so that an onlooker would have thought that the praise came from my mouth.

Having done, he said: "No doubt you wish to make my son's acquaintance, so go to the concert hall, that's where you'll find him. My son is a well-loved man, all the doors are open to him, not only the doors of music but the doors of all the important houses in town. Why, if my son desired, let's say, to ride on a mouse, why, the animal would rush up to him with its tail between its legs and beg him to take a ride. Truly, I myself would love to go to that concert, all the best members of our intelligentsia will be there, the trouble is they won't let you in if you haven't got a ticket." Saying this, he rubbed two fingers together and made a noise with his lips, as if to say, you need real coins for that.

I kept quiet and did not say a word. It was some years now that I hadn't gone to a concert. I could never understand how a crowd of people could assemble at a fixed date and hour, in a special hall, just to hear some singing. Nor could I understand how it was that the singers were ready to lift up their voices in song at the exact hour the ticket holders were filling the hall, ready to listen.

I'm just a small-town boy; I can grasp that someone is singing because his heart is full; but this singing in front of an audience rich enough to buy tickets, because some impresario organized it all, was beyond me. So when I saw how much this man wanted to go to the concert, I asked myself whether I should help him, and decided to buy him a ticket. He saw what I was thinking, and said, "I won't go without you." I asked myself whether to go with him, and then I said, "All right, I'll buy two tickets, and we'll go together." He started feeling the air, as if it were full of tickets. Again he rubbed two fingers together, and made a popping noise, like a cork coming out of a bottle.

So we walked together, and he kept praising the concert hall, where there was so much music one could almost drown in it. Then he told me about this violinist whose violin was so precious that even the case he carried it in was worth more than the instruments of other violinists. Then he returned to his son, to whom poetical rhymes came for the sole purpose of the matching of words. Then he returned to the subject of the tickets, out of respect for which the doors used to open themselves. Suddenly he began worrying, as it occurred to him that he could be wasting his time, for, although I seemed willing enough to buy him a ticket, what if every seat was sold out, or supposing there was only one single ticket left wouldn't I buy it for myself, and leave him standing outside. Thus we came to my hotel.

I said to him: "Wait here, I'm going in to change, and then we're off to the concert." He poked his stick into the ground, leaned on it with both hands, and stood there.

I left him outside and told the doorman I wanted two tickets for the concert. The doorman said: "I have two good tickets, which were ordered by the Duke of Ilivio, but he left them with me, as he cannot come since he has been called to the Emperor." Here the doorman whispered to me that the Emperor had arrived secretly in town, with most of his retinue, dukes, lords, and officers, and that some of them were actually staying at our hotel.

I took the tickets and went up to my room, leaving the door open so that I could change by the light in the corridor, and not have to turn on the light in the room, which would have awakened my wife. I walked in on tiptoe, noiselessly, and to my surprise and distress I found a strange man in the room. Who was that who dared to enter my room in the dark of the night? Should the earth refuse to open at his feet and swallow him, then I would be forced to throw him out myself, and not too politely, either.

As I approached him, I saw that it was Moshele, a relative of mine. This Moshele and I had grown up together, and we went through difficult times together, until one day he was caned up into the army, where he stayed until he was wounded and dismissed. We thought that he had been burned in the gas chambers of Auschwitz, but here he stood, alive, in my room.

I said, "What brought you here?" He said, "My troubles

brought me here. I have been shuffling from one mound of refuse to another without a roof over my head, and when I heard you were here I came running, for I was sure that you would put me up."

I said to him: "Do I have a home that you should ask to sleep here? As you can see, I'm myself but a guest for the night."

He said: "All I'm asking is a place on the floor."

I began laughing. A hotel where dukes and lords live, and he wants to sleep on the floor.

I don't know if his brain succeeded in grasping what I meant and if his heart accepted my words. In any case, he got up and left.

I went to the window to watch him go, and I saw him in the street, cowering as he was hit by the whips of the coachmen who drove the coaches of the nobility. I called to him, but he didn't answer me; I called to him again and he didn't answer, probably being too busy trying to evade the whips to hear my voice. I decided to call louder, but then I remembered that my wife was sleeping, so I didn't. And it is probably just as well, for, had I shouted, all the other coachmen would have seen him too, and joined in beating him.

I looked after Moshele until he disappeared from view. Then I went to the wardrobe to change. Two small children came in and started walking around me in circles. As I opened the door of the wardrobe to take some clothes, one of them jumped in, and his brother jumped after him, and they shut the wardrobe door behind them. I was somewhat perplexed; as they were probably the sons of a duke or a lord, I couldn't very well be rude to them. On the other hand, I couldn't let them go on playing, as they were liable to wake my wife.

Their governess came and helped me out of this trouble. She said to them: "If I may be so bold as to say, it behooves not the princes to enter the room of a strange person."

I apologized to the governess for having left the door of my room open and caused the two king's sons to enter my room. I added that I was going to the concert and had only come to dress.

The governess examined my clothes with her eyes and said: "You can't show yourself in that collar you're wearing." I said to her: "Yes, you're quite right." She said: "Surely, you can find another collar."

"Probably," I said. She said: "Go on, put it on." I said to her: "I am afraid that when the king's son did me the honor of jumping into my wardrobe, he trampled on my collars, and they got soiled." She said: "In that case, I'll tie your tie. Your gracious highnesses, would you be so kind as to leave the room until I finish tying the tie of this gentleman, who is the brother of your teacher." The little boys stood there and looked very surprised that this creature, which had been created to serve them, should now wish to serve a simple mortal.

The graciousness of the young lady and the envy of the king's sons put me into a much better mood. I stuttered somewhat and said: "It is not my custom to go to concerts, but what is a custom worth if you're not ready to disregard it for the sake of another person." The young lady didn't pay much attention to my words; she was too busy tying and then untying every knot she tied, saying, "It wasn't such a knot I meant to tie, now I shall tie one that is much handsomer." Finally, she stroked my arm and said: "Look in the mirror and see how beautifully tied your tie is." I said to her: "I cannot look in the mirror." "Why?" "Because the mirror is screwed onto the inside of the wardrobe door, and if I opened it wide it would squeak and wake my wife." "Your wife?" screamed the young lady in a rage. "And here you were talking to me as if we were alone in the room. If your wife is here, then go and be happy with her." With that the young lady went away.

"Who were you talking to," asked my wife. I said to her: "No one." She said: "I must have been dreaming." I said to her: "Dream or not, I'm going out for a walk, and won't be back till after midnight."

I went looking for the man who was waiting for me in front of the hotel, but he was nowhere to be seen. I asked the doorman about him; he answered: "Some time ago I did see a person loitering in front of the hotel. Had I known he was a friend of yours, sir, I would have looked at him more carefully." I said to the doorman: "Where could he be now?" "Where? I really don't know." "Which way did he go?" "Well," said the doorman, "I seem to remember that he turned right, or maybe it was left, people like these have round shoulders and one never knows quite which way they turn." I gave him a tip. He bowed low and said: "If your excellency would care to listen to my advice, he would visit the servants' quarters in the hotel, as the serfs of the nobles have brought a Jewish clown with them, and it is quite possible that the man your excellency is looking for has gone there to see the fun."

I went to the servants' quarters of the hotel, and saw the serfs sitting like masters, their bellies shaking with laughter, and a small man, shrunken and beautiful, standing on the big stage doing tricks, and talking all the while. When the tricks were funny, his voice was sad, and when they were sad, his voice was funny. I wondered whether he did it on purpose. It seemed to me to be great art, being funny in a sad voice, and being sad in a funny voice. I looked around and found the man I was searching for. I waved the two tickets at him, but he pretended not to see me, and left. It seemed as if his leaving were only temporary, because of me, that is, and he was likely to return as soon as I had gone.

Another man came up to me; he had a long face and a cheerful beard. He stroked his beard and said: "Who are you looking for?" I told him. He said: "I could manage to go with you to the concert." I threw a look at him and shouted in amazement: "What! You?" He shook his beard and said: "Why not?" I repeated what I had said before, only with a great deal of sarcasm: "What! You?" He disappeared, and so did his beard. "What do we do now?" I thought to myself. I waved the tickets in the air, but nothing happened. The man I was waving at didn't show up. So I said to myself: Not only can't I give him the pleasure of a concert, I'm even preventing him from the pleasure of seeing the clown, as he won't show his face in the audience as long as I'm here. I got up and left.

As this man didn't wish to come, I gave up the idea of going to the concert; but, having told my wife that I wouldn't be in before midnight, not until the singer had finished his recital, I had time to take a walk. I began thinking about what had happened, about these incidents which seemed to grow each out of the other, and yet there was no connection between them. I started from the beginning, from the ladder in the bookstore, *The Poem of Jerusalem Liberated*, and that small creature whose garb is a part of him.

After skipping over some matters, I got to thinking of Moshele, my own flesh and blood, who had escaped the fires of cremation and now was shuffling from one mound of refuse to another. As the concert had not yet come to an end and it was not yet time for me to return to my room, I was able to think a great many thoughts. As I strolled along I thought: If only I could find Moshele now that I am just strolling and have nothing else to do, I would talk to him and let him tell me all his troubles; I would appease him and bring him to the inn, give him food and drink and order a soft, warm bed, and we would part from each other with a hearty goodnight. As I was strolling and thinking such thoughts, it suddenly dawned on me that there could be nothing finer. But favors do not come at all times, or to anyone. Moshele had been saved from cremation, and as an added favor it had been given him to find his own flesh and blood. Whereas I, who was his flesh and blood—no favors at all were granted to me, and I couldn't find Moshele again.

Finally, the singer ended his song and the audience went home. I too returned to the room at the hotel and closed the door behind me carefully, as an open door calls to uninvited guests. But there are guests who come no matter how tightly one's door is shut, as they are the thoughts surrounding our actions. So many guests came that the air in the room got fouler and fouler, and I was afraid I was going to choke. I then untied the knot which the young lady had made in my tie, and that helped a little. Now there was more air to breathe, and the guests brought some more guests, and very soon I was choking again.

Translated by Yoram Matmor

First Kiss

Friday afternoon; Sabbath eve. Father was out of town on business and had left me alone, like a kind of watchman, to take care of the store. Dusk. Time to lock up, I said to myself, time to go home and change my clothes. Time to go to the House of Prayer.

I took down the keys from where we keep them hidden, but as I went outside to lock the door, three monks appeared. They were bareheaded and wore heavy, dark robes and sandals on their feet. "We want to talk with you," they said.

I thought to myself, If they've come to do business, Friday afternoon close to sunset is no time to do business; and if they've come to have a talk, I'm not the man for them. But they saw that I was hesitant to reply, and they smiled.

"Don't be afraid," one of them said, "we're not about to delay you from your prayers."

"Look to the heavens and see," added the second. "The sun has yet to go down, we still have time."

The third one nodded his head, and in the same words, or in different words, repeated what the first two had already said. I locked the door and walked along with them. It so happened that we came out opposite my house. One of the monks raised his left hand.

"Isn't this your house?"

"This is his house," answered the second.

"Of course it's his house," added the third. "This is his house." And he pointed three fingers at Father's house.

"If you'd like, we can go in," I said.

They nodded their heads: "By your leave."

We made a circuit of the entire street and walked down a short incline that took us below street level. I forgot to say that there are two entrances to Father's house, one onto the street, where his shop is, and another onto an alleyway, opposite his House of Study. Both entrances are kept open on weekdays, but at dusk on Friday afternoon we close the door that gives onto the street and unlock the one to the House of Study.

I pushed open the door and we went in. I brought them into the parlor. They sat on chairs that in preparation for the Sabbath meal had been arranged around a table set for the Sabbath. Their robes dragged behind their sandals over the special rug that Mother lays out in honor of the Sabbath.

The eldest of the three, who sat at the head of the table, was fat and fleshy. The others sat on either side of him: one was long and thin, with pale hair and a small wound that glowed red on the back of his head where the monks leave a round spot without hair. The other had no distinguishing marks except for a large Adam's apple. Myself—I didn't sit down, but remained standing, as is only reasonable for a man who is in a hurry but has had to receive guests.

They began to talk; I kept quiet. When they saw the two candlesticks on the table they said, "There are three of you, aren't there? There's you, your father, and your mother. Why doesn't your mother light a third candle for her son?"

"Mother is simply continuing a custom she began on the first Sabbath after her marriage," I told them, "which is to light two candles only."

They started discussing the various regulations that pertain to the ritual of candle-lighting, and what each one of them means.

"No," I broke in, "it's not for any of the reasons you've mentioned, it's just that one candle is for the Written Law and one is for the Oral Law. And the two are actually one, which is why we refer to the Sabbath candles in the singular. But, anyway, I see you're all quite expert in Jewish custom."

They smiled, but the smile disappeared into the wrinkles in their faces.

"Well, and why shouldn't we be experts in Jewish custom," said the one that I've been calling the third. "After all, we belong to the order of—"

I thought he said they were Dominicans; but outside the monastery Dominicans don't usually wear their habits, and these three had their habits on. So he must have named a different order, but his Adam's apple got in the way and I didn't catch what he said.

The conversation was preventing me from keeping track of time, and I forgot that a man has to make himself ready to greet the Sabbath. I asked the maid to serve refreshments. She brought in the special delicacies that we prepare in honor of the Sabbath. I put a flask of brandy in front of them. They ate and drank and talked. Since I was agitated about the time, I didn't hear anything they said.

Two or three times it occurred to me that the hour had come to welcome the Sabbath. But when I looked out the window, the sun was in the same place it had been when the monks first accosted me. Now you can't say there was some kind of black magic here, because I had mentioned the name of God any number of times during the conversation; and you can't say that I'd made a simple mistake in time, because the sexton had not yet called for prayers. The whole thing was quite astonishing: when the monks first came, the sun was close to setting, and all this time they'd been eating and drinking and talking, yet the sun was precisely where I'd last seen it before they ever appeared. And it's even harder, for that matter, to explain away the problem of our clock, because even if you claim that I was so preoccupied with my guests I didn't think to set it for the Sabbath, all the same I assure you it's a fine instrument, and would keep proper time even without a daily winding.

Mother came in to light the candles. The monks stood up, and in the selfsame movement walked out.

I got up to accompany them. In the street, one of them shoved me aside.

I was stunned. After all the honor I'd shown him, to be treated like that—while the other two, who saw him push me, didn't even bother to rebuke him.

I didn't want Mother to notice that something had happened to me, so I decided not to return home. And I didn't go to the House of Prayer, because, by the time I could have washed myself from the touch of the monk's hand, they would have already finished the prayers. I stood there like a man with nothing to do, neither here nor there.

Two young novices came along.

"Where did the Fathers go," they said.

I was dumbfounded by what I heard. Men like that they call Father. Before I could rouse myself to answer, one of the novices disappeared. Vanished, right before my eyes. He left the other one behind.

I just stood there, shocked and speechless. For a while it was as if no one else existed. Then I glanced at him and saw that he was very young, about the height of a small youth, with black eyes. If it hadn't been for the commandment that tells us not to show them grace, which also means not to impute grace to them, I would even have said that his eyes were graceful, and sweet. His face was quite smooth, without the slightest trace of a beard. He had the kind of beauty you used to be able to see in every Jewish town, the beauty of young Jewish boys who have never tasted the taste of sin. And beyond that there was something else about him that imparted all the more grace to his graceful features.

I began talking with him so that I could examine him more closely. As I talked, I laid my hand on his shoulder and I said to him, "Listen my brother, aren't you a Jew?"

I felt his shoulders tremble beneath my hand; I felt his

eyes tremble; he lowered his head on his chest and I felt his heart tremble.

"Tell me," I repeated my question, "aren't you a Jew?"

He raised his head from his heart: "I am a Jew."

I said to him, "If you're a Jew, what are you doing with them?"

He bowed his head.

"Who are you," I said, "and where are you from?"

He stood in silence before me.

I brought my face close to his, as if to transfer my sense of hearing to my mouth.

He lifted his head, and I could see how his heart was shuddering, and my heart too began to shudder. I felt his black, sweet eyes upon me. He looked at me with such loving grace, with such tender faith, such glorious kindness, and above all with such grief— like a man trying to control himself before he finally reveals a long-kept secret.

I said to myself, What is all this?

As much time went by as went by, and still he said nothing.

"Is it so hard for you to tell me where you're from?"

He whispered the name of a city.

I said, "If I heard you correctly you're from the town of Likovitz."

He nodded his head.

"If you're from Likovitz," I said, "then you must certainly know the Tzaddik of Likovitz, I was in his House of Prayer once on New Year's Day, and the Tzaddik himself led the prayers. Let me tell you, when he came to the verse 'And all shall come to serve Thee,' I imagined that I heard the approaching footsteps of all the nations of the world who fail to recognize the people of Israel or their Father in Heaven.

And when he sang 'And the wayward shall learn understanding,' I imagined they were all bowing down as one to worship the Lord of Hosts, the God of Israel.... My brother, are you in pain?"

He shook with sobs.

"What are you crying about?"

Tears flooded his eyes. He wiped them away. Still weeping, he said, "I am his daughter. His youngest daughter. The daughter of his old age."

My heart thundered and my mouth fastened to hers, and her mouth to mine. And the purest sweetness flowed from her mouth to mine and—it is possible—from my mouth to hers. We call this in Hebrew "the kiss of the mouth," and it must be the same in other languages too. I should say here that this was the first time I ever kissed a young girl, and it seems almost certain to me that it was her first kiss as well: a kiss of innocence that carries with it no pain, but goodness and blessing, life, grace, and kindness, whereby a man and a woman live together till calm old age.

Translated by Neal Kozodoy

Notes

Agunot

39/ *"It is said"* This first passage is an example of what Gershon Shaked calls a pseudoquotation, that is, a passage presented as a citation from classical sources but which is in fact made up by Agnon. This allegorical midrash about the relations between God and Israel evokes the midrash on the Song of Songs (Shir Hashirim Rabbah) but is not found there.

39/ *"Behold thou art fair…"* Song of Songs 1:15; *"Strike me, wound me…"* Song of Songs 5:7; *"If ye find my beloved…"* Song of Songs 5:8.

42/ *Ben Uri* In the Book of Exodus, Bezalel Ben Uri is the master craftsman called by God to build the tabernacle and fashion its implements.

44/ *Her breasts—the Tables of the Covenant* In the rabbinic interpretation of the Song of Songs, the female beloved represents the people Israel and the parts of her body different aspects of the Torah. The Tables of the Covenant are the tablets of the Ten Commandments.

49/ *"Lo, thou are sanctified unto me"* The binding formula pronounced by the groom to the bride during the marriage ceremony. *"Lo, I cast thee forth"* The formula pronounced by the husband to the wife at the divorce ceremony.

50/ *He put the best possible interpretation on his dream…made good his dream* A reference to a set of ritual practices suggested by the rabbis for neutralizing the predictive power of bad dreams.

51/ *The "world of confusion"* According to Jewish mysticism, the realm in which lost souls wander.

The Kerchief

61/ *Lashkowitz fair* A large annual trade fair in Galicia where merchants went to buy merchandise for the year.

62/ *"She is become like a widow"* The figurative description of Jerusalem destroyed in Lamentations 1:1. In his gloss on this verse, Rashi, the great medieval commentator, softens the image by making the woman's loss temporary; she is not a widow but only *like* a widow.

63/ *Only yesterday he was binding his wounds* In talmudic legend (Sanhedrin 98a), the Messiah is described as disguised among the beggars at the gates of Rome (the seat of impurity) awaiting God's call to redeem the world.

63/ *"Every man under his…fig tree"* Micah 4:4.

63/ *Fringed garment* A ritual undergarment with knotted fringes on each of its four corners.

66/ *The dust of Abraham our father, which turned into swords* Sanhedrin 108b.

67/ *"Peace be unto you, angels of peace"* According to legend, good angels and bad angels accompany the Jew home from the synagogue on Friday evening; if Sabbath preparations have been adequately performed, the good angels are vindicated, and vice versa.

68/ *"A woman of valor who shall find?"* Proverbs 21, which is read at the Sabbath table before the sanctification of the wine.

68/ *"He maketh the winds His messengers"* Psalm 104:4.

68/ *A black satin robe and a round shtreimel of sable* This was the special garb of pious householders in Eastern Europe for the Sabbath. The shtreimel is a hat with fur trim.

69/ *"The Lord is my shepherd..."* Psalm 23; *"The earth is the Lord's..."* Psalm 24, both recited at the beginning of the noontime Saturday meal.

69/ *Like that child in the Talmud* Shabbat 119a.

72/ *When I reached the house I walked around it on all four sides* An allusion to the pious custom of walking around the walls of Jerusalem, based on the fact that the house as a domestic dwelling and the Temple in Jerusalem are represented by the same Hebrew word *bayit*.

Two Pairs

76/ *Dead...raised by the prophet Ezekiel* The rabbinic comment on Ezekiel 37 is found in Sanhedrin 92b.

76/ *King Saul's daughter Michal* Eruvin 96a; Yerushalmi Berakhot 1 (p. 4c); Mekhilta Bo 17.

77/ *Tana Devei Eliyahu* A midrashic work of uncertain date.

79/ *Maimonides…Book of Love* The second of the fourteen divisions in the Mishneh Torah, the great twelfth-century law code written by Moses Maimonides. Its contents cover the laws of blessings and prayers.

80/ *Bind them as a sign upon your arm* Deuteronomy 11:18.

81/ *When all the synagogues…reassembled in the Land of Israel* Megillah 29a.

81/ *The conflagration* In 1924 fire destroyed Agnon's home in Homburg, Germany, destroying his collection of rare books as well as manuscripts of unpublished writings. This traumatic event echoes within Agnon's work; see "A Whole Loaf" in this volume.

82/ *King/fing* The Hebrew letter *khaf* in *malkenu* (king) has been changed to *peh*.

Hill of Sand

97/ *Nevei Tsedek* At the time of the Second Aliyah, Nevei Tsedek was one of the Jewish quarters of Jaffa. It later became part of Tel Aviv.

97/ *It's a Rembrandt* The picture is most likely a reproduction of Rembrandt's *The Bride and Groom (1665)*.

98/ *Poem by Heine* Heinrich Heine (1779–1856), German poet and essayist, born a Jew, converted to Christianity, but returned to a positive view of Judaism toward the end of his life. The poet Hayim Nahman Bialik translated some of Heine's work into Hebrew.

100/ *"Your words uphold the stumbler"* See Job 4:4.

100/ *Bialik* Hayim Nahman Bialik (1873–1934), a major Hebrew writer of the modern period who became known as the Hebrew national poet; he was born in Russia and lived in Odessa, Berlin, and Tel Aviv.

101/ *Sanin* The main character in the Russian novel of the same name, written by Mikhail Petrovich Artzybashev (1878–1927). The novel, first published in 1907, created a sensation and was considered by many to be pornographic.

102/ *Forel* Auguste-Henri Forel (1848–1931), Swiss psychiatrist, known for his investigations of brain structure.

104/ *Ninth Zionist Congress* Held in Hamburg, December 26–30, 1909. The decision to begin cooperative settlement in the Land of Israel was taken at this congress, the first to be held in Germany.

105/ *Mrs. Ilonit* Ilonit is a term applied to a woman who is unable to bear children.

106/ *Rabbi Nahman of Bratslav* (1772–1811) A hasidic Tzaddik who became known for mystical teachings that took the form of enigmatic tales. These were collected and recorded by his disciple Nathan ben Naphtali Hertz Sternhartz. Rabbi Nahman's tales constitute a major influence on modern writers, including Agnon.

111/ *Dr. Pikchin* His name is fashioned from the adjective *pikhi*, meaning someone who keeps his eyes open.

116/ *Jacobsen's Niels Lyhne* Jens Peter Jacobsen (1847–1885), Danish botanist and writer. *Niels Lyhne* (1880) is a novella about a young man who wants to be a poet. Full of longing for a full life, he remains a dreamer who fails to grasp the reality around him. *Niels Lyhne* was translated into Hebrew by P. Ginsburg in 1921.

118/ *"A land wherein you will eat bread without scarcity"* Deuteronomy 8:9.

122/ *The complete Brockhaus* The lexicon, a model for later ency-
clopedias, that was developed in the course of the nineteenth cen-
tury through the efforts of the German publisher Friedrich Arnold
Brockhaus (1772–1823). By 1890, the lexicon, known as *Der Grosse
Brockhaus,* had gone through many editions and was available in a
Russian translation.

124/ *Yaakov Malkov's inn* This is a reference to an actual person who
owned a hotel in Jaffa in the early years of this century. Malkov
appears as well in Agnon's novel *Temol Shilshom* (Only Yesterday).

126/ *The founding of Tel Aviv* The growth of Jaffa's Jewish population
during the Second Aliyah necessitated expansion beyond the city's
limits and its existing Jewish communities. On April 11, 1909, the
Ahuzzat Bayit (Housing Property) Society assigned lots for a new
development, intended originally as a suburb of Jaffa. On May 21,
1910, the suburb was named Tel Aviv.

Knots Upon Knots

131/ *Joseph Eibeschütz* Agnon gives to this figure one of his own given
names and the family name of the famous rabbi Jonathan Eibeschütz
(1690/95–1764), a kabbalist and talmudist. Eibeschütz was suspected
of leanings toward Sabbateanism, the cult that developed around
the false messiah Sabbatai Zvi. His opponent in a rift that divided
Ashkenazic Jewry was Jacob Emden (see note below).

132/ *Gates of Mercy* Shaarei Hesed, one of the Jewish quarters of Jerusalem (outside the Old City) that existed prior to World War 1.

132/ *Heshvan* The eighth month of the Jewish calendar (shortened
from the original name Marheshvan), falling within the range of
October to November. On the seventh of Heshvan, the prayer for
rain is inserted into the Amidah portion of the service in the Land

of Israel. The rains that fall at the end of the story are thus seasonal, as well as indicative of the narrator's isolation.

132/ *Samuel Emden* Here too Agnon gives the character one of his own given names and the family name of a great rabbi, Jacob Emden (1697–1776), an authority on Jewish law, a kabbalist, and an anti-Sabbatean poiemicist. In a drawn-out feud Emden argued that Jonathan Eibeschütz had circulated Sabbatean amulets.

A Book That Was Lost

137/ *Shulhan Arukh, Orah Hayyim* The Shulhan Arukh is a code of laws compiled by Joseph Caro. It was first printed in Venice in 1565 and became accepted over time as the standard code of Jewish law. The section of it known as Orah Hayyim concerns the daily commandments, the Sabbath, and festivals.

137/ *Magen Avraham* A commentary on the Shulhan Arukh, Orah Hayyim, written by Abraham A. Gombiner (ca. 1637–83).

138/ *Rabbi Samuel Kolin…Mahazit Hashekel* Samuel Kolin (1720–1806) wrote *Mahazit Hashekel* as a commentary on the Shulhan Arukh, Orah Hayyim. The section of Kolin's book on Orah Hayyim is actually a commentary on the Magen Avraham that simplifies its difficult language. The *Mahazit Hashekel* was widely used as a source for decisions in Jewish law.

139/ *Tartars who came to wage war on the town* A reference to invasions that occurred between 1655 and 1667.

139/ *Hamizpeh* "The Watchtower," a Hebrew weekly newspaper with a religious Zionist orientation, published in Cracow by Simon Menahem Laser. Laser was one of the first to publish Agnon (still known at that time as Czaczkes).

139/ *Ginzei Yosef Library and the Jewish National and University Library* The Ginzei Yosef Library is the collection established by Dr. Joseph Chasanowitsch (see note below) that formed the basis for the Jewish National and University Library at the Hebrew University of Jerusalem.

140/ *Those little books that God does not deign to look upon* Books that belong to secular culture rather than Jewish learning.

143/ *Dr. Joseph Chasanowitsch* (1844–1919) Russian Zionist who studied medicine in Konigsberg and settled in Bialystok. He collected ancient and rare books for a national Jewish library in Jerusalem. His collection, *Ginzei Yosef*, consisted of 63,000 books, of which 20,000 were in Hebrew, and formed the basis of the Jewish National and University Library, first at Mount Scopus and then at the Givat Ram campus of the Hebrew University.

On One Stone

145/ *Rabbi Adam Baal Shem* A legendary kabbalist whose miraculous deeds gave rise to many tales during the seventeenth century. The nineteenth-century compiler of the *Shivehi Habesht*, the collection of stories about the founder of Hasidism, the Baal Shem Tov, took these stories of Rabbi Adam Baal Shem and transformed them to show him as an esoteric kabbalist who was close in time and place to the Baal Shem Tov.

147/ *The permitted domain* According to Jewish law, this is the permitted distance (2,000 cubits) that one may walk beyond an established community on the Sabbath.

The Sense of Smell

149/ *"Behold thou art beautiful"* Song of Songs 1:15.

149/ *"Let me hear your voice"* Song of Songs 2:14.

149/ *"The Lord builds Jerusalem"* Psalm 147:2–3.

150/ *Balaam the Wicked* Chapters 22–25 of Numbers describe how Balak, the king of Moab, commissioned the prophet Balaam to curse the Israelites, who were about to travel through his territory. Balaam praised them instead; a section of his poetic prophecy ("How goodly are thy tents, O Jacob!" [Numbers 24:5])is included at the beginning of daily morning liturgy.

151/ *Edom* An epithet for Christendom.

151/ *Like one exiled from his father's palace* Based on a midrashic theme.

152/ *The book called Perfect Treatise* Ketav Tamim, by the thirteenth-century German sage Moses Taku.

153/ *Rabbi Jacob of Lissa* R. Jacob Lorbeerbaum (ca. 1760–1832), rabbi of Leszno (Lissa) from 1809, commentator on the Shulhan Arukh and author of Derekh Ha-hayyim, a frequently reprinted digest of ritual law often printed with the prayer book.

154/ *Javetz* Jacob Emden (1697–1776), rabbi of Hamburg and well-known author in many fields of Jewish learning. Javetz was his pen name. (See "Knots upon Knots" in this volume.)

155/ *Psalm for the Chief Musician upon Lilies* Psalm 45.

From Lodging to Lodging

161/ *"A man should never change his quarters"* Arakhin 10b.

164/ *Followers of Korah* Numbers 16.

The Tale of the Scribe

178/ *Fashioning crowns for his Creator* In addition to the figurative sense, the reference is also to ornamental calligraphic crowns that the scribe places at the top of certain Hebrew letters.

179/ *Path of Life* The Orah Hayyim, one of the four orders of the Shulhan Arukh, the great sixteenth-century code of Jewish law.

179/ *Book of Splendor* The Zohar, the classic text of Jewish mysticism, written in the thirteenth century in Spain by Moses de Leon.

181/ *Reb Gadiel, the infant* A tiny scholar, a creation of Agnon's who also appears in another story; the character is based on medieval Jewish mystical legend.

181/ *"The earth is the Lord's"* Psalm 24:1.

181/ *"I have set the Lord always before me"* Psalm 16:8.

182/ *A bundle of twigs* On Hoshana Rabbah, which is the last day of Sukkot and the eve of Shemini Atzeret, seven circuits are made in the synagogue and willow branches are beaten against the reader's lectern.

182/ *The Seer of Lublin* Jacob Isaac Ha-Hozeh Mi-Lublin (1748–1815), a founder of the hasidic movement in Poland and Galicia.

183/ *The Torah portion Ki tavo* Chapters 26–29:8 of the Book of Deuteronomy, read in the synagogue as part of the yearly cycle around the month of September.

184/ *When Miriam visits the bathhouse* Immersion in a ritual bath (mikvah) is required after a woman's menstrual flow so that she may resume relations with her husband.

188/ *"And Aaron did so"* Numbers 8:3.

189/ *"And now ye shall write down"* Deuteronomy 31:24.

191/ *The seventh round of the procession* On the eve of Simhat Torah, the Torah scrolls are carried around the pulpit seven times.

191/ *Rabbi Akiba of whom it is told* Berakhot 31a.

That Tzaddik's Etrog

195/ *Reb Mikheleh the Holy Preacher of Zloczow* The founder of Hasidism in eastern Galicia and a contemporary of the Baal Shem Tov.

196/ *A beautiful etrog and...kosher* In addition to the numerous laws about the ritual fitness of the citron, there is great store set on its physical beauty.

Fable of the Goat

200/ *"Until the day breathe and the shadows flee away"* Song of Songs 2:17.

200/ *Men like angels, wrapped in white shawls* The kabbalists in sixteenth-century Safed, who created the Kabbalat Shabbat service, would welcome the Sabbath by going out into the fields dressed in white.

201/ *Not be able to return* Travel is forbidden after sunset on Friday.

201/ *"An evil beast has devoured him."..."I will go down to the grave in mourning for my son"* The words of Jacob in Genesis 37:33–35 when informed of Joseph's fate.

Paths of Righteousness,
or the Vinegar Maker

204/ *Mondays and Thursdays he would fast* These are the two weekdays on which part of the weekly portion is read from the Torah in synagogue; it is the custom of the especially pious to fast on these days.

204/ *That man* The euphemistic locution used in rabbinic literature to refer to Jesus of Nazareth.

206/ *An unworthy son born of a worthy father* Translation of *hometz ben yayin*, literally, vinegar made from wine.

206/ *Like the early mystics* In late antiquity, mystics would induce trances by putting their heads between their legs while meditating on the mysteries of the divine chariot.

208/ *Kolel* A communal organization in Jerusalem that distributed charitable funds collected in the Diaspora.

208/ *Not to hold over the dead* It is the custom in Jerusalem to bury the dead on the day of death rather than the next day.

The Lady and the Peddler

213/ *She broiled the meat in butter* Mixing meat and milk is forbidden according to Jewish dietary laws.

Tears

223/ *Baal Shem* Israel Baal Shem Tov, the founder of Hasidism (ca. 1700–1760).

Buczacz

235/ *Sound of a dog* The previous paragraph specified "horses"; the inconsistency is Agnon's.

237/ *Without the reading of the Torah and without communal prayer* Reading the Torah from a scroll requires a quorum of ten, as does the recitation of certain prayers.

238/ *Barekhu and Kedushah* These two prayers must be omitted when praying in private.

238–239/ *Disaster had overtaken the people of God* In 1096, these three communities in the Rhine Valley were the scene of massacres against Jews by bands of Crusader zealots. See the story "On the Road" in this volume.

239/ *Chmielnicki's thugs* In 1648 hundreds of Jewish communities were destroyed in the Ukraine in an insurrection against Polish landowners led by Cossack bands under Bogdan Chmielnicki.

The Tale of the Menorah

241/ *The Tale of the Menorah* In the Hebrew title, "Ma'aseh Hamenorah," *ma'aseh* denotes a historical occurrence, not a fictional story; *menorah* refers not to the Hanukkah lamp but to the candelabrum that originally stood before the tabernacle in the Temple courtyard.

242/ *"Blessed be the Lord who has shared His wonderful counsel"* Isaiah 28:29.

242/ *Words that Jacob our forefather spoke to Esau* Genesis 32:11.

242/ *Chmielnicki* See note to "Buczacz," above.

245/ *The Twentieth of Sivan* The date commemorating the Chmiel-nicki massacres.

247/ *Blood libel* The false allegation that Jews murder non-Jews, especially Christians, in order to use their blood for Passover and other rituals. From the early Middle Ages through modern times, accusations of blood libels led to trials and massacres of Jews.

248/ *Related in my tale "My Sabbath."* The story is found in *Eilu Ve'eilu* pp. 341–42. In the story, Yisrael is imprisoned for counterfeiting seven copper pennies so that he can buy food for the Sabbath and not desecrate the holy day; during the time of his imprisonment, a mysterious stranger, who is later revealed to be the spirit of the Sabbath (and whose name is Shabbati, "My Sabbath"), surreptitiously brings his wife seven copper pennies every Friday for her to buy food for herself.

254/ *"O Lord! Have pity on Your people"* Joel 2:17.

254/ *"How long shall they direct us"* Proverb 21:1.

Pisces

256/ *Eglon, the king of Moab* Judges 3:17: "Eglon was a very fat man."

257/ *Leviathan and Wild Ox* The term leviathan occurs in the Bible and Talmud and refers to a serpentine sea-creature. According to Jewish folklore, the flesh of the Leviathan and of the Wild Ox, a huge, mythical beast, are a delicacy to be consumed by the righteous in the afterlife.

261/ *Delayed by saying prayers for divine mercy* A petitionary prayer called Tahanun is omitted in the synagogue service when there is a celebration at hand.

261/ *Purim and the Fast of Esther* Purim falls on the 14th of Adar (the carnival month whose sign is Pisces); the celebration is preceded by the Fast of Esther, commemorating the fast Esther undertook before going to see the king. Those who prepare the delicacies for the celebration often have to do so while fasting.

261/ *Sabbath during the nine days of mourning* Although meat is not eaten during the nine days preceding the summer fast of the Ninth of Av, it is permitted on the Sabbath that falls during that period.

262/ *A rooster…slaughtered for Yom Kippur* In place of the penitential sacrifices once offered in the Jerusalem Temple, it was customary on the eve of Yom Kippur to wave a rooster over the head, which would later be slaughtered, and to declare that one's sins were transferred to the animal.

263/ *The place is too narrow for me* Isaiah 49:20.

263–4/ *Kedushah and Barekhu* Parts of the service that cannot be said without a quorum of ten.

266/ *Karpl Shleyen…Fishl Fisher…Fishl Hecht…Fishl Fishman* These are names for fish in Yiddish.

267/ *"And he prayed"* Jonah 2:2.

267/ *"And Thou didst cast me into the deep"* Jonah 2:4.

268/ *"Who teaches us by the beasts of the earth"* Job 35:11.

270/ *5423 or 5424* Corresponds to the years 1663 or 1664.

274/ *Ascent That Is Descent* Refers to the hasidic concept of the Tzaddik's descent into impurity in order to raise himself up to a higher spiritual level.

277/ *Someone who puts on two pair of tefillin* There are two kinds of tefillin, resulting from a difference of opinion between two medieval sages; some pious Jews wear two pair of tefillin at the same time in order to practice both approaches.

277/ *Hok Leyisrael, Hovot Halevavot, Reshit Hokhmah* Popular moralistic manuals and commentaries.

278/ *"I have deprived my soul of good"* Ecclesiastes 4:8.

279/ *"And even the fish of the sea"* Hoshea 4:3.

280/ *"For the earth was full of knowledge"* Isaiah 11:9.

283/ *Just as Yitzhak Kummer drew on Balak's skin* A reference to characters in Agnon's novel *Temol Shilshom* about the early years of Zionist settlement in Palestine.

290/ *"As the birds fly"* Isaiah 31:5.

296/ *The Twelve Tribes are compared to animals* The quotations are taken from Jacob's blessing of his sons in Genesis 49.

297/ *"And they drew water"* 1 Samuel 7:6; the reference is to Pseudo-Jonathan, an Aramaic translation of the Bible with many midrashic additions.

297/ *"Let them curse it"* Job 3:7.

298/ *"And they shall abound"* See Genesis 48:16. Agnon draws out a pun by finding the Hebrew word for fish—dag—in the verb *vayidgu* ("to abound").

On the Road

338/ *The day of the great slaughter…the blood of the martyrs who slaughtered themselves* At the end of the eleventh and the beginning of the twelfth centuries, Jews in the Rhineland communities of Worms, Speyer, and Mainz were attacked by zealots assembling for the Crusades. Many Jews killed themselves and their families rather than convert to Christianity or be killed by the Crusaders.

339/ *"The dead praise not the Lord"* Psalm 115:17.

339/ *Until after the Day* The Day is rabbinic parlance for Yom Kippur, the Day of Atonement; see the story "At the Outset of the Day" in this volume.

341/ *The descendants of the priestly family* Descendants of the Levite tribe, the family of Aaron, constitute the priestly class in Israel and are forbidden to have any contact with the dead.

341/ *Song of Songs* 8:13; *"Flee my beloved"* Song of Songs 8:14.

343/ *Casting away sins* A custom ordinarily performed on the first day of the New Year in which sins are symbolically cast into water.

343/ *"O my dove, that art in the clefts of the rock"* Song of Songs 2:14.

343/ *"Every firstborn"* Deuteronomy 15:19.

344/ *"Ye are sons to the Lord"* Deuteronomy 14:1.

344/ *"Many daughters"* Proverb 31:29.

344/ *Seventh of Adar* The traditional date of Moses' death, which was observed in some communities as a fast followed by a feast for the members of the Hevra Kadisha, the burial society.

344/ *"And Moses went up…"* Deuteronomy 34.

Between Two Towns

348/ *Der Israelit* The leading Orthodox weekly in Germany, widely read in western Europe.

348/ *Das Familienblatt Das Israelitisches Familienblatt,* a Jewish newspaper published in Hamburg.

353/ *Two thousand cubits…the distance one is permitted to walk on the Sabbath* According to Jewish law, this is the distance one is permitted to walk beyond an established community on the Sabbath.

To the Doctor

370/ *Mr. Andermann* This character's name is German for the "other one," suggestive of the *Sitra Ahra,* the evil side of human nature.

371/ *"And because of our sins"* This line opens the collective confession that all members of the community recite together on the Day of Atonement.

A Whole Loaf

373/ *I had nothing to eat on the Sabbath* See Shabbat 117b: "He who observes [the practice of] three meals on the Sabbath is saved from three evils: the travails of the Messiah, the retribution of Gehinnom, and the wars of Gog and Magog." (See also Avodah Zarah 3a.)

373/ *The floor was as hot as glowing fire, the roof fevered like piercing fire* The rather stylized form of this paragraph, including the repetition of "fire," suggests the form of a medieval piyyut.

374/ *The Mahaneh Yehudah Quarter…Street of the Prophets* The narrator traces a map of Jerusalem's neighborhoods in this passage.

375/ *The Lord* (….) In an earlier edition of the story, the ellipsis consisted of three dots. The change to four prompts the association of this unseen Lord with the tetragrammaton, the four-letter unpronounceable name of God.

376/ *The mourning of Moses* According to traditional belief, the 7th of Adar is considered the yahrzeit or anniversary of the death of Moses.

379/ *Mr. Gressler* The name suggests a German or Yiddish term for crassness or crudeness.

379/ *My house was burned down* Agnon lost his home in Homburg, Germany, in 1924 to a fire that destroyed all his possessions (see the reference to this fire in "Two Pairs").

379/ *Mr. Gressler sat playing cards with my neighbor* Avraham Holtz points out that this recalls the talmudic warning "The house in which the words of Torah are not heard at night shall be consumed by fire" (Sanhedrin 92a).

382/ *Dusting himself with the dust of the horses' feet* This phrase suggests an ironic reversal of the talmudic injunction to dust yourself with the dust of the feet of the sages, i.e., to sit at their feet and absorb their wisdom (from Pirke Avot, Ethics of the Fathers).

383/ *But I want a whole loaf* At the Sabbath table, the blessing of the bread can only be recited over a loaf that is whole, rather than cut into slices. Critics have attempted to connect the "whole loaf" here to a variety of talmudic injunctions concerning Sabbath requirements.

385/ *The post office doors were already closed* The three-letter verb for "closed," *n-'a-l,* also forms the root for the noun Neilah, the title of the closing prayer on the Day of Atonement that signals the closing of the gates of heaven.

At the Outset of the Day

389/ *My little daughter* The standard epithet for the soul in medieval Jewish philosophical writing.

389/ *The Great Synagogue* In the town of Buczacz where Agnon was born and spent his boyhood.

390/ *The memorial candle* Memorial candles are lit on the eve of the Day of Atonement in memory of those who have died. In eastern Europe, because of the fear of fire at home, it was the custom to bring the candles to the synagogue and leave them in the lobby.

391/ *The storeroom...where torn sacred books are hidden away* The geniza, a room usually attached to a synagogue, where books and ritual objects containing the name of God would be preserved.

391/ *When books were read, they were rent* The translation here reproduces the wordplay in the Hebrew *(nikra'im,* meaning "read," and *nikrai'm,* meaning "torn").

392/ *Reb Alter had circumcised me, and a covenant of love bound us together* Circumcision is considered the sign of the covenant through which the male child enters the Jewish community. Reb Alter appears elsewhere in Agnon's writing—in the novel *Temol Shilshom* (Only Yesterday), for example—as the mohel (ritual circumciser) and the keeper of the *pinkas,* the communal record of all those he has circumcised.

394/ *Ritual gowns* This is a reference to the "kittel," the white garment that is worn by worshippers in the Ashkenazi tradition during the prayer service of the High Holidays.

394/ *"At times she takes the form of an old woman"* The identity of "she" here is not specified. We may read it as a further reference to the soul as a feminine image.

394/ *The fool substitutes the form for the need; the wise man substitutes will for need* The Hebrew plays on the guttural assonance of the nouns *tsurah* (form), *tsorekh* (need), and *ratson* (will).

396/ *Scroll...in memory* The narrator here identifies himself as a scribe who has written a scroll in memory of the souls of days that had departed. This may be interpreted as a rather solipsistic reference on Agnon's part to his own body of work written in memory of the past. (See "The Tale of the Scribe" for an account of the inscription of a Torah scroll in memory of someone who has died.)

396/ *My soul fainted within me* The verb *nit'atfah*, translated here as "fainted," also means "covered itself." The sentence thus also reads: "My soul covered itself," with *nefesh* as the feminine noun for soul.

The Sign

397/ *The disturbances of 1929* In 1929, widespread Arab uprisings against Jewish settlement occurred, during which Agnon's home in Talpiyot was destroyed.

397/ *My wife and I remained alive in Jerusalem...and there built a house and made a garden* The phrasing here recalls Isaiah 4:3: "And those who...are left in Jerusalem" and Ecclesiastes 2:5: "I laid out gardens and groves, in which I planted every kind of fruit and tree."

400/ *liturgical poems* These are piyyutim, poems intended to embellish prayer and religious ceremony. Certain piyyutim are associated with particular parts of the liturgy and with particular holidays.

401/ *"I shall bear you on the wings of eagles and bring you unto Me"*
Exodus 19:4.

401/ *"There shall be seven full weeks"* Lev. 23:15.

401/ *"And Moses declared the festivals of the Lord"* This formula is part
of the festival kiddush (blessing over wine).

402/ *"Because of you, the soul liveth"* Genesis 12:13.

402/ *"Who has given us life"* The Sheheheyanu blessing, recited on the
first day of the festival.

402/ She *"brings her bread from afar"* Proverbs 31:14.

403/ *They gave off a good aroma* The phrase recalls Agnon's reference
to the sukkah that actively gives off its fragrance, a wording that
brought Agnon the reprimand of a member of the National Committee on Language. (See "The Sense of Smell" for the literary version of this controversy.)

404/ *"The heavens are the heavens of God, but the earth hath He given
to the children of men"* Psalm 115:16.

405/ *The moment when the sky splits open* According to Jewish mysticism, the heavens open up at midnight on the eve of Shavuot.

407/ *Rabbi Solomon Ibn Gabirol* (ca. 1020–ca. 1057) Spanish poet and
philosopher, generally acknowledged as the greatest of the medieval
Spanish religious poets. With great virtuosity, he drew on a knowledge of biblical Hebrew and Arabic poetry.

407/ *The book of hymns…on the six hundred and thirteen commandments*
A reference to the category of liturgical poems for Shavuot, known
as Azharot, in which the 613 commandments are enumerated. Ibn

Gabirol composed a book of Azharot. (The numerical value of the letters of the word *azharot* is 613.)

408/ *"At the dawn I seek Thee, my rock and tower"; "Before Thy greatness I stand and am confounded"* From the liturgical poem recited at the beginning of the Shaharit (morning) service in the German Ashkenazic rite.

408/ *"O poor captive in a foreign land"* From the opening line of "A Song of Redemption" by Ibn Gabirol, a Sabbath morning hymn, recited between Passover and Sukkot.

411/ *The Dead Sea on one side and the Temple Mount on the other* This was the view from Agnon's house in Talpiyot.

412/ *A kind of heralding voice* The Balfour Declaration, November 2, 1917, announcing British support for a Jewish national homeland.

413/ *The neighborhood was finally built* The suburb of Talpiyot was first established in 1922.

413/ *The horrors that began in 1936 and lasted until World War II began* Arab strikes intended to pressure the British government to stop Jewish emigration and eruptions of violence against Jews occurred frequently during these years.

415/ *The tremors of 1927* An earthquake in 1927 caused damage in Jerusalem, particularly to the Augusta Victoria Hospital and the Church of the Holy Sepulcher.

416/ *"We cannot go up and be seen there because of the hand which has cast itself into our Temple"* Recited in the Additional Service for festivals.

420/ *Conversations of Rabbi Nahman of Bratslav* (1772–1811) The hasidic

Tzaddik who became known for mystical teachings that took the form of enigmatic tales. His teachings and his tales were collected and recorded by his disciple Nathan ben Naphtali Hertz Sternhartz.

422/ *For it was the eve of the New Moon, and he was rolling the scroll to the reading for that day* A reference to the additional readings in the Torah for the New Moon.

423/ *"Small Yom Kippur"* An observance begun by the kabbalists of Safed in the late sixteenth century. The eves of eight new months are observed by the very pious as a day of fast and repentance.

423/ *The first destruction* World War I.

424/ *"May God give strength to His people; may God bless His people with peace"* Psalm 29:11.

425/ *Trees of life* The wooden dowels around which the Torah scrolls are wound.

425/ *The Order of Shavuot night* The *tikkun leyl Shavuot,* the vigil held on the eve of Shavuot at which selections from classical Jewish texts are studied.

Notes on Additional Stories

To Father's House

Unable to do his work, the narrator decides to go to his home town, to his father's house, i.e., to renew contact with his childhood. There are distracting elements in the way: the narrator's hesitance to interrupt his father's celebration of the feast; a twice-beheld enigmatic candle suspended in the air; meeting the eighteenth-century enlightener Isaac Euchel; the inn that tries to replace the home. Finally, a child—innocence—points the way.

The Document

Here the helpless individual, conscious of himself and his memories, aware of his surroundings, and there a mindless bureaucratic machine, moving automatically, blindly disregarding the petitioner. And between the two: hordes of people, pushing, squeezing, shoving; seemingly composed of individuals, they are in effect part of the machine.

Friendship

The narrator leaves his home in order not to be bothered by clinging neighbors; but having left it, he cannot find his way back and has even forgotten the address. Who will help? Not Mrs. Klingel (Jingle), whose jokes are insulting; not Dr. Rischel, whose linguistic discourse the narrator seems to interrupt; the narrator's wife, who had come "home" when the story started, has walked off. The unfriendly, uncommunicative situation (of which the narrator is a part!) is suddenly changed when a former friend appears after an absence of many years. His kind though half-hearted readiness to help leads the narrator to find his home (he was standing right beside it)—and himself.

Metamorphosis

Divorce ended the meaningless marriage between Toni and Hartmann—and initiated a new phase of communication, concern, awareness of the other person, and tenderness. Will the couple be reunited? The story does not reveal this, only that Hartmann's "spirit began to hover in the world of dreams, where no partition separated them."

The Face and the Image

The Hebrew title of the story is taken from Proverbs 27: 19, which the standard translations render as, "As in the water face answereth to face, so the heart of man to man." The narrator is quietly planning a study on mirrors (in which face is "answered" by face). This plan is strangely counteracted (or challenged?) by a call to visit his sick mother. A series of absurd interferences prevents this homecoming. The story ends with the narrator's surprised look into a mirror that reflected his face "without partiality."

S.Y. Agnon

The Orchestra

The narrator, a writer, tries to prepare himself for the awesome New Year's Day. The attempt fails. In A.J. Band's view, the two figures Charni (Black) and Ora (Light) represent traditional faith and artistic involvement, respectively, while the orchestra is "nothing but a projection of [the writer's] guilt-stricken imagination, his remorse at having allowed his artistic preoccupations to distract him from repentance" (*Nostalgia and Nightmare,* pp. 338f.).

Fernheim

The name signifies "distant home" or "home is distant." Such is the experience of the hero, a soldier and prisoner of war, who, returning "home," finds his wife and family estranged. His quest for human contact fails. Home is not merely distant; it is non-existent.

The Night

The time: the period shortly after World War II. The place: Jerusalem, to which many refugees from the death camps of Europe flocked. The central episode: the arrival of Moshele, the narrator's relative, believed to have perished in Auschwitz. In awe of some nobility that have taken up quarters at the hotel where the narrator rented a room (he has no home), he refuses hospitality to Moshele. Soon, however, remorse sets in, and the narrator sets out to find his relative, to involve himself in his fate rather than relishing childhood memories (the bookseller Halbfried), the luxury of going to a concert, and the enticing graciousness of a young governess.

571

First Kiss

The Sabbath transforms secular, natural time into sacred time; on that day time reaches fulfillment, presaging life eternal. (Note the references to "time" in the first part of the story.) Here, the Jew is in his very own sphere; an intrusion from the outside cannot but create a disturbance in the innermost sense. But the outside world does intrude, consciously; the three monks (note the number) are no innocent visitors; they suggest there should be three Sabbath candles, only to be informed that the two candles are "actually one." The three monks are followed by two novices, one of whom confesses to be a woman (conversion—perversion). In fact, she is "the daughter of old age" of a hasidic master whose mighty New Year's prayer for the unity of mankind in the service of the one God led his listeners to imagine this union to be a reality. The narrator, representing this tradition of Israel, and the "novice," representing the return of the wayward, become one in a holy kiss. The transforming power of the Sabbath is restored.

Glossary

AMIDAH A sequence of nineteen petitionary prayers recited three times a day; also known as the Shemoneh Esreh or the Eighteen Benedictions. Together with the Shema, it is the most important Jewish prayer.

ARK, OR HOLY ARK *(aron kodesh)* An ornate cabinet in which the Torah scrolls are kept in the synagogue.

BAREKHU The beginning of the morning and evening statutory prayer, which can only be recited in the presence of the quorum of ten.

CHALLAH (pl. challot): The braided loaf of bread that is prepared specially for the Sabbath and for holidays.

COMMANDMENTS (*mitzvot*) The obligations of Jewish life as ordained in the Torah or derived from it by the rabbis.

DAYAN A respected rabbi who serves as a judge in matters of communal, religious, and legal disputes.

DAY OF ATONEMENT See Yom Kippur.

DAYS OF AWE The solemn holiday season including Rosh Hashanah (New Year) and Yom Kippur (Day of Atonement).

DAYS OF JOY The festive holiday season immediately following Yom Kippur, including Sukkot, Shemini Atzeret, and Simhat Torah.

EIGHTEEN BENEDICTIONS See Amidah.

ERETZ YISRAEL The Land of Israel.

ETERNAL LIGHT (*ner tamid*) A perpetually burning lamp hung over the ark containing the Torah scrolls in synagogues; it is a remembrance of the daily sacrifice offered in the Jerusalem temple.

ETROG A citron (a fruit resembling a lemon), one of the "four species" used in the celebration of the Sukkot holiday.

FOUR SPECIES Leaves from the palm, myrtle, and willow trees, together with the citron (etrog), are used to celebrate the holiday of Sukkot.

GEMARA The commentary on the Mishnah; another name for the Talmud, the compendium of post-biblical legal and scriptural interpretation.

HALACHA The corpus of Jewish law and jurisprudence; literally "the way" of life of the observant Jew.

HALLEL A liturgy of praise included in the synagogue service on festivals and New Moons.

HANUKKAH An eight-day winter holiday, observed by lighting lamps, which commemorates the repurification of the Jerusalem Temple after the successful revolt of the Maccabees in the second century B.C.E.

HAVDALAH A ceremony employing a candle, spices, and wine that marks the conclusion of the Sabbath and the reentry into the workaday week.

HEDER A private one-room schoolhouse for boys which was the basis of Jewish education in eastern Europe.

HOSHANA RABBAH A semi-festival that concludes the week of Sukkot; it is marked by beating willow branches against the synagogue altar.

INTERMEDIATE FESTIVAL DAYS (*hol hamo'ed*) The days that fall between the first two and the last two days of Passover and Sukkot; they have the status of semiholidays.

KADDISH A litany of praise for God; among other purposes, it is recited by mourners after the death of a parent or child or on the anniversary of their deaths.

KEDUSHAH A portion of the Amidah prayer that can only be recited in the presence of a quorum of ten.

KIDDUSH The sanctification of the wine that is recited when the Sabbath is ushered in Friday night and again at the midday meal on Saturday.

KING OF ISHMAEL The leader of Islam.

KOSHER The state of ritual fitness; often applied to foods permitted by Jewish law and the rules governing their preparation.

LAG B'OMER A day for picnicking and outings that occurs thirty-three days after the beginning of Passover.

MAARIV The evening service in the daily liturgy.

MAHZOR A collection of prayers and sacred poems used on holidays, especially Rosh Hashanah and Yom Kippur.

MEN OF THE GREAT ASSEMBLY The high court of sages that legislated matters of Jewish law in Second Temple times.

MENORAH (*pl. menorot*) A lamp, usually with seven branches, that is placed in the synagogue in remembrance of the candelabrum that stood in the ancient tabernacle and Temple.

MEZUZAH (*pl. mezuzot*) A piece of parchment containing biblical passages affixed to the doorposts of Jewish homes as a visual reminder of spiritual obligations.

MIDRASH The rabbinic interpretations of Scripture.

MIKVAH A ritual bath in which married women immerse themselves after menstruation.

MINHAH The brief afternoon service in the daily liturgy.

MINYAN A quorum of ten adult males required for public worship.

MISHNAH The code of post biblical Jewish law compiled around 200 C.E.

MUSAF The additional service offered on the Sabbath and the festivals.

NEW MOON The first day of the new month in the Hebrew calendar and sometimes the last day of the old month are celebrated as semiholidays, with special additions to the liturgy.

NEW YEAR See Rosh Hashanah.

NINTH OF AV (*Tisha b'Av*) A solemn summer fast day commemorating the destruction of the Jerusalem Temples and other historic calamities.

NOVELLA (*pl. novellae; Hebrew: hiddush, hiddushim*) Innovative interpretations of Jewish legal traditions.

OMER The forty-nine days that are counted between Passover and Shavuot, marking the passage from the liberation from Egypt to the giving of the Torah.

PASSOVER The spring holiday that commemorates the exodus from Egypt.

PESAH See Passover.

PILGRIMAGE FESTIVALS (*shalosh regalim*) The holidays of Sukkot, Passover, and Shavuot, during which pilgrimages were made to the Jerusalem Temple during biblical times.

PURIM A late-winter feast day that commemorates the saving of Persian Jewry from destruction as described in the Scroll of Esther.

RABBIS, THE The postbiblical sages who produced the midrash and the Talmud.

REB A title of respect for a man; the equivalent of "Mister" or "Master."

REBBE A hasidic rabbi.

REBBETZIN The wife of a rabbi.

ROSH HASHANAH The New Year festival, the first two days of the Hebrew month of Tishrei, which falls in early autumn.

SABBATH QUEEN (*shabbat hamalkah*) A symbolic personification of the spirit of the Sabbath.

SCROLL OF ESTHER A short biblical book recited on the holiday of Purim which recounts a threat to the Jews of Persia and its happy reversal.

SELIHOT Penitential poems and prayers recited early in the morning on the days preceding and following the New Year.

SHAMMASH A functionary of the community or synagogue who performs tasks such as awakening the congregants for morning prayer and caring for ceremonial objects.

SHAVUOT A festival in the late spring (forty-nine days after Passover) that celebrates the giving of the Torah on Sinai and the offering of the first fruits. One of the three pilgrimage festivals.

SHEKHINAH In rabbinic lore, the immanent aspect of the divine represented as a feminine figure; the Shekhinah dwelt in the sanctuary while the Temple stood and went into exile with Israel following the destruction.

SHEMA The central, statutory prayer affirming God's unity recited by a Jew several times a day.

SHEMONEH ESREH See Amidah.

SHOFAR A ram's horn that is blown on Rosh Hashanah as a call to repentance.

SHOHET A learned and pious Jew who is trained in the proper slaughtering of animals according to Jewish law.

SHTETL The small Jewish market towns of Eastern Europe.

SHULHAN ARUKH A medieval codification of practical Jewish law that was regarded as authoritative by most Jewish communities.

SIMHAT TORAH The second day of Shemini Atzeret and the last day of the Sukkot holidays; on it the Torah is both concluded and begun again by reading the end of Deuteronomy and then immediately the beginning of Genesis. The Torah scrolls are paraded around the pulpit seven times.

SUKKOT One of the three pilgrimage festivals, which falls in early autumn and is celebrated by dwelling in huts or booths (sukkah; pl. sukkot) and making blessings over the etrog and palm fronds.

TALLIT (*pl. tallitot*) A shawl with ritually knotted fringes (tsitsit) worn by males during worship.

TALMUD The Mishnah and Gemara together; often an inclusive term for the study of rabbinic law.

TEFILLIN (*sing. tefillah*) A set of black leather boxes with thongs, worn on the arm and the head by men at morning prayers; the boxes contain scriptural passages written by a scribe (sofer) on parchment.

TEN DAYS OF PENITENCE A period of reflection and contrition between the New Year and the Day of Atonement.

TISHA B'AV The ninth day of the month of Av, observed as a day of mourning to commemorate the destruction of the First and Second Temples in Jerusalem.

TORAH The Five Books of Moses (the Pentateuch) written by a scribe in the form of a parchment scroll; the first five books of the Jewish Bible; in a broader sense, the way of Jewish life and practice as ordained in the Bible and rabbinic sources.

TSITSIT The knotted fringes of the tallit.

TZADDIK In Hasidism, a sage and a charismatic spiritual leader endowed with special powers of intercession.

YAHRZEIT The anniversary of the death of a close relative, marked by special prayers and the lighting of a memorial candle or lamp.

YOM KIPPUR The Day of Atonement; the solemn fast day that falls in the early autumn ten days after Rosh Hashanah.

Bibliographic Note

There have been a number of previous translations of Agnon into English. The novella form, in which Agnon excelled, is represented in English by *Two Tales: "Betrothed" and "Ido and Enam"* (New York: Schocken Books, 1966) and *In the Heart of the Seas* (New York: Schocken Books, 1948). "In the Prime of Her Life" appeared in 1983 in the collection *Eight Great Hebrew Novellas*, edited by Alan Lelchuk and Gershon Shaked (reissued *The* Toby Press, 2005). Among the novels, there are a number of English translations, beginning with *The Bridal Canopy* (New York: Schocken Books, 1967), a translation in need of updating since it is based on a Hebrew version of the novel that Agnon subsequently revised. The major novel *Oreah Nata Lalun* was published in English as *A Guest for the Night*, in a 1968 translation by Misha Louvish (New York: Schocken Books). *A Simple Story*, Hillel Halkin's translation of *Sippur Pashut*, appeared in a Schocken edition in 1985. This novel of eastern Europe focuses on a young man whose difficulties in adjusting to his life are symptomatic of larger-scale conflicts of direction in Jewish life of the time. *Shira*, translated by Zeva Shapiro and published in Schocken Books in 1989, presents its middle-aged protagonist, Manfred Herbst, and his infatuation with the nurse Shira, against the background of the academic community of Jerusalem in the 1940s.

For critical work on Agnon in English, readers might begin with Arnold Band's study of the life and work, *Nostalgia and Nightmare: A Study of the Fiction of S.Y. Agnon,* published in 1968 (Berkeley and Los Angeles: University of California Press). Early studies also include Baruch Hochman's *The Fiction of S.Y. Agnon,* published by Cornell University Press in 1970. Robert Alter has produced insightful essays over the years. More recently, Gershon Shaked has provided an analytic overview of genres and themes in *Shmuel Yosef Agnon: A Revolutionary Traditionalist* (New York: New York University Press, 1989). Anne Golomb Hoffman's critical study, *Between Exile and Return: S.Y. Agnon and the Drama of Writing* (Albany: State University of New York Press, 1991), examines themes of writing and text for insight into Agnon's unique position as a Jewish modernist who transformed traditional themes and sources. Over the last ten years, *Prooftexts: A Journal of Jewish Literary History* has published many articles on Agnon, including a special issue in 1987 celebrating the centenary of his birth with critical studies by Nitza Ben-Dov, Yael Feldman, Alan Mintz, Dan Miron, and others.

For readers who want to locate the originals of the stories contained in this anthology, we offer the following information on the publication of Agnon's works in Hebrew. *Eilu Ve'eilu,* volume 2 in *The Collected Works,* is the source for the following stories: "Agunot," "The Tale of the Scribe," "Two Pairs," "The Kerchief," "On One Stone," "A Sense of Smell," "Tears," "Fable of the Goat," "Paths of Righteousness, or The Vinegar Maker." From *Al Kapot Haman'ul,* volume 3 in *The Collected Works,* we have taken "Hill of Sand" and "The Doctor's Divorce." *Samukh Venir'eh,* volume 6 in *The Collected Works,* supplied the following stories: "Between Two Towns," "The Lady and the Peddler," "Knots upon Knots," "From Lodging to Lodging," "On the Road," "To the Doctor," and "A Whole Loaf." "At the Outset of the Day" is taken from *Ad Hena,* volume 7 in *The Collected Works.* "That Tzaddik's Etrog" comes from *Ha'esh Veha'etsim,* volume 8 in *The*

Collected Works. The posthumously published *Ir Umeloah* (Tel Aviv: Schocken Publishing House Ltd., 1973) is the source for the following stories: "Buczacz," "The Tale of the Menorah," "Pisces," "The Sign," and "A Book That Was Lost."

Permissions Acknowledgments

A number of people were generous with advice and counsel in the course of our work on this volume. We would like to express our gratitude to Arnold Band, Avraham Holtz, Dan Laor, Chaim Milikowsky, Dan Miron, Gershon Shaked, and Emuna Yaron.

Grateful acknowledgment is made for permission to reprint the following stories:

"A Book That Was Lost" and "Paths of Righteousness, or The Vinegar Maker," translated by Amiel Gurt. First published in *Ariel* 45–46 (1978). Reprinted by permission of the publisher and the translator.

"Hill of Sand," translated by Hillel Halkin. Copyright © 1995 by The Fund for the Translation of Jewish Literature. Used by permission of The Fund for the Translation of Jewish Literature.

"Knots upon Knots," translated by Anne Golomb Hoffman. First published in *Conservative Judaism* 37 (1983–84). Reprinted by permission of the translator.

"The Lady and the Peddler," translated by Robert Alter. First published in *Commentary* (1966). Copyright © 1966 by Robert Alter. Reprinted by permission of the publisher and the translator.

About the Editors

Nahum N. Glatzer (1903–1990) was a noted American literary scholar, theologian, and editor. Born in Lemberg, he received his Ph.D. from the University of Frankfurt. In 1938 he emigrated to the United States. He taught at Chicago, New York, Brandeis and Boston Universities during his long career. He was the editor of *Judaism: A Quarterly Journal of Jewish Life and Thought*, and a consulting editor of Schocken Books, an American publishing house where he was responsible, in part, for the publication of Kafka's writings in English translation.

He is known for seminal anthologies of Jewish sources in English translation; for his study of *The Loves of Franz Kafka* (New York, Schocken Books, 1986), and for his influential biography of Franz Rosenzweig, *Franz Rosenzweig: His Life and Thought*. He was also the author of a vast array of other books.

Anne Golomb Hoffman is Professor of English and Comparative Literature at Fordham University and author of *Between Exile and Return: S.Y. Agnon and the Drama of Writing* (SUNY Press, 1991) as well as many articles on Agnon and other writers of modern Hebrew fiction. She also teaches and writes on the relationship of psychoanalytic writing to literature, with a particular interest in the history of representations of the body in literary and theoretical texts.

Alan Mintz is the Chana Kekst Professor of Hebrew Literature and chair of the Department of Hebrew Language at The Jewish Theological Seminary. Dr. Mintz joined the JTS faculty in June 2001 after ten years at Brandeis University as Professor of Modern Hebrew Literature. Dr. Mintz is the author, most recently, of *Popular Culture and the Shaping of Holocaust Memory in America* and *Translating Israel: The Reception of Hebrew Literature in America*, and editor of *Reading Hebrew Literature*. His major academic works include *Hurban: Responses to Catastrophe in Hebrew Literature*, and *Banished from Their Father's Table: Loss of Faith and Hebrew Autobiography* Dr. Mintz was the founder of *Response* magazine, which he edited from 1967 through 1970. In 1981, Dr. Mintz cofounded *Prooftexts: A Journal of Jewish Literary History* with professor of Literature David Roskies.

Jonathan Rosen is the editorial director of Nextbook, where he edits the Nextbook\Schocken "Jewish Encounters" series. He is the author of two novels, *Eve's Apple* and *Joy Comes in the Morning*, and two works of non-fiction, *The Talmud and the Internet* and *The Life of the Skies: Birding at the End of Nature*. His essays have appeared in the *New York Times*, the *New Yorker* and the *American Scholar*, as well as several anthologies.

About the Author

S.Y. Agnon was born Shmuel Yosef Halevi Czaczkes in Buczacz, Eastern Galicia. In 1908 he immigrated to Ottoman Palestine, there to publish his first story, "Agunot," ("Forsaken Wives"), under the pen name "Agnon"—a surname he later adopted legally. After an extended stay in Germany from 1913 to 1924, he returned to Jerusalem, where he remained until his death in 1970.

Called "a man of unquestionable genius" and "one of the great storytellers of our time," S.Y. Agnon is among the most effusively praised and widely translated of Hebrew authors. Extolled for the uniqueness of his style and the beauty of his language, as well as his comic mastery, Agnon's contribution to the renewal of Hebrew literature has been seminal for all subsequent Israeli writing. While much of his work attempts to recapture the lives and traditions of a former time, his stories are never a simple act of preservation, but rather deal with the most important psychological and philosophical problems of his generation, touching on the spiritual desolation of a world standing on the threshold of a new age.

The winner of numerous Israeli prizes (Bialik Prize, 1934 and 1950; Israel Prize, 1954 and 1958), Agnon was awarded the Nobel Prize for Literature in 1966.

The fonts used in this book are from the Garamond family